# THE RUNAWAY PRINCESS

RH
GRAPHIC

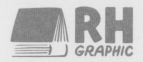

# THE RUNAWAY P

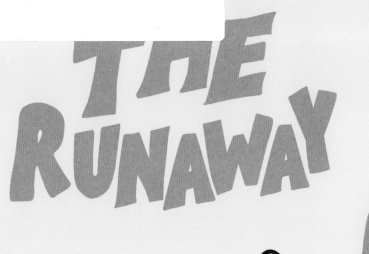

Johan Troïanowski

Translation copyright © 2020 by Makaka Editions
Cover art and interior art copyright © 2015, 2016, 2017, 2020 by Makaka Editions

All rights reserved. Published in the United States by RH Graphic, an imprint of Random House Children's Books, a division of Penguin Random House LLC, New York. The titles in this work were originally published in three separate volumes in France and in the French language by Makaka Editions, Saint-Etienne-de-Fontbellon as *Rouge, Petite Princesse Punk* by Johan Troïanowski in 2015, copyright © 2015 by Makaka Editions; *Rouge et la Sorcière D'Automne* by Johan Troïanowski in 2016, copyright © 2016 by Makaka Editions; and *Rouge L'île des Gribouilleurs* by Johan Troïanowski in 2017, copyright © 2017 by Makaka Editions.

RH Graphic with the book design is a trademark of Penguin Random House LLC.

Visit us on the Web! rhkidsgraphic.com • @RHKidsGraphic

Educators and librarians, for a variety of teaching tools, visit us at RHTeachersLibrarians.com

*Library of Congress Cataloging-in-Publication Data*
Names: Troïanowski, Johan, author, illustrator. | Smith, Anne Collins, translator. | Smith, Owen (Owen M.), translator. | Troïanowski, Johan. Rouge, petite princesse punk. English. | Troïanowski, Johan. Rouge et la sorcière d'automne. English. | Troïanowski, Johan. Rouge l'île des gribouilleurs. English.
Title: The runaway princess / Johan Troïanowski; translation by Anne and Owen Smith.
Description: New York : RH Graphic, [2020] | Originally published in three separate volumes in French by Makaka Editions, Saint-Etienne-de-Fontbellon, in 2015–2017 under the titles Rouge, petite princesse punk, Rouge et la sorcière d'automne, and Rouge l'île des gribouilleurs.
Identifiers: LCCN 2019018080 | ISBN 978-0-593-11840-5 (trade pbk.) | ISBN 978-0-593-12416-1 (hardcover) | ISBN 978-0-593-11842-9 (ebook) | ISBN 978-0-593-11841-2 (lib. bdg.)
Subjects: LCSH: Graphic novels. | CYAC: Graphic novels. | Princesses—Fiction. | Adventure and adventurers—Fiction. | France—Fiction. | Fairy tales—Fiction.
Classification: LCC PZ7.7.T76 Run 2020 | DDC 741.5/944—dc23

Designed by Patrick Crotty
Translation by Anne and Owen Smith

MANUFACTURED IN CHINA
10 9 8 7 6 5 4 3 2 1
First American Edition

RH
GRAPHIC

**A comic on every bookshelf.**

This book was drawn with India ink and a nib pen on 180g a4 sheets of paper, then colored directly with crayon and inks. This edition was lettered with Stanton ICG.

For Mathilde, Lou, Camille, and Pome

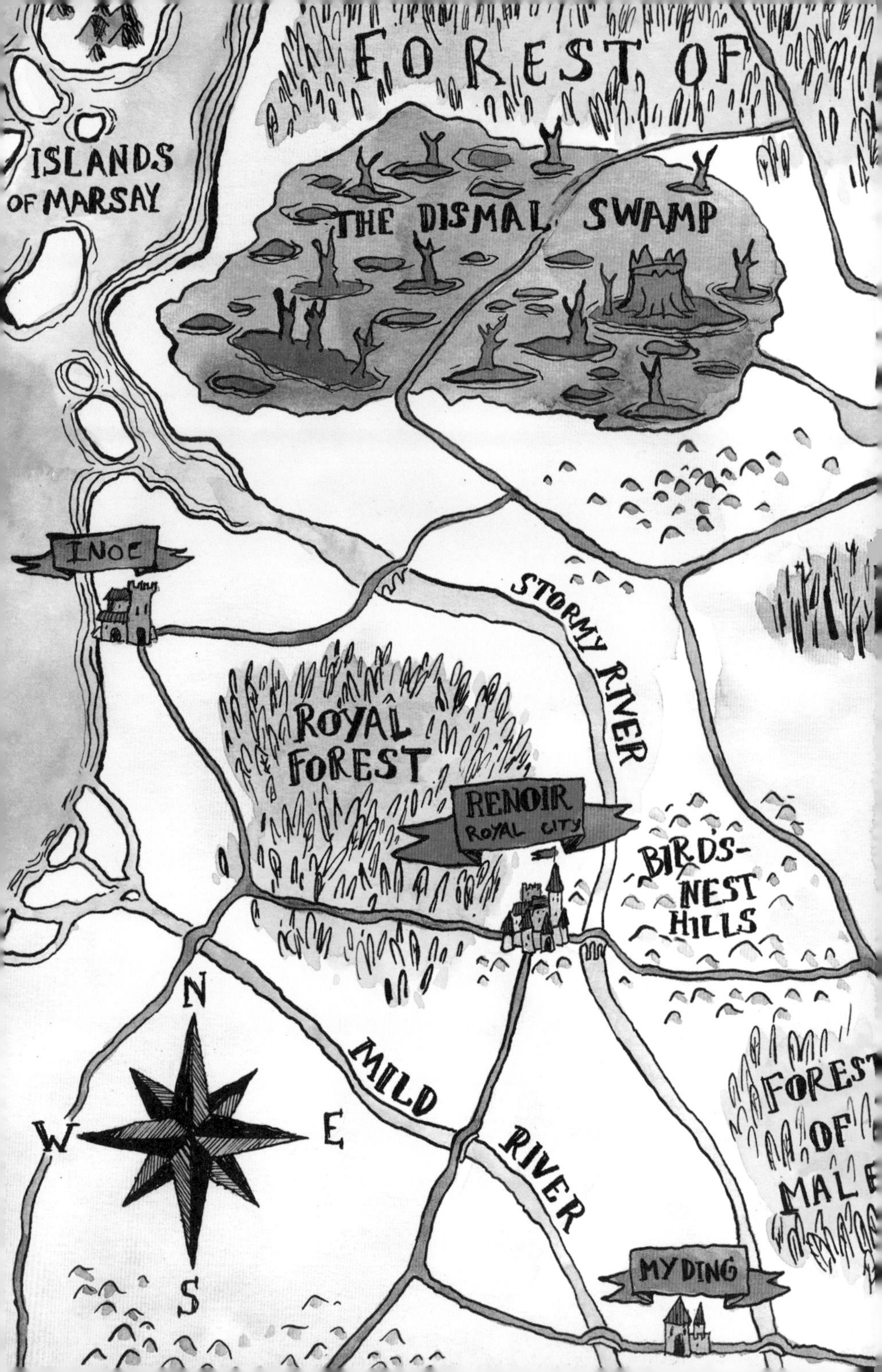
FOREST OF
ISLANDS OF MARSAY
THE DISMAL SWAMP
INOE
STORMY RIVER
ROYAL FOREST
RENOIR
ROYAL CITY
BIRDS-NEST HILLS
N
W
E
S
MILD RIVER
MYDING

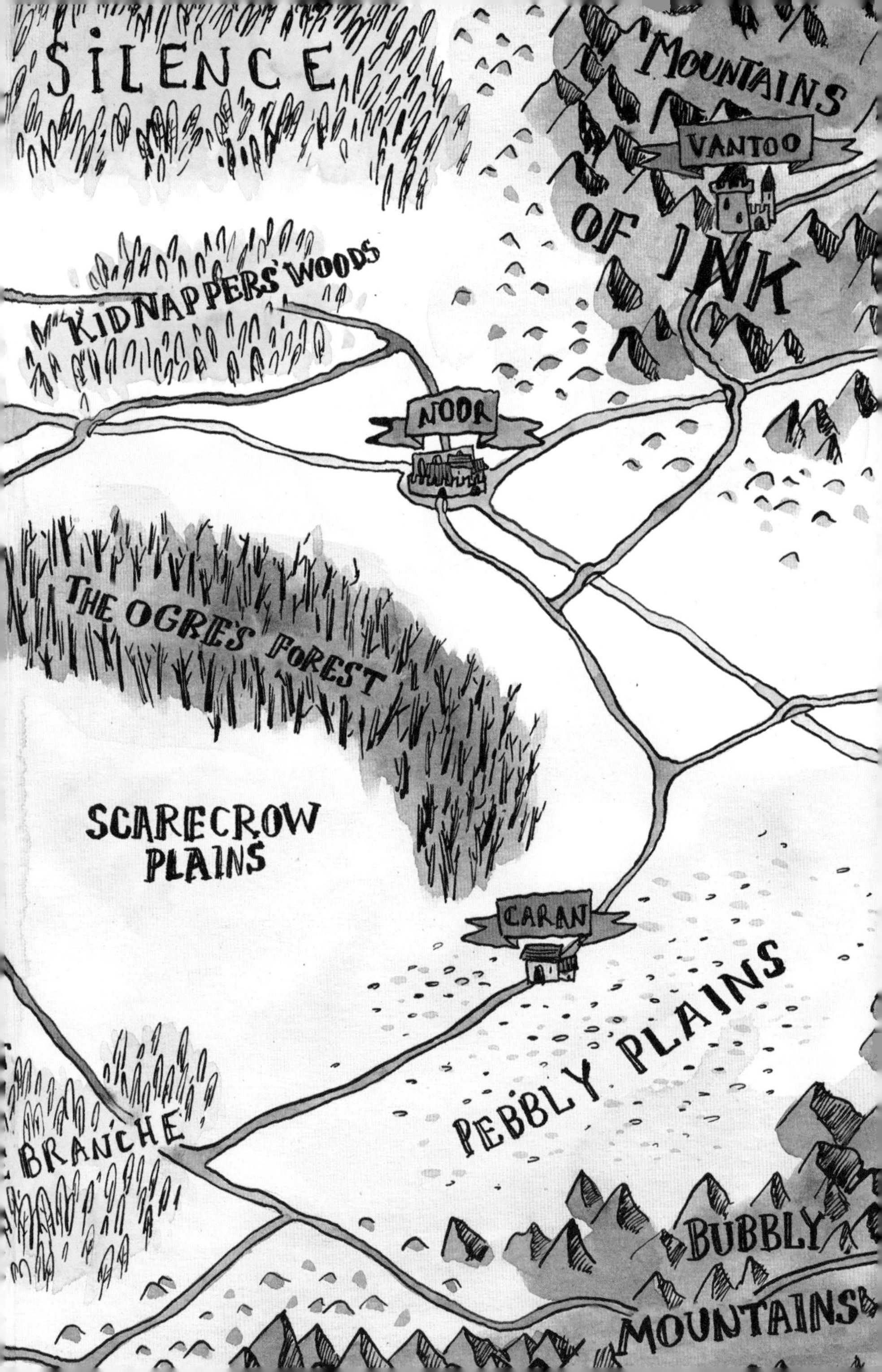
SILENCE
MOUNTAINS
VANTOO
OF INK
KIDNAPPERS' WOODS
NOOR
THE OGRE'S FOREST
SCARECROW PLAINS
CARAN
PEBBLY PLAINS
BRANCHE
BUBBLY
MOUNTAINS

# THE PRINCESS RUNS AWAY

### (AND MAKES SOME FRIENDS)

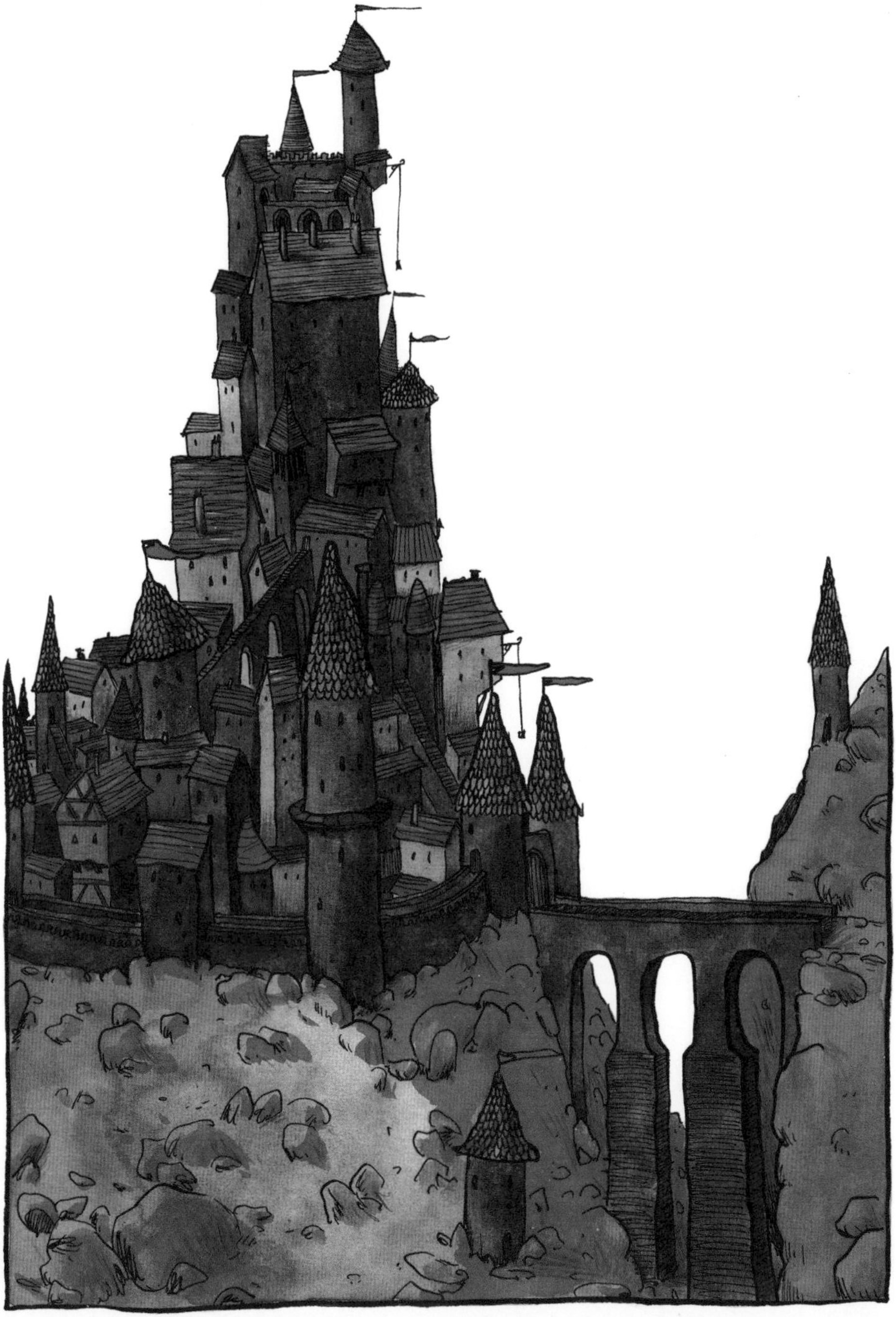

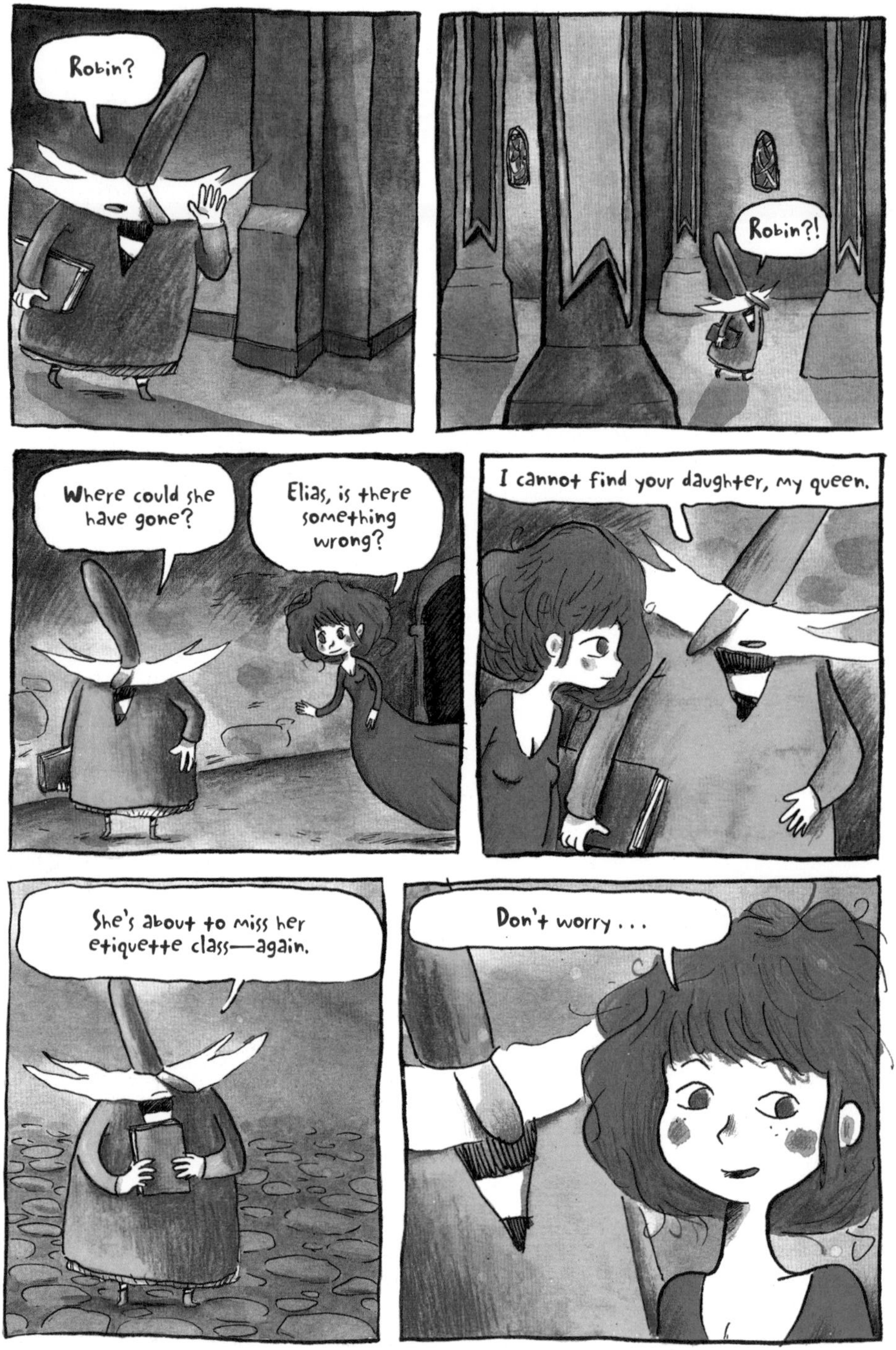
Robin?
Robin?!
Where could she have gone?
Elias, is there something wrong?
I cannot find your daughter, my queen.
She's about to miss her etiquette class—again.
Don't worry . . .

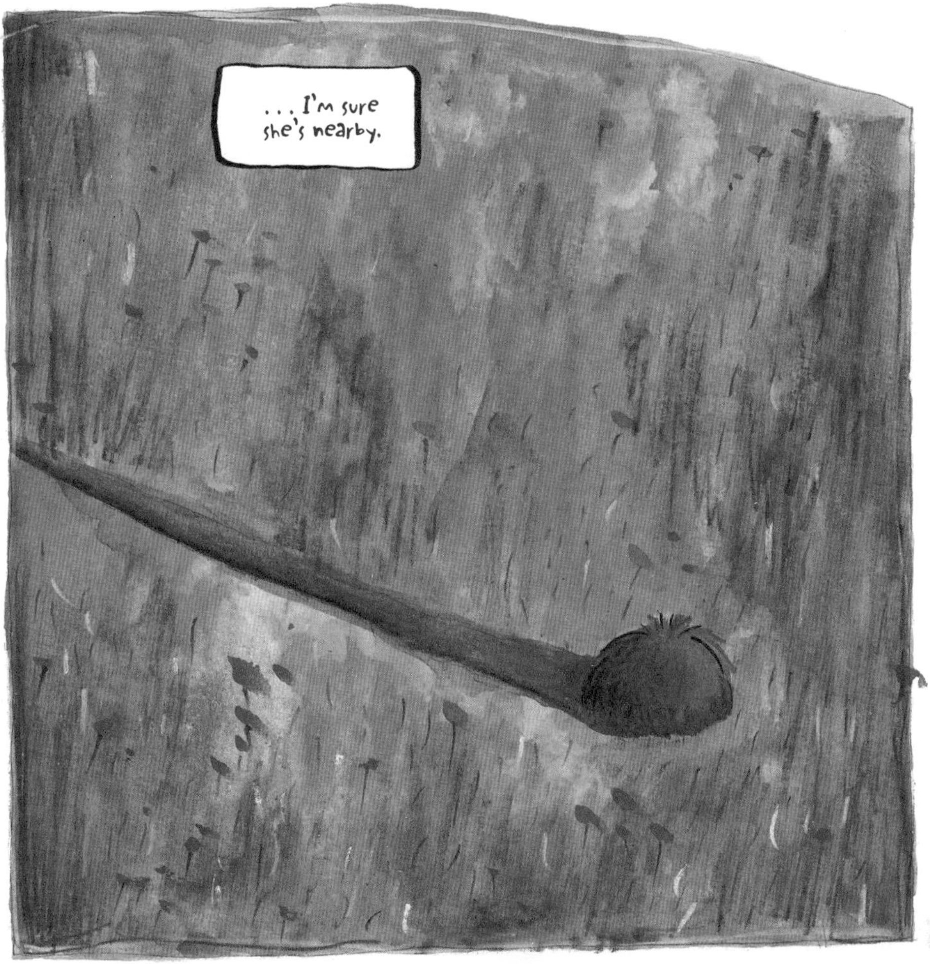
. . . I'm sure she's nearby.

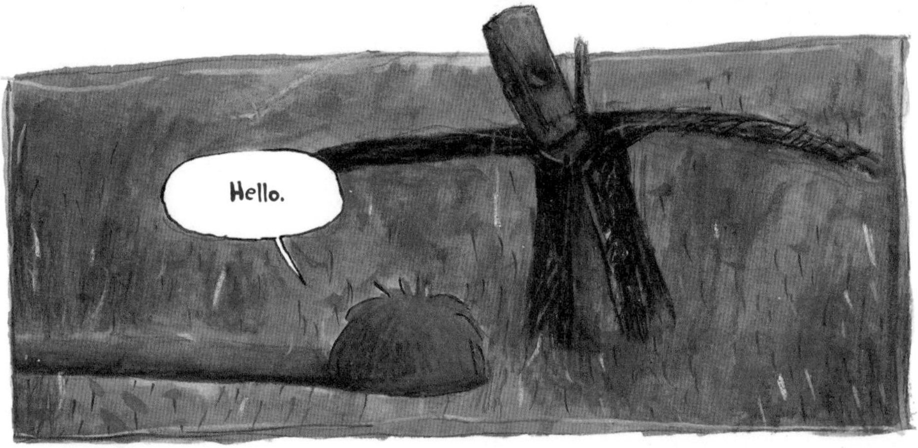
Hello.

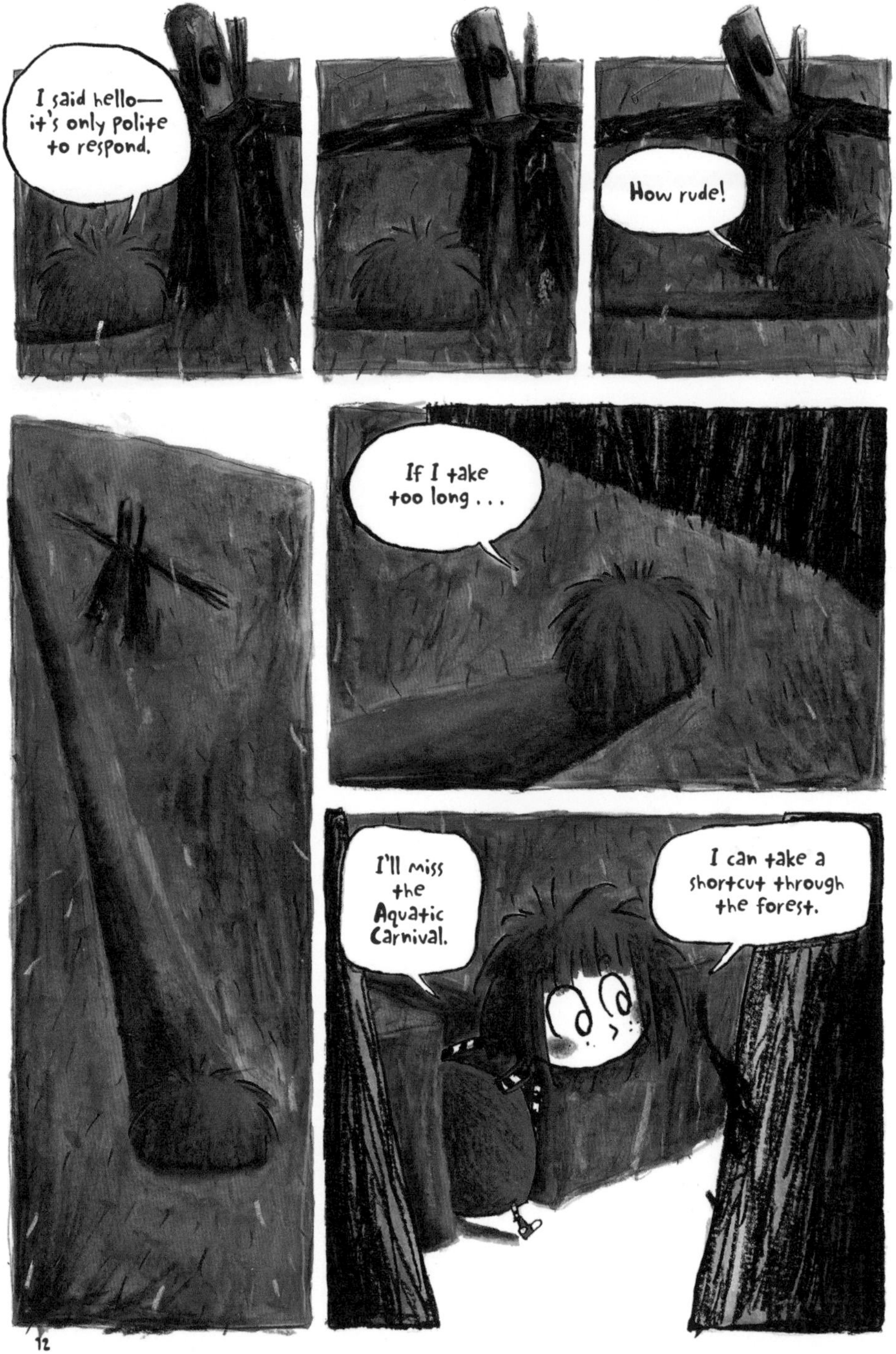
I said hello—it's only polite to respond.
How rude!
If I take too long . . .
I'll miss the Aquatic Carnival.
I can take a shortcut through the forest.

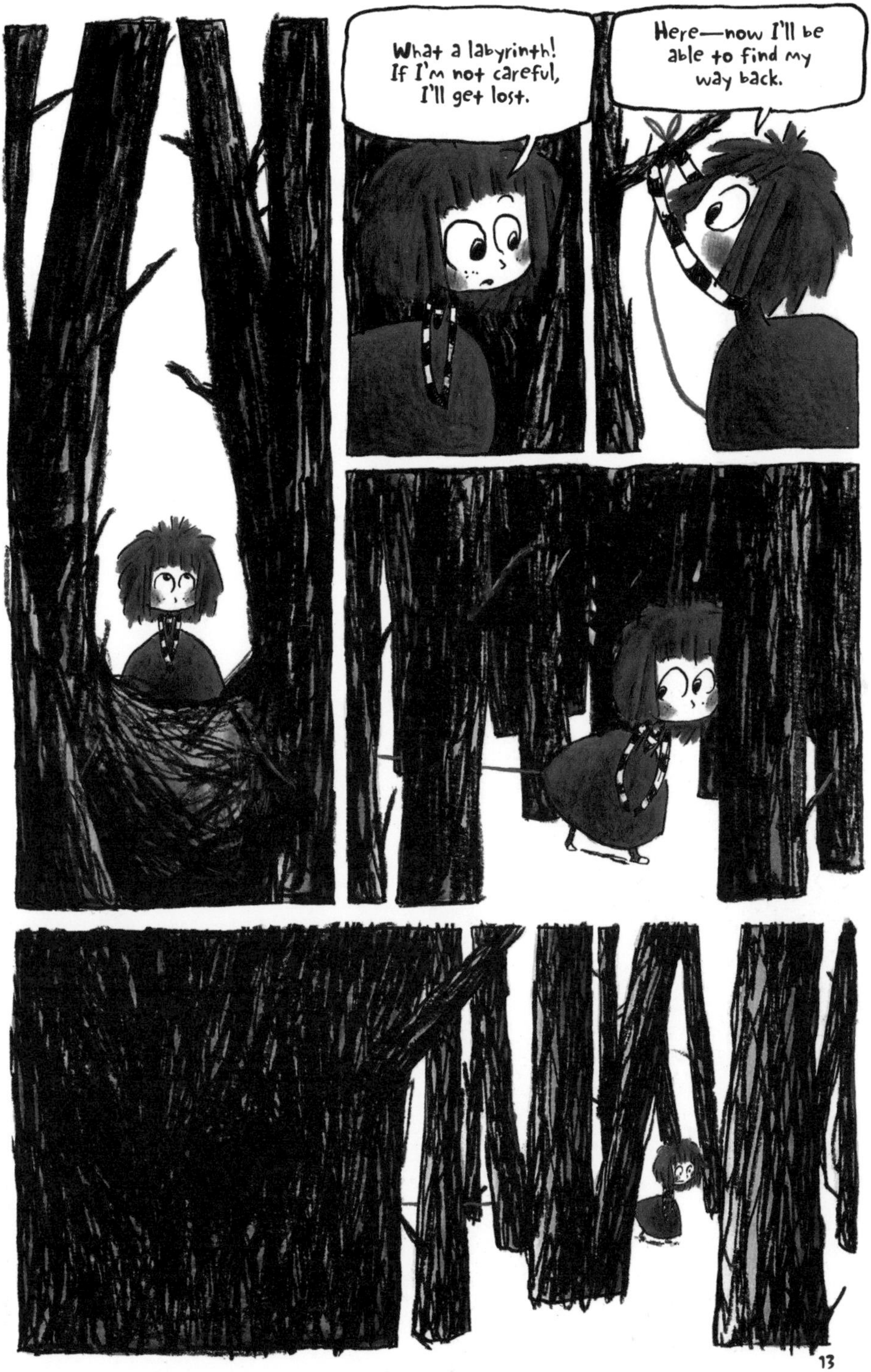
What a labyrinth! If I'm not careful, I'll get lost.
Here—now I'll be able to find my way back.

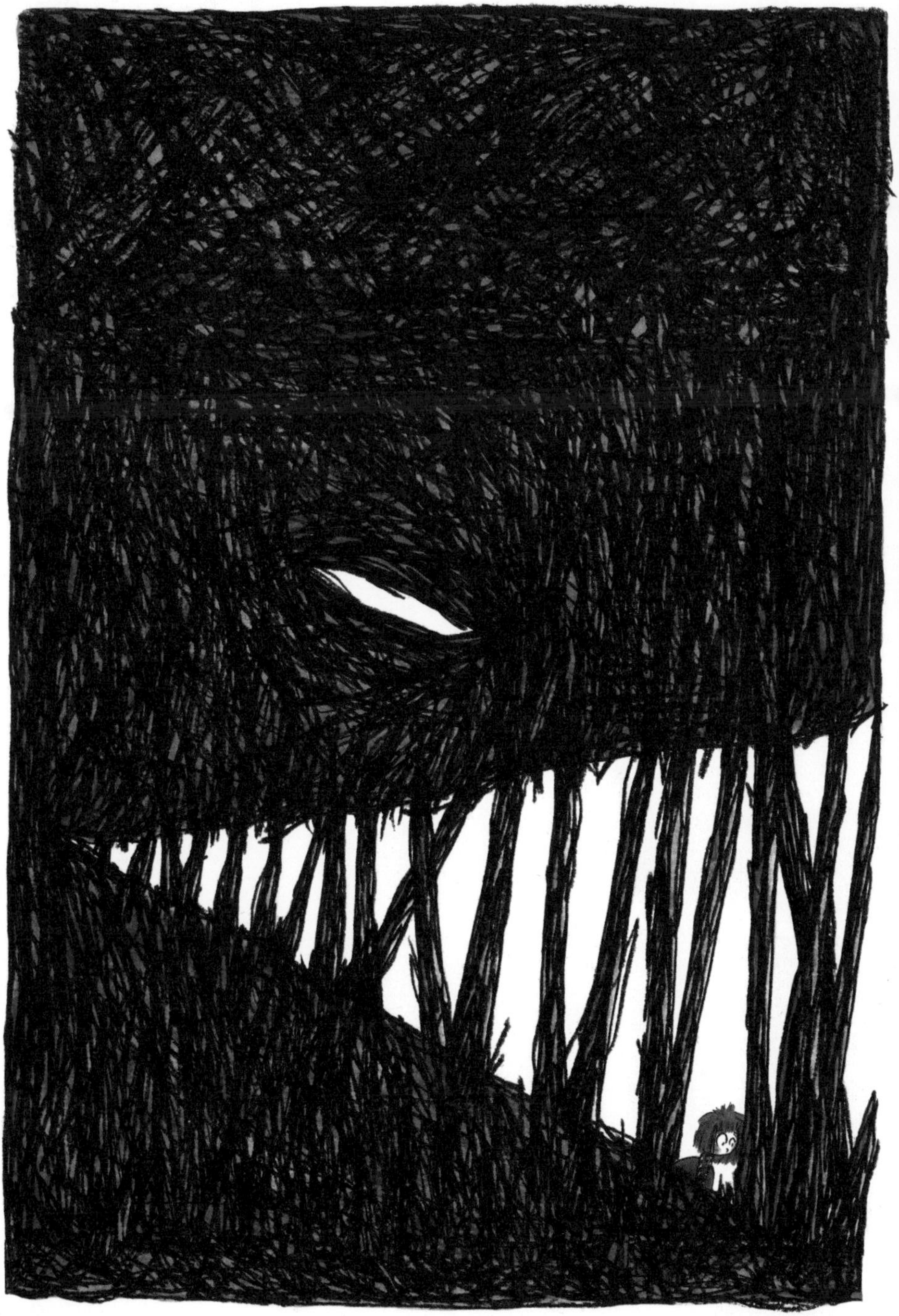

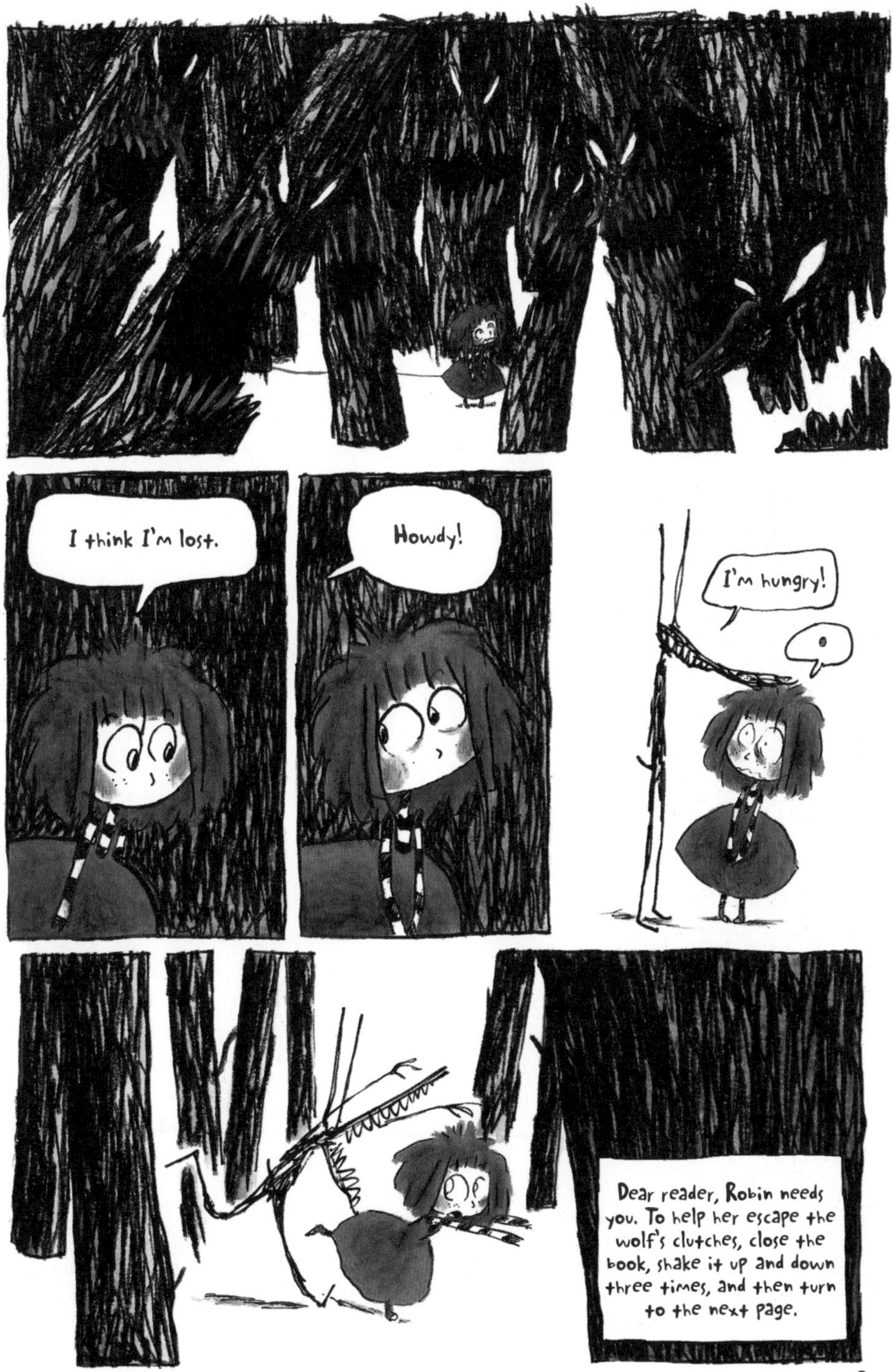

I think I'm lost.
Howdy!
I'm hungry!
?
Dear reader, Robin needs you. To help her escape the wolf's clutches, close the book, shake it up and down three times, and then turn to the next page.

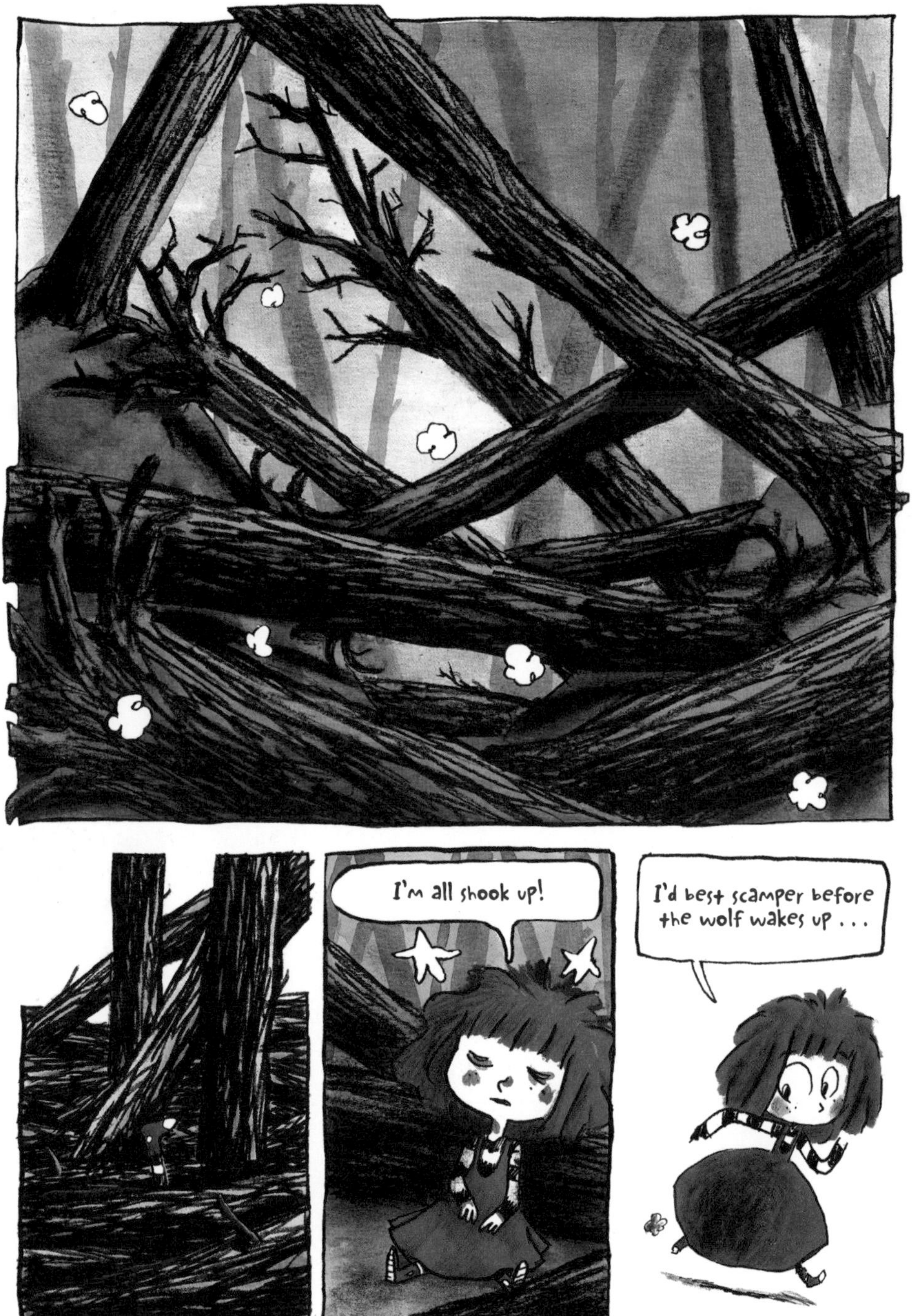
I'm all shook up!
I'd best scamper before the wolf wakes up . . .

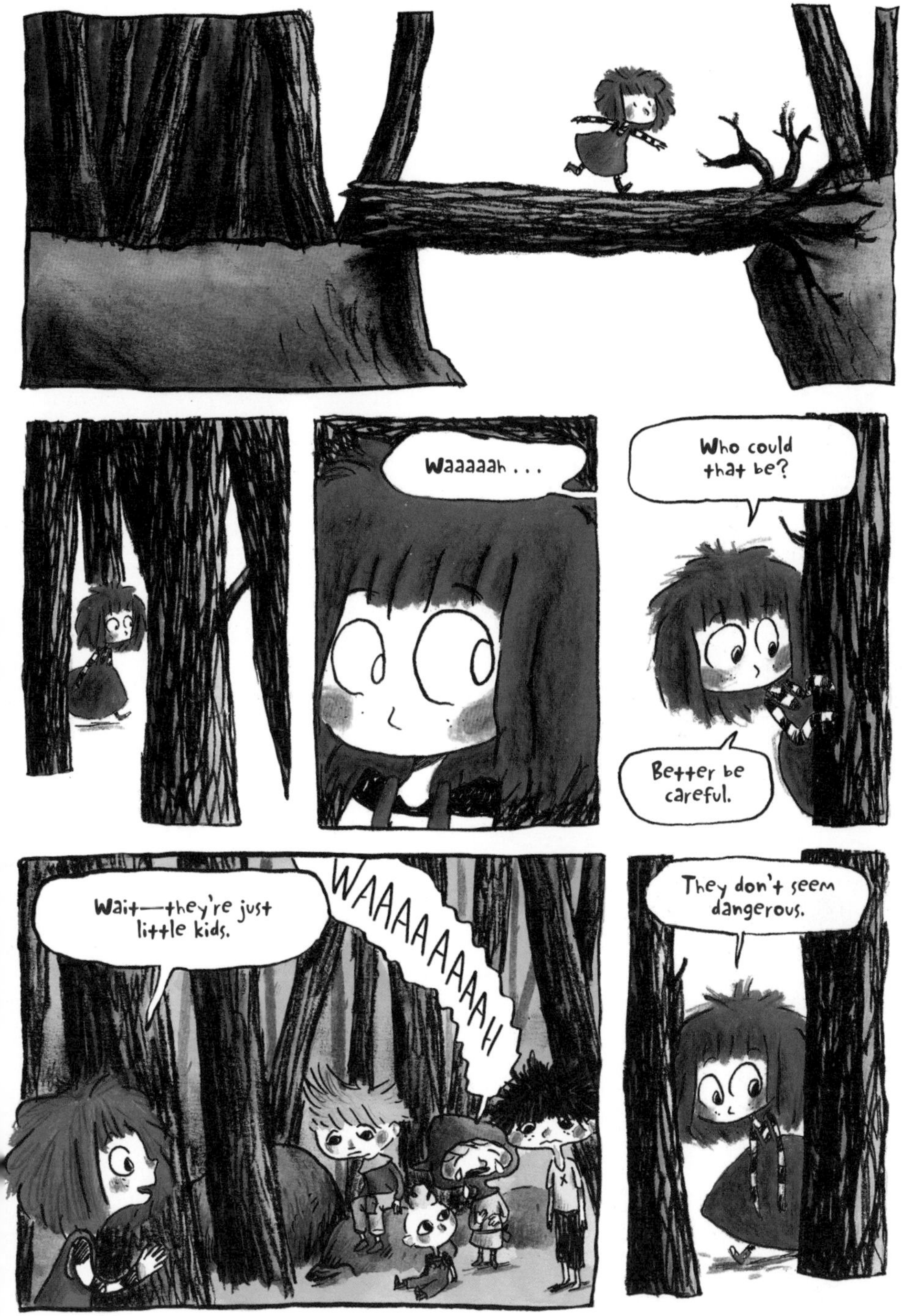
Waaaaah . . .
Who could that be?
Better be careful.
Wait—they're just little kids.
WAAAAAAAAAH
They don't seem dangerous.

Hello.

Eeeek!

Is it an ogre?

Worse! It's a girl!

Nice . . . and I was going to give you a hand.

But if I'm not welcome . . .

No, wait!

I'm sorry. We're lost.

Our father abandoned us in the woods—all because of him.

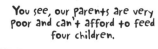

You see, our parents are very poor and can't afford to feed four children.

And now the ogre is going to eat us.

The ogre?

The ogre who devours little children!

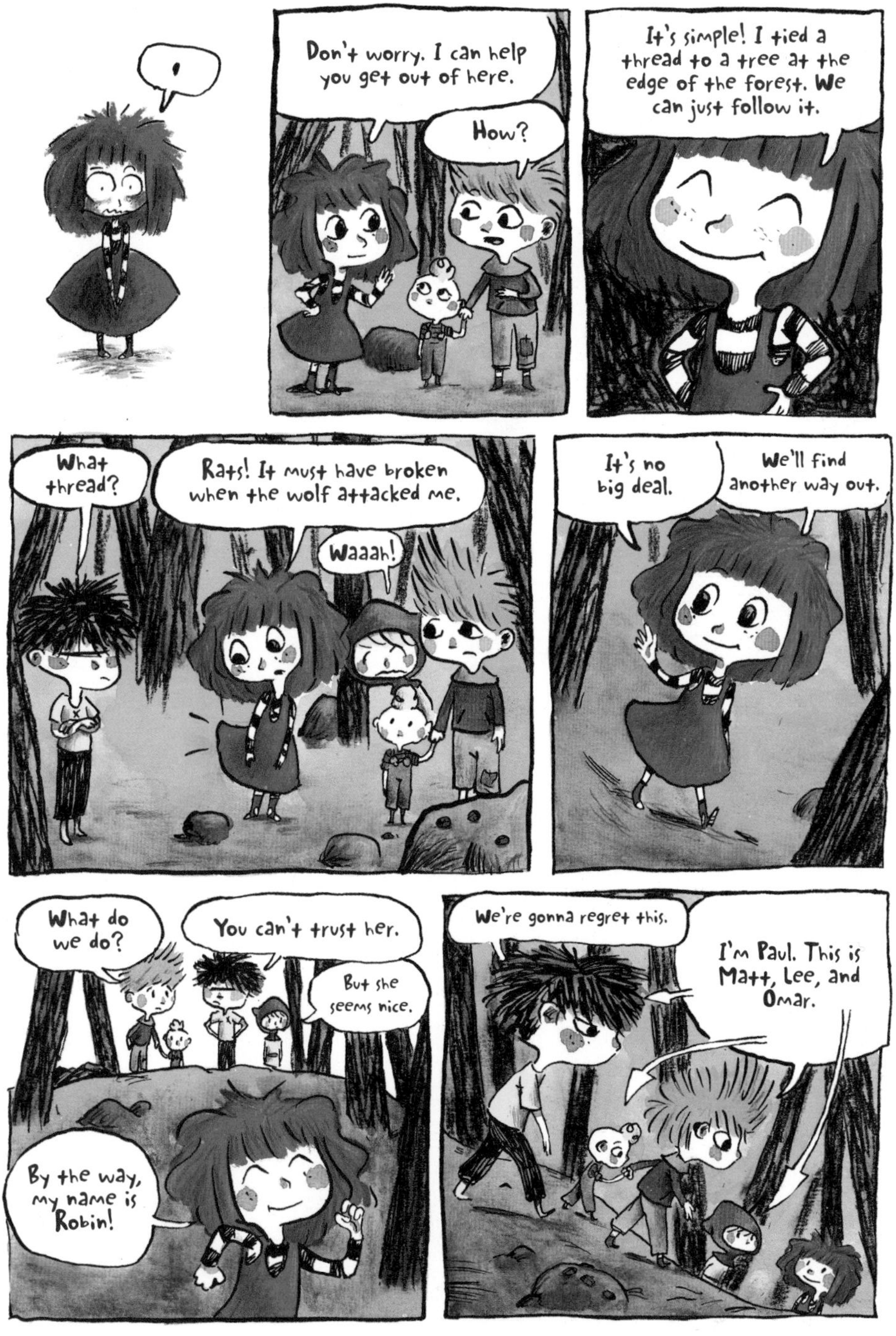
!
Don't worry. I can help you get out of here.
How?
It's simple! I tied a thread to a tree at the edge of the forest. We can just follow it.
What thread?
Rats! It must have broken when the wolf attacked me.
Waaah!
It's no big deal.
We'll find another way out.
What do we do?
You can't trust her.
But she seems nice.
By the way, my name is Robin!
We're gonna regret this.
I'm Paul. This is Matt, Lee, and Omar.

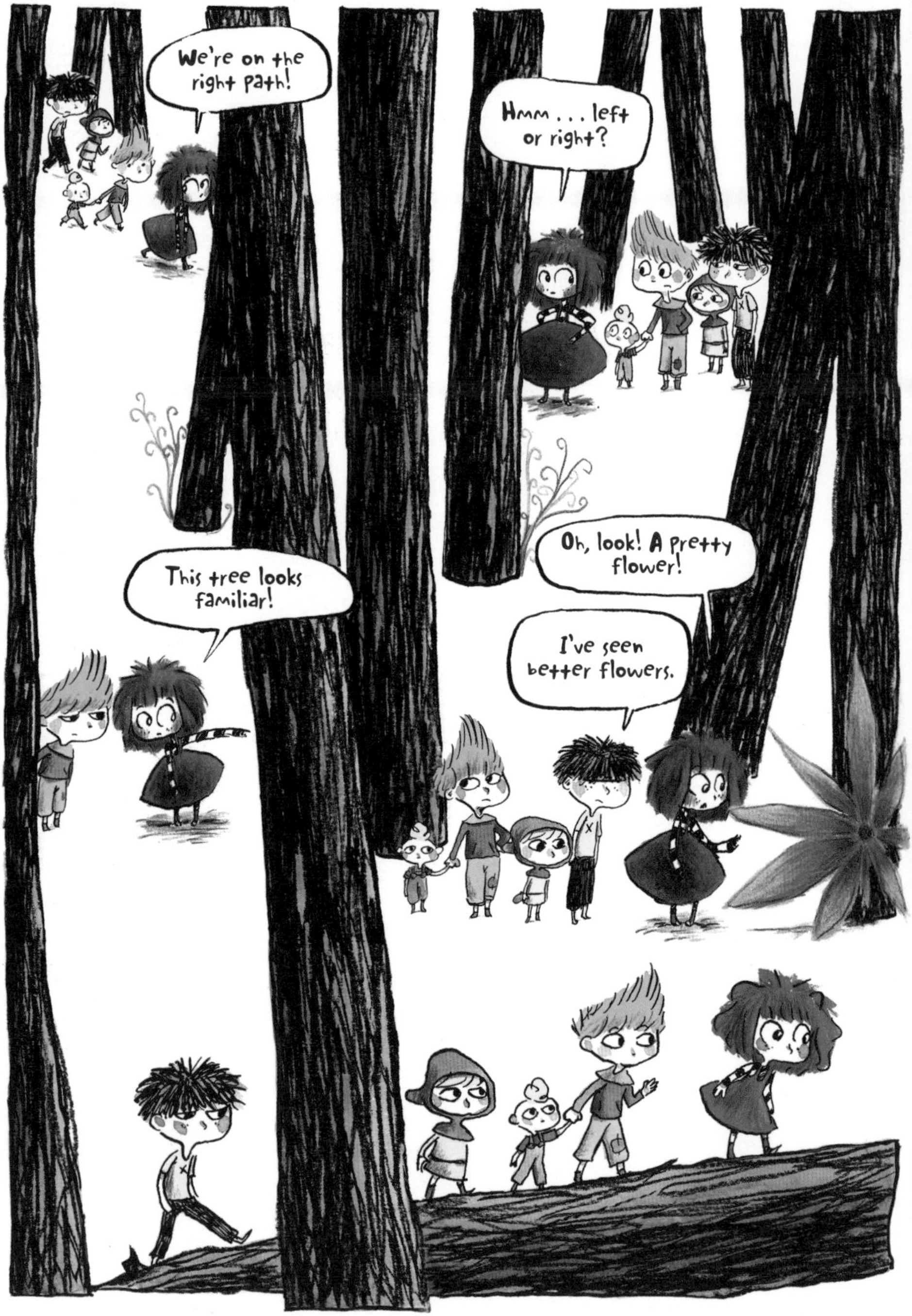
We're on the right path!
Hmm . . . left or right?
This tree looks familiar!
Oh, look! A pretty flower!
I've seen better flowers.

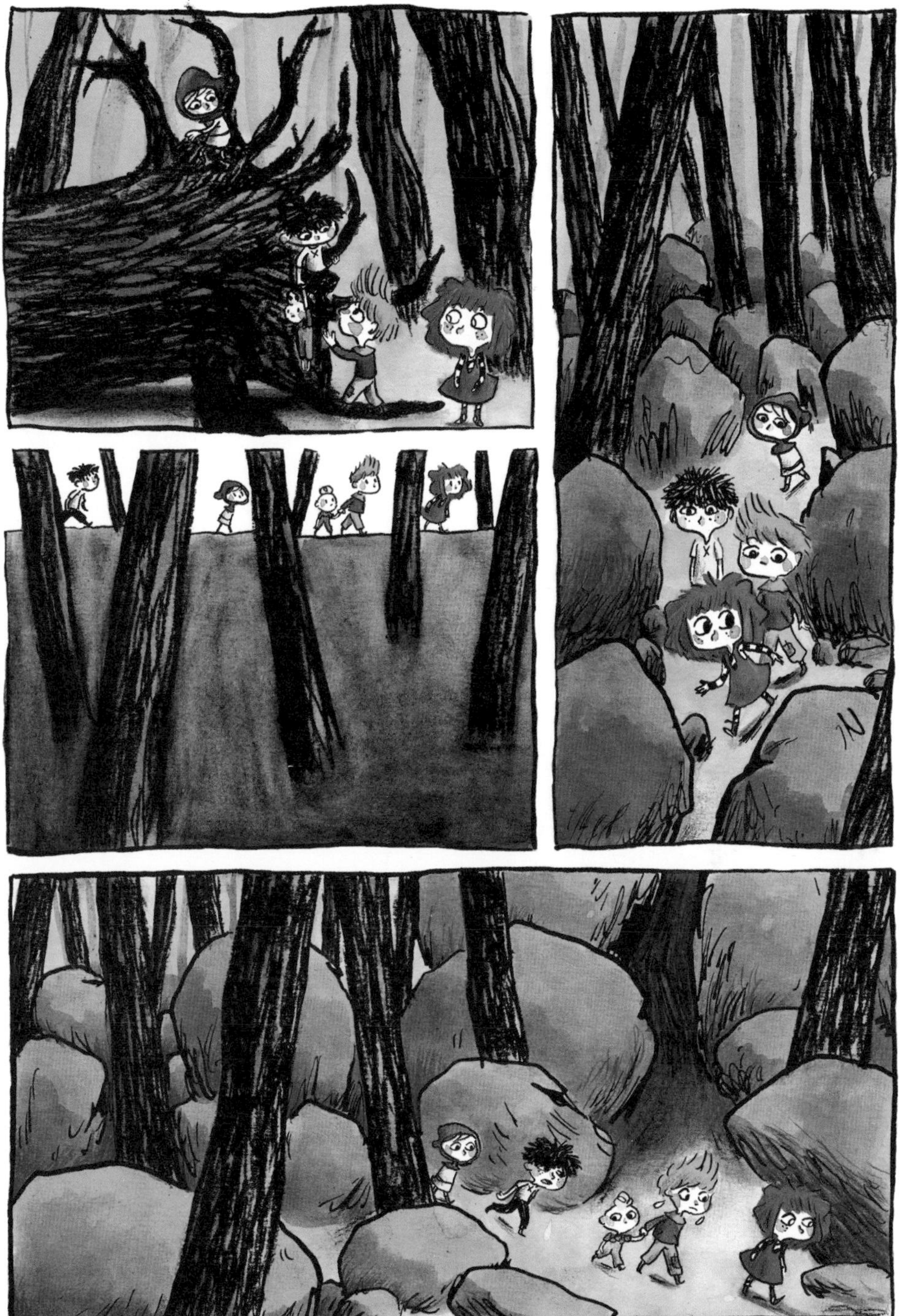

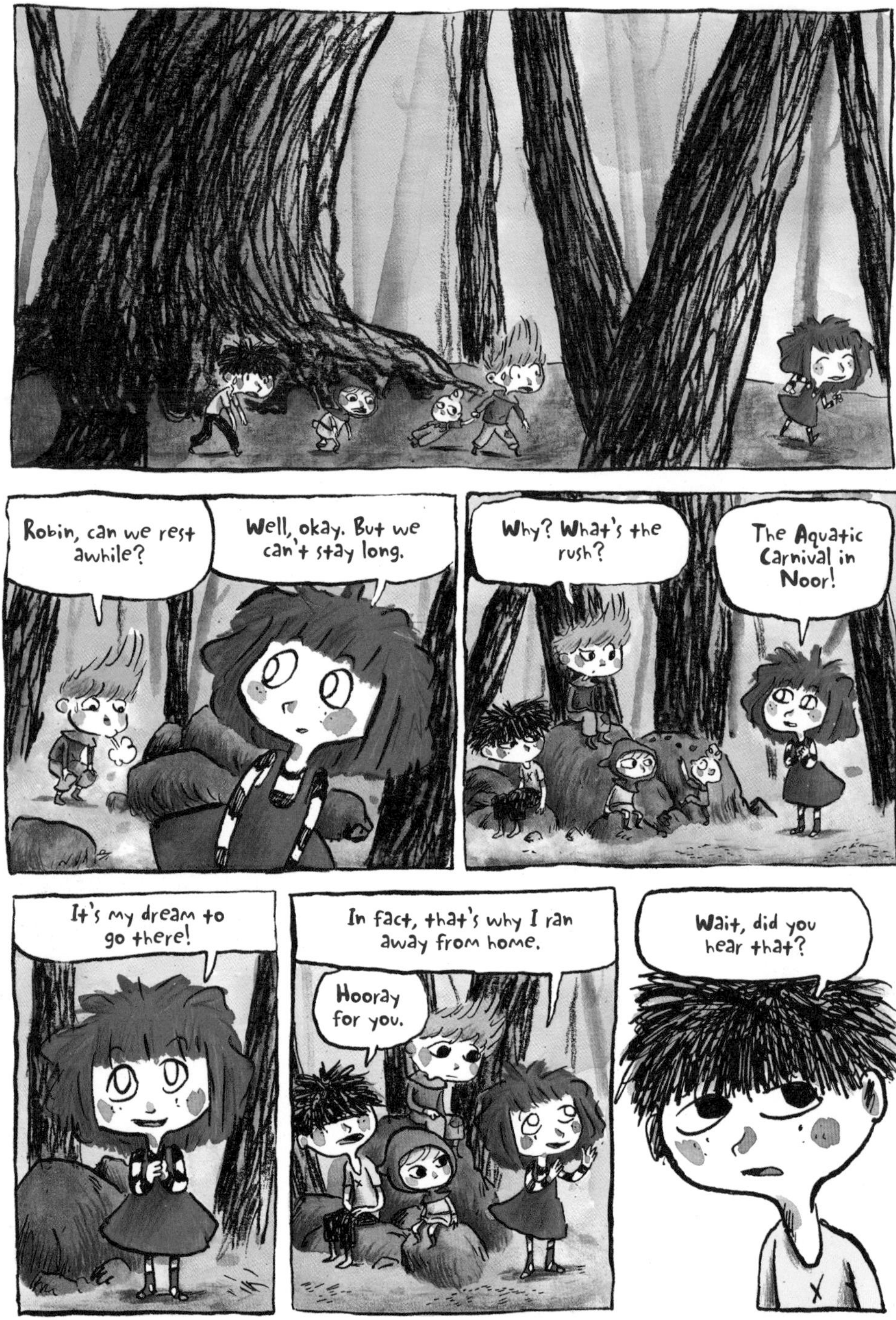
Robin, can we rest awhile?
Well, okay. But we can't stay long.
Why? What's the rush?
The Aquatic Carnival in Noor!
It's my dream to go there!
In fact, that's why I ran away from home.
Hooray for you.
Wait, did you hear that?

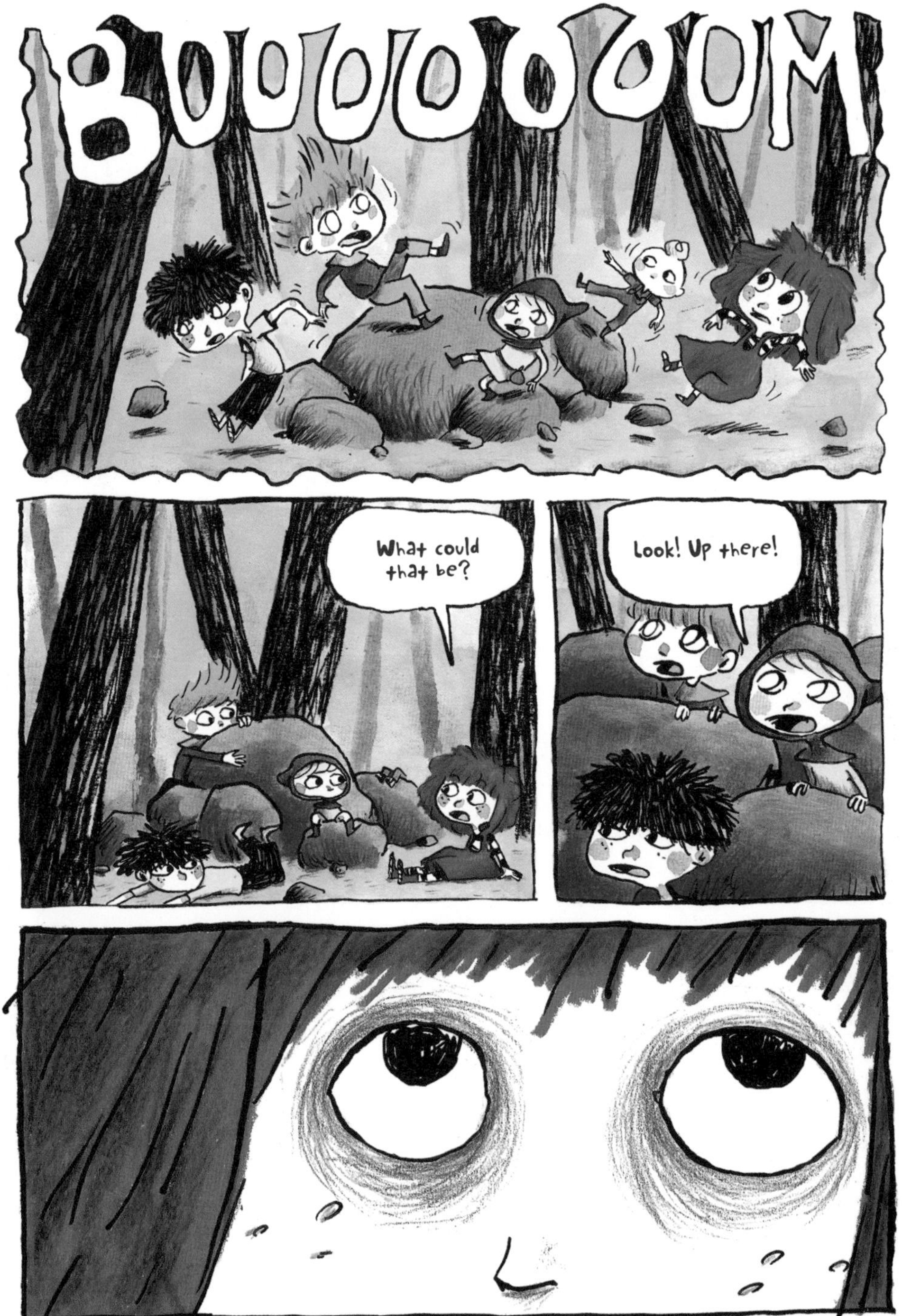
BOOOOOOOOOM!
What could that be?
Look! Up there!

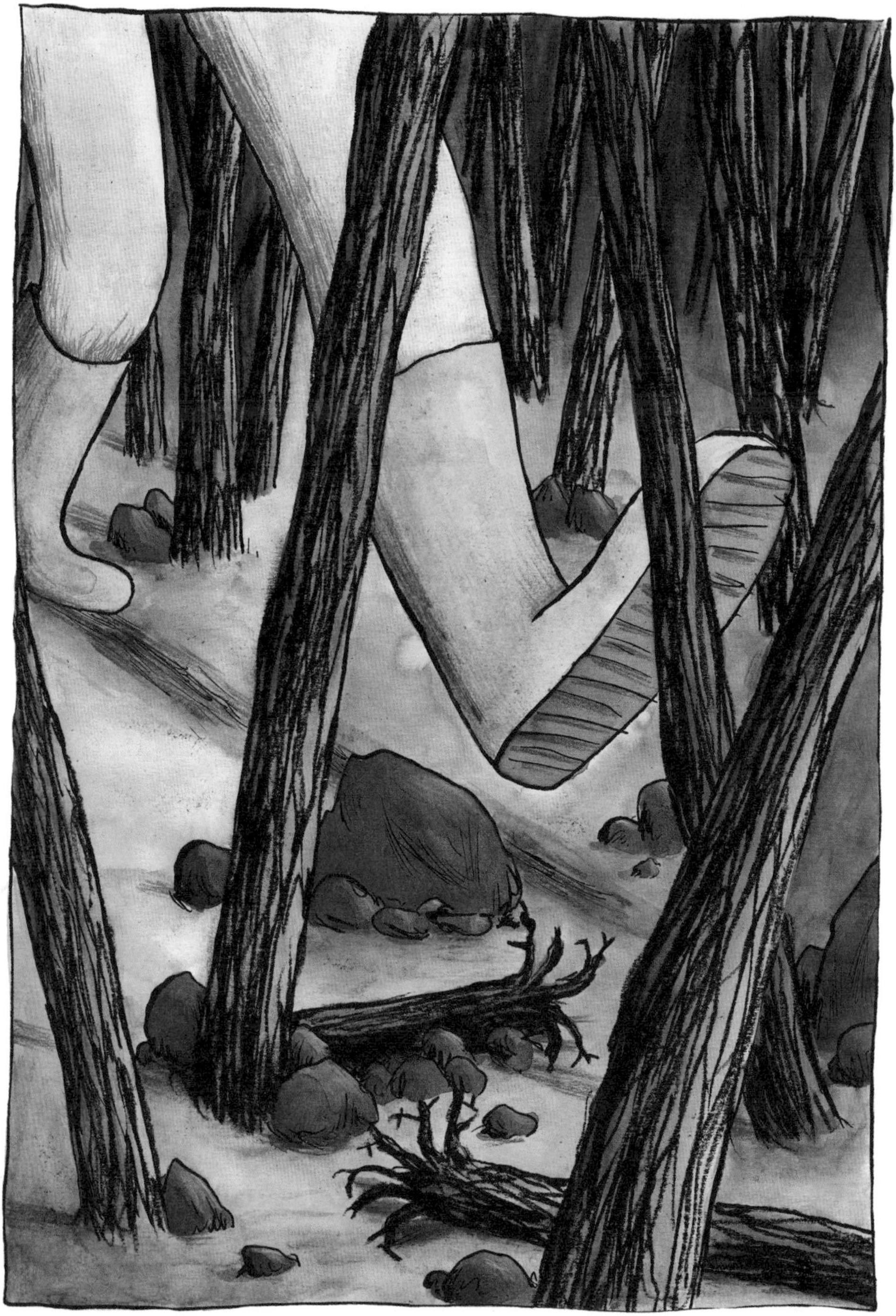

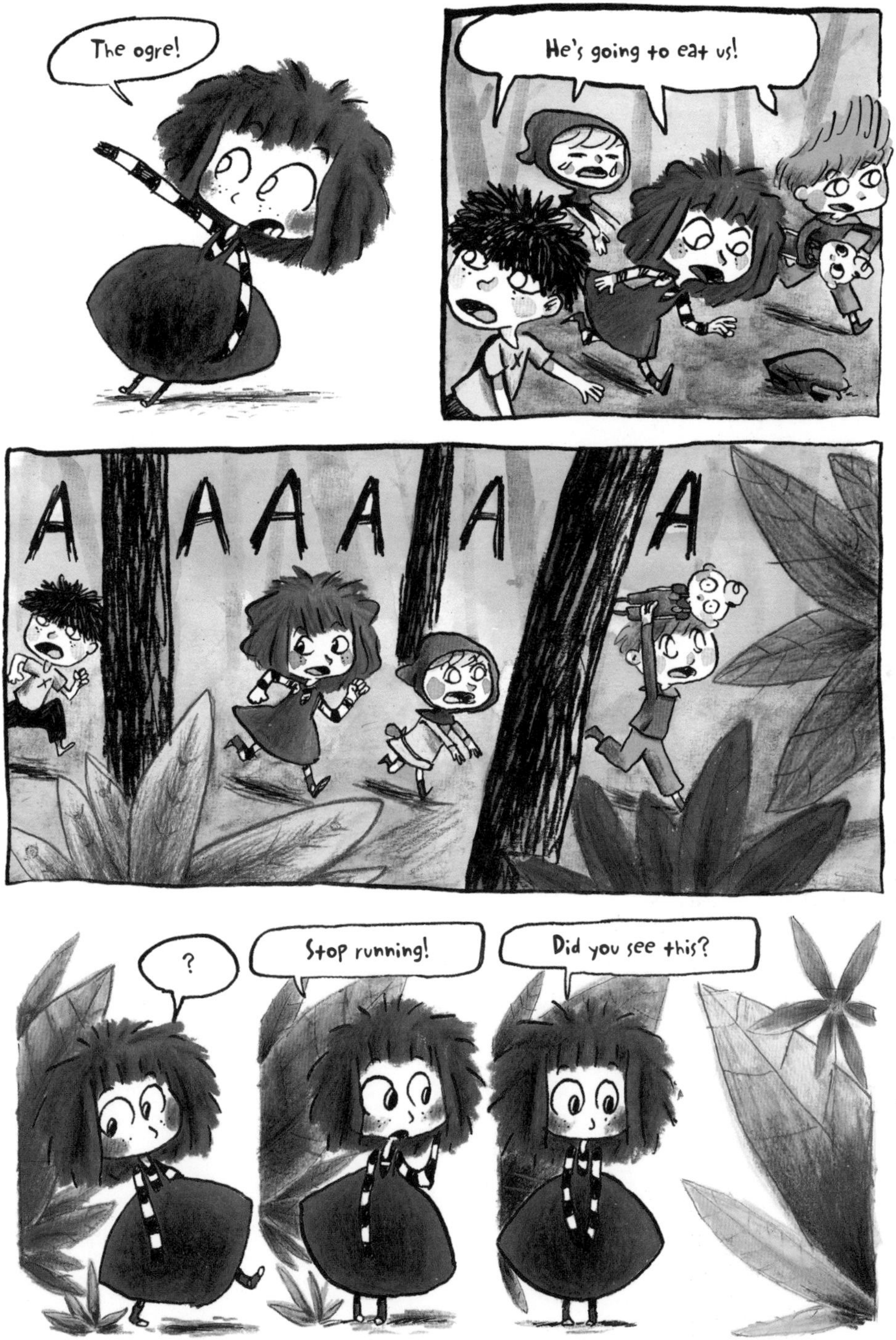
The ogre!
He's going to eat us!
AAAAAA
?
Stop running!
Did you see this?

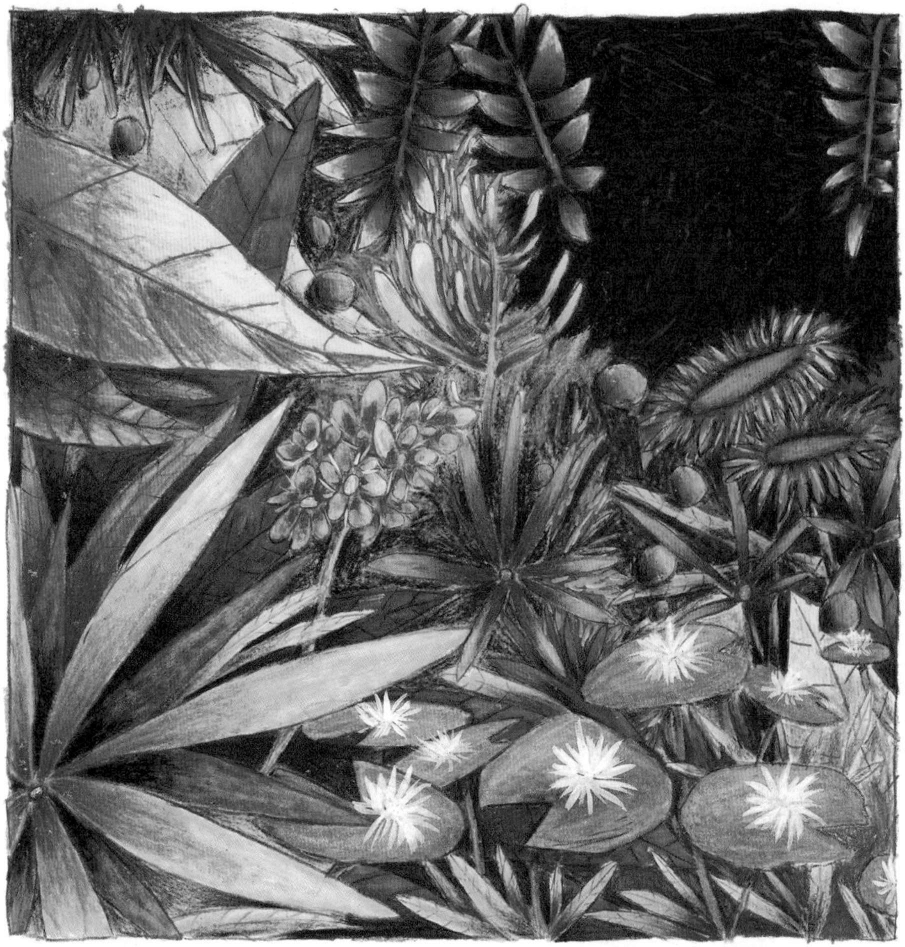

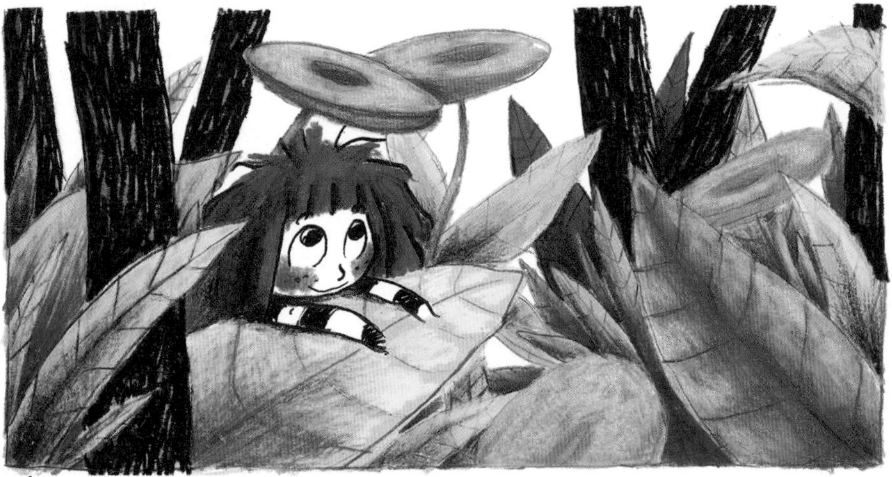

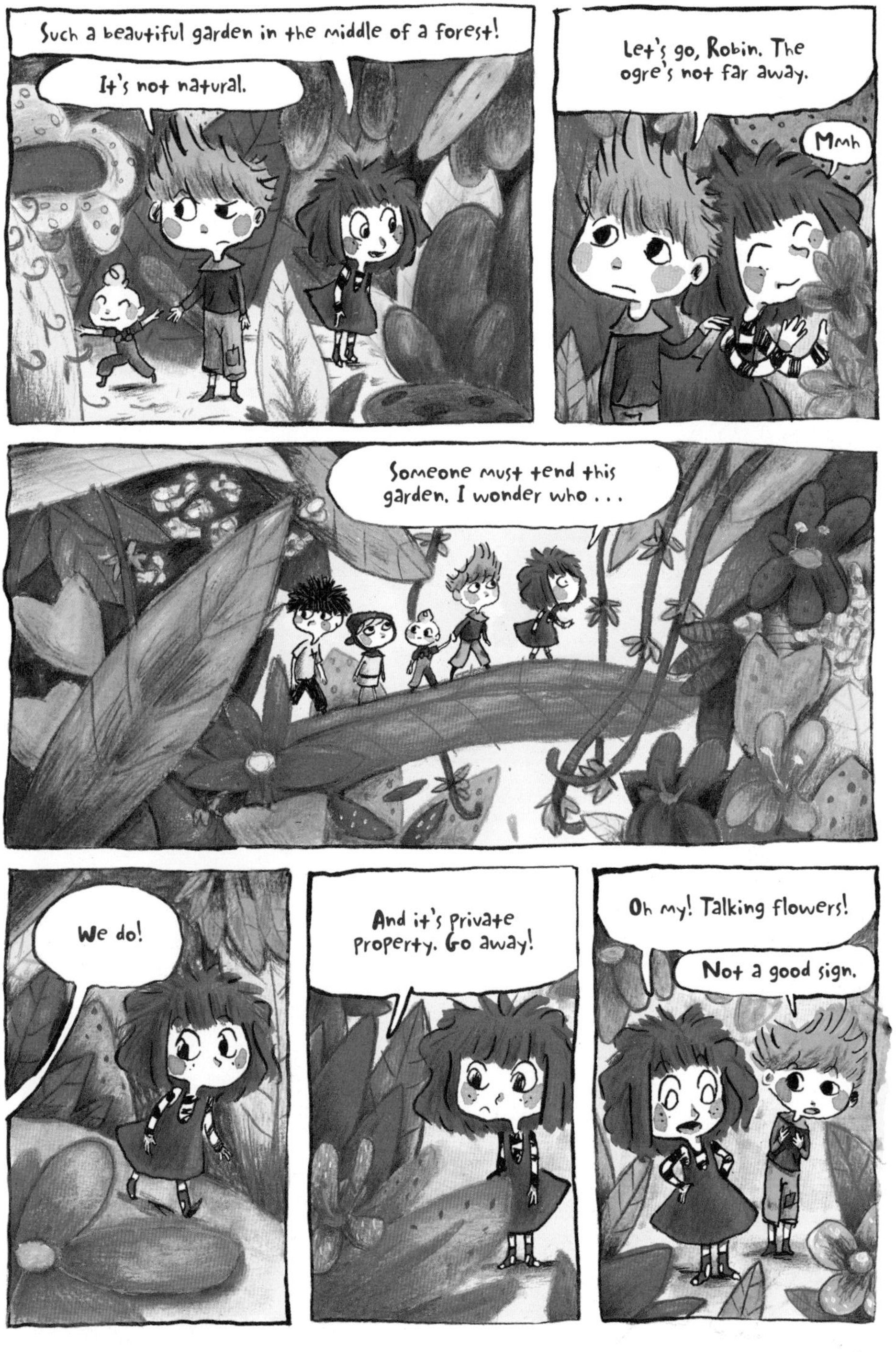

Such a beautiful garden in the middle of a forest!
It's not natural.
Let's go, Robin. The ogre's not far away.
Mmh
Someone must tend this garden. I wonder who . . .
We do!
And it's private property. Go away!
Oh my! Talking flowers!
Not a good sign.

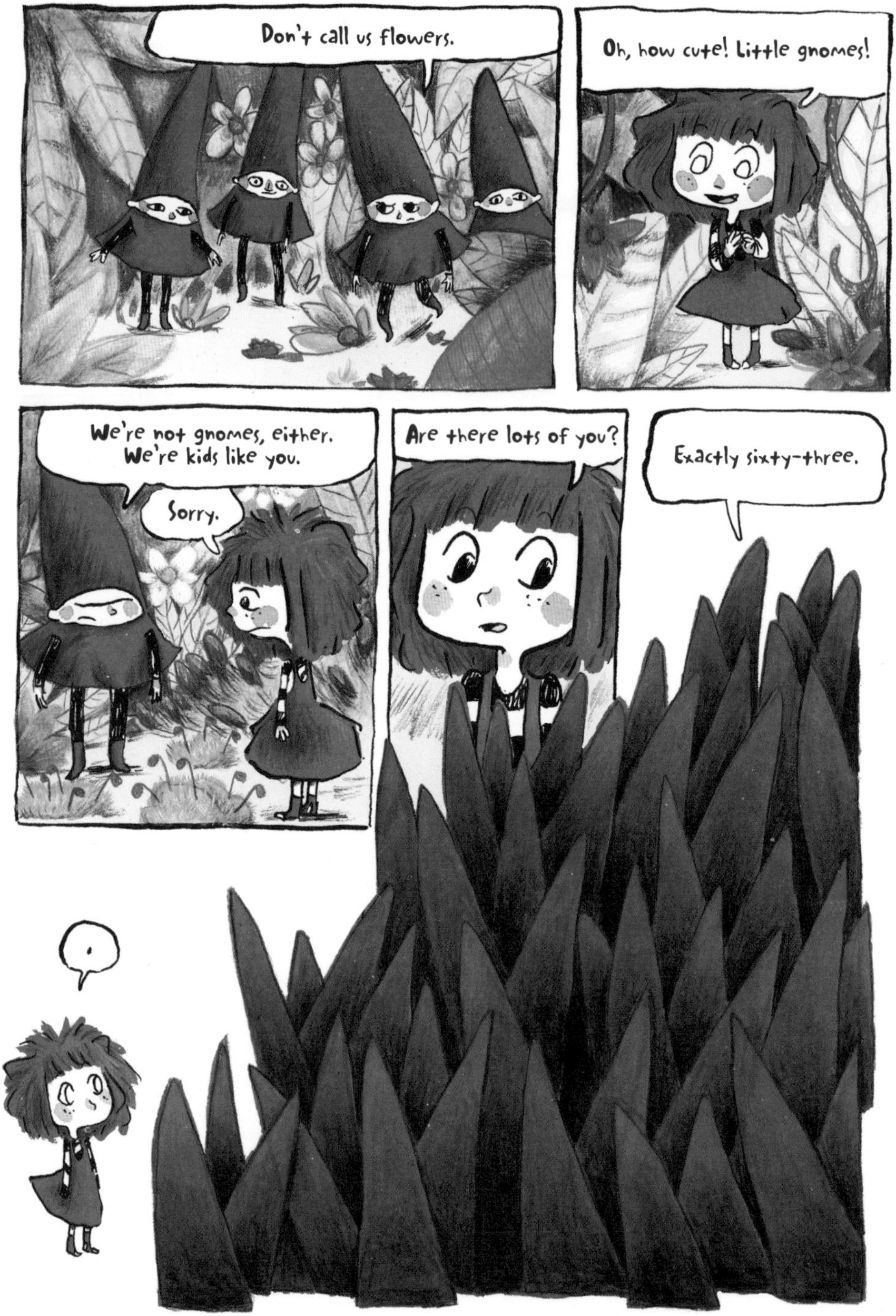

Don't call us flowers.
Oh, how cute! Little gnomes!
We're not gnomes, either. We're kids like you.
Sorry.
Are there lots of you?
Exactly sixty-three.

It's just gorgeous!

Thanks.

Each of us has a special task.

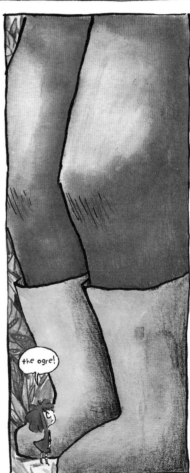

the ogre!

What a paradise!

But aren't you afraid of . . .

29

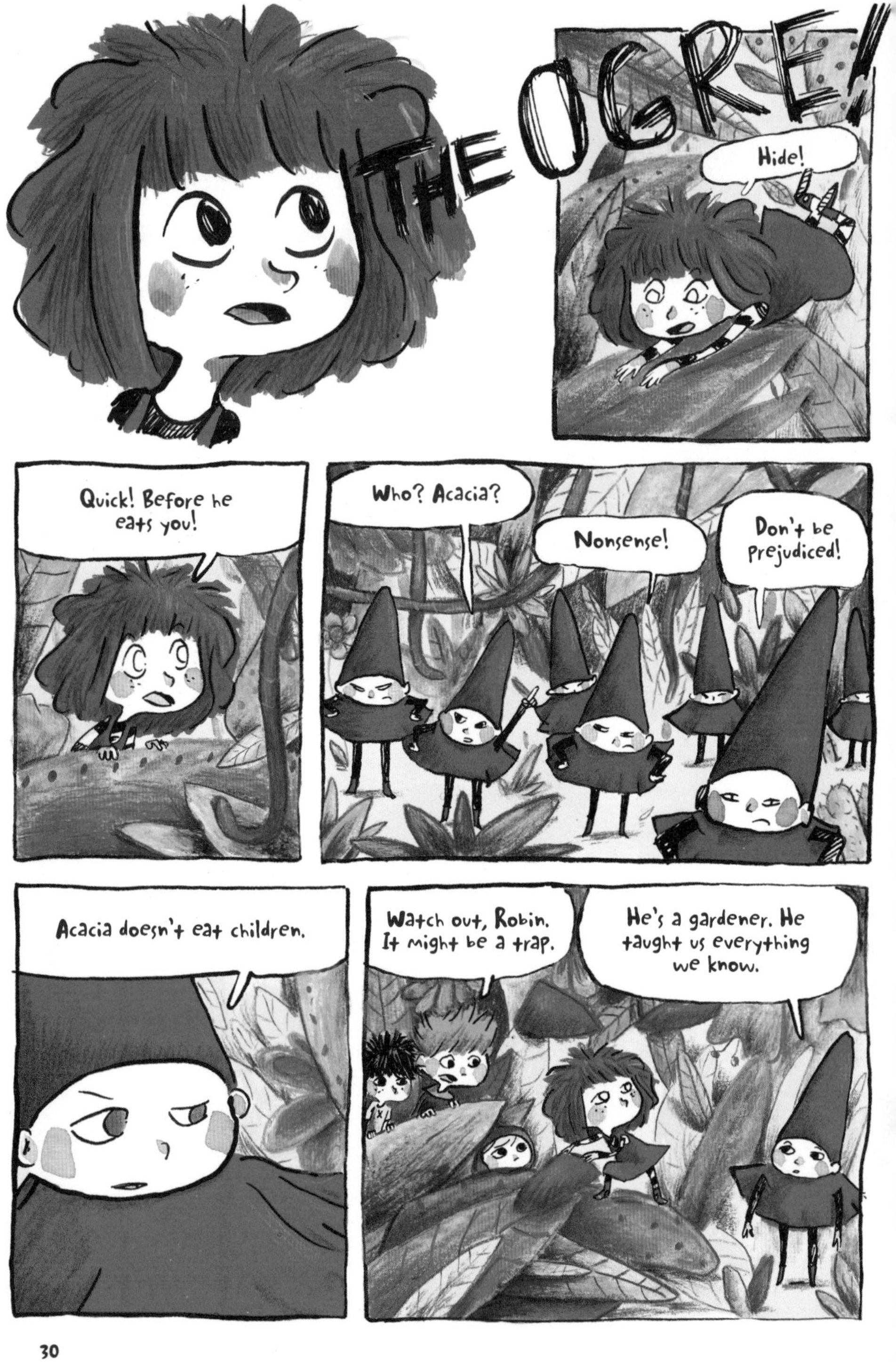
THE OGRE!
Hide!
Quick! Before he eats you!
Who? Acacia?
Nonsense!
Don't be prejudiced!
Acacia doesn't eat children.
Watch out, Robin. It might be a trap.
He's a gardener. He taught us everything we know.

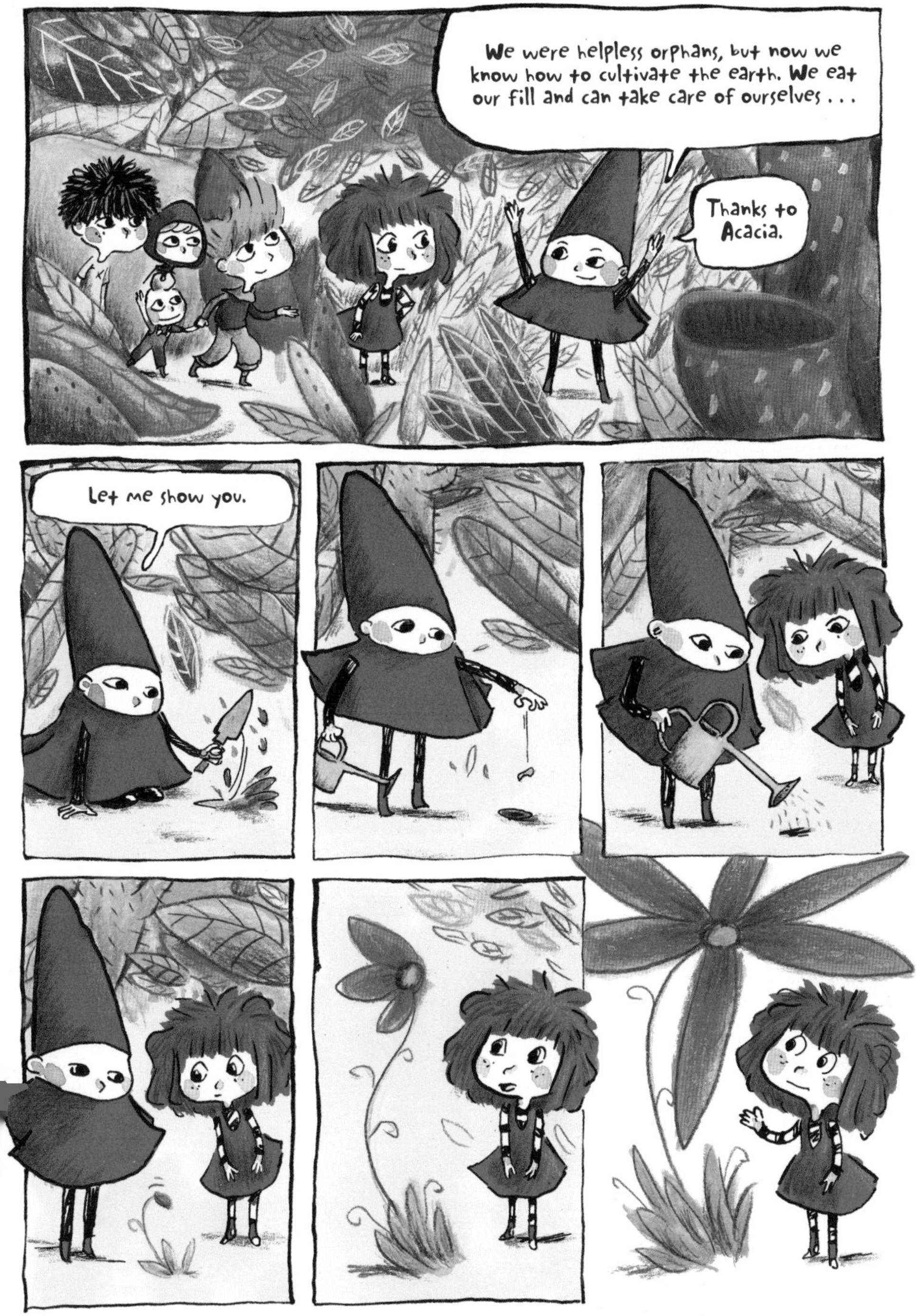
We were helpless orphans, but now we know how to cultivate the earth. We eat our fill and can take care of ourselves . . .
Thanks to Acacia.
Let me show you.

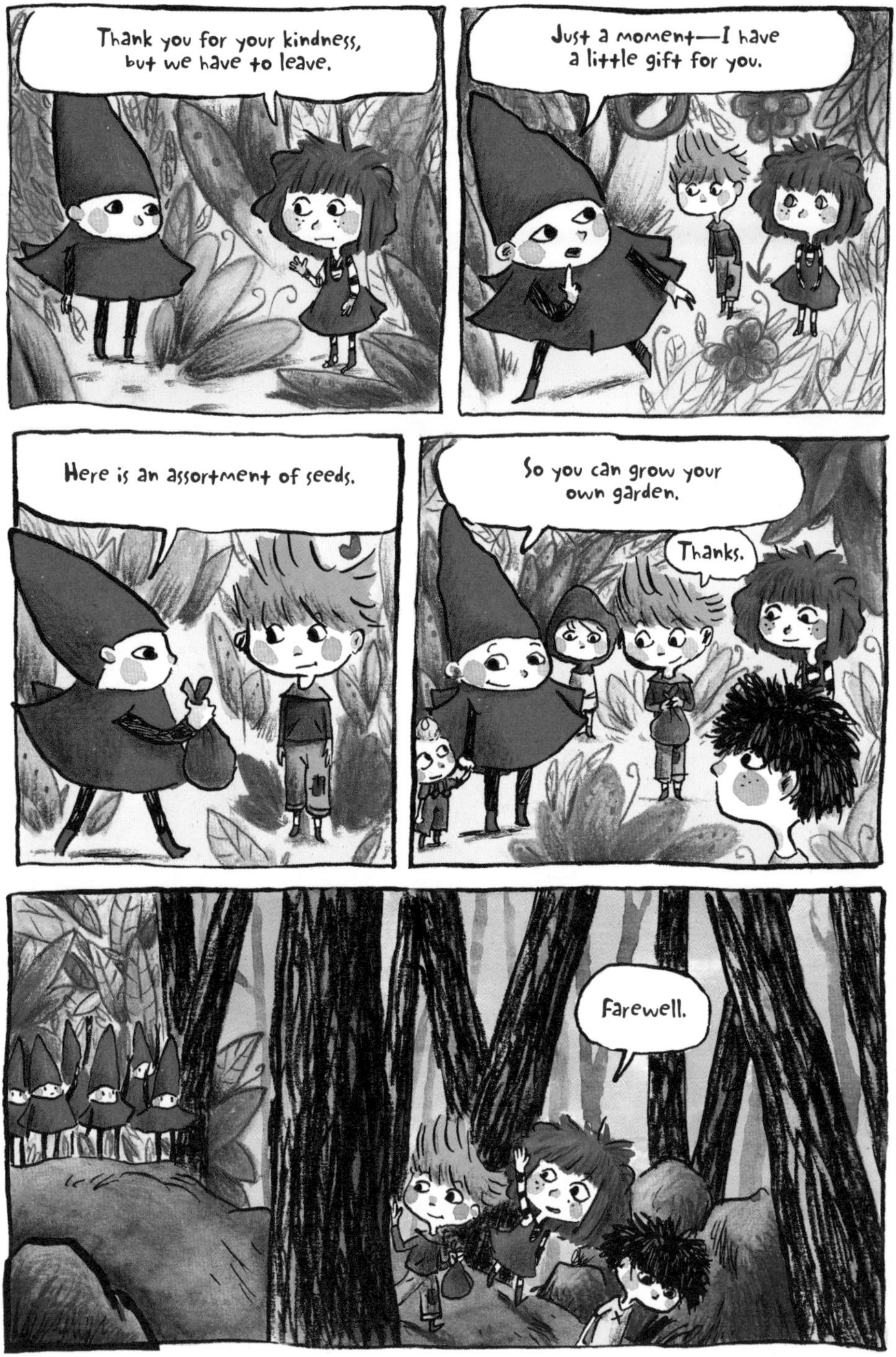
Thank you for your kindness, but we have to leave.
Just a moment—I have a little gift for you.
Here is an assortment of seeds.
So you can grow your own garden.
Thanks.
Farewell.

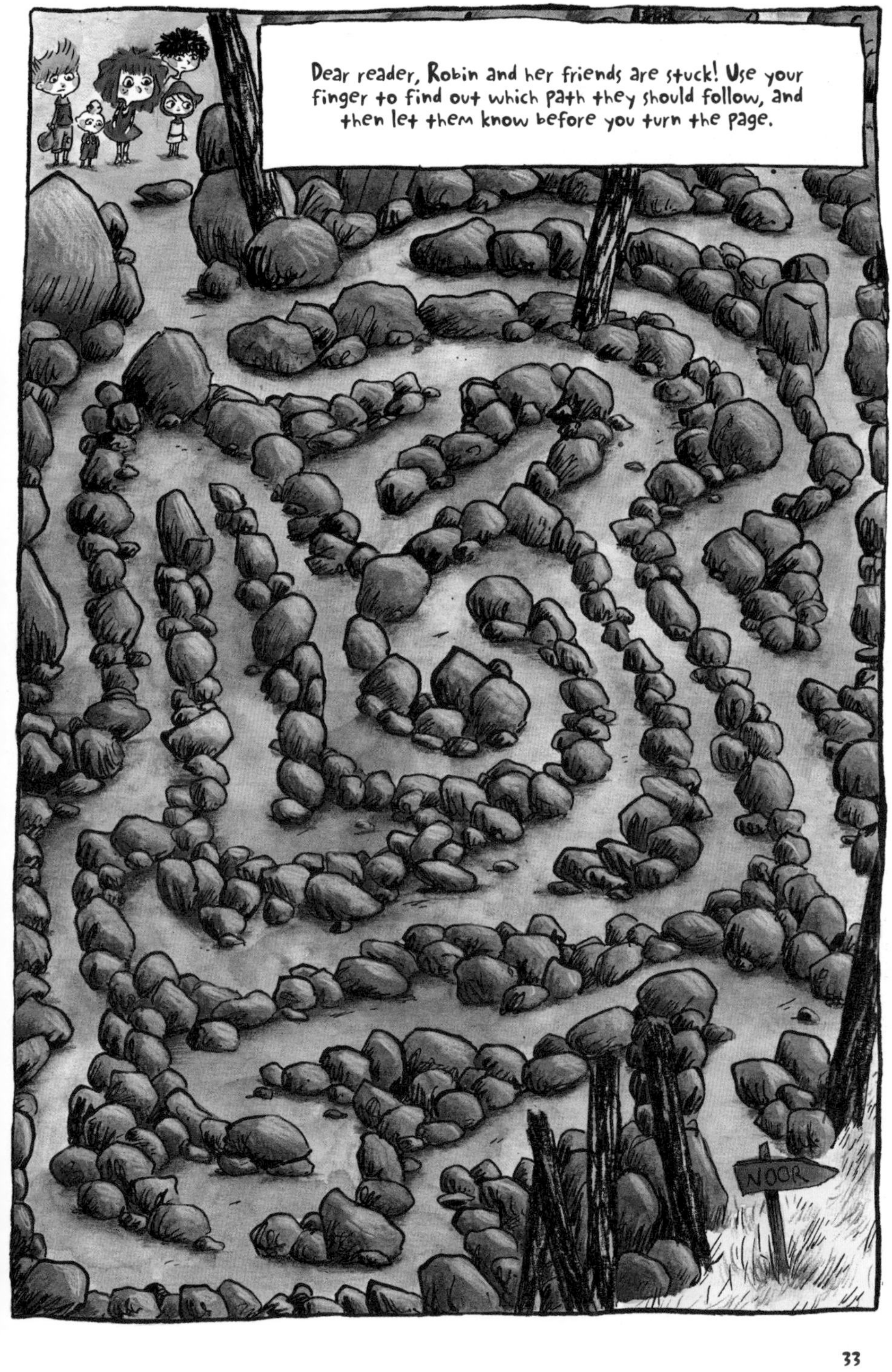
Dear reader, Robin and her friends are stuck! Use your finger to find out which path they should follow, and then let them know before you turn the page.
NOOR

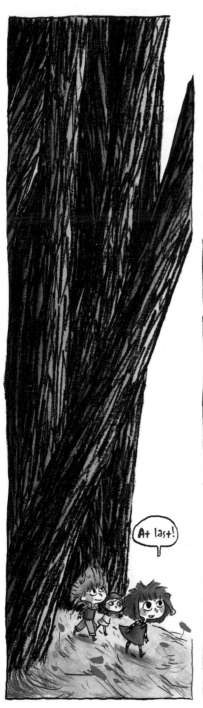

Hurry up! We don't want to miss anything.

Doesn't she ever get tired?

At last!

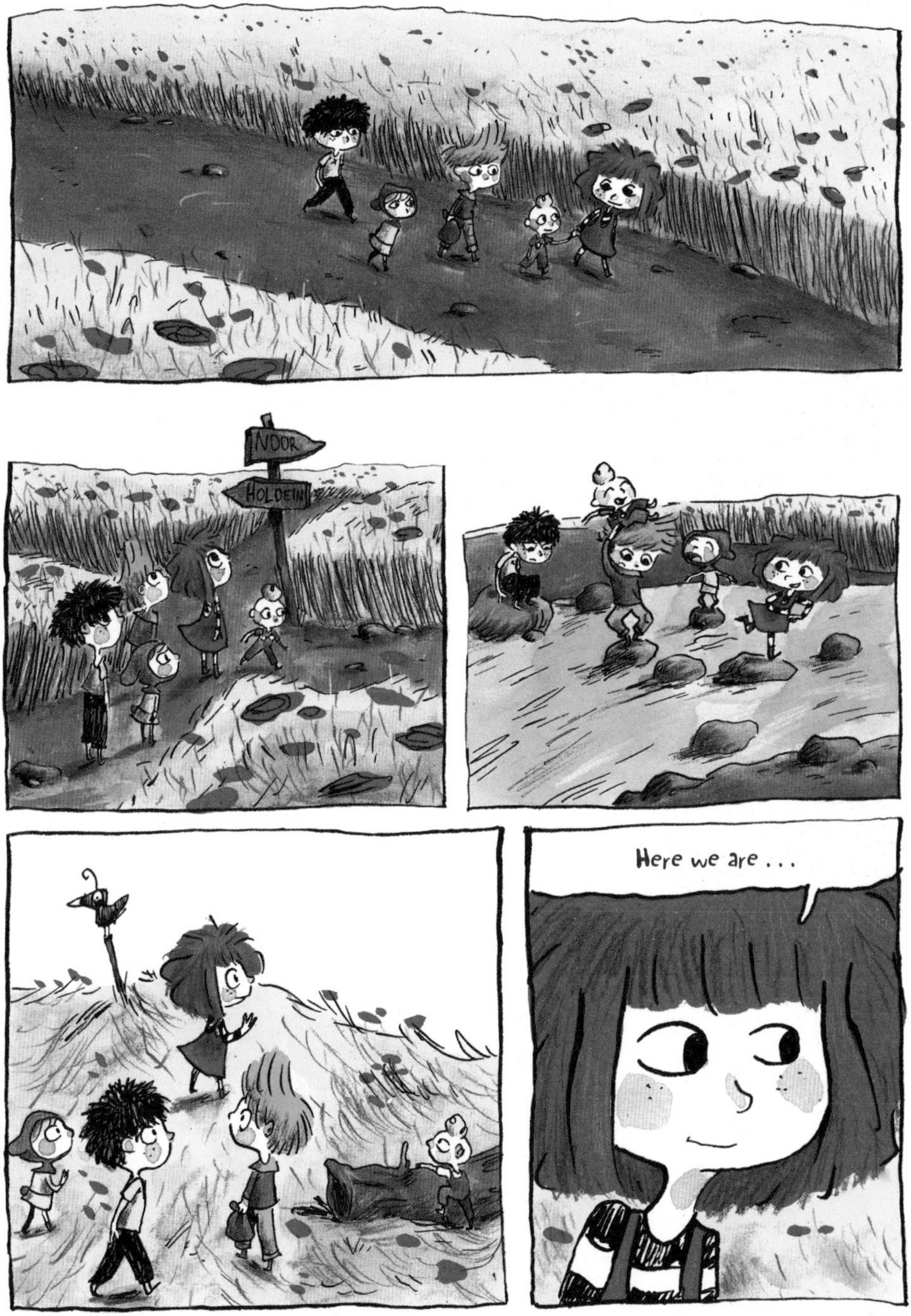
NOOR
HOLDEIN
Here we are . . .

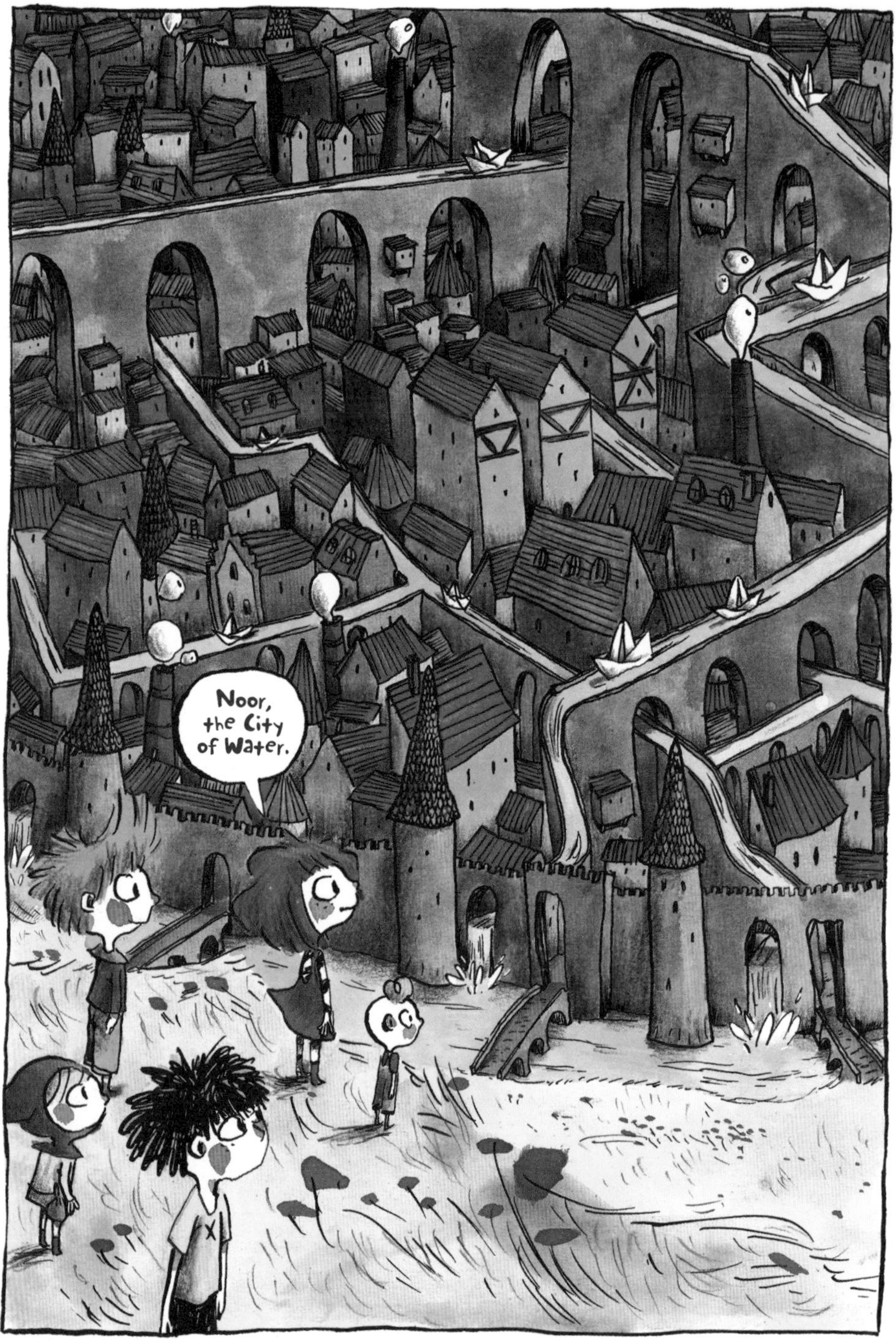
Noor, the City of Water.

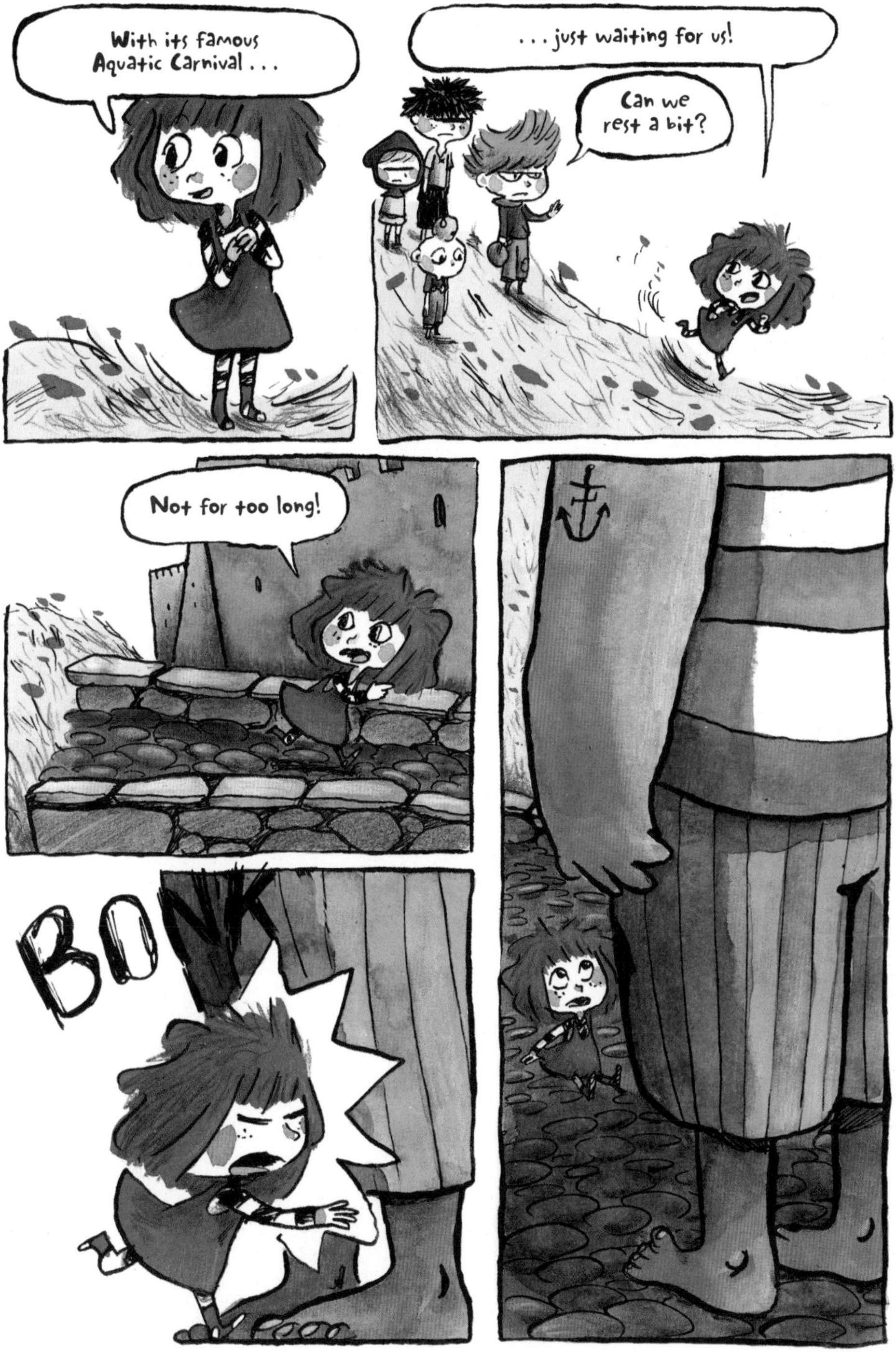
With its famous Aquatic Carnival . . .
. . . just waiting for us!
Can we rest a bit?
Not for too long!
BONK

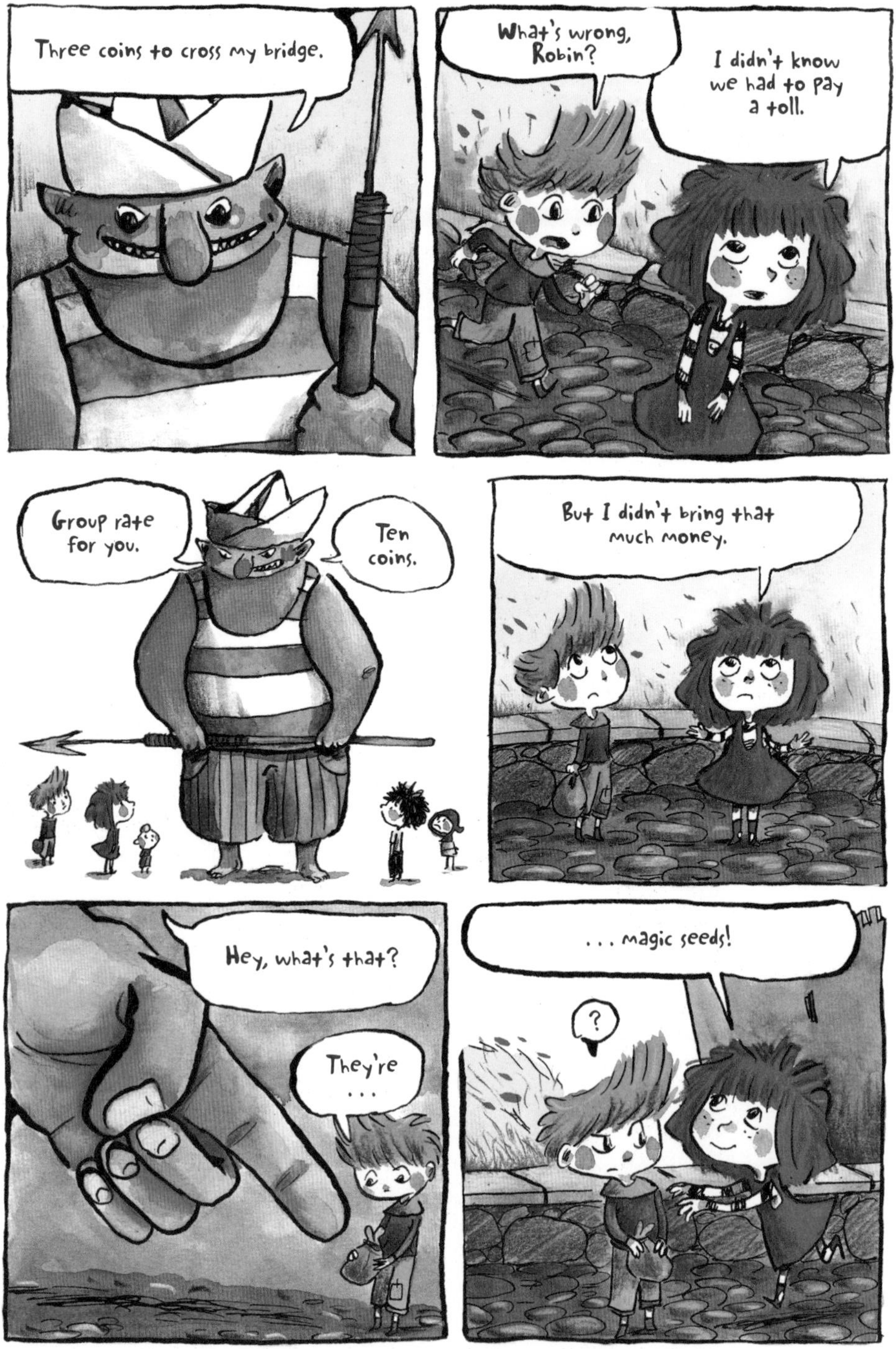
Three coins to cross my bridge.
What's wrong, Robin?
I didn't know we had to pay a toll.
Group rate for you.
Ten coins.
But I didn't bring that much money.
Hey, what's that?
They're . . .
?
. . . magic seeds!

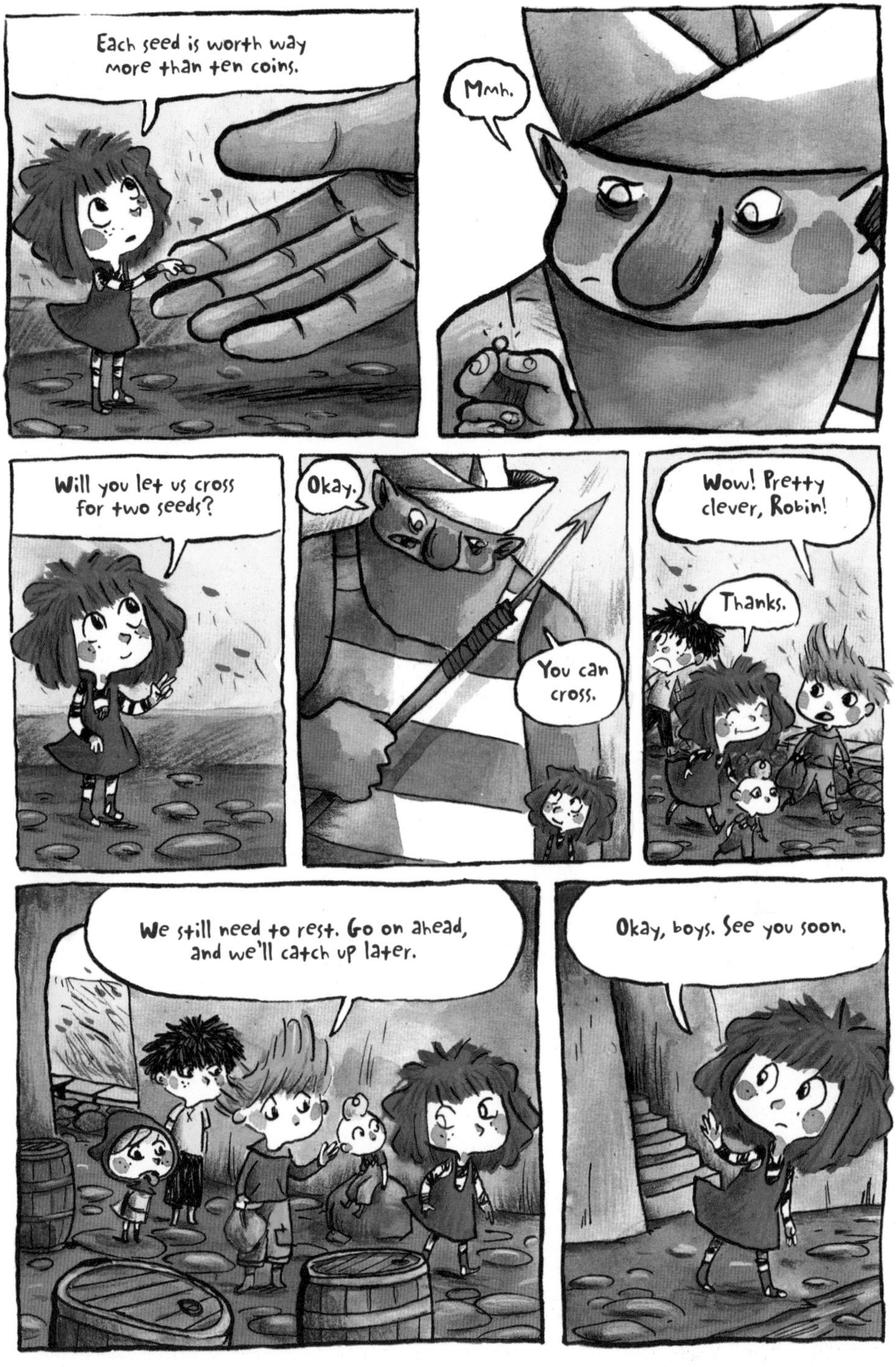
Each seed is worth way more than ten coins.
Mmh.
Will you let us cross for two seeds?
Okay.
You can cross.
Wow! Pretty clever, Robin!
Thanks.
We still need to rest. Go on ahead, and we'll catch up later.
Okay, boys. See you soon.

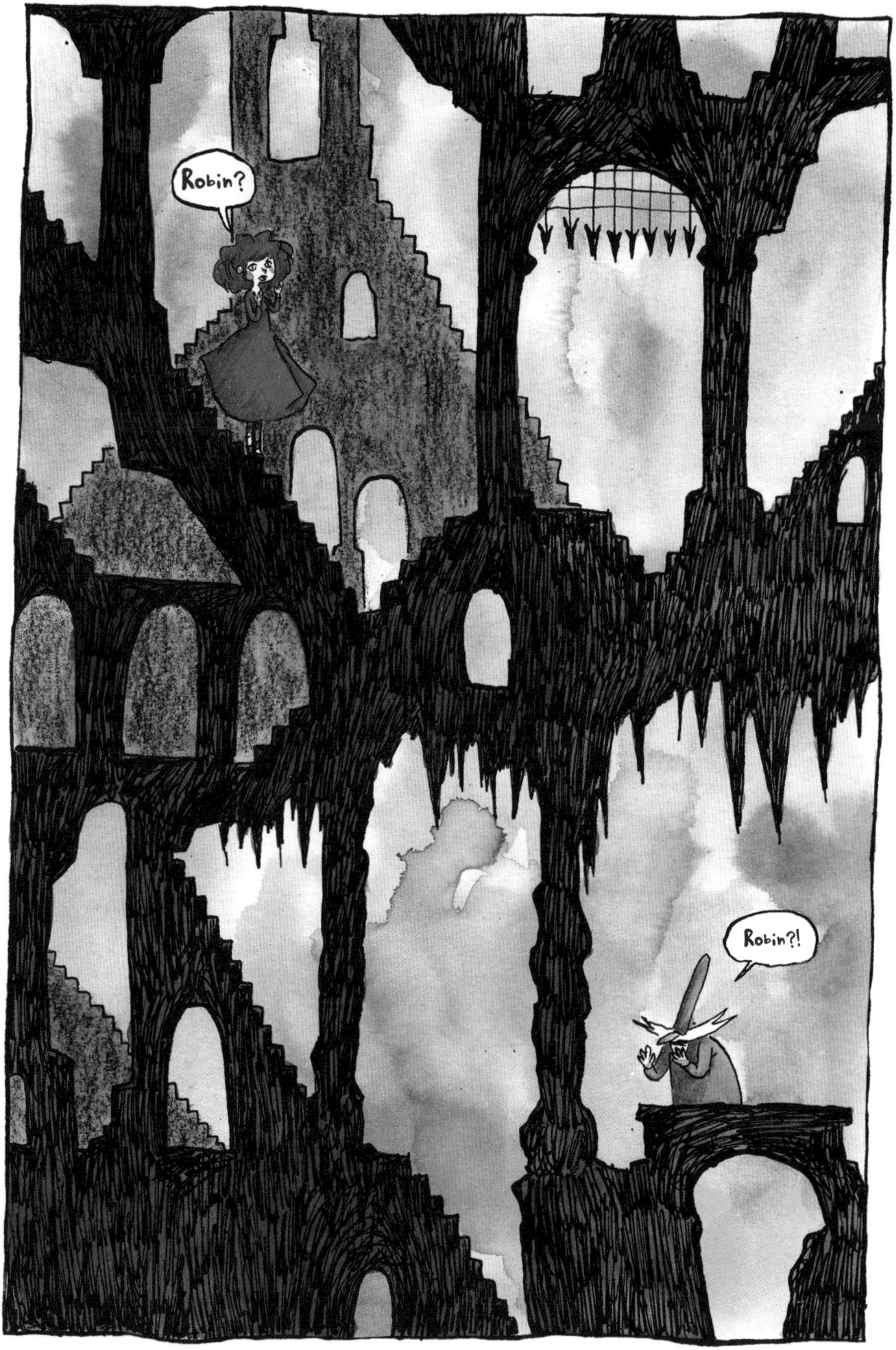
Robin?
Robin?!

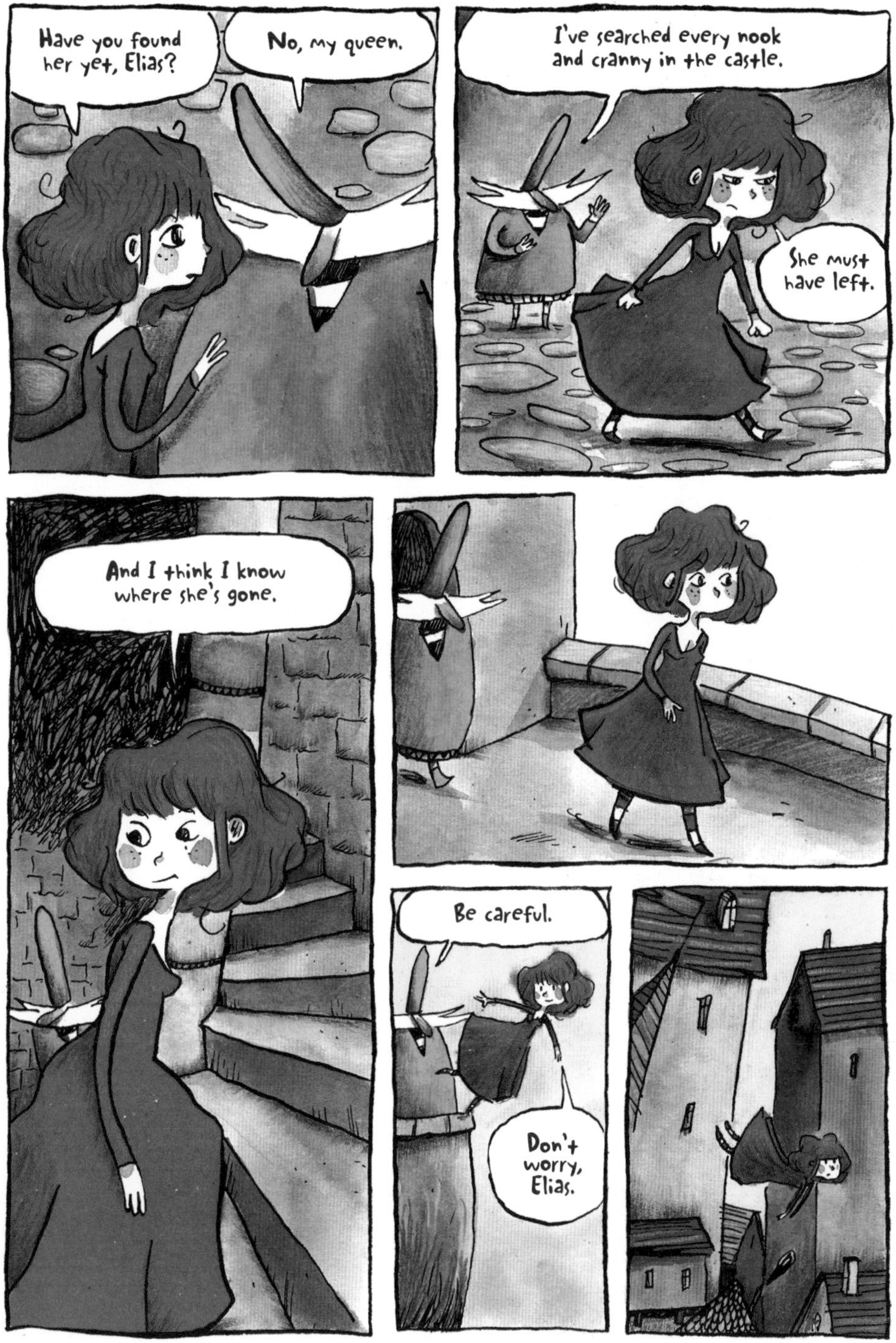
Have you found her yet, Elias?
No, my queen.
I've searched every nook and cranny in the castle.
She must have left.
And I think I know where she's gone.
Be careful.
Don't worry, Elias.

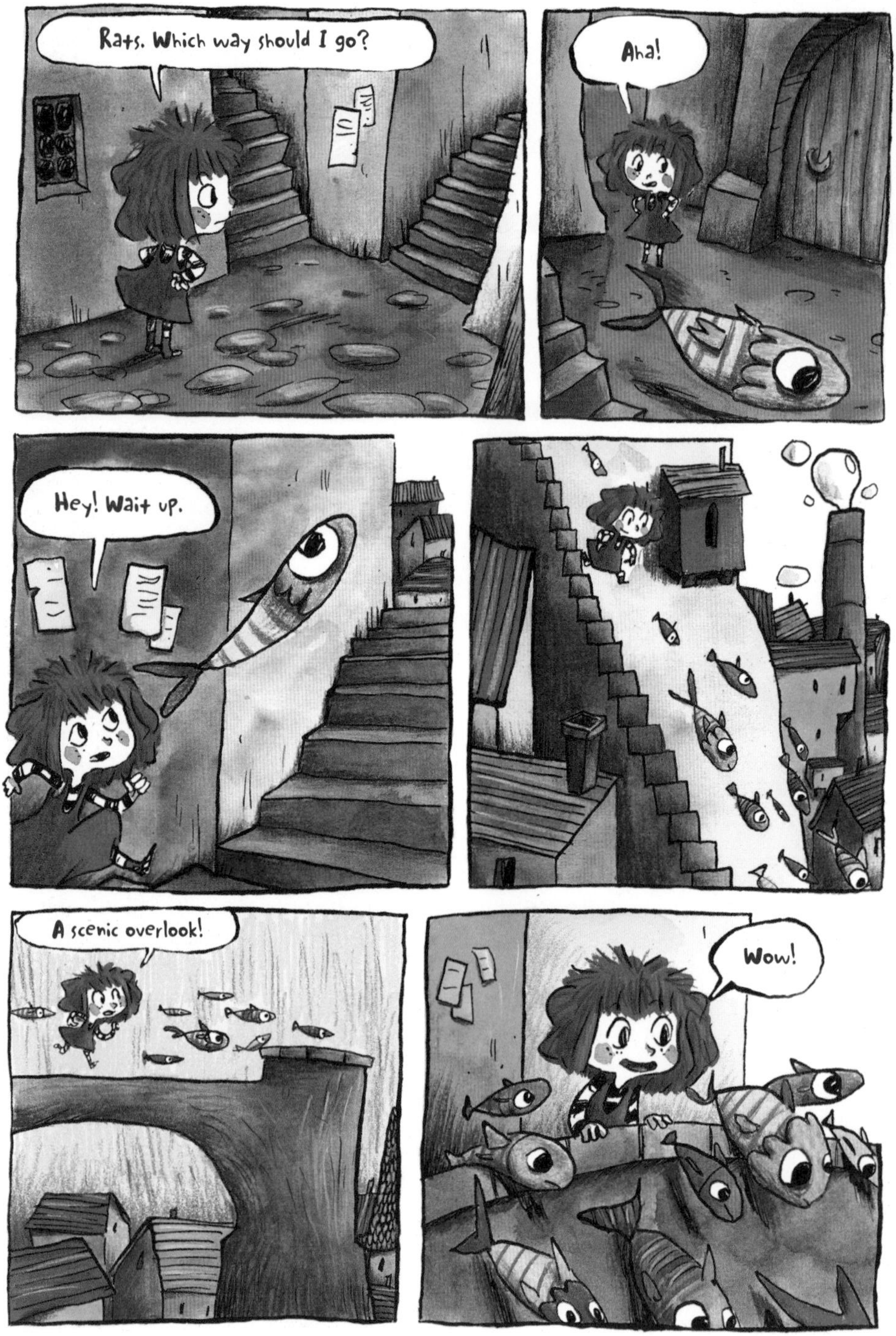

Rats. Which way should I go?
Aha!
Hey! Wait up.
A scenic overlook!
Wow!

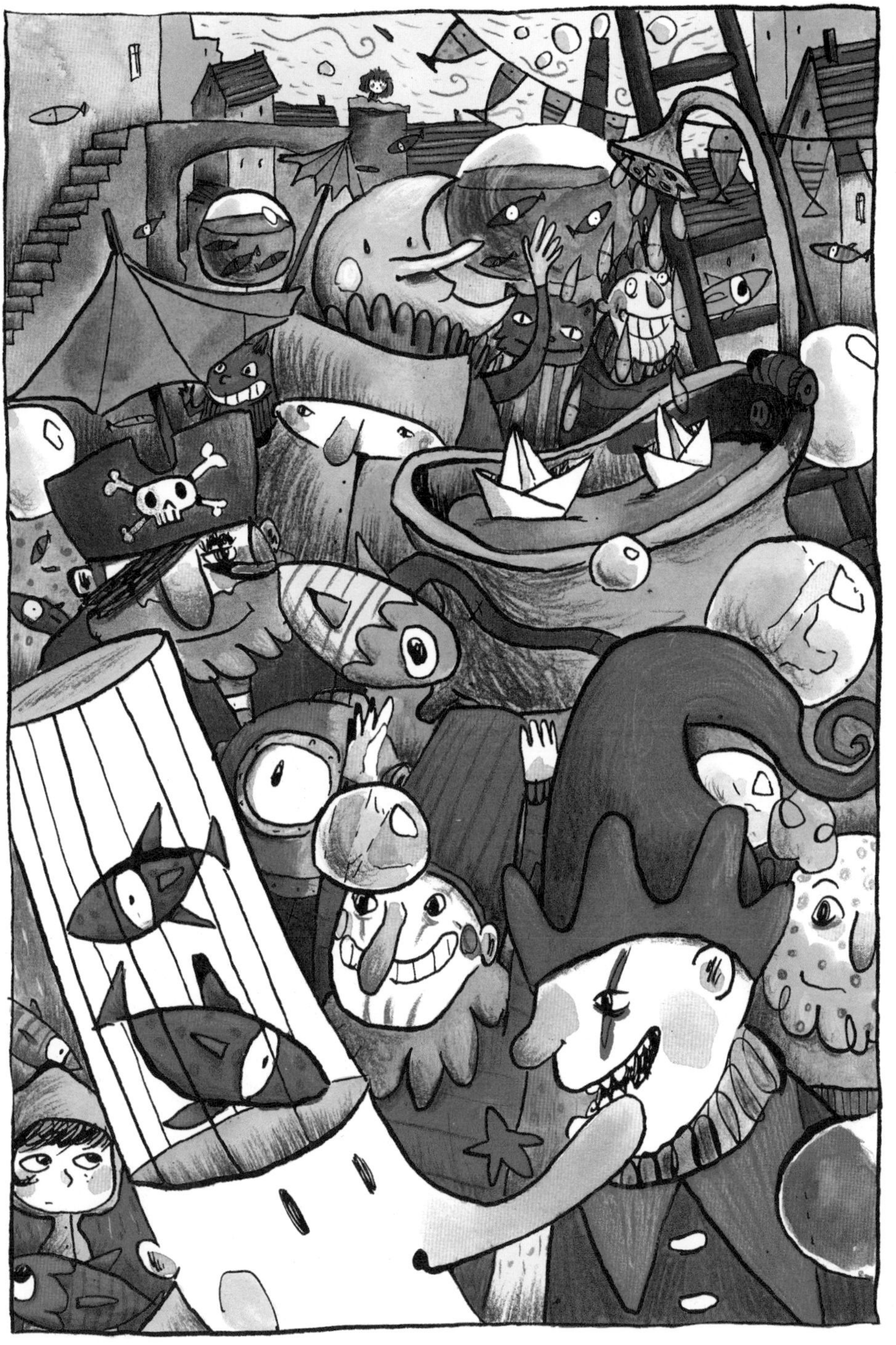

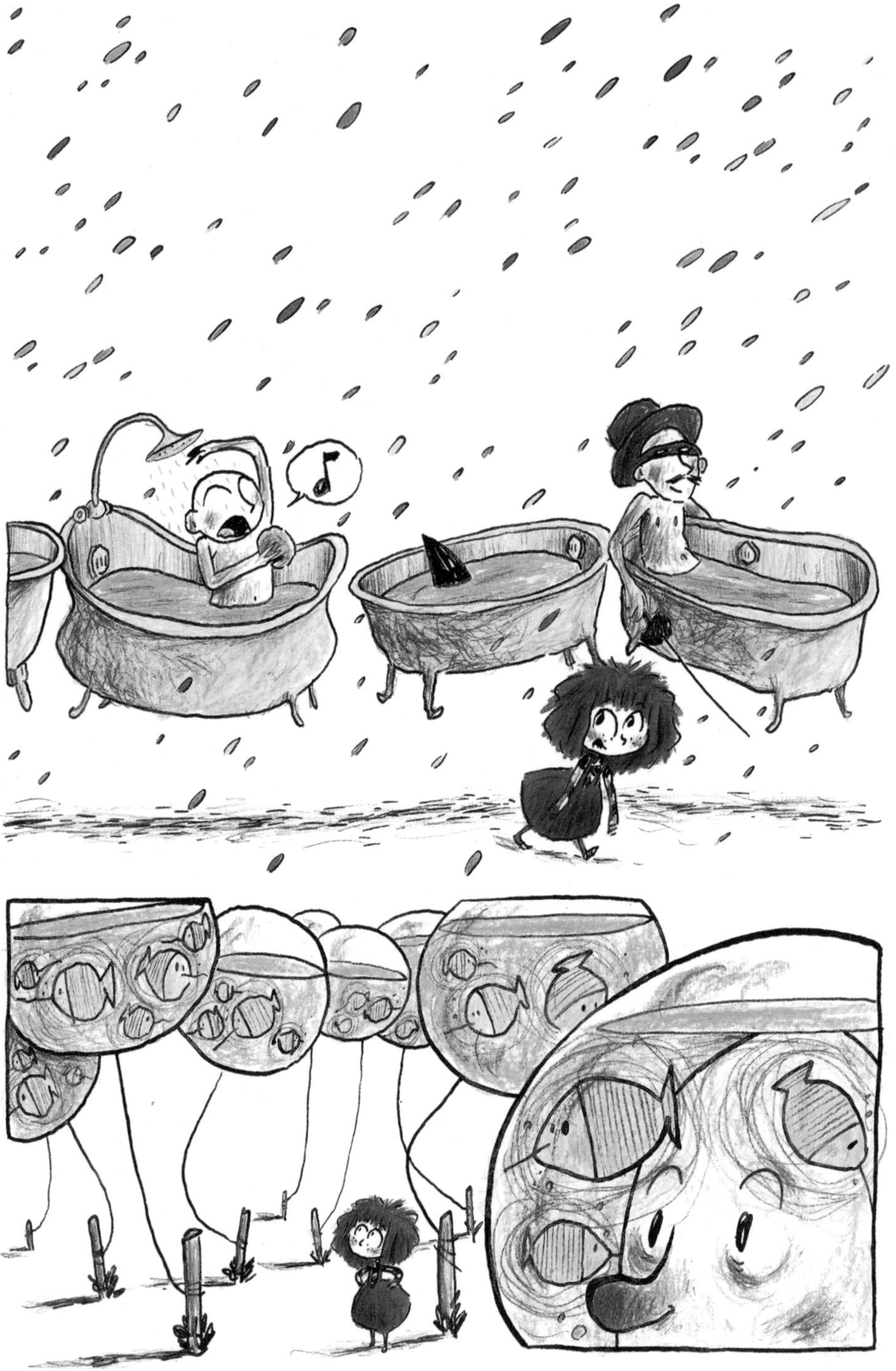

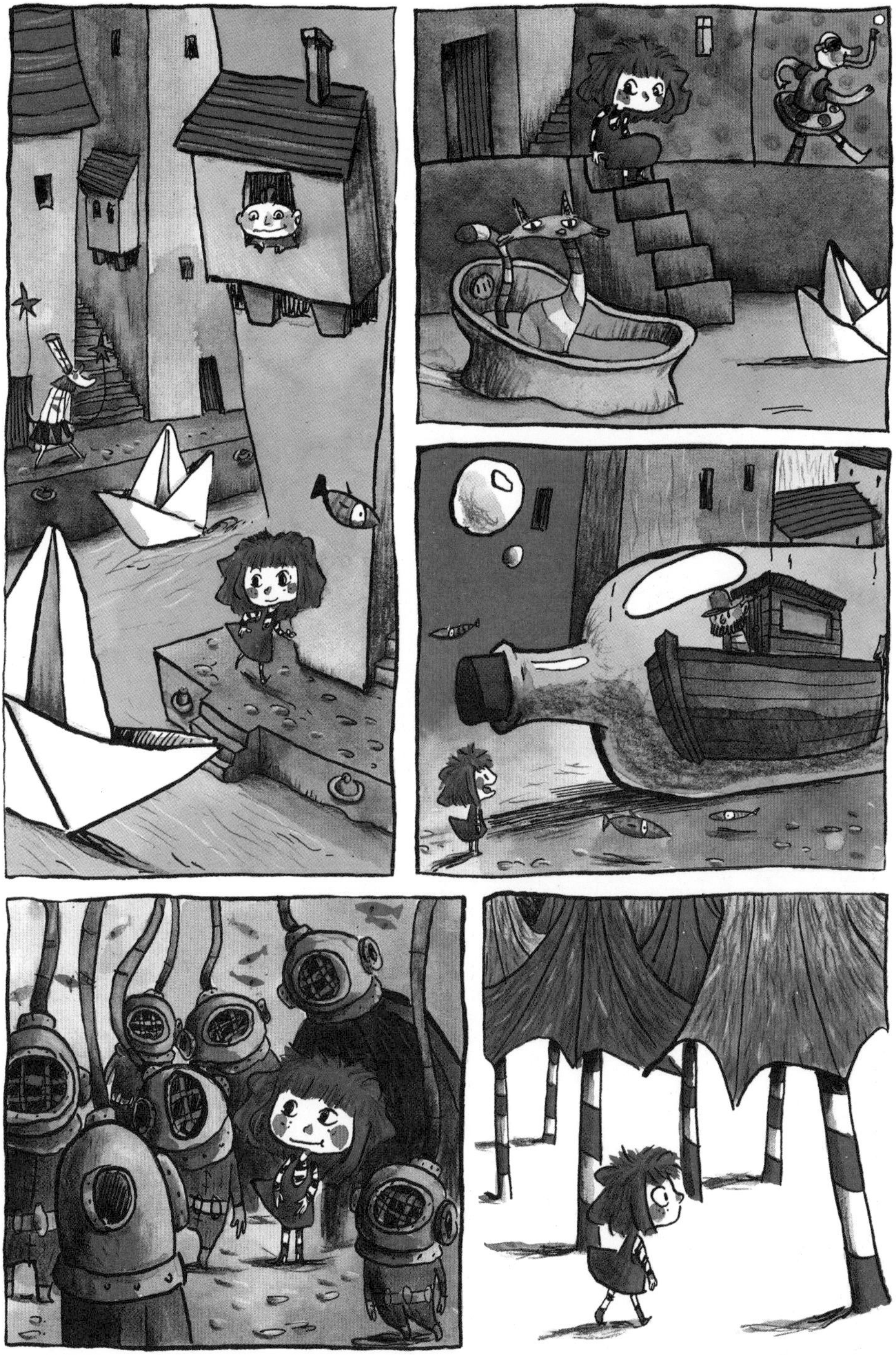

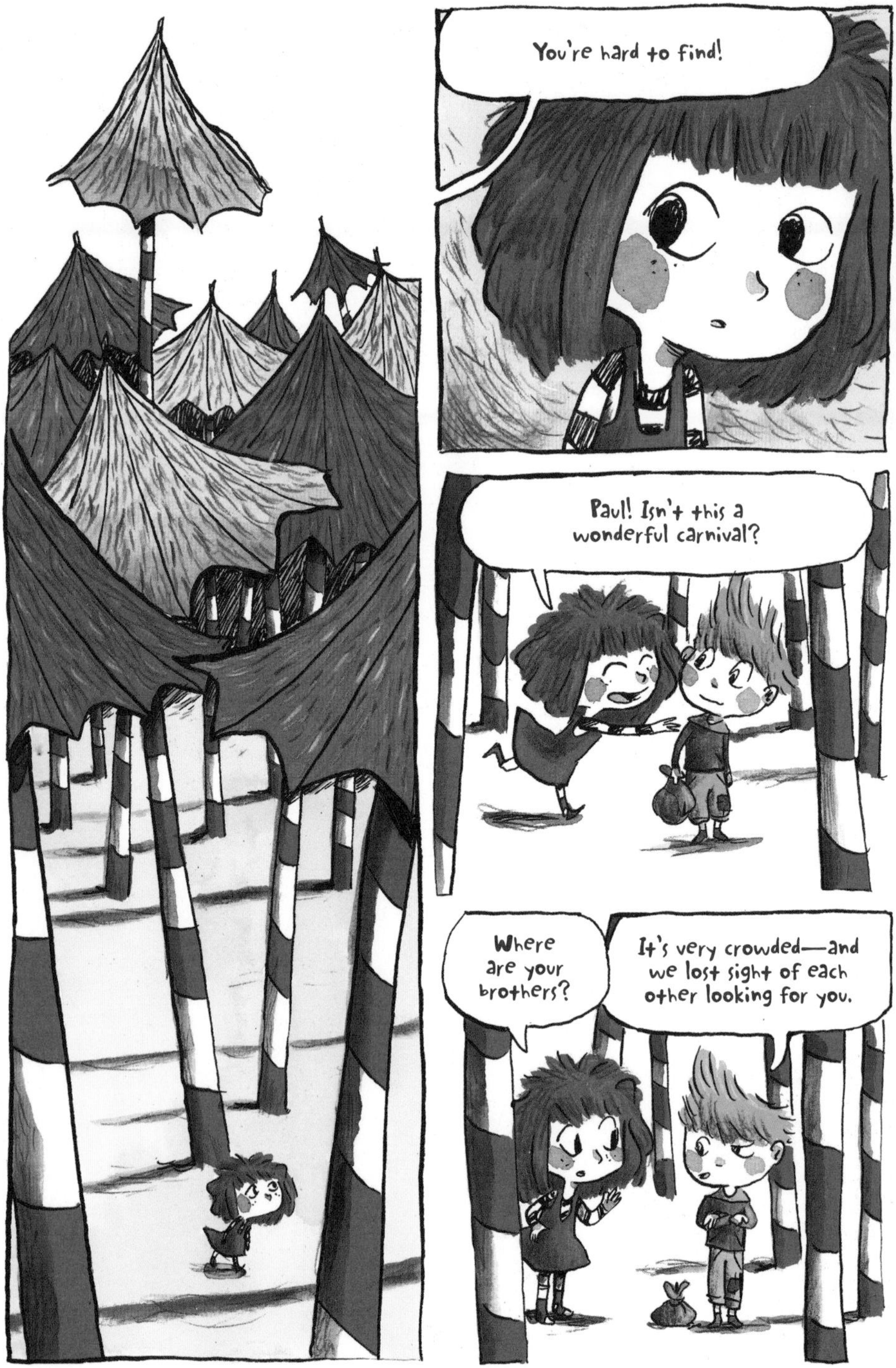
You're hard to find!
Paul! Isn't this a wonderful carnival?
Where are your brothers?
It's very crowded—and we lost sight of each other looking for you.

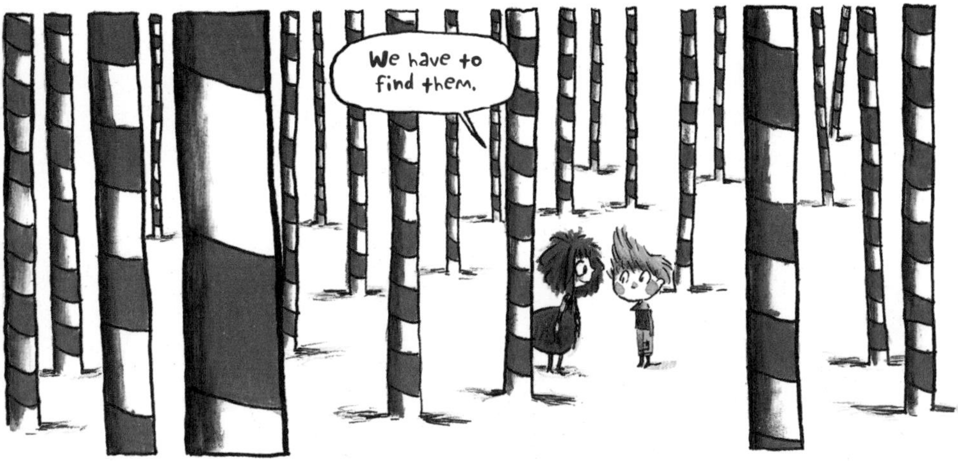
We have to find them.

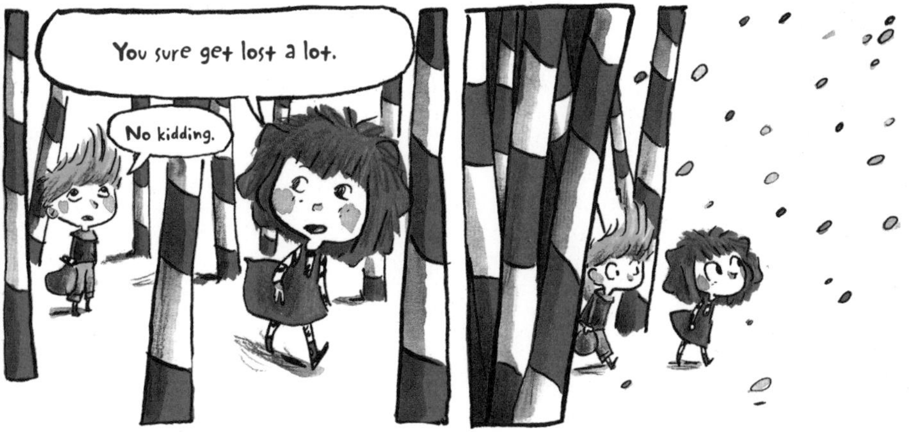
You sure get lost a lot.
No kidding.

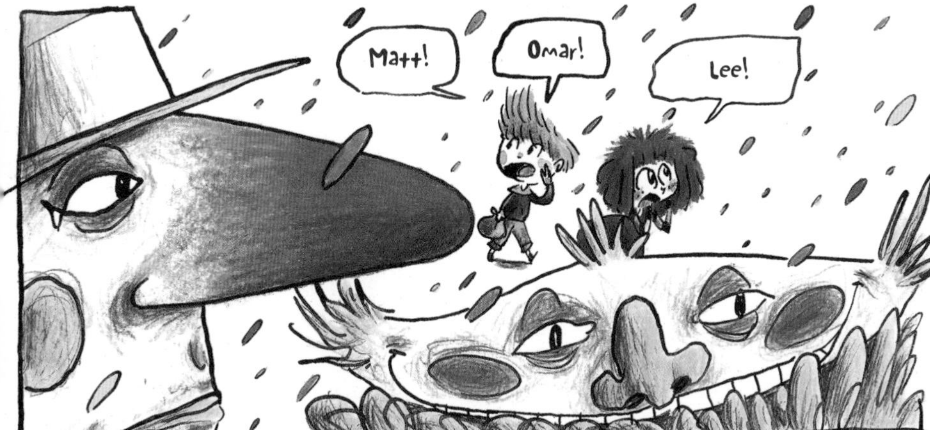
Matt!
Omar!
Lee!

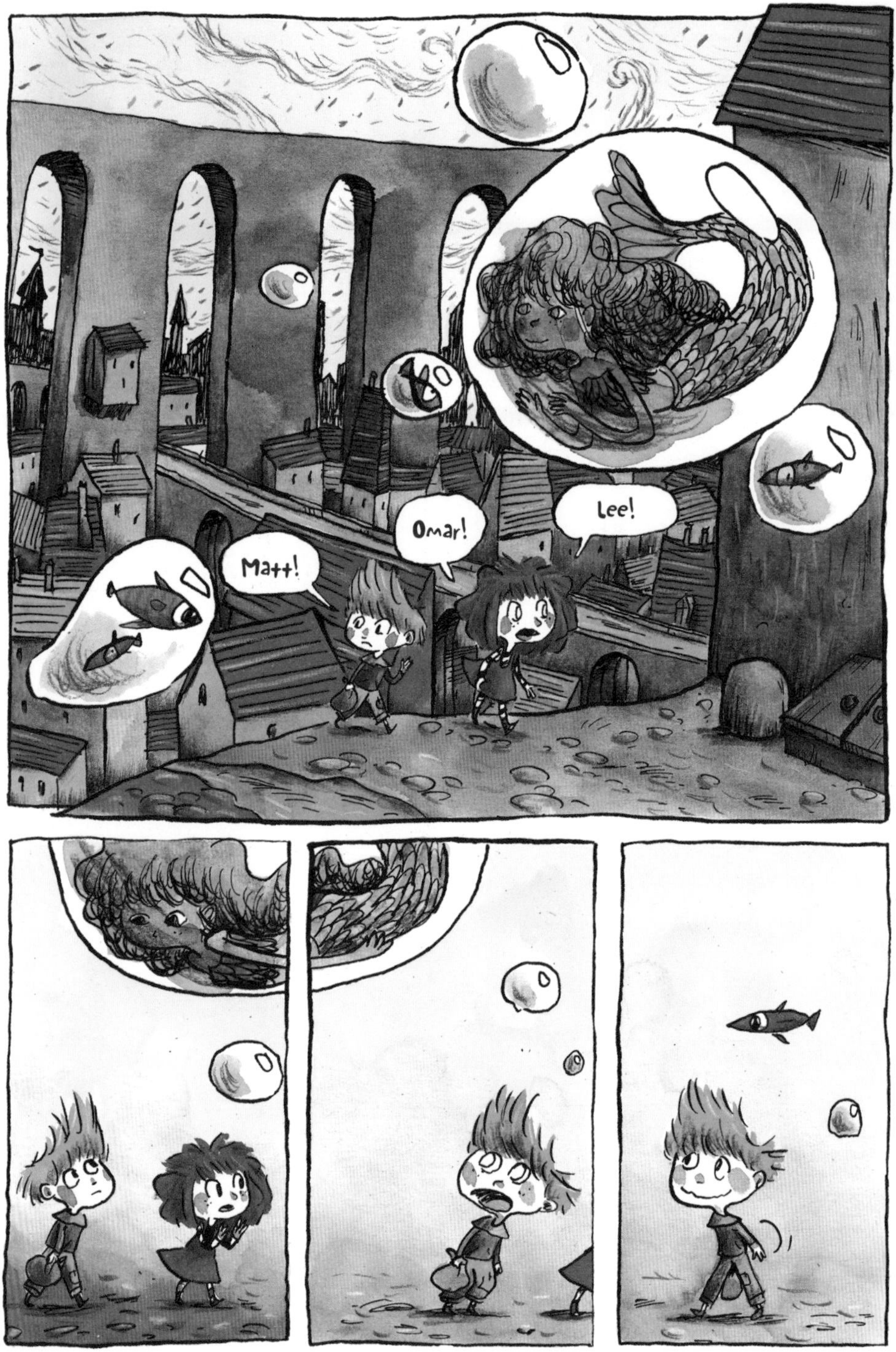
Matt!
Omar!
Lee!

I don't see them anywhere. How about you?

Paul?

What are you doing?

I've never seen anything so beautiful.

It's just a fish.

Come on—we have to find your brothers.

Mmh.

Hey, Paul—snap out of it!

Dear reader, Paul is completely under the mermaid's spell. Help Robin set him free by turning the page and shouting his name as loudly as possible.

49

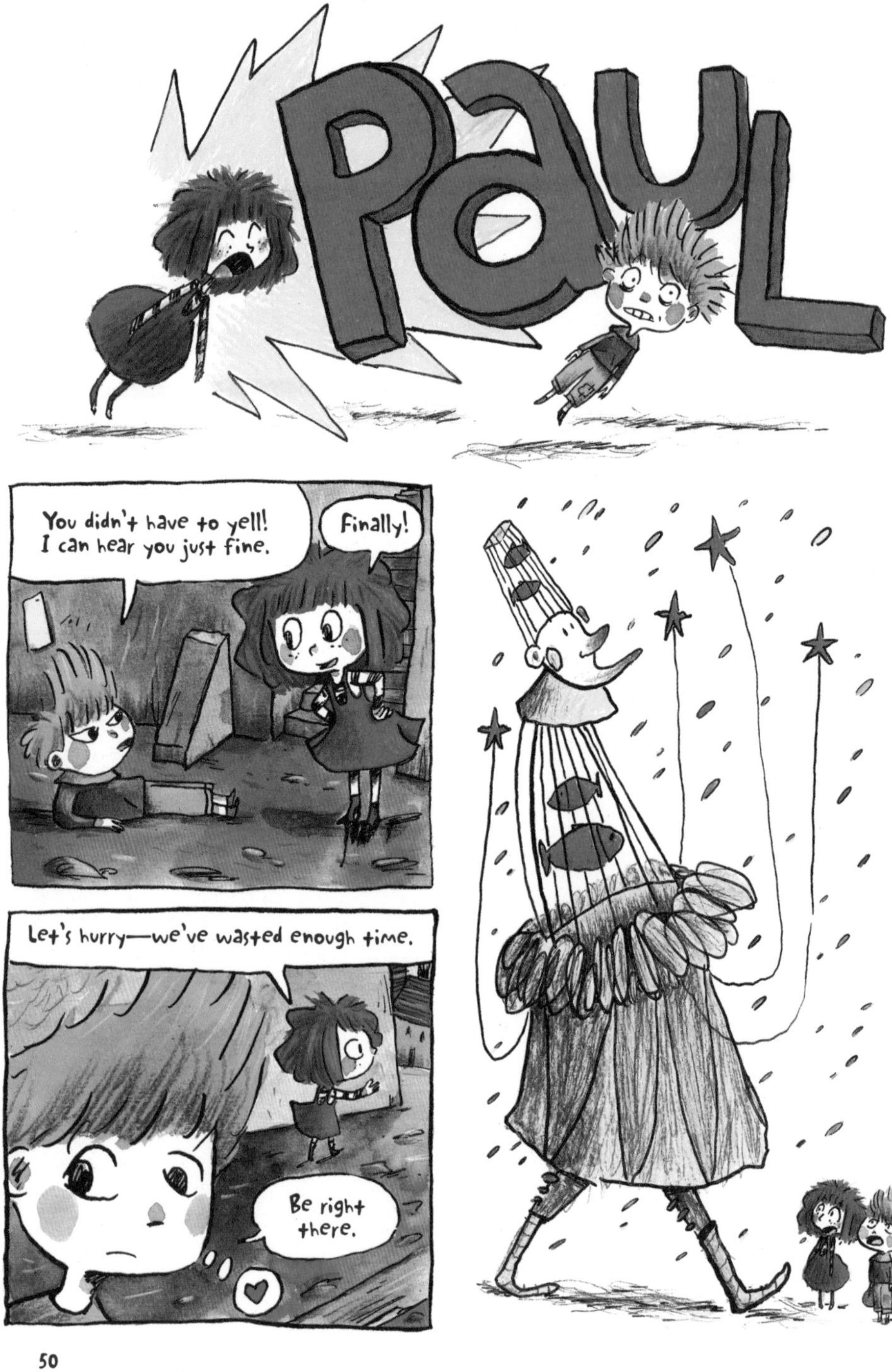
PAUL
You didn't have to yell! I can hear you just fine.
Finally!
Let's hurry—we've wasted enough time.
Be right there.

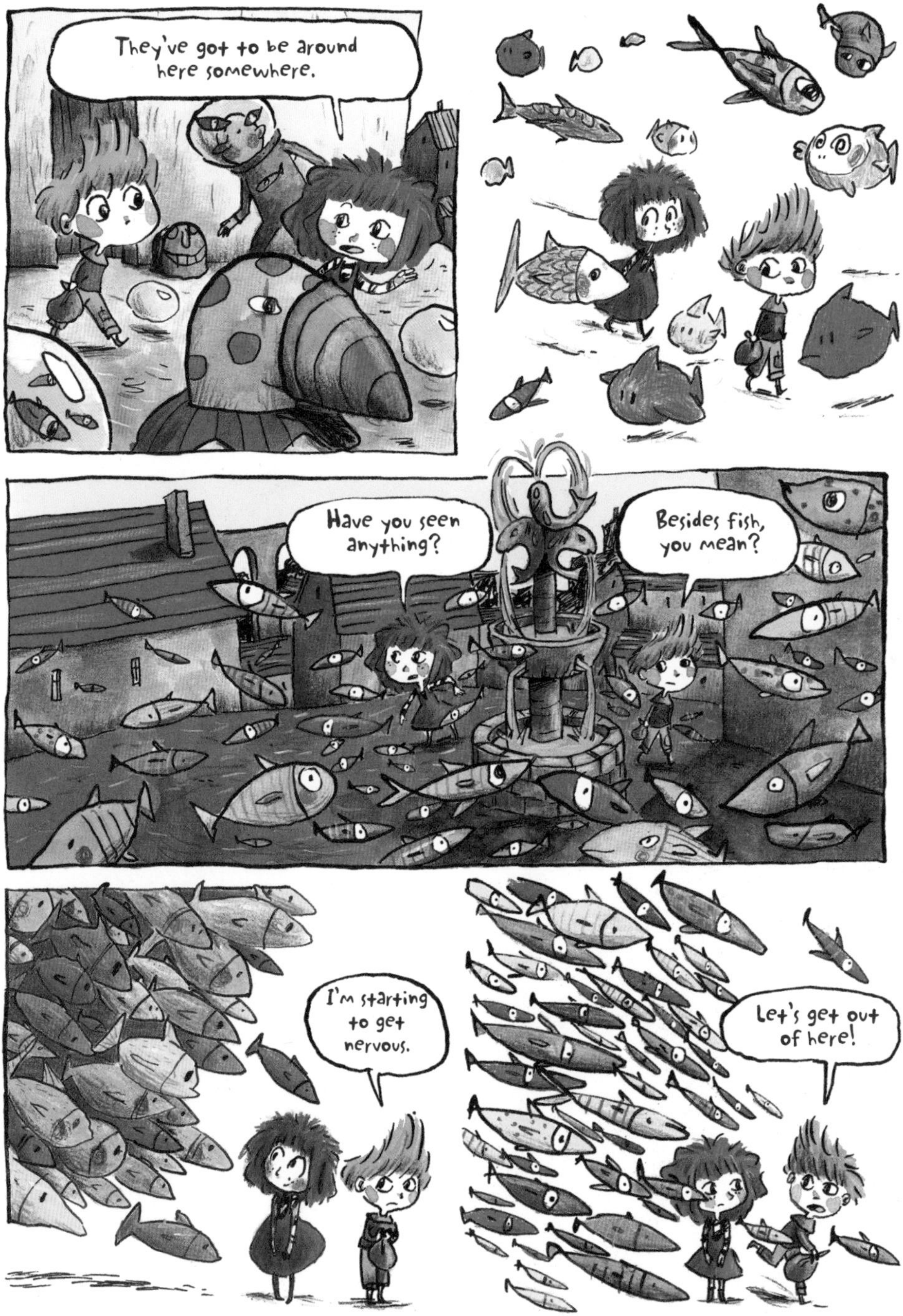
They've got to be around here somewhere.
Have you seen anything?
Besides fish, you mean?
I'm starting to get nervous.
Let's get out of here!

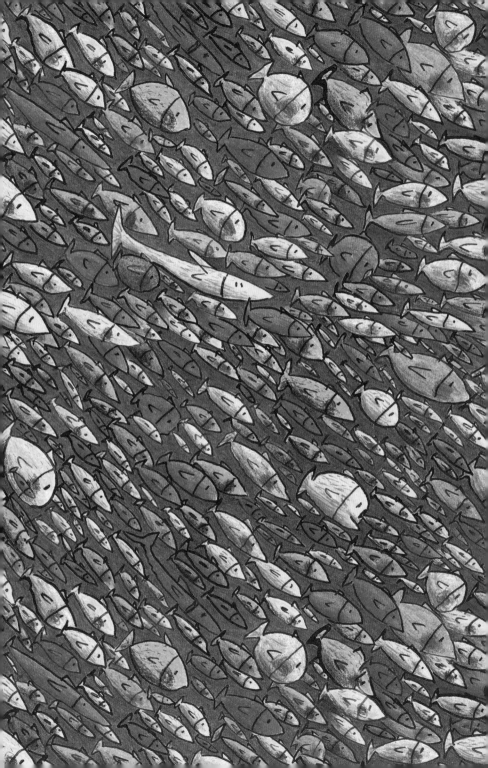

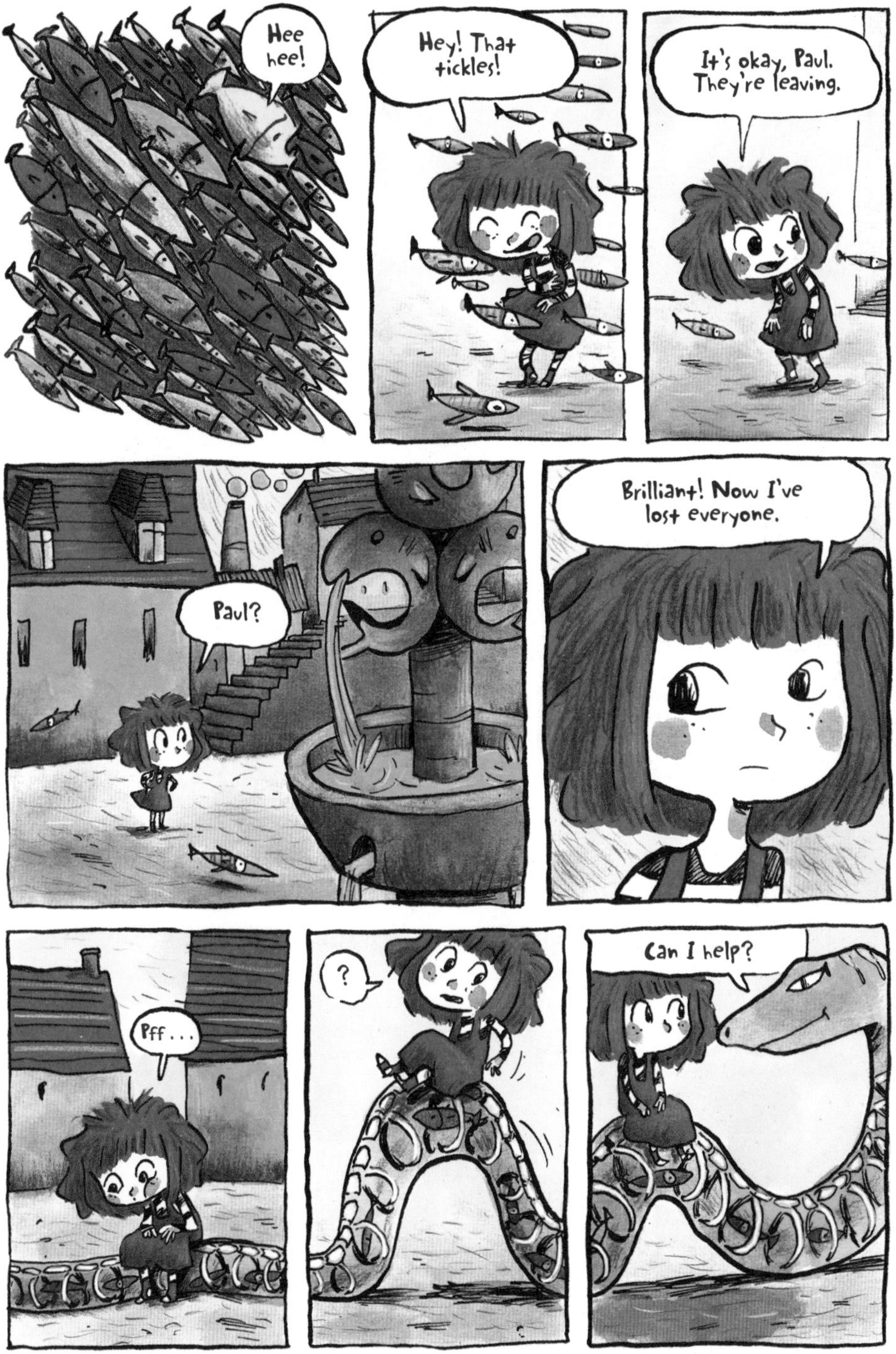
Hee hee!
Hey! That tickles!
It's okay, Paul. They're leaving.
Paul?
Brilliant! Now I've lost everyone.
Pff...
?
Can I help?

Dear reader, the queen has finally arrived in **Noor**. But she doesn't know where to go. Would you help her find the carnival? Go to panel 1. Each direction has a number. Pick a direction, and take her to the panel with that number. Keep going until she finds the carnival.

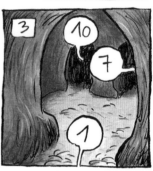

Mmh, this is no place for a queen.

What a lovely view of **Noor**! Unfortunately, there's no way down.

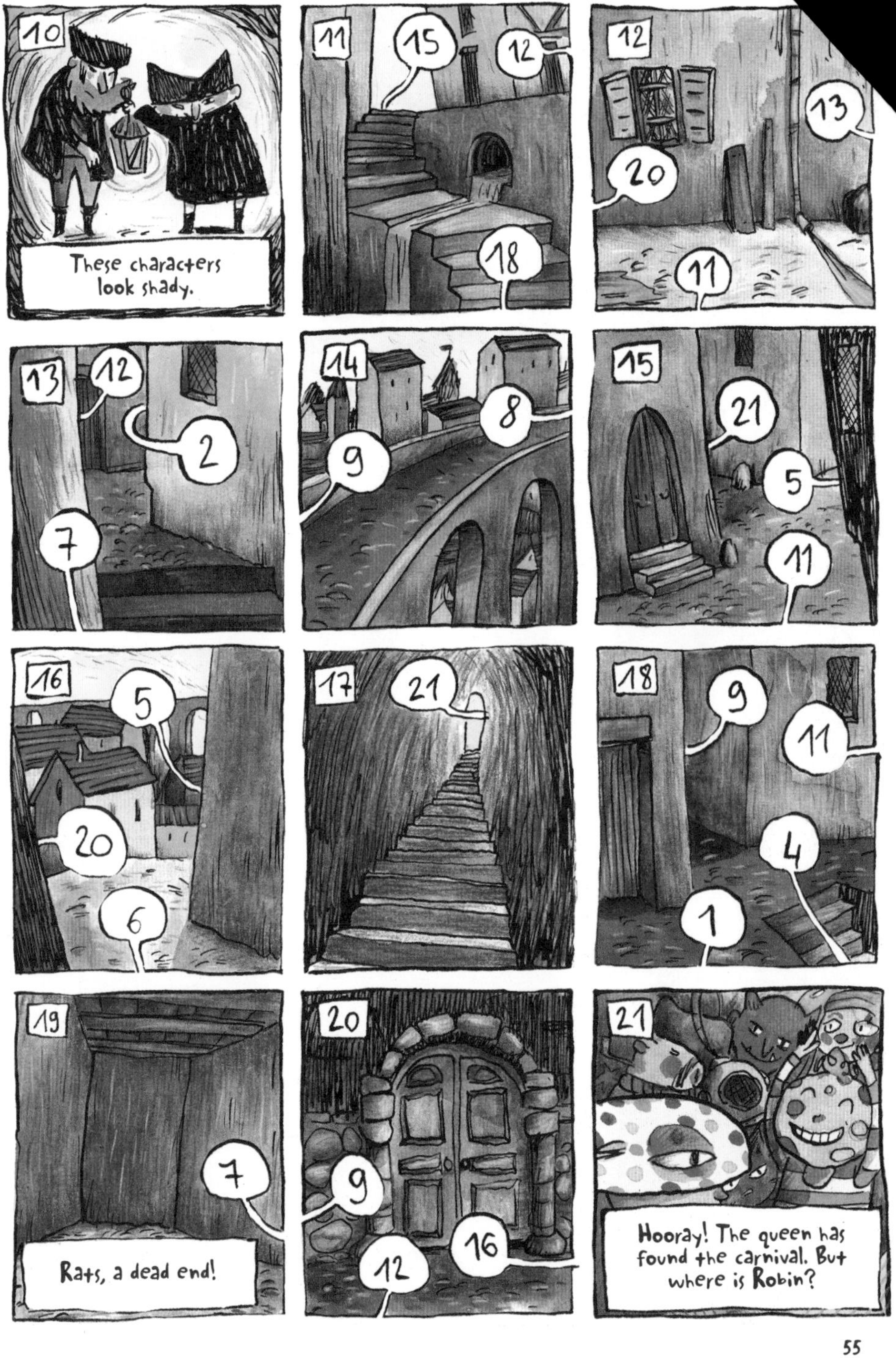
10
These characters look shady.
11
15
12
18
12
13
20
11
13
12
2
7
14
8
9
15
21
5
11
16
5
20
6
17
21
18
9
11
4
1
19
7
Rats, a dead end!
20
9
16
12
21
Hooray! The queen has found the carnival. But where is Robin?

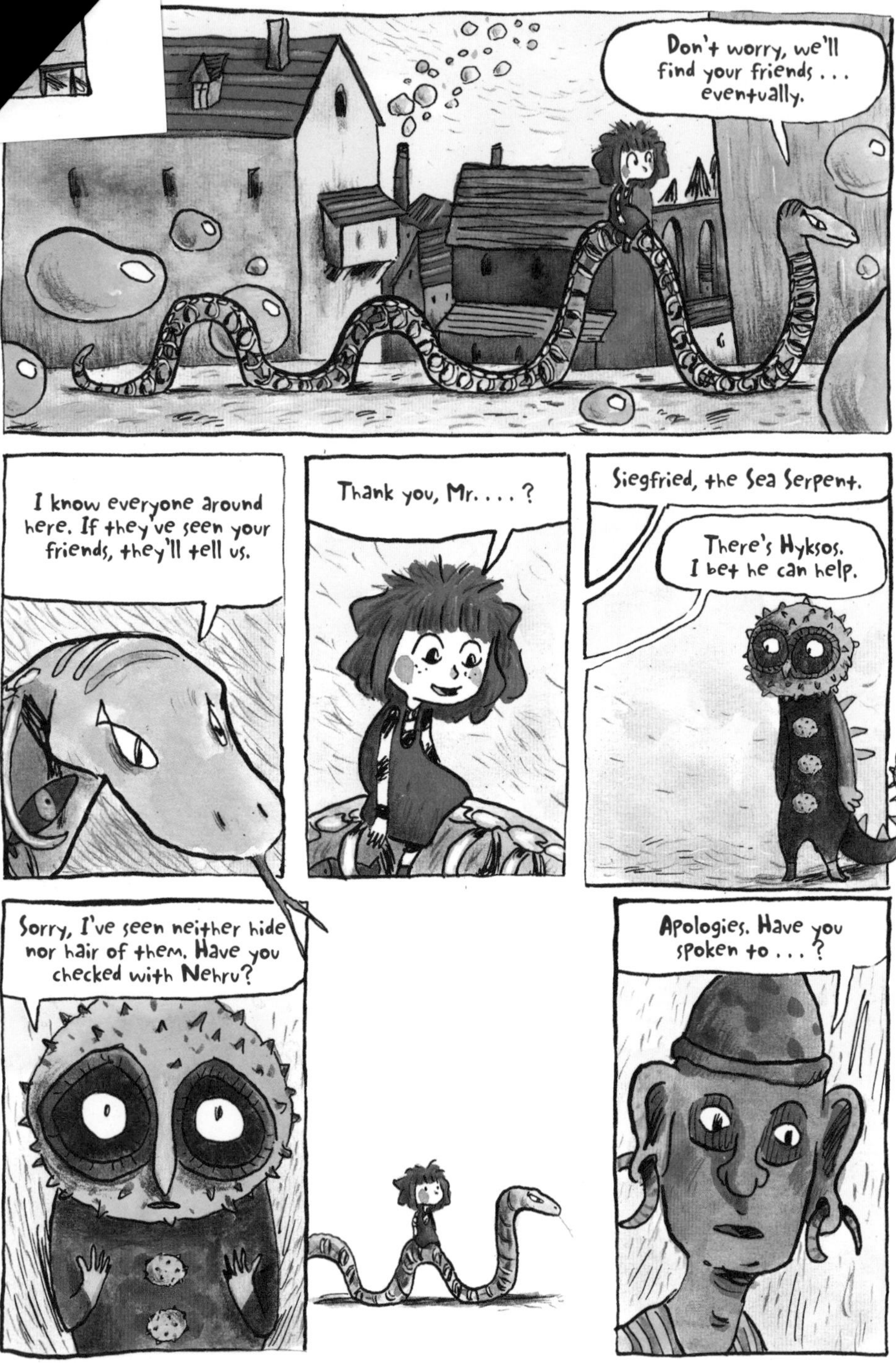

Don't worry, we'll find your friends . . . eventually.
I know everyone around here. If they've seen your friends, they'll tell us.
Thank you, Mr. . . . ?
Siegfried, the Sea Serpent.
There's Hyksos. I bet he can help.
Sorry, I've seen neither hide nor hair of them. Have you checked with Nehru?
Apologies. Have you spoken to . . . ?

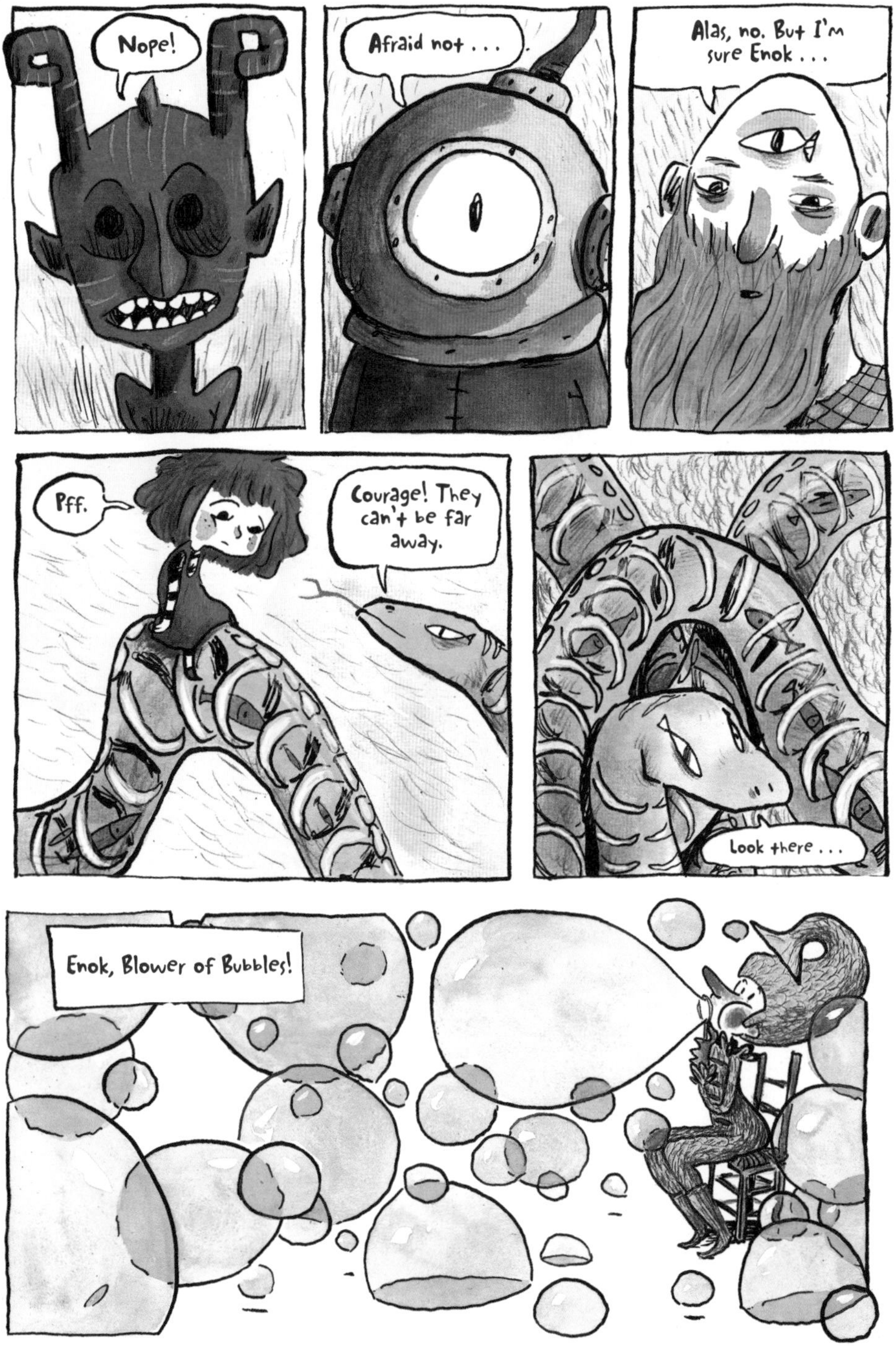
Nope!
Afraid not . . .
Alas, no. But I'm sure Enok . . .
Pff.
Courage! They can't be far away.
Look there . . .
Enok, Blower of Bubbles!

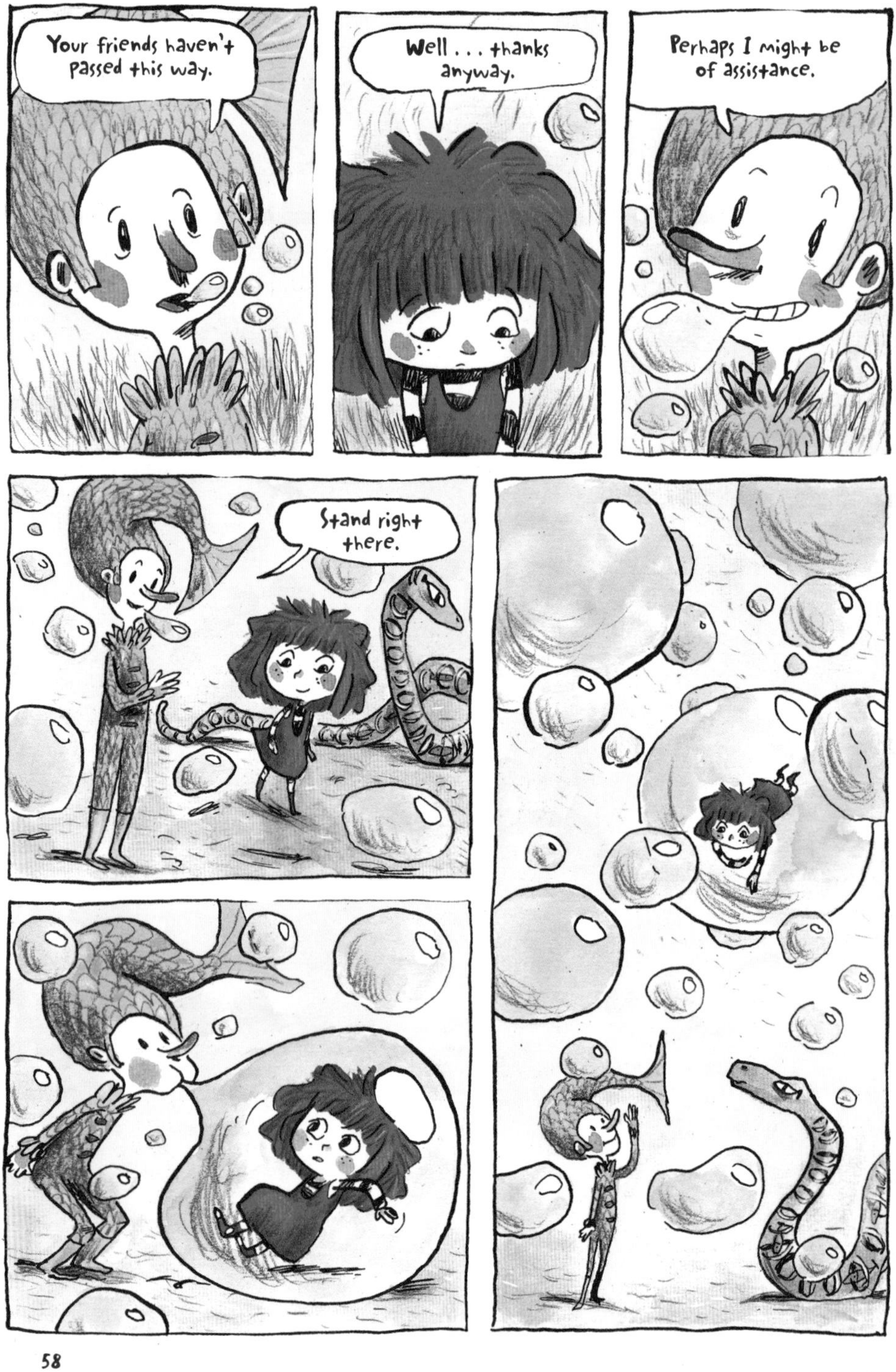
Your friends haven't passed this way.
Well . . . thanks anyway.
Perhaps I might be of assistance.
Stand right there.

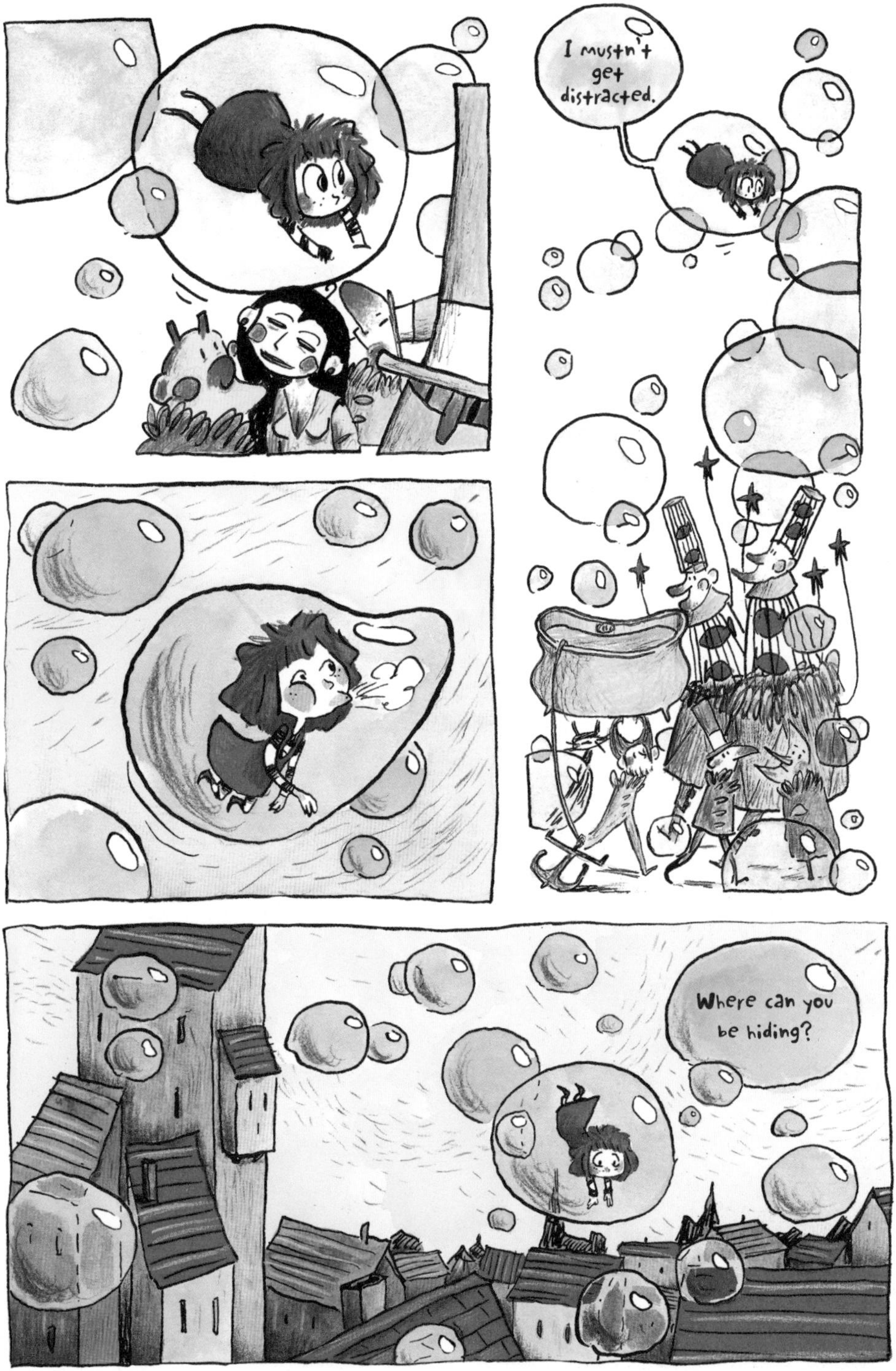
I mustn't get distracted.
Where can you be hiding?

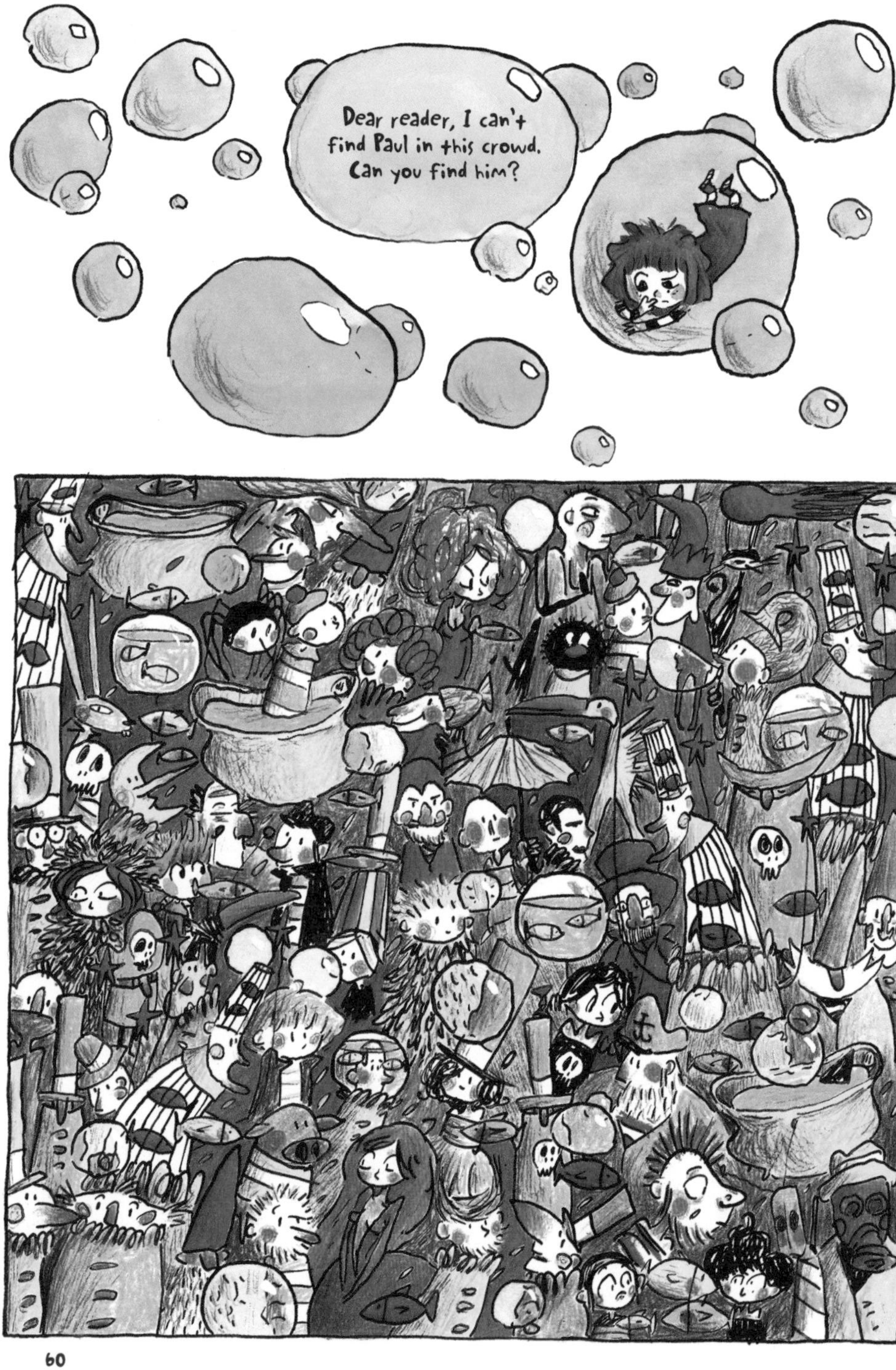
Dear reader, I can't find Paul in this crowd. Can you find him?

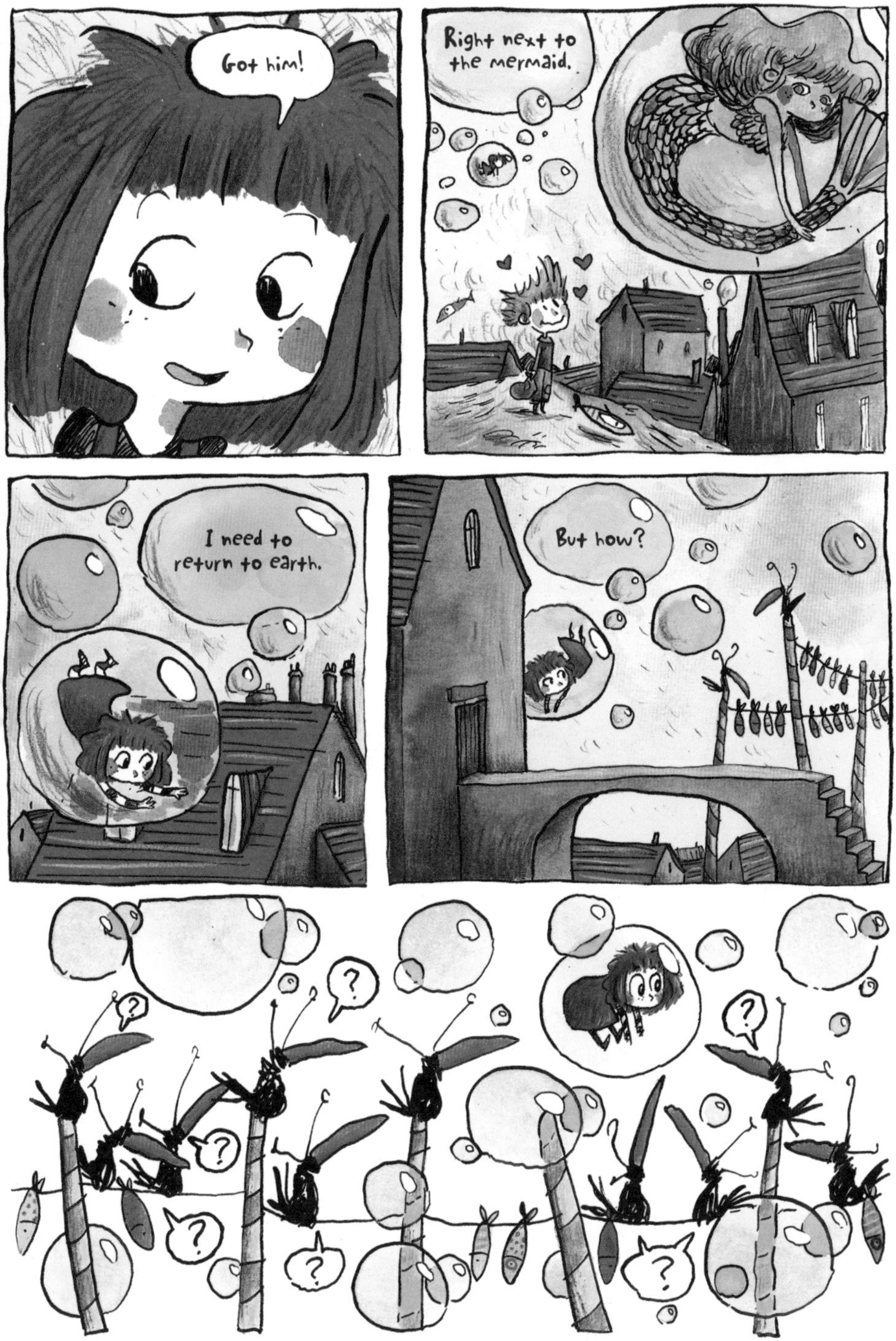
Got him!
Right next to the mermaid.
I need to return to earth.
But how?
?
?
?
?
?
?
?

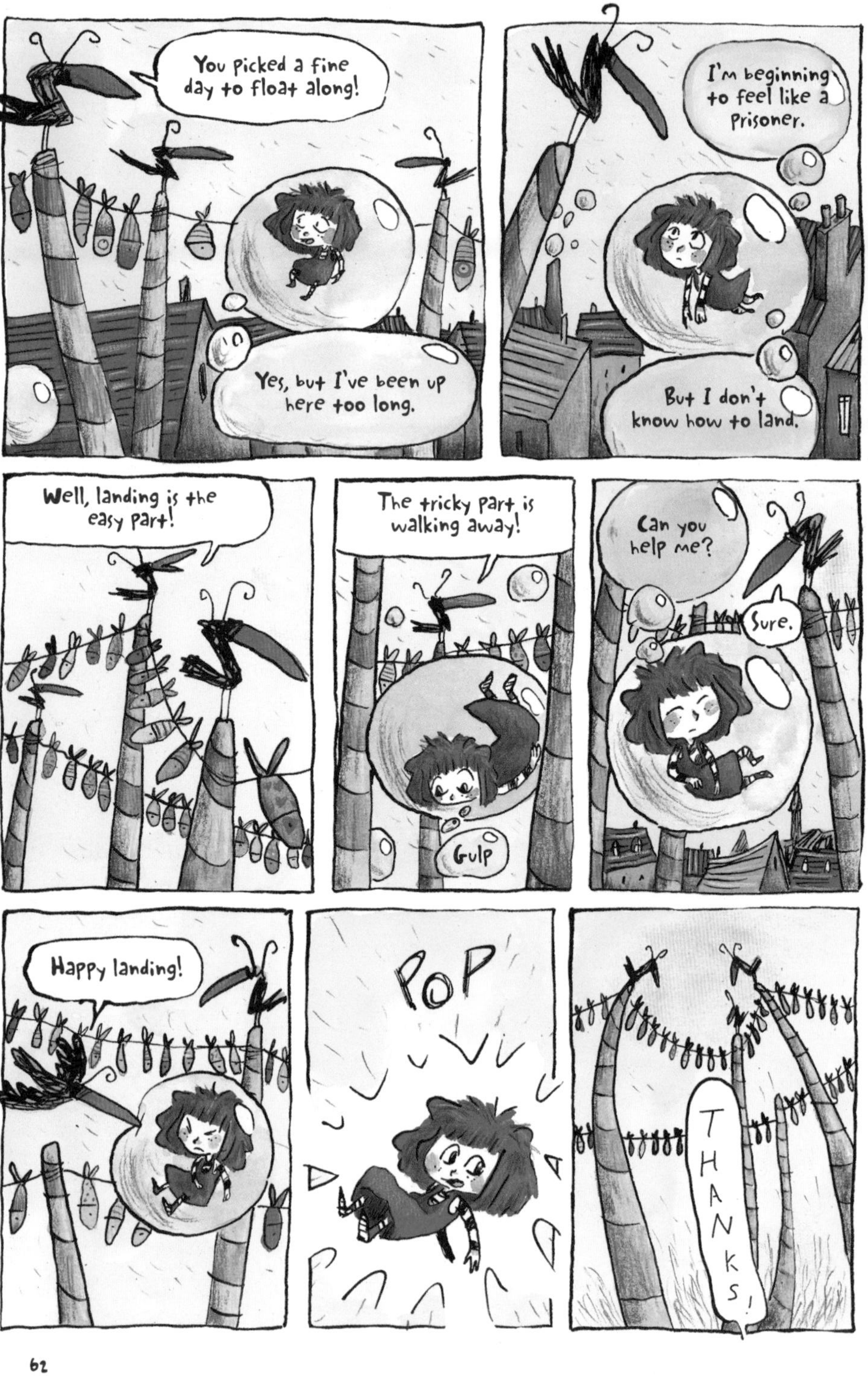
You picked a fine day to float along!
Yes, but I've been up here too long.
I'm beginning to feel like a prisoner.
But I don't know how to land.
Well, landing is the easy part!
The tricky part is walking away!
Gulp
Can you help me?
Sure.
Happy landing!
POP
THANKS!

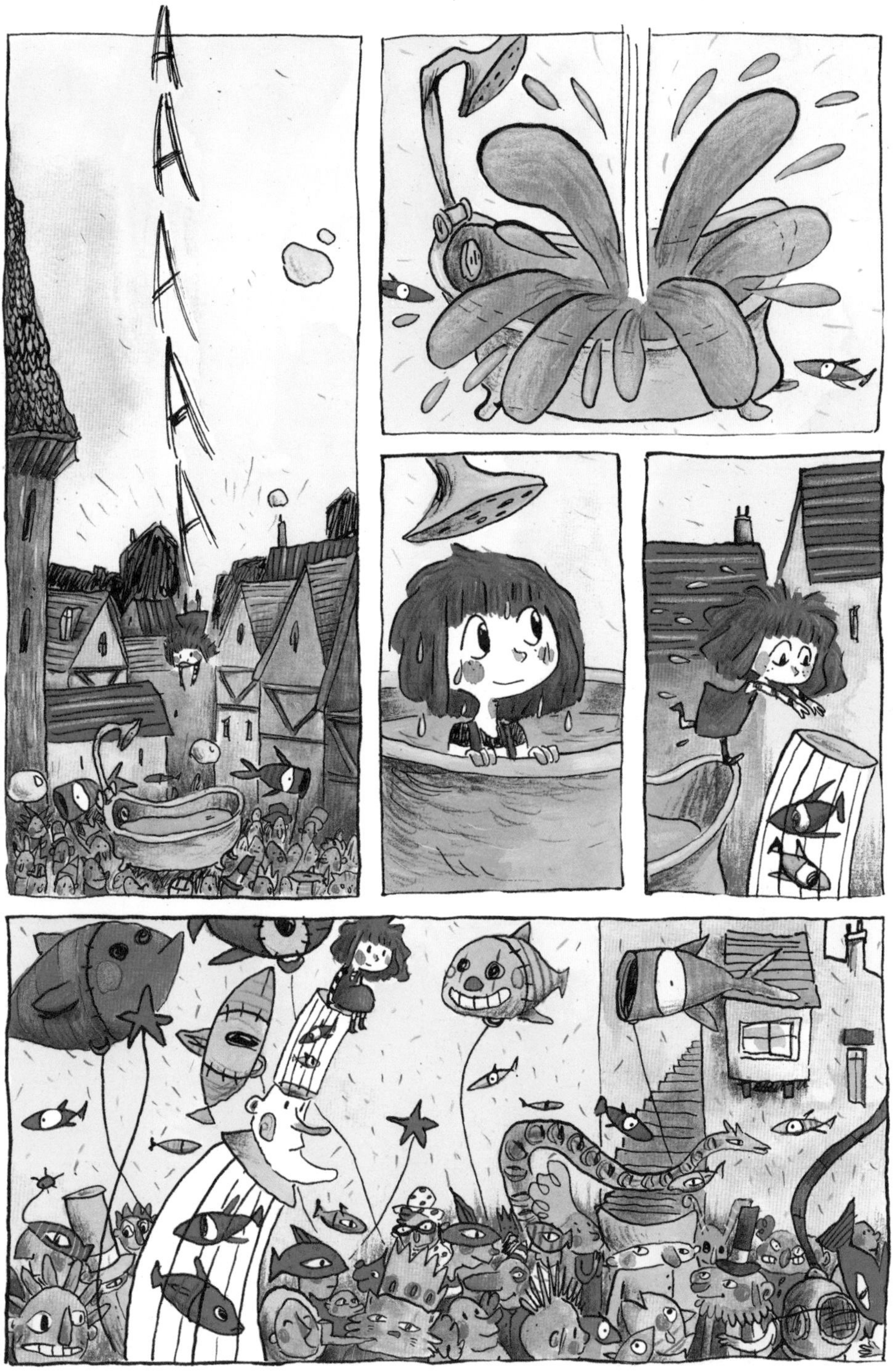
AAAAA

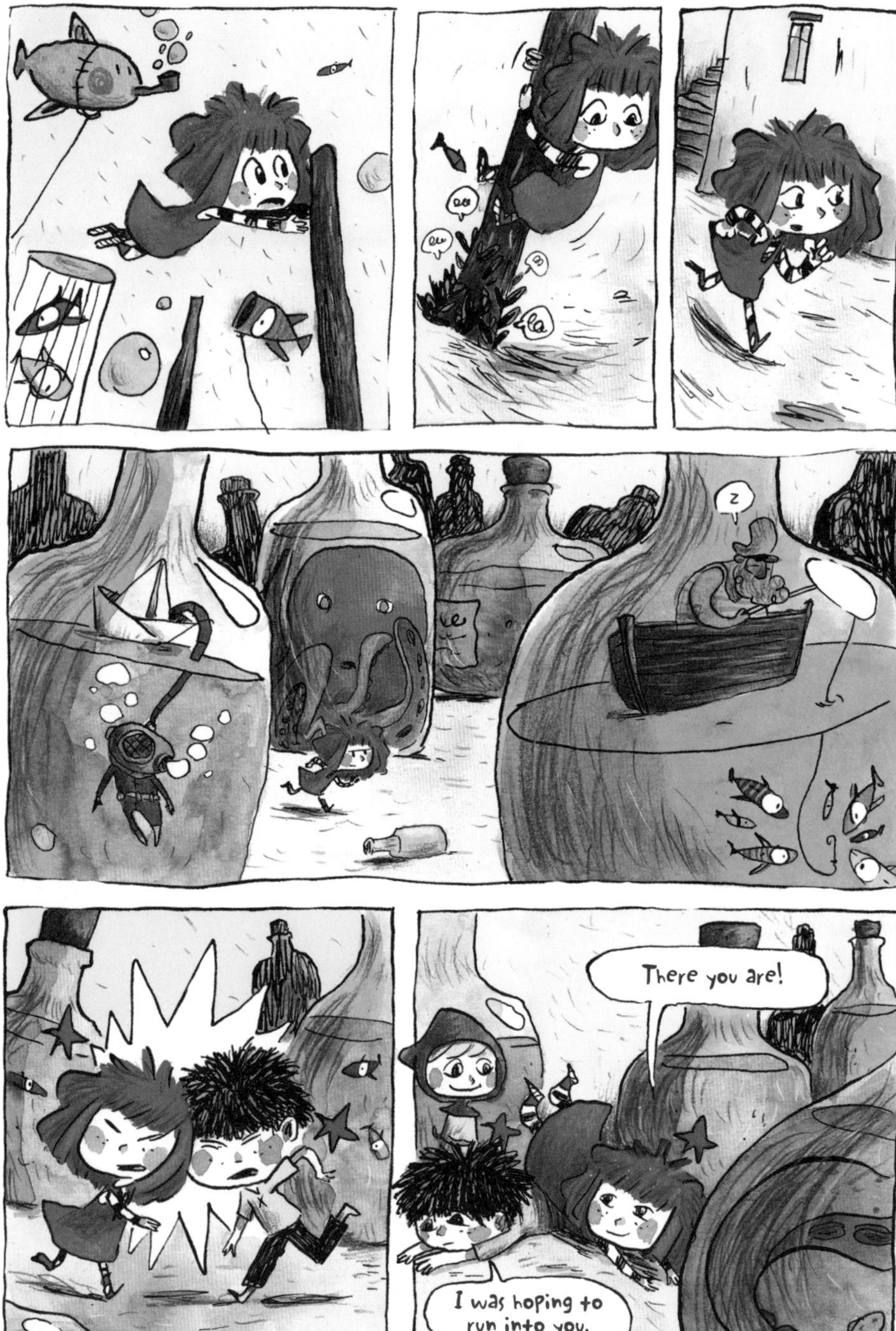
There you are!
I was hoping to run into you.

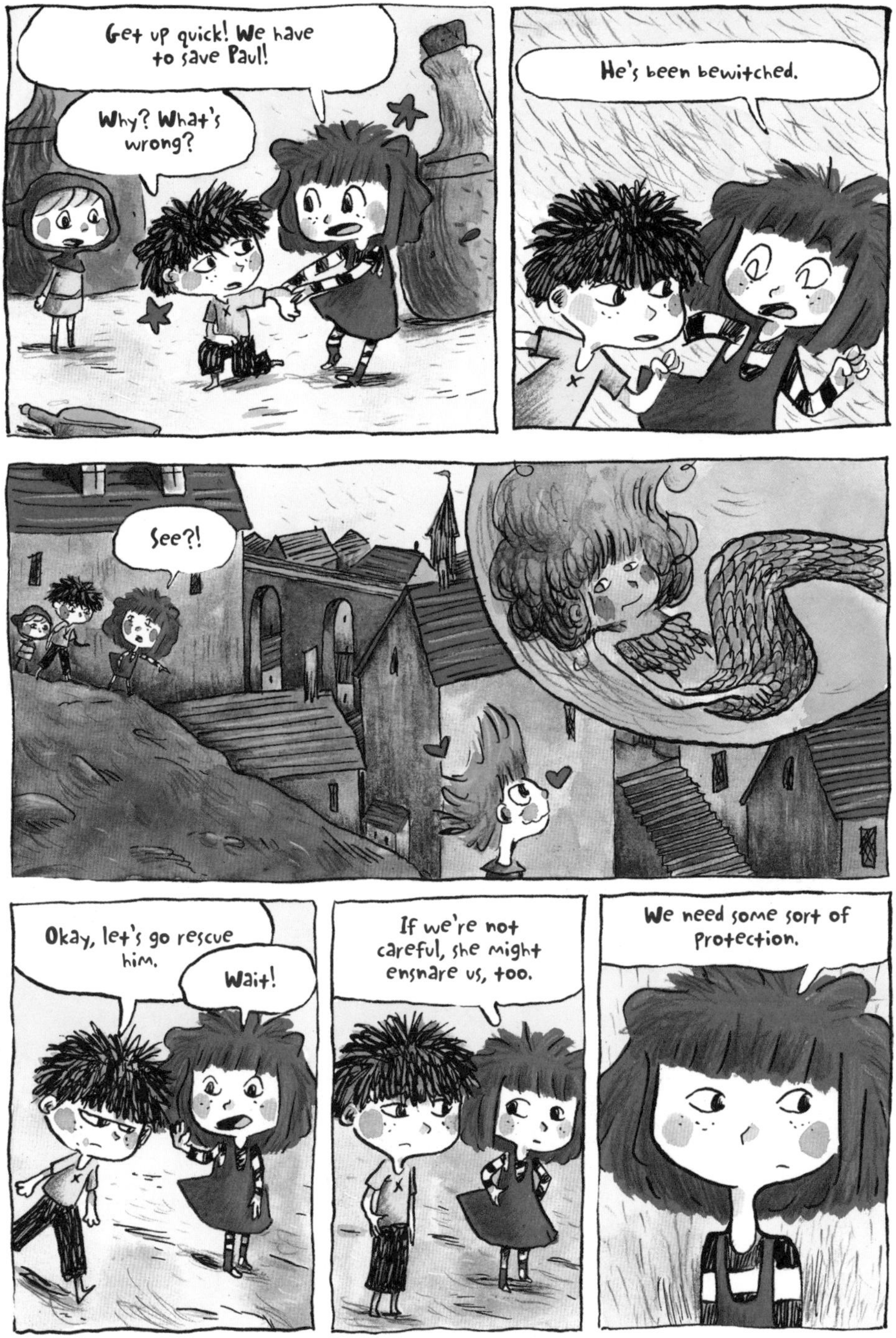
Get up quick! We have to save Paul!
Why? What's wrong?
He's been bewitched.
See?!
Okay, let's go rescue him.
Wait!
If we're not careful, she might ensnare us, too.
We need some sort of protection.

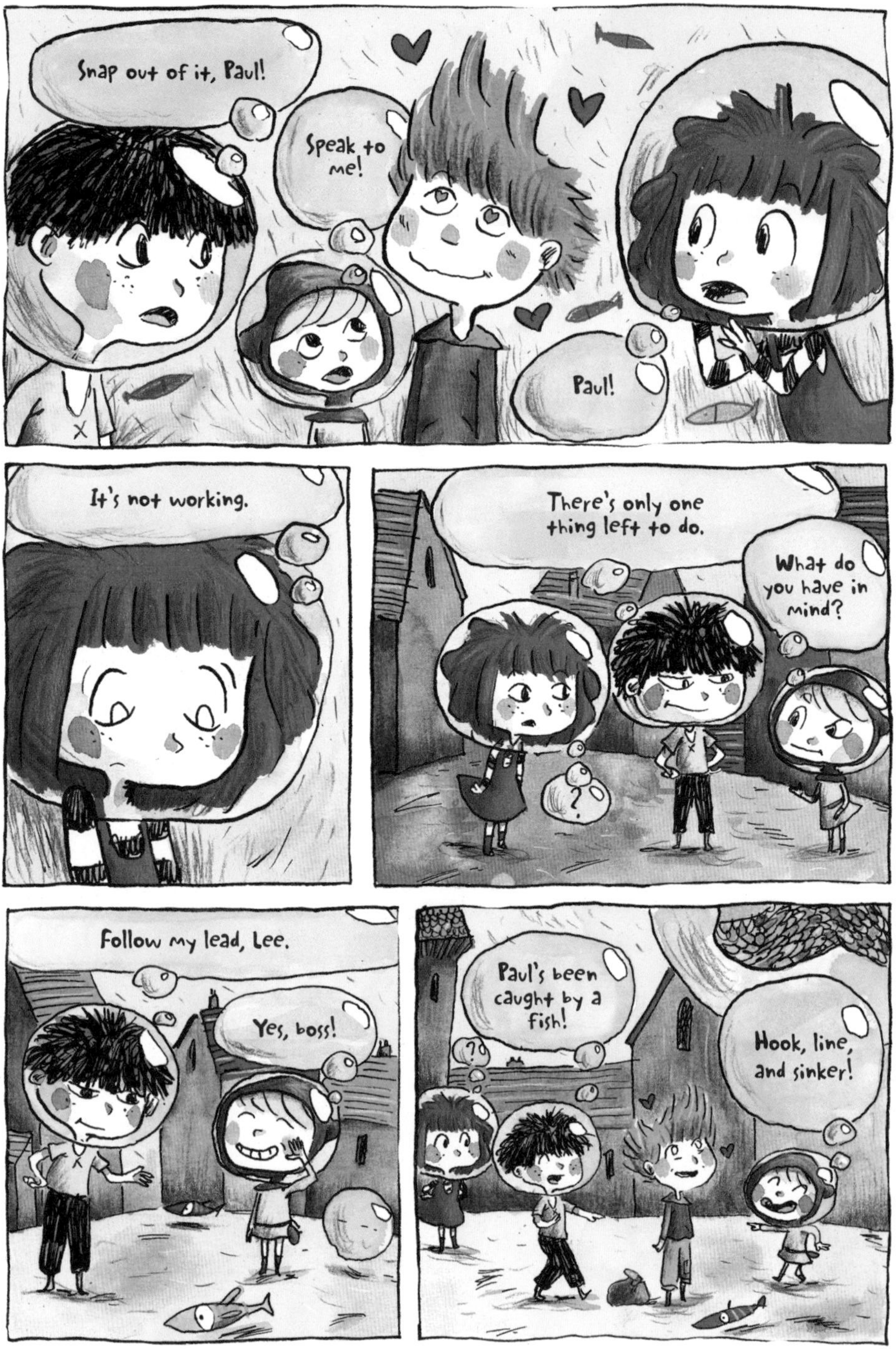
Snap out of it, Paul!
Speak to me!
Paul!
It's not working.
There's only one thing left to do.
What do you have in mind?
?
Follow my lead, Lee.
Yes, boss!
Paul's been caught by a fish!
Hook, line, and sinker!

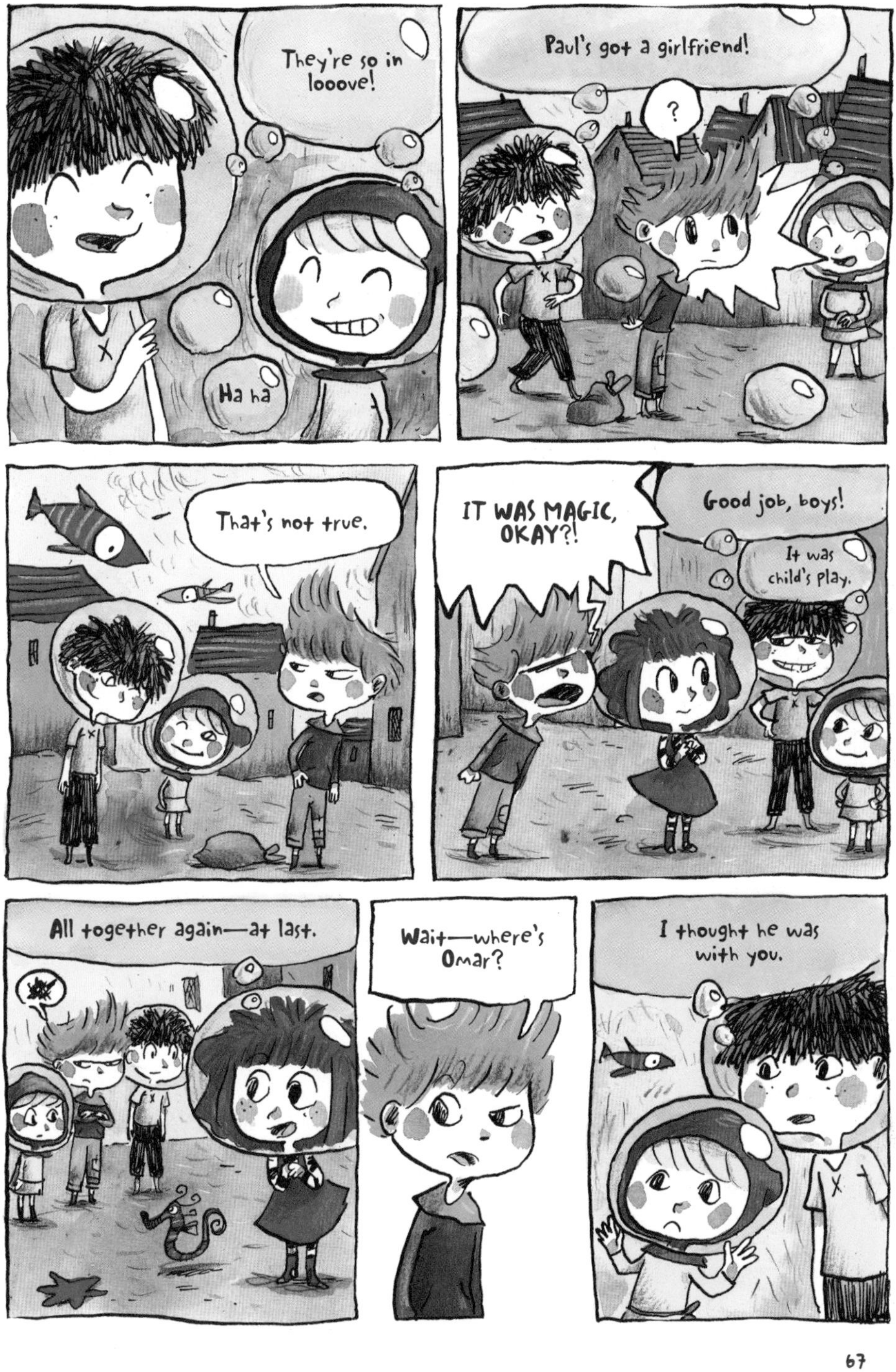
They're so in looove!
Ha ha
Paul's got a girlfriend!
?
That's not true.
IT WAS MAGIC, OKAY?!
Good job, boys!
It was child's play.
All together again—at last.
Wait—where's Omar?
I thought he was with you.

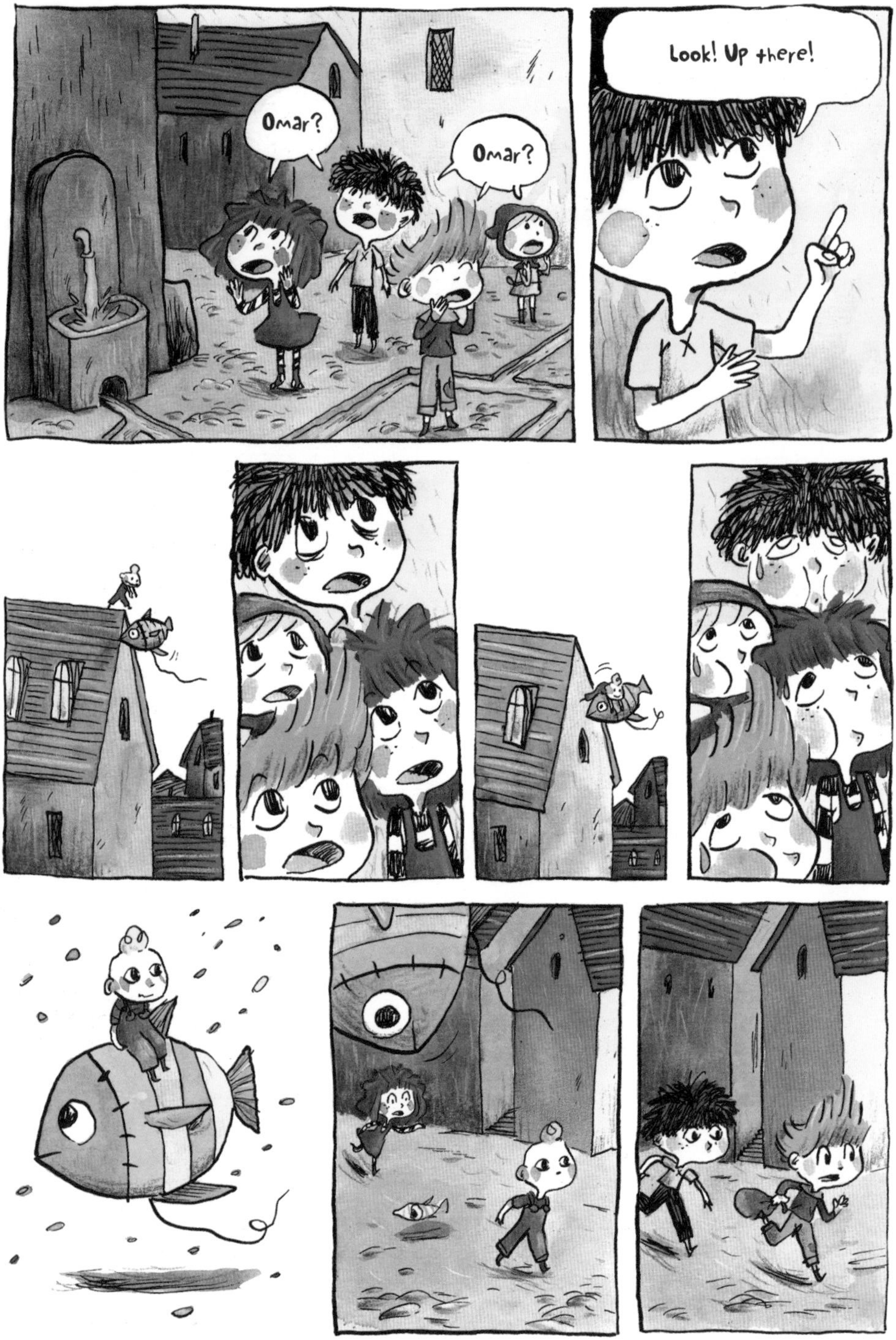
Omar?
Omar?
Look! Up there!

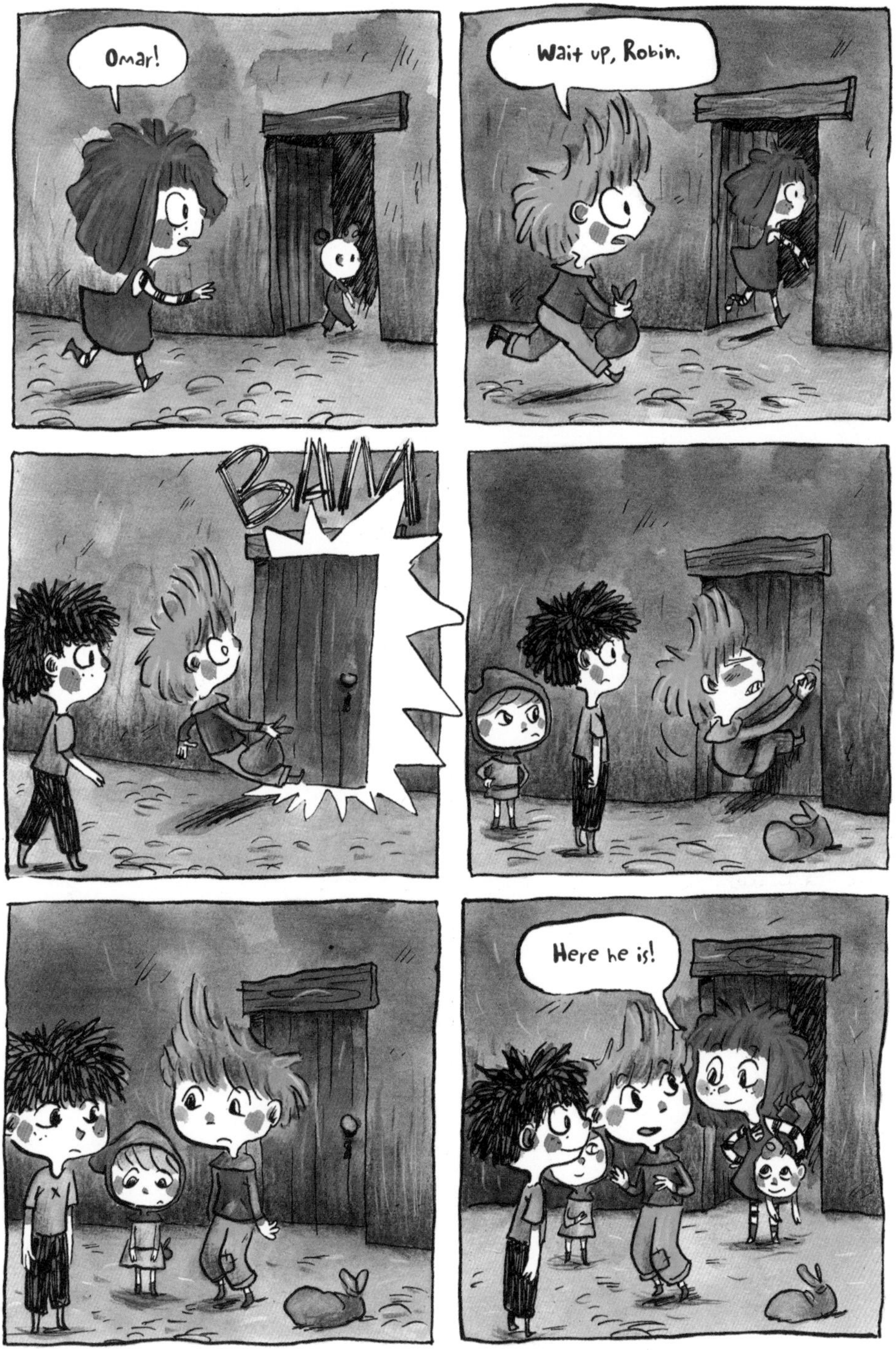
Omar!
Wait up, Robin.
BAM
Here he is!

To find out what happened on the other side of the door...

...read from right to left.

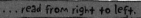

I'm going to catch you!

BAM

Gotcha, you little rascal!

HA! HA!

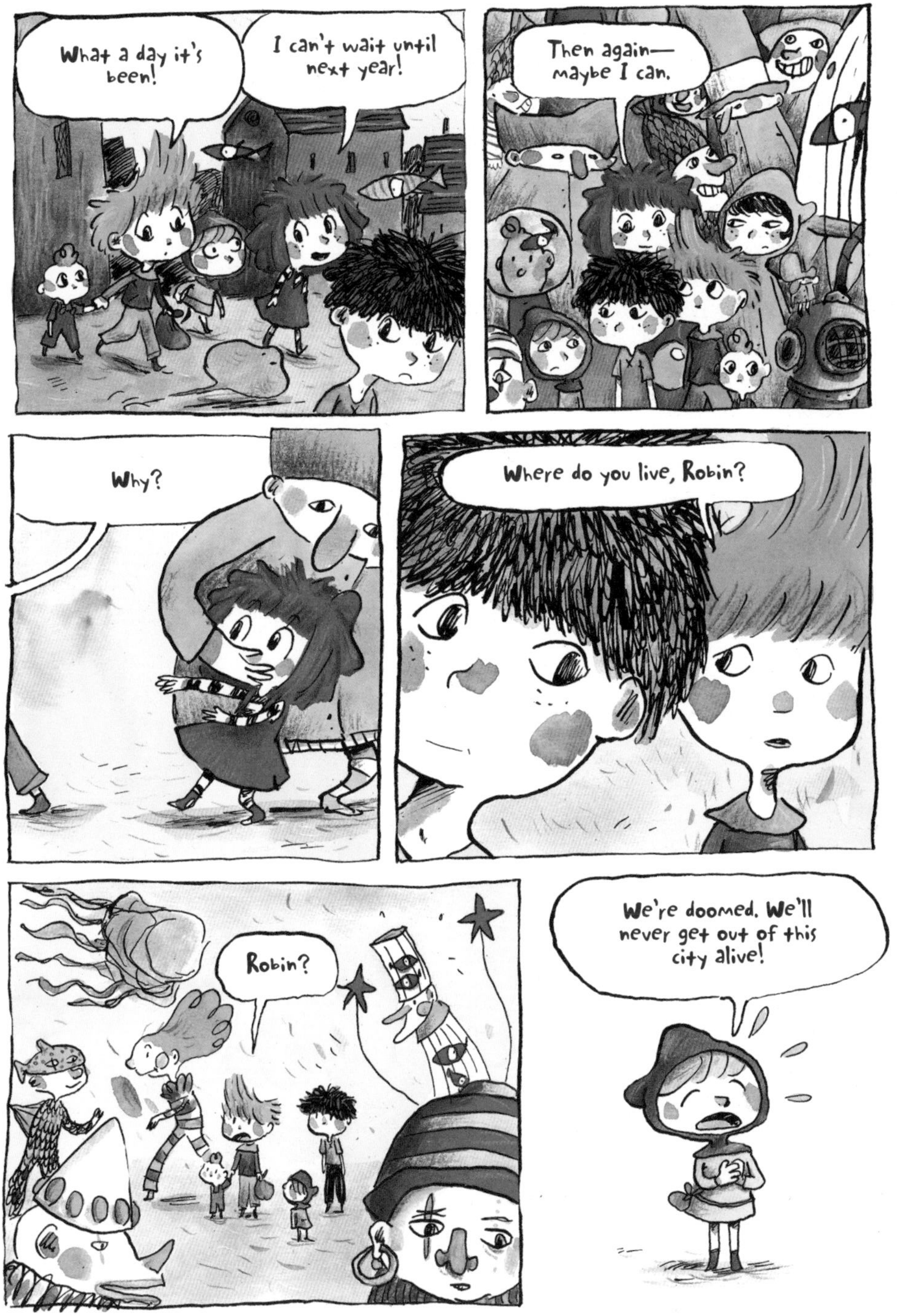
What a day it's been!
I can't wait until next year!
Then again—maybe I can.
Why?
Where do you live, Robin?
Robin?
We're doomed. We'll never get out of this city alive!

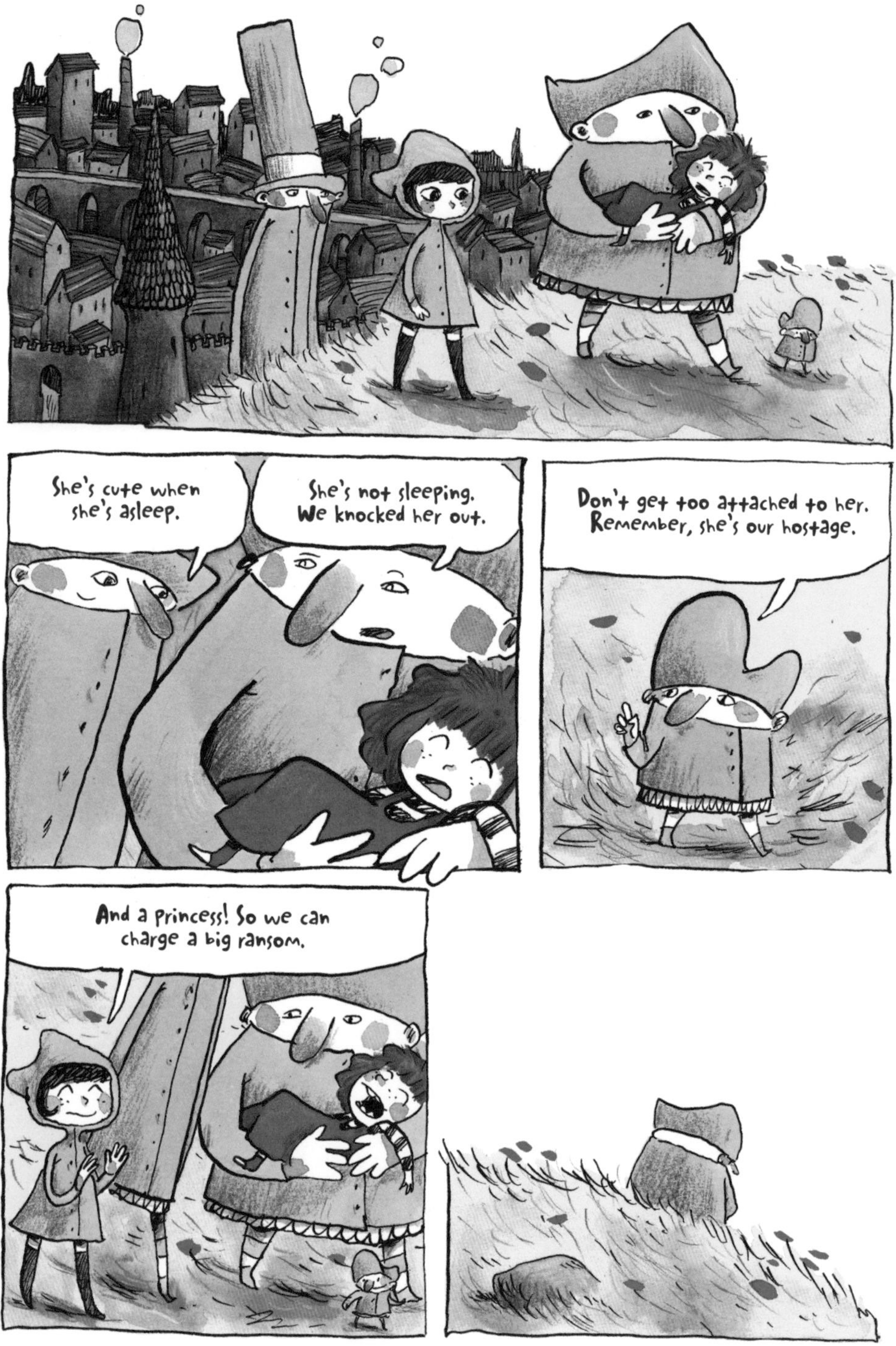
She's cute when she's asleep.
She's not sleeping. We knocked her out.
Don't get too attached to her. Remember, she's our hostage.
And a princess! So we can charge a big ransom.

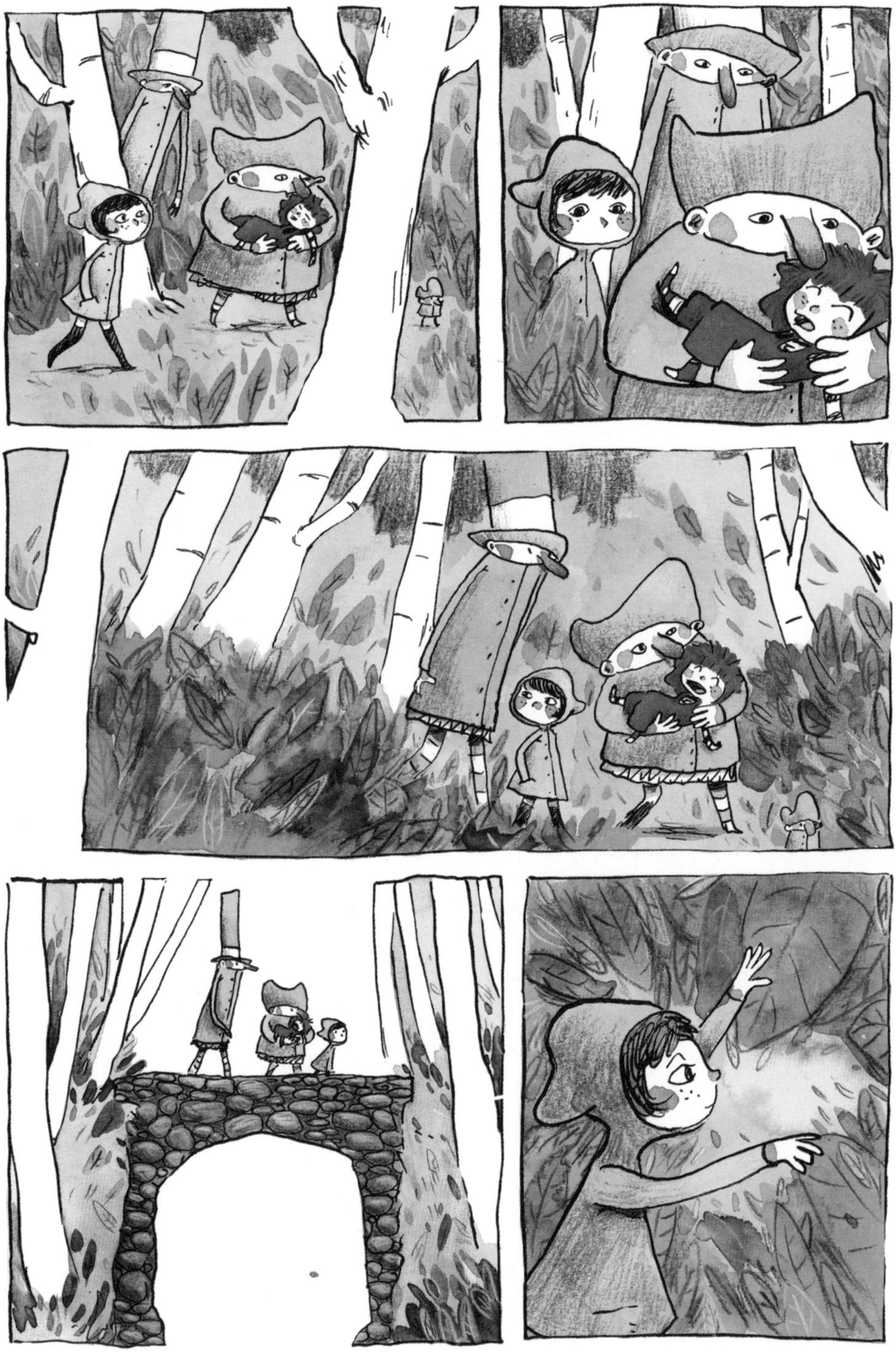

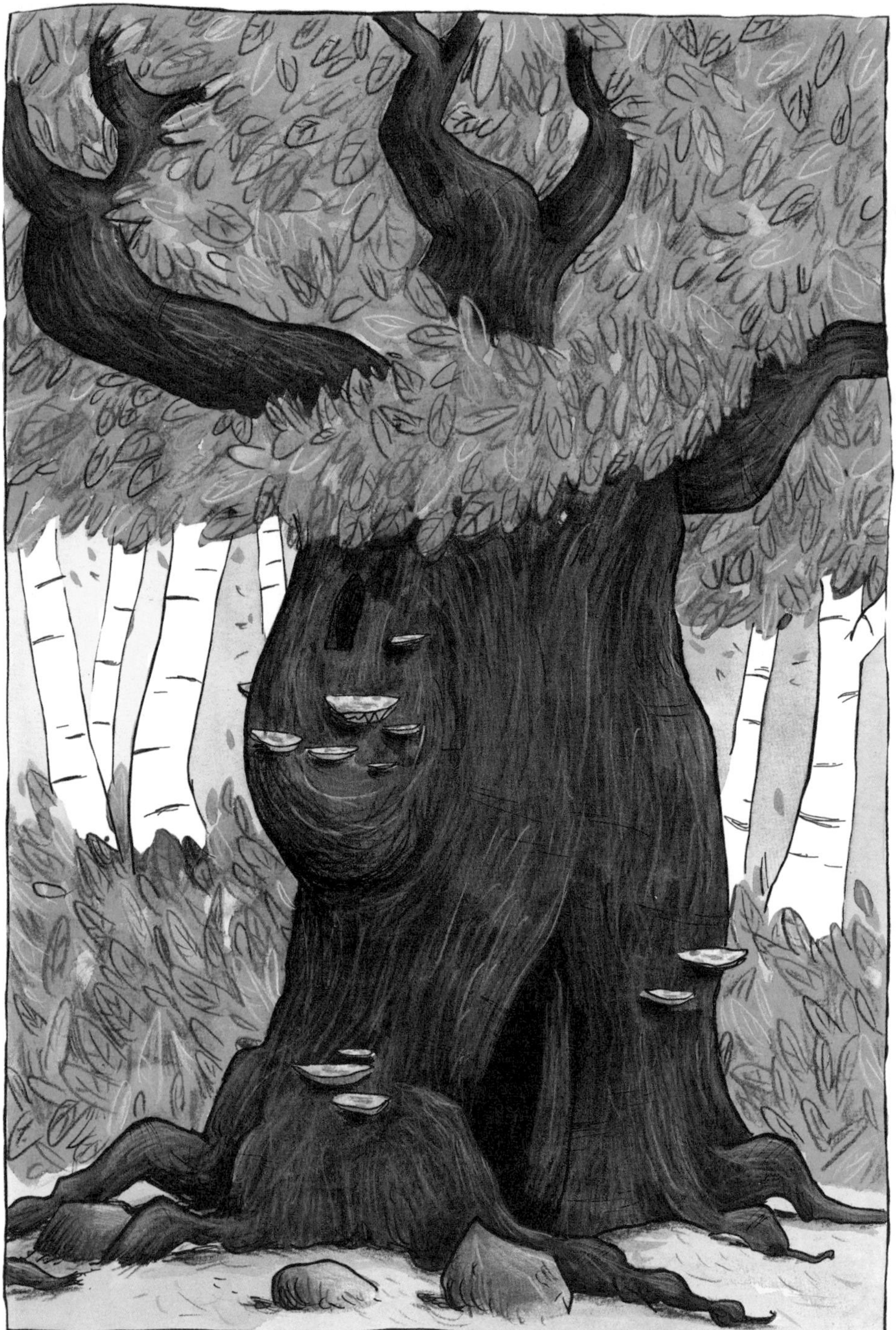

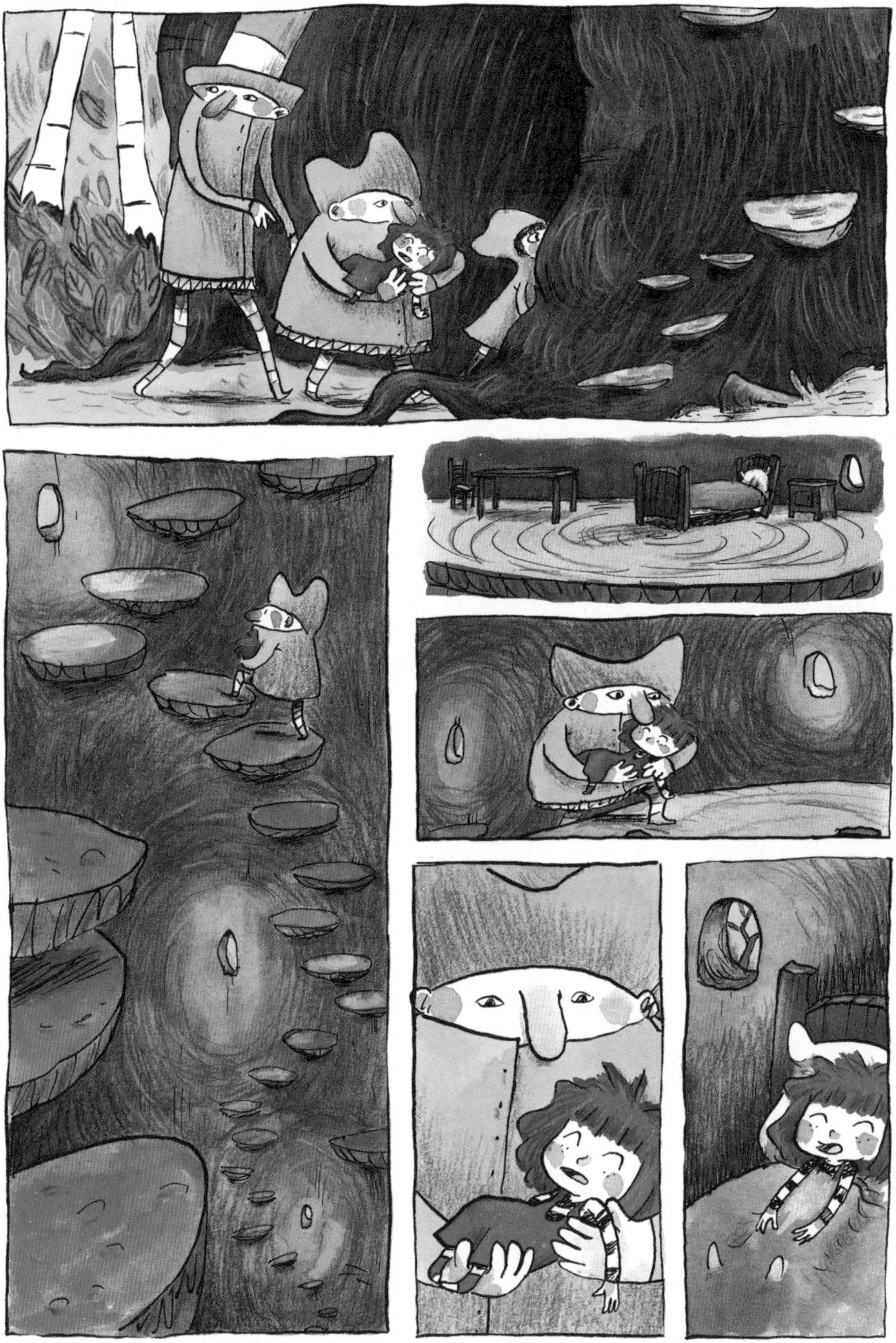

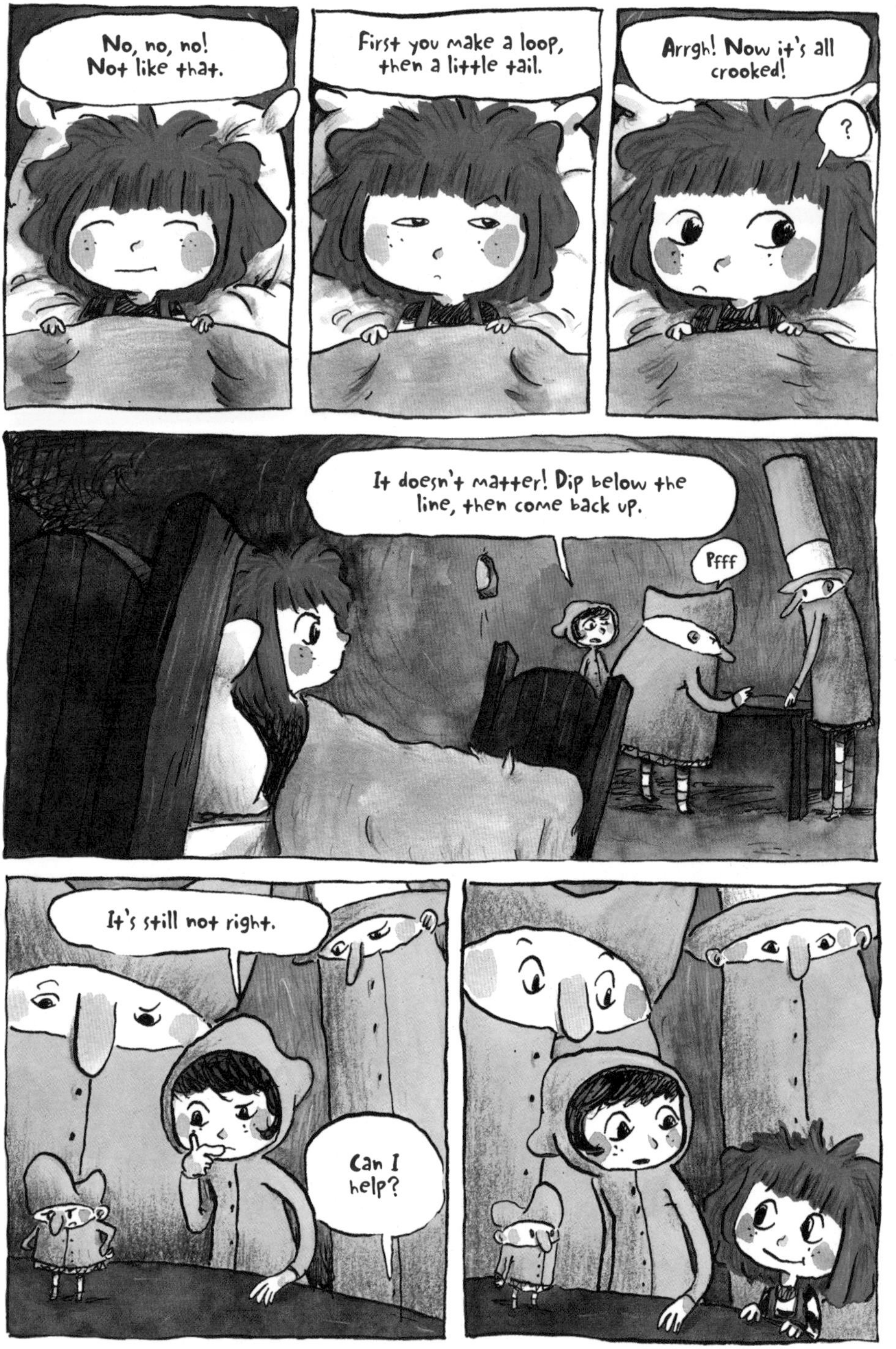
No, no, no!
Not like that.
First you make a loop, then a little tail.
Arrgh! Now it's all crooked!
?
It doesn't matter! Dip below the line, then come back up.
Pfff
It's still not right.
Can I help?

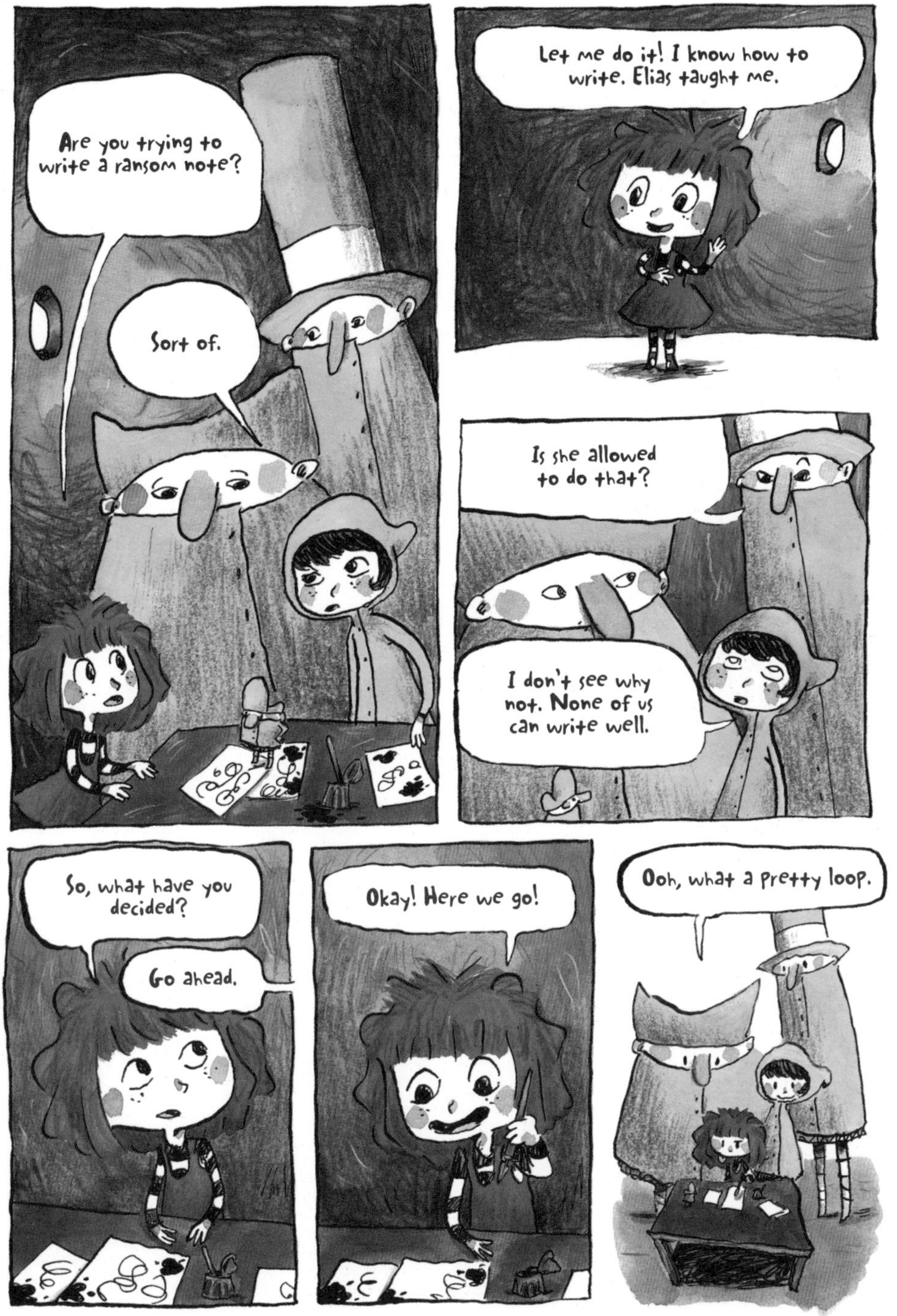
Are you trying to write a ransom note?
Sort of.
Let me do it! I know how to write. Elias taught me.
Is she allowed to do that?
I don't see why not. None of us can write well.
So, what have you decided?
Go ahead.
Okay! Here we go!
Ooh, what a pretty loop.

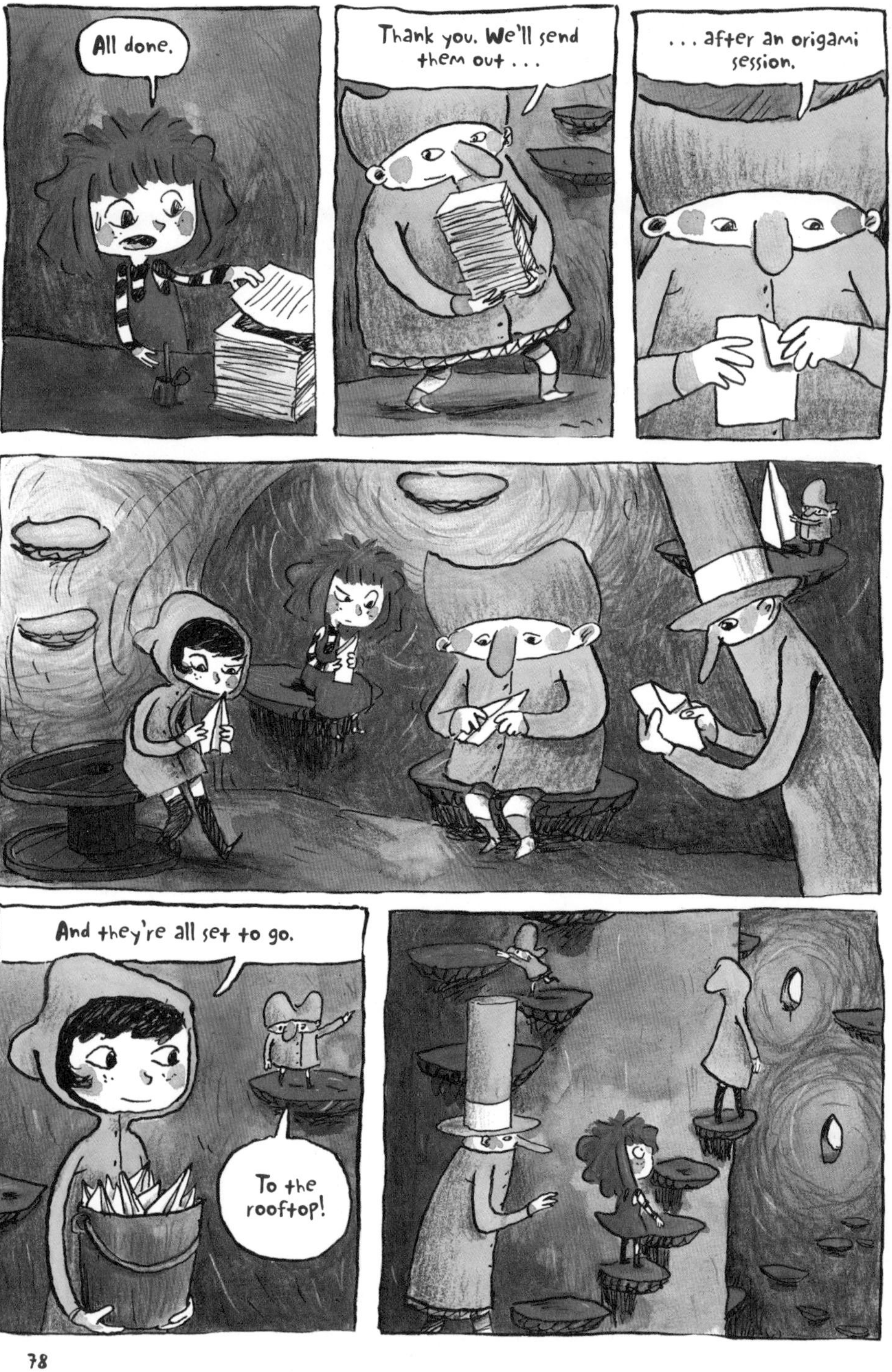
All done.
Thank you. We'll send them out . . .
. . . after an origami session.
And they're all set to go.
To the rooftop!

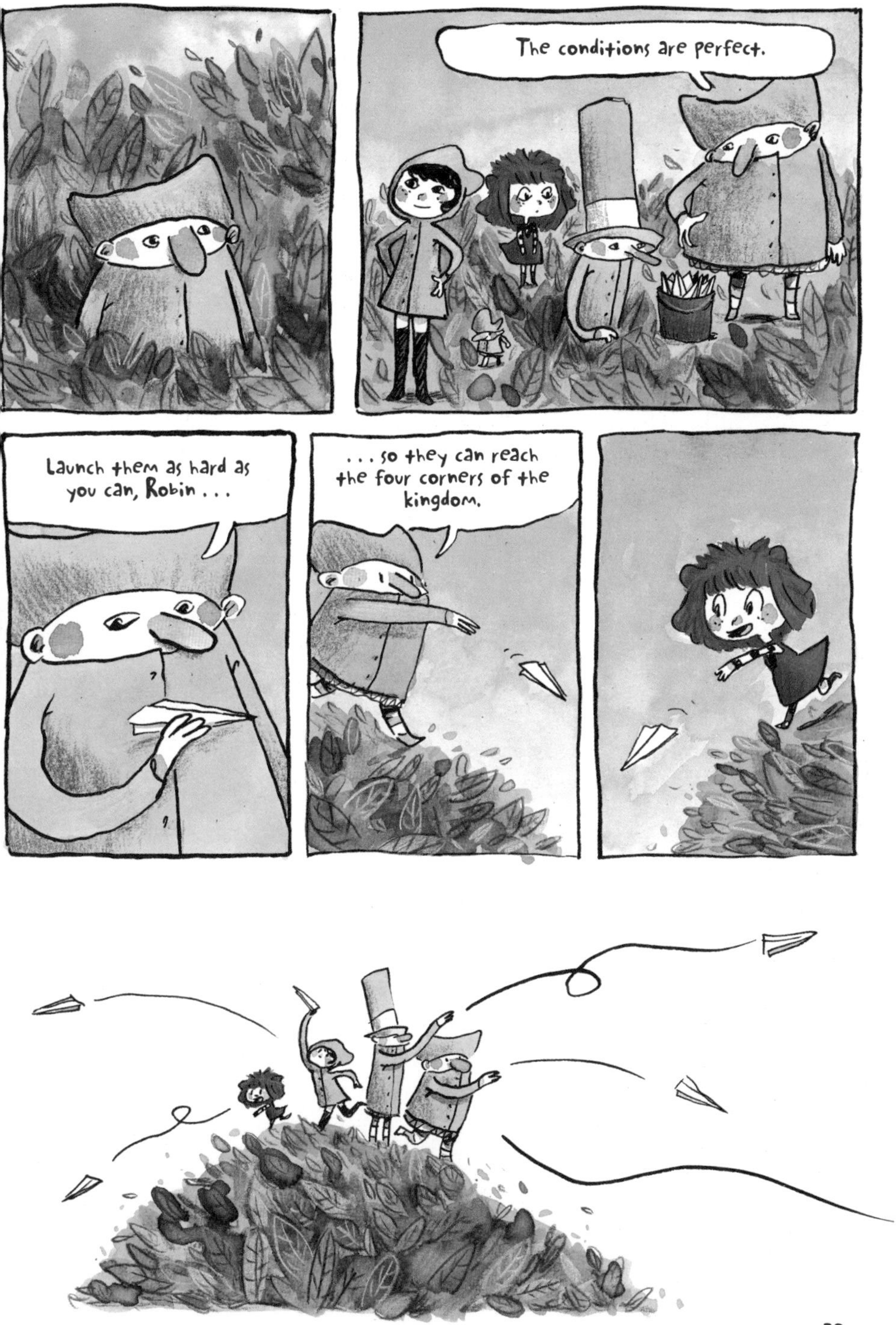
The conditions are perfect.
Launch them as hard as you can, Robin . . .
. . . so they can reach the four corners of the kingdom.

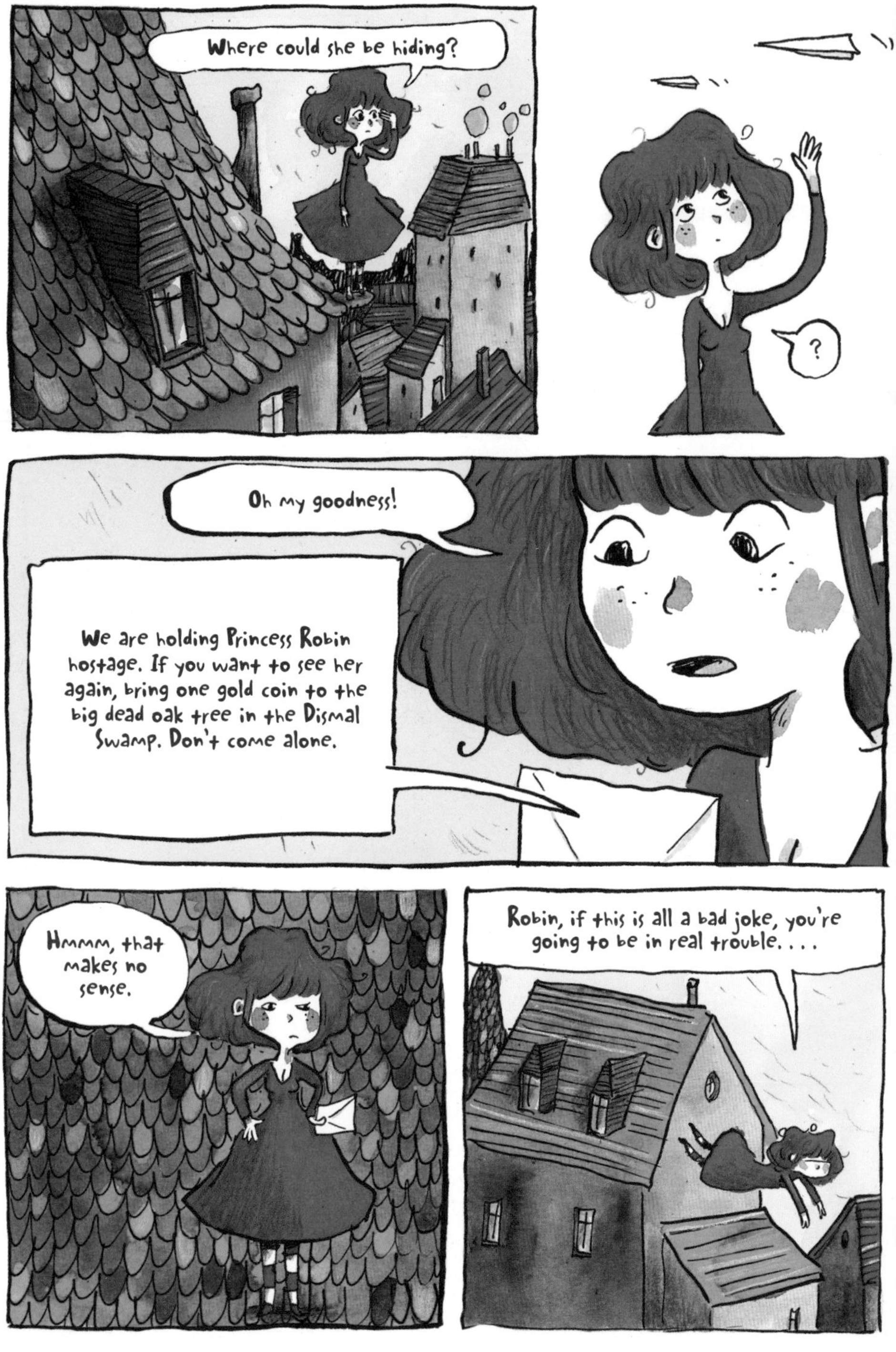
Where could she be hiding?
?
Oh my goodness!
We are holding Princess Robin hostage. If you want to see her again, bring one gold coin to the big dead oak tree in the Dismal Swamp. Don't come alone.
Hmmm, that makes no sense.
Robin, if this is all a bad joke, you're going to be in real trouble. . . .

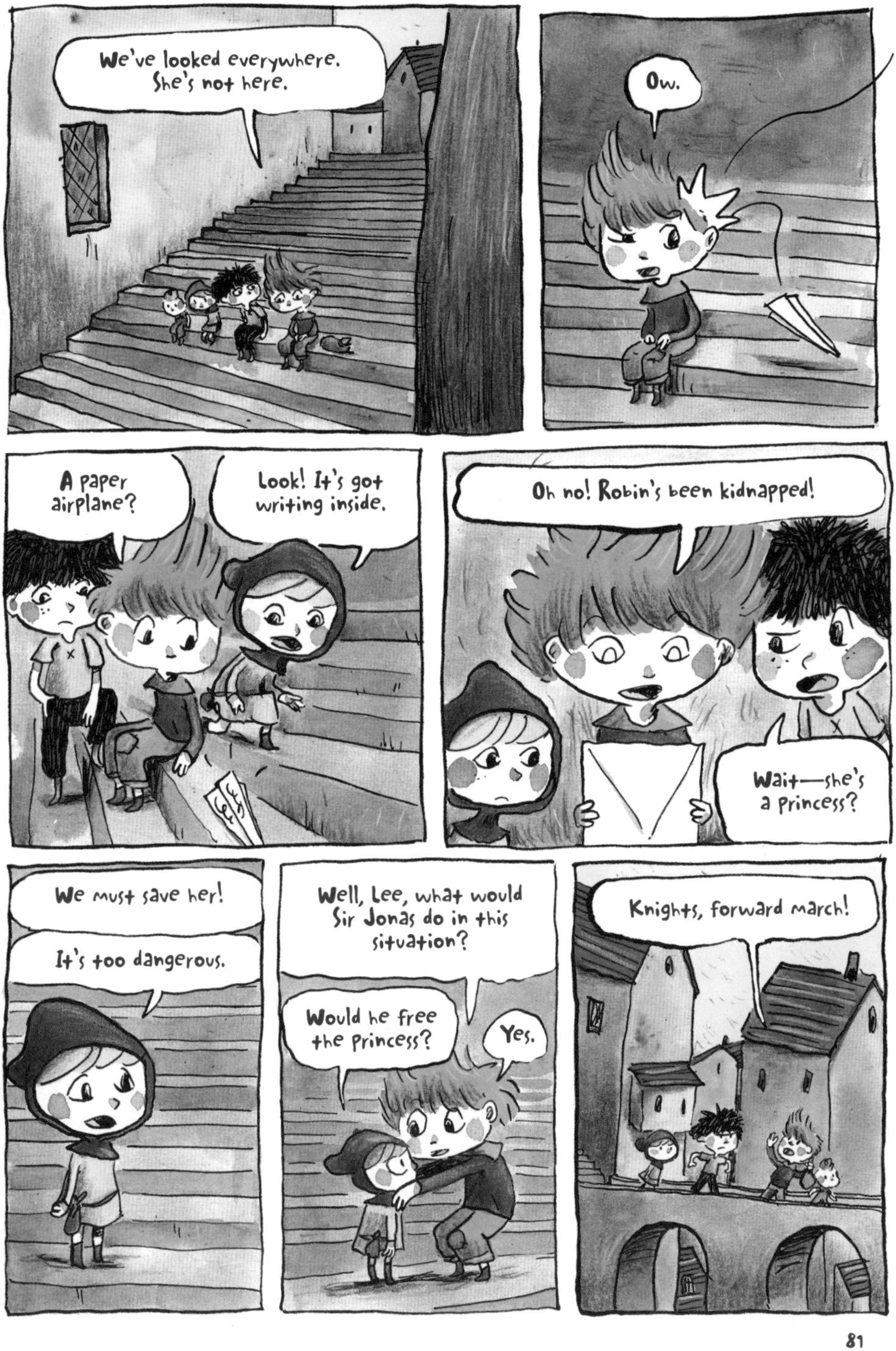
We've looked everywhere. She's not here.
Ow.
A paper airplane?
Look! It's got writing inside.
Oh no! Robin's been kidnapped!
Wait—she's a princess?
We must save her!
It's too dangerous.
Well, Lee, what would Sir Jonas do in this situation?
Would he free the princess?
Yes.
Knights, forward march!

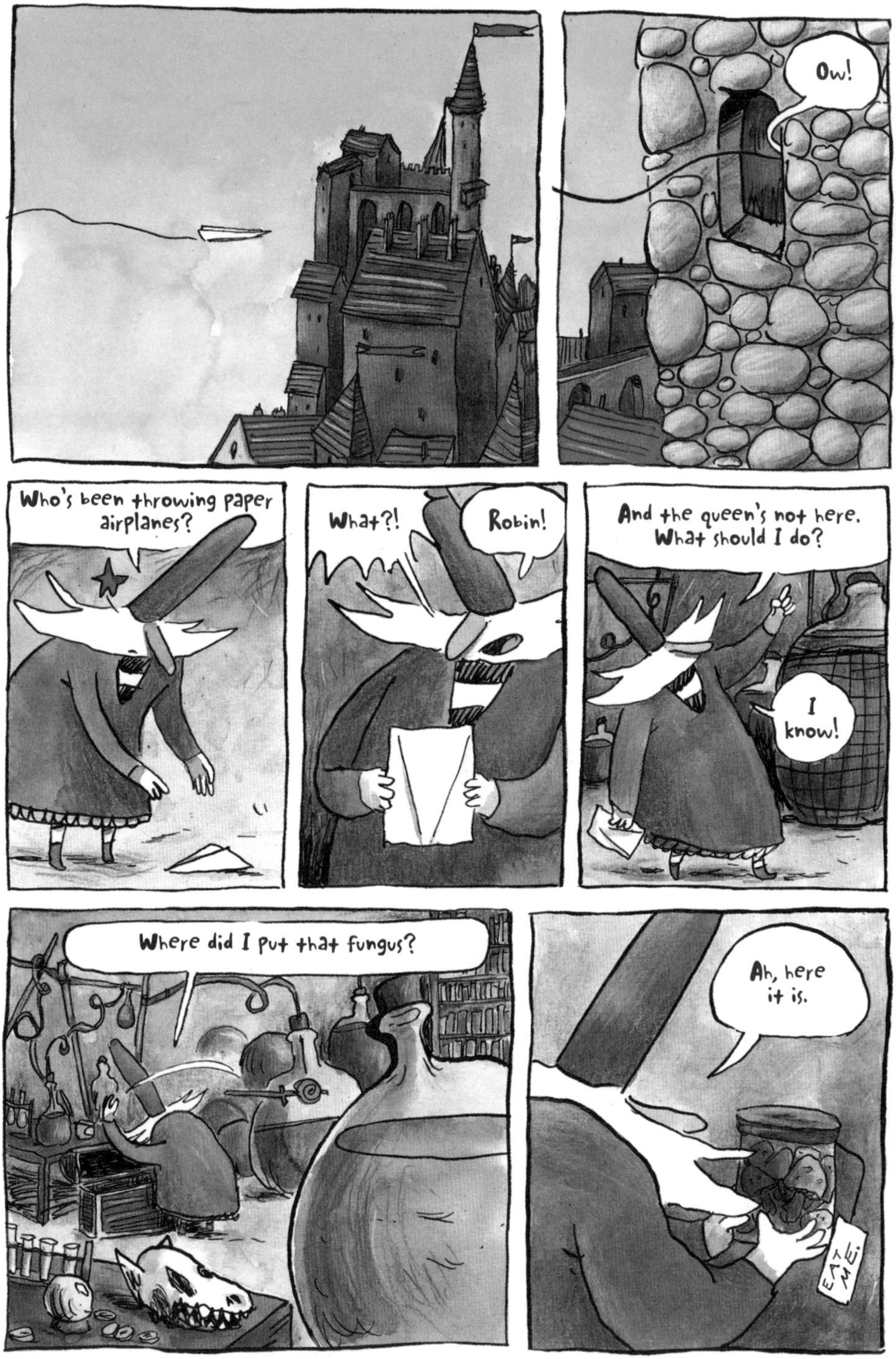
Ow!
Who's been throwing paper airplanes?
What?!
Robin!
And the queen's not here. What should I do?
I know!
Where did I put that fungus?
Ah, here it is.
EAT ME.

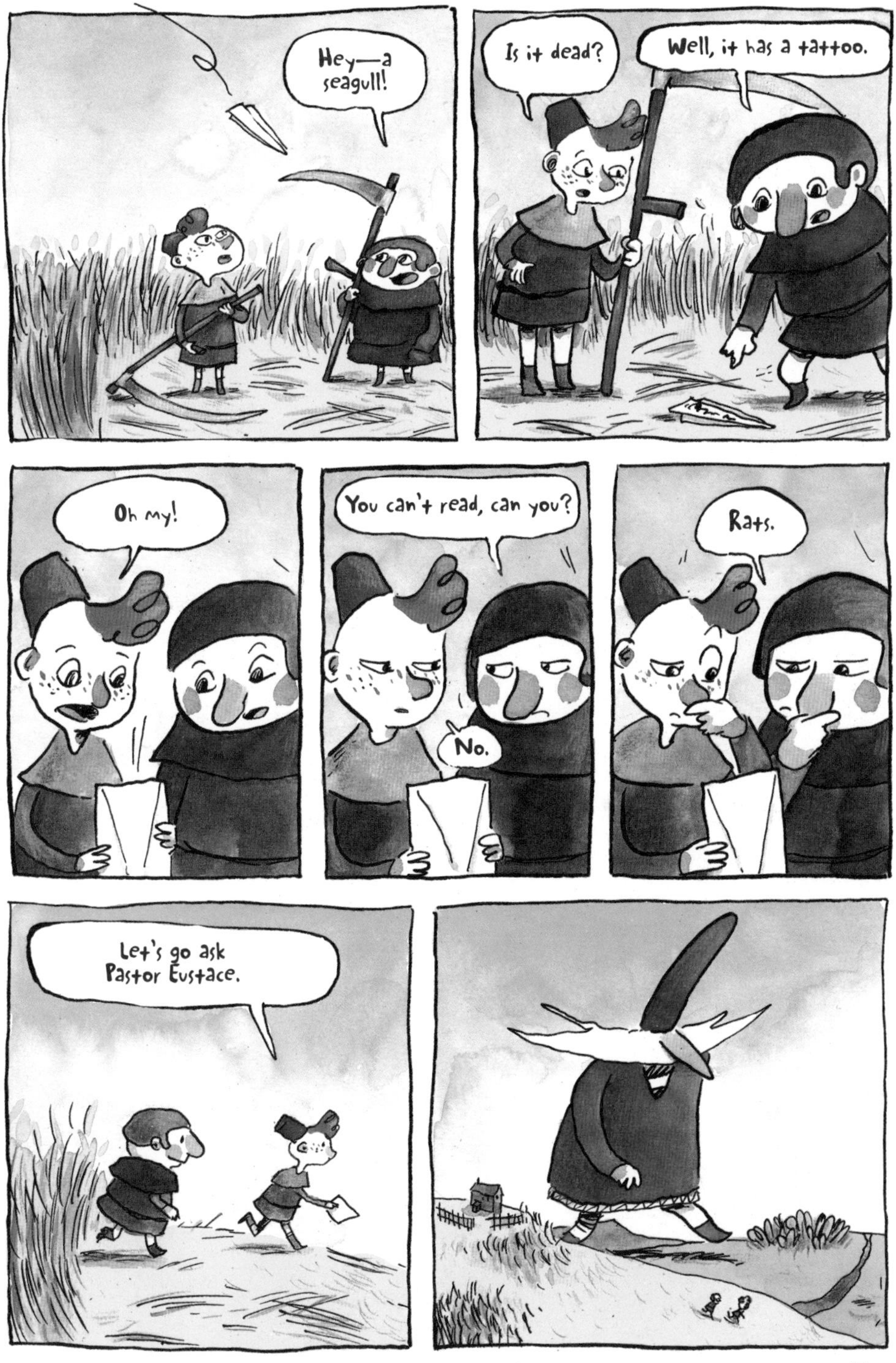
Hey—a seagull!
Is it dead?
Well, it has a tattoo.
Oh my!
You can't read, can you?
No.
Rats.
Let's go ask Pastor Eustace.

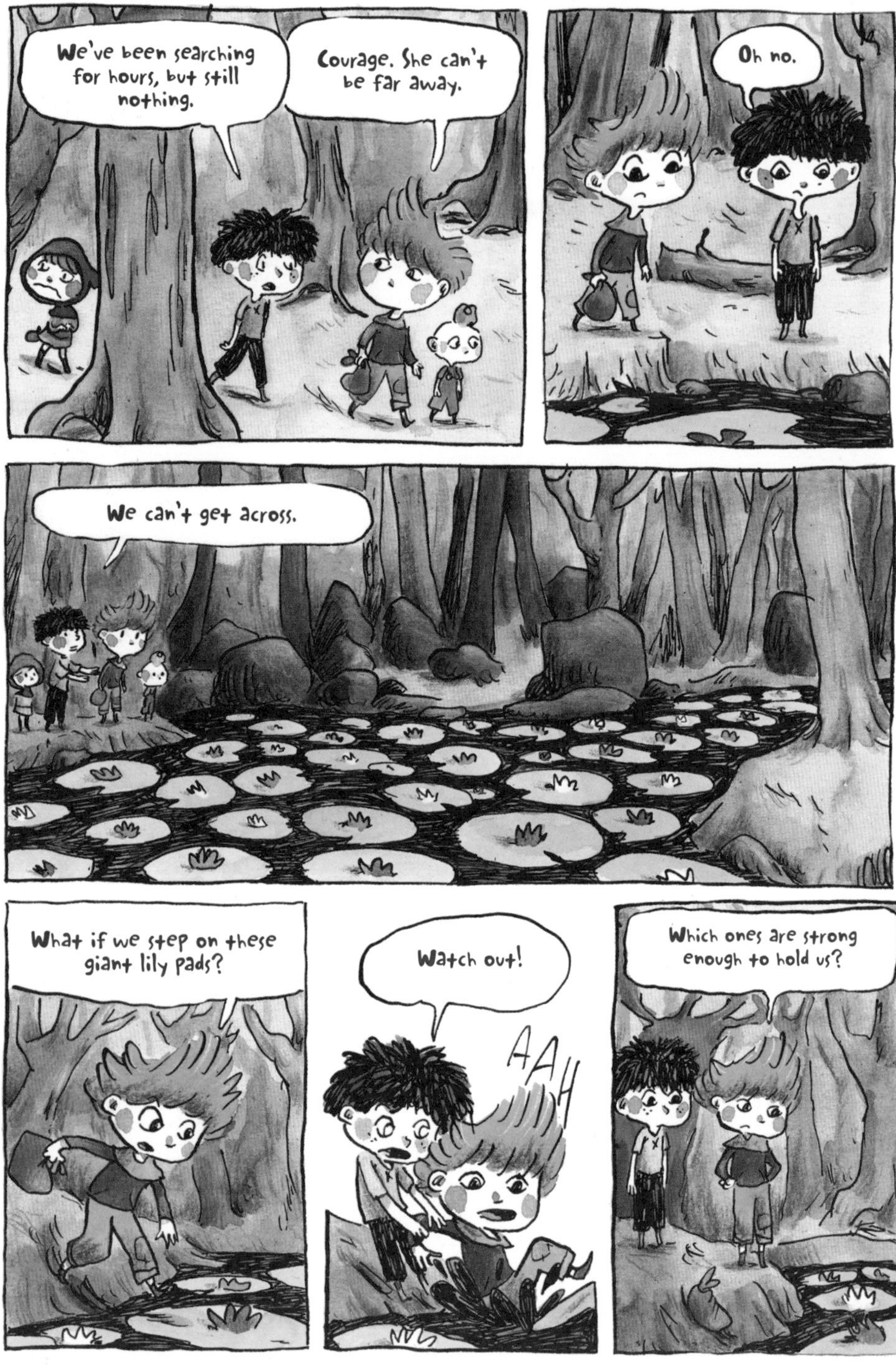

We've been searching for hours, but still nothing.
Courage. She can't be far away.
Oh no.
We can't get across.
What if we step on these giant lily pads?
Watch out!
AAH
Which ones are strong enough to hold us?

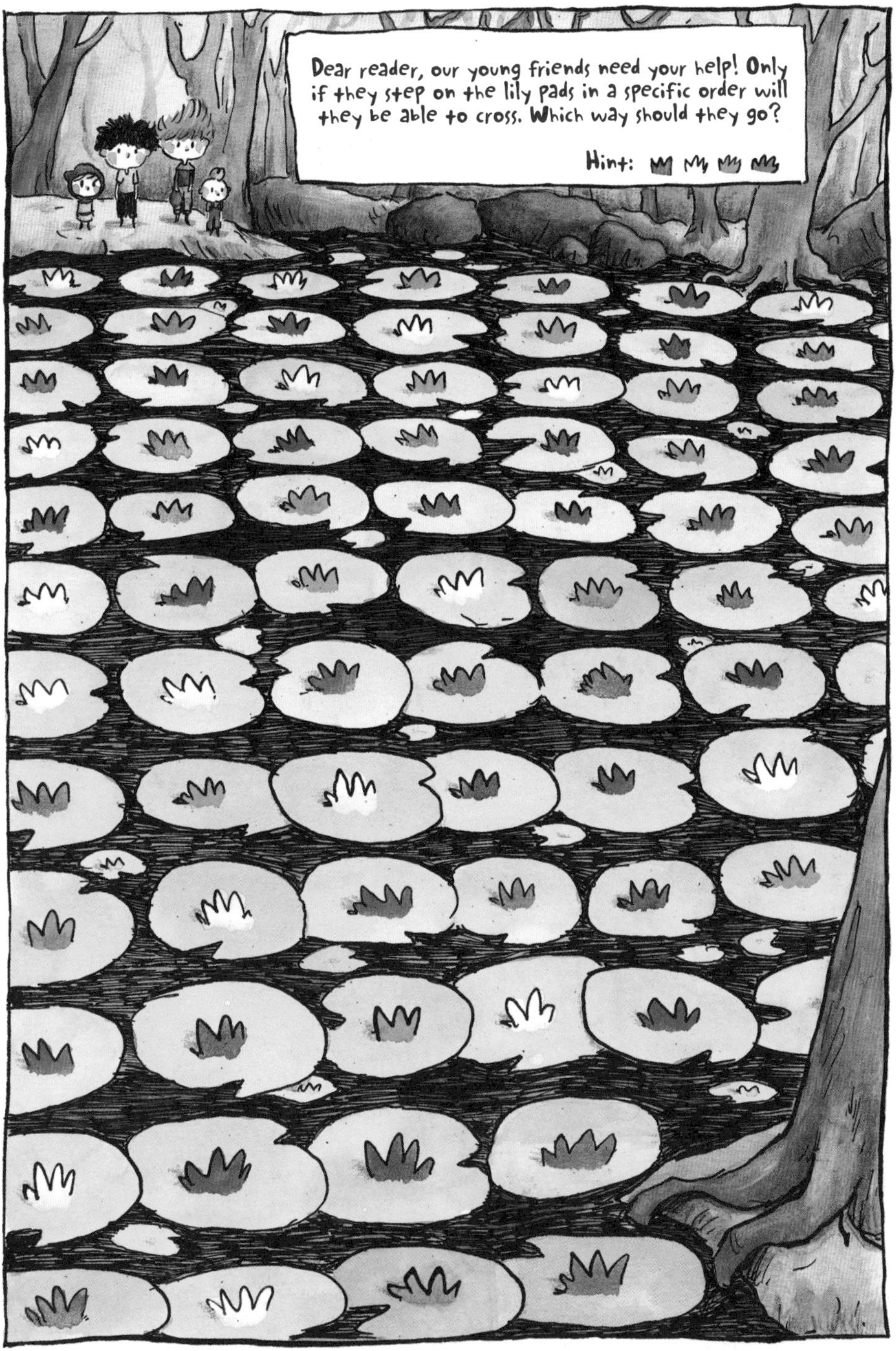
Dear reader, our young friends need your help! Only if they step on the lily pads in a specific order will they be able to cross. Which way should they go?
Hint:

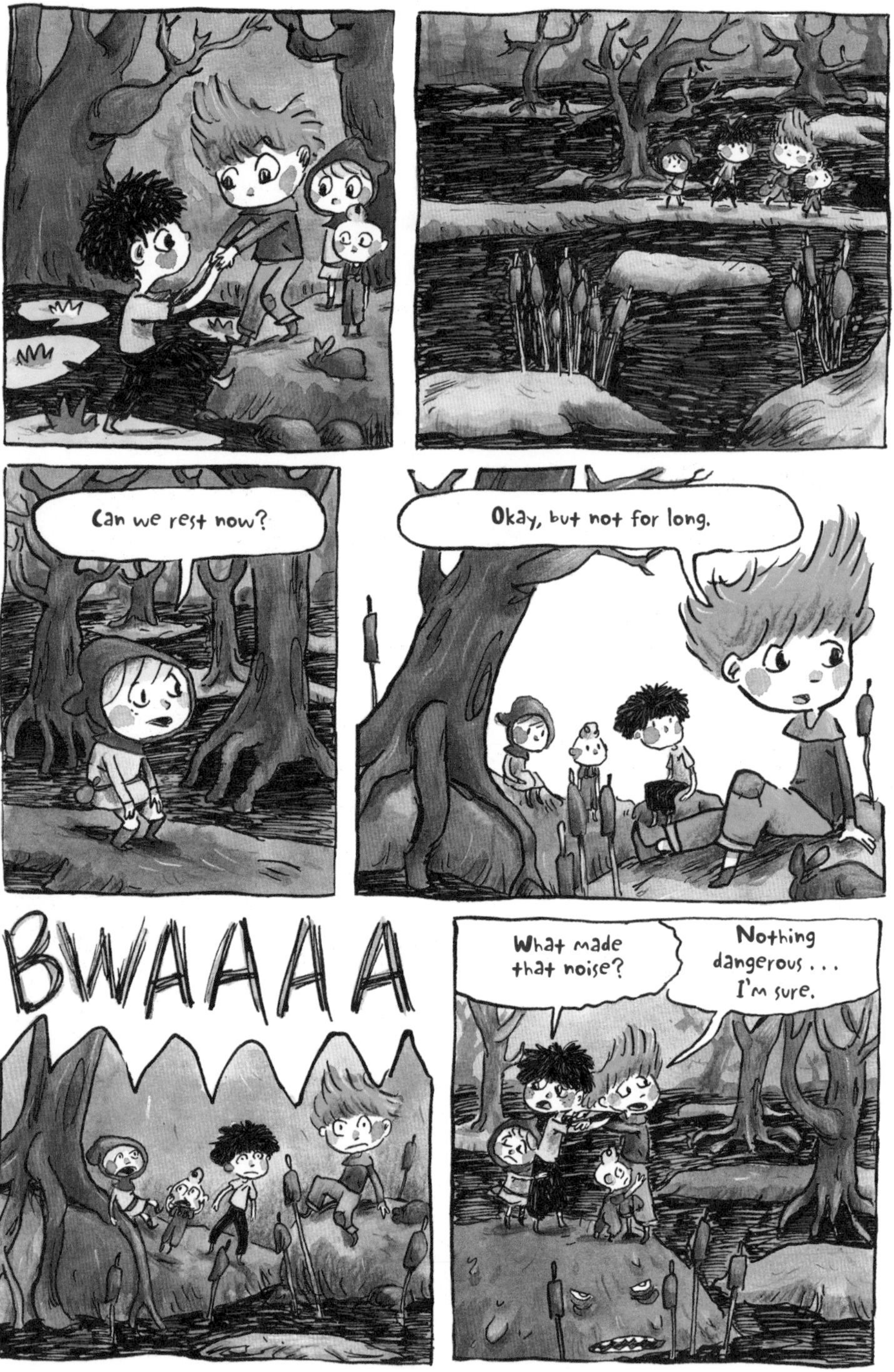
Can we rest now?
Okay, but not for long.
BWAAAA
What made that noise?
Nothing dangerous . . . I'm sure.

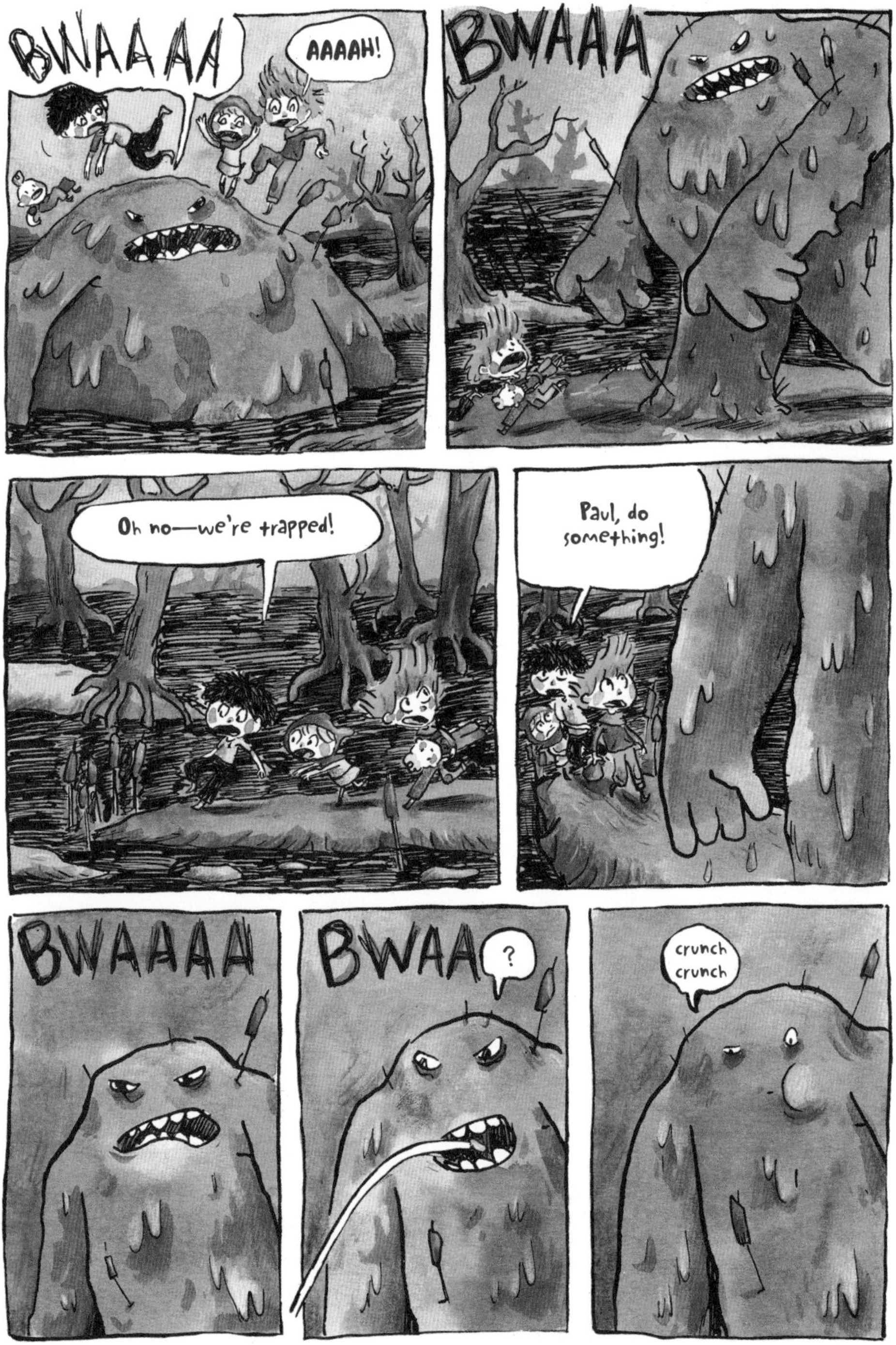
BWAAAAA
AAAAH!
BWAAAA
Oh no—we're trapped!
Paul, do something!
BWAAAAA
BWAA
?
crunch crunch

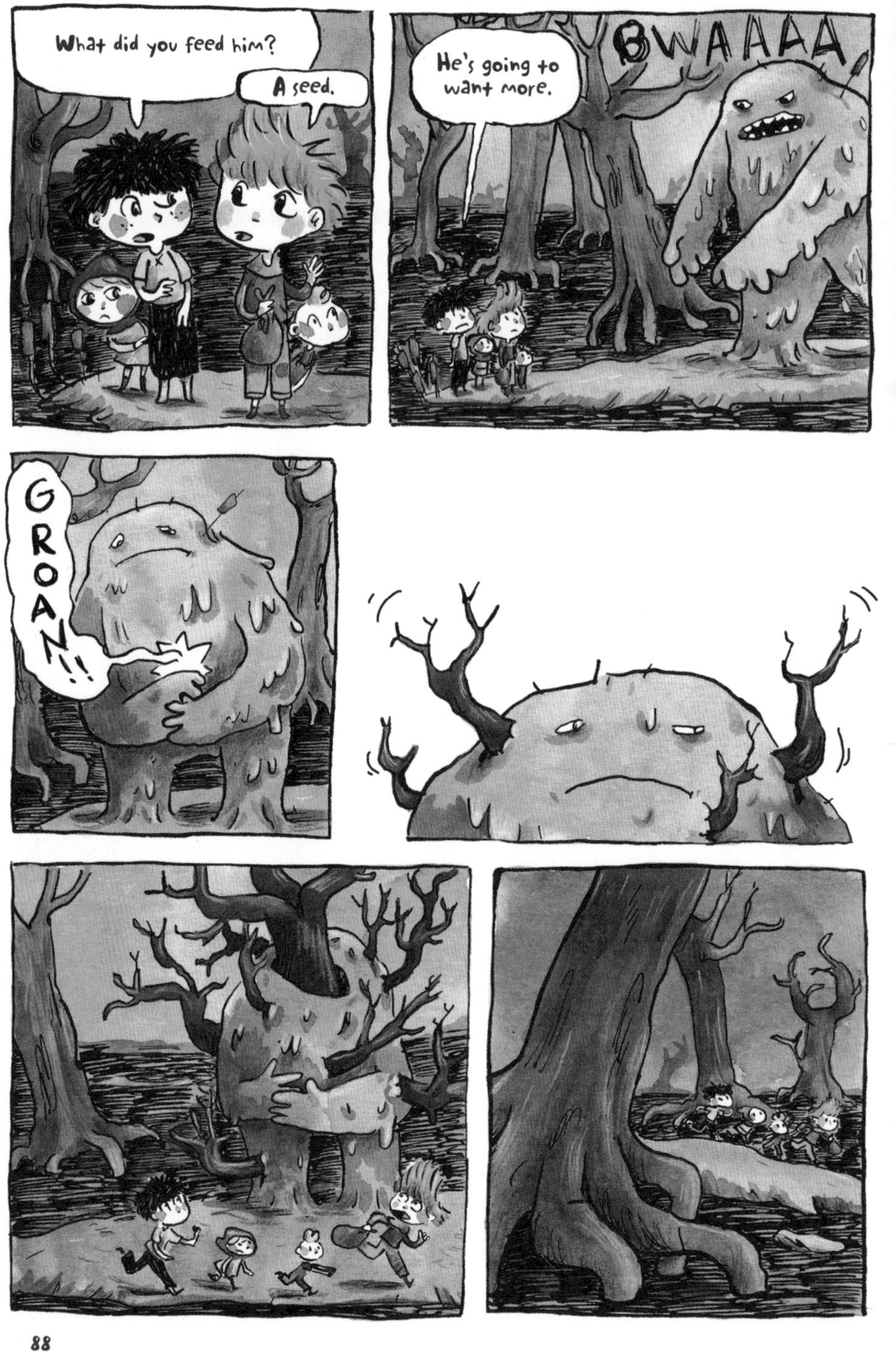
What did you feed him?
A seed.
He's going to want more.
BWAAAA
GROAN!!

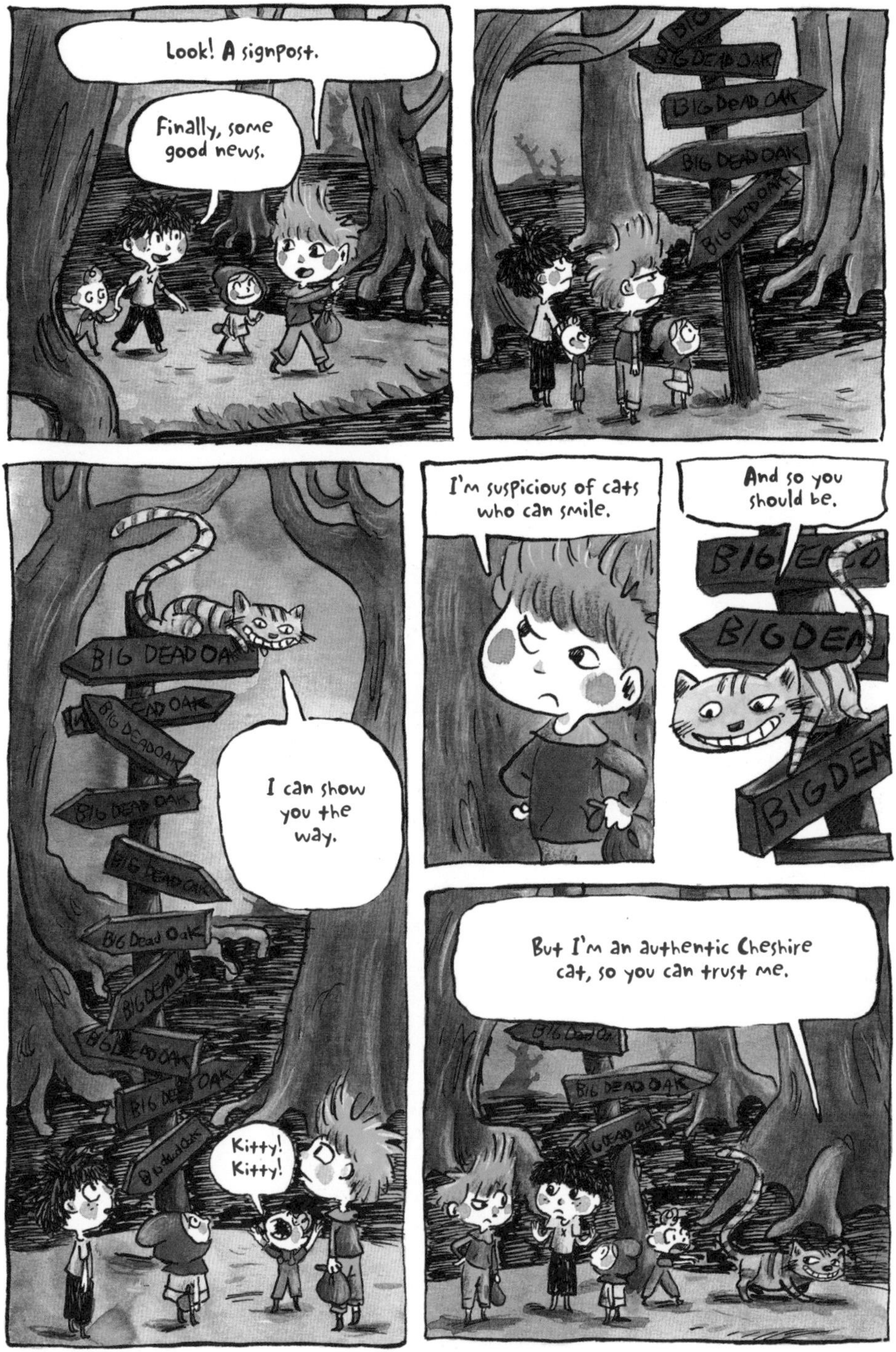
Look! A signpost.
Finally, some good news.
BIG DEAD OAK
BIG DEAD OAK
BIG DEAD OAK
BIG DEAD OAK
I can show you the way.
Kitty! Kitty!
I'm suspicious of cats who can smile.
And so you should be.
But I'm an authentic Cheshire cat, so you can trust me.

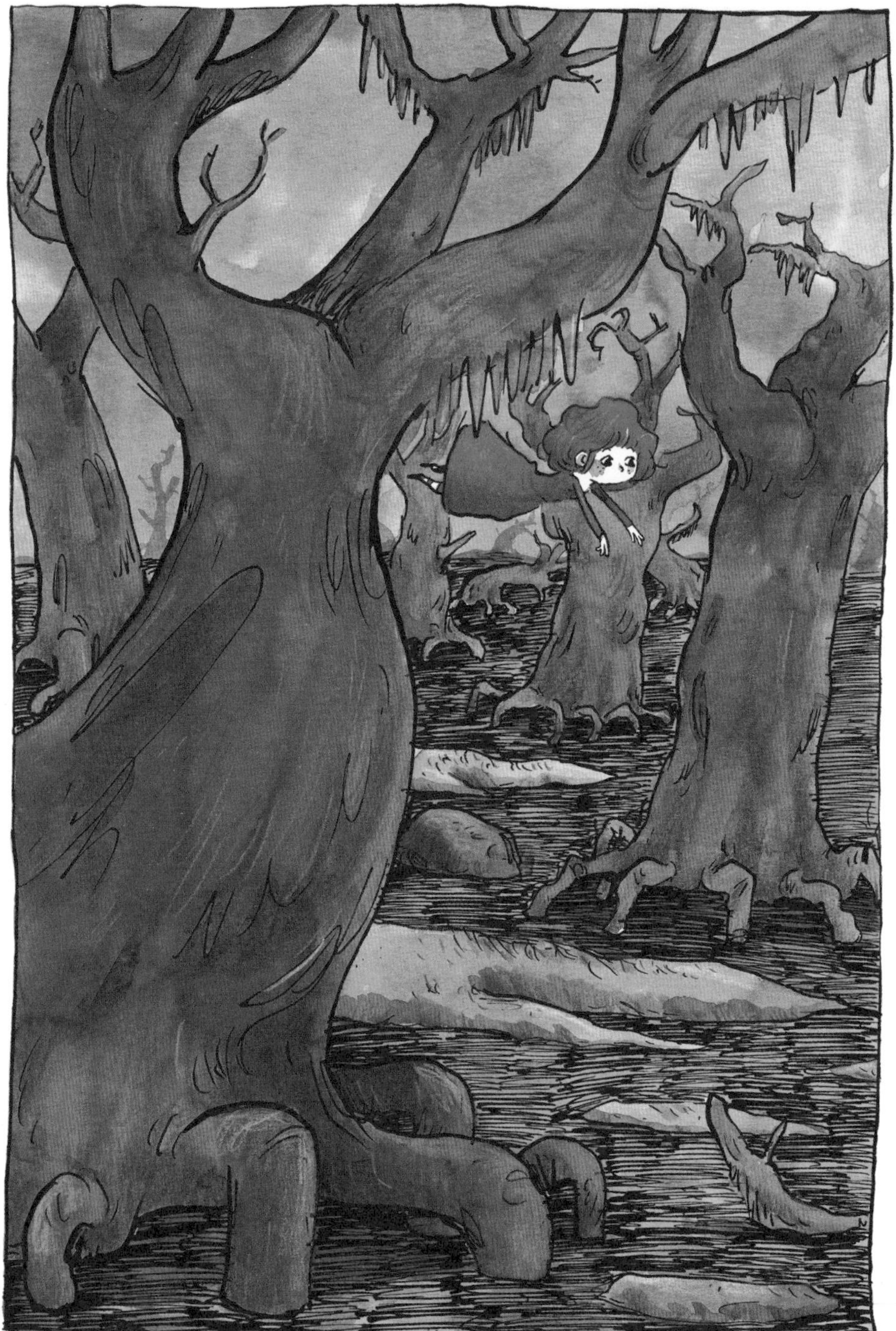

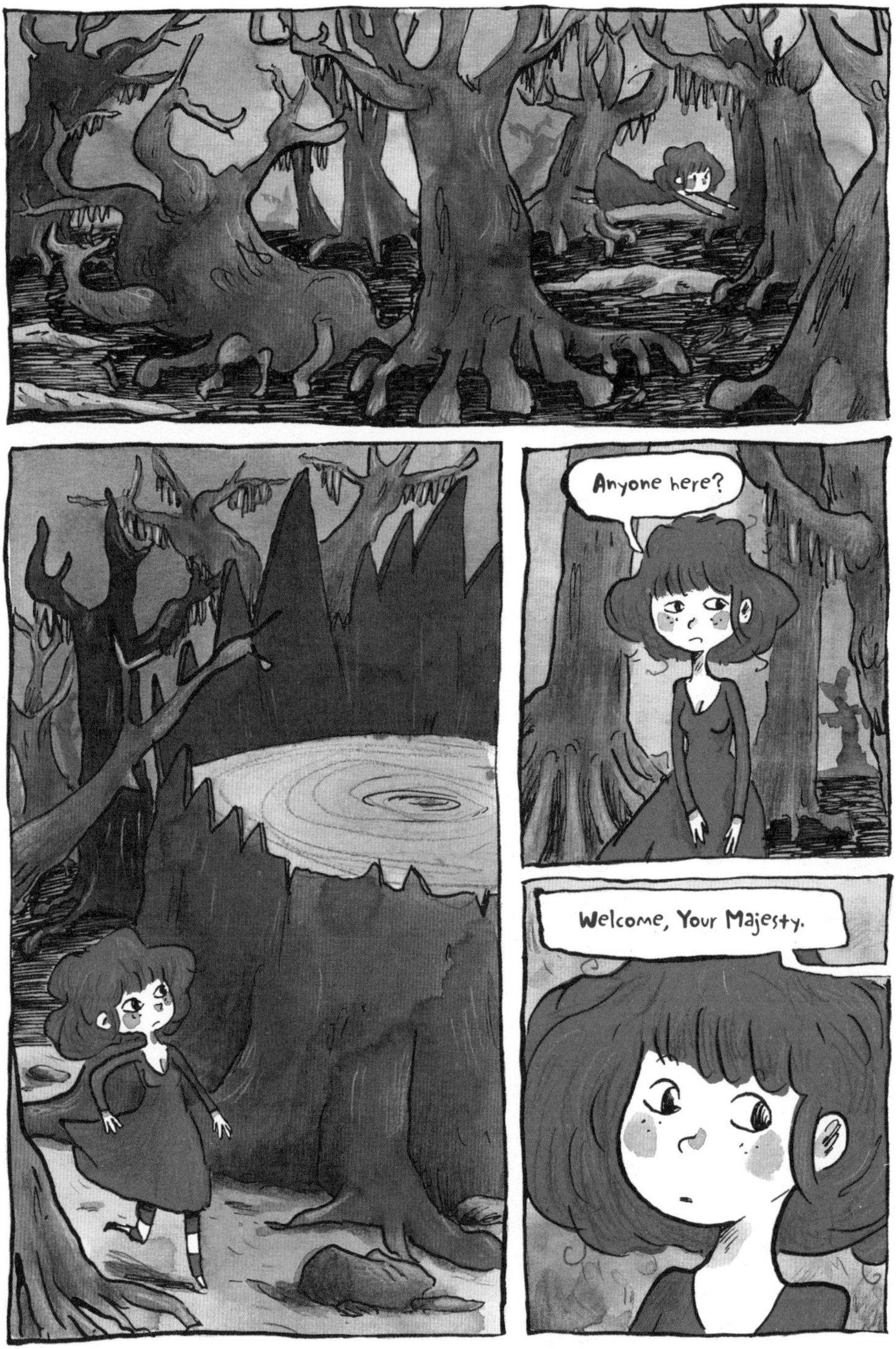
Anyone here?
Welcome, Your Majesty.

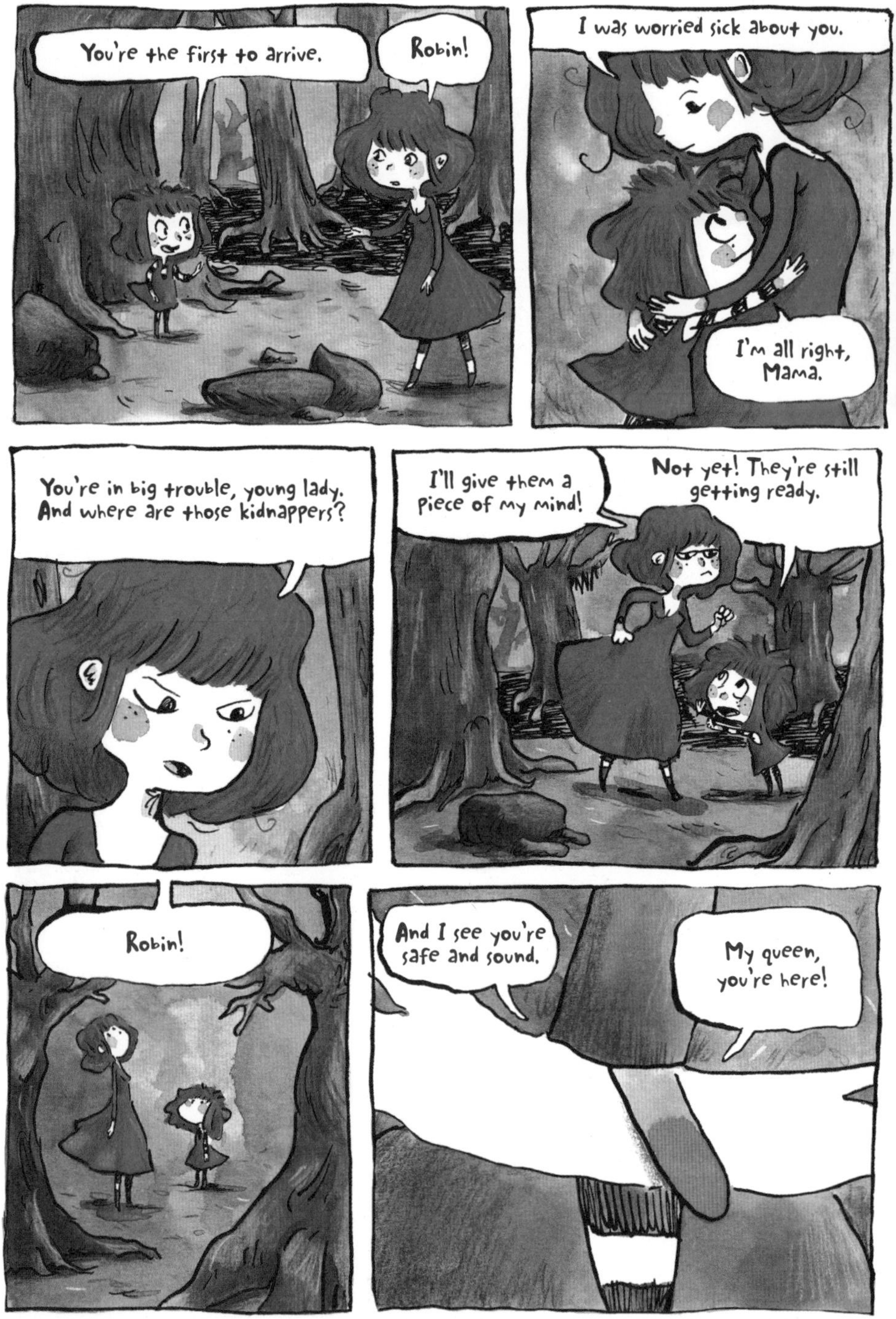
You're the first to arrive.
Robin!
I was worried sick about you.
I'm all right, Mama.
You're in big trouble, young lady. And where are those kidnappers?
I'll give them a piece of my mind!
Not yet! They're still getting ready.
Robin!
And I see you're safe and sound.
My queen, you're here!

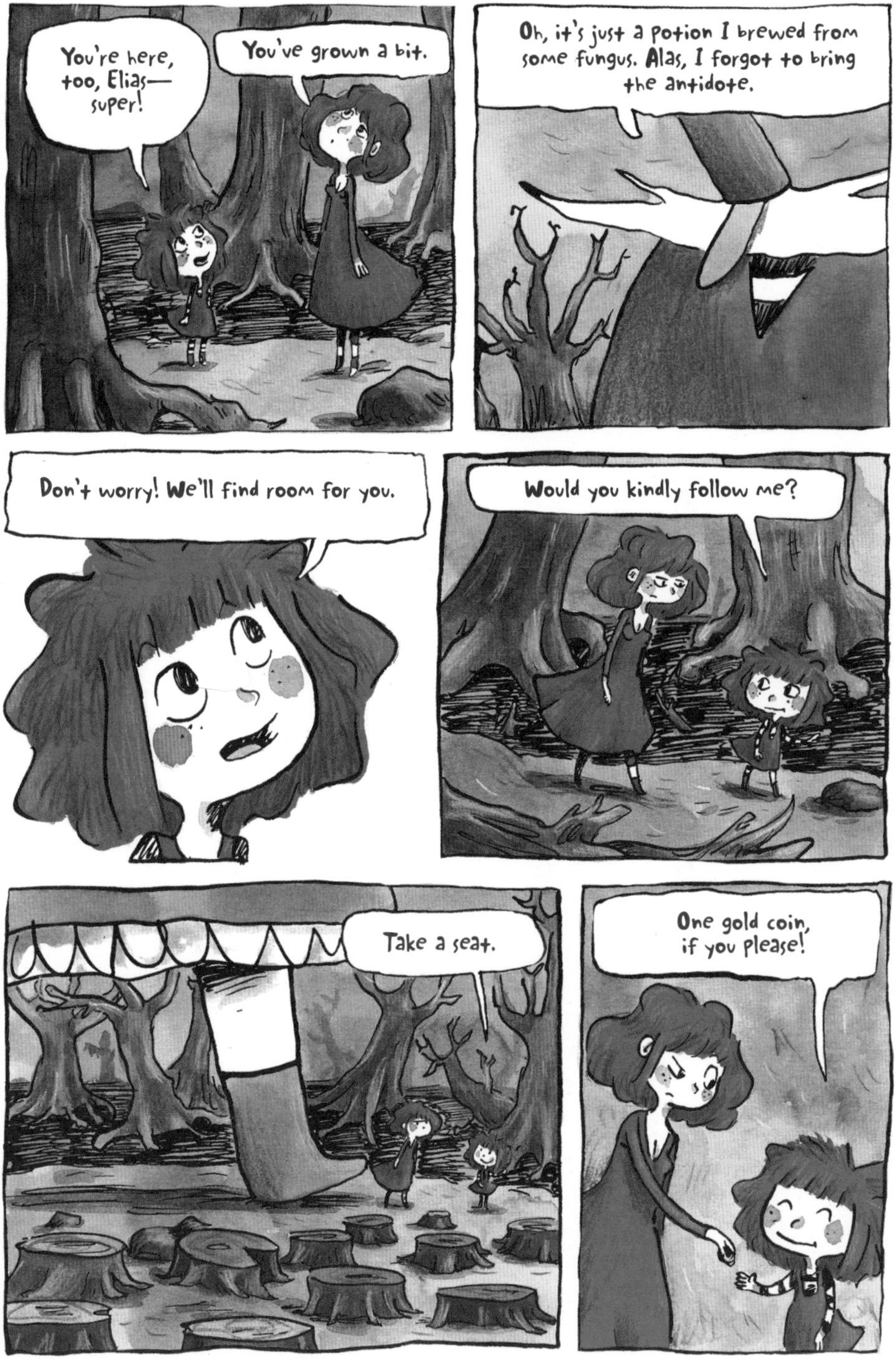

You're here, too, Elias—super!
You've grown a bit.
Oh, it's just a potion I brewed from some fungus. Alas, I forgot to bring the antidote.
Don't worry! We'll find room for you.
Would you kindly follow me?
Take a seat.
One gold coin, if you please!

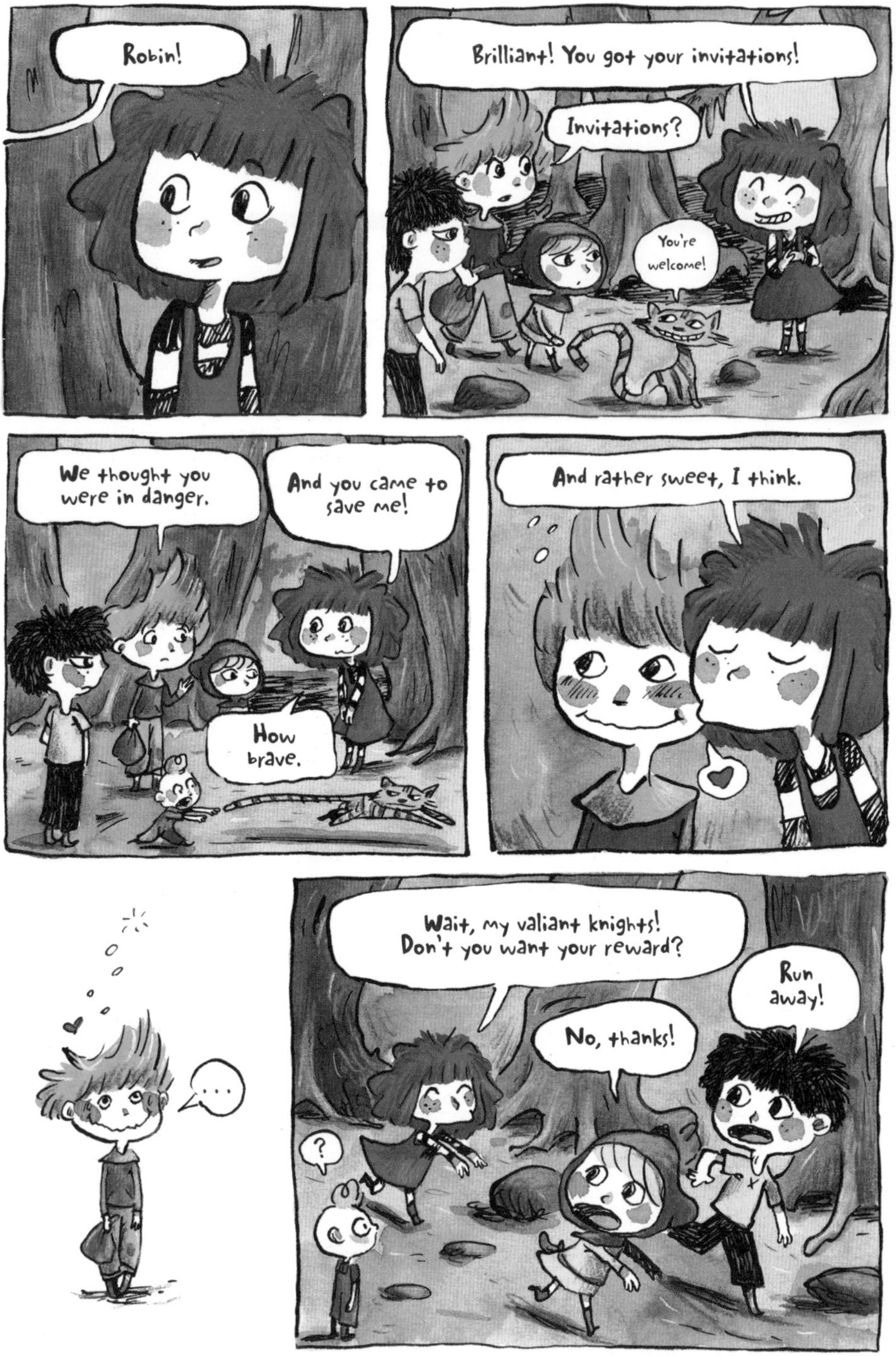
Robin!
Brilliant! You got your invitations!
Invitations?
You're welcome!
We thought you were in danger.
And you came to save me!
How brave.
And rather sweet, I think.
...
Wait, my valiant knights! Don't you want your reward?
?
No, thanks!
Run away!

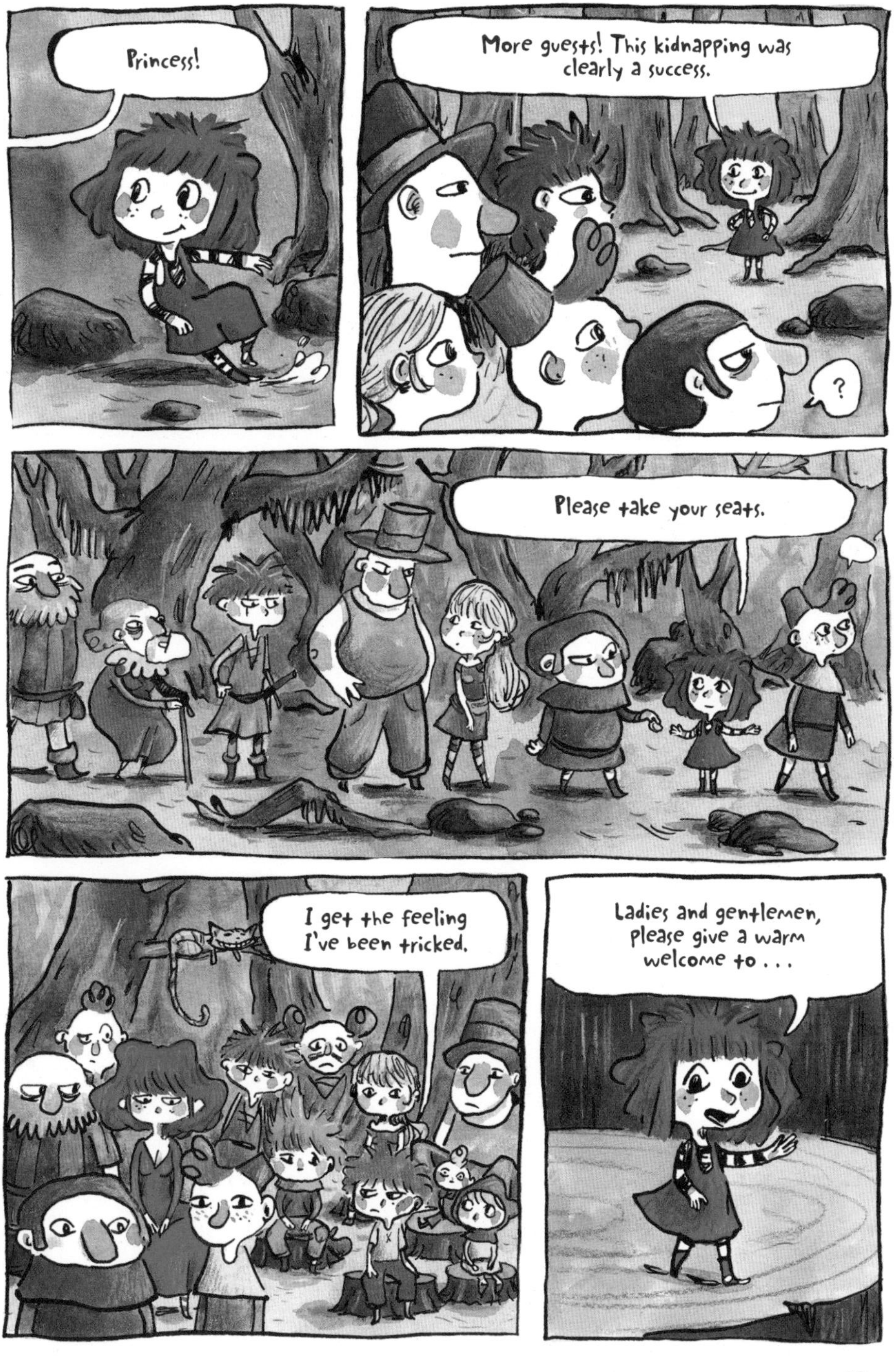
Princess!
More guests! This kidnapping was clearly a success.
?
Please take your seats.
I get the feeling I've been tricked.
Ladies and gentlemen, please give a warm welcome to . . .

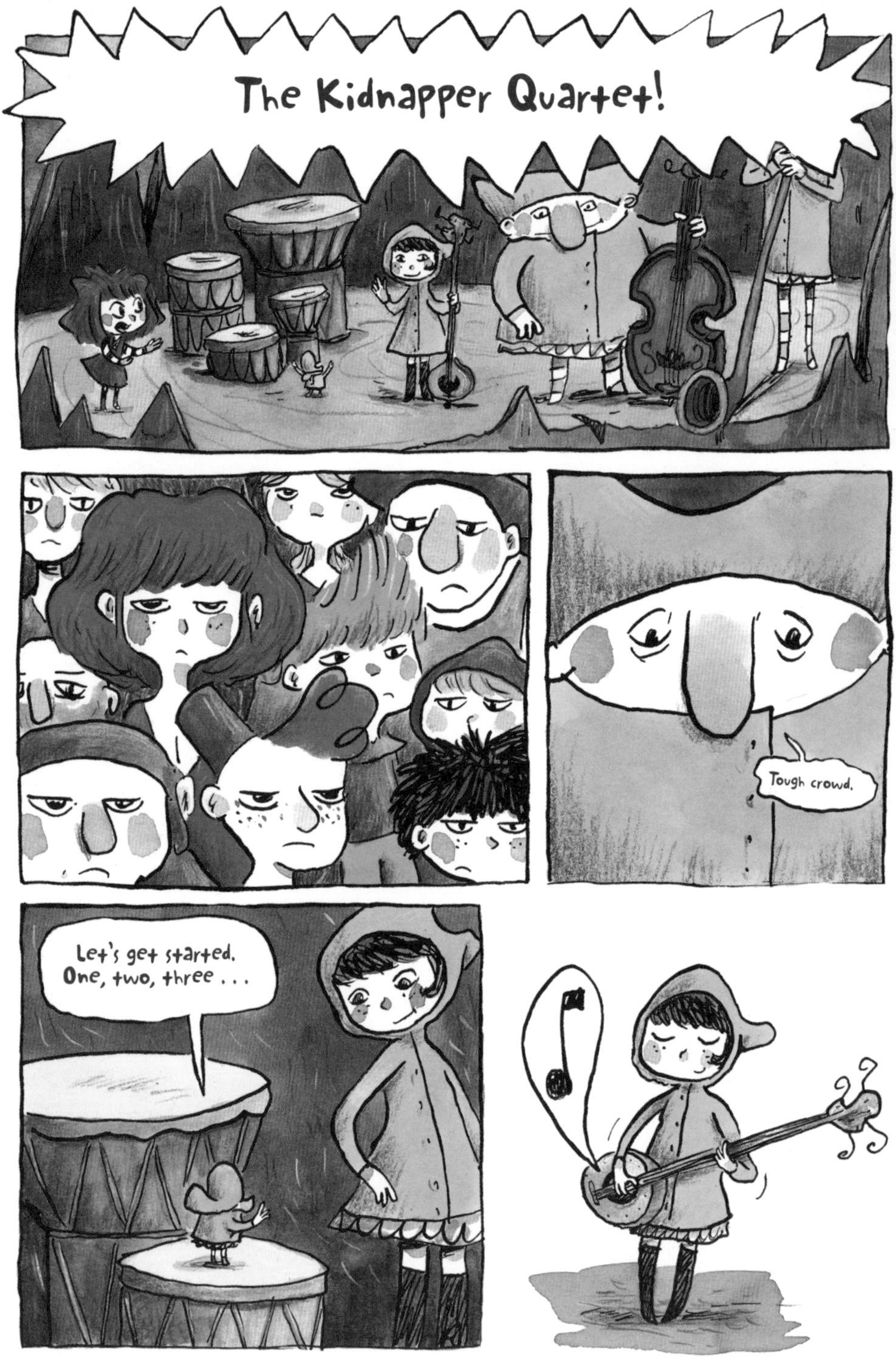
The Kidnapper Quartet!
Tough crowd.
Let's get started.
One, two, three . . .

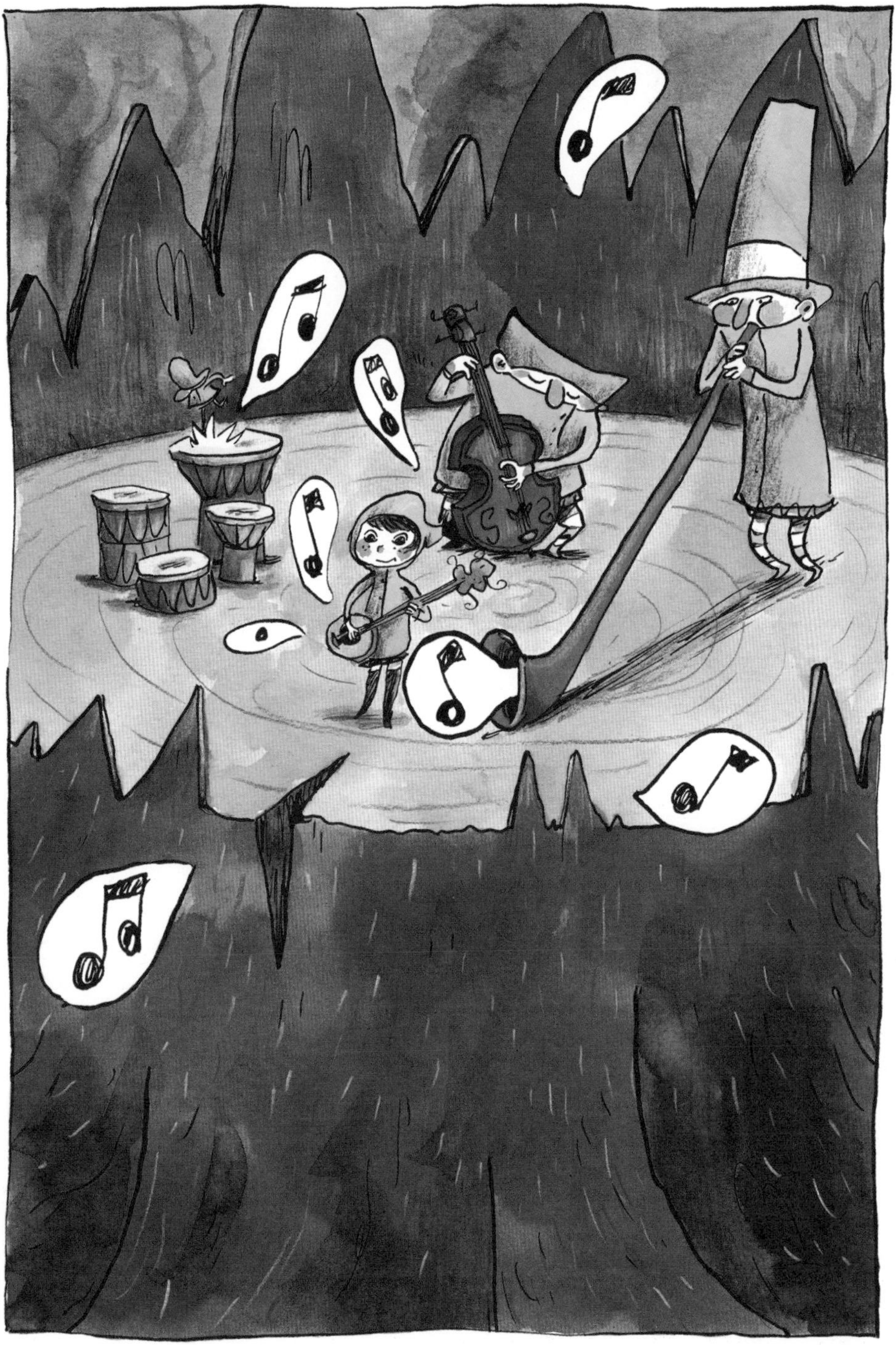

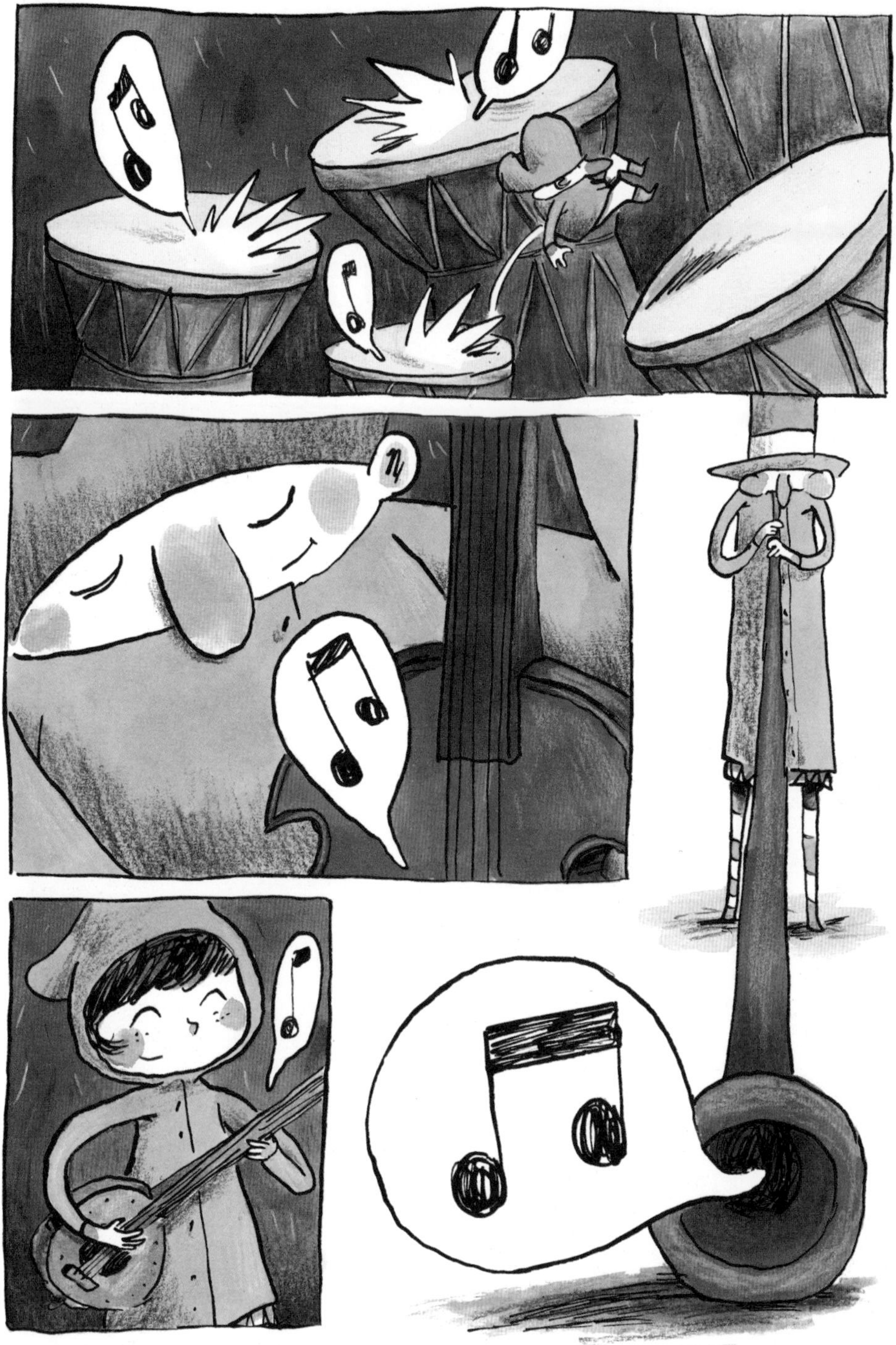

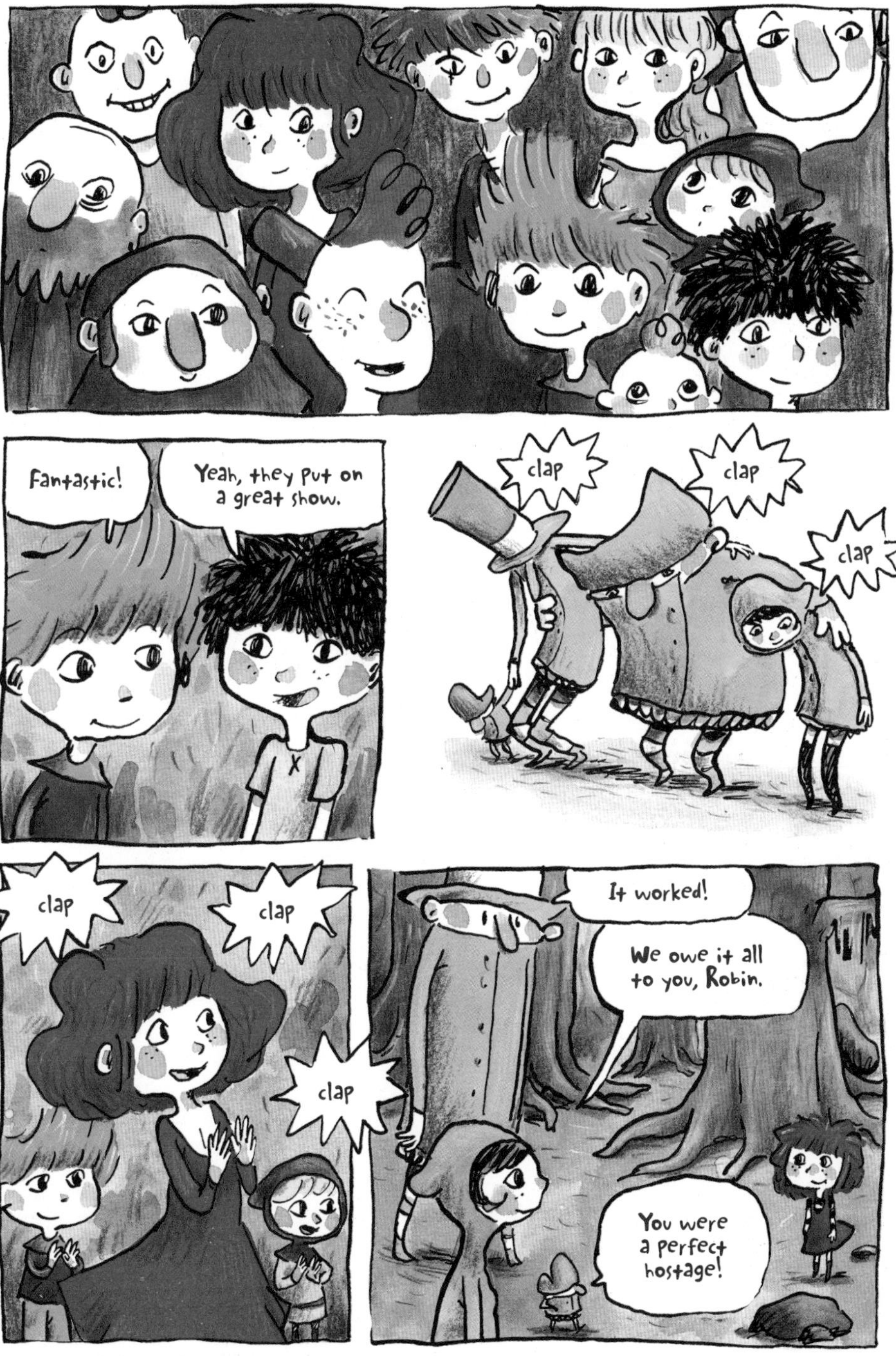
Fantastic!
Yeah, they put on a great show.
clap
clap
clap
clap
clap
clap
It worked!
We owe it all to you, Robin.
You were a perfect hostage!

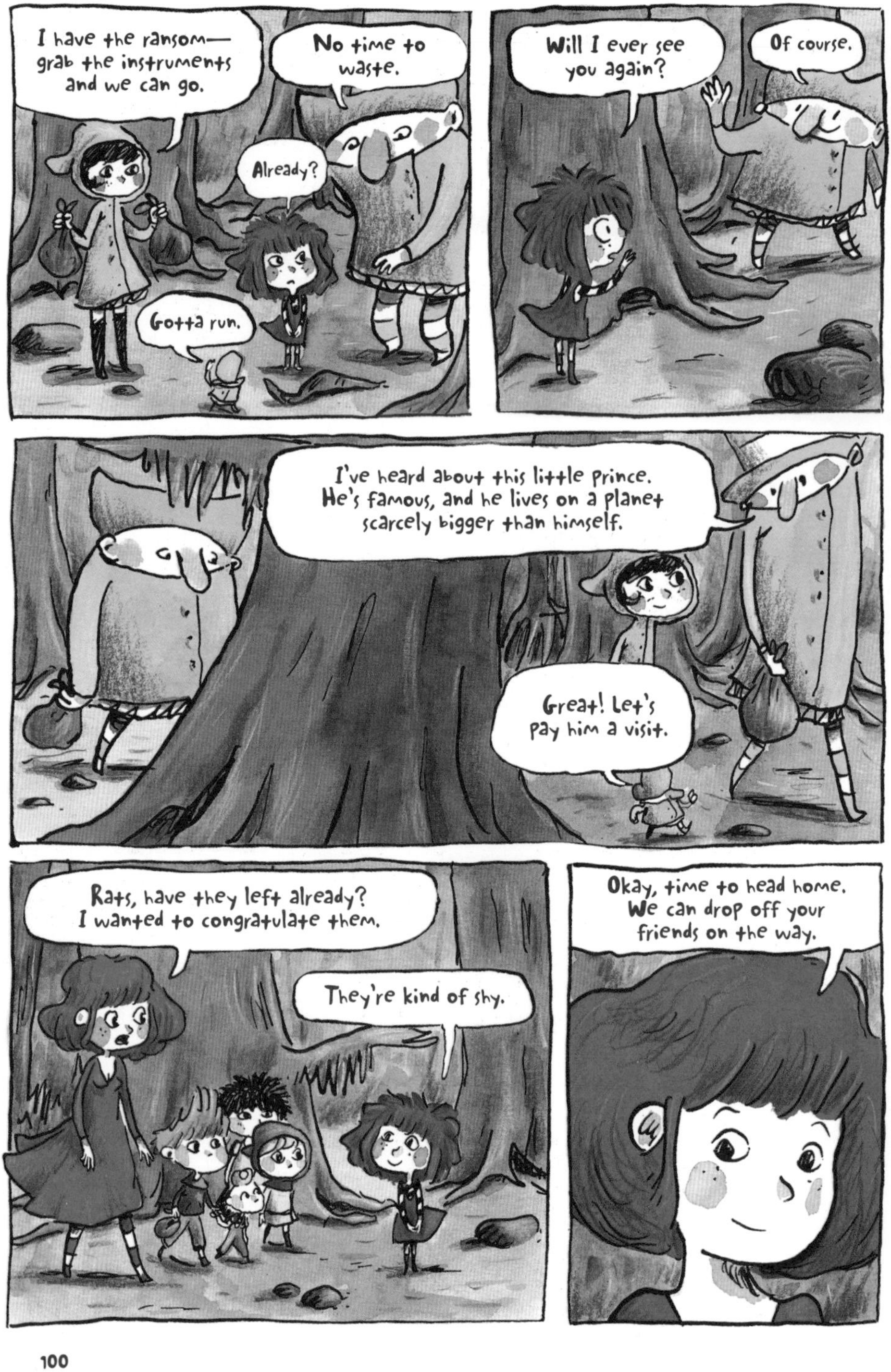
I have the ransom—grab the instruments and we can go.
No time to waste.
Already?
Gotta run.
Will I ever see you again?
Of course.
I've heard about this little prince. He's famous, and he lives on a planet scarcely bigger than himself.
Great! Let's pay him a visit.
Rats, have they left already? I wanted to congratulate them.
They're kind of shy.
Okay, time to head home. We can drop off your friends on the way.

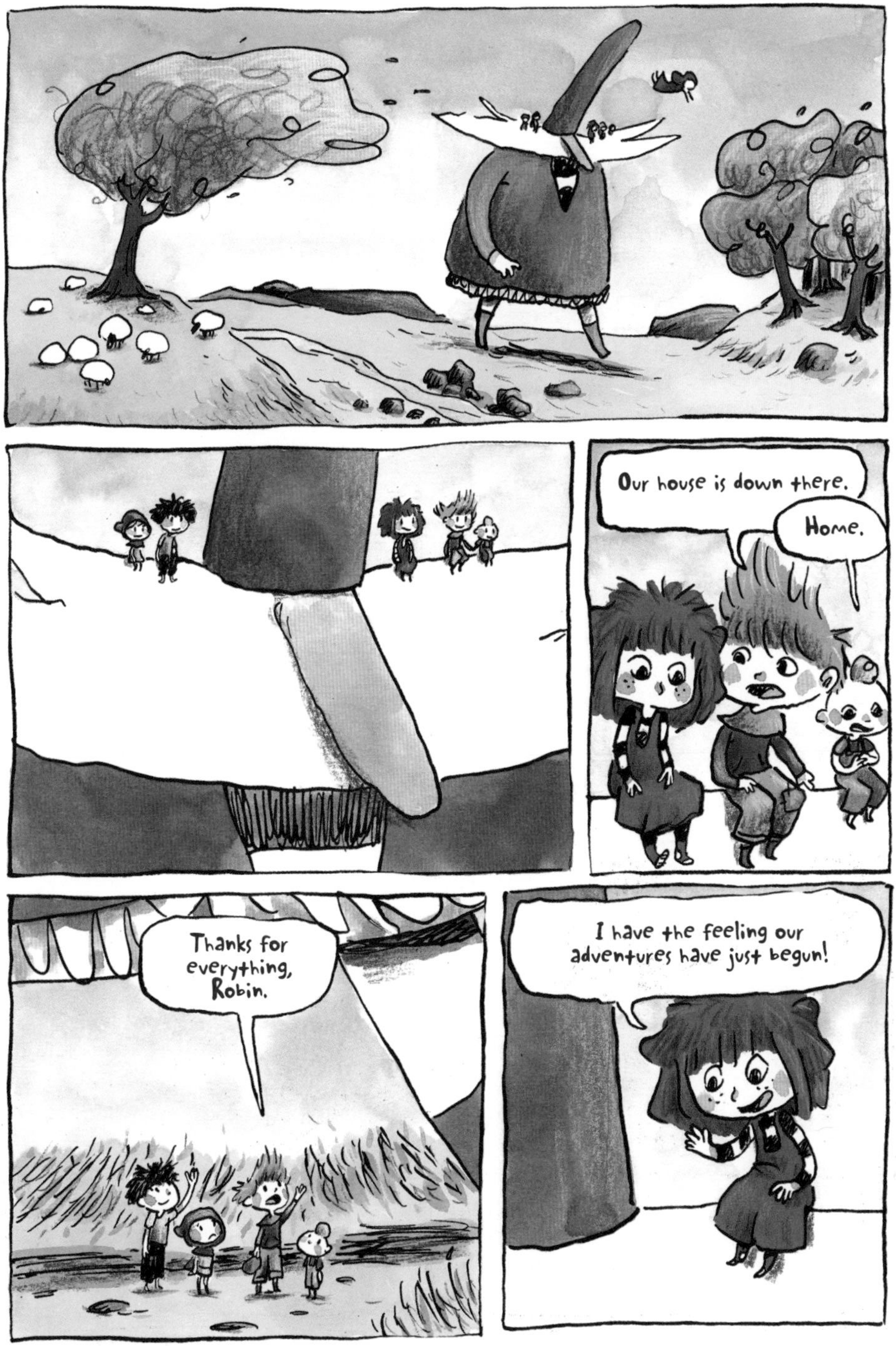

Our house is down there.
Home.
Thanks for everything, Robin.
I have the feeling our adventures have just begun!

Paul, Matt, Lee, and Omar went home and showed their parents the bag of seeds. Immediately, the boys began to plant a garden and were soon able to feed the whole family.

TROIA1SNOWSKI

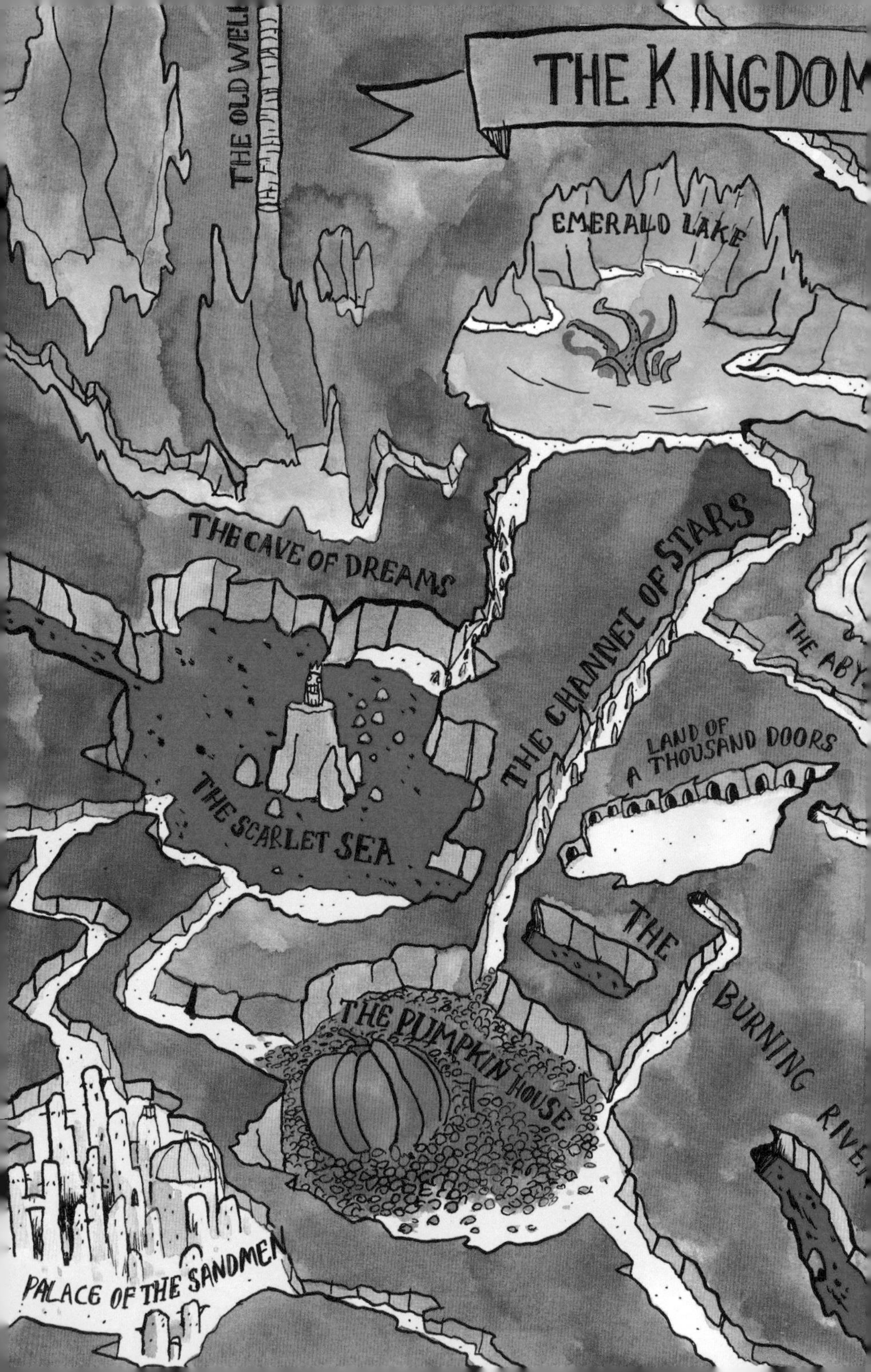
THE KINGDOM
THE OLD WELL
EMERALD LAKE
THE CAVE OF DREAMS
THE CHANNEL OF STARS
THE ABY
LAND OF A THOUSAND DOORS
THE SCARLET SEA
THE BURNING RIVE
THE PUMPKIN HOUSE
PALACE OF THE SANDMEN

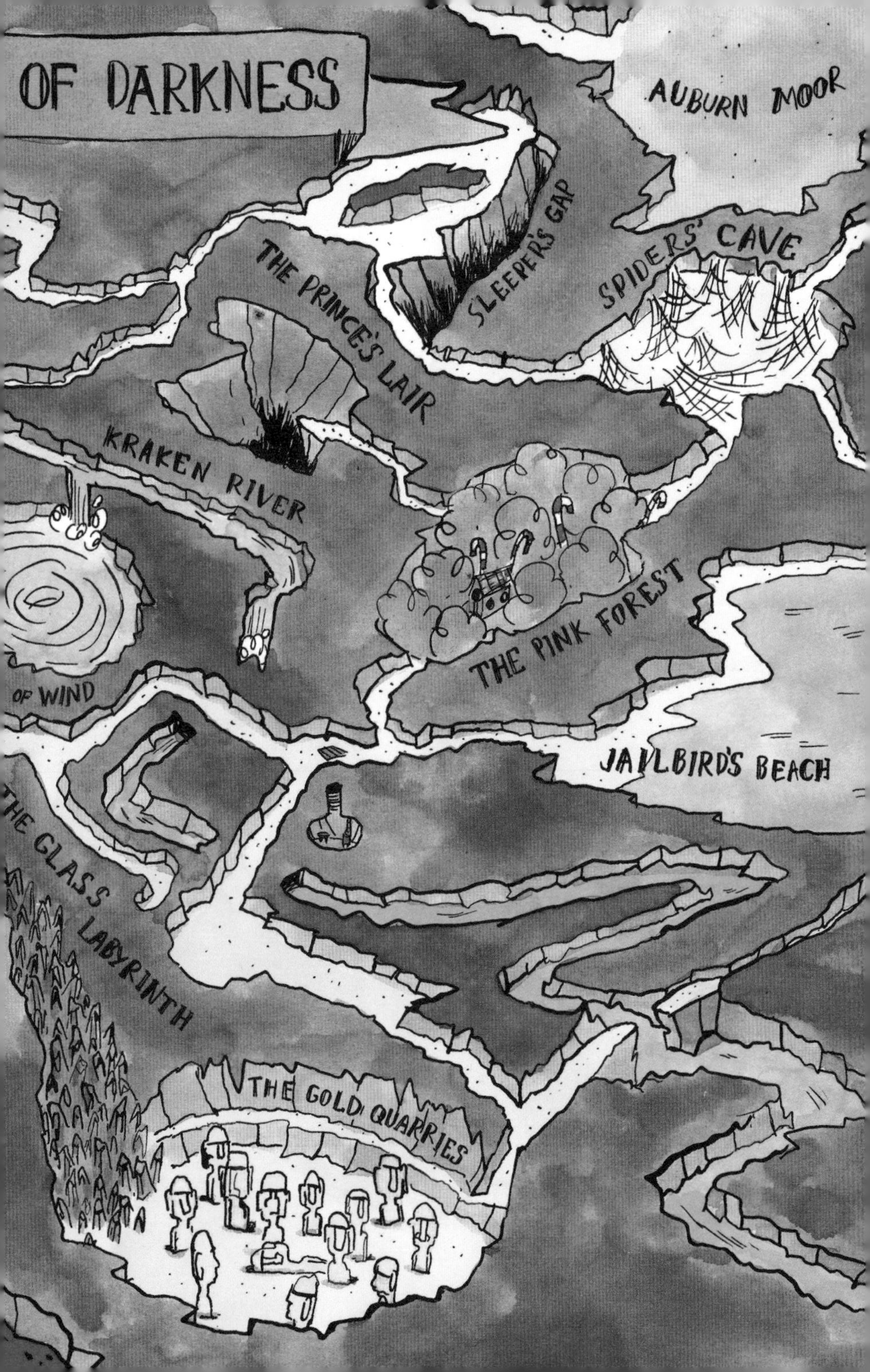
OF DARKNESS
AUBURN MOOR
SLEEPER'S GAP
SPIDERS' CAVE
THE PRINCE'S LAIR
KRAKEN RIVER
THE PINK FOREST
OF WIND
JAILBIRD'S BEACH
THE GLASS LABYRINTH
THE GOLD QUARRIES

# THE PRINCESS RUNS AWAY AGAIN

(BY ACCIDENT THIS TIME)

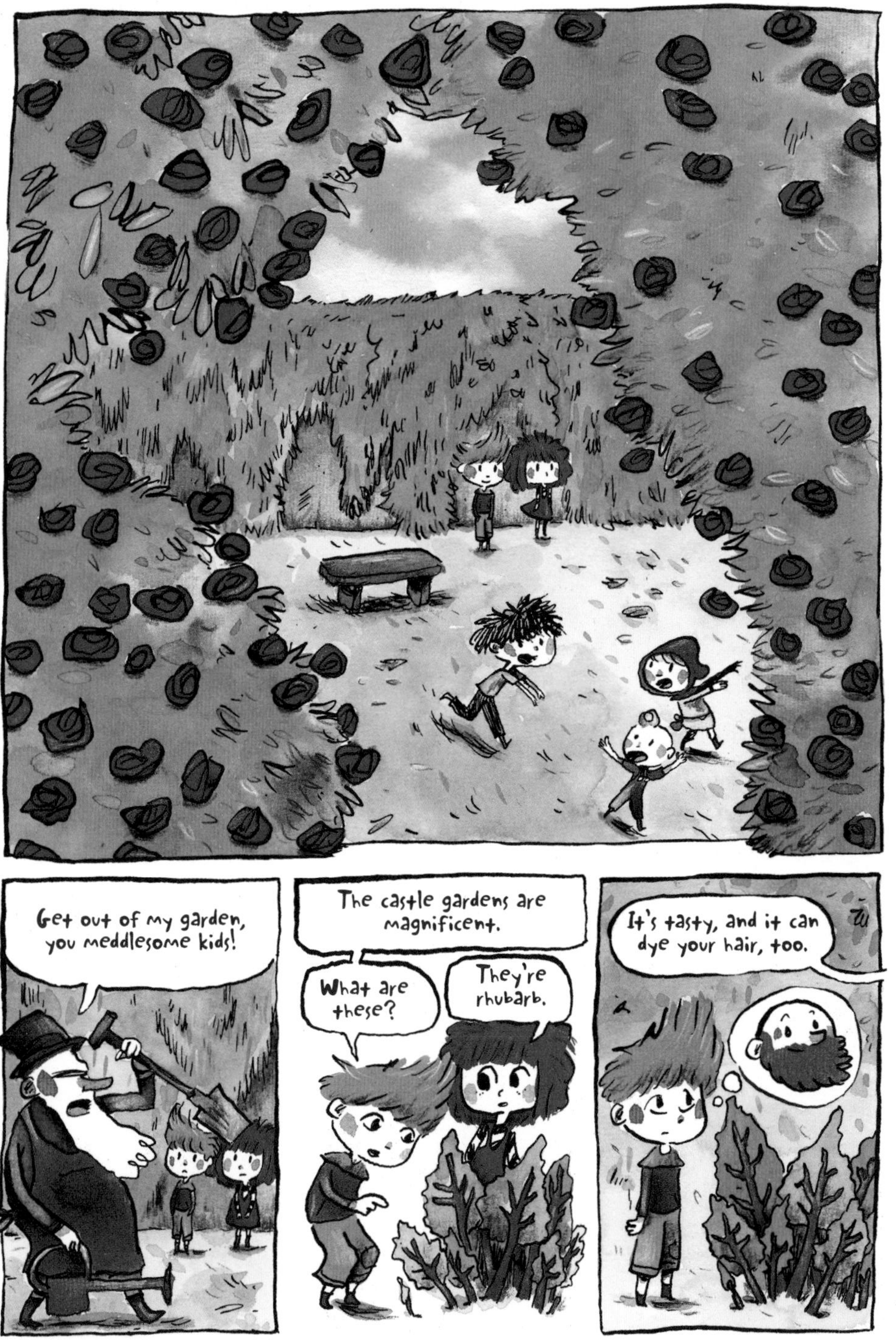
Get out of my garden, you meddlesome kids!
The castle gardens are magnificent.
What are these?
They're rhubarb.
It's tasty, and it can dye your hair, too.

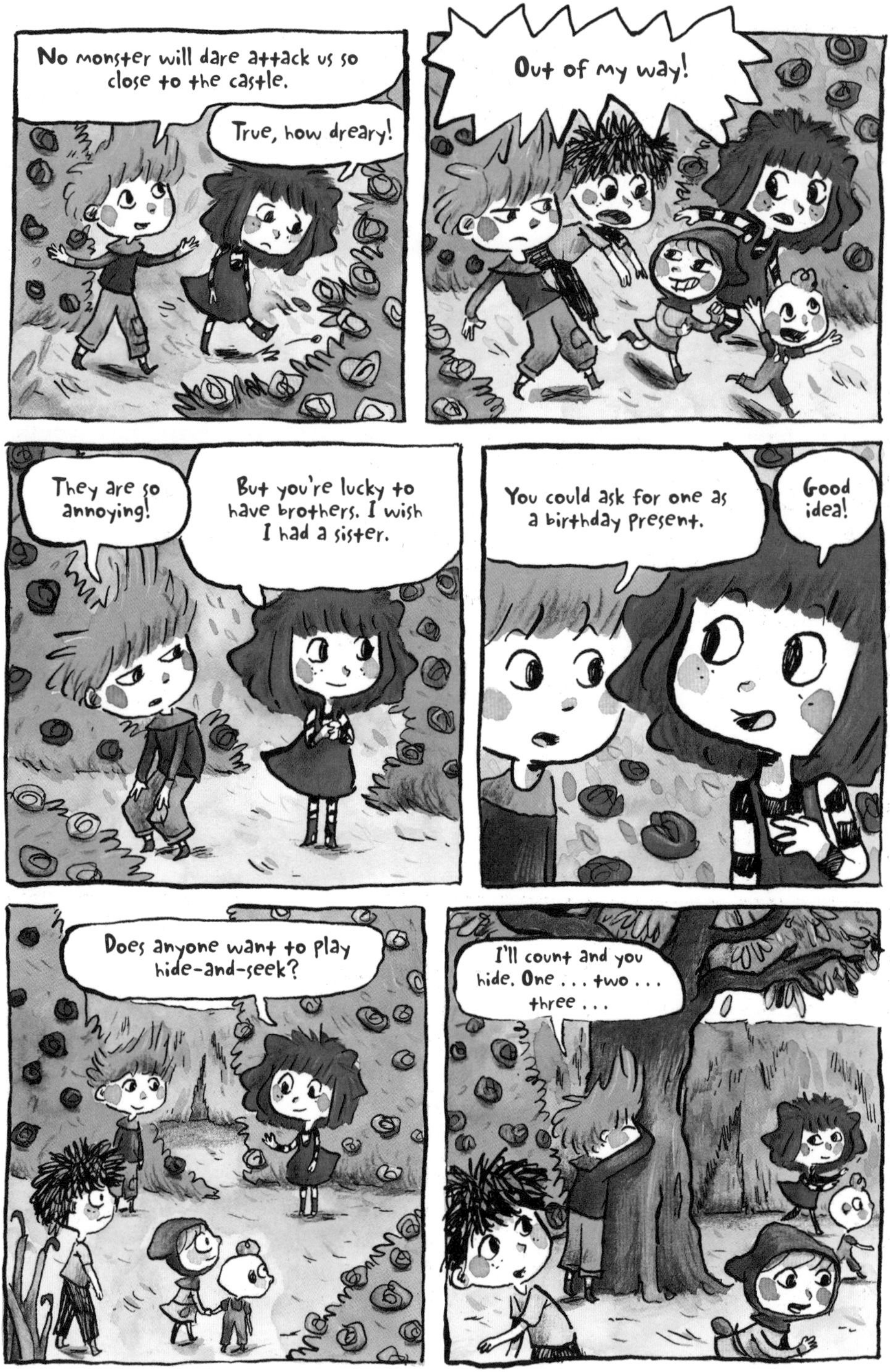
No monster will dare attack us so close to the castle.
True, how dreary!
Out of my way!
They are so annoying!
But you're lucky to have brothers. I wish I had a sister.
You could ask for one as a birthday present.
Good idea!
Does anyone want to play hide-and-seek?
I'll count and you hide. One . . . two . . . three . . .

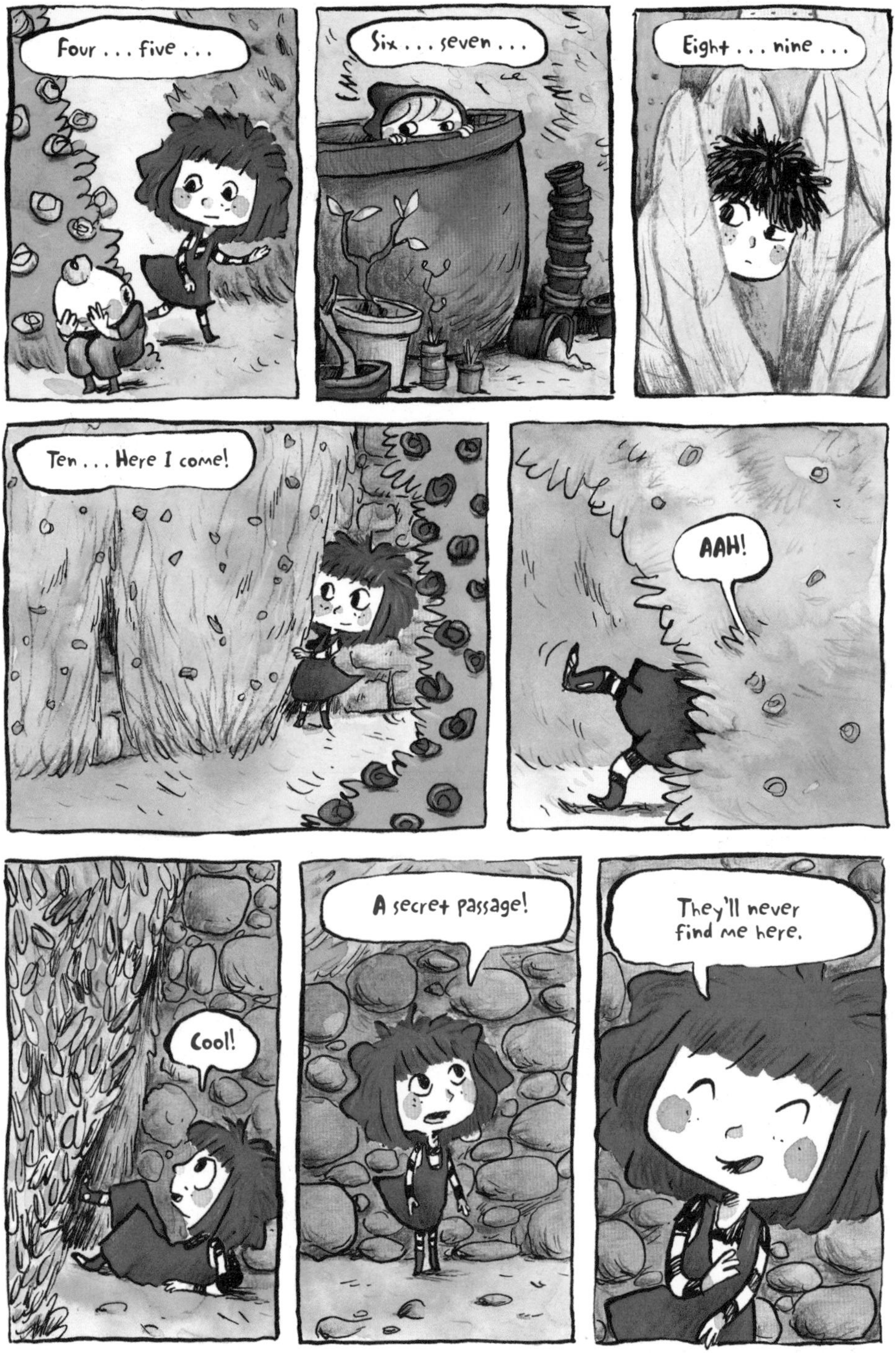
Four . . . five . . .
Six . . . seven . . .
Eight . . . nine . . .
Ten . . . Here I come!
AAH!
Cool!
A secret passage!
They'll never find me here.

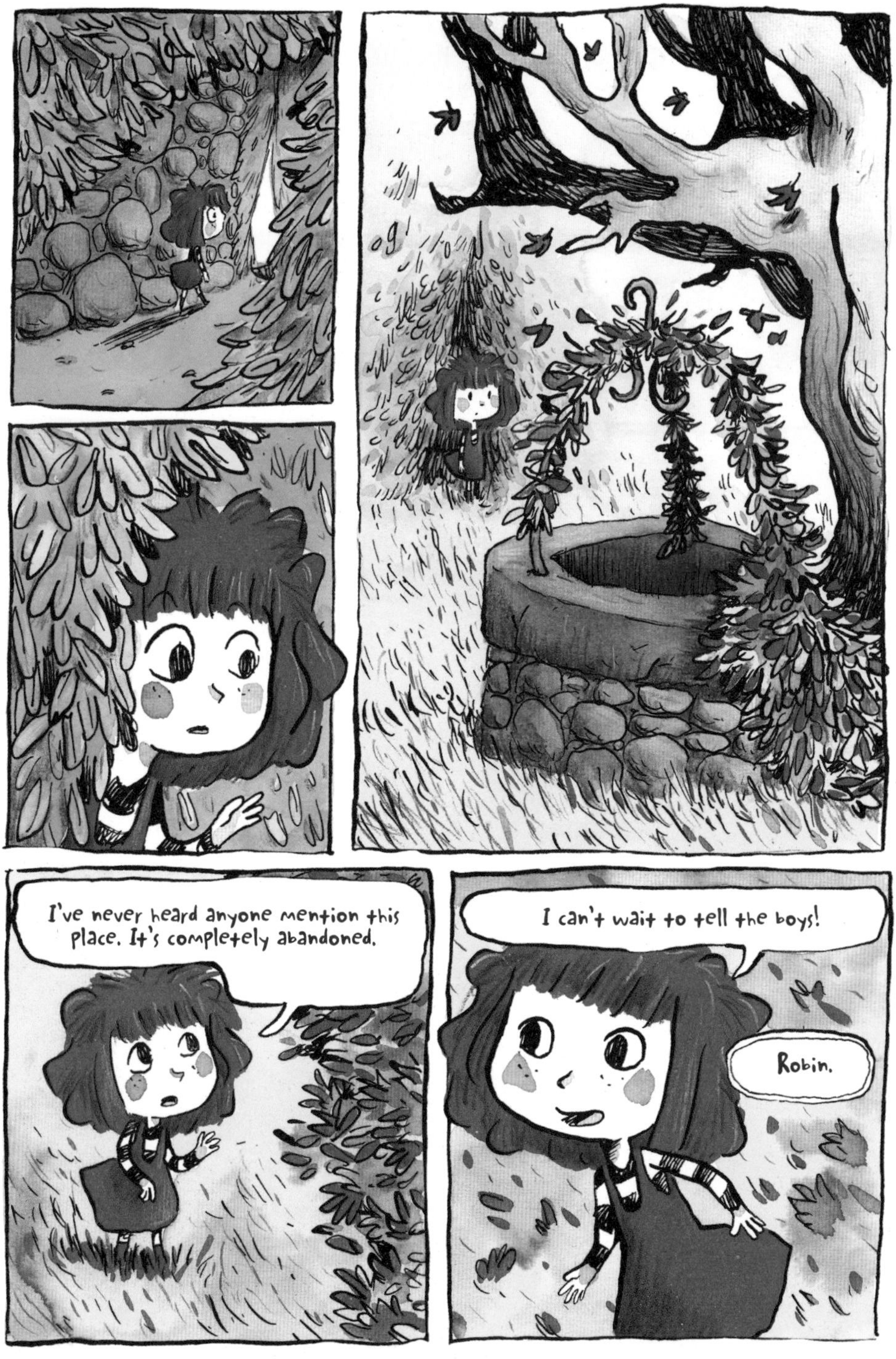
I've never heard anyone mention this place. It's completely abandoned.
I can't wait to tell the boys!
Robin.

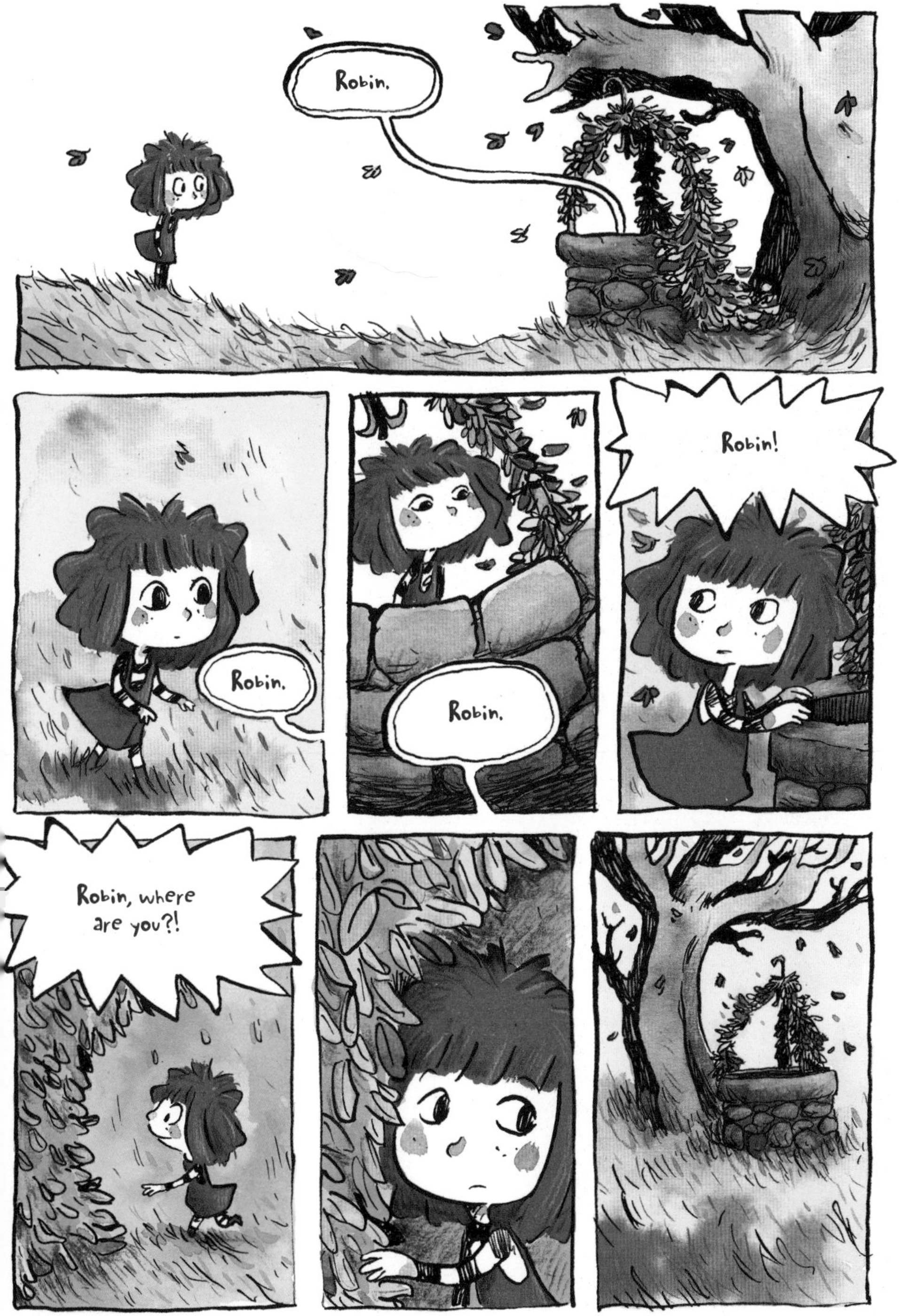
Robin.
Robin.
Robin.
Robin!
Robin, where are you?!

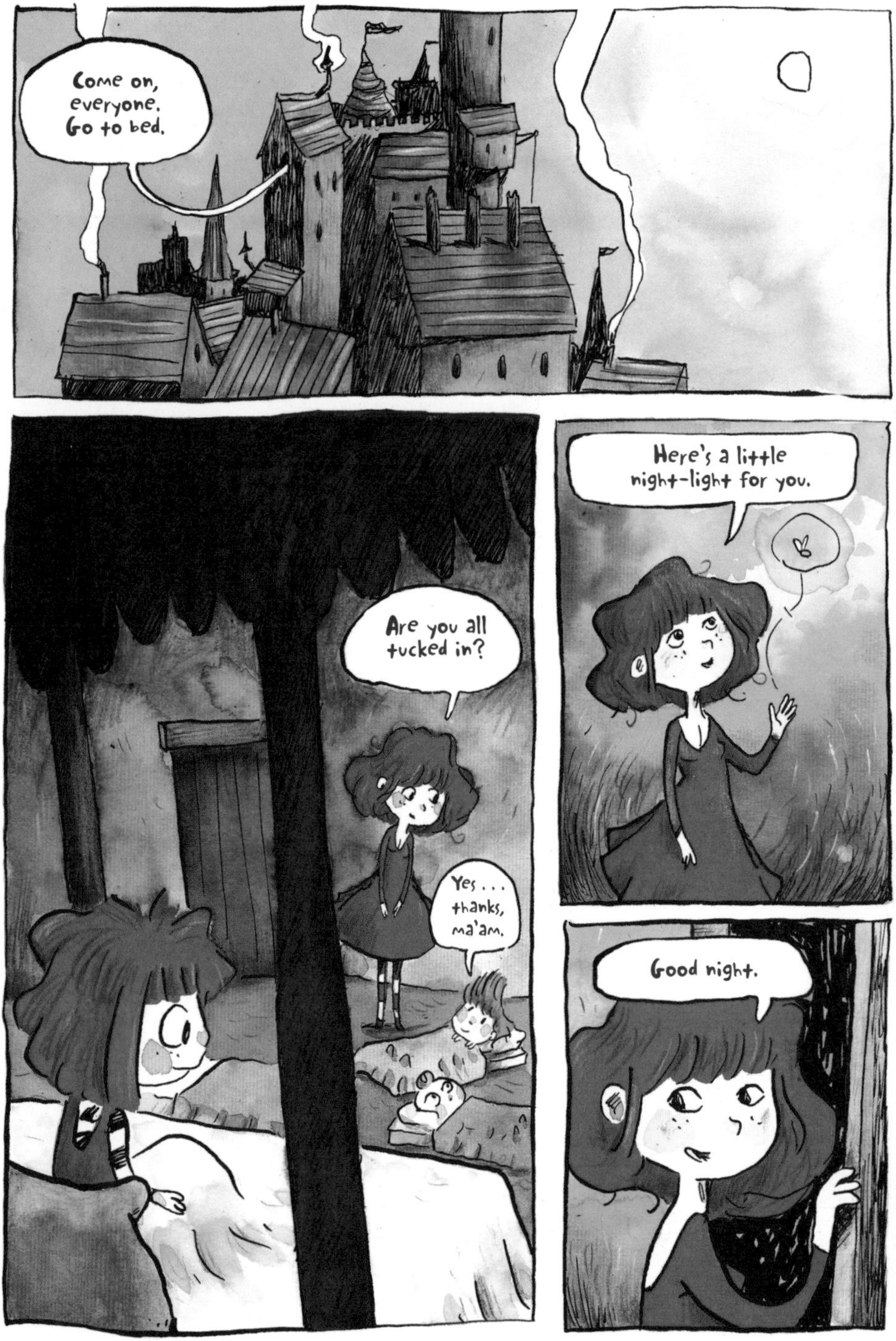
Come on, everyone. Go to bed.
Are you all tucked in?
Yes . . . thanks, ma'am.
Here's a little night-light for you.
Good night.

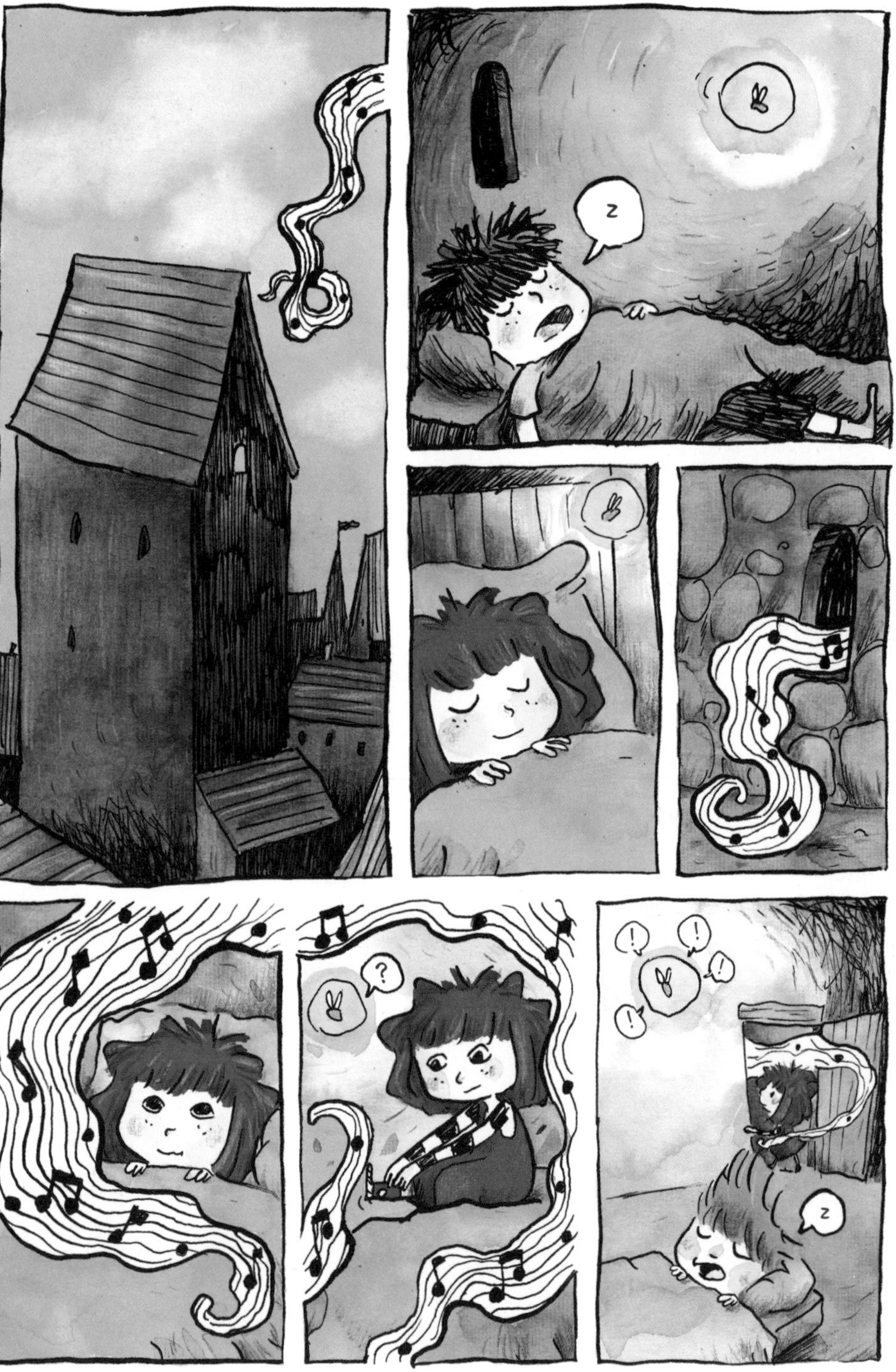
z
?
!
!
!
!
z

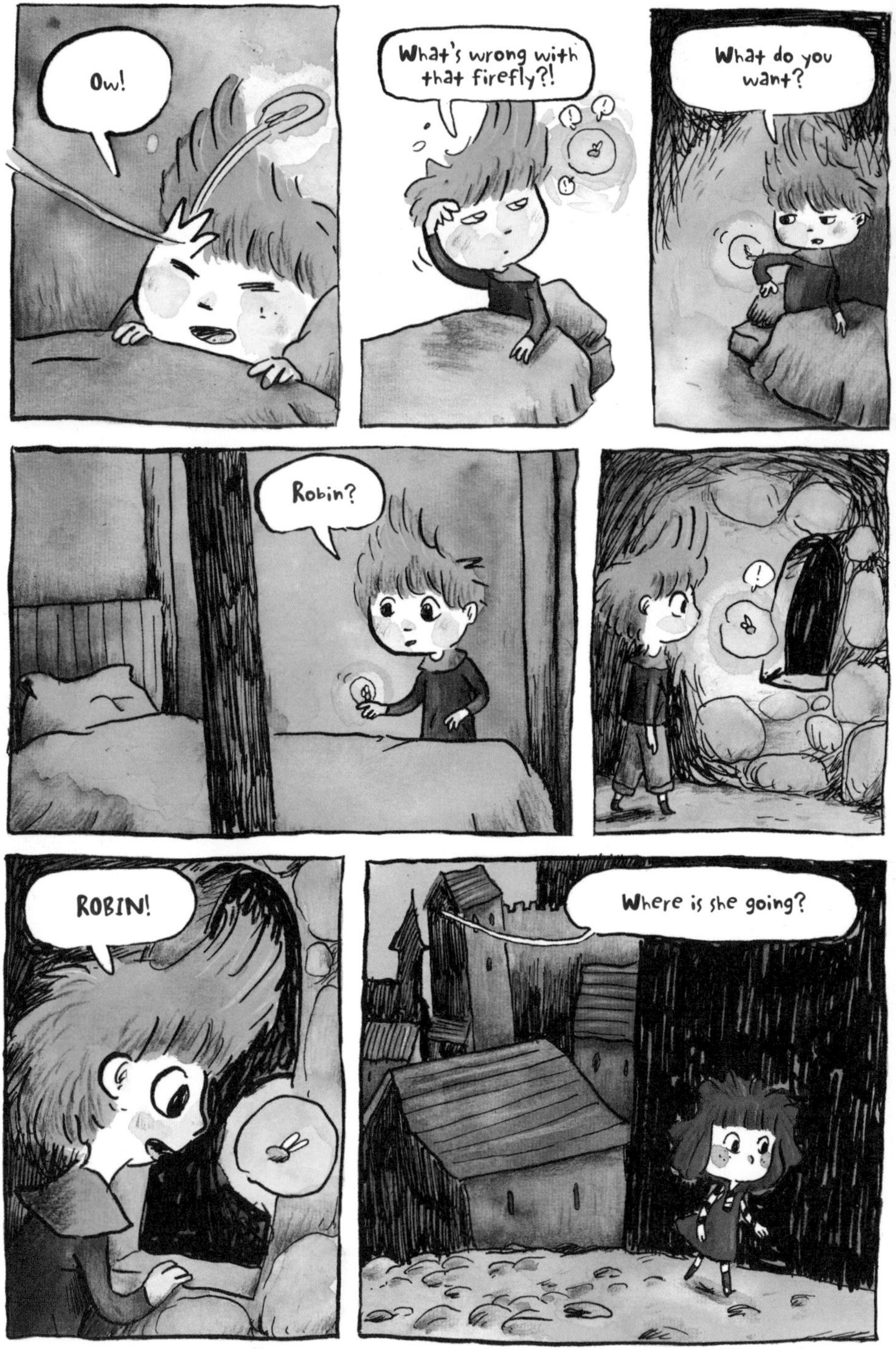
Ow!
What's wrong with that firefly?!
!
!
!
What do you want?
Robin?
!
ROBIN!
Where is she going?

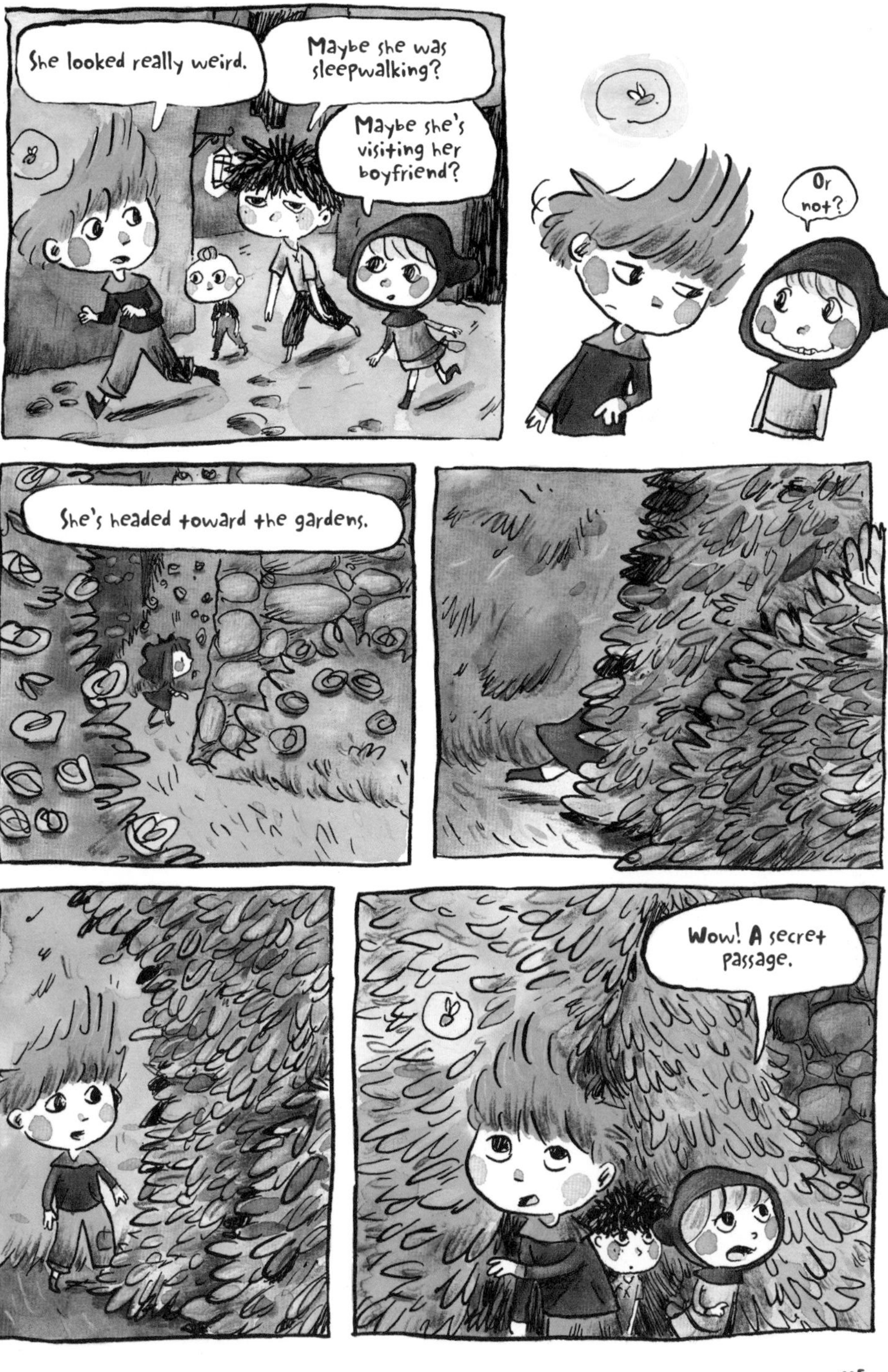
She looked really weird.
Maybe she was sleepwalking?
Maybe she's visiting her boyfriend?
Or not?
She's headed toward the gardens.
Wow! A secret passage.

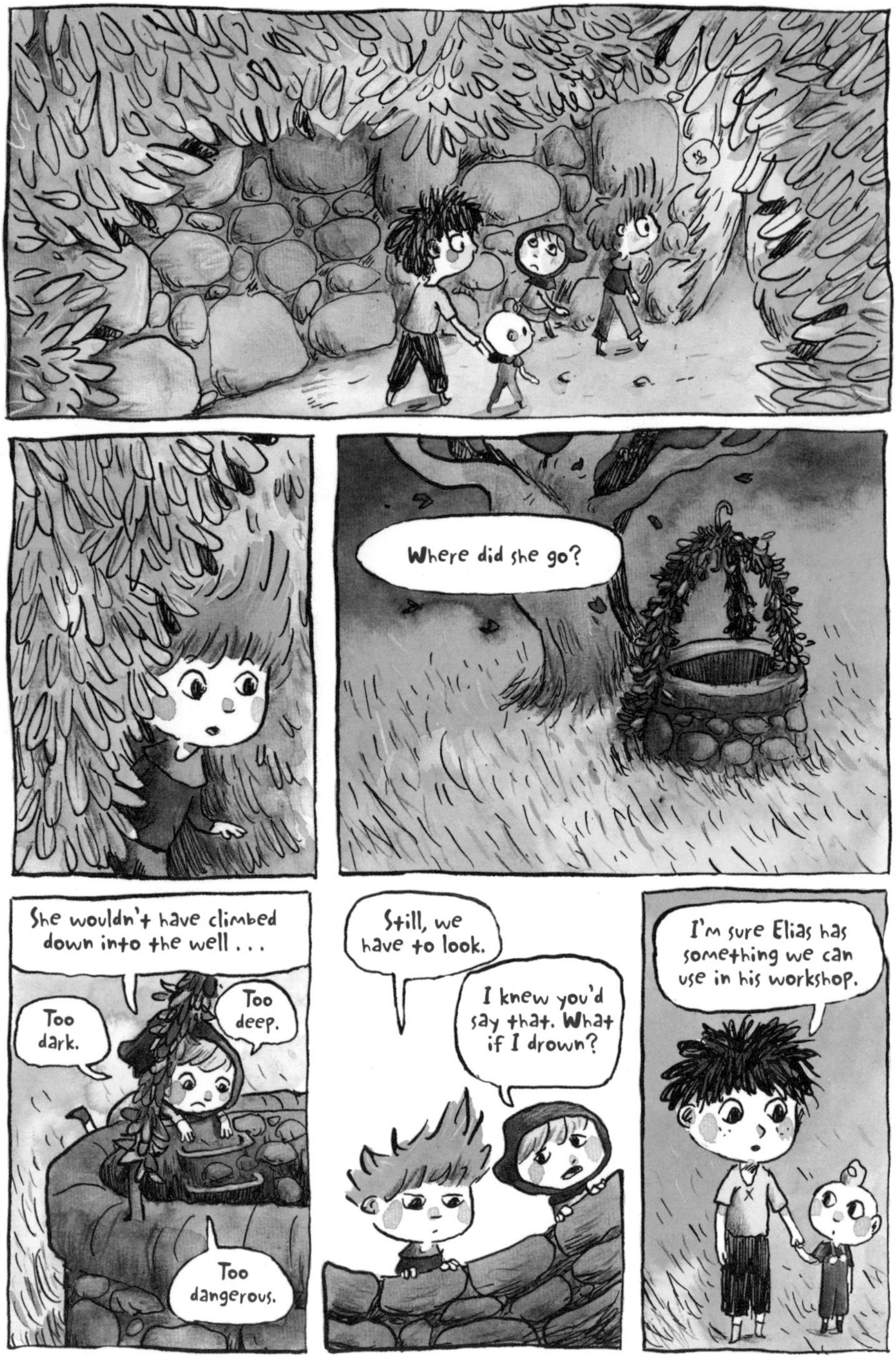
Where did she go?
She wouldn't have climbed down into the well . . .
Too dark.
Too deep.
Too dangerous.
Still, we have to look.
I knew you'd say that. What if I drown?
I'm sure Elias has something we can use in his workshop.

Perfect!

Let's go explore the very dark, very deep, and very dangerous well!

...

All set?

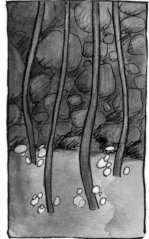

117

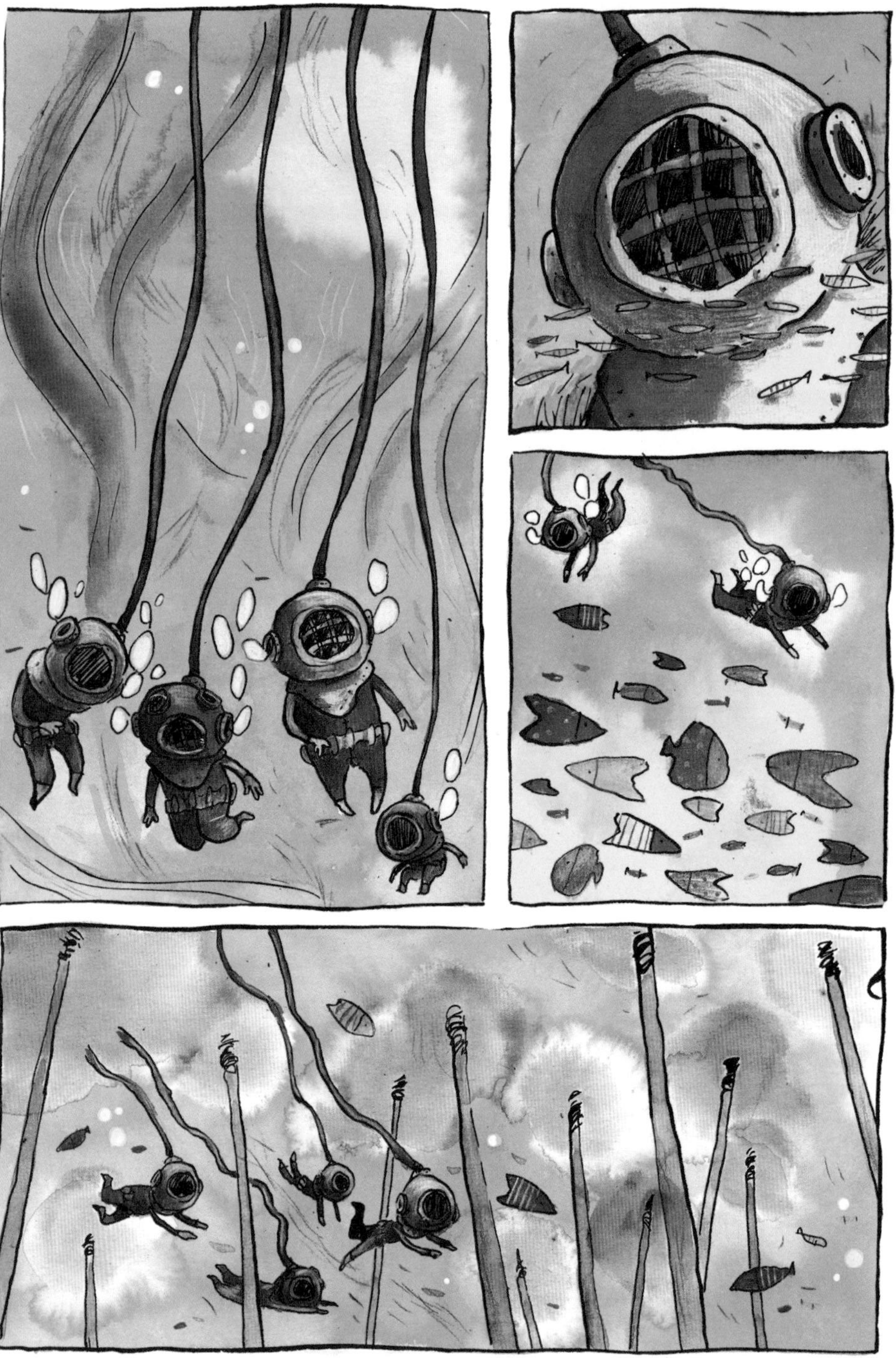

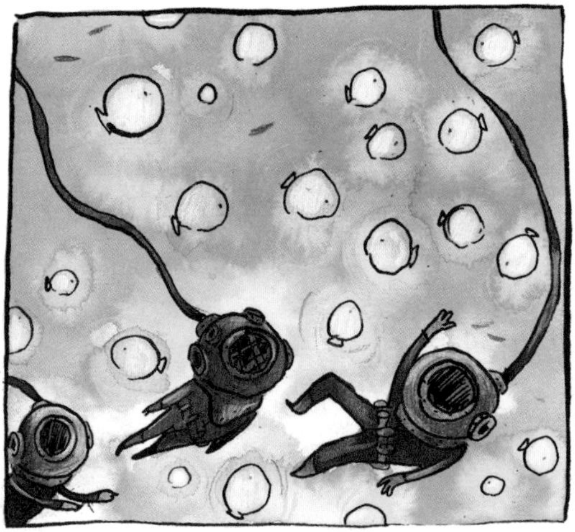

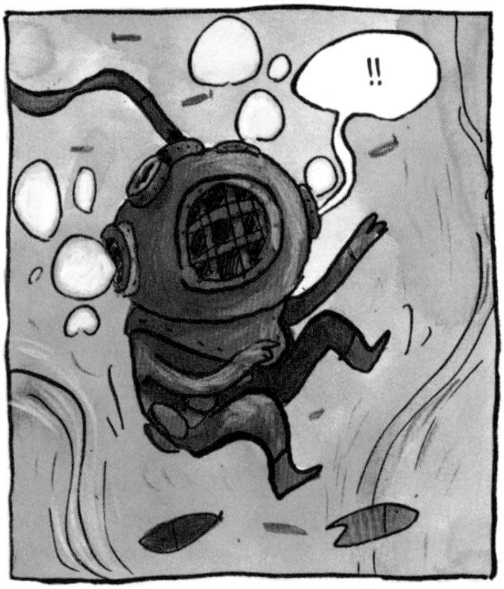
!!

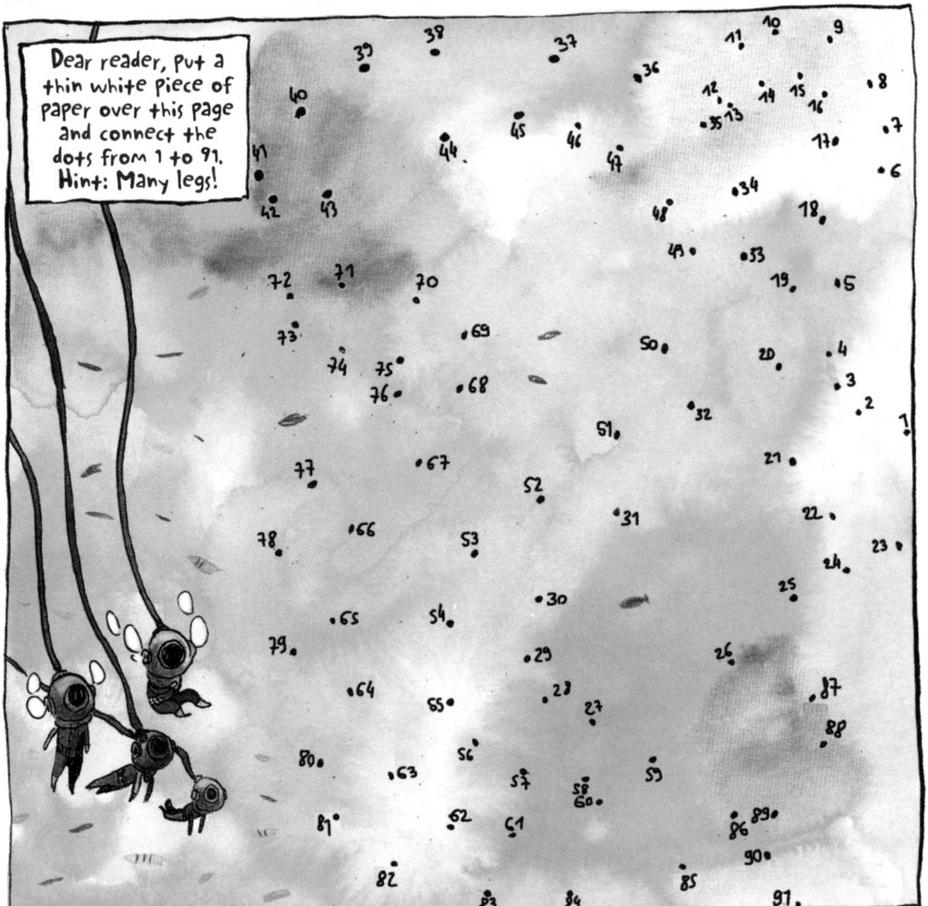
Dear reader, put a thin white piece of paper over this page and connect the dots from 1 to 91. Hint: Many legs!

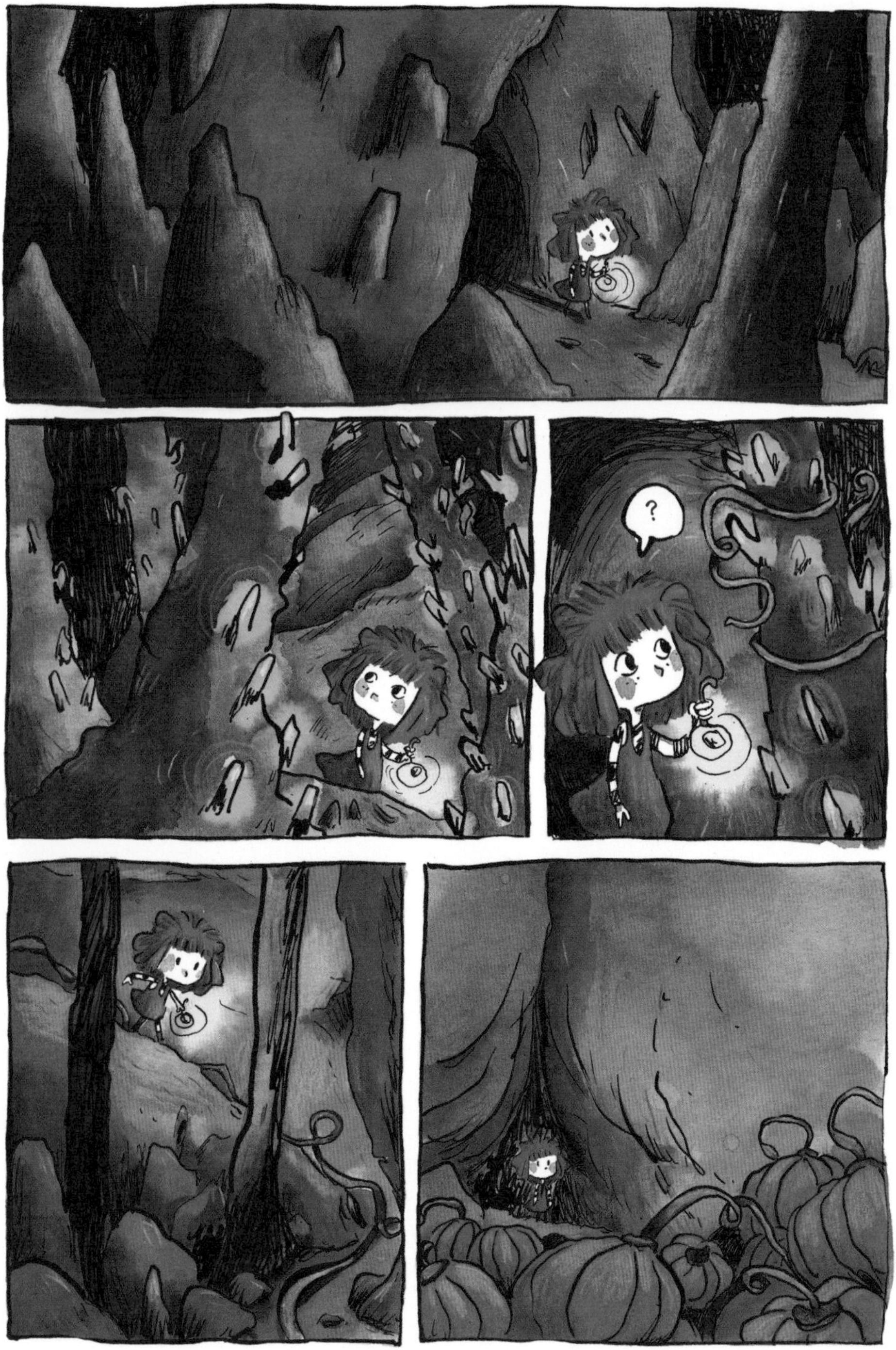
?

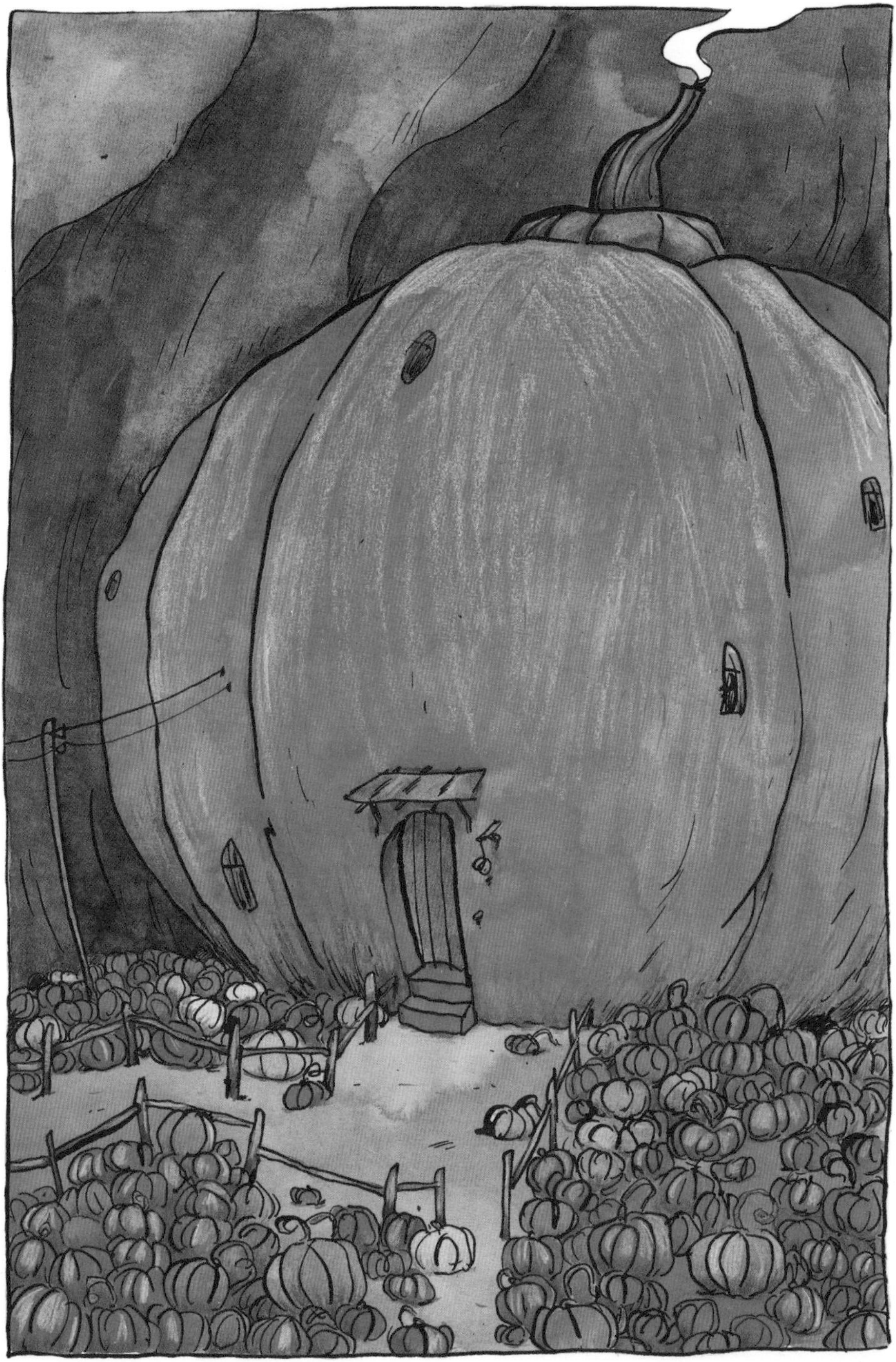

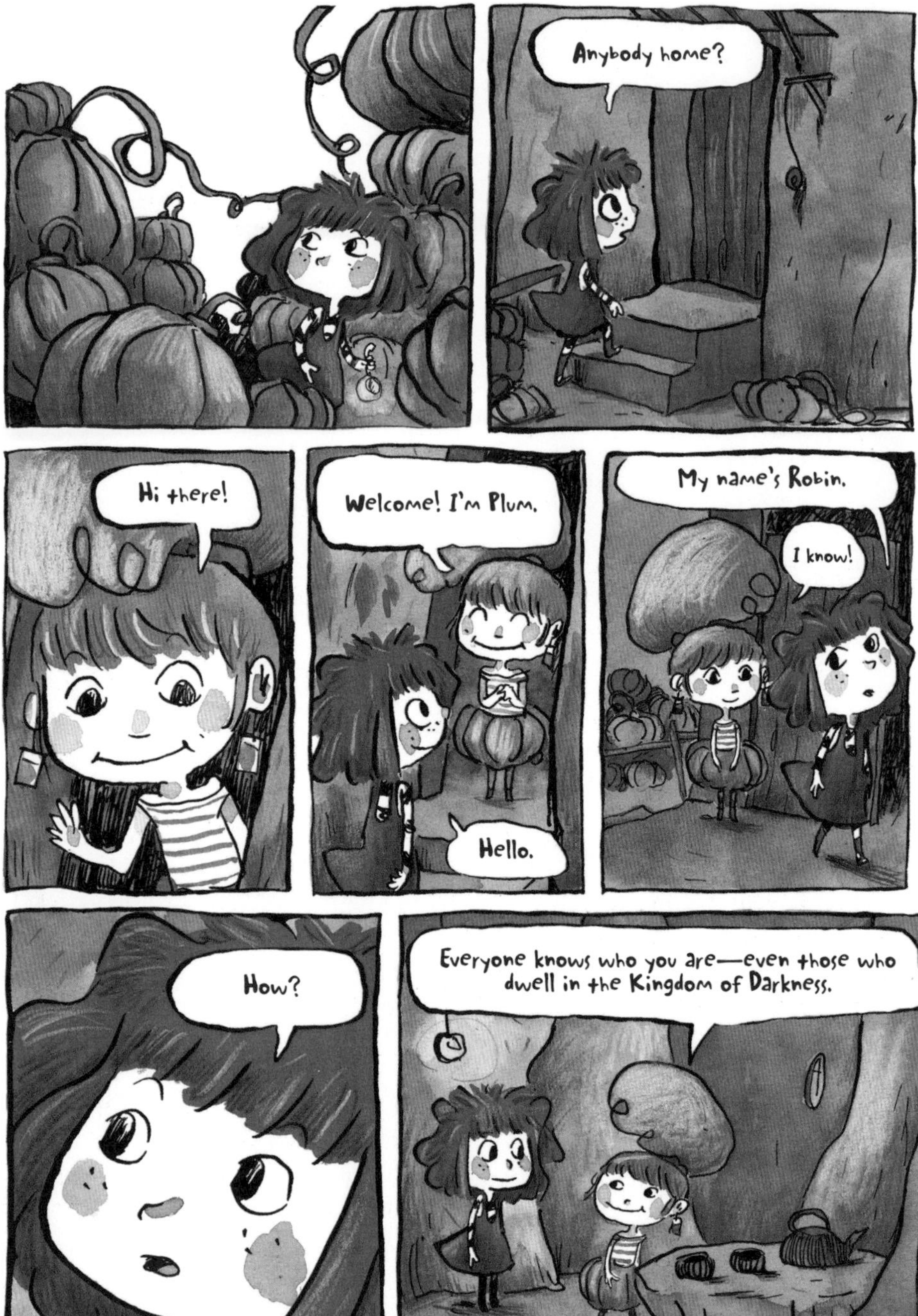
Anybody home?
Hi there!
Welcome! I'm Plum.
Hello.
My name's Robin.
I know!
How?
Everyone knows who you are—even those who dwell in the Kingdom of Darkness.

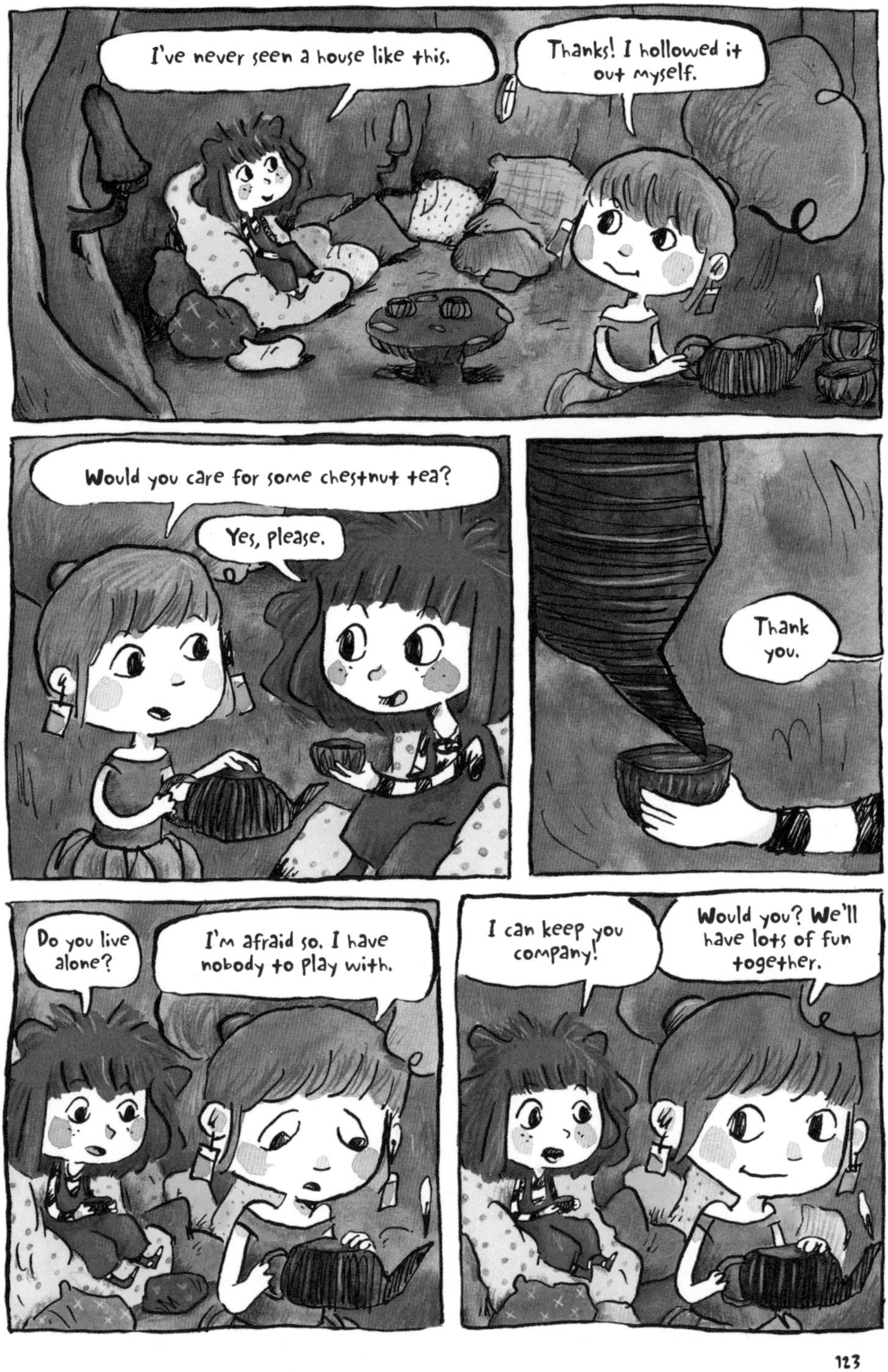

I've never seen a house like this.
Thanks! I hollowed it out myself.
Would you care for some chestnut tea?
Yes, please.
Thank you.
Do you live alone?
I'm afraid so. I have nobody to play with.
I can keep you company!
Would you? We'll have lots of fun together.

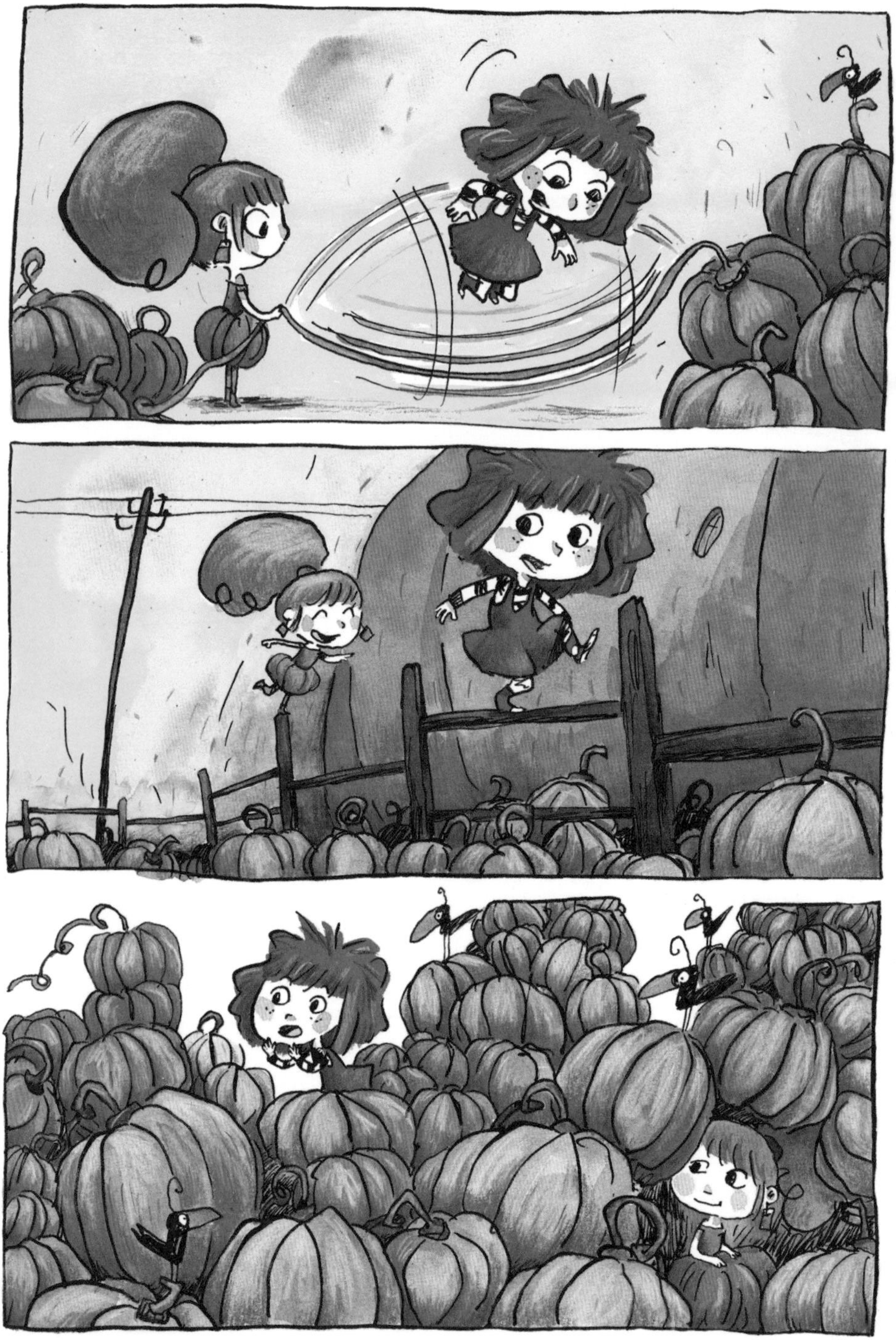

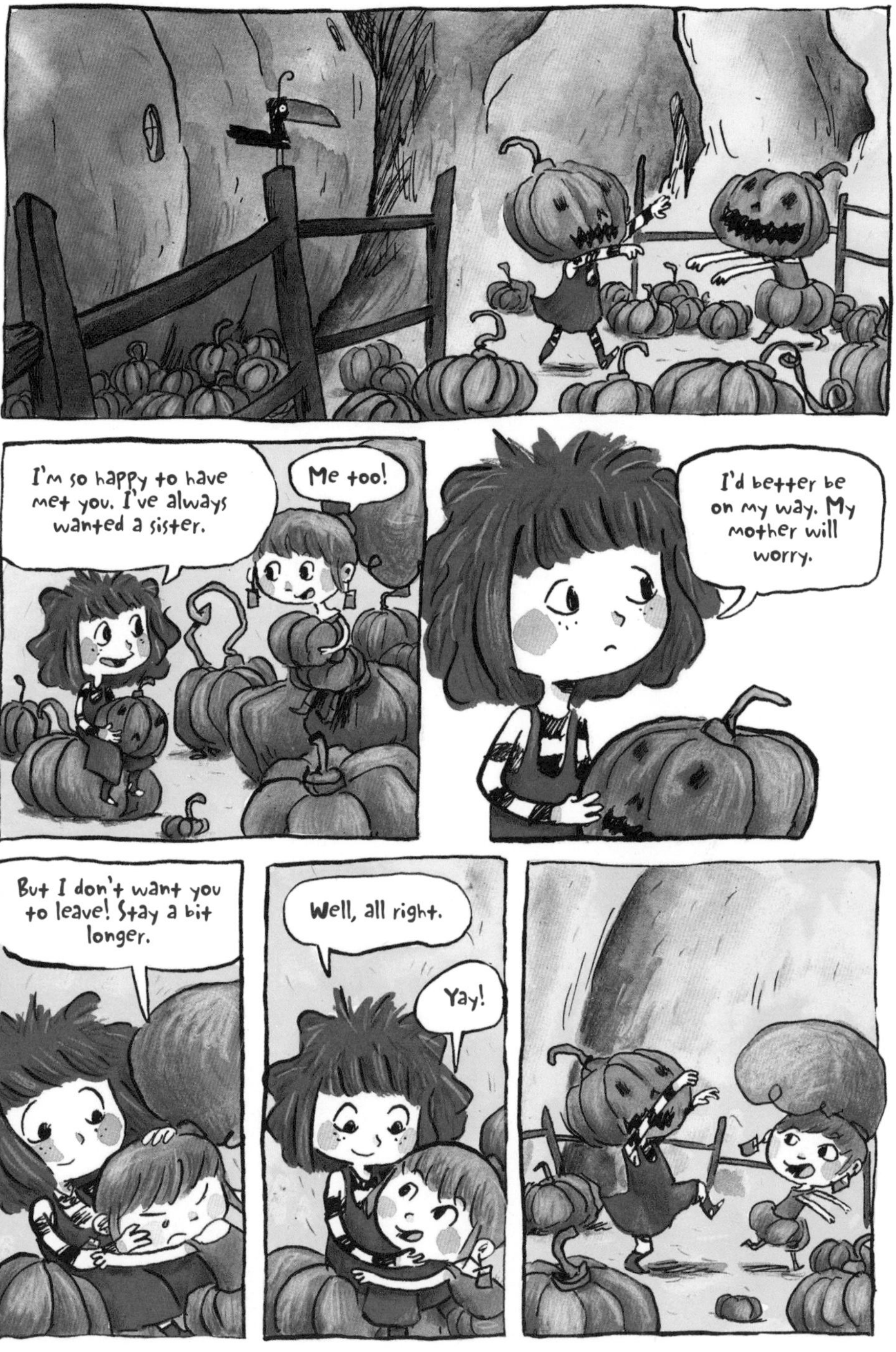
I'm so happy to have met you. I've always wanted a sister.
Me too!
I'd better be on my way. My mother will worry.
But I don't want you to leave! Stay a bit longer.
Well, all right.
Yay!

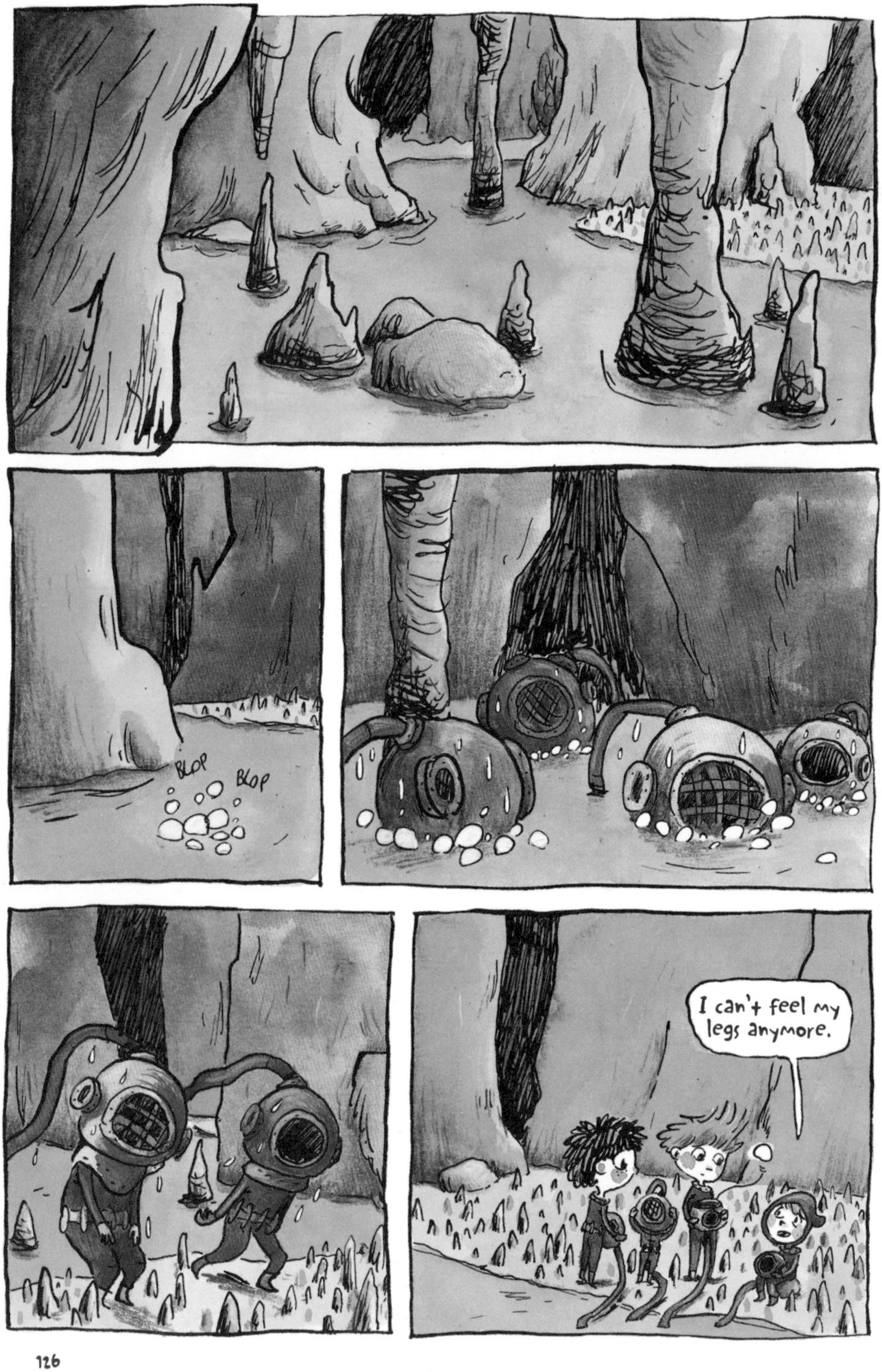
BLOP
BLOP
I can't feel my legs anymore.

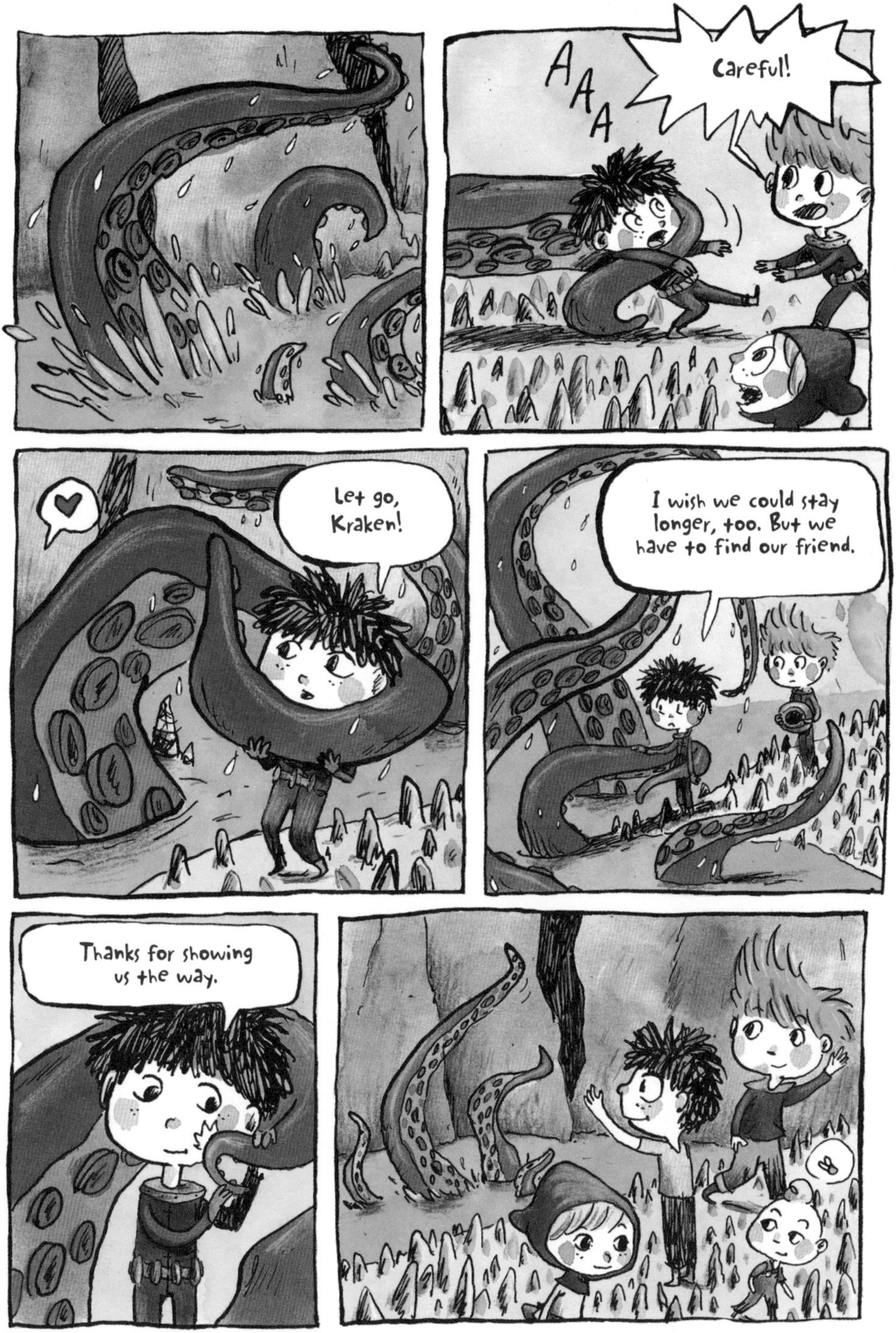
AAA
Careful!
Let go, Kraken!
I wish we could stay longer, too. But we have to find our friend.
Thanks for showing us the way.

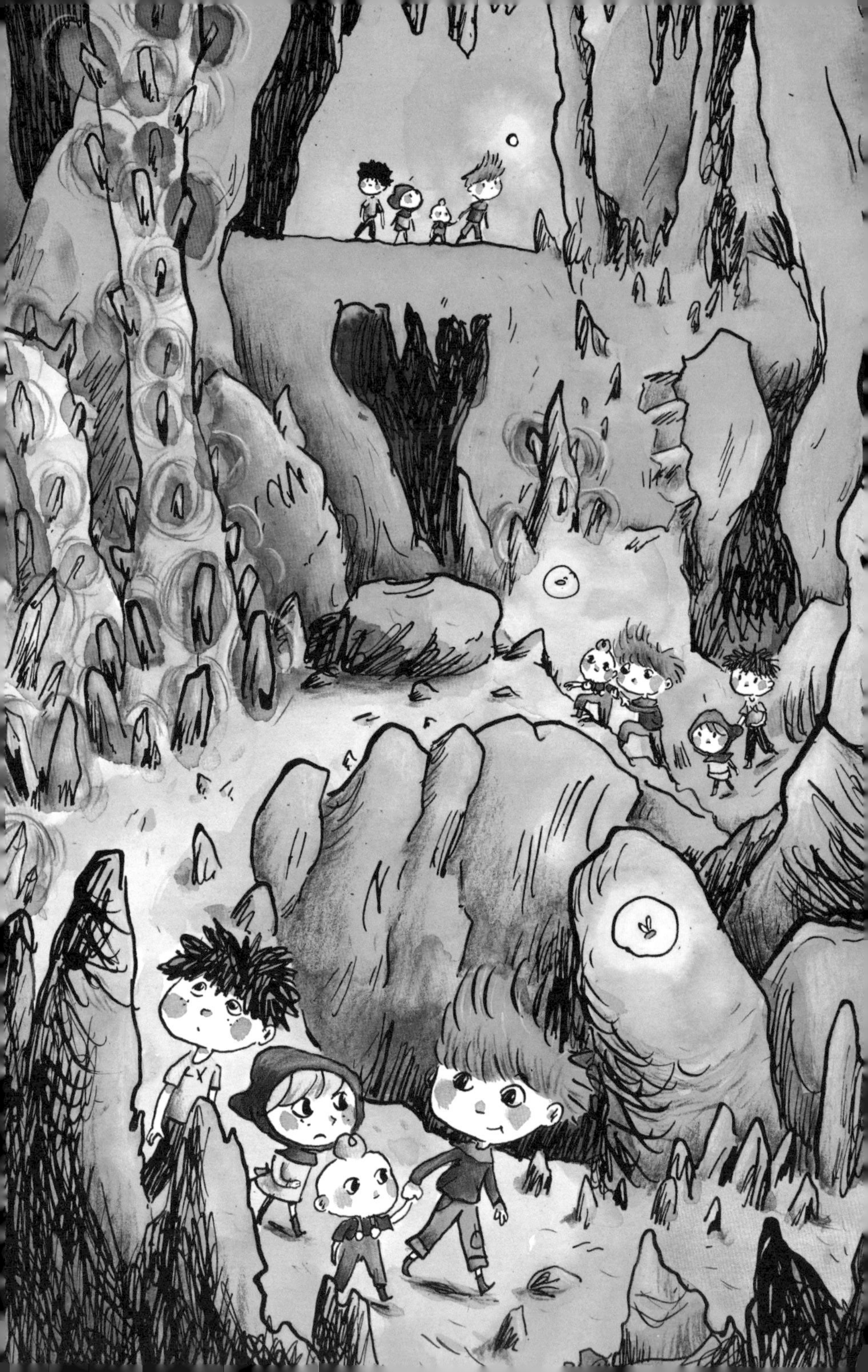

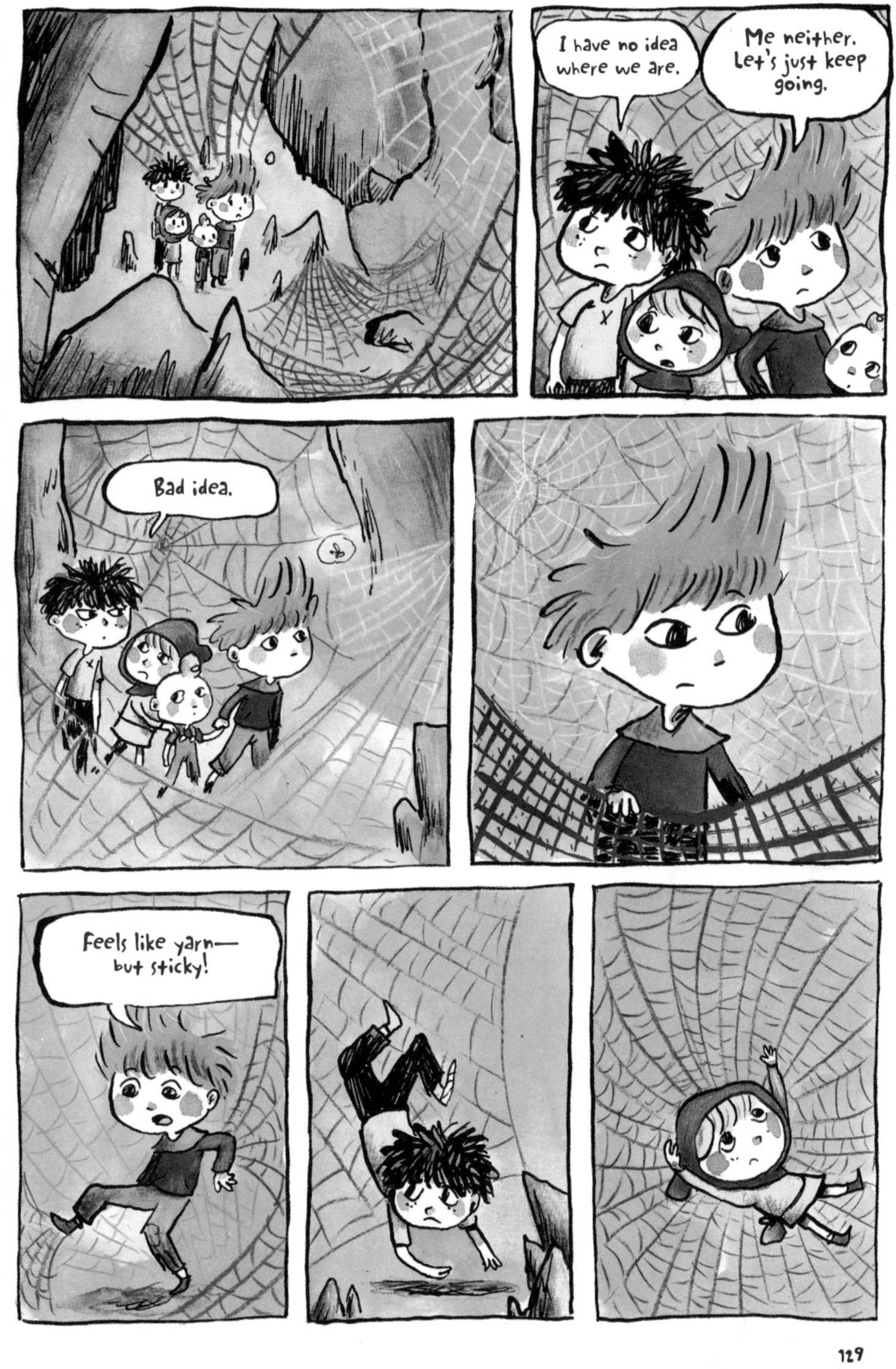
I have no idea where we are.
Me neither. Let's just keep going.
Bad idea.
Feels like yarn— but sticky!

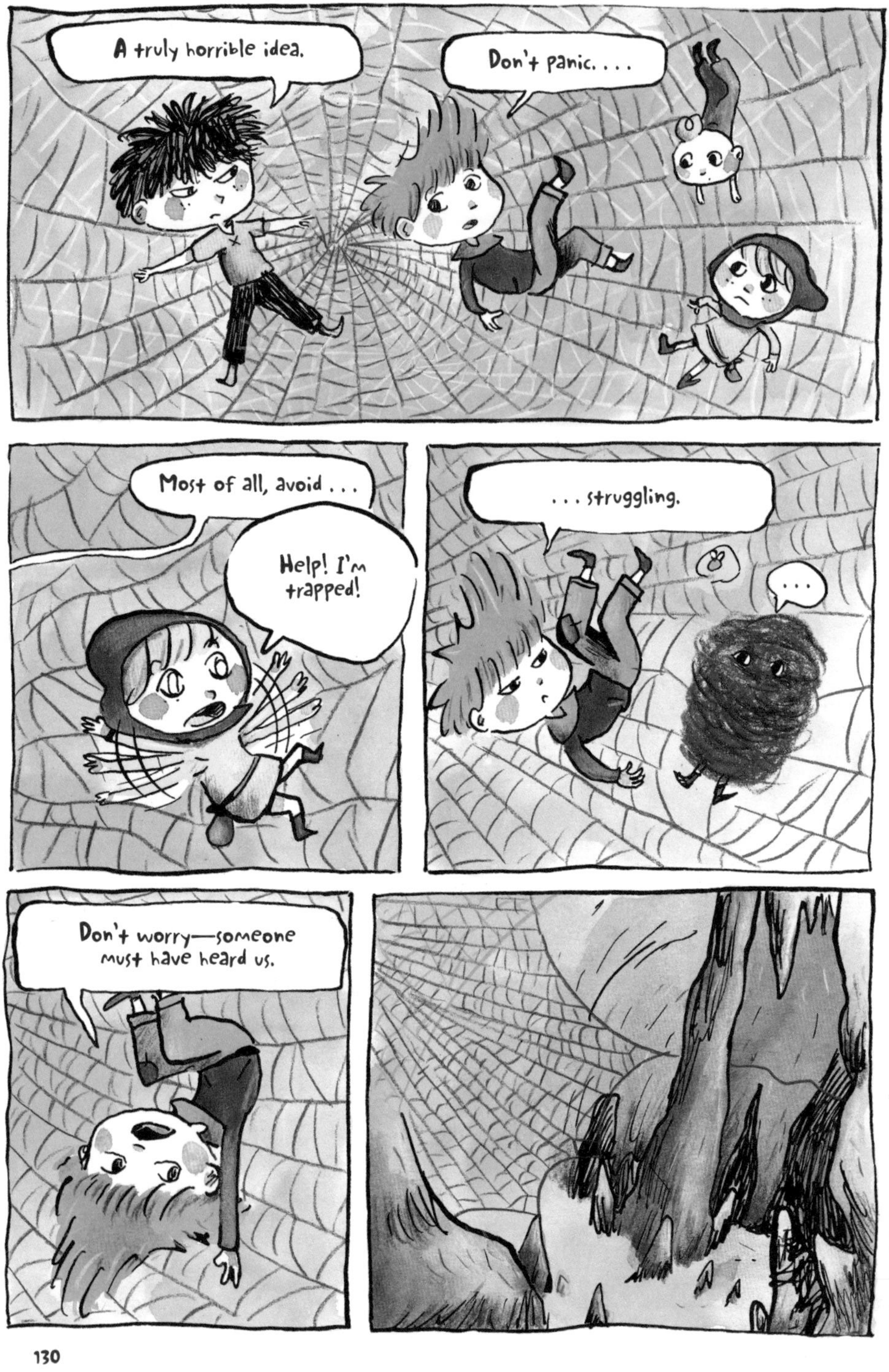
A truly horrible idea.
Don't panic. . . .
Most of all, avoid . . .
Help! I'm trapped!
. . . struggling.
. . .
Don't worry—someone must have heard us.

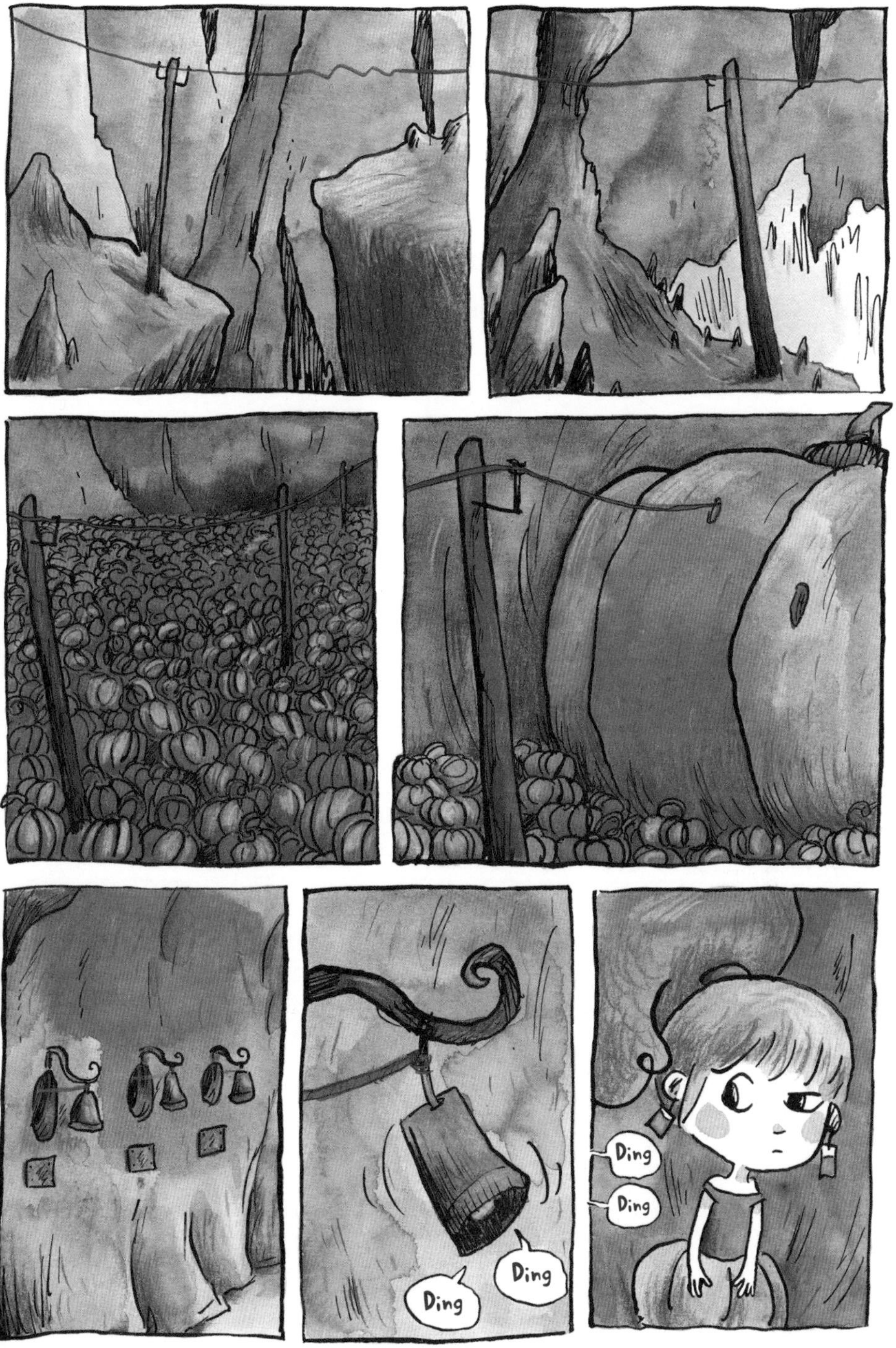
Ding
Ding
Ding
Ding

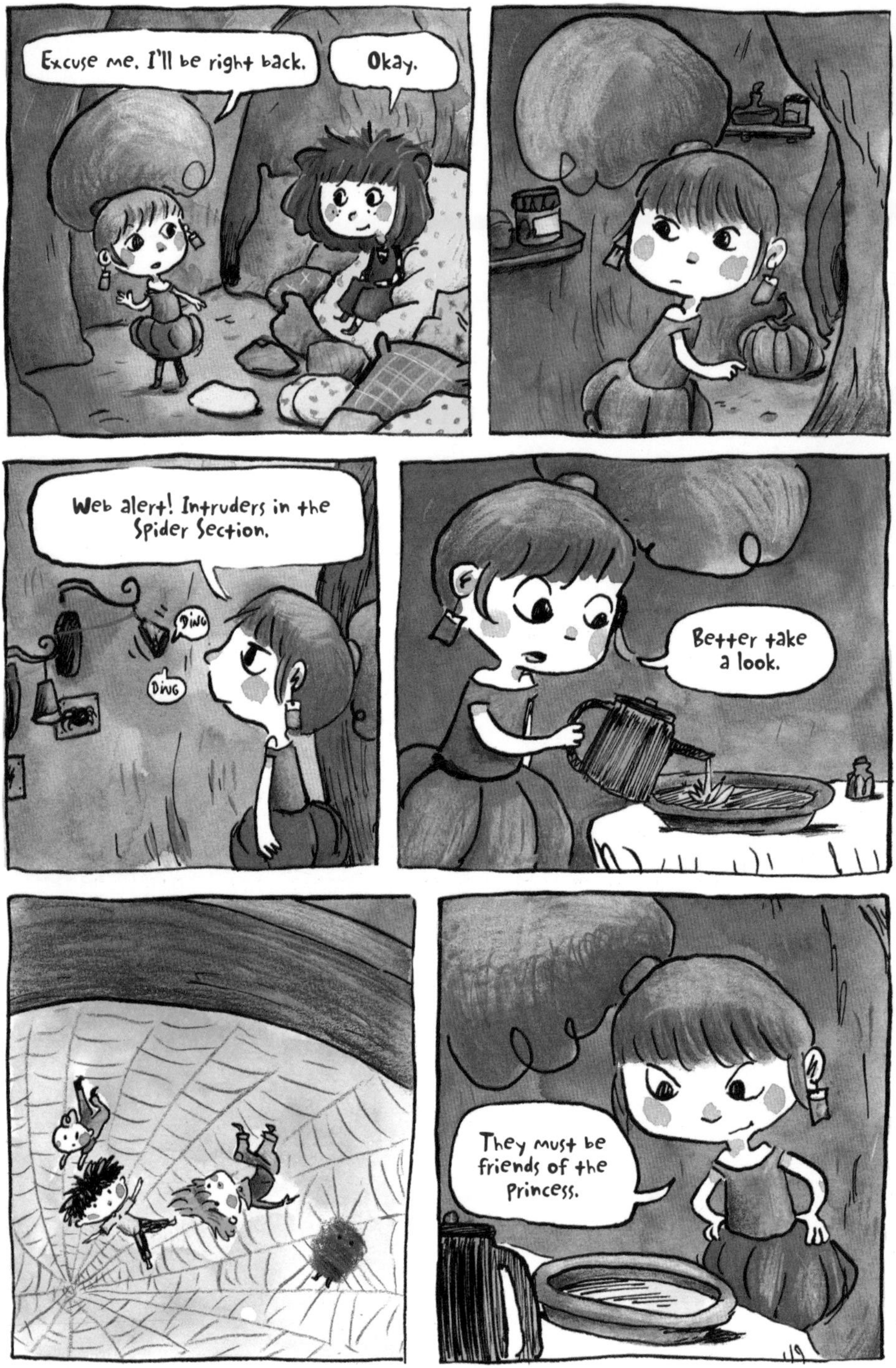
Excuse me. I'll be right back.
Okay.
Web alert! Intruders in the Spider Section.
DING
DING
Better take a look.
They must be friends of the Princess.

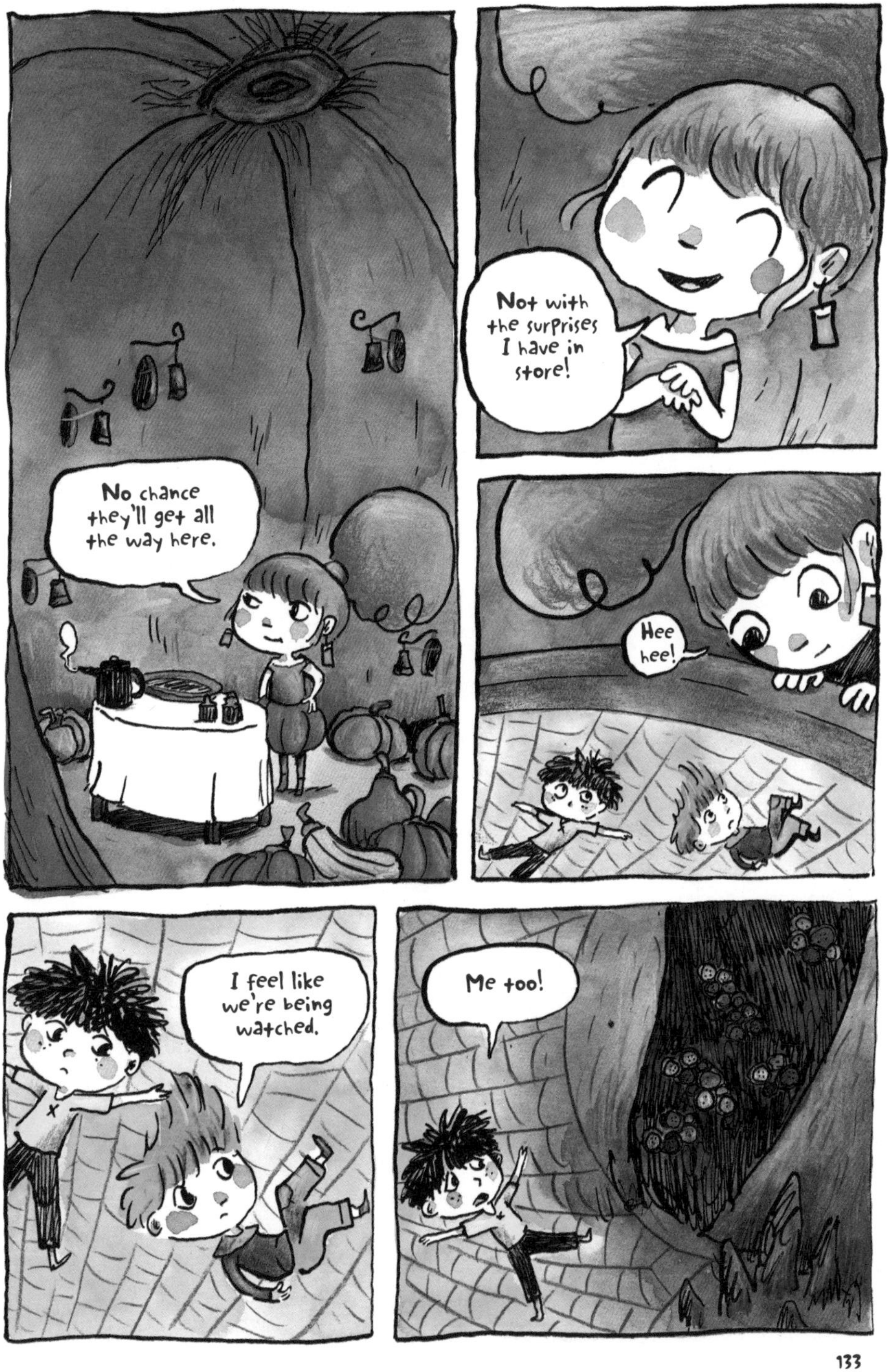
No chance they'll get all the way here.
Not with the surprises I have in store!
Hee hee!
I feel like we're being watched.
Me too!

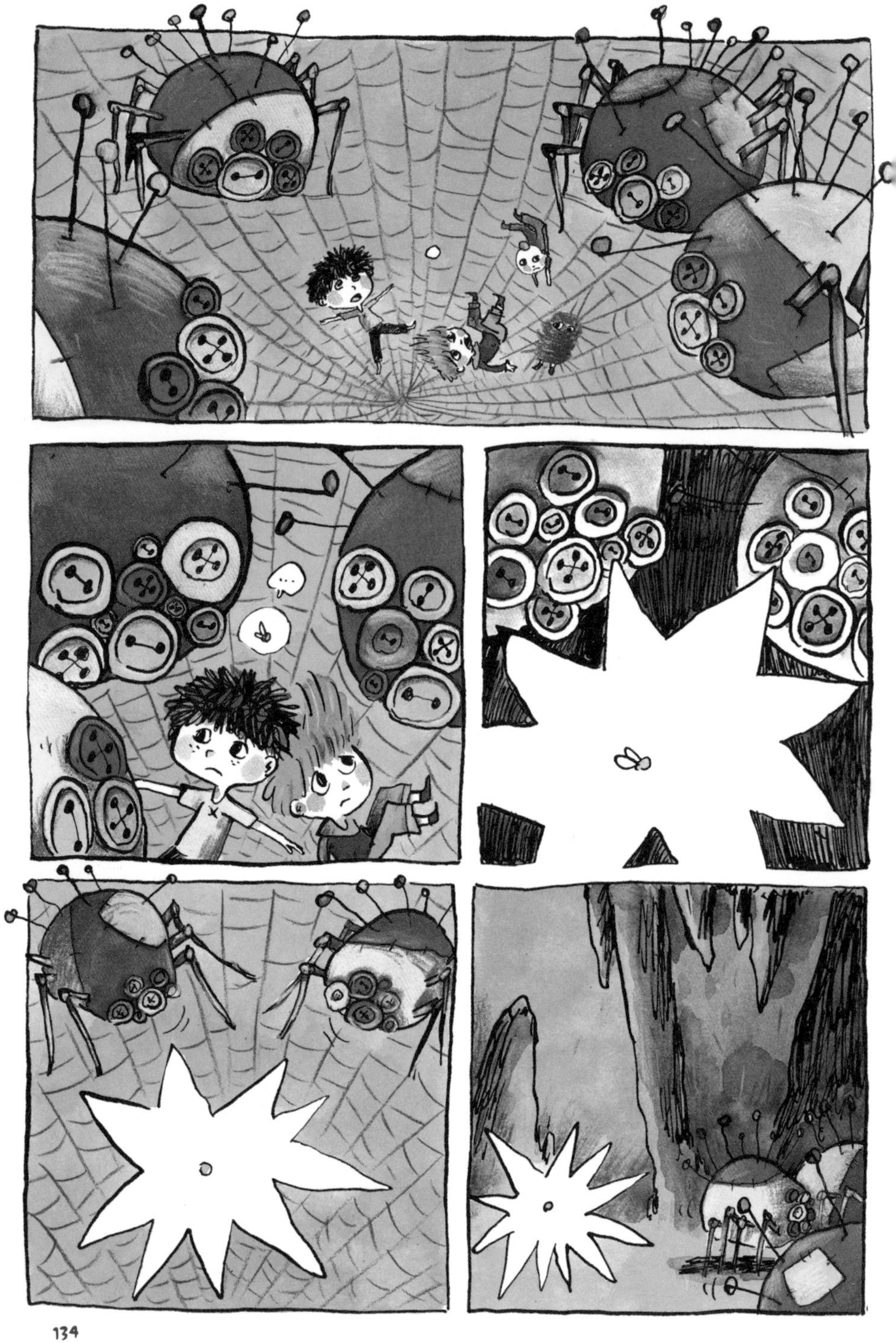
...

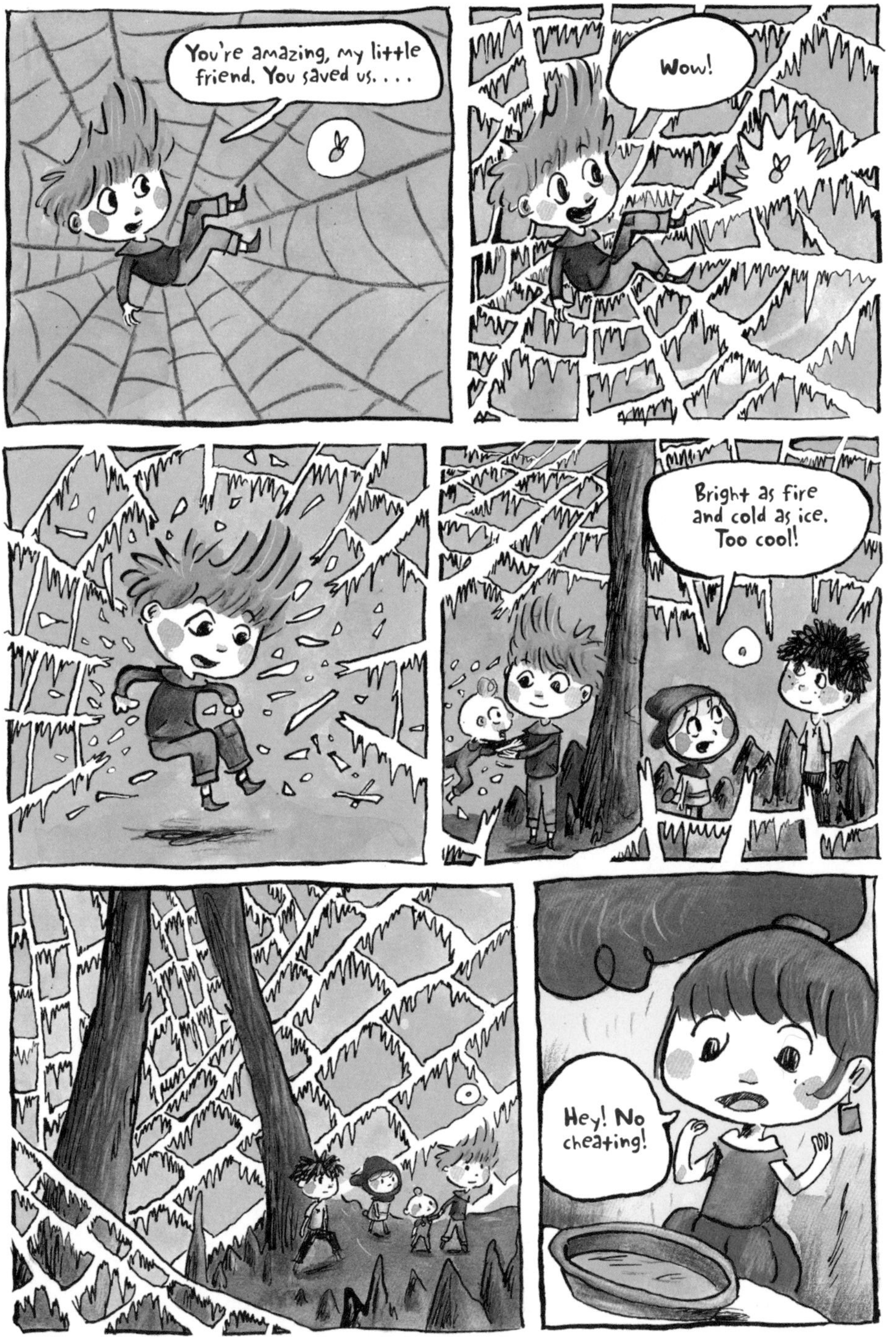
You're amazing, my little friend. You saved us. . . .
Wow!
Bright as fire and cold as ice. Too cool!
Hey! No cheating!

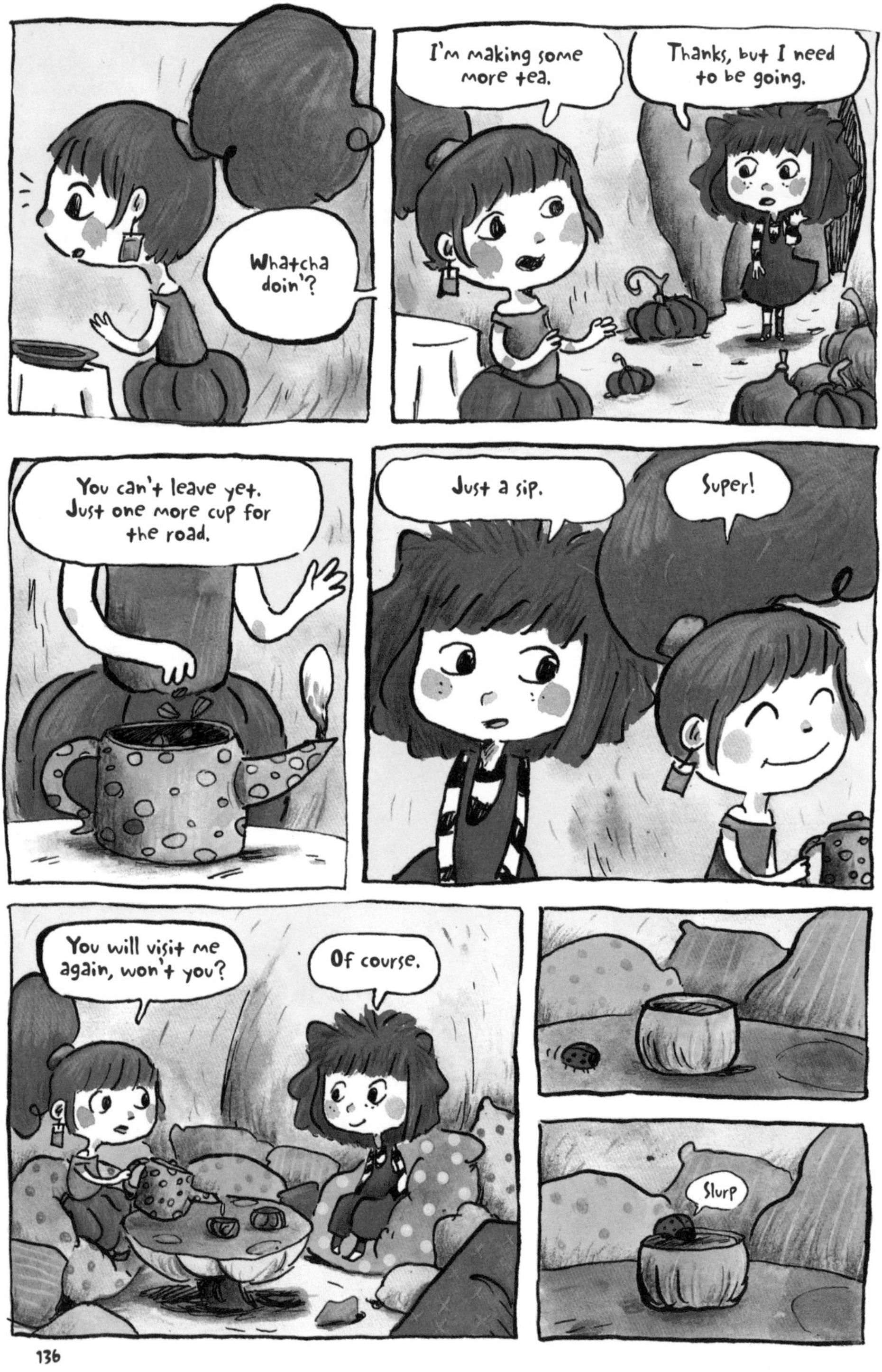
Whatcha doin'?
I'm making some more tea.
Thanks, but I need to be going.
You can't leave yet. Just one more cup for the road.
Just a sip.
Super!
You will visit me again, won't you?
Of course.
Slurp

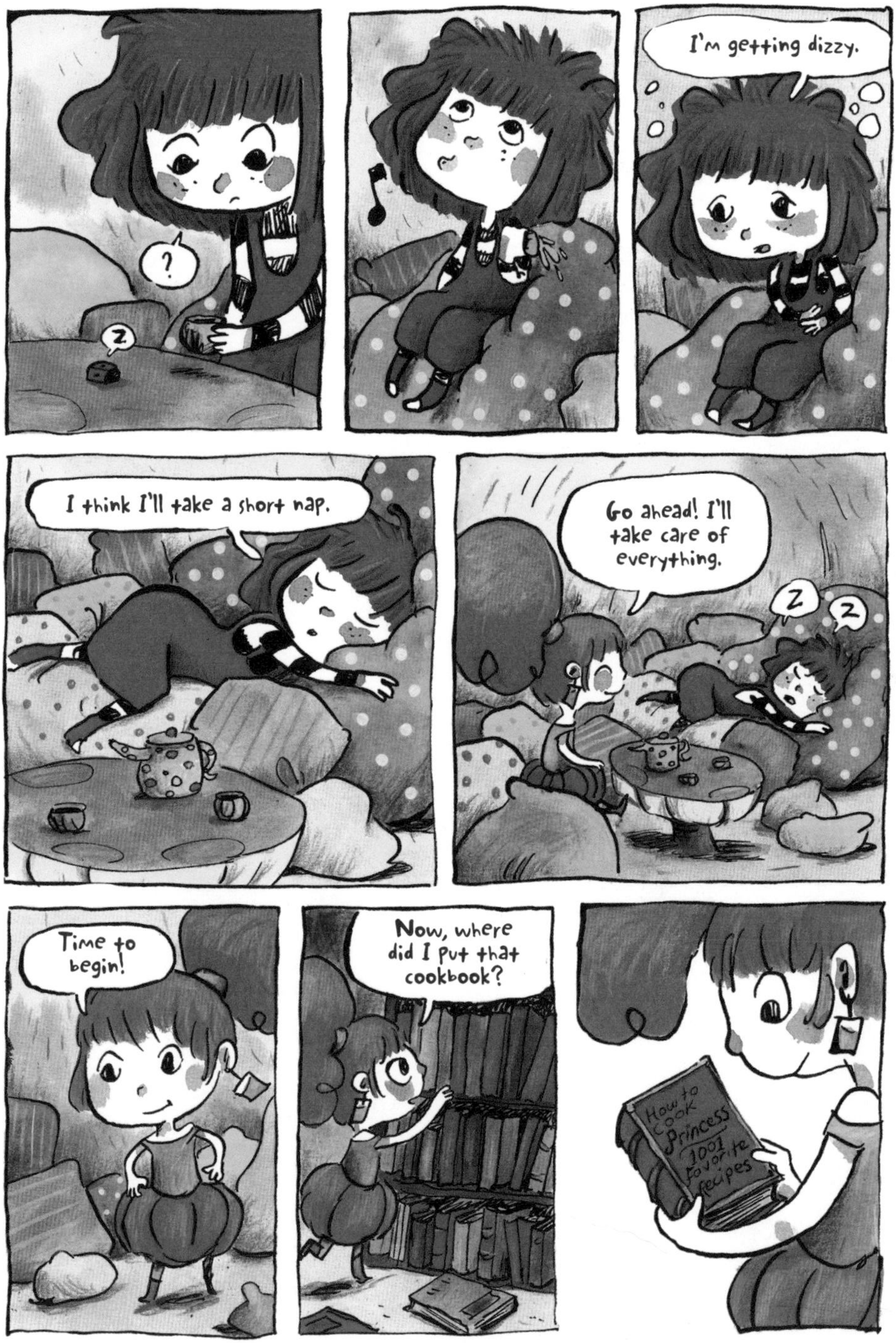
?
Z
I'm getting dizzy.
I think I'll take a short nap.
Go ahead! I'll take care of everything.
Z
Z
Time to begin!
Now, where did I put that cookbook?
How to Cook Princess
1001 favorite recipes

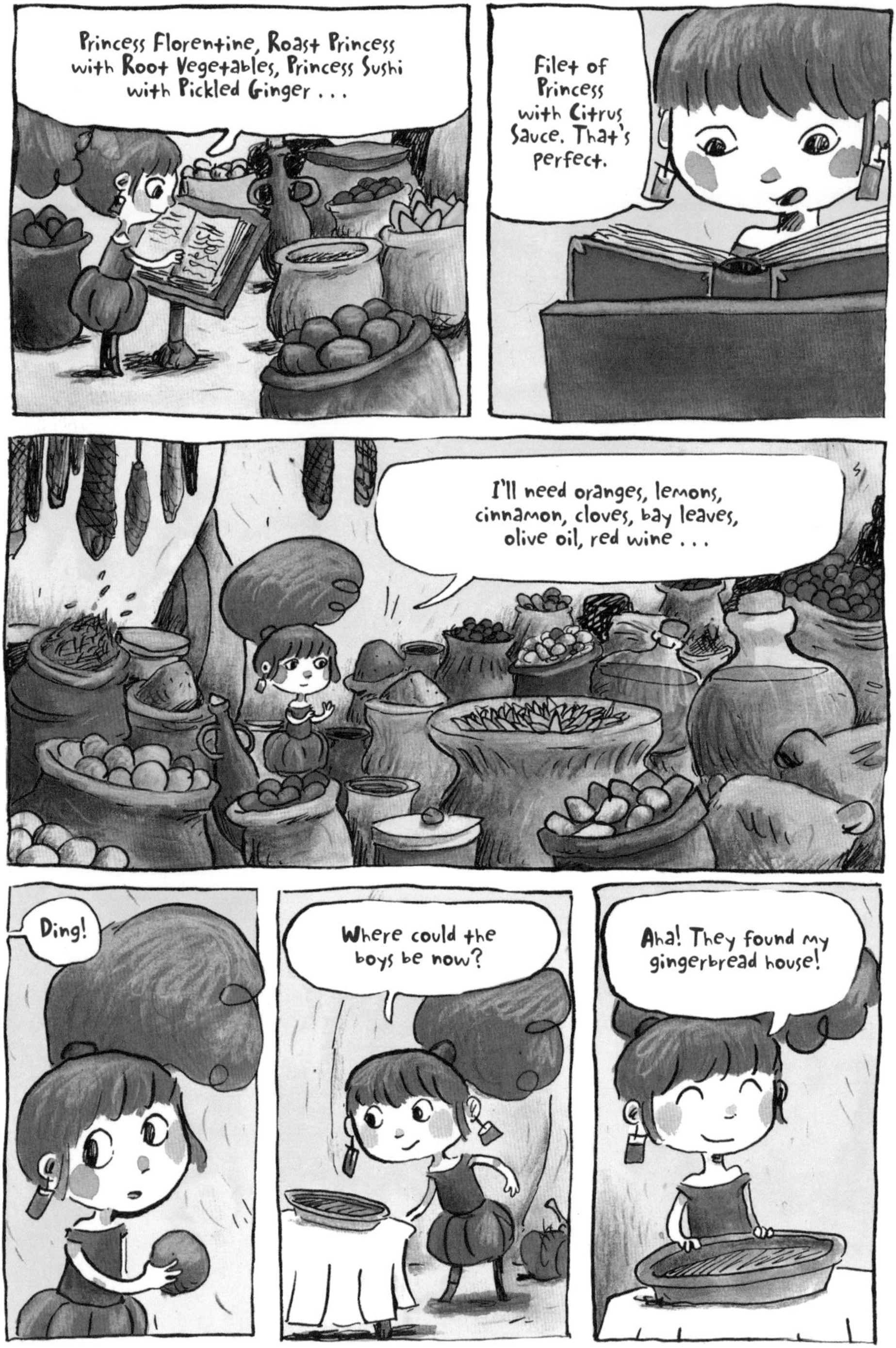

Princess Florentine, Roast Princess with Root Vegetables, Princess Sushi with Pickled Ginger . . .
Filet of Princess with Citrus Sauce. That's perfect.
I'll need oranges, lemons, cinnamon, cloves, bay leaves, olive oil, red wine . . .
Ding!
Where could the boys be now?
Aha! They found my gingerbread house!

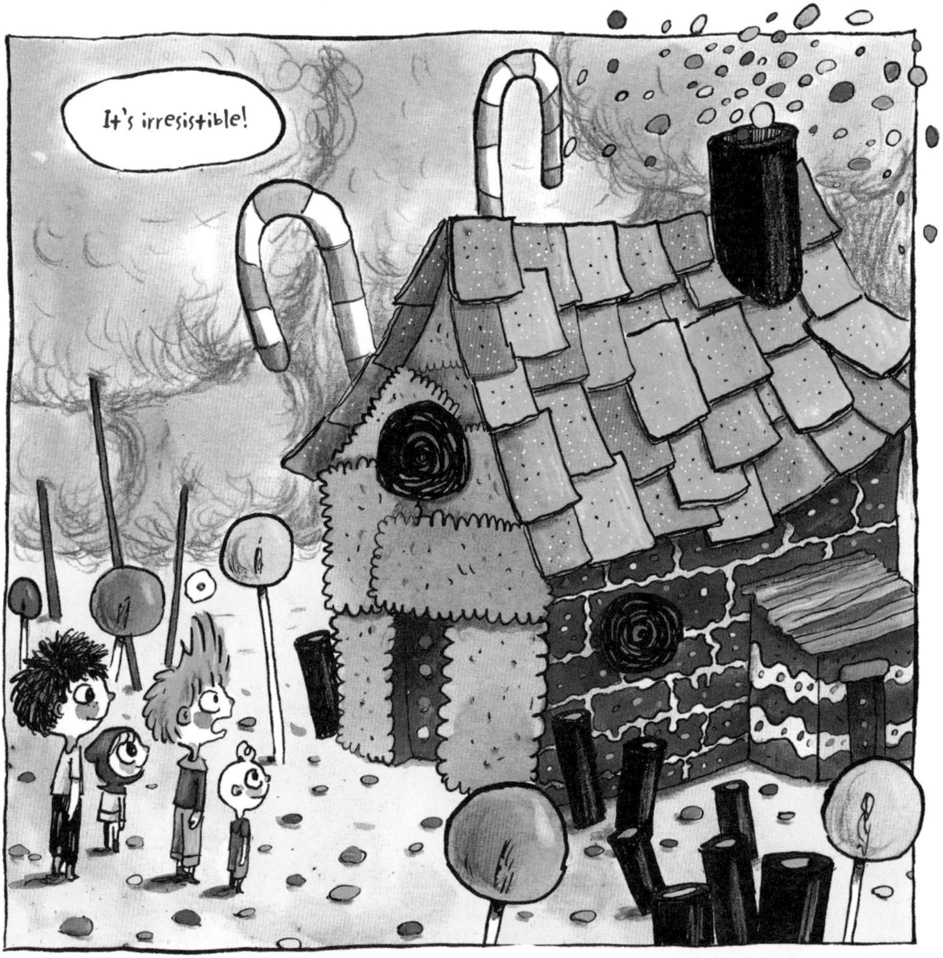
It's irresistible!

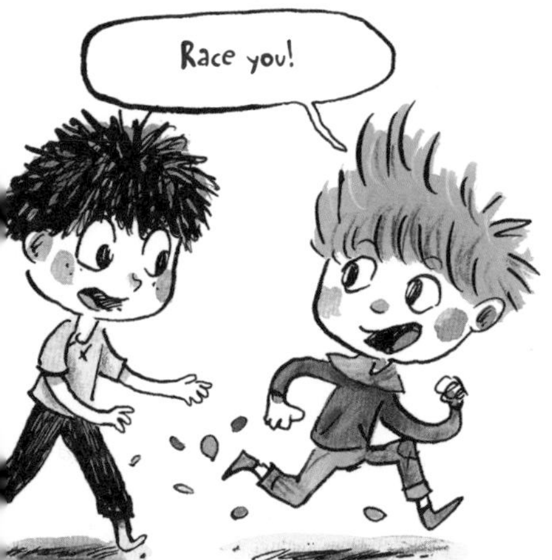
Race you!

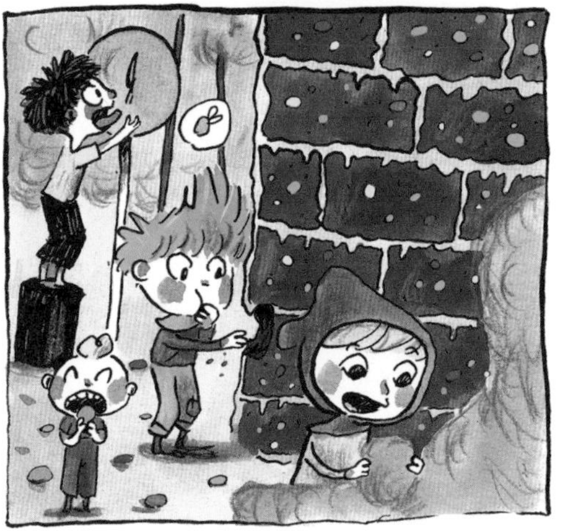

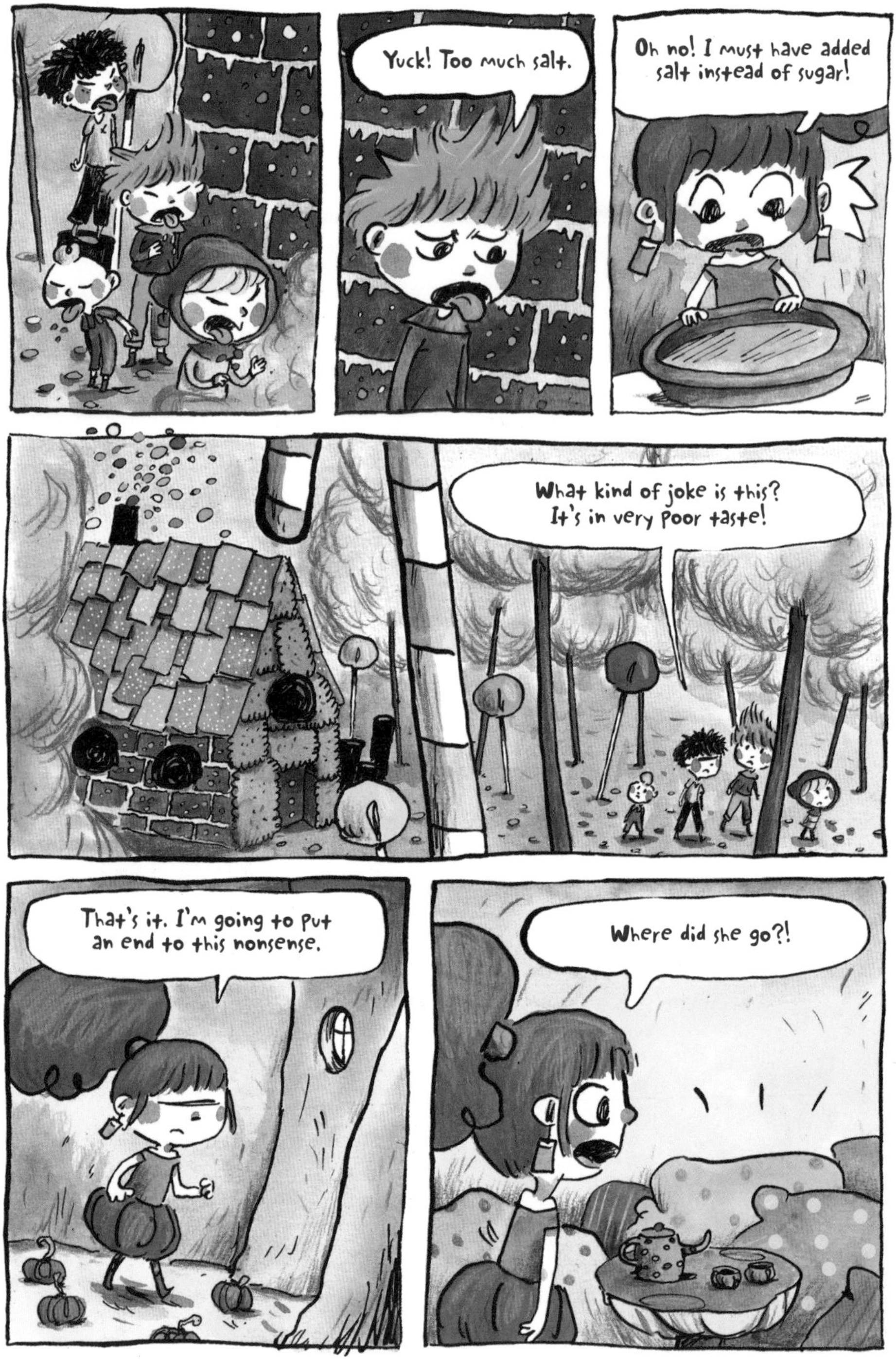

Yuck! Too much salt.
Oh no! I must have added salt instead of sugar!
What kind of joke is this? It's in very poor taste!
That's it. I'm going to put an end to this nonsense.
Where did she go?!

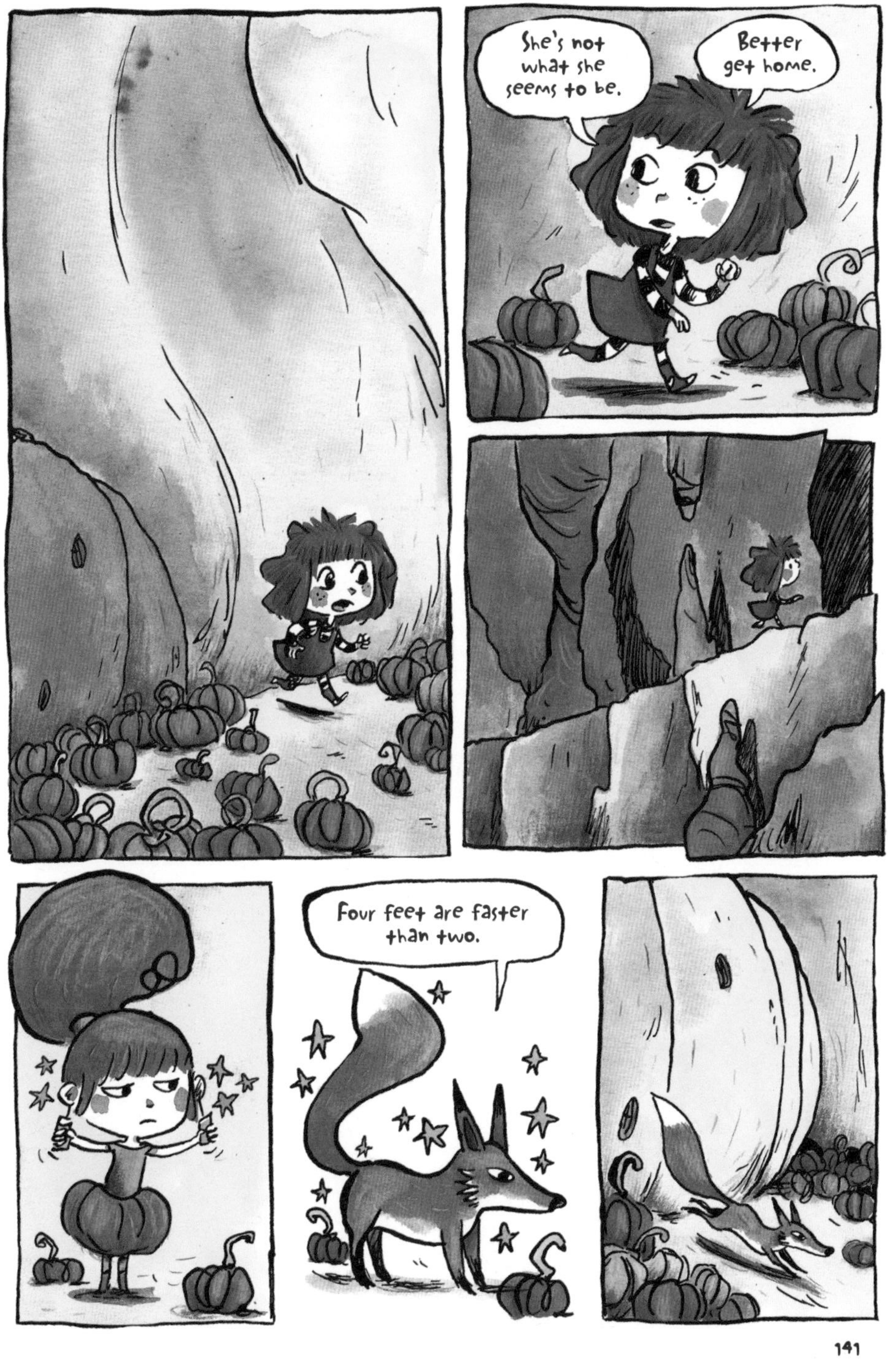
She's not what she seems to be.
Better get home.
Four feet are faster than two.

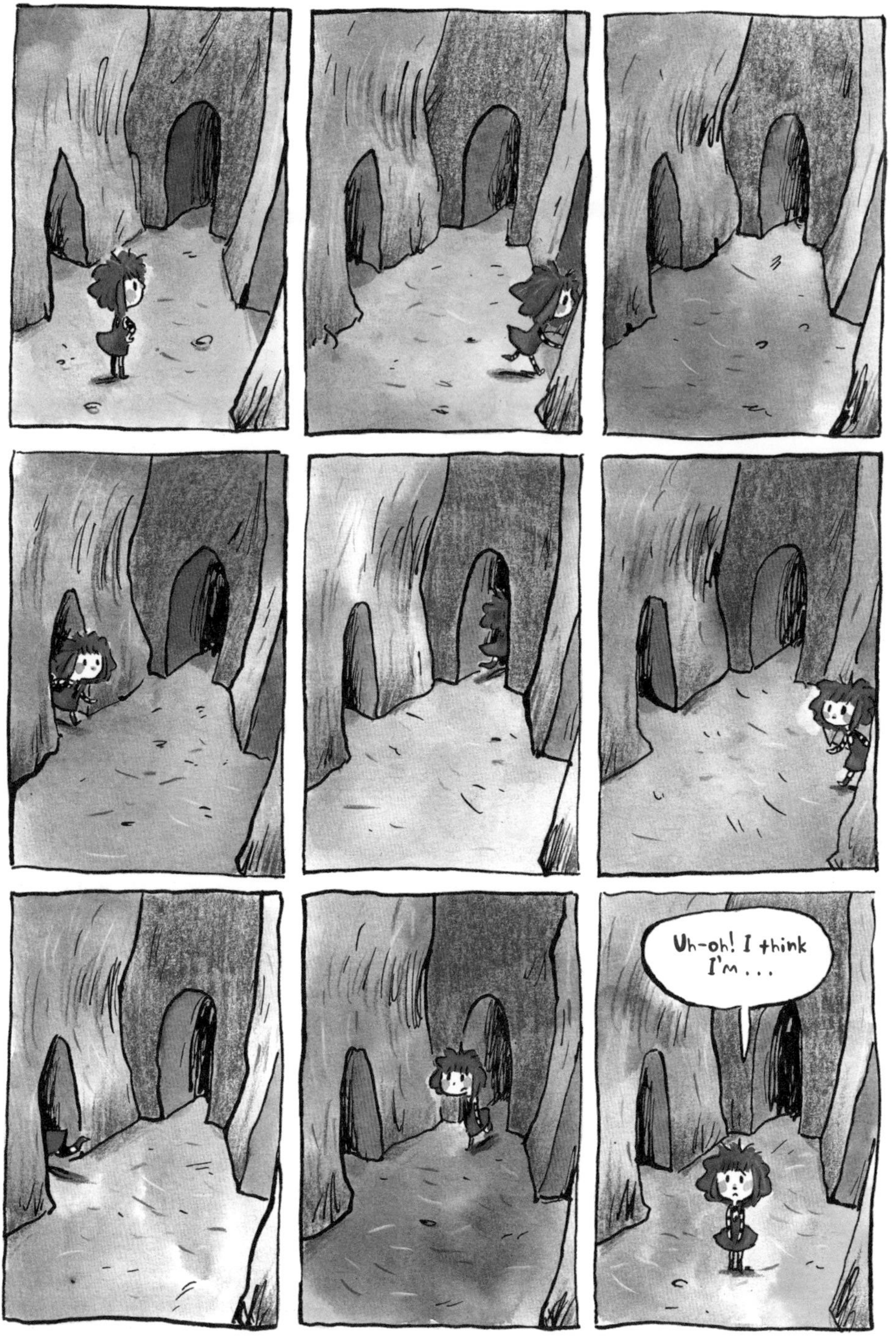
Uh-oh! I think I'm . . .

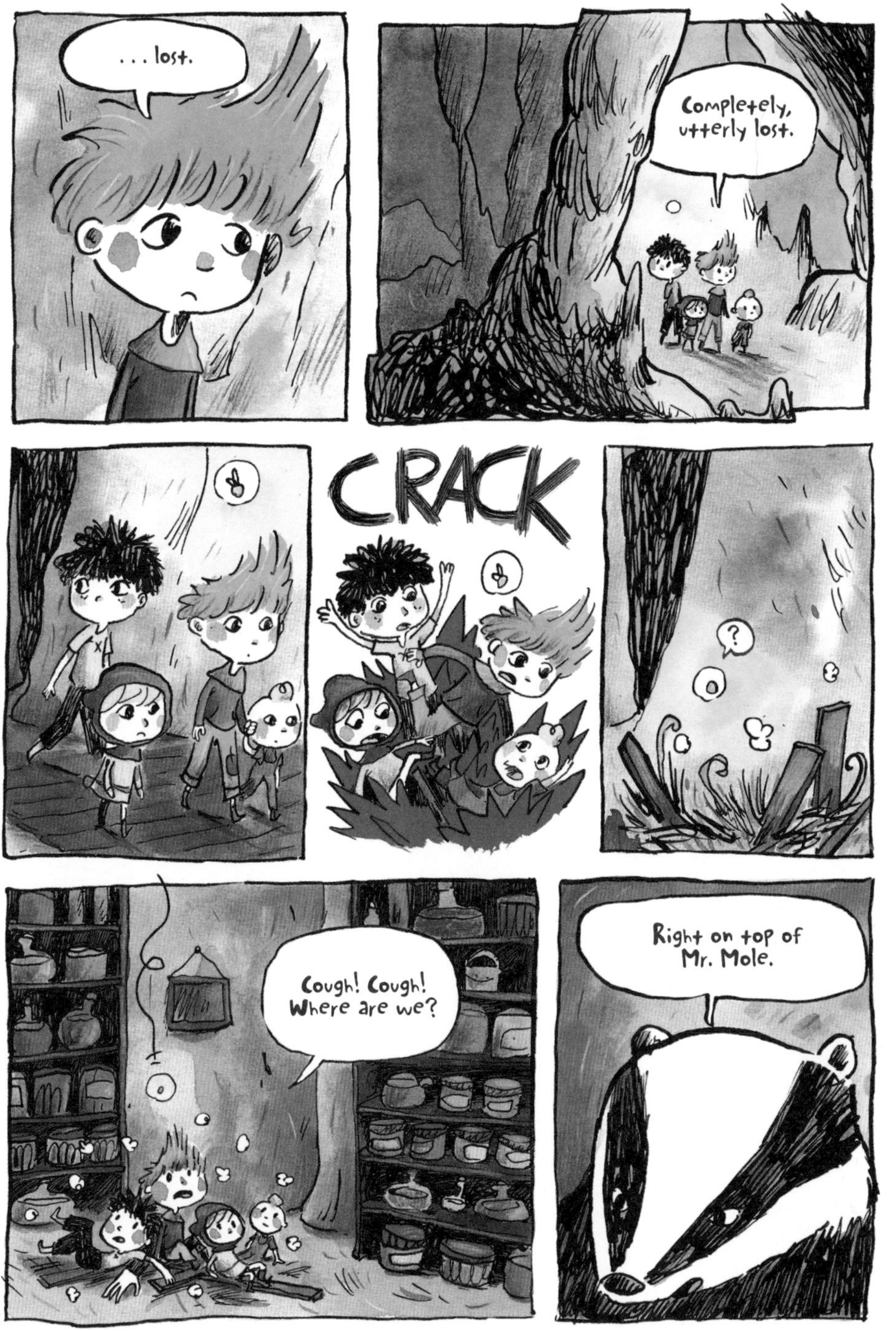
. . . lost.
Completely, utterly lost.
CRACK
Cough! Cough! Where are we?
Right on top of Mr. Mole.

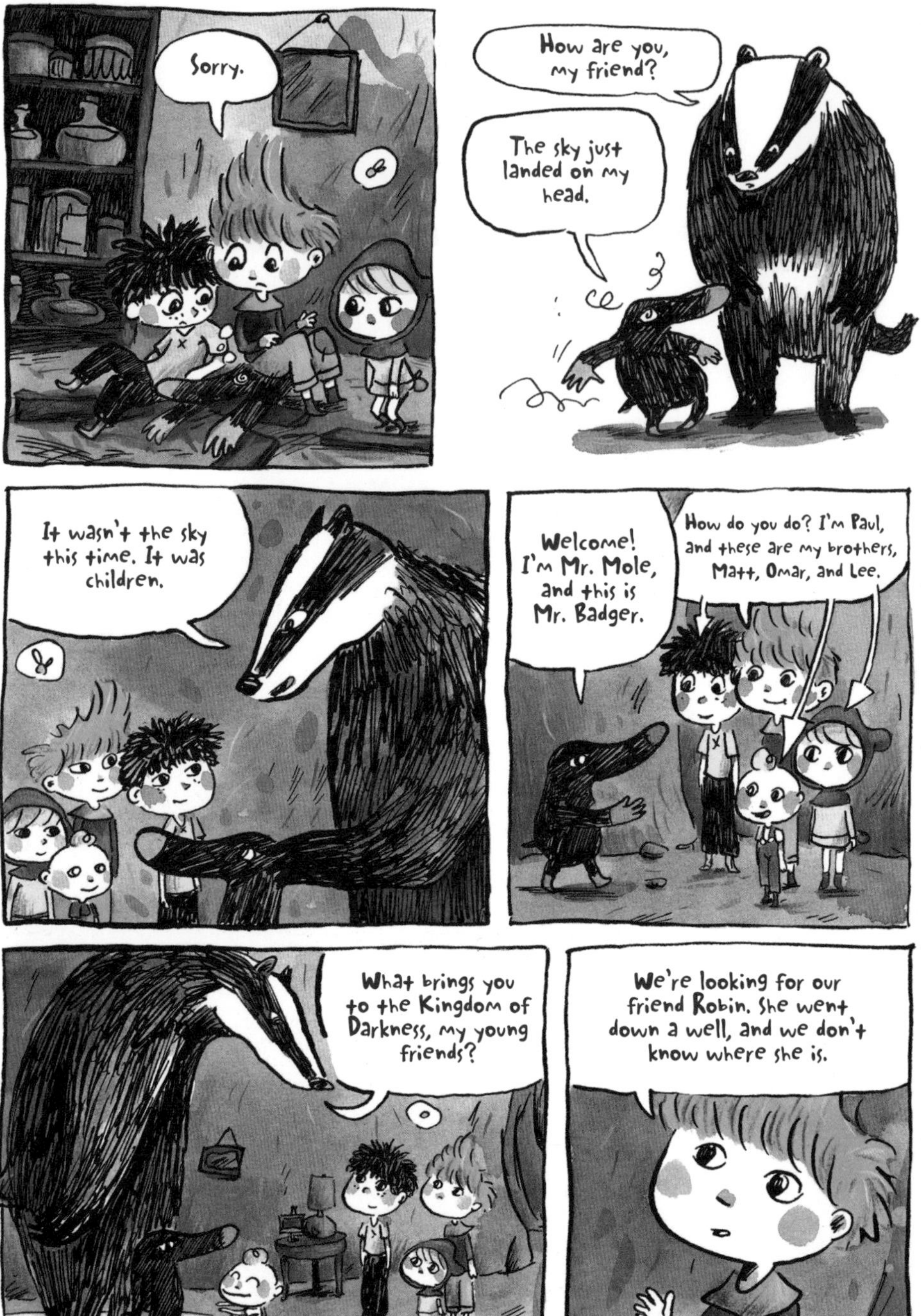
Sorry.
How are you, my friend?
The sky just landed on my head.
It wasn't the sky this time. It was children.
Welcome! I'm Mr. Mole, and this is Mr. Badger.
How do you do? I'm Paul, and these are my brothers, Matt, Omar, and Lee.
What brings you to the Kingdom of Darkness, my young friends?
Binky!
We're looking for our friend Robin. She went down a well, and we don't know where she is.

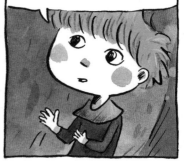

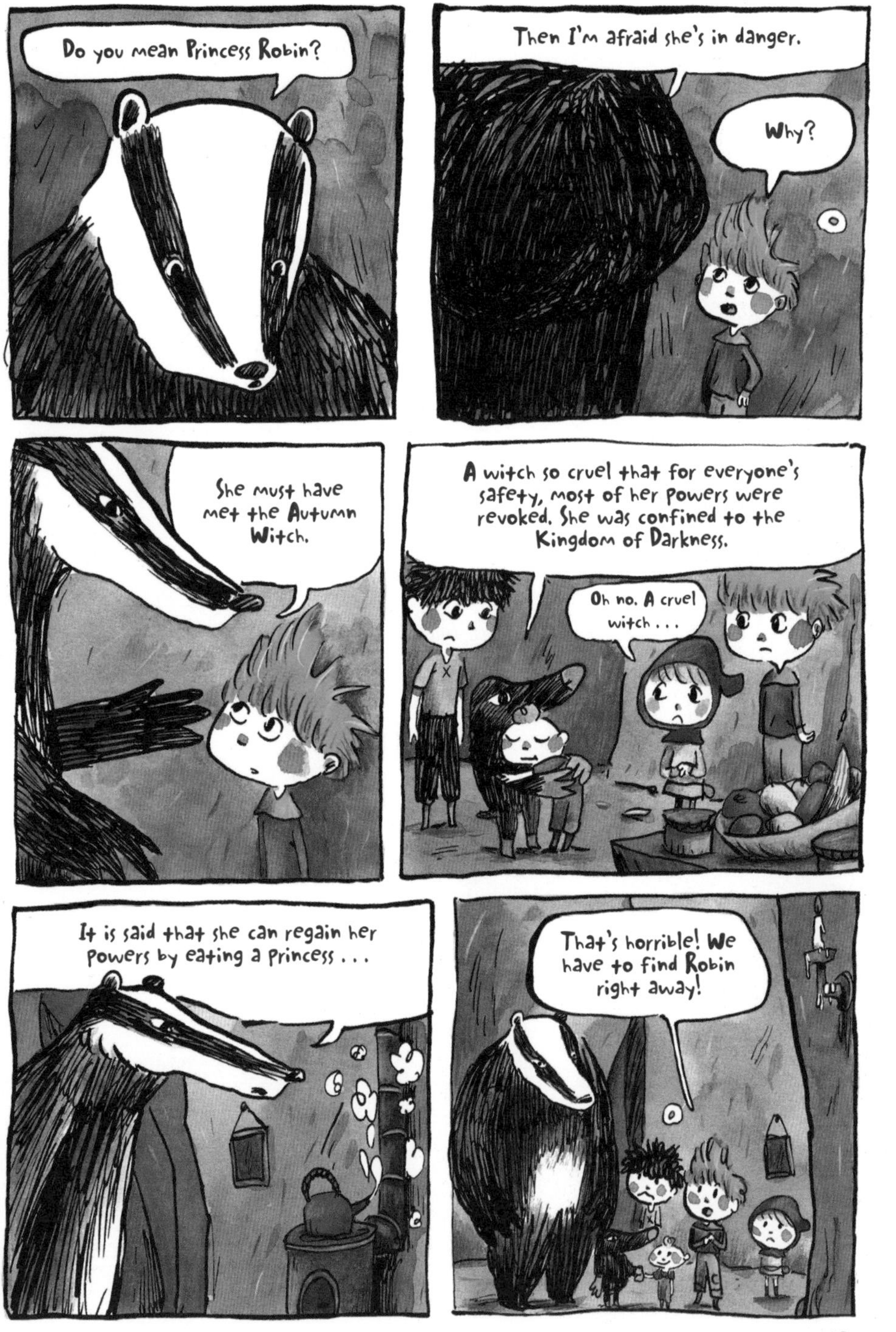
Do you mean Princess Robin?
Then I'm afraid she's in danger.
Why?
She must have met the Autumn Witch.
A witch so cruel that for everyone's safety, most of her powers were revoked. She was confined to the Kingdom of Darkness.
Oh no. A cruel witch . . .
It is said that she can regain her powers by eating a princess . . .
That's horrible! We have to find Robin right away!

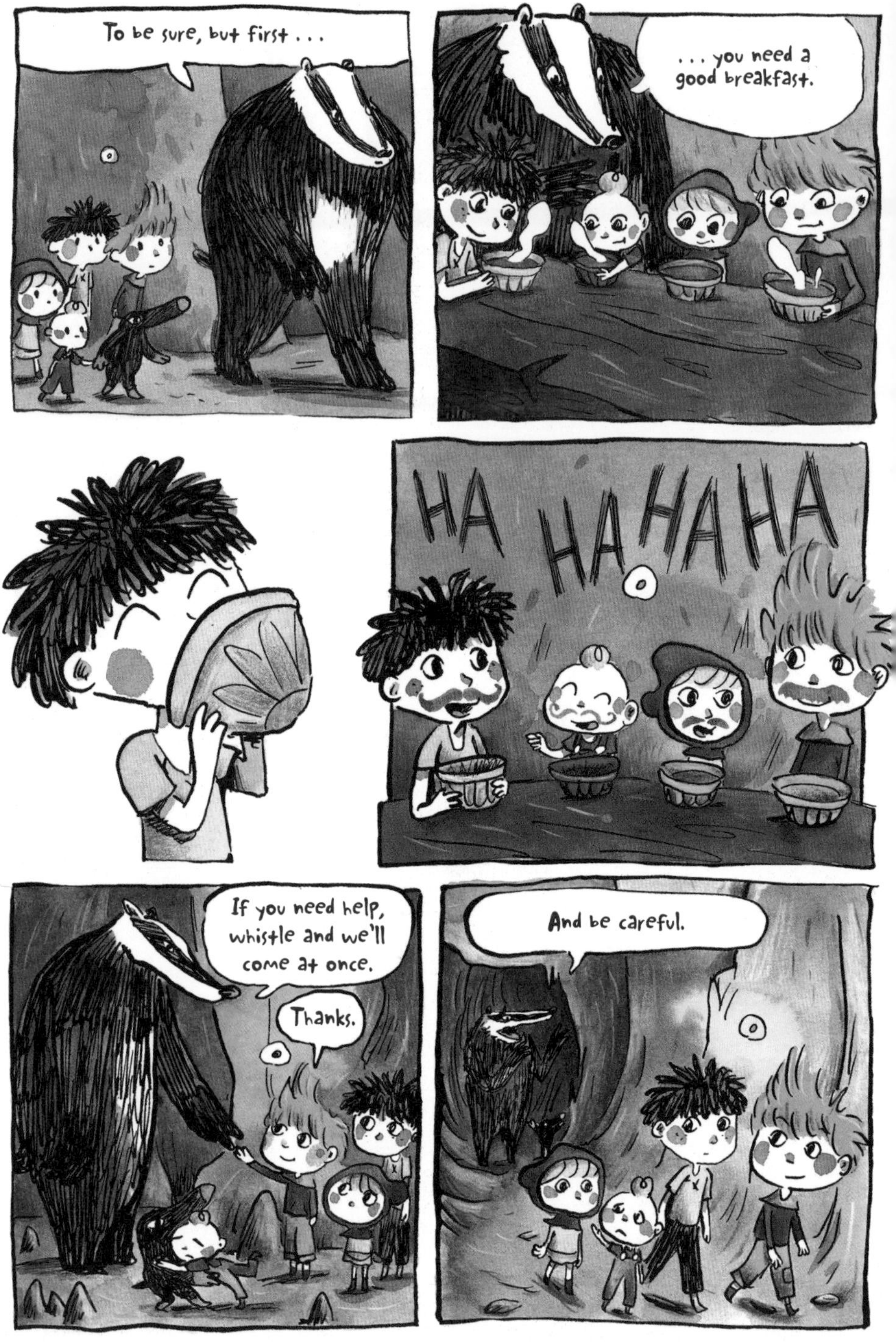
To be sure, but first . . .
. . . you need a good breakfast.
HA HA HA HA HA
If you need help, whistle and we'll come at once.
Thanks.
And be careful.

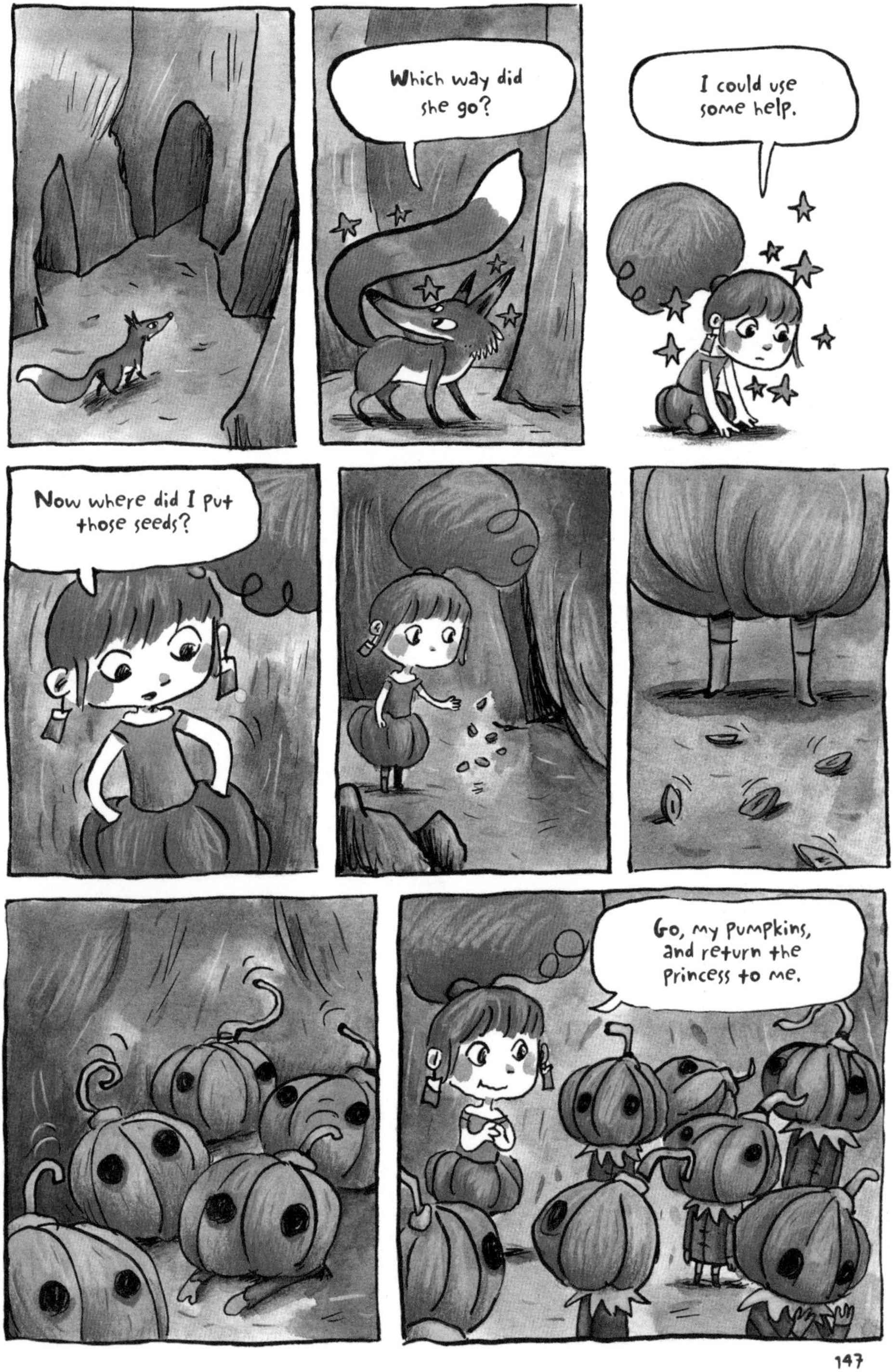
Which way did she go?
I could use some help.
Now where did I put those seeds?
Go, my pumpkins, and return the Princess to me.

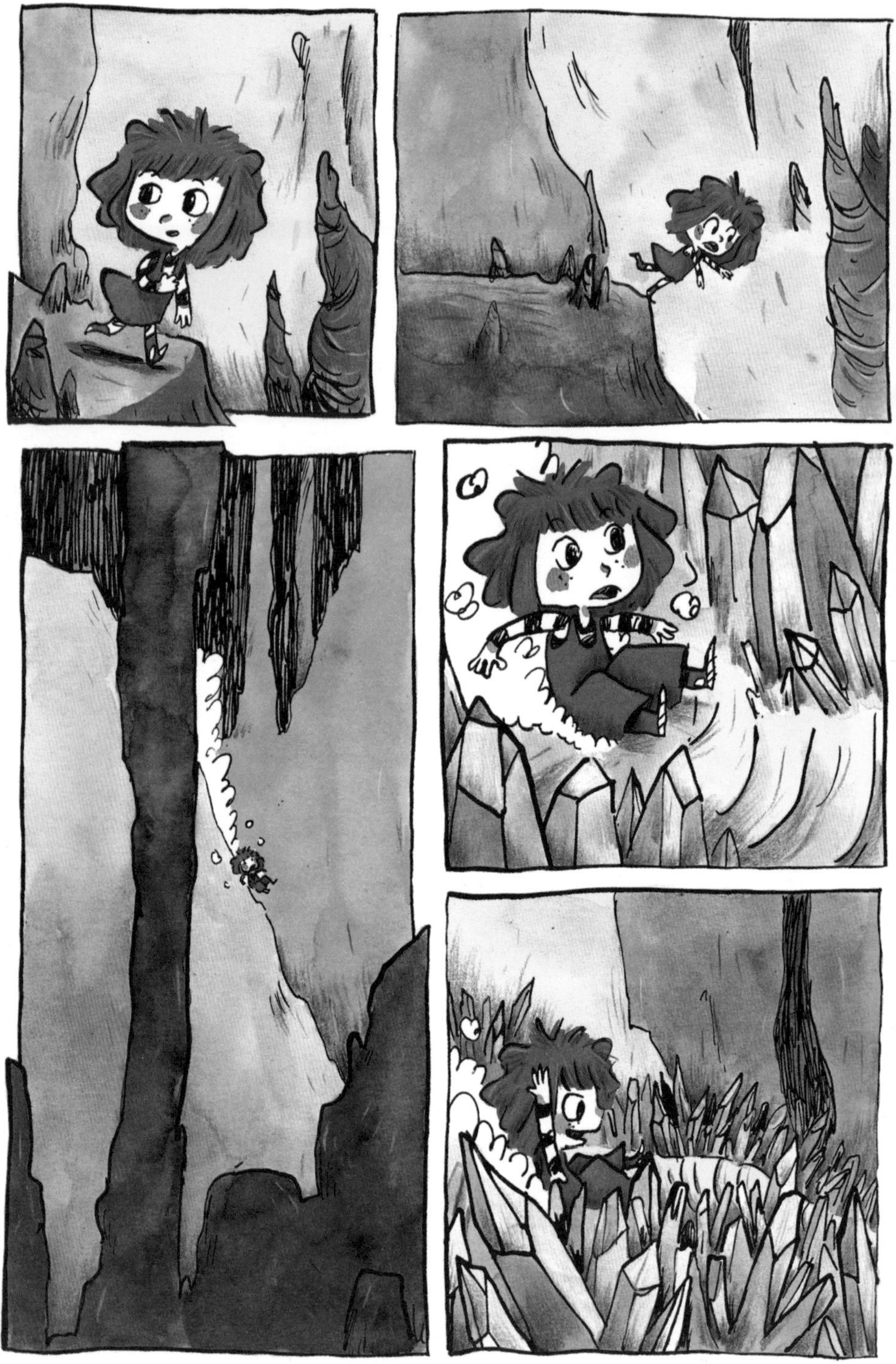

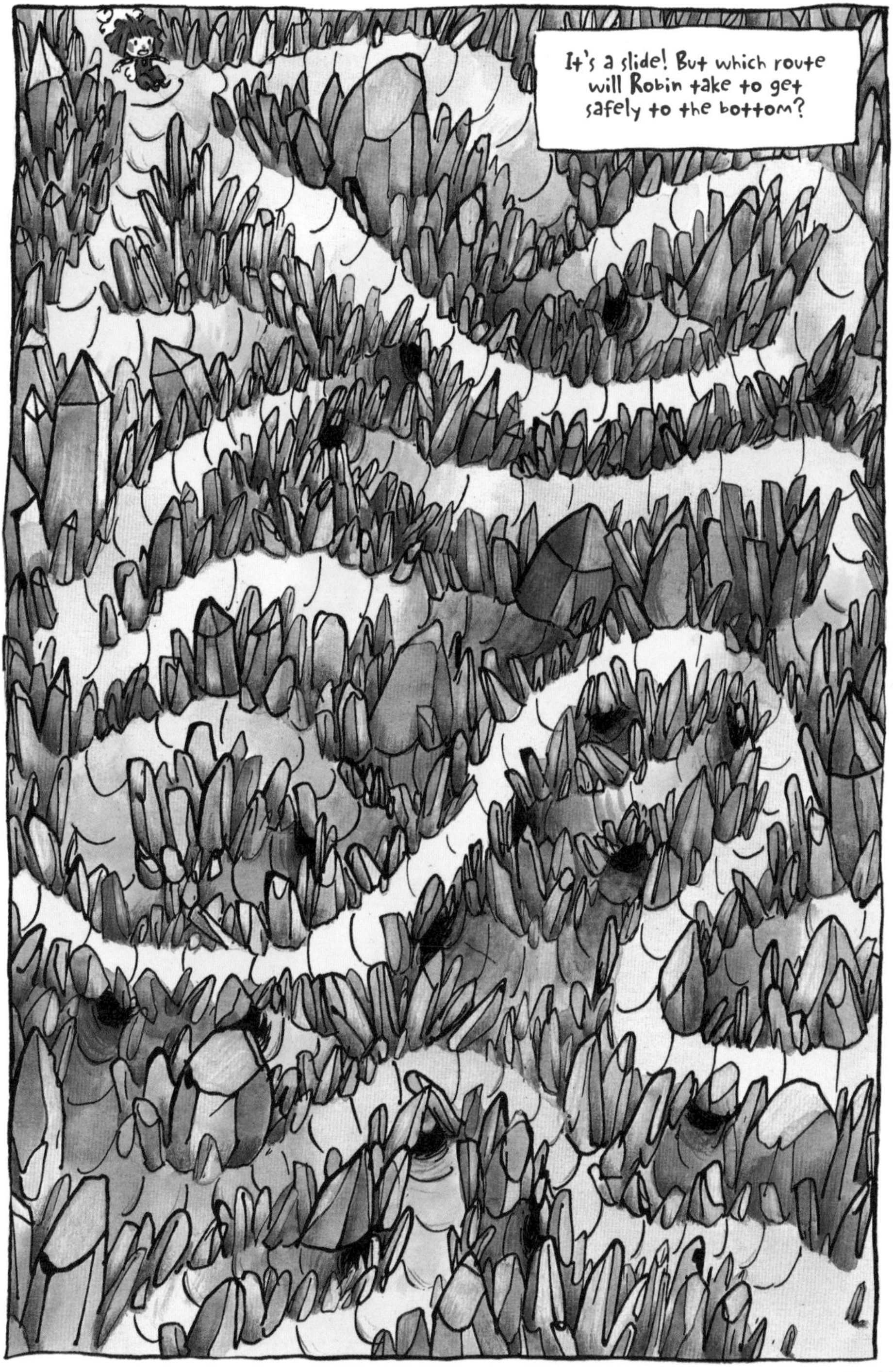
It's a slide! But which route will Robin take to get safely to the bottom?

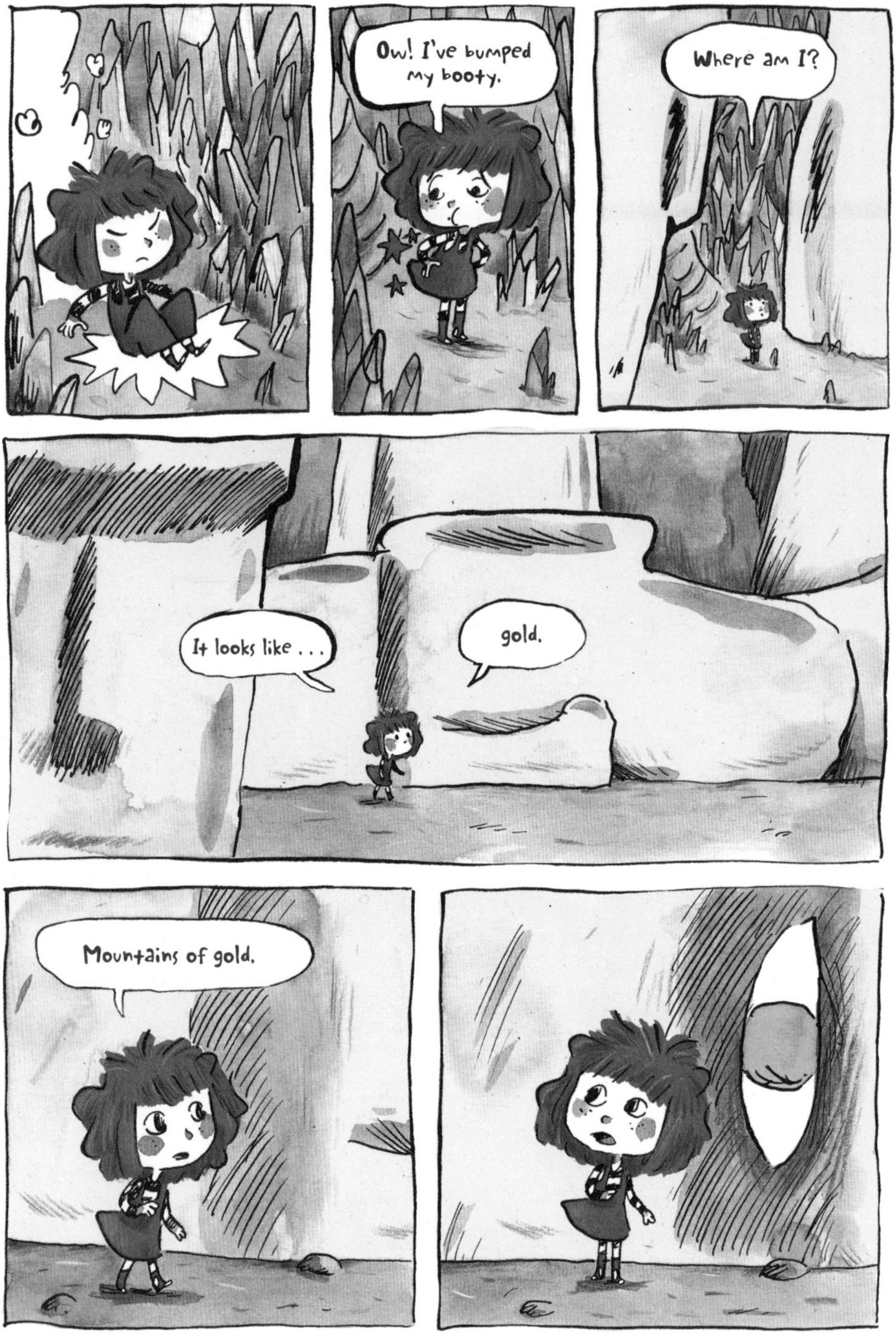
Ow! I've bumped my booty.
Where am I?
It looks like . . .
gold.
Mountains of gold.

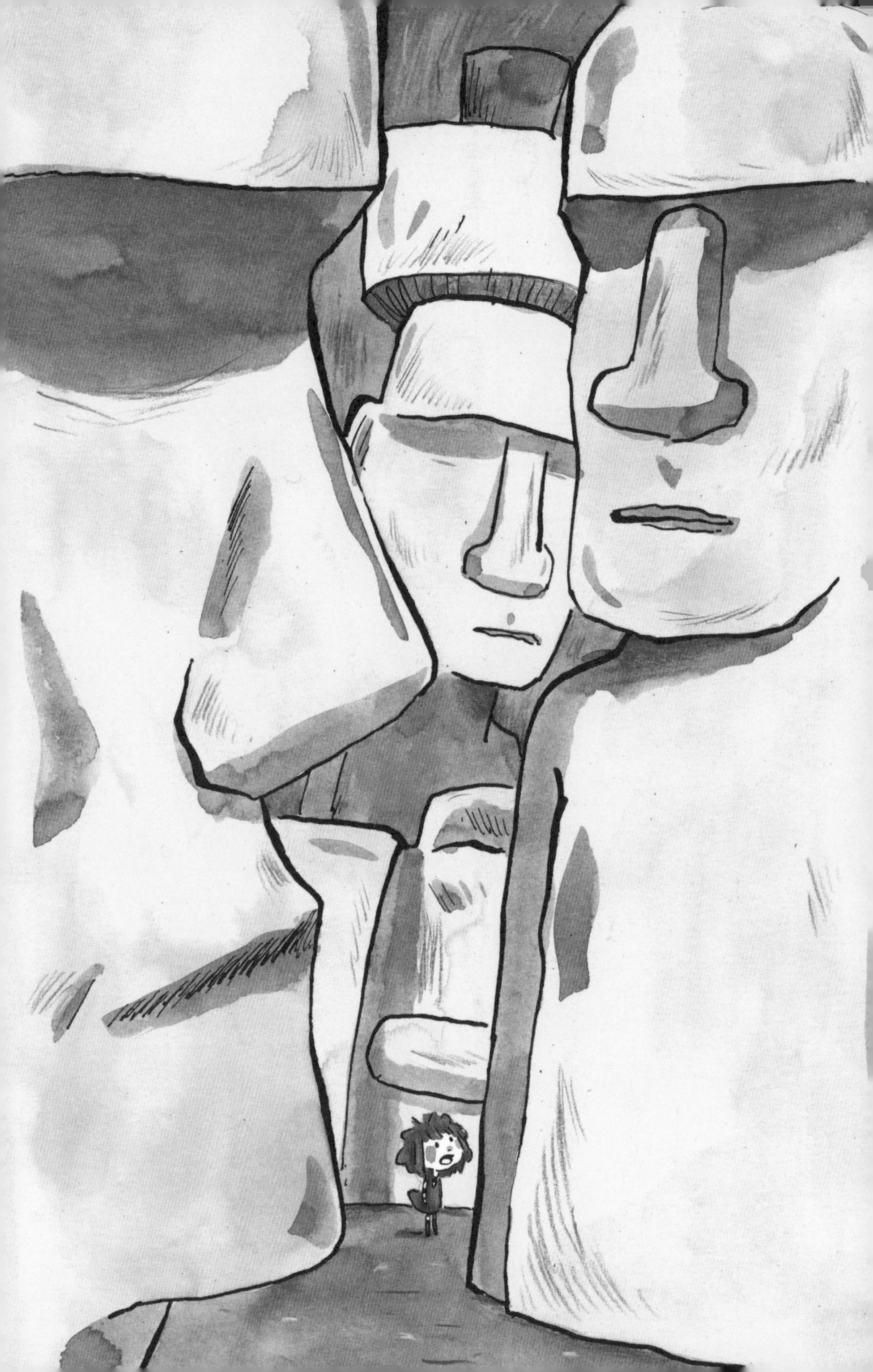

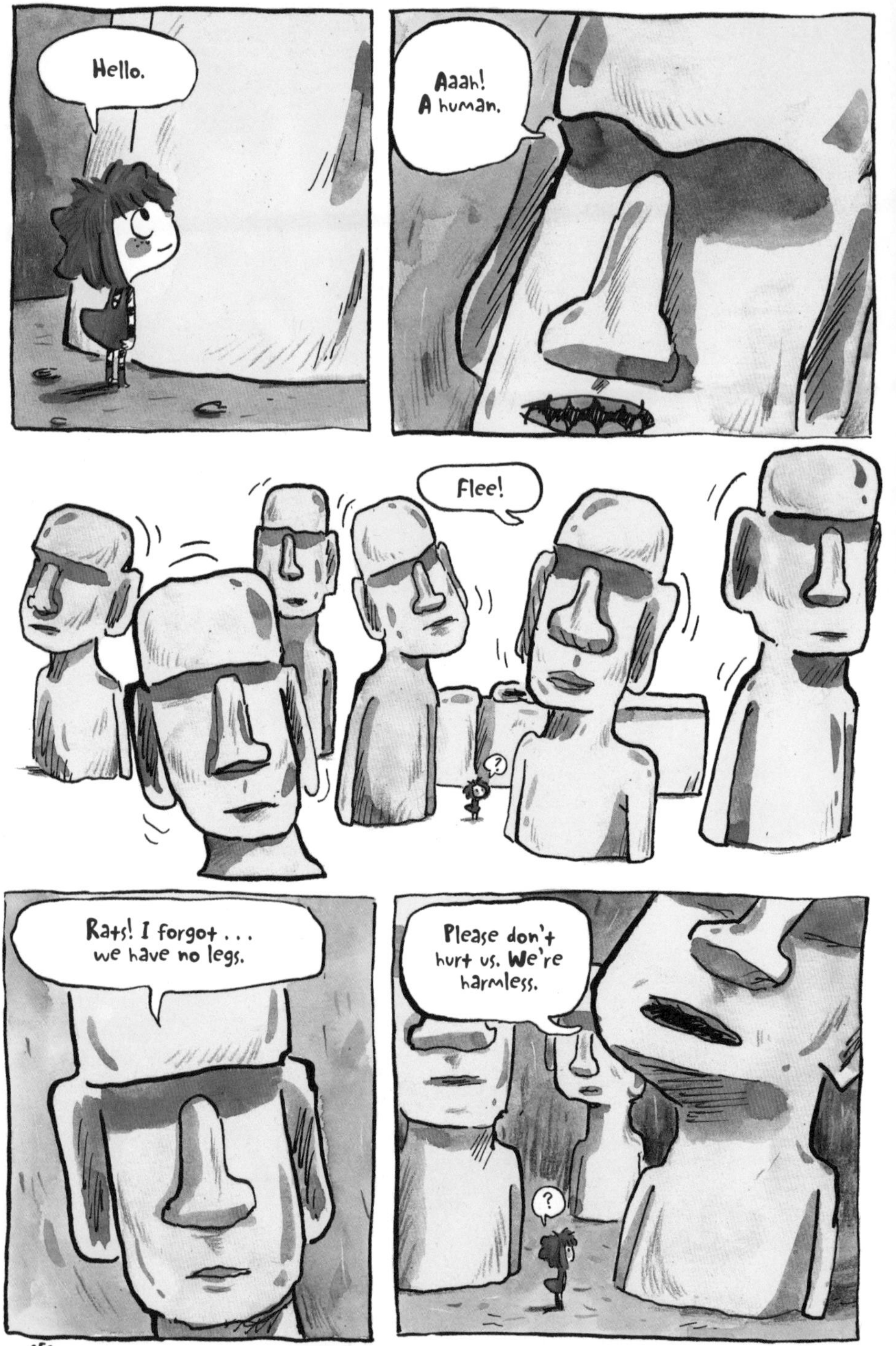
Hello.
Aaah! A human.
Flee!
?
Rats! I forgot . . . we have no legs.
Please don't hurt us. We're harmless.
?

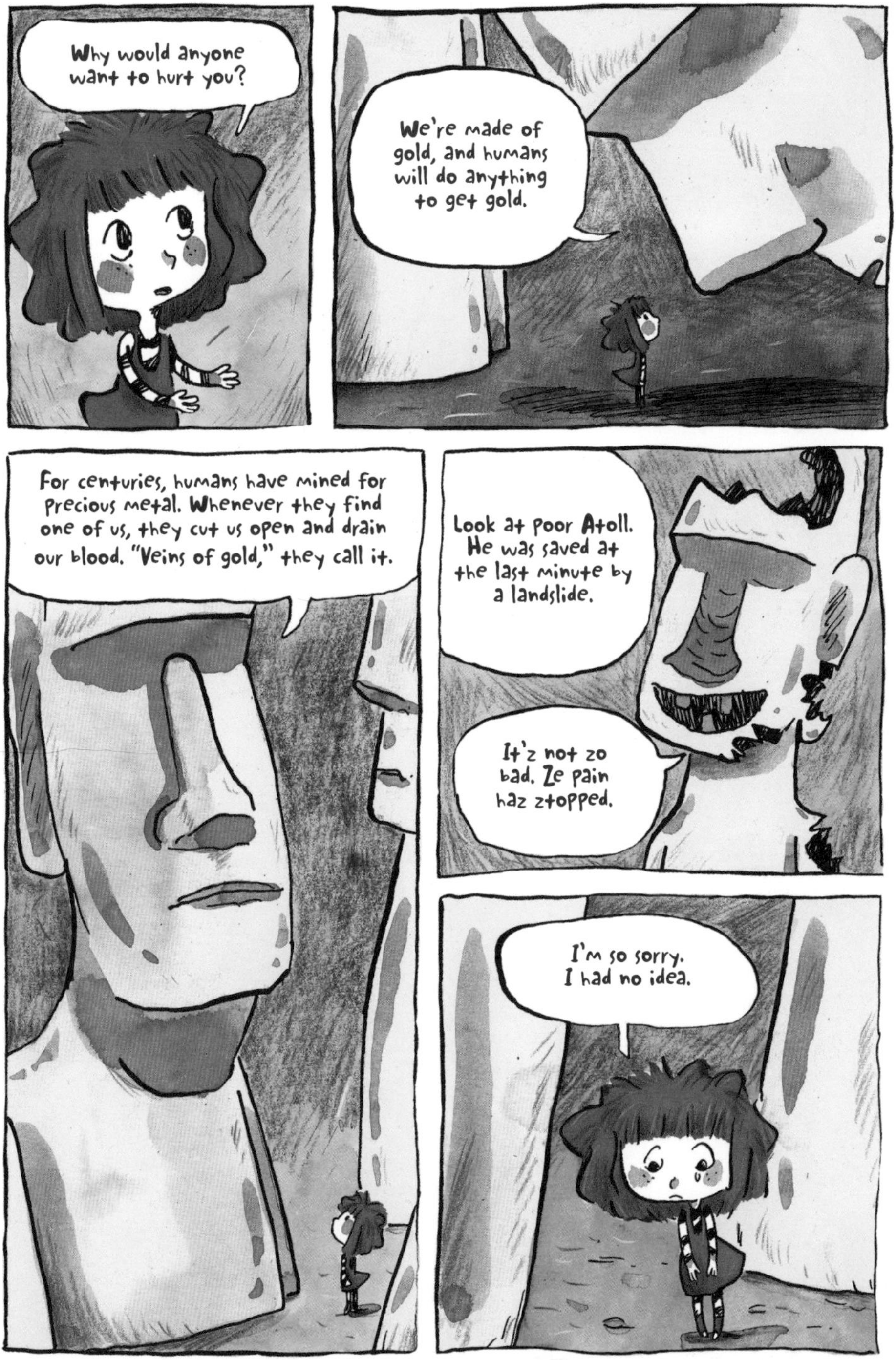
Why would anyone want to hurt you?
We're made of gold, and humans will do anything to get gold.
For centuries, humans have mined for precious metal. Whenever they find one of us, they cut us open and drain our blood. "Veins of gold," they call it.
Look at poor Atoll. He was saved at the last minute by a landslide.
It'z not zo bad. Ze pain haz ztopped.
I'm so sorry. I had no idea.

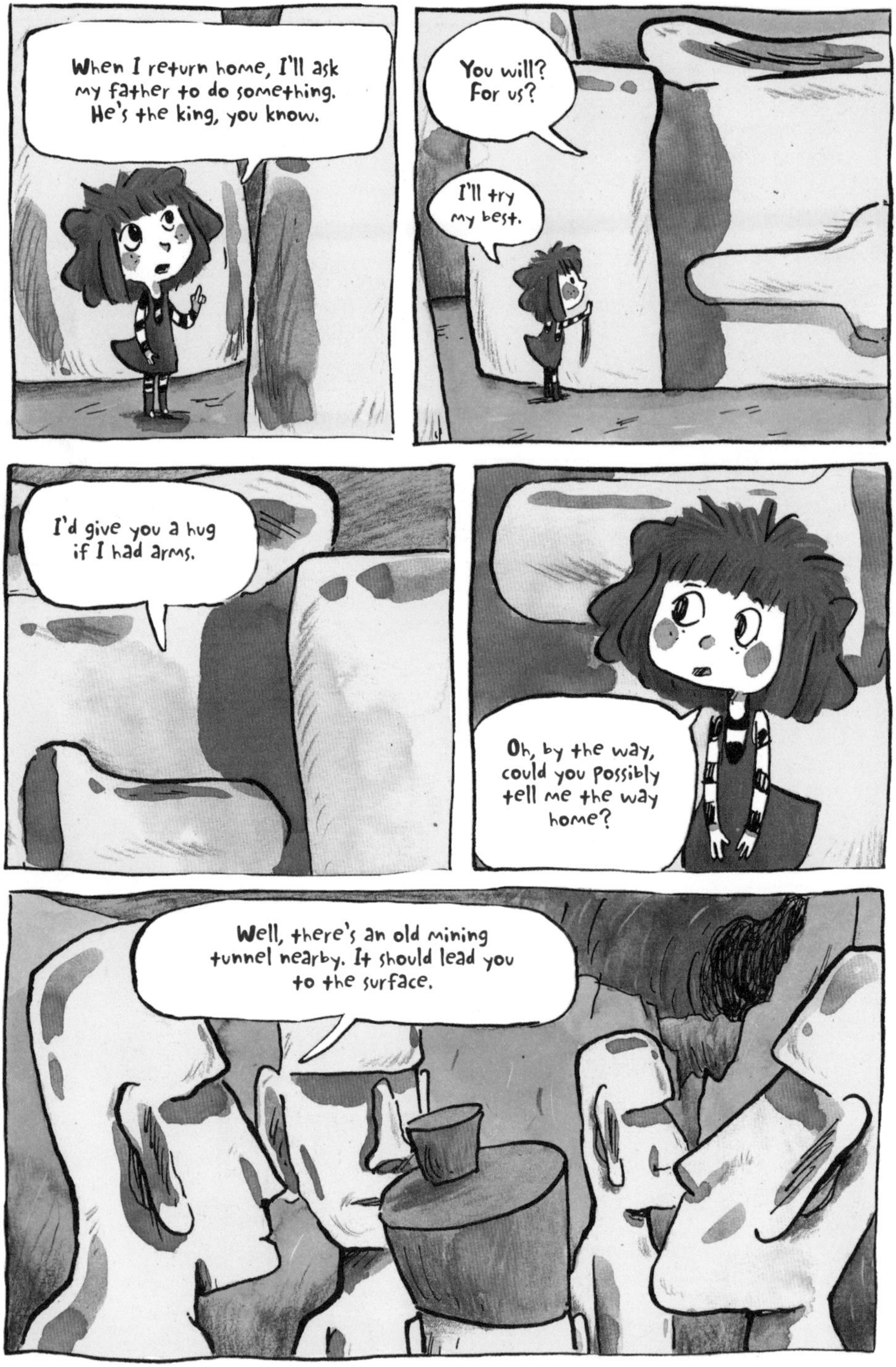

When I return home, I'll ask my father to do something. He's the king, you know.
You will? For us?
I'll try my best.
I'd give you a hug if I had arms.
Oh, by the way, could you possibly tell me the way home?
Well, there's an old mining tunnel nearby. It should lead you to the surface.

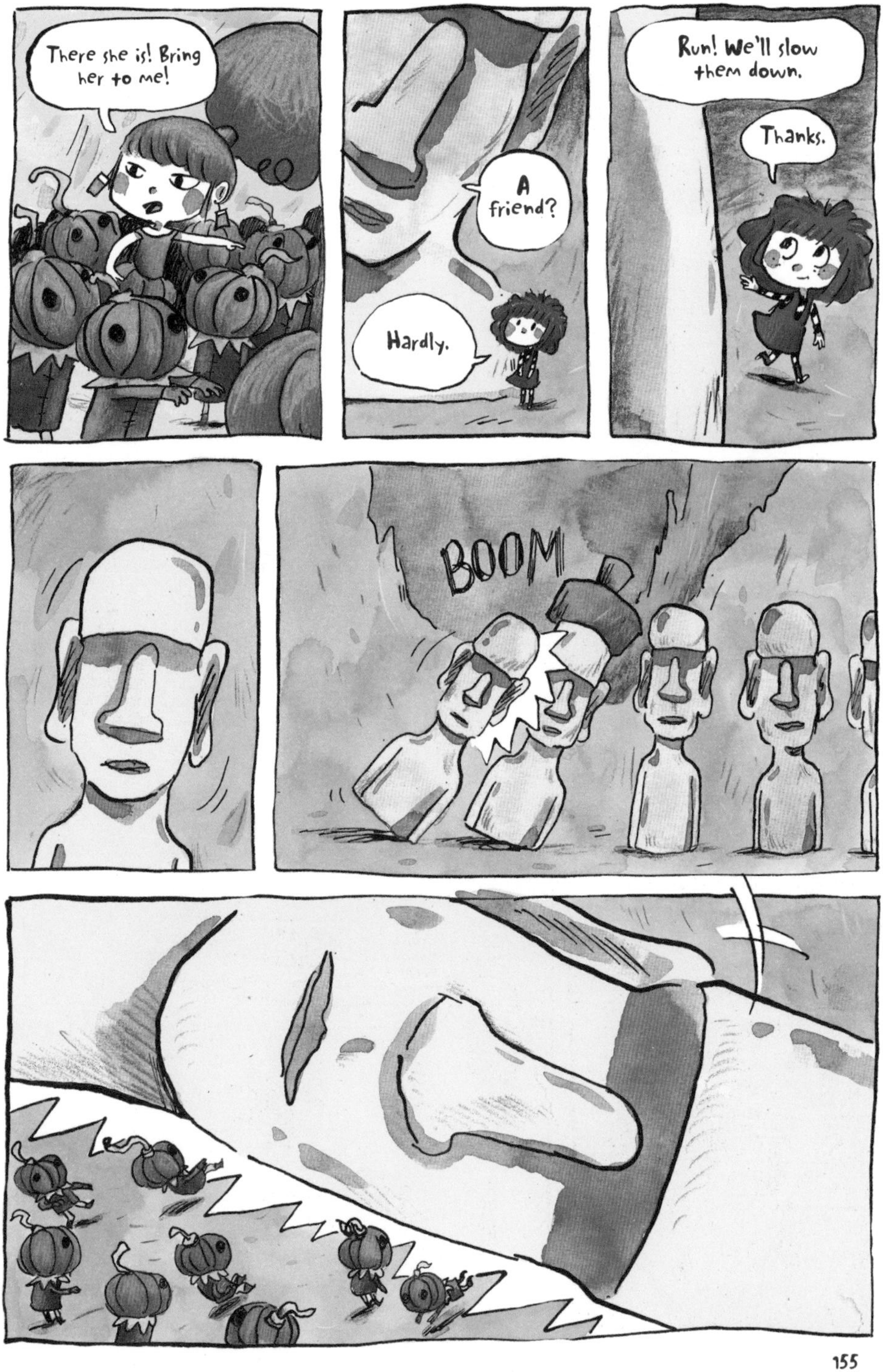
There she is! Bring her to me!
A friend?
Hardly.
Run! We'll slow them down.
Thanks.
BOOM

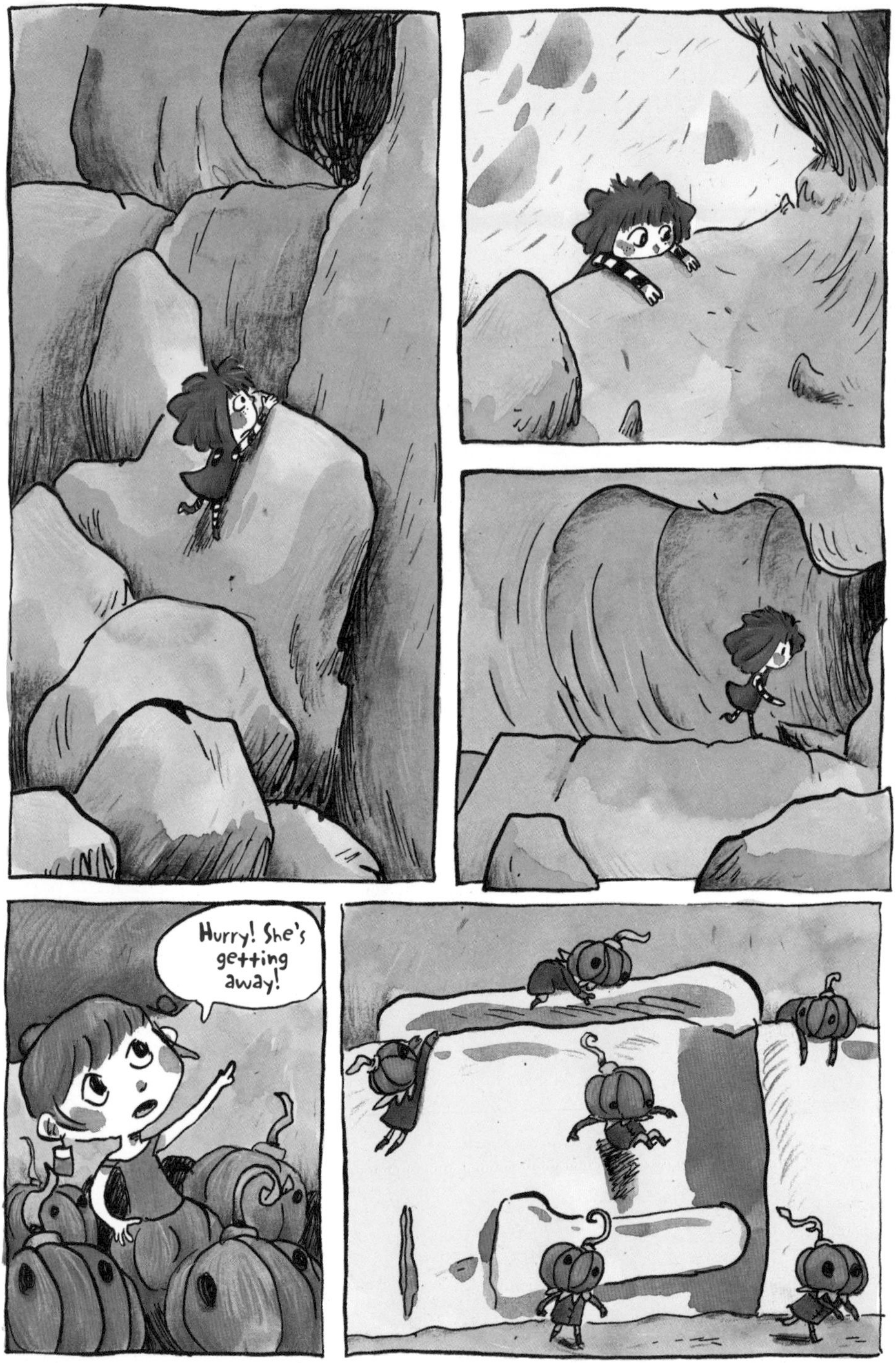
Hurry! She's getting away!

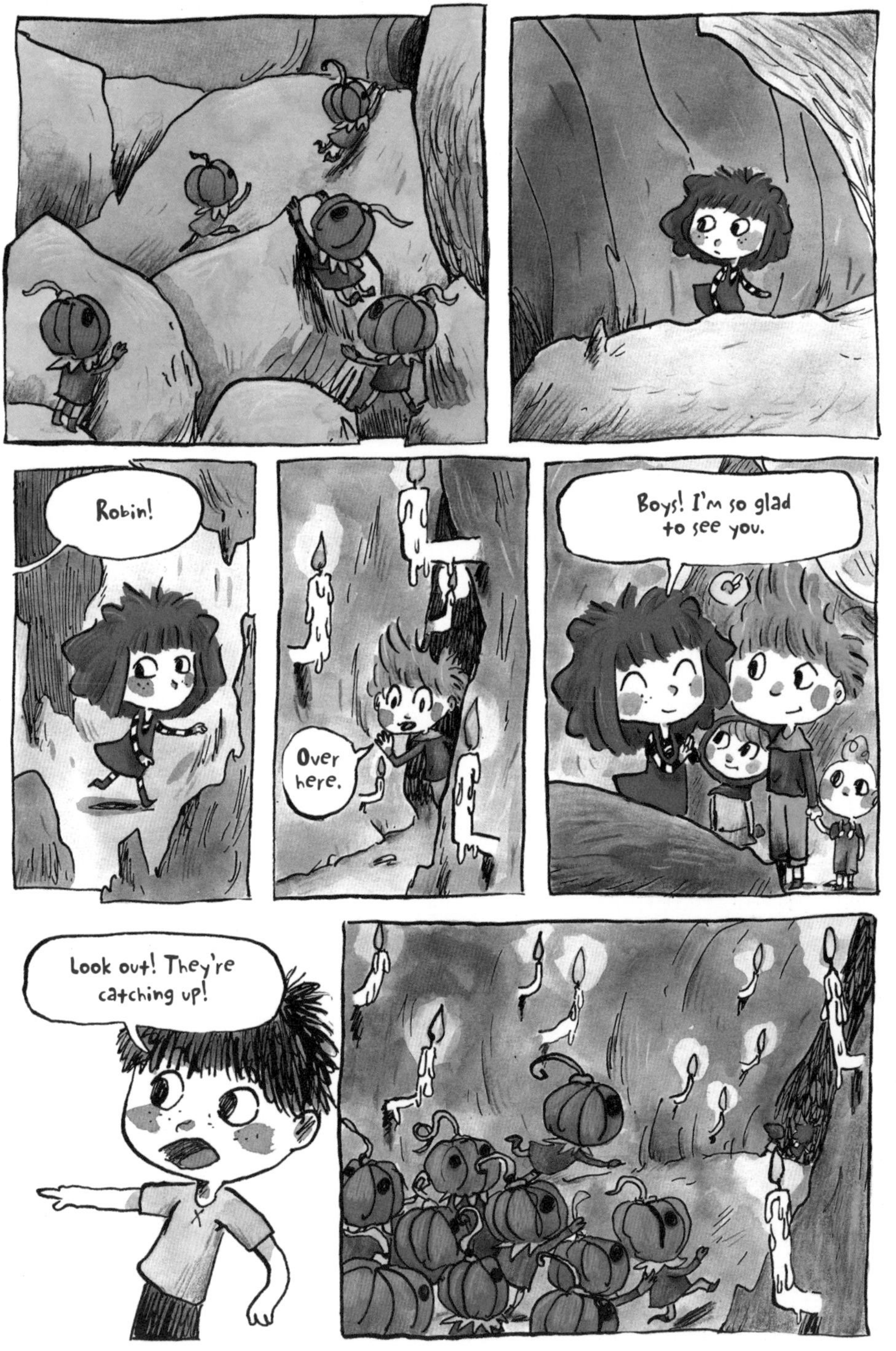

Robin!
Over here.
Boys! I'm so glad to see you.
Look out! They're catching up!

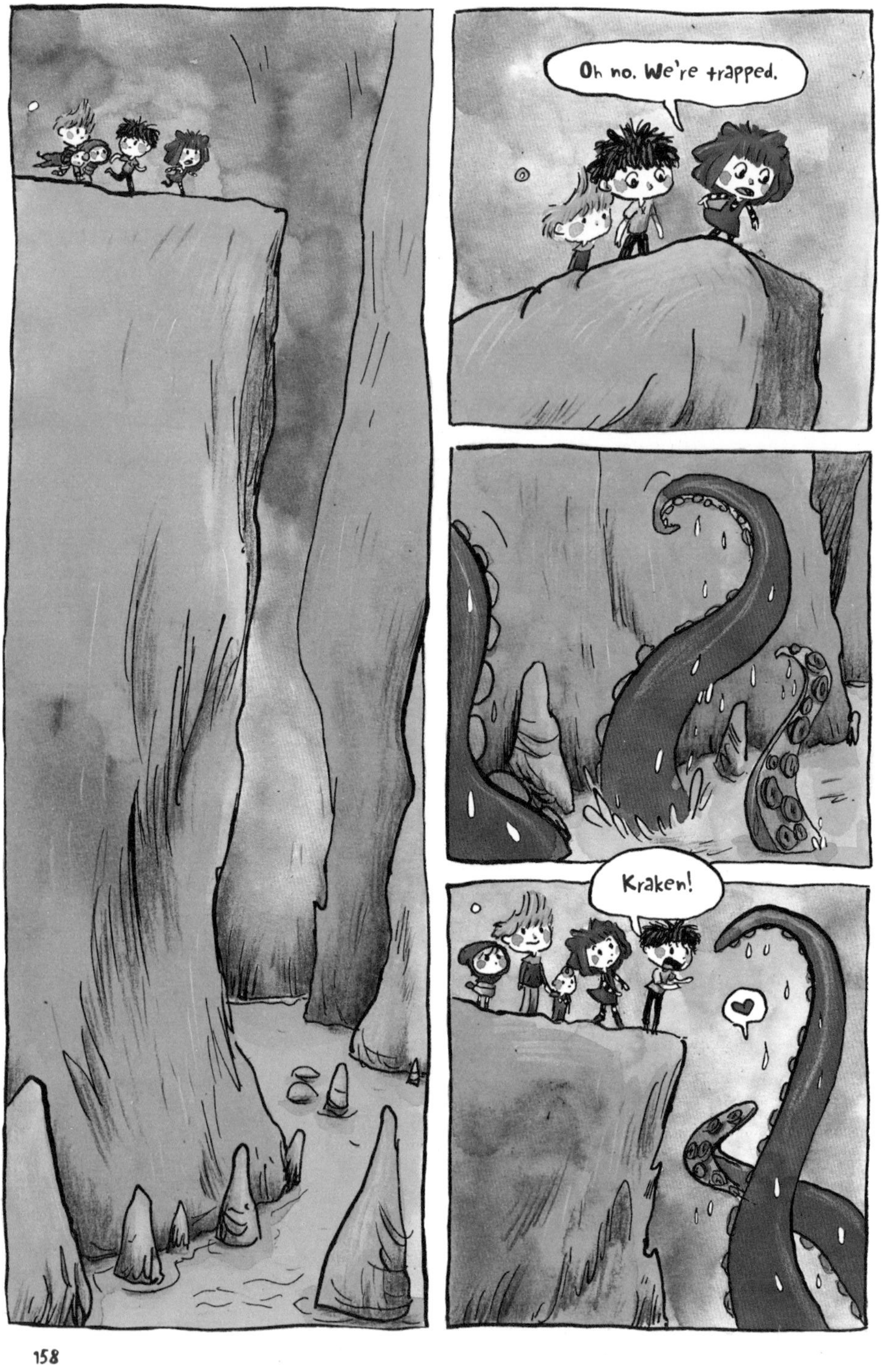
Oh no. We're trapped.
Kraken!

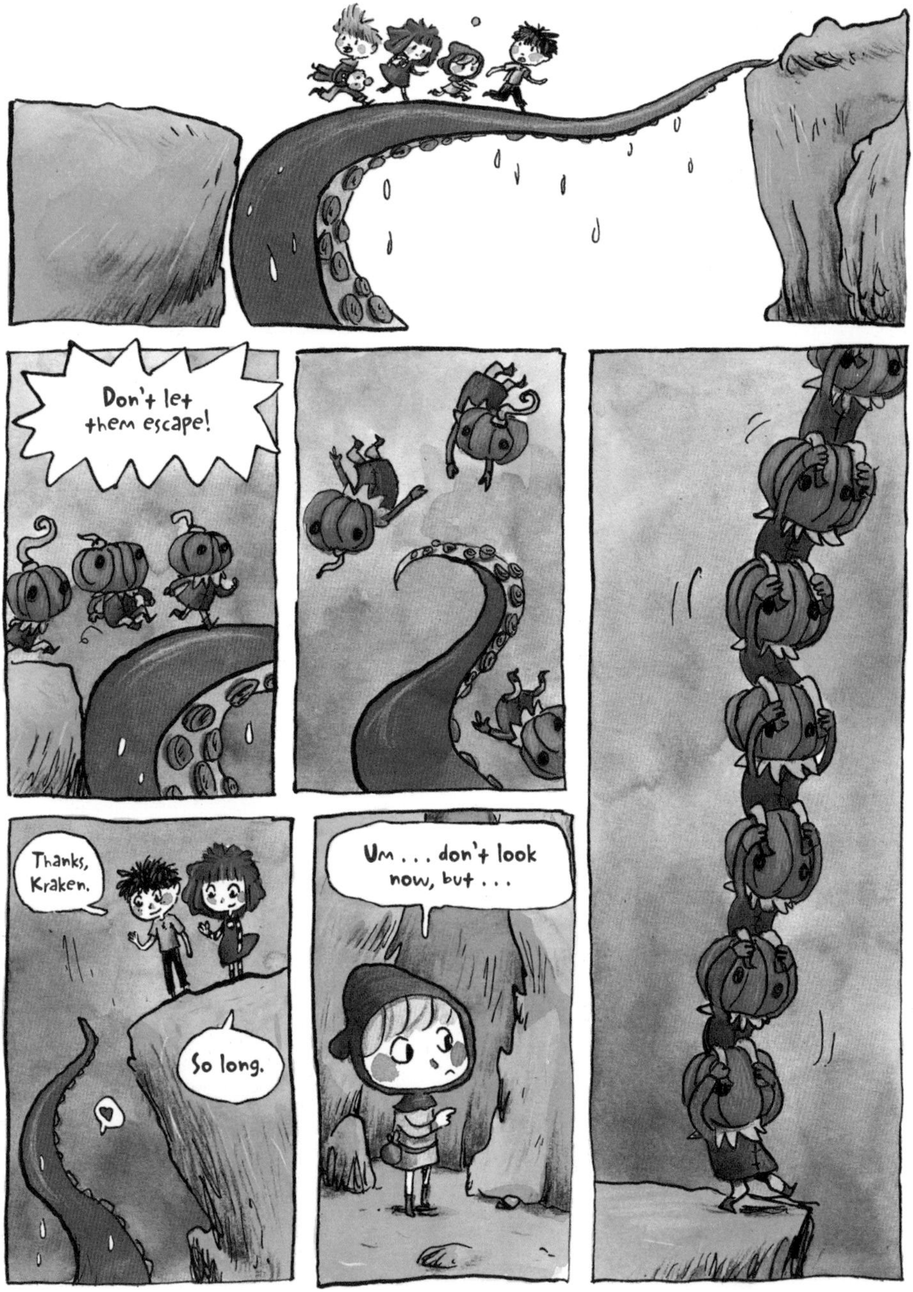
Don't let them escape!
Thanks, Kraken.
So long.
Um . . . don't look now, but . . .

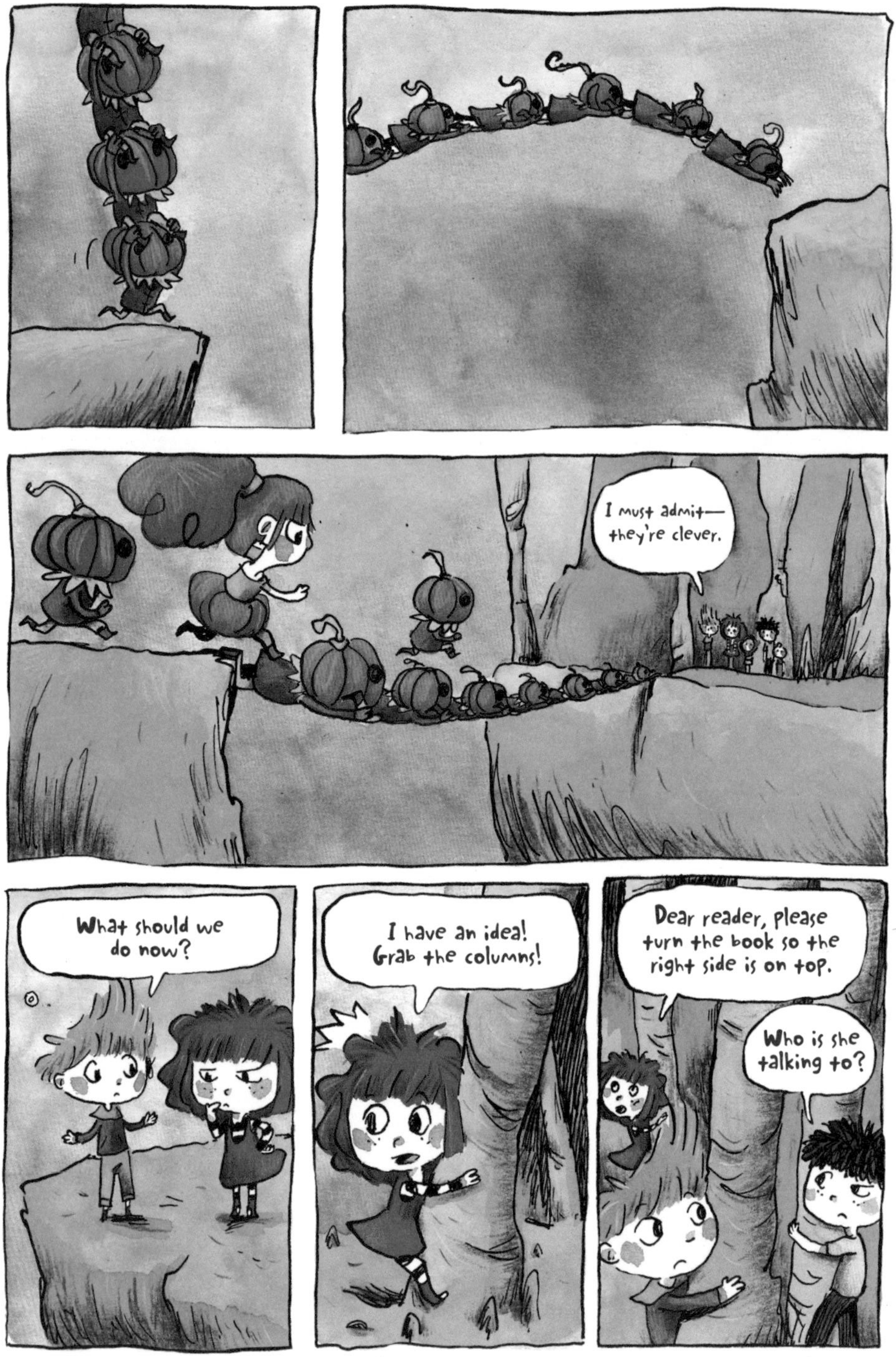
I must admit—
they're clever.
What should we do now?
I have an idea! Grab the columns!
Dear reader, please turn the book so the right side is on top.
Who is she talking to?

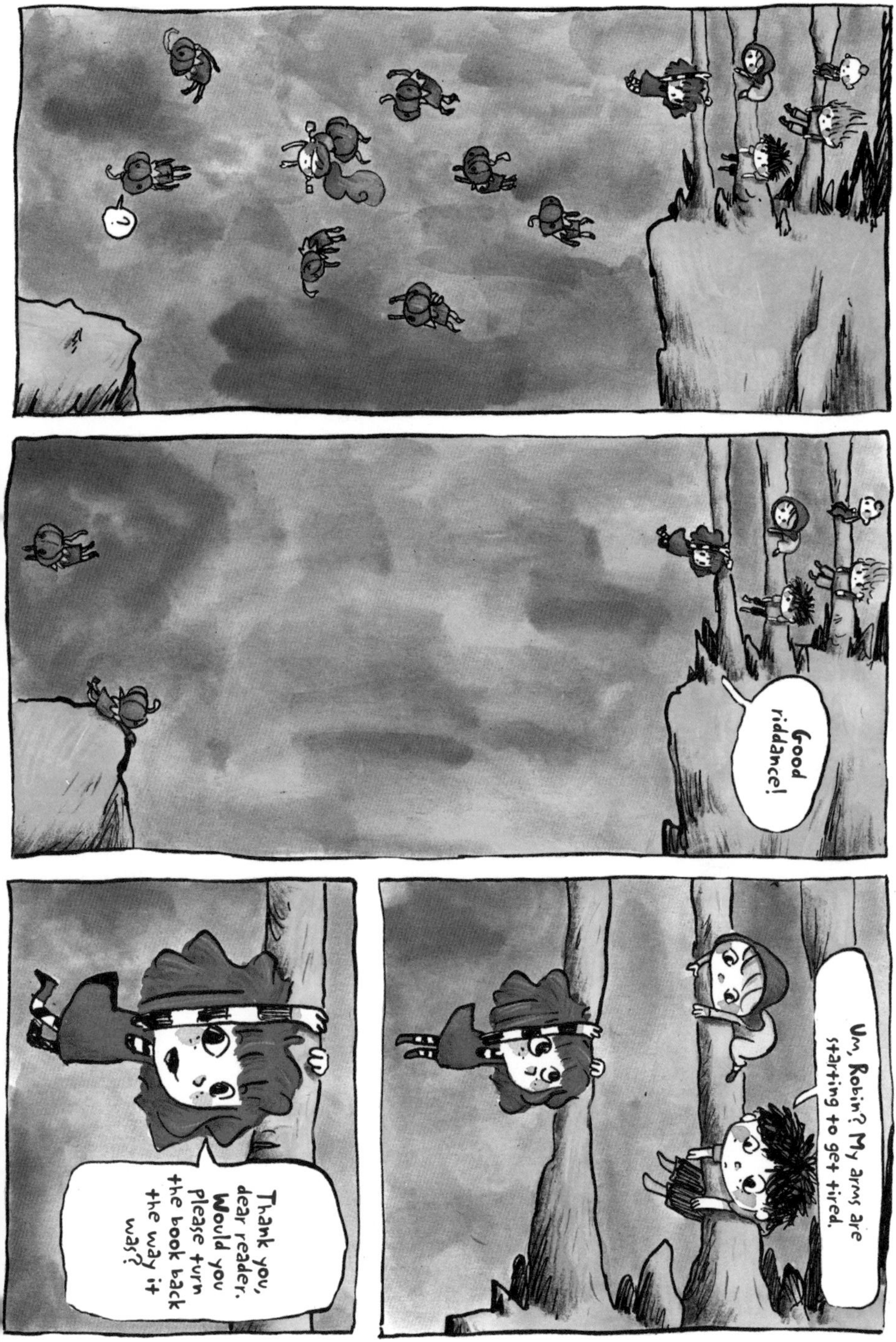
?
Good riddance!
Um, Robin? My arms are starting to get tired.
Thank you, dear reader. Would you please turn the book back the way it was?

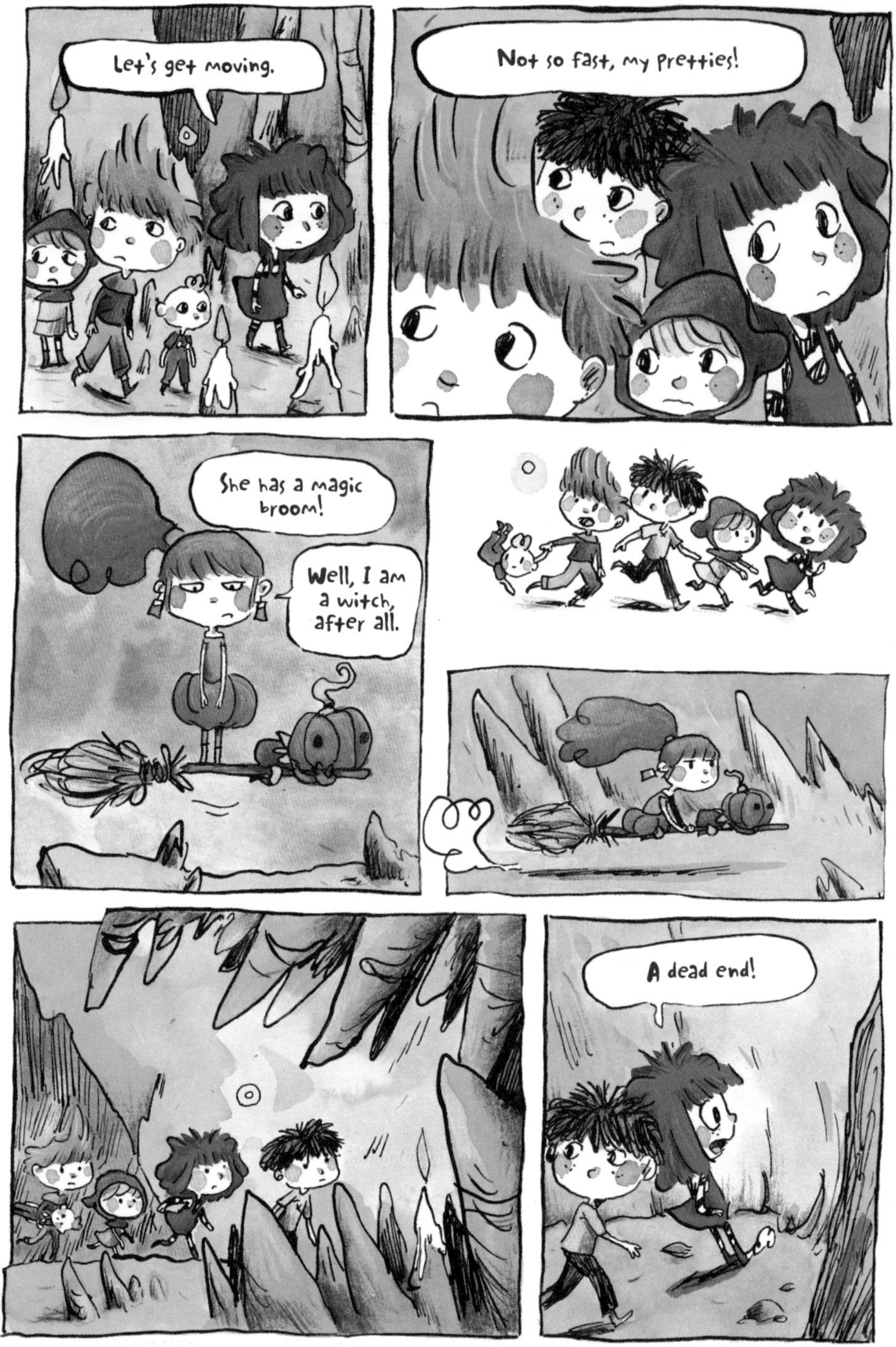
Let's get moving.
Not so fast, my pretties!
She has a magic broom!
Well, I am a witch, after all.
A dead end!

I'm sorry I dragged you into this adventure, boys.

Might as well give up.

Not without a fight.

Look! Mr. Badger's whistle.

...

Great.

?

Did I hear you whistle, children?

Mr. Mole!

The Autumn Witch is about to capture us.

Follow me.

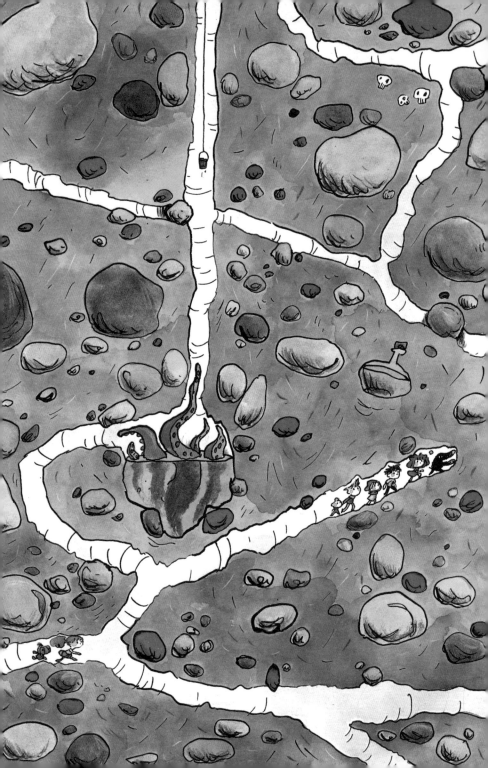

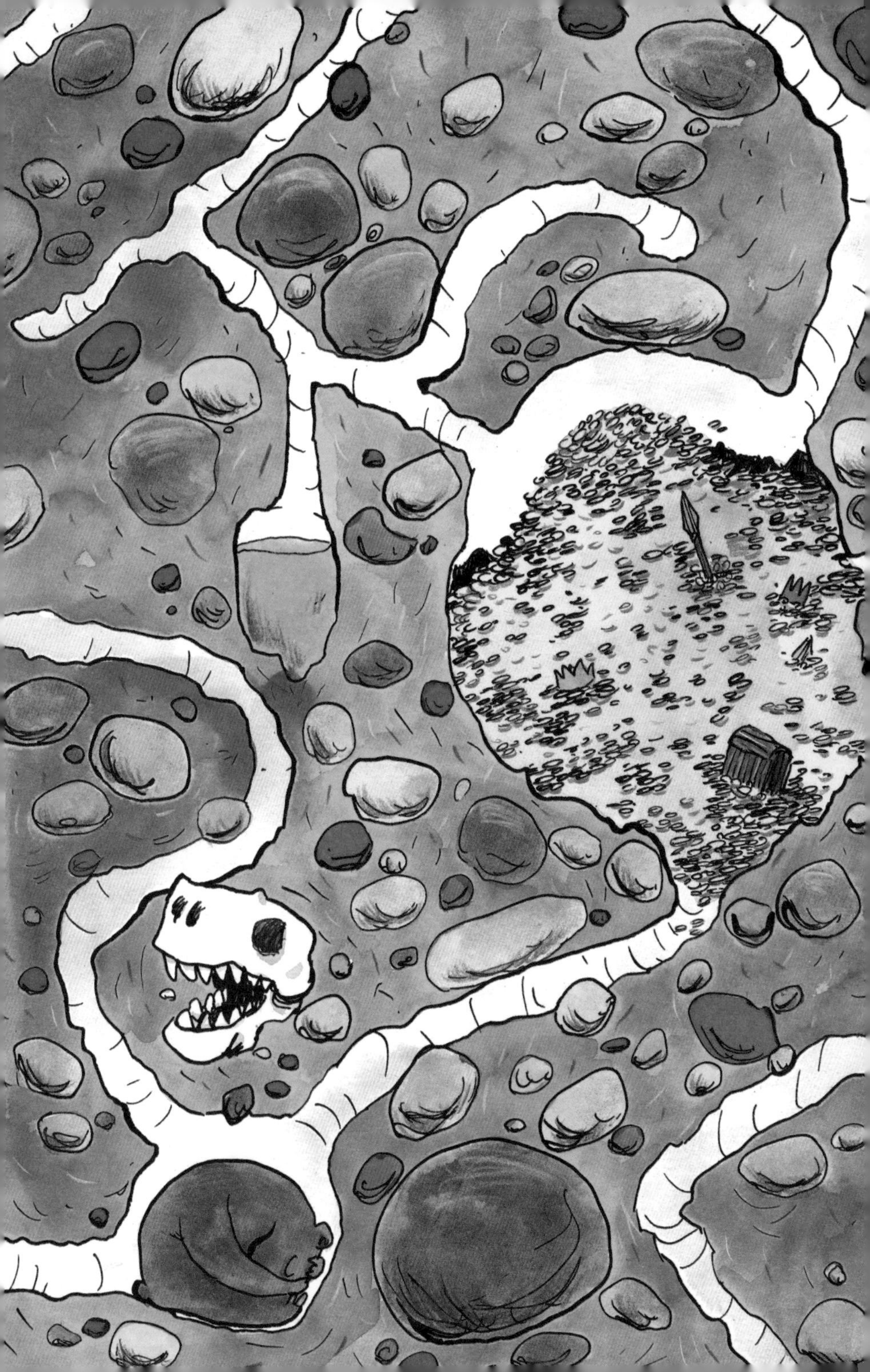

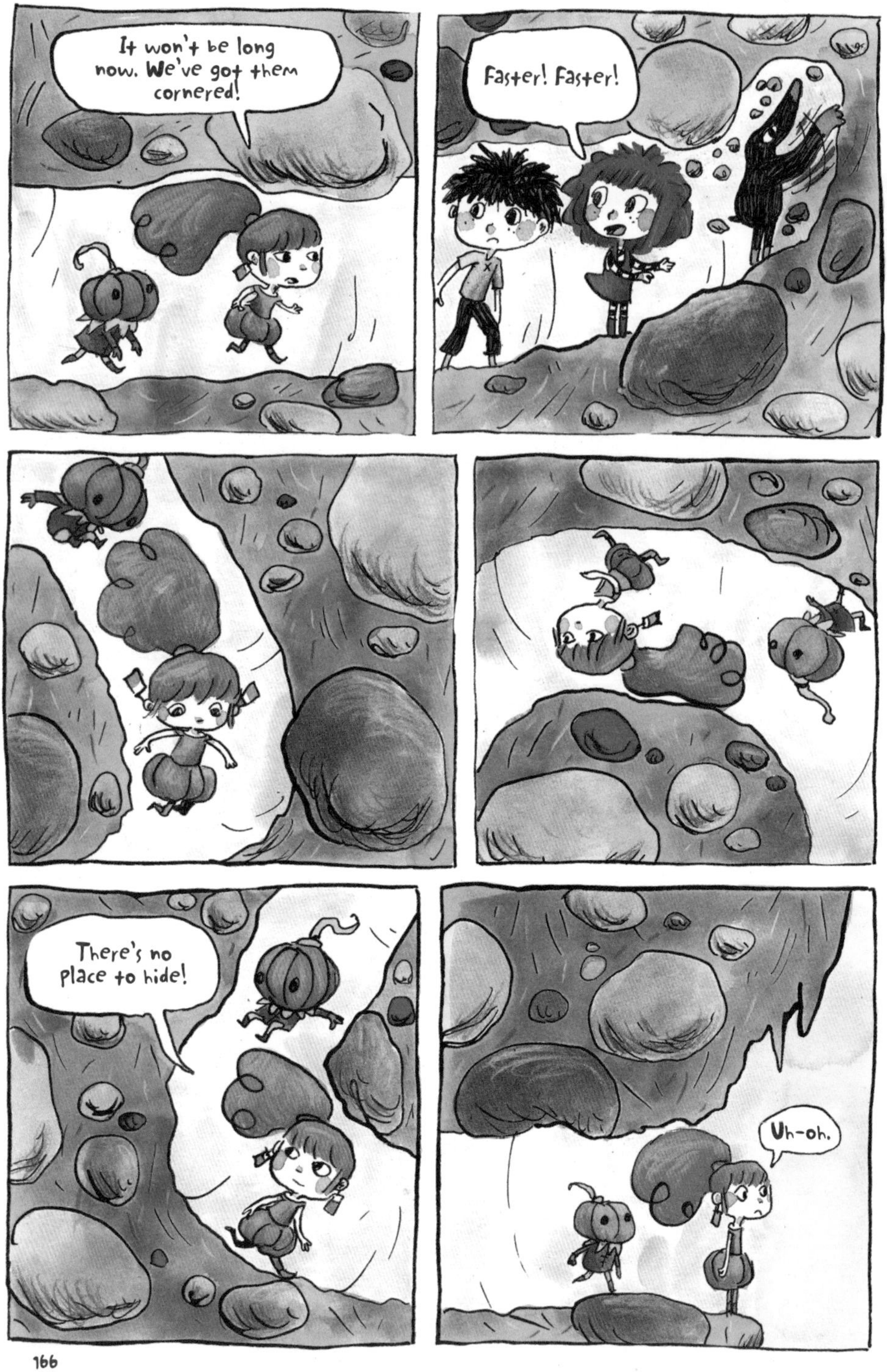
It won't be long now. We've got them cornered!
Faster! Faster!
There's no place to hide!
Uh-oh.

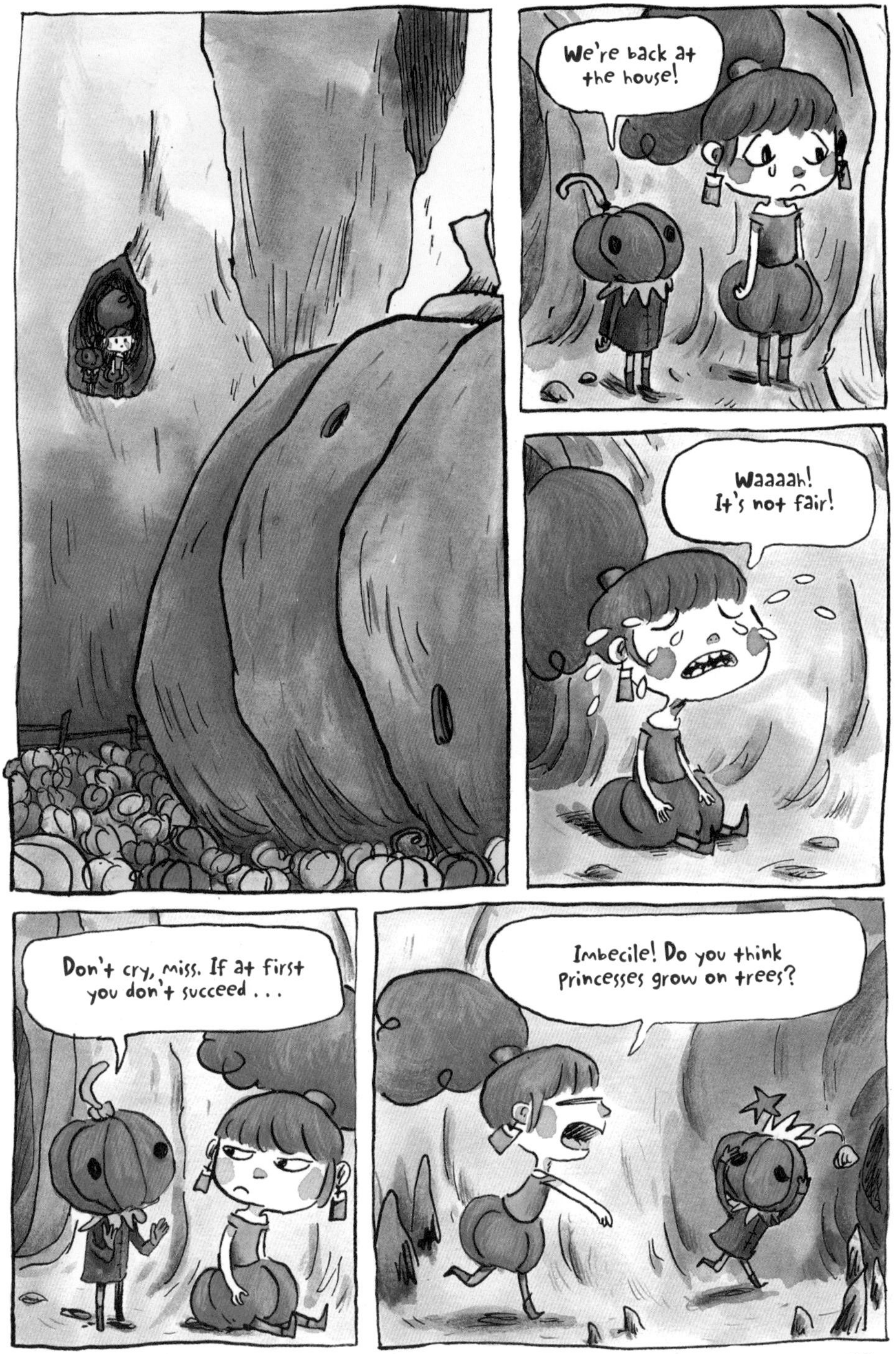
We're back at the house!
Waaaah! It's not fair!
Don't cry, miss. If at first you don't succeed . . .
Imbecile! Do you think Princesses grow on trees?

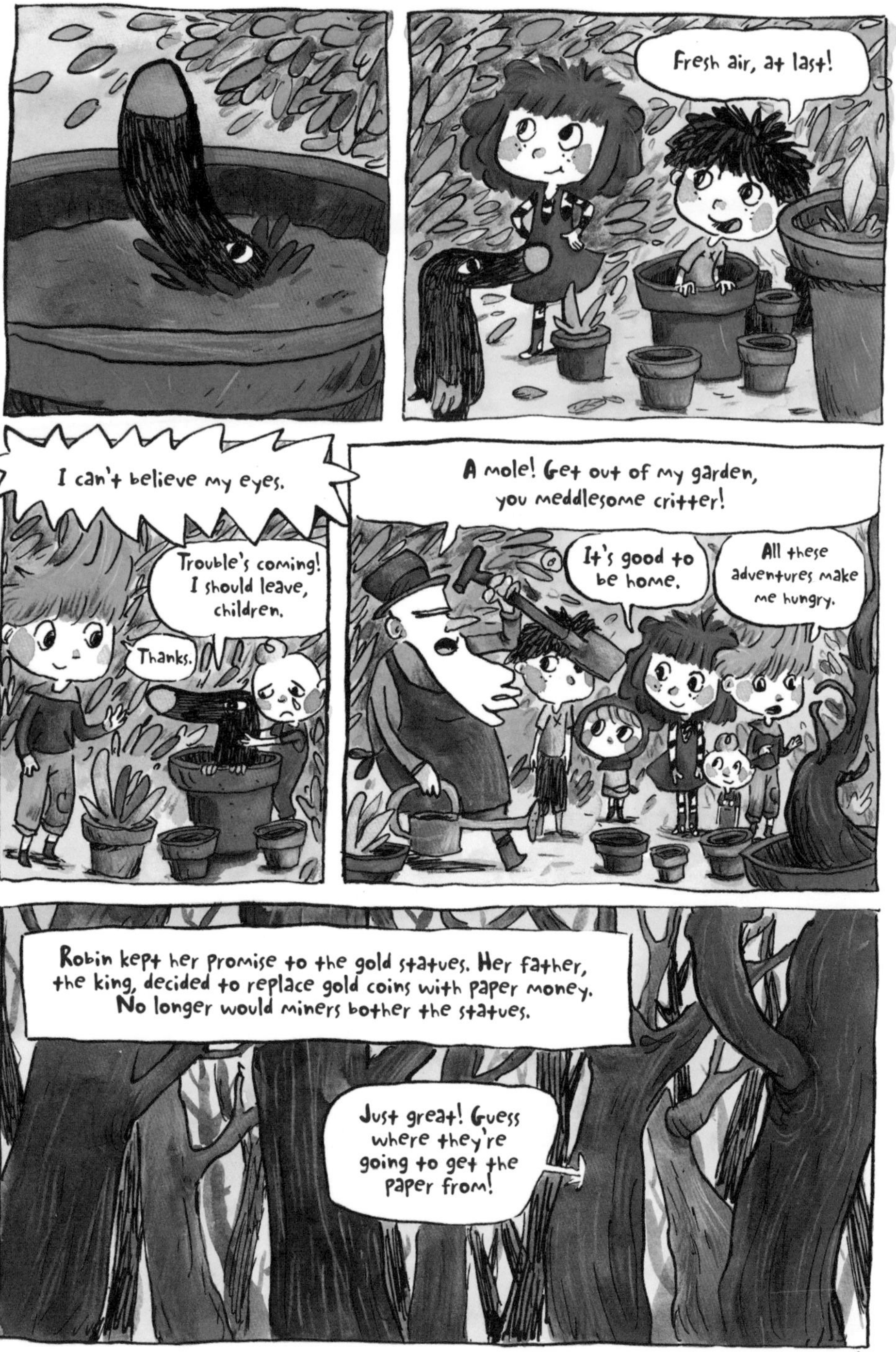
Fresh air, at last!
I can't believe my eyes.
Trouble's coming! I should leave, children.
Thanks.
A mole! Get out of my garden, you meddlesome critter!
It's good to be home.
All these adventures make me hungry.
Robin kept her promise to the gold statues. Her father, the king, decided to replace gold coins with paper money. No longer would miners bother the statues.
Just great! Guess where they're going to get the paper from!

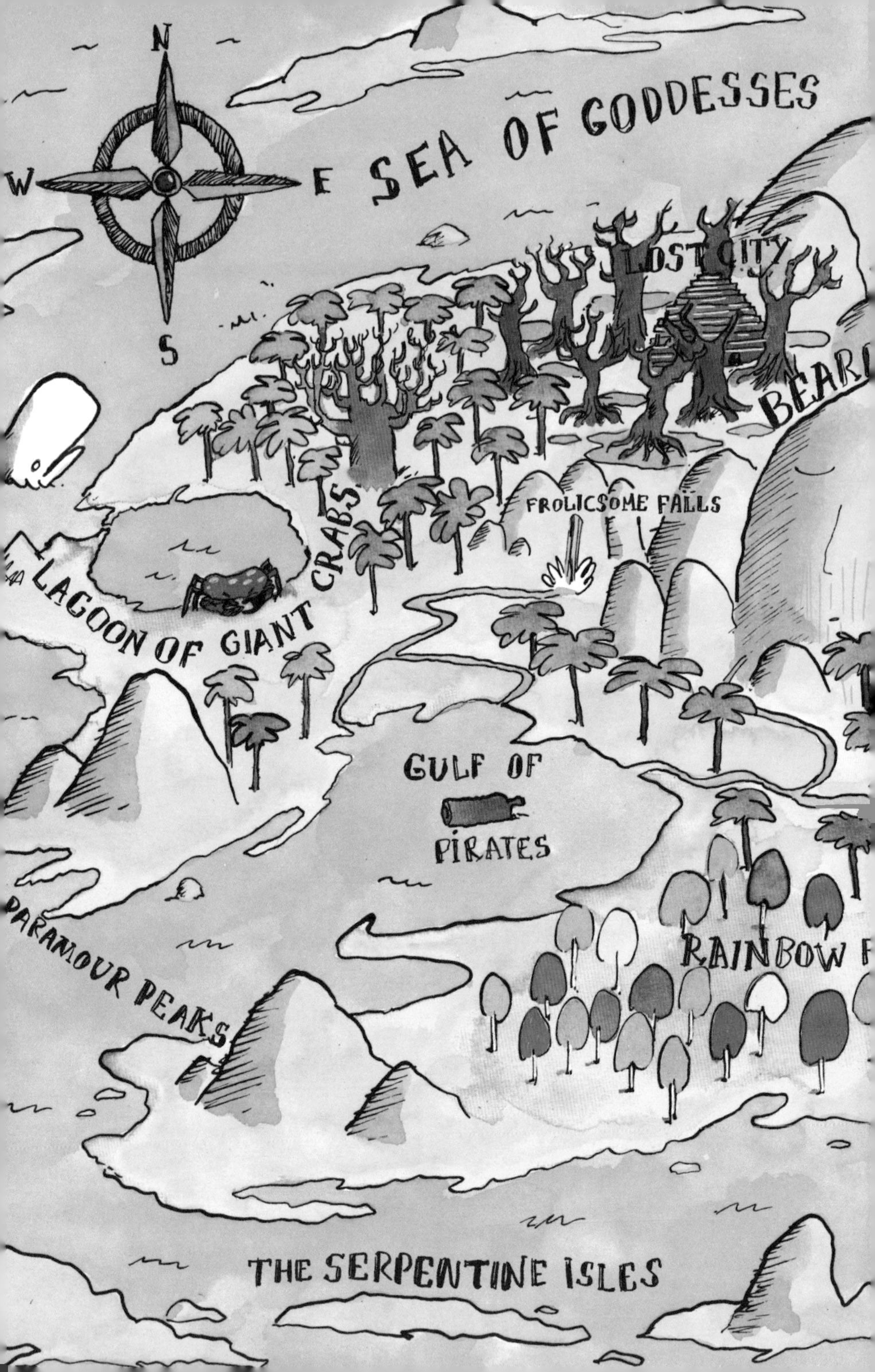
N
W
E
S
SEA OF GODDESSES
LOST CITY
BEAR
FROLICSOME FALLS
CRABS
LAGOON OF GIANT
GULF OF
PIRATES
RAINBOW F
PARAMOUR PEAKS
THE SERPENTINE ISLES

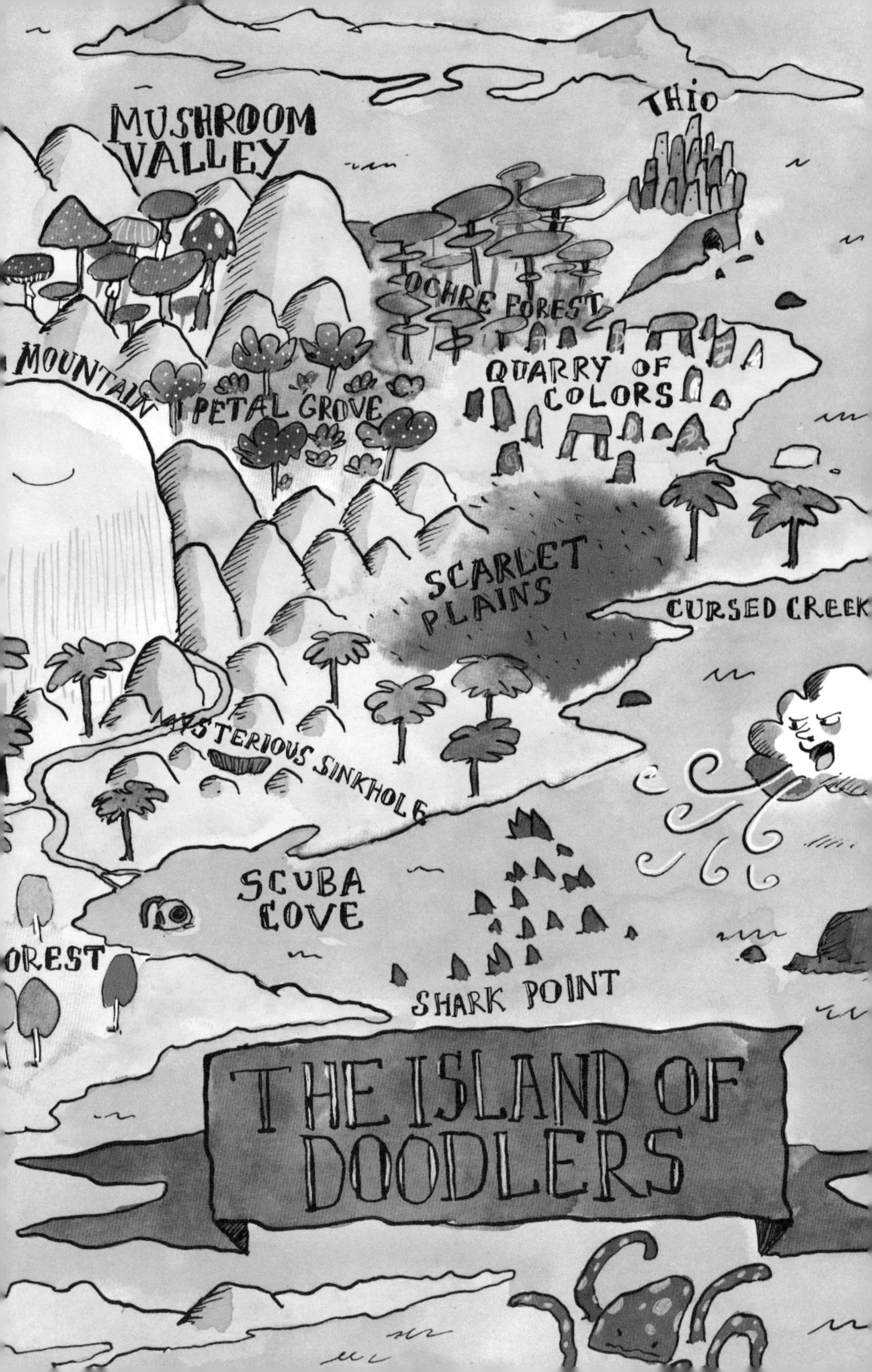
MUSHROOM VALLEY
THIO
OCHRE FOREST
QUARRY OF COLORS
MOUNTAIN
PETAL GROVE
SCARLET PLAINS
CURSED CREEK
MYSTERIOUS SINKHOLE
SCUBA COVE
OREST
SHARK POINT
THE ISLAND OF DOODLERS

# THE PRINCESS

## TRIES TO STAY IN ONE PLACE

(BUT THE WEATHER DOESN'T COOPERATE)

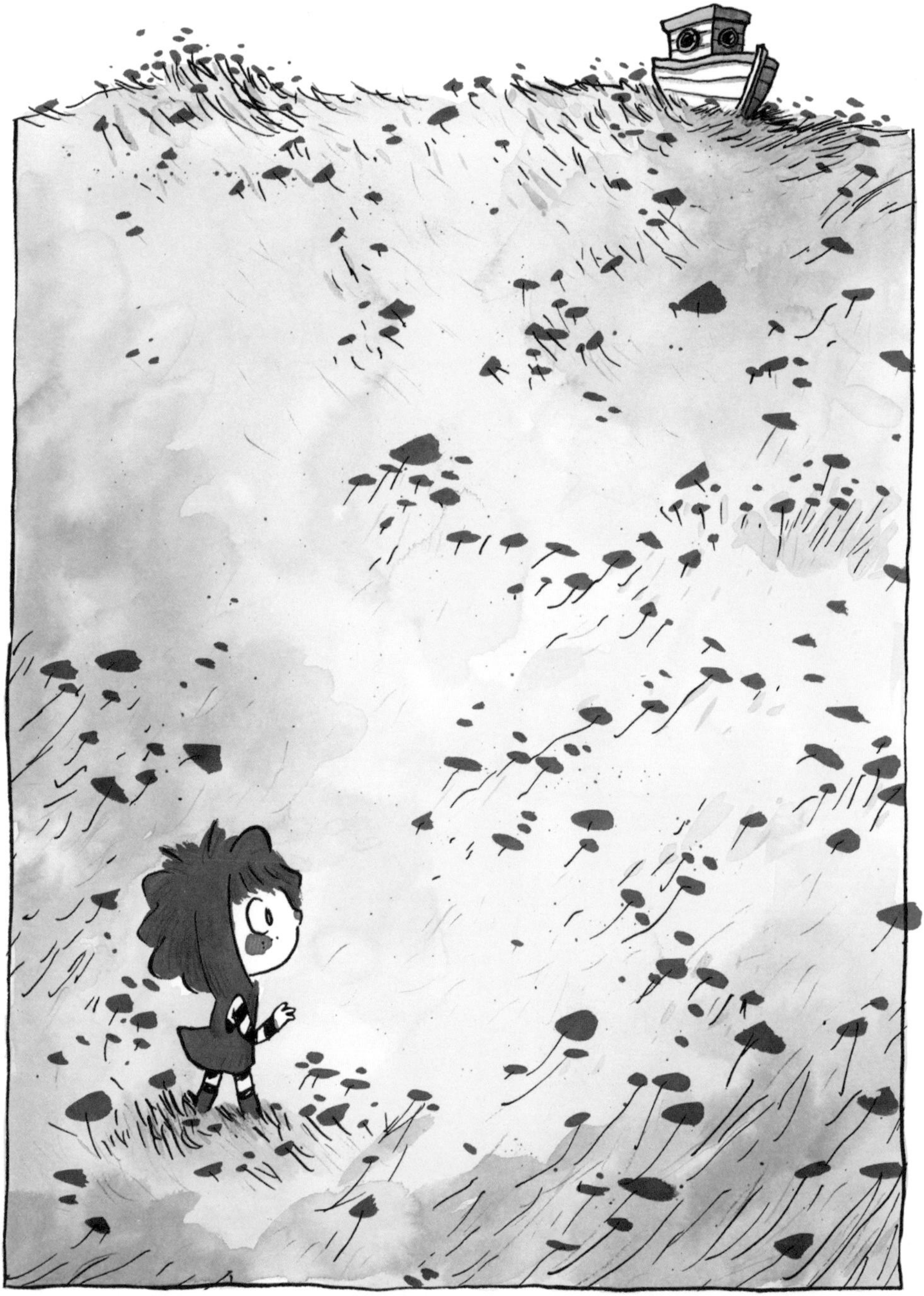

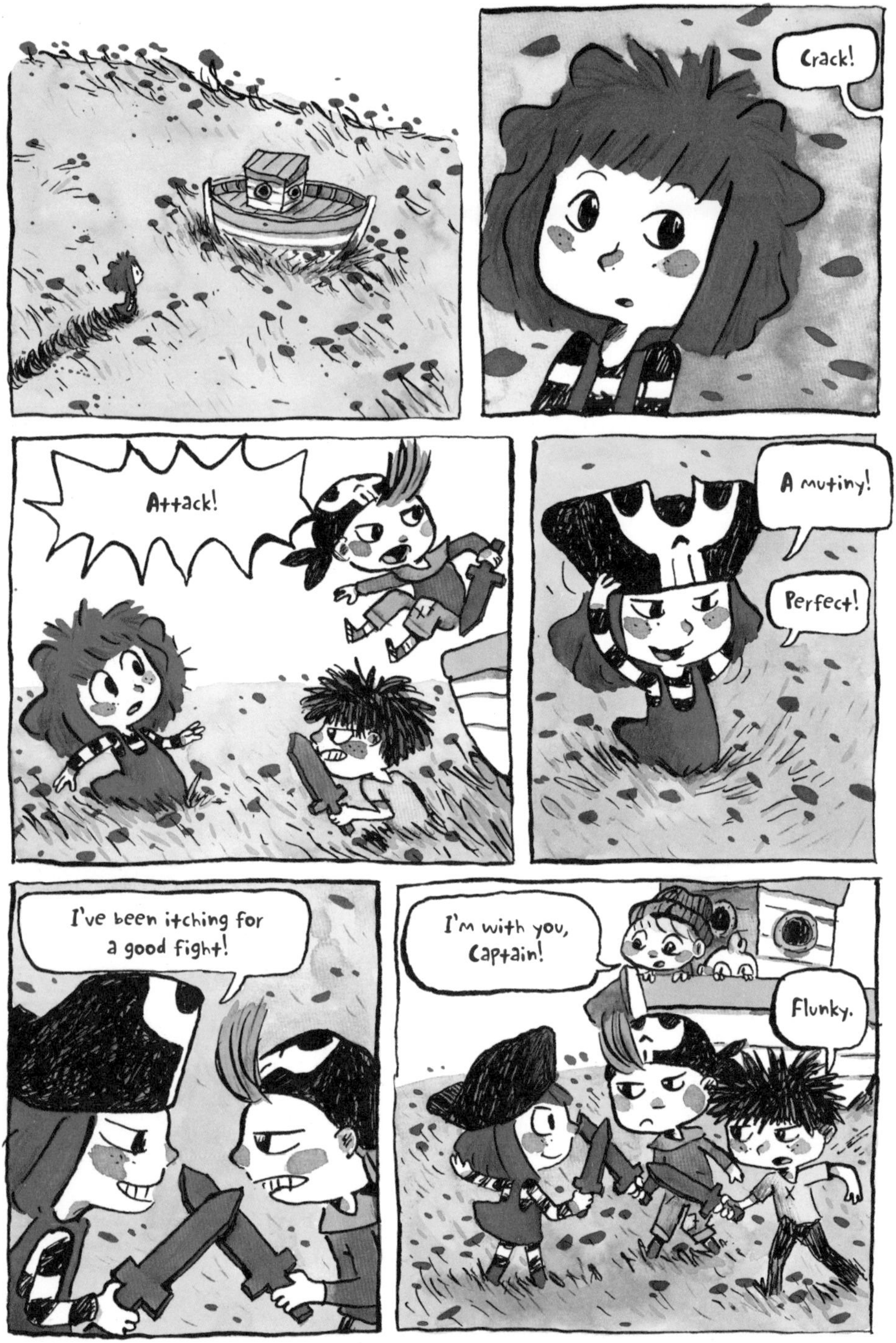
Crack!
Attack!
A mutiny!
Perfect!
I've been itching for a good fight!
I'm with you, Captain!
Flunky.

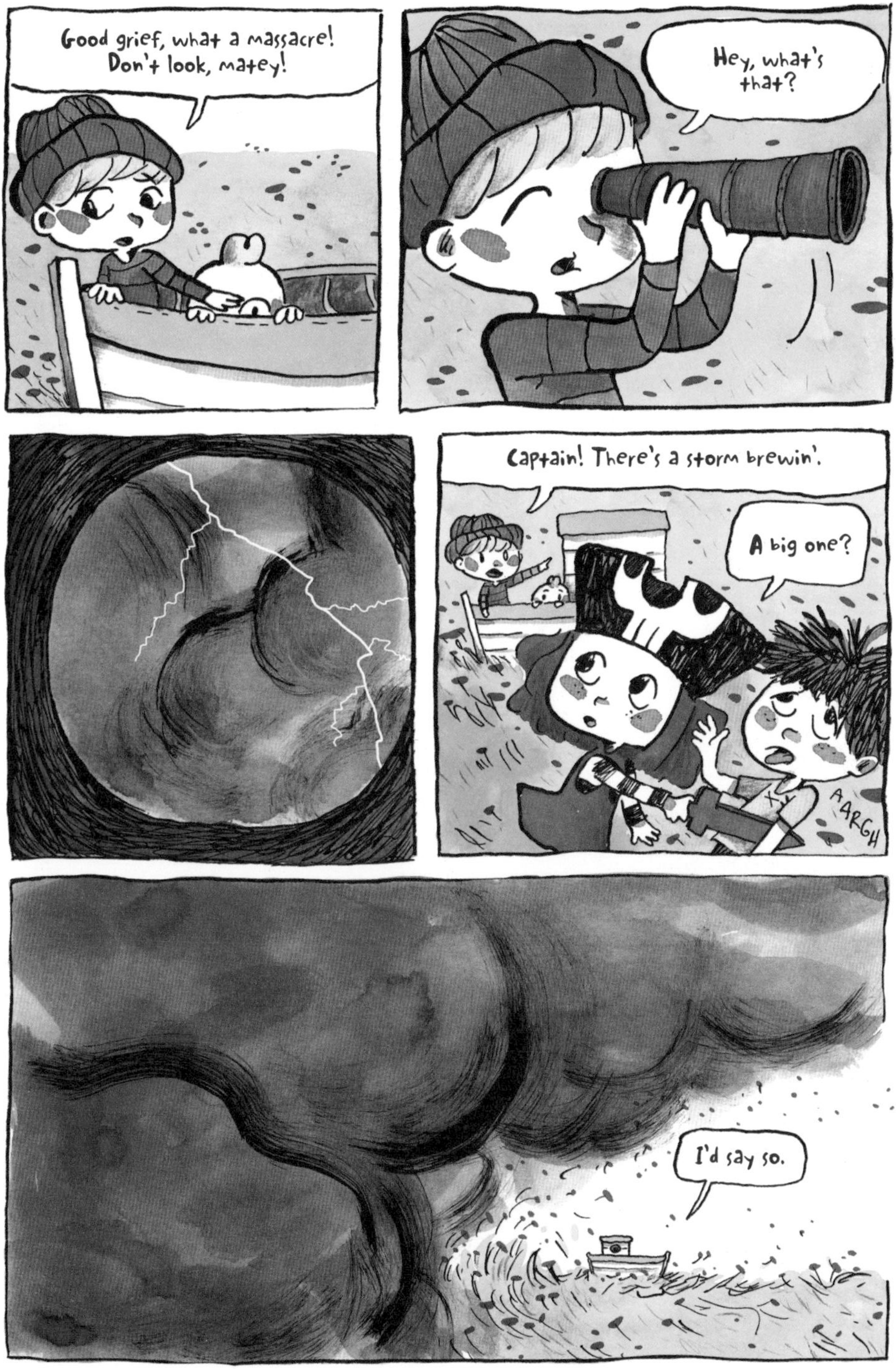
Good grief, what a massacre! Don't look, matey!
Hey, what's that?
Captain! There's a storm brewin'.
A big one?
AARGH
I'd say so.

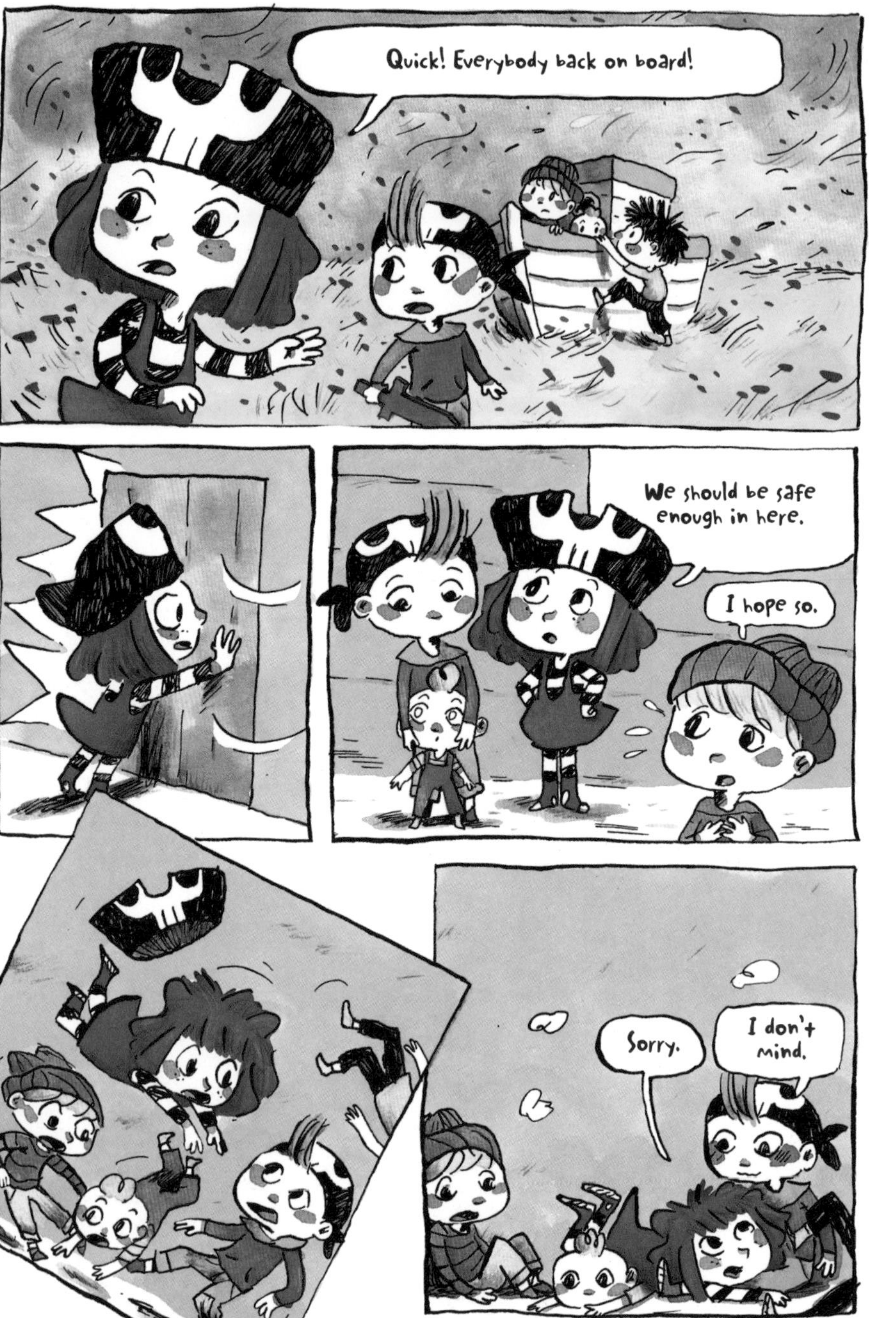
Quick! Everybody back on board!
We should be safe enough in here.
I hope so.
Sorry.
I don't mind.

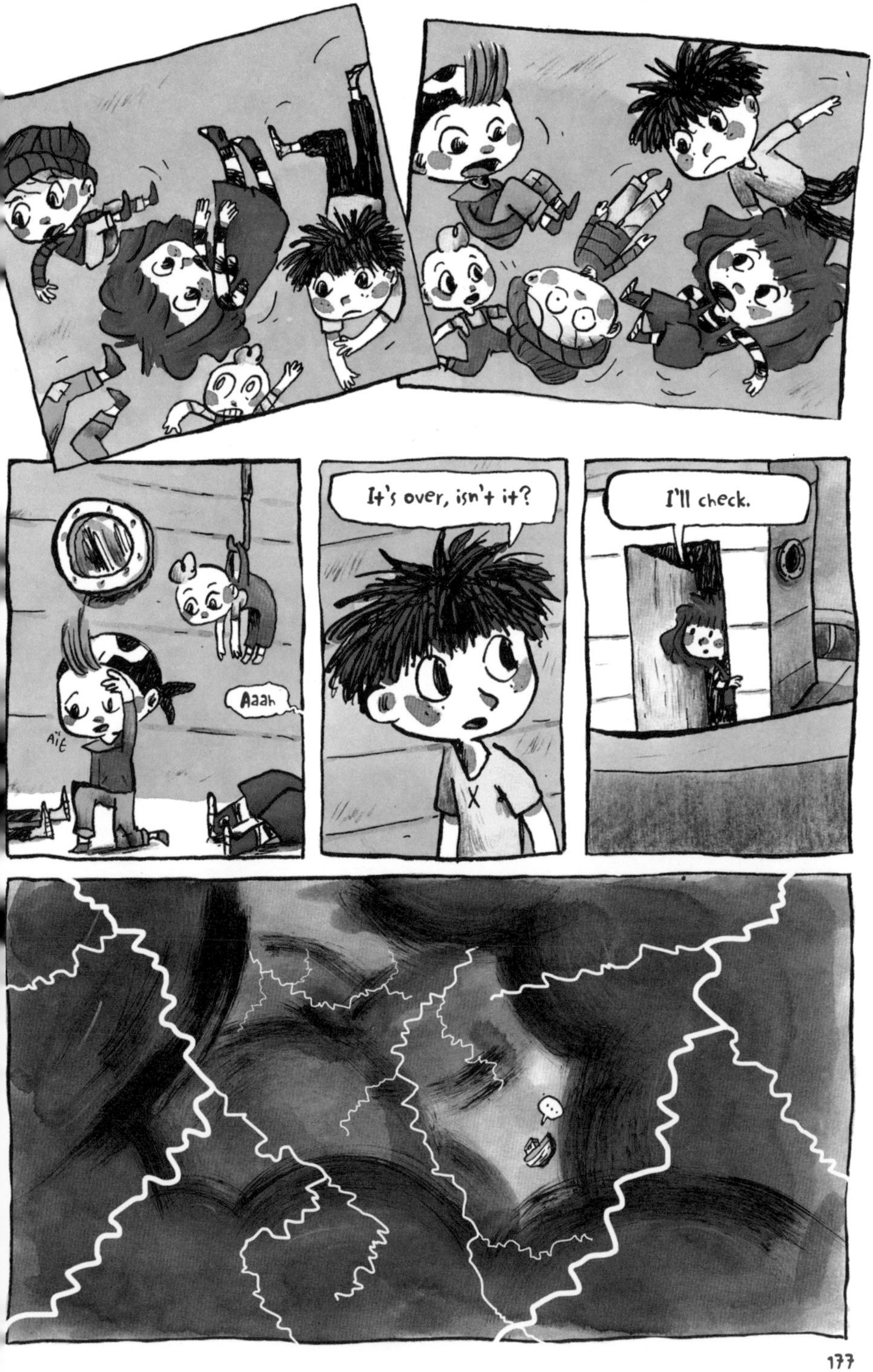
Ait
Aaah
It's over, isn't it?
I'll check.

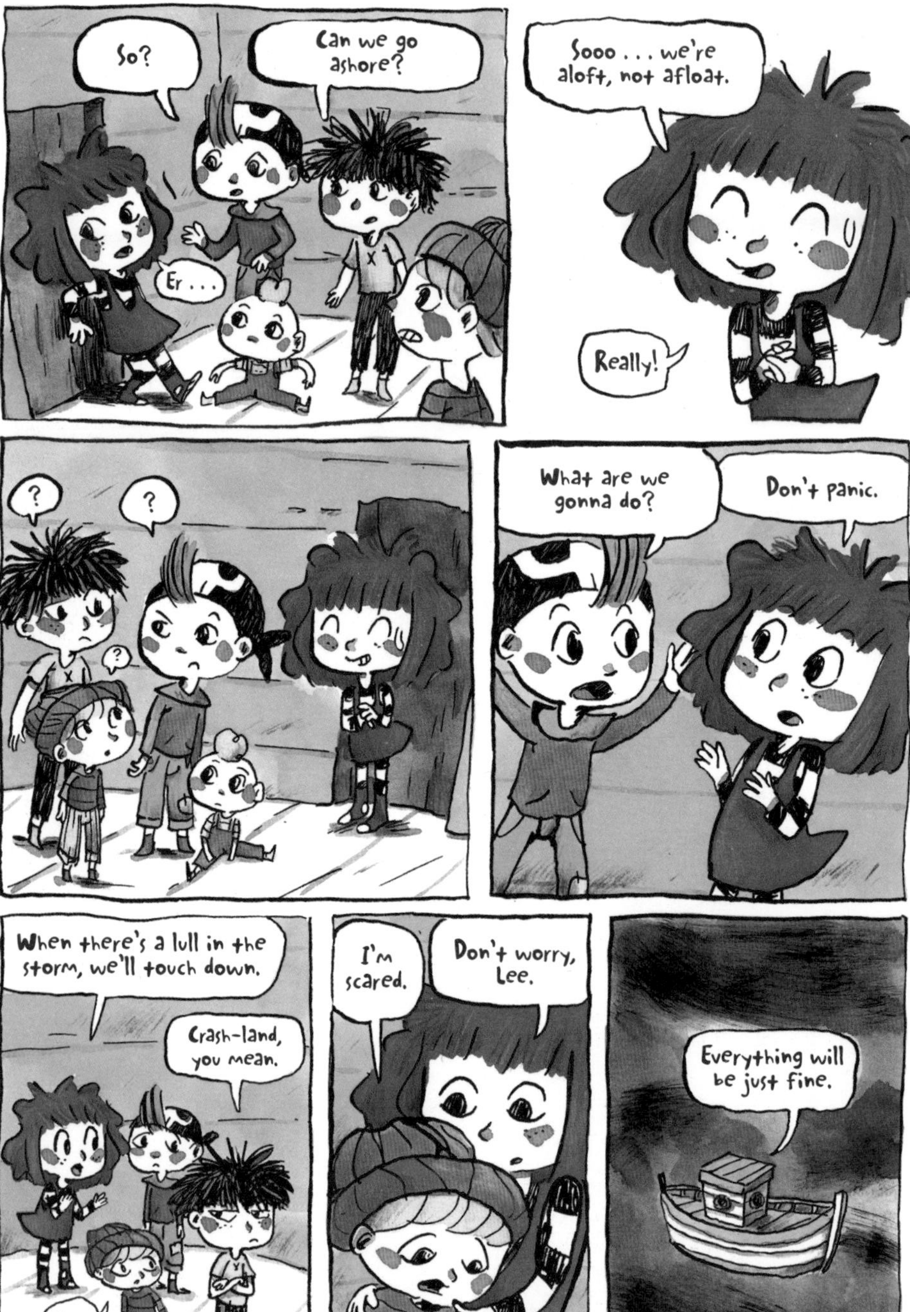
So?
Can we go ashore?
Er . . .
Sooo . . . we're aloft, not afloat.
Really!
?
?
?
What are we gonna do?
Don't panic.
When there's a lull in the storm, we'll touch down.
Crash-land, you mean.
Huh?
I'm scared.
Don't worry, Lee.
Everything will be just fine.

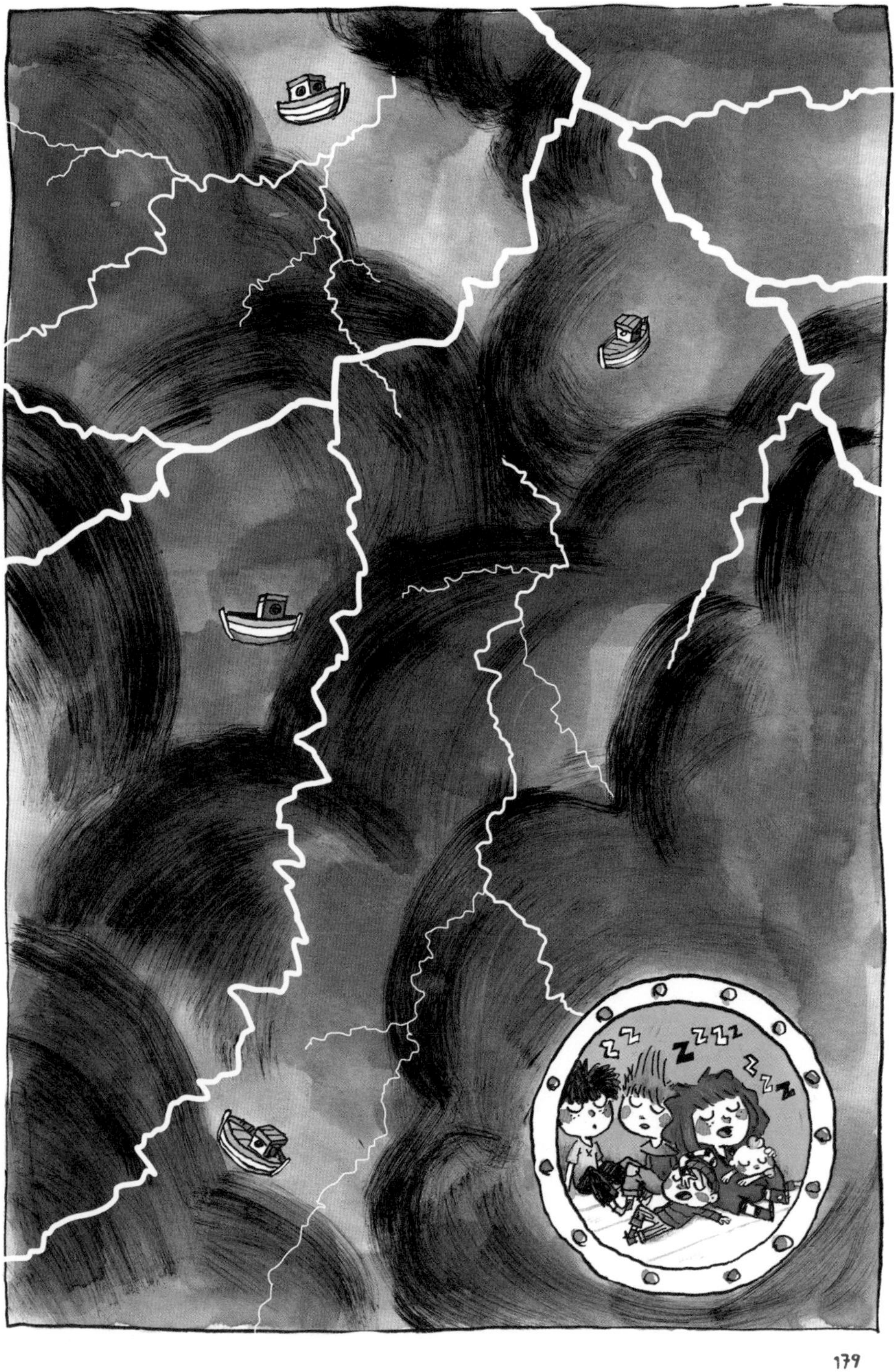
Z Z
Z Z Z Z
Z Z Z

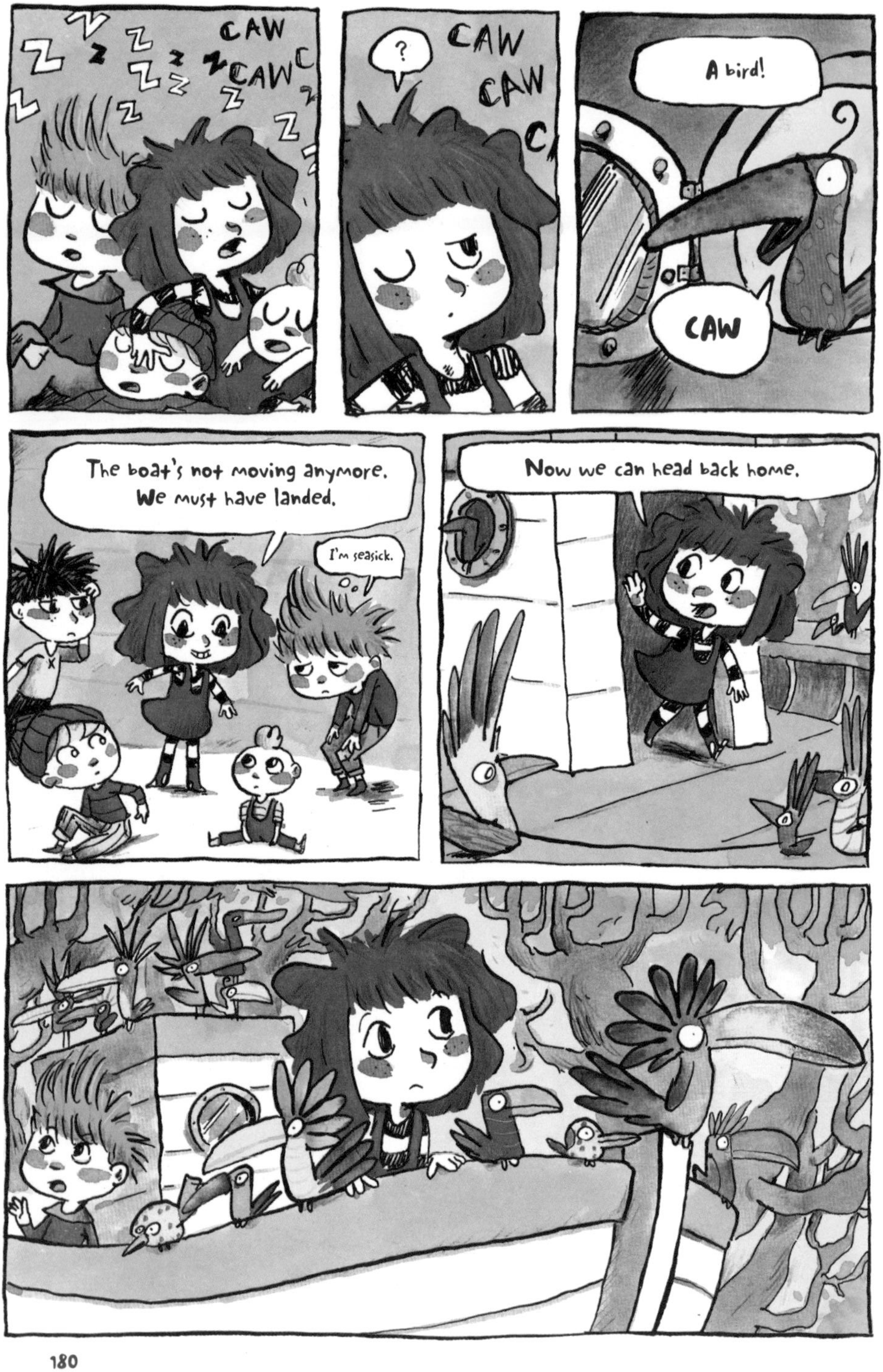
Z Z Z Z Z Z Z Z Z
CAW CAW C
?
CAW CAW C
A bird!
CAW
The boat's not moving anymore. We must have landed.
I'm seasick.
Now we can head back home.

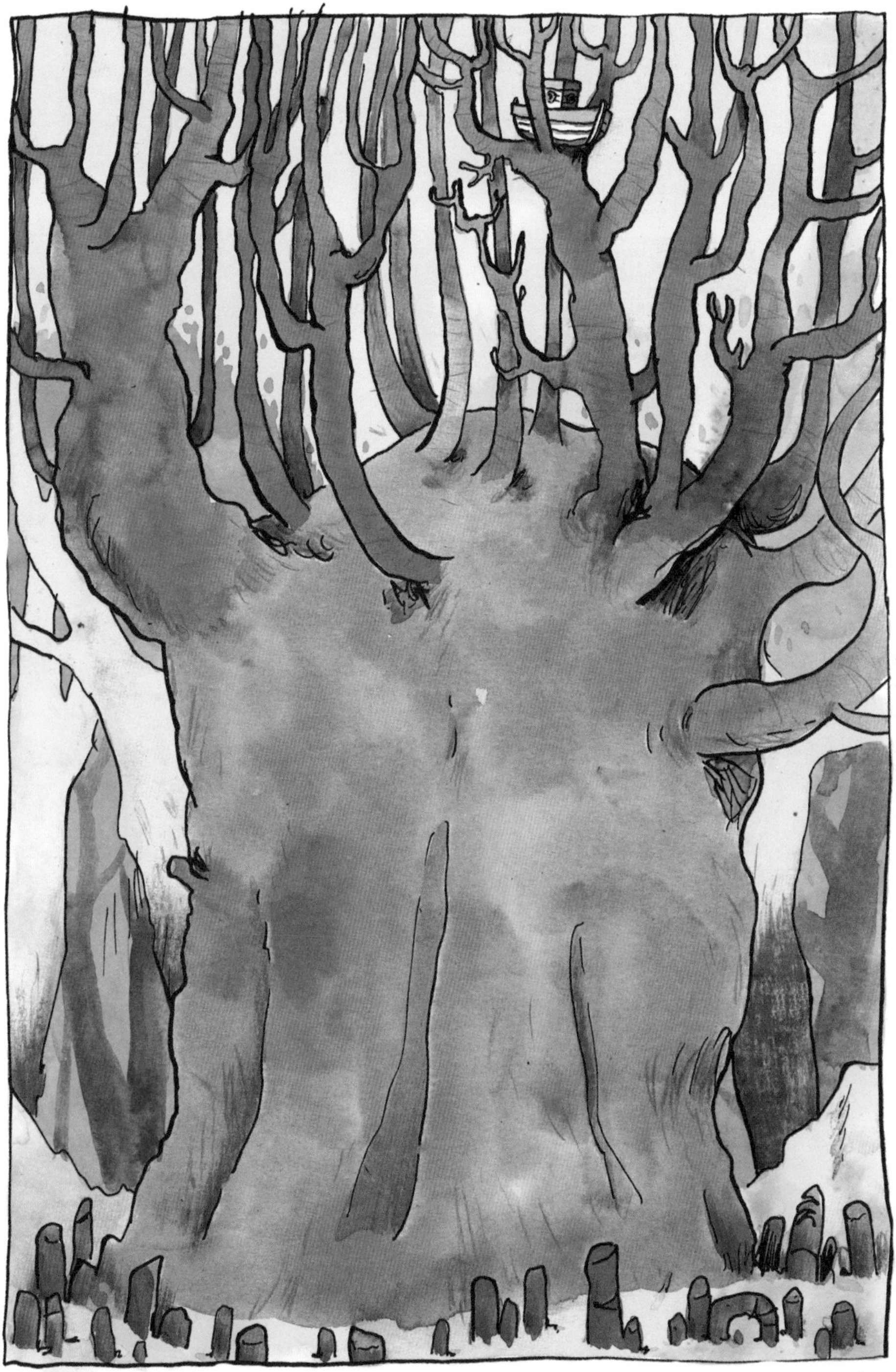

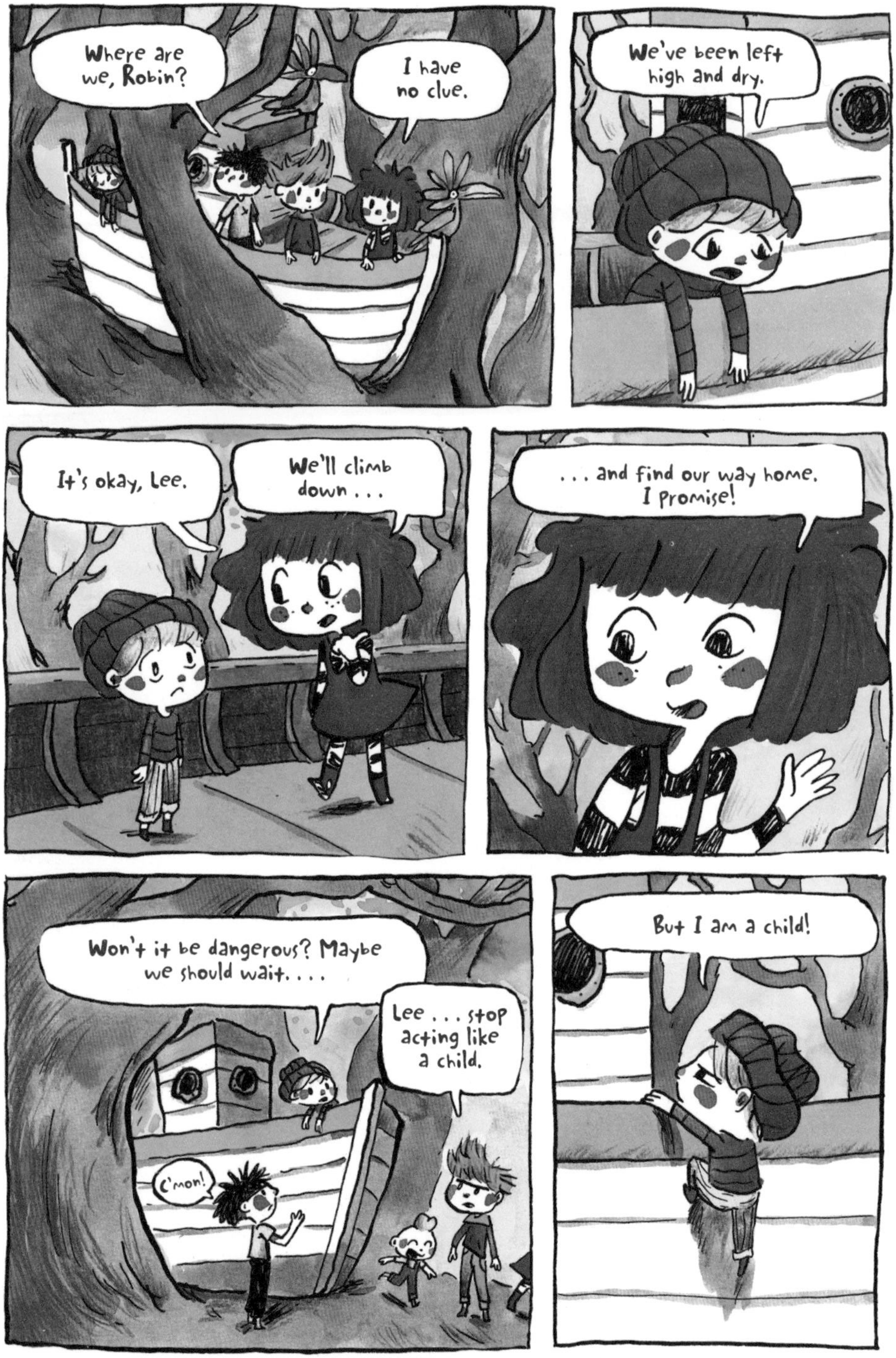
Where are we, Robin?
I have no clue.
We've been left high and dry.
It's okay, Lee.
We'll climb down . . .
. . . and find our way home. I promise!
Won't it be dangerous? Maybe we should wait. . . .
Lee . . . stop acting like a child.
C'mon!
But I am a child!

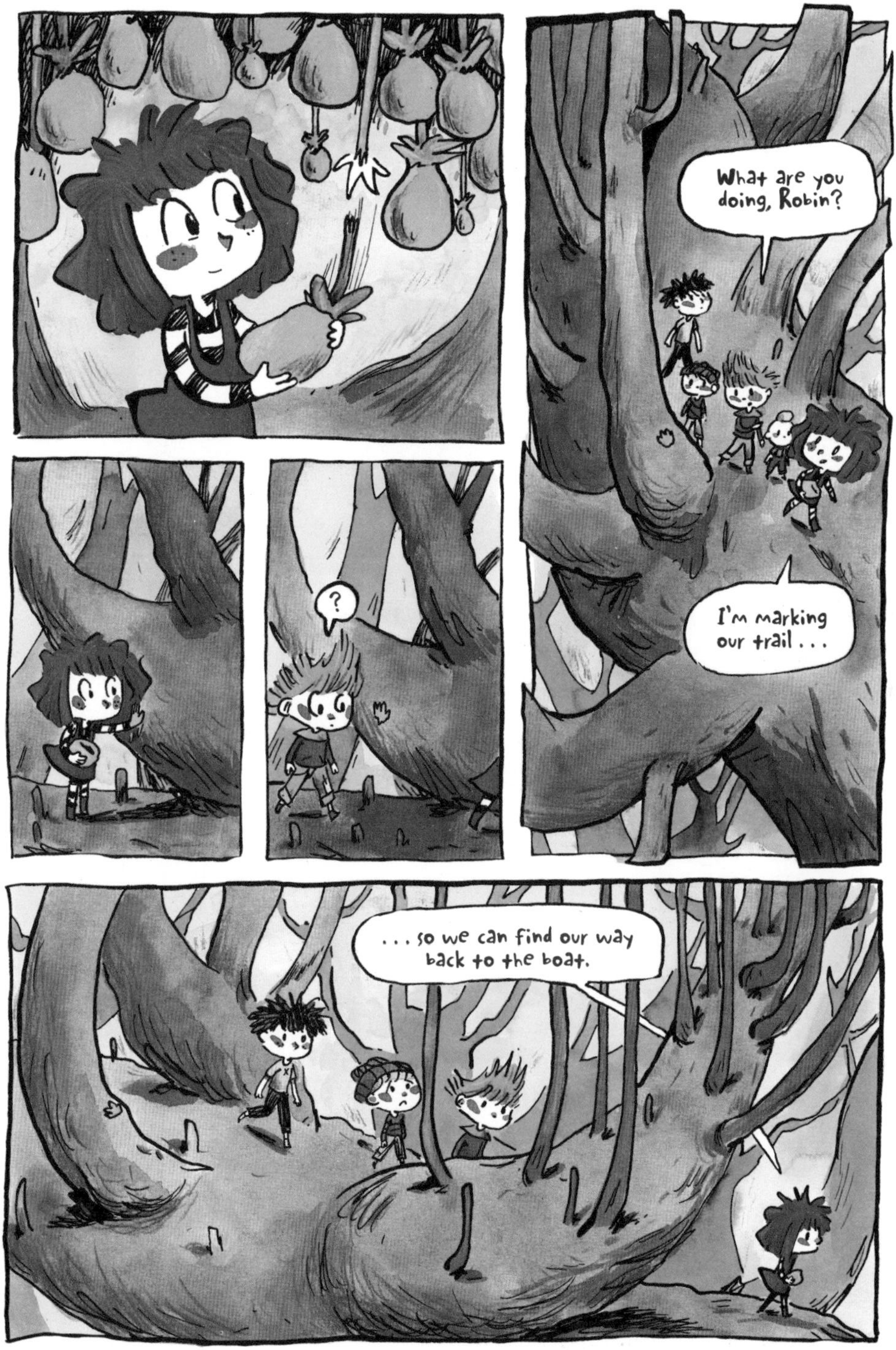
?
What are you doing, Robin?
I'm marking our trail . . .
. . . so we can find our way back to the boat.

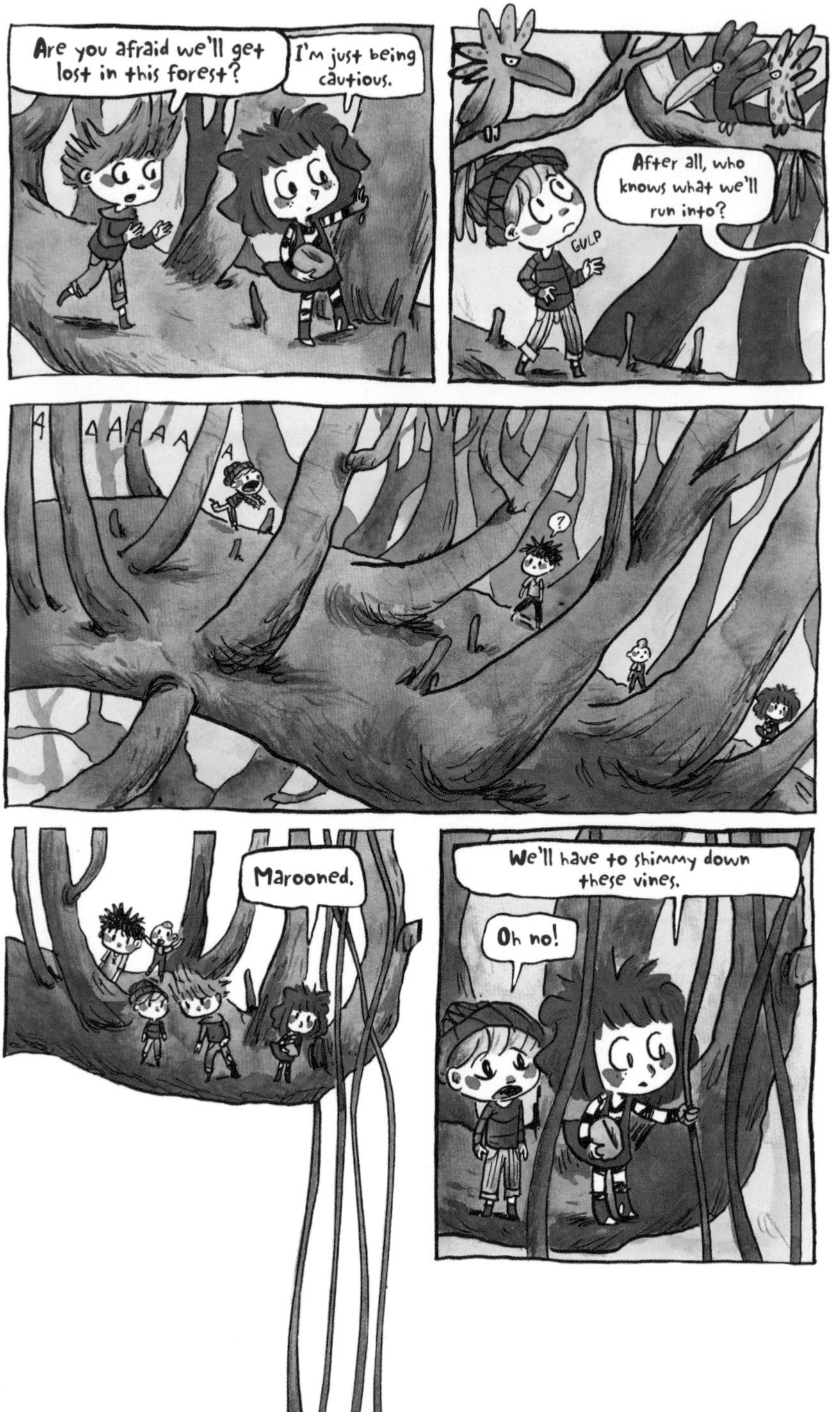
Are you afraid we'll get lost in this forest?
I'm just being cautious.
After all, who knows what we'll run into?
GULP
AAAAAAAA
?
Marooned.
We'll have to shimmy down these vines.
Oh no!

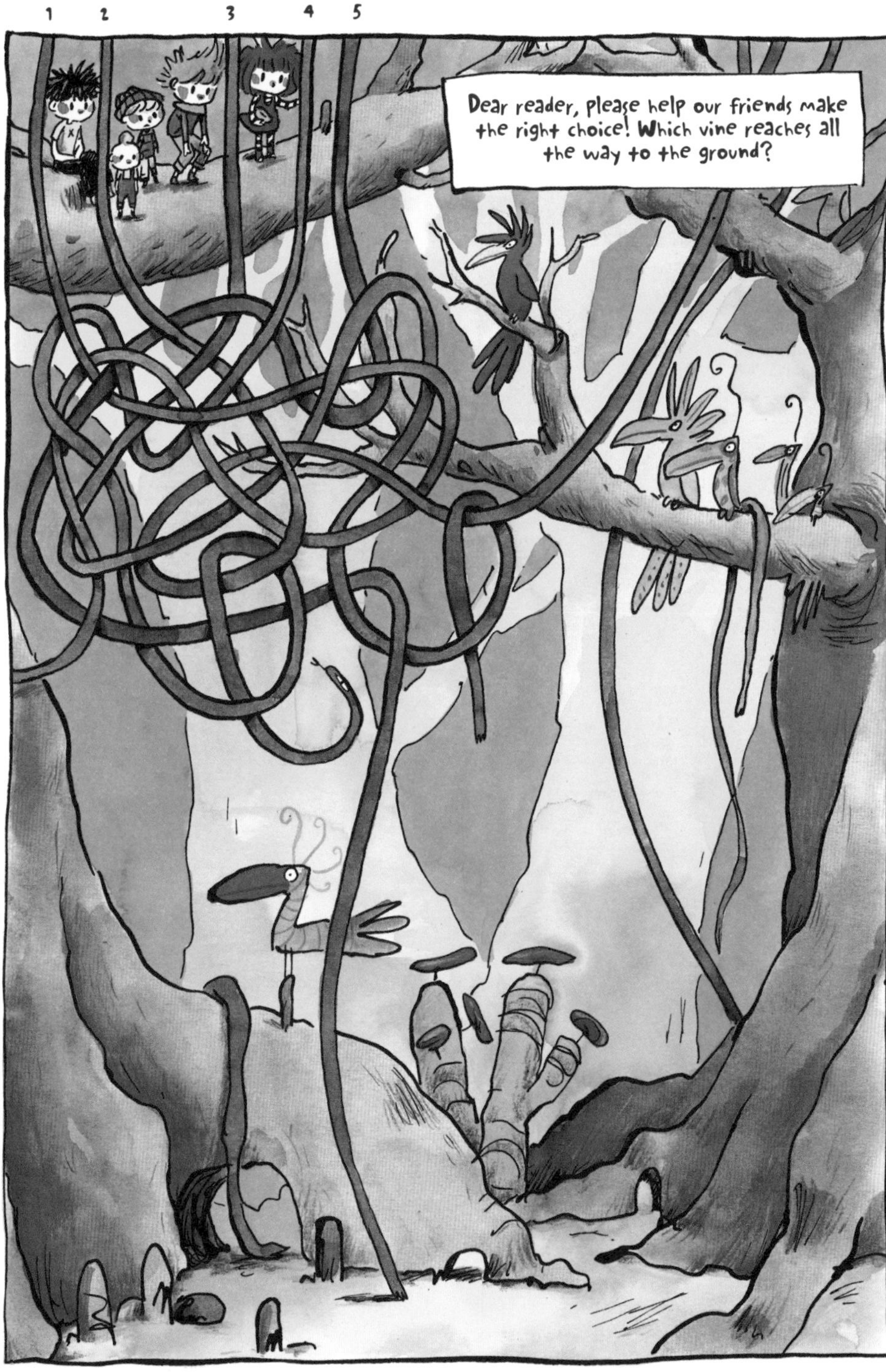
1
2
3
4
5
Dear reader, please help our friends make the right choice! Which vine reaches all the way to the ground?

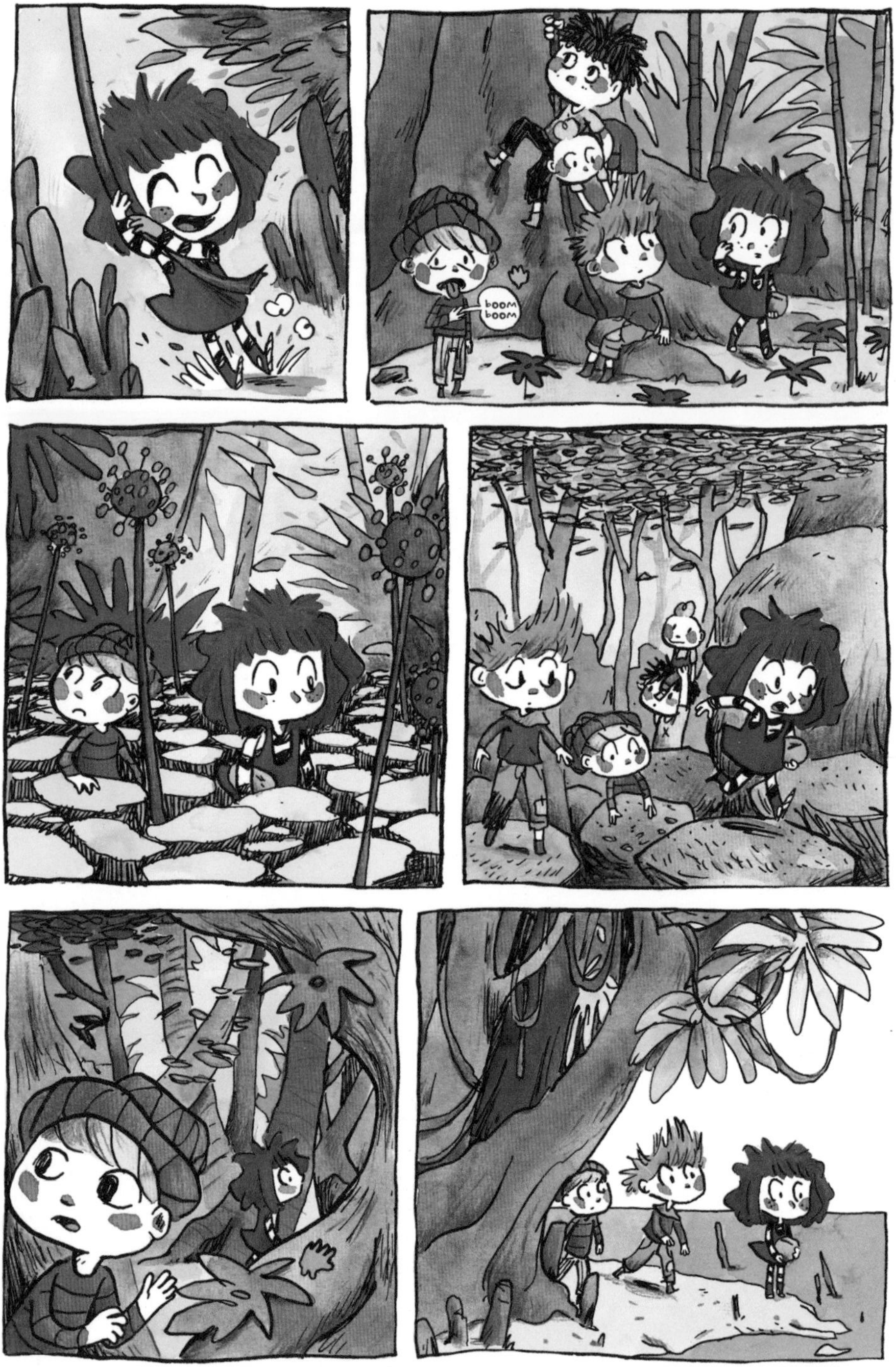
boom boom

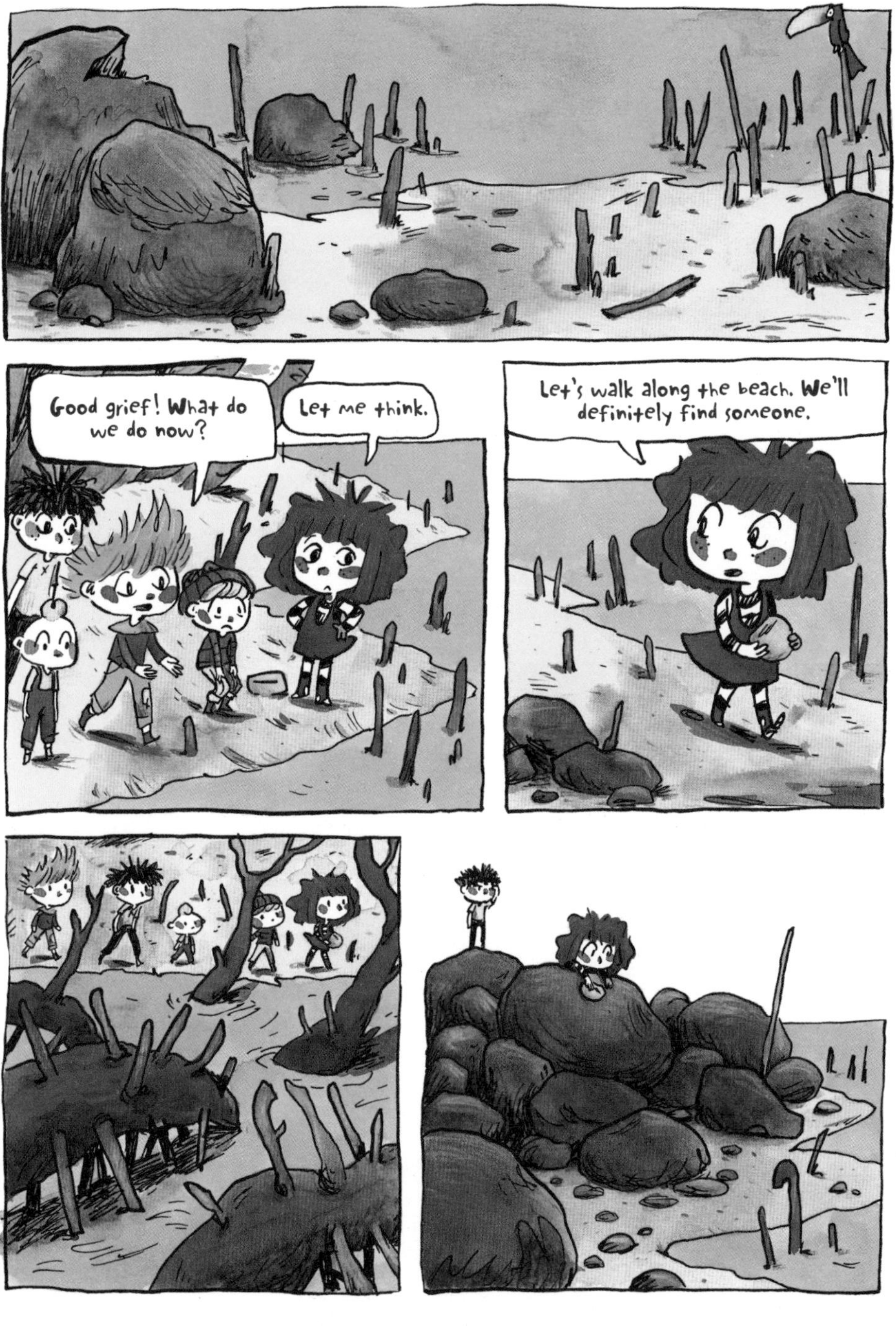
Good grief! What do we do now?
Let me think.
Let's walk along the beach. We'll definitely find someone.

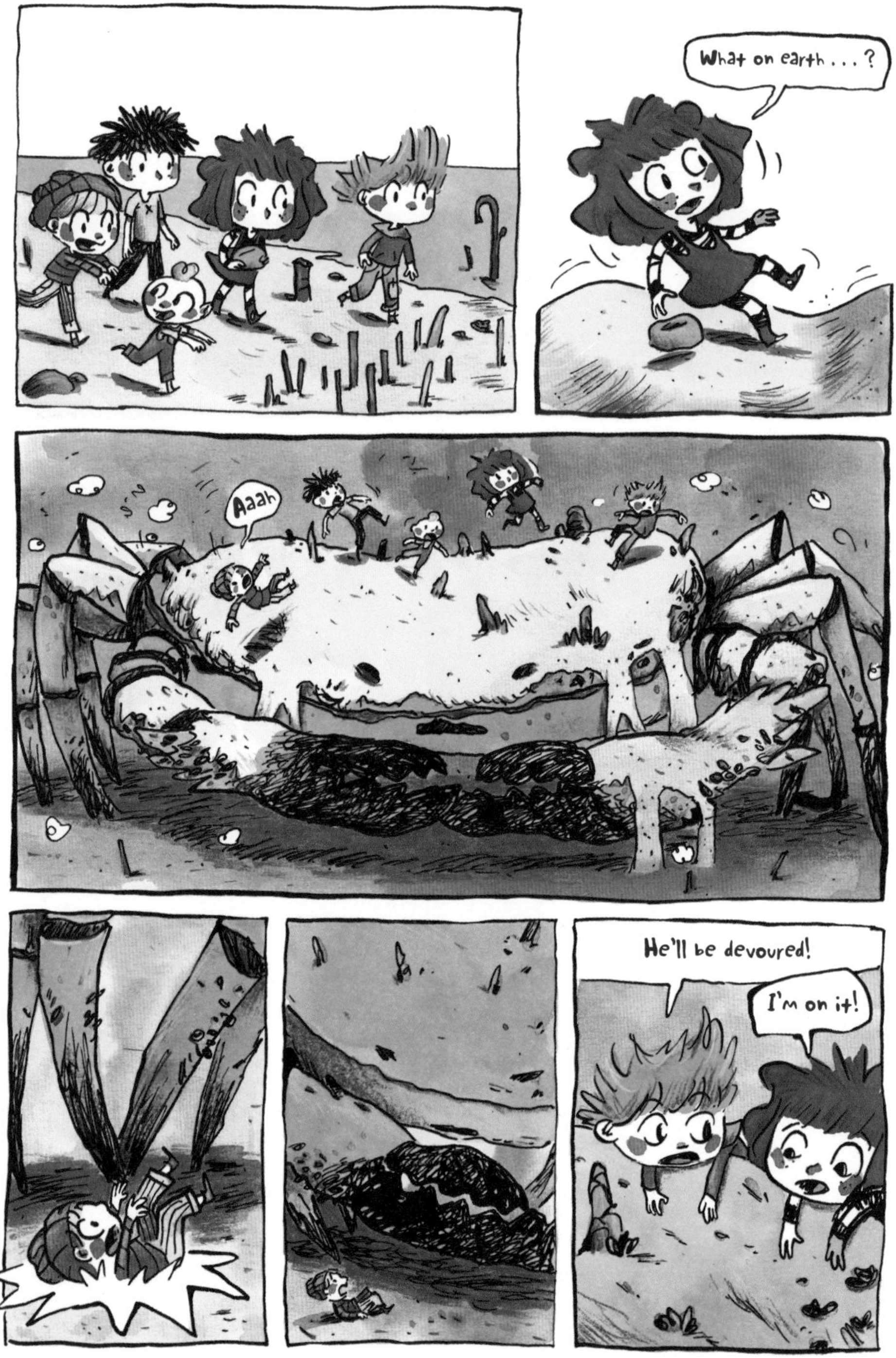
What on earth . . . ?
Aaah
He'll be devoured!
I'm on it!

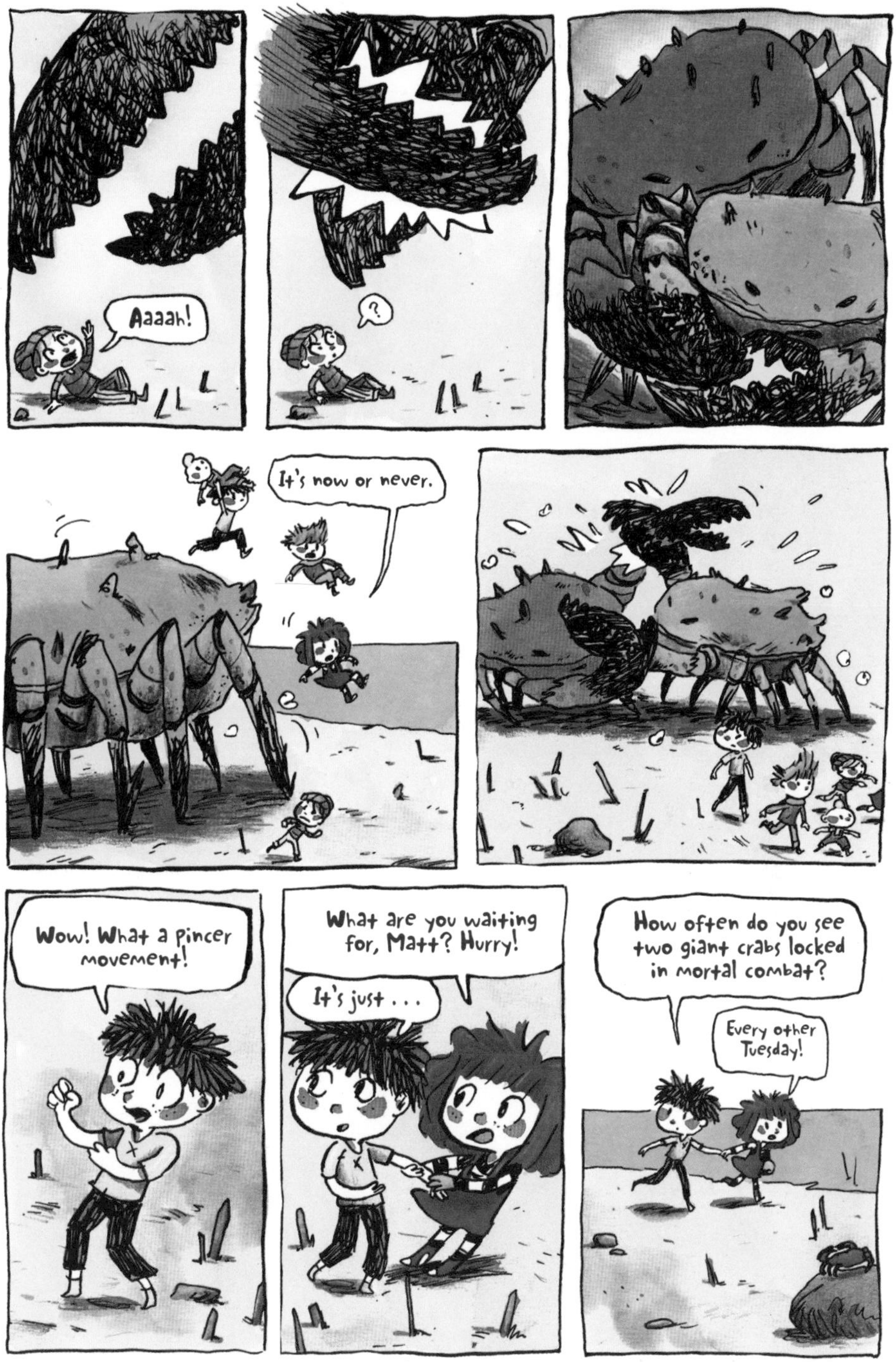
Aaaah!
?
It's now or never.
Wow! What a pincer movement!
What are you waiting for, Matt? Hurry!
It's just . . .
How often do you see two giant crabs locked in mortal combat?
Every other Tuesday!

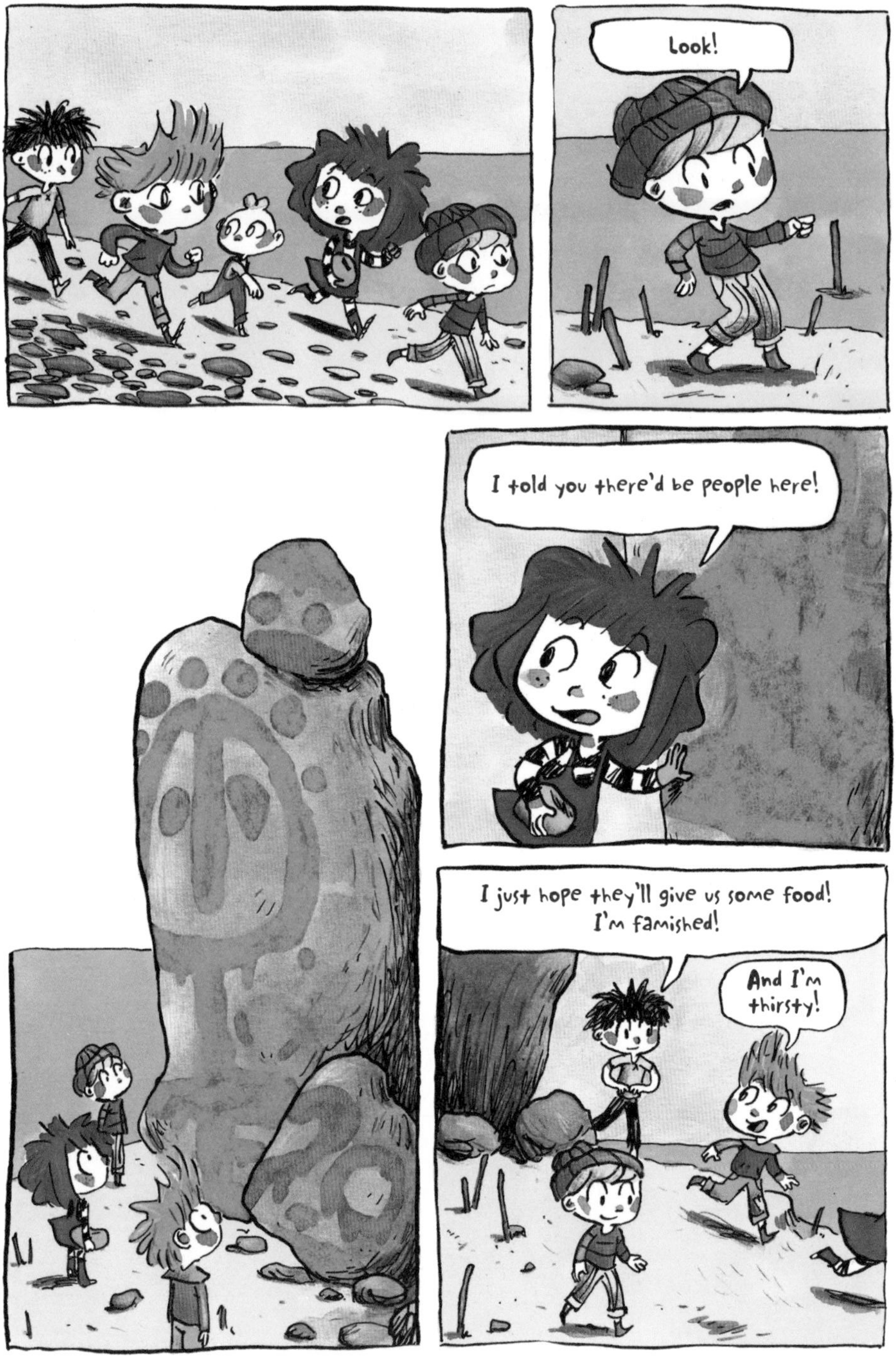
Look!
I told you there'd be people here!
I just hope they'll give us some food! I'm famished!
And I'm thirsty!

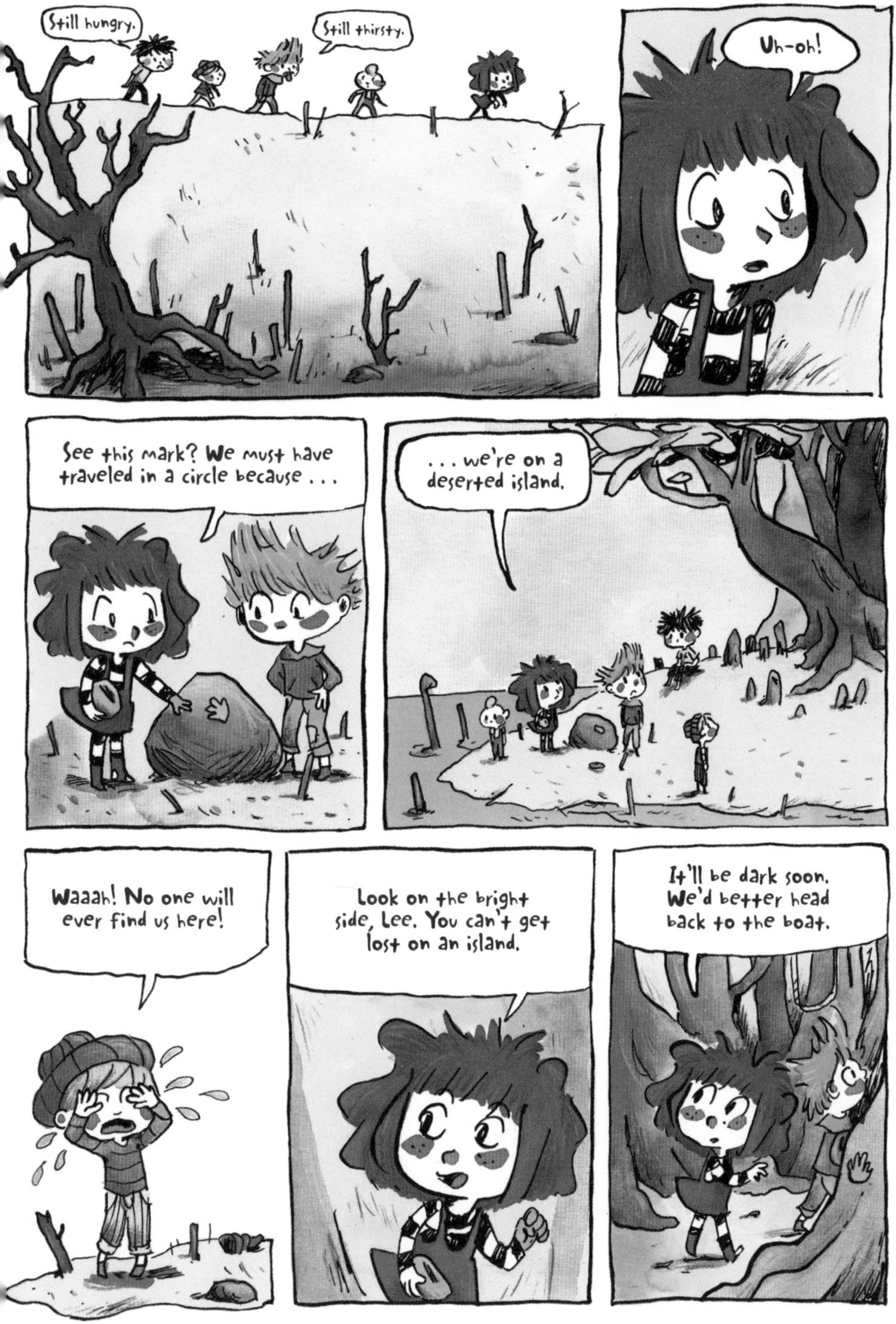
Still hungry.
Still thirsty.
Uh-oh!
See this mark? We must have traveled in a circle because . . .
. . . we're on a deserted island.
Waaah! No one will ever find us here!
Look on the bright side, Lee. You can't get lost on an island.
It'll be dark soon. We'd better head back to the boat.

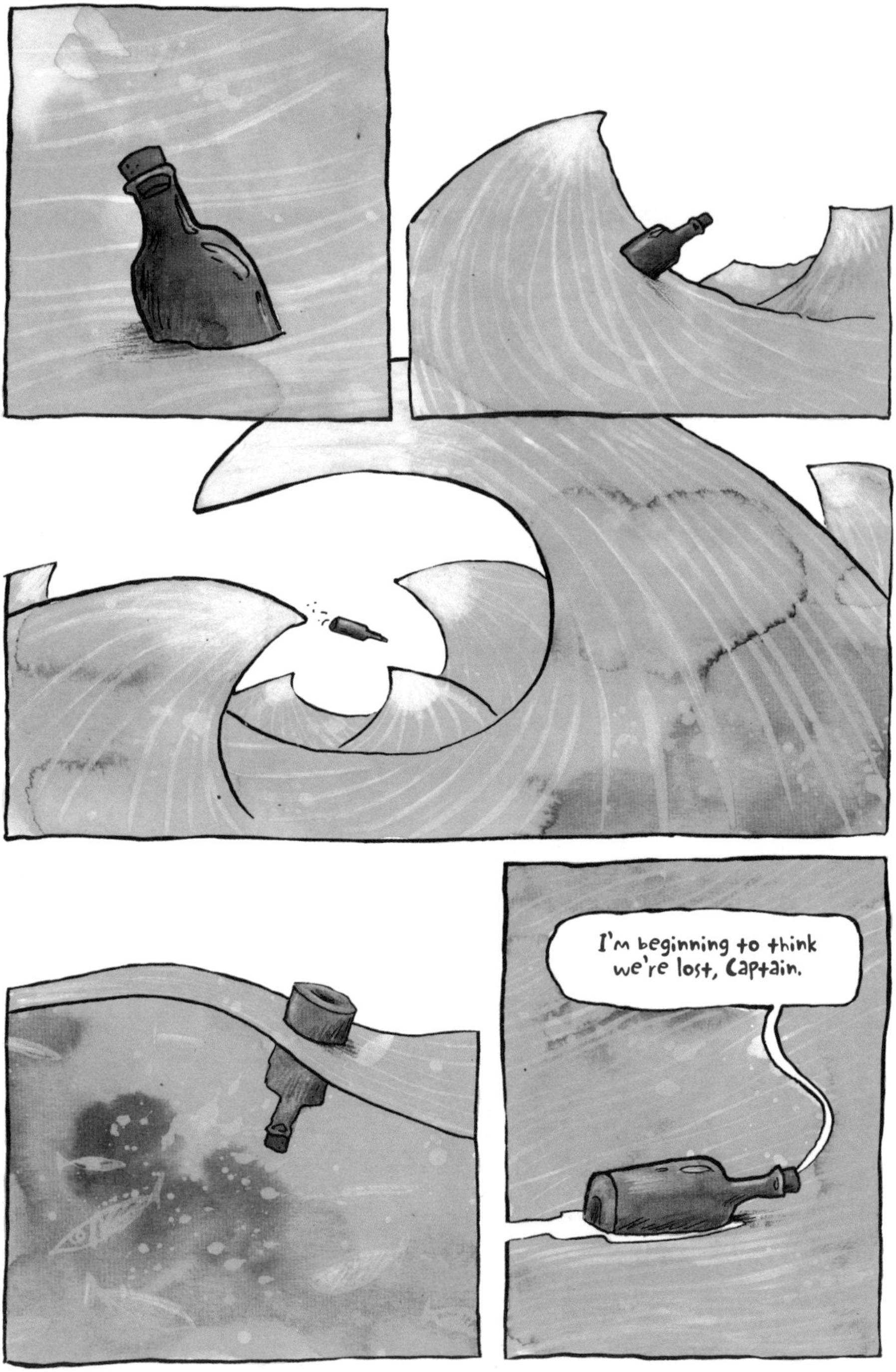
I'm beginning to think we're lost, Captain.

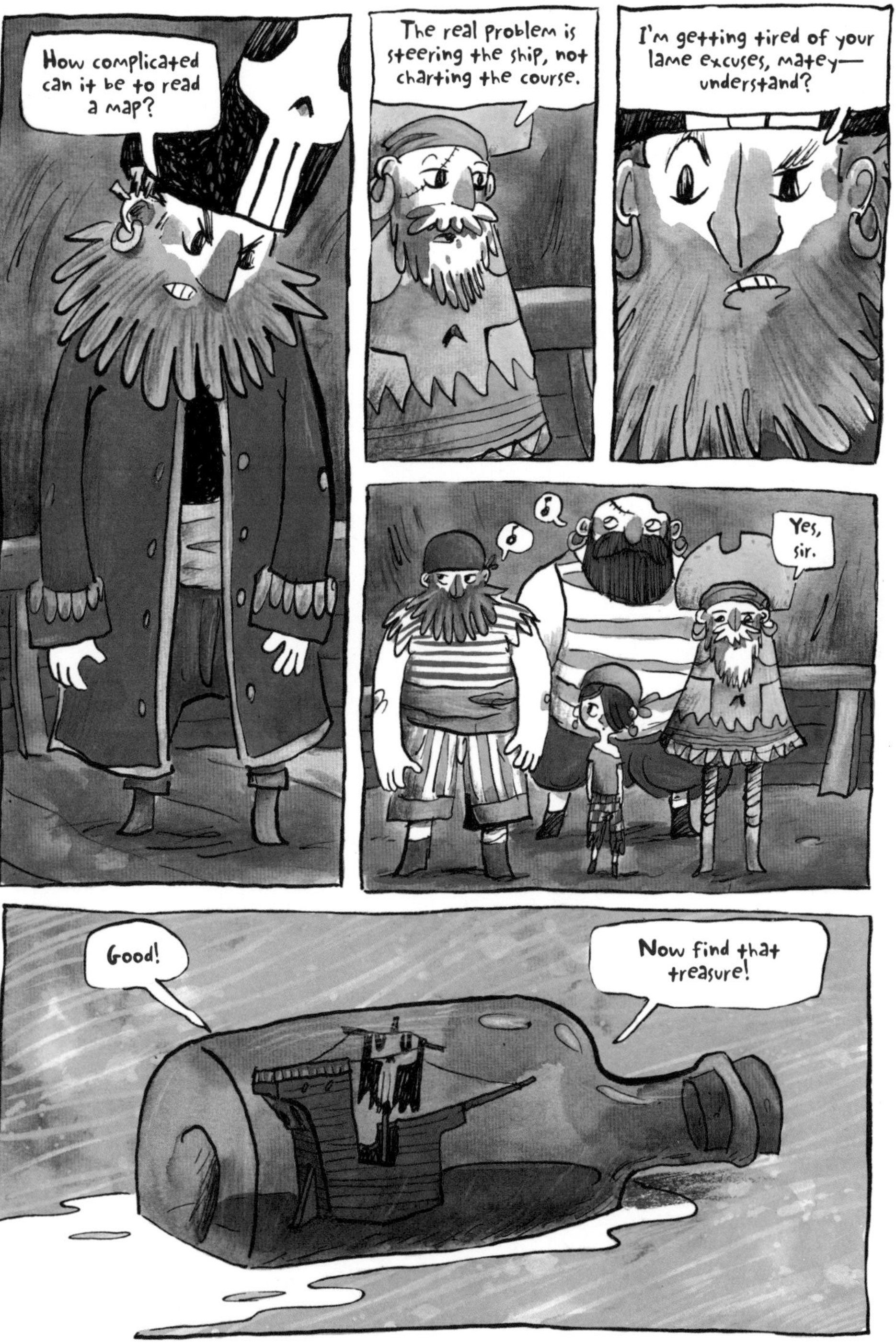
How complicated can it be to read a map?
The real problem is steering the ship, not charting the course.
I'm getting tired of your lame excuses, matey— understand?
Yes, sir.
Good!
Now find that treasure!

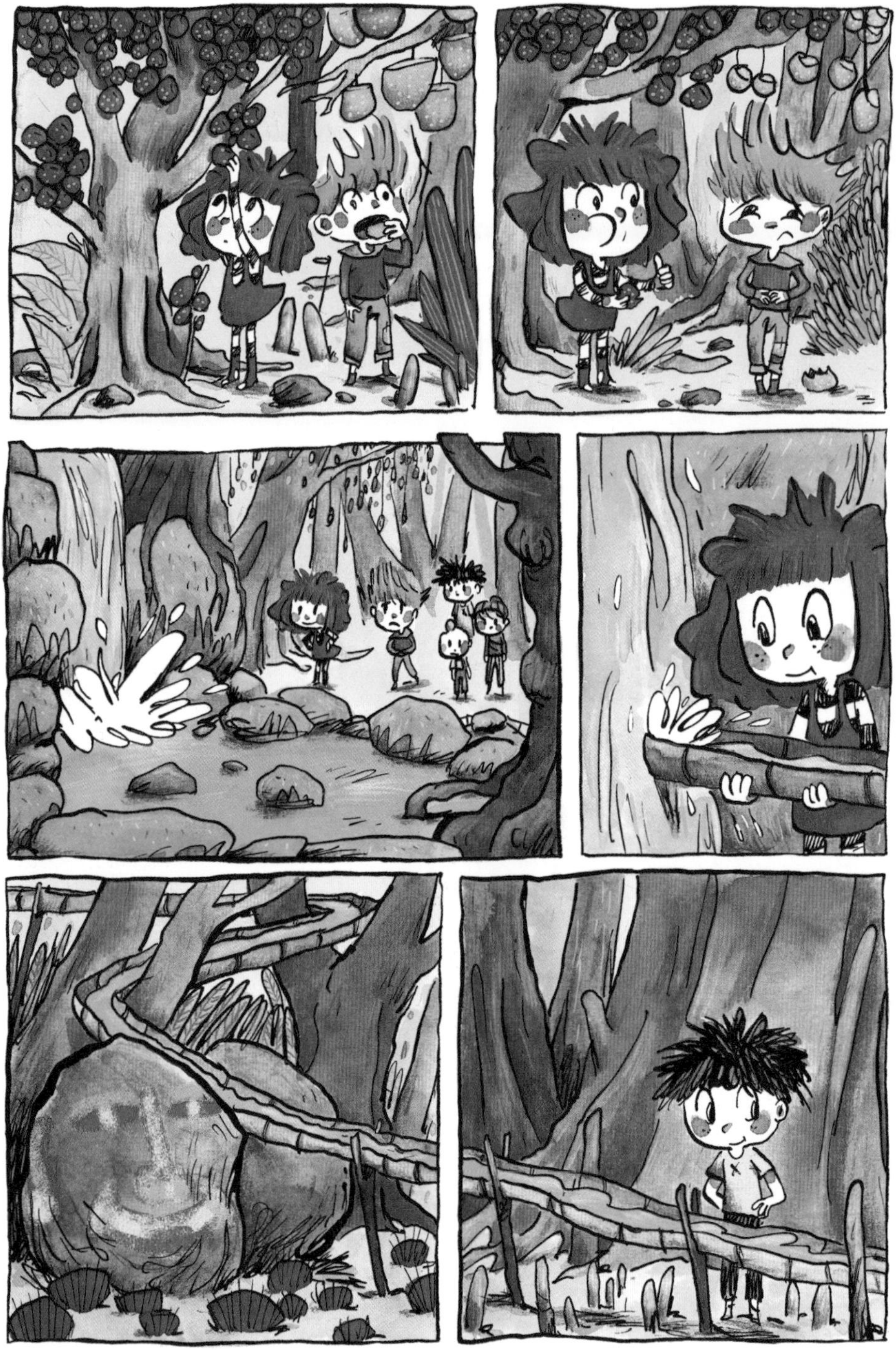

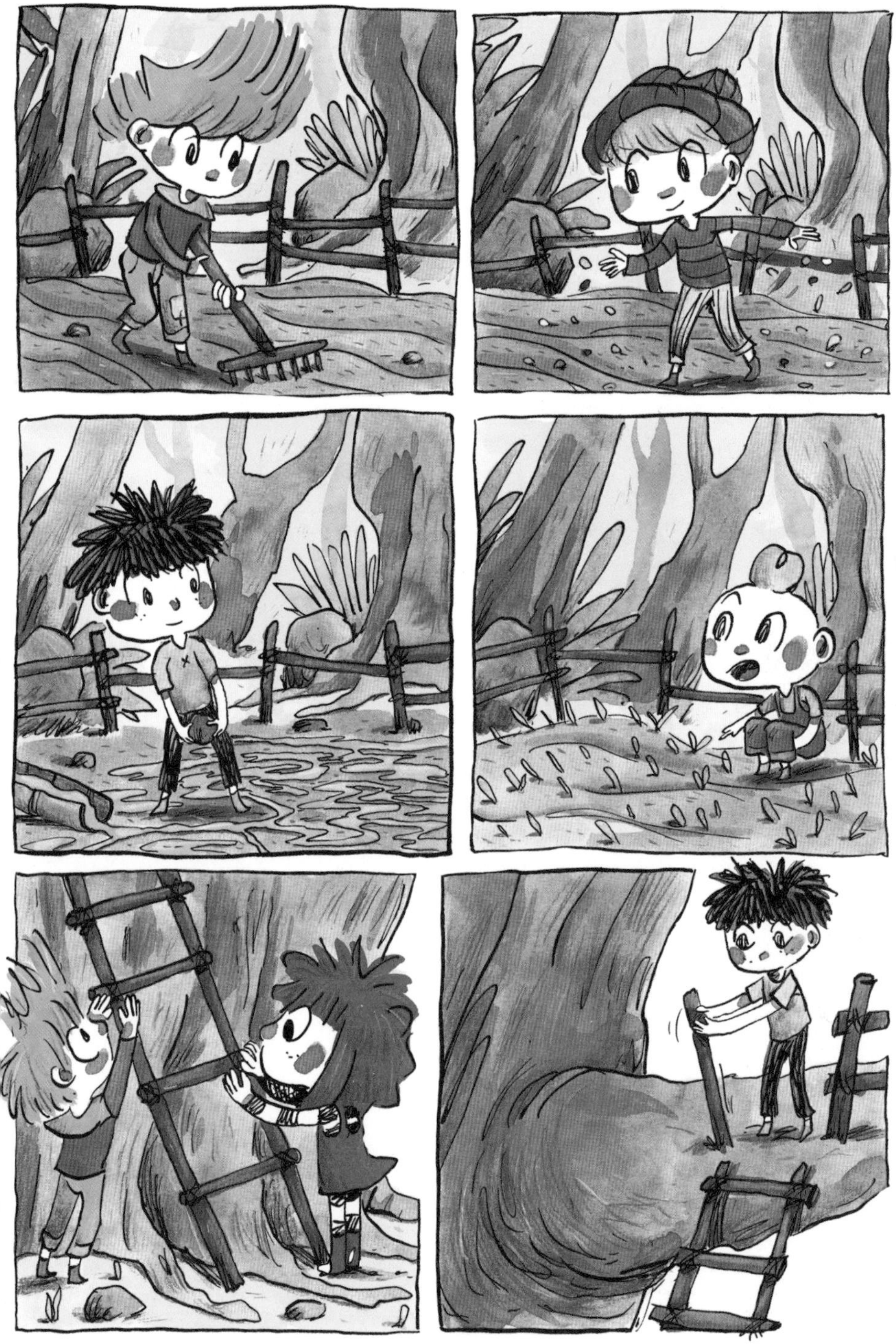

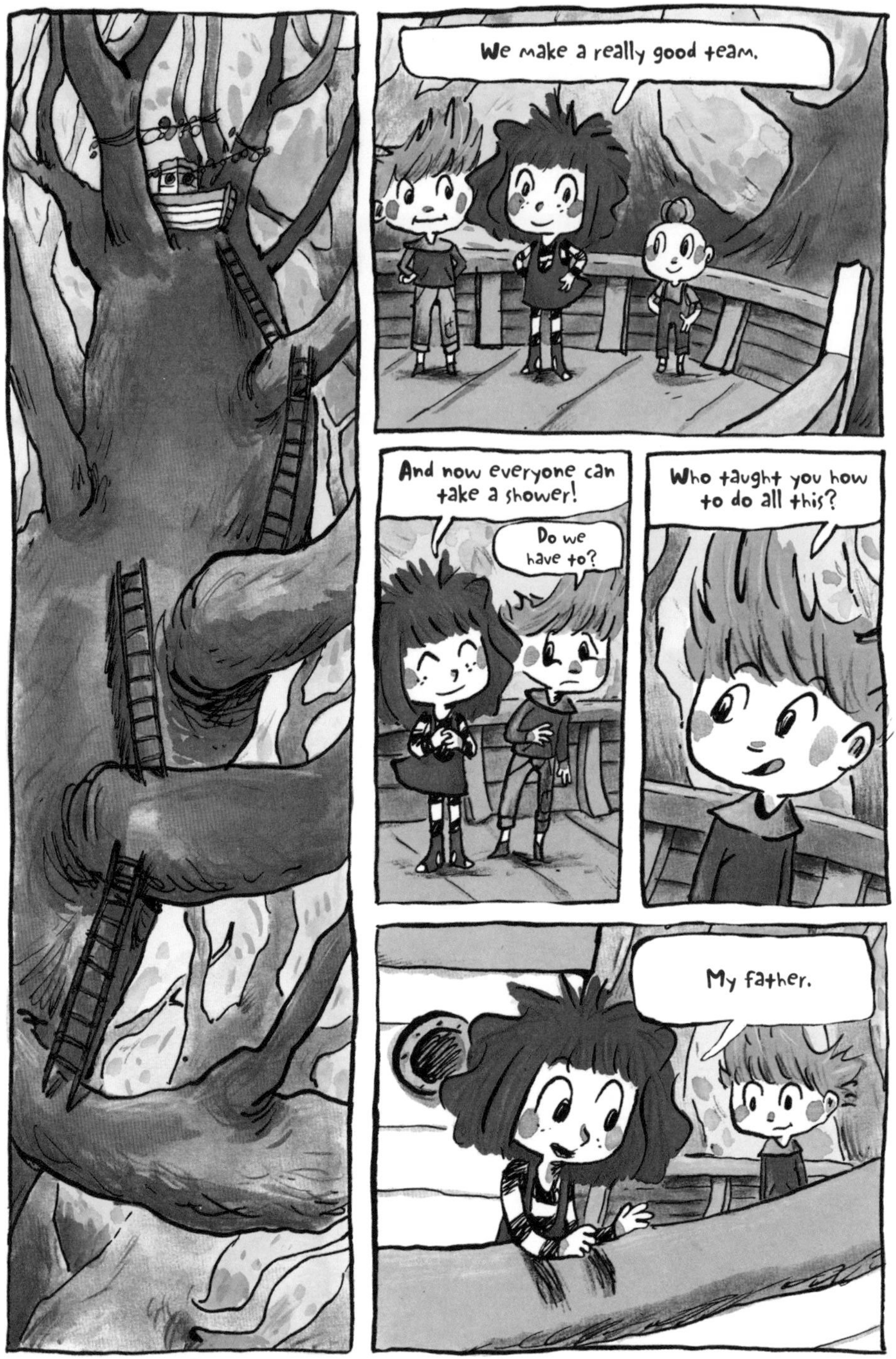
We make a really good team.
And now everyone can take a shower!
Do we have to?
Who taught you how to do all this?
My father.

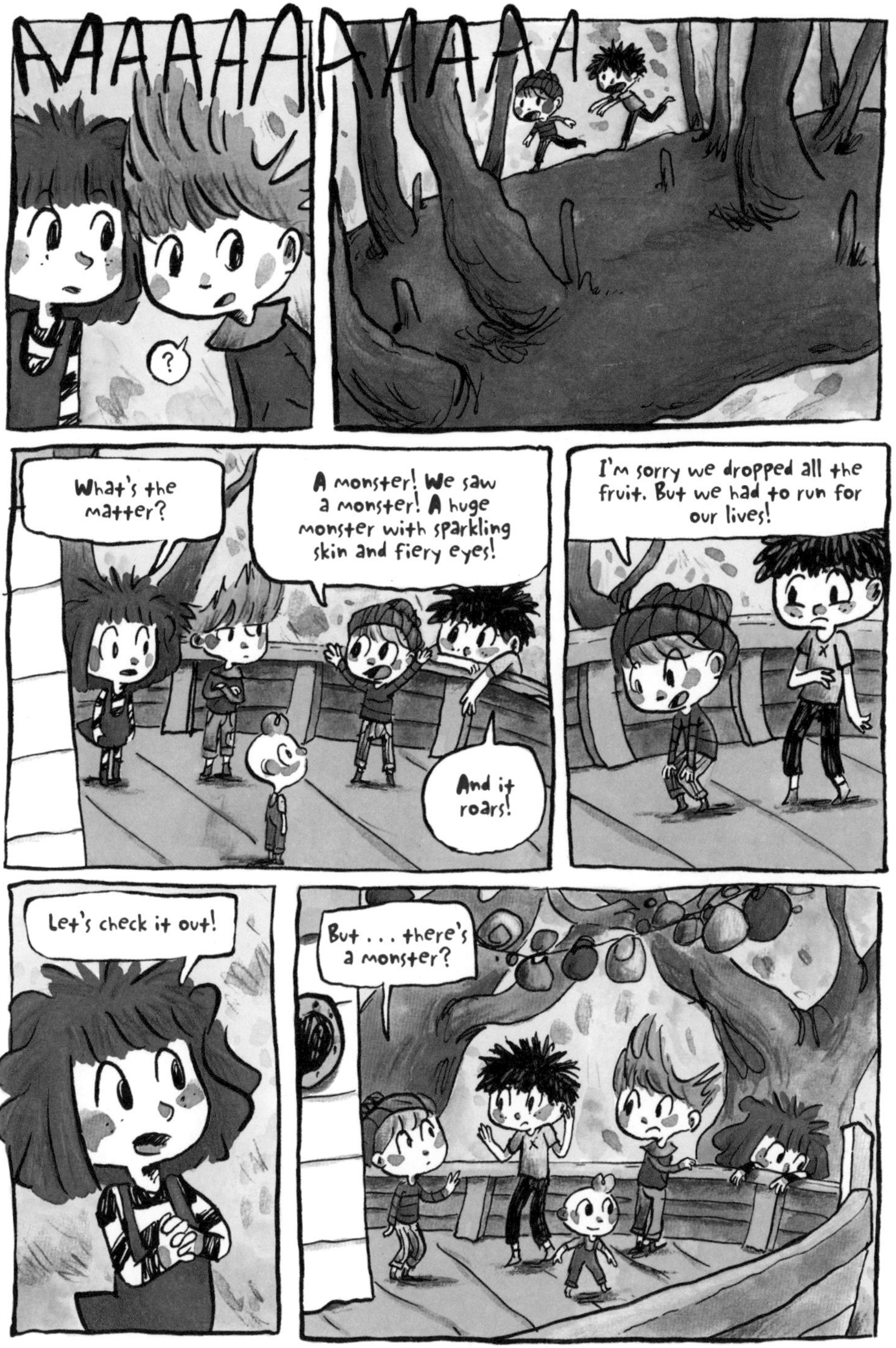
AAAAAAAAAAA
?
What's the matter?
A monster! We saw a monster! A huge monster with sparkling skin and fiery eyes!
And it roars!
I'm sorry we dropped all the fruit. But we had to run for our lives!
Let's check it out!
But . . . there's a monster?

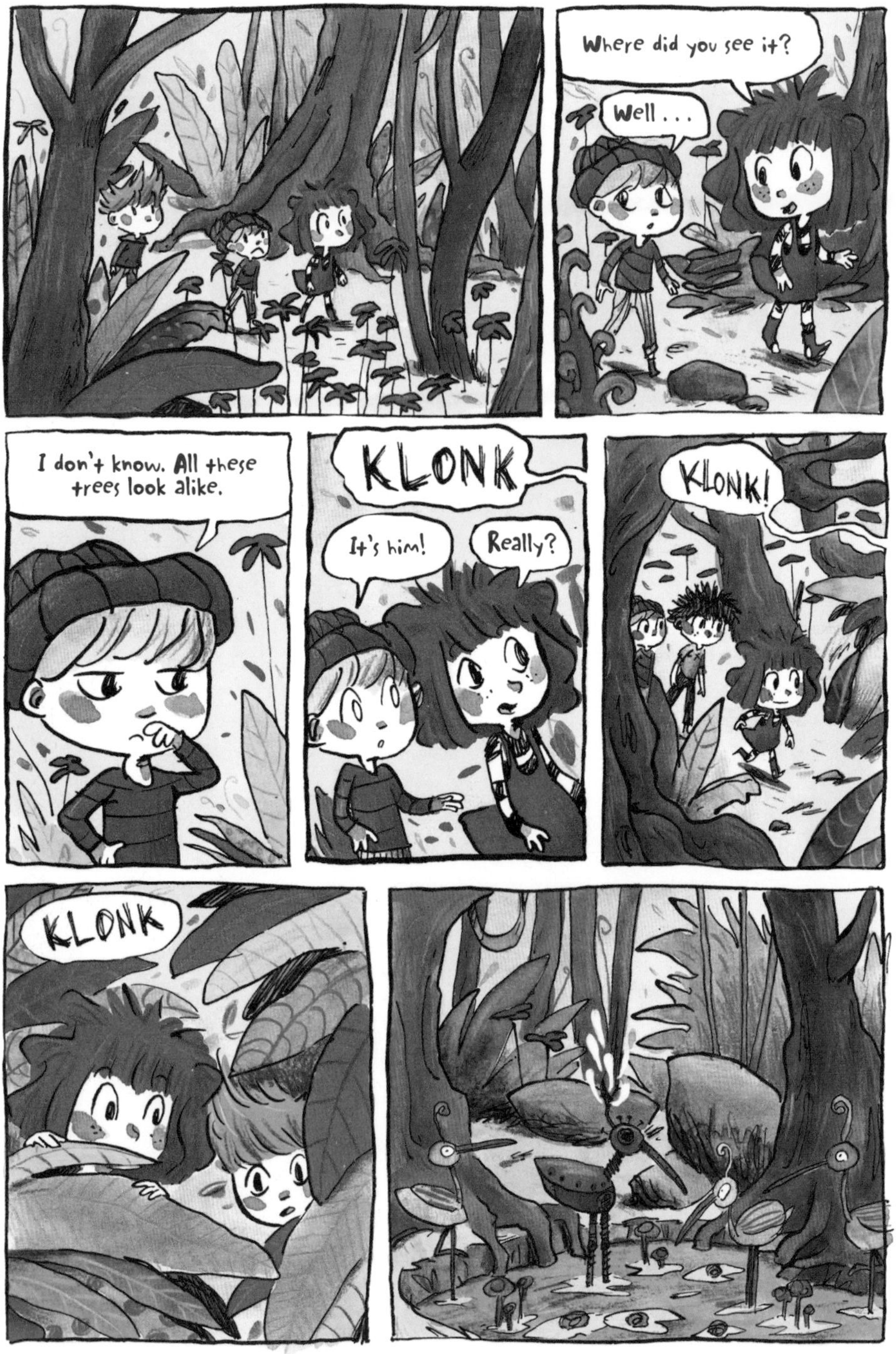

Where did you see it?
Well . . .
I don't know. All these trees look alike.
KLONK
It's him!
Really?
KLONK!
KLONK

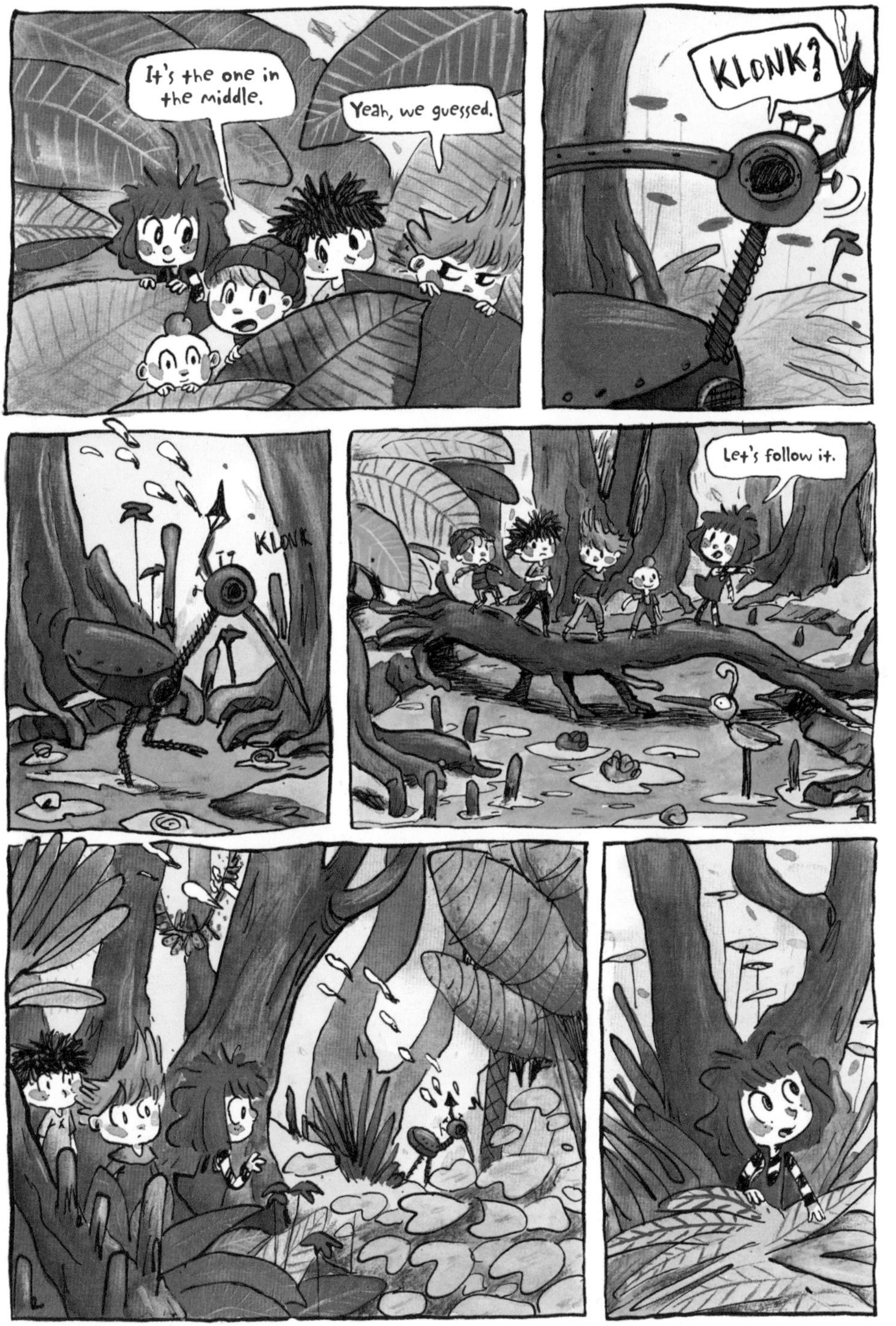
It's the one in the middle.
Yeah, we guessed.
KLONK?
KLONK
Let's follow it.

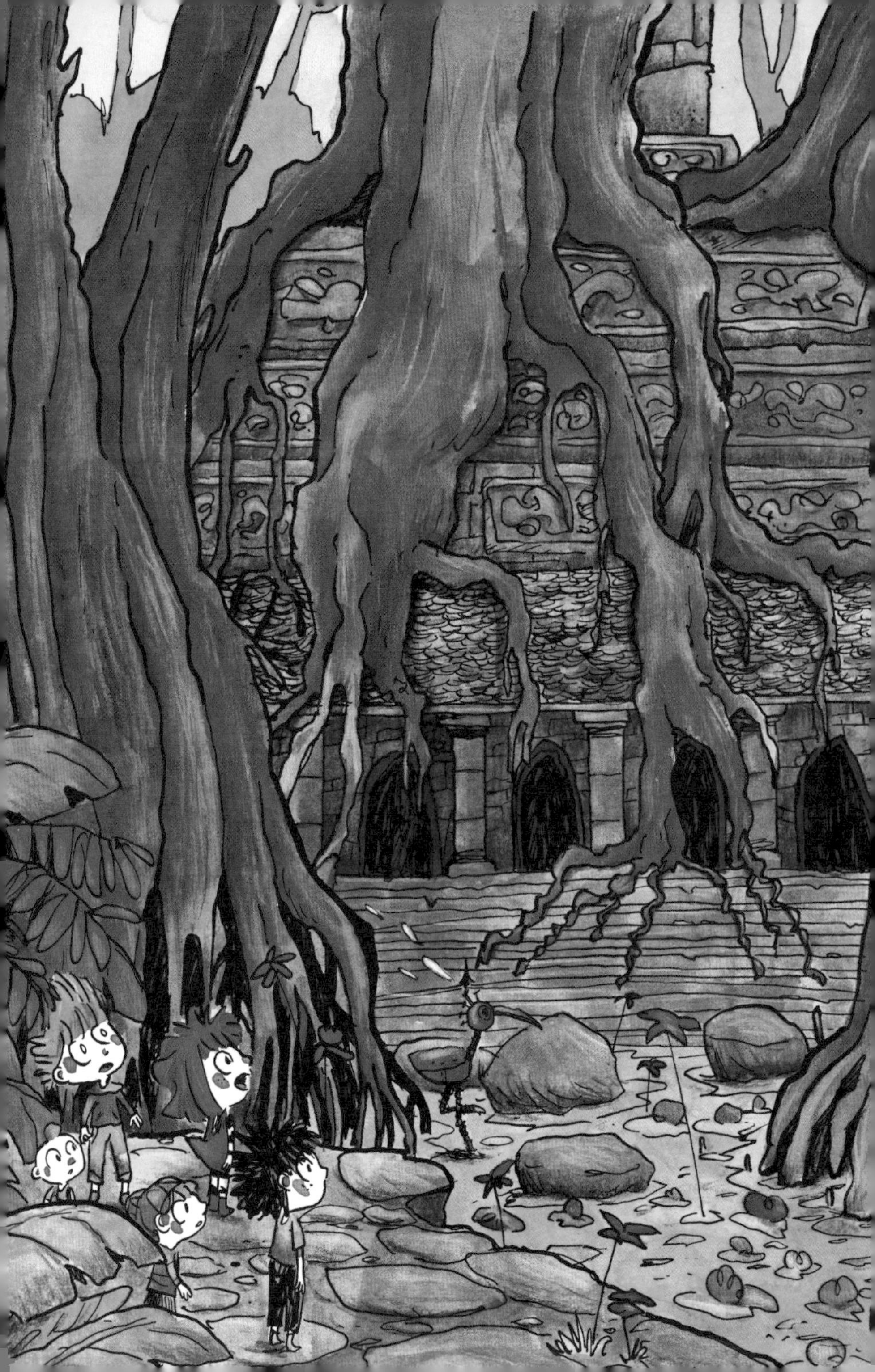

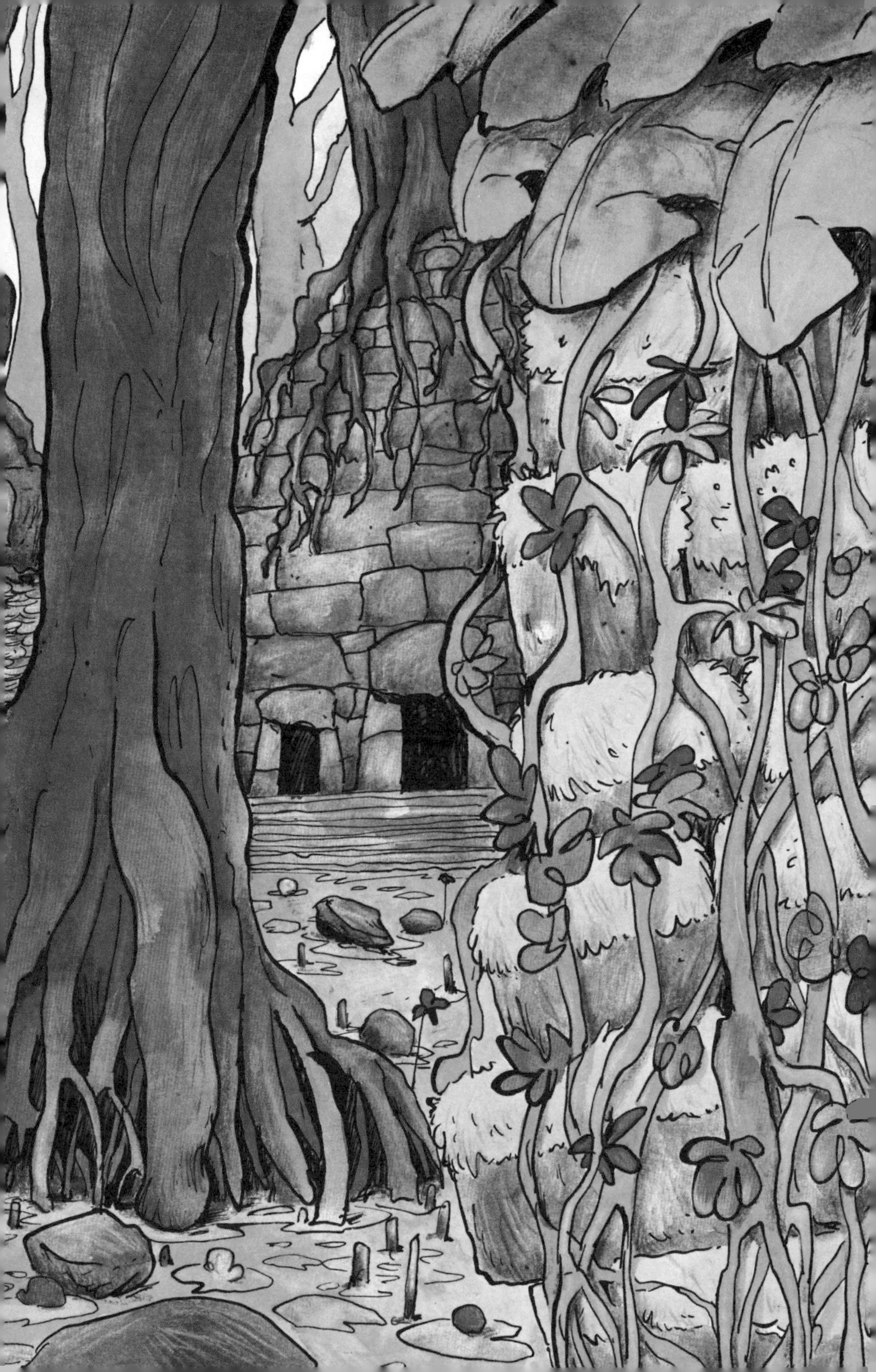

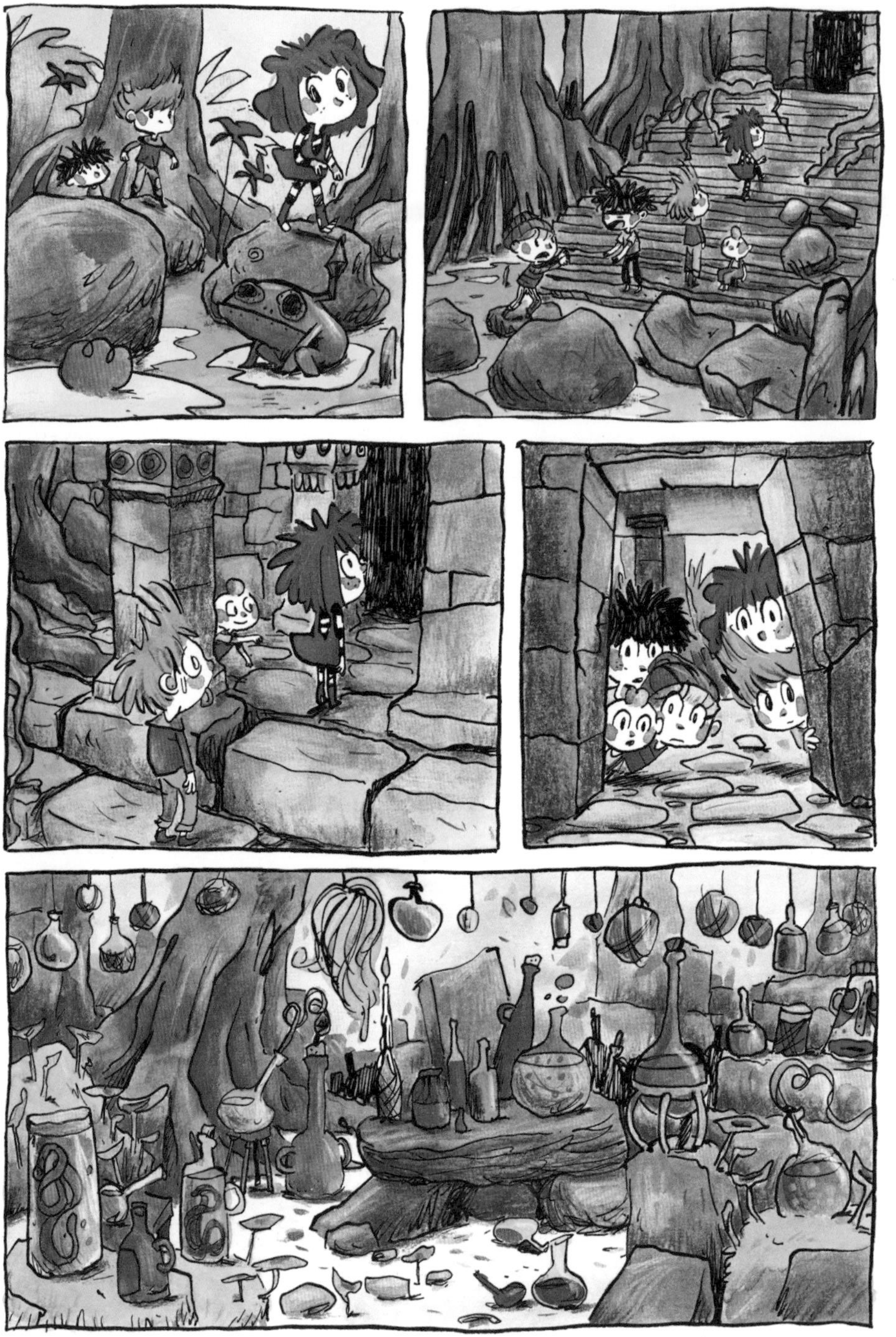

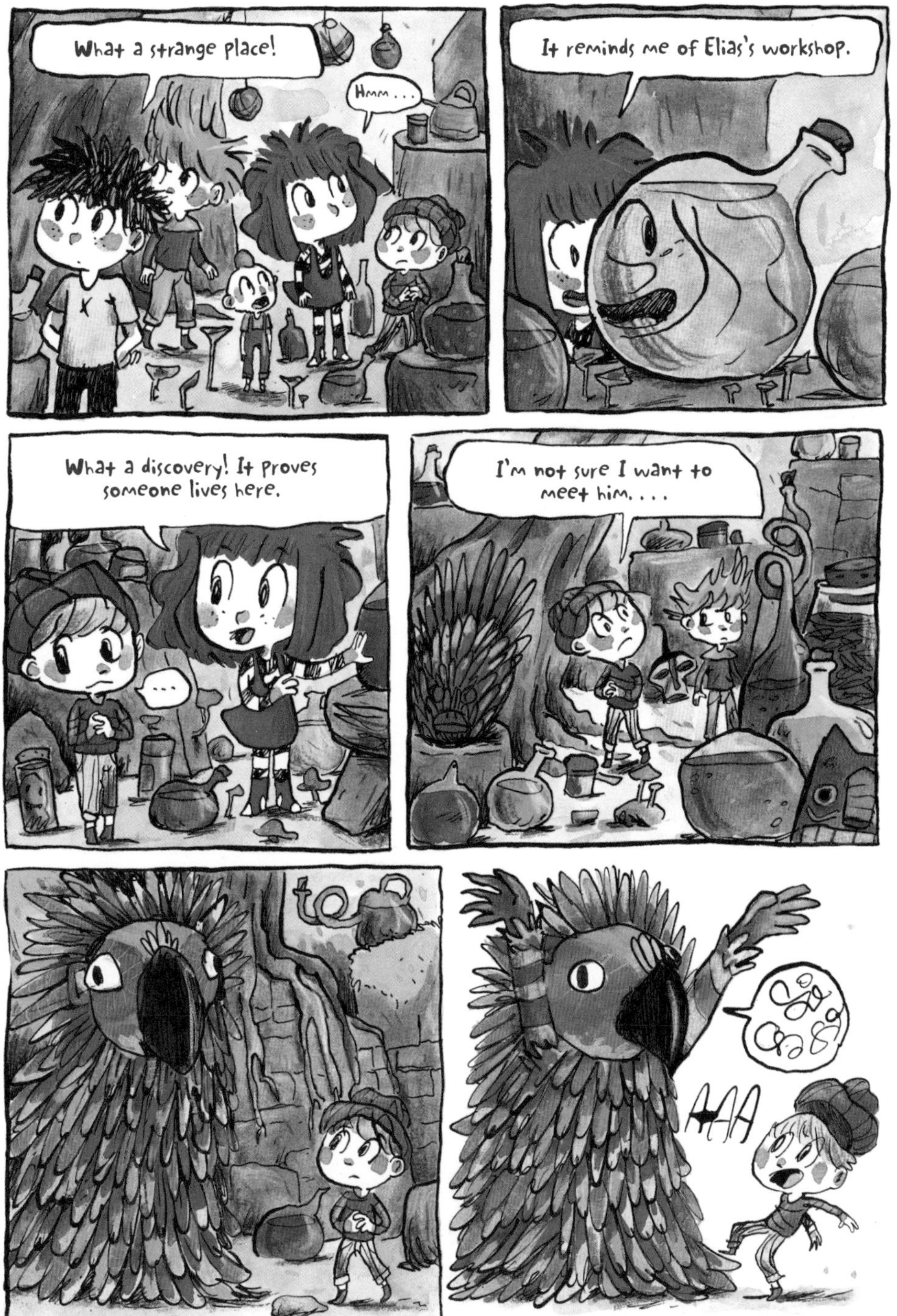
What a strange place!
Hmm . . .
It reminds me of Elias's workshop.
What a discovery! It proves someone lives here.
. . .
I'm not sure I want to meet him. . . .
AAA

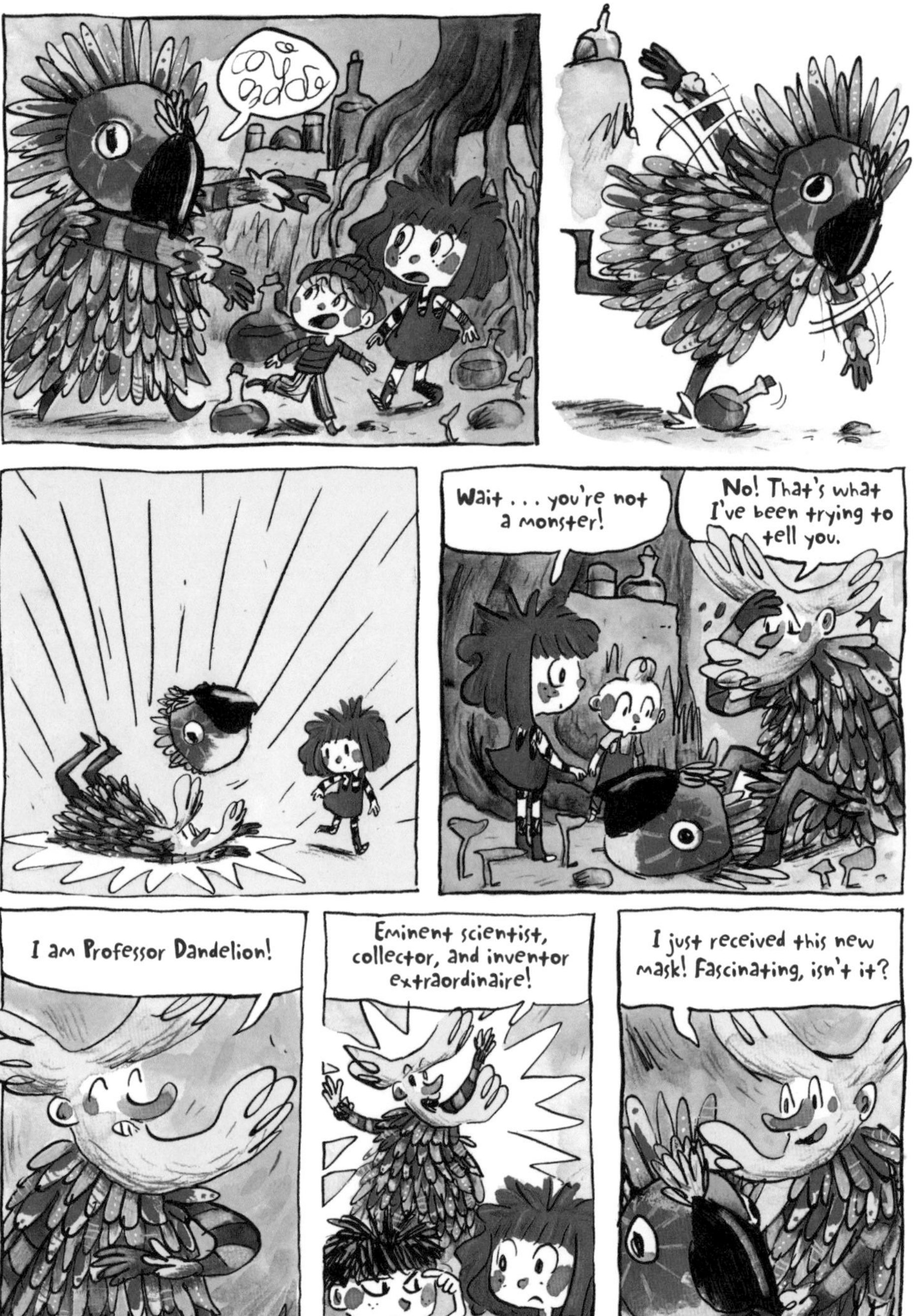
Wait . . . you're not a monster!
No! That's what I've been trying to tell you.
I am Professor Dandelion!
Eminent scientist, collector, and inventor extraordinaire!
I just received this new mask! Fascinating, isn't it?

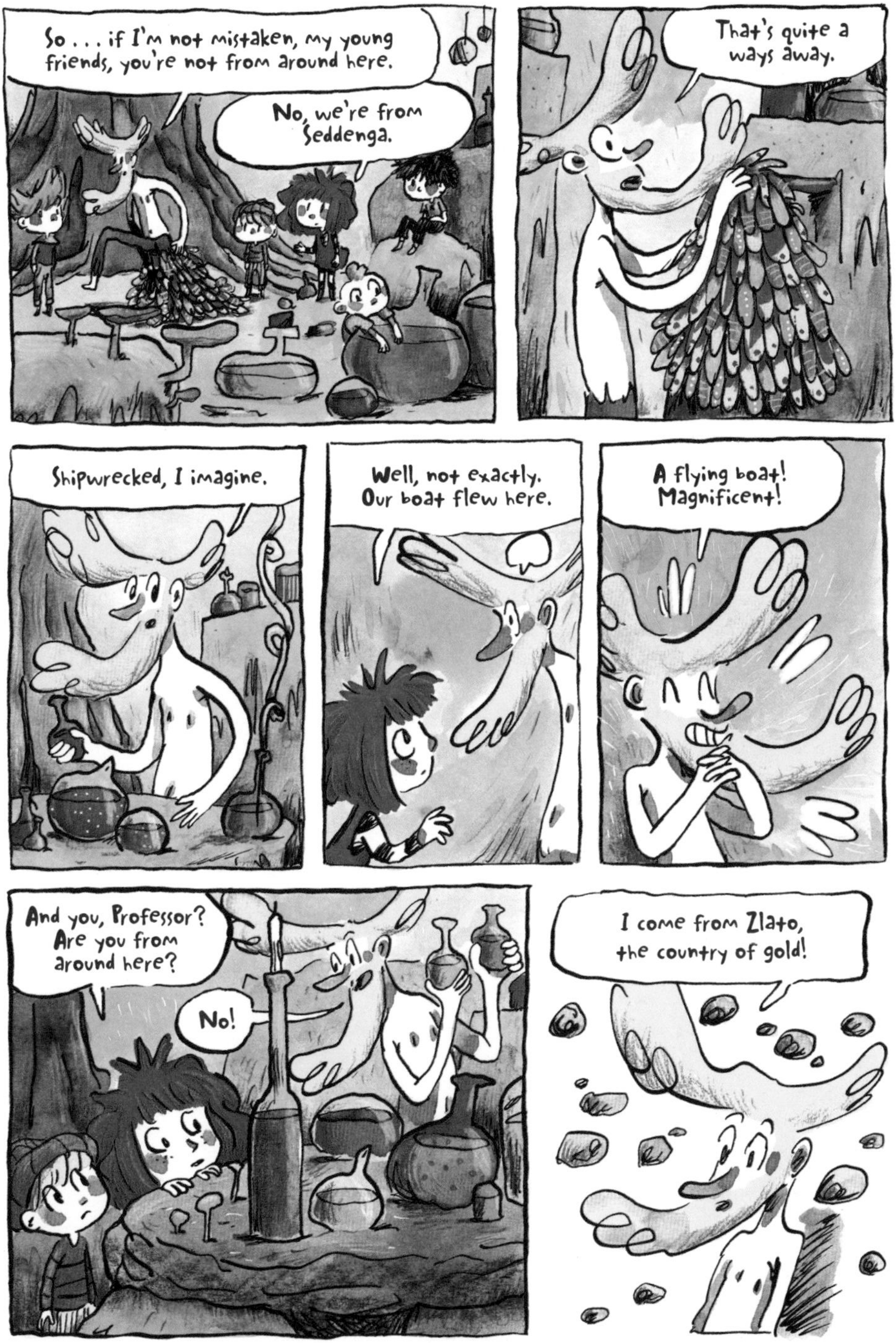
So . . . if I'm not mistaken, my young friends, you're not from around here.
No, we're from Seddenga.
That's quite a ways away.
Shipwrecked, I imagine.
Well, not exactly. Our boat flew here.
A flying boat! Magnificent!
And you, Professor? Are you from around here?
No!
I come from Zlato, the country of gold!

I was a scientist in the palace of King Croesus.

He was so obsessed with gold that he even powdered his beard with gold dust.

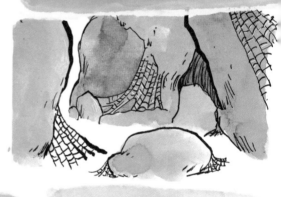

But he spent his wealth so lavishly that the royal gold mines were soon exhausted.

Since he couldn't unearth any more gold, he decided to manufacture it using the legendary Philosopher's Stone . . .

. . . but none of his scientists or scholars knew the formula for making one!

Like all the other scholars in the kingdom, I searched high and low for the secret of the Stone . . .

. . . but without success.

With each failure, the king's wrath grew.

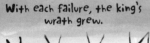

He executed several of my colleagues as an example to the rest of us. So I decided to escape.

Fortunately, I had invented a giant cannon . . .

. . . which enabled me to travel for several days.

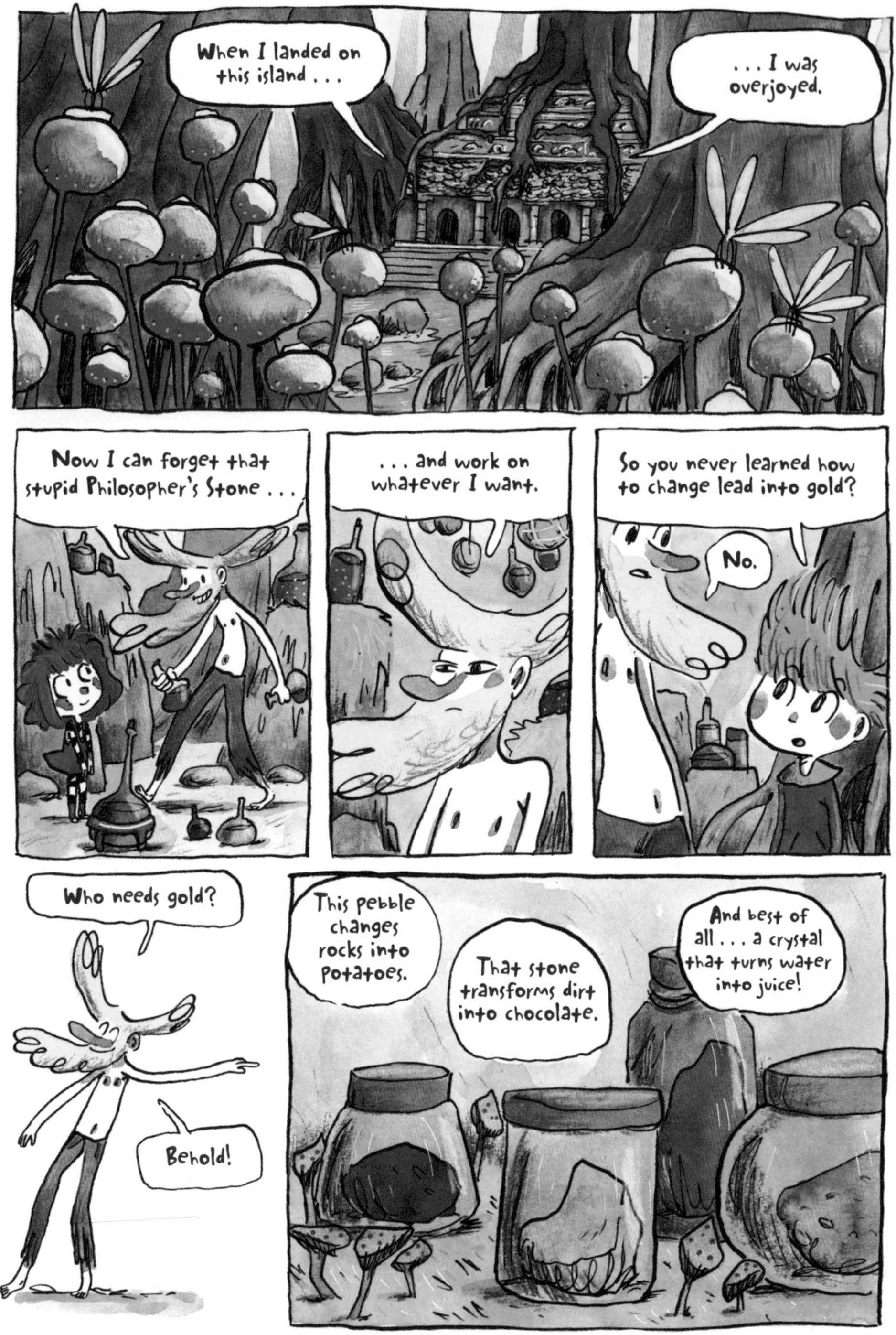

When I landed on this island . . .
. . . I was overjoyed.
Now I can forget that stupid Philosopher's Stone . . .
. . . and work on whatever I want.
So you never learned how to change lead into gold?
No.
Who needs gold?
Behold!
This pebble changes rocks into potatoes.
That stone transforms dirt into chocolate.
And best of all . . . a crystal that turns water into juice!

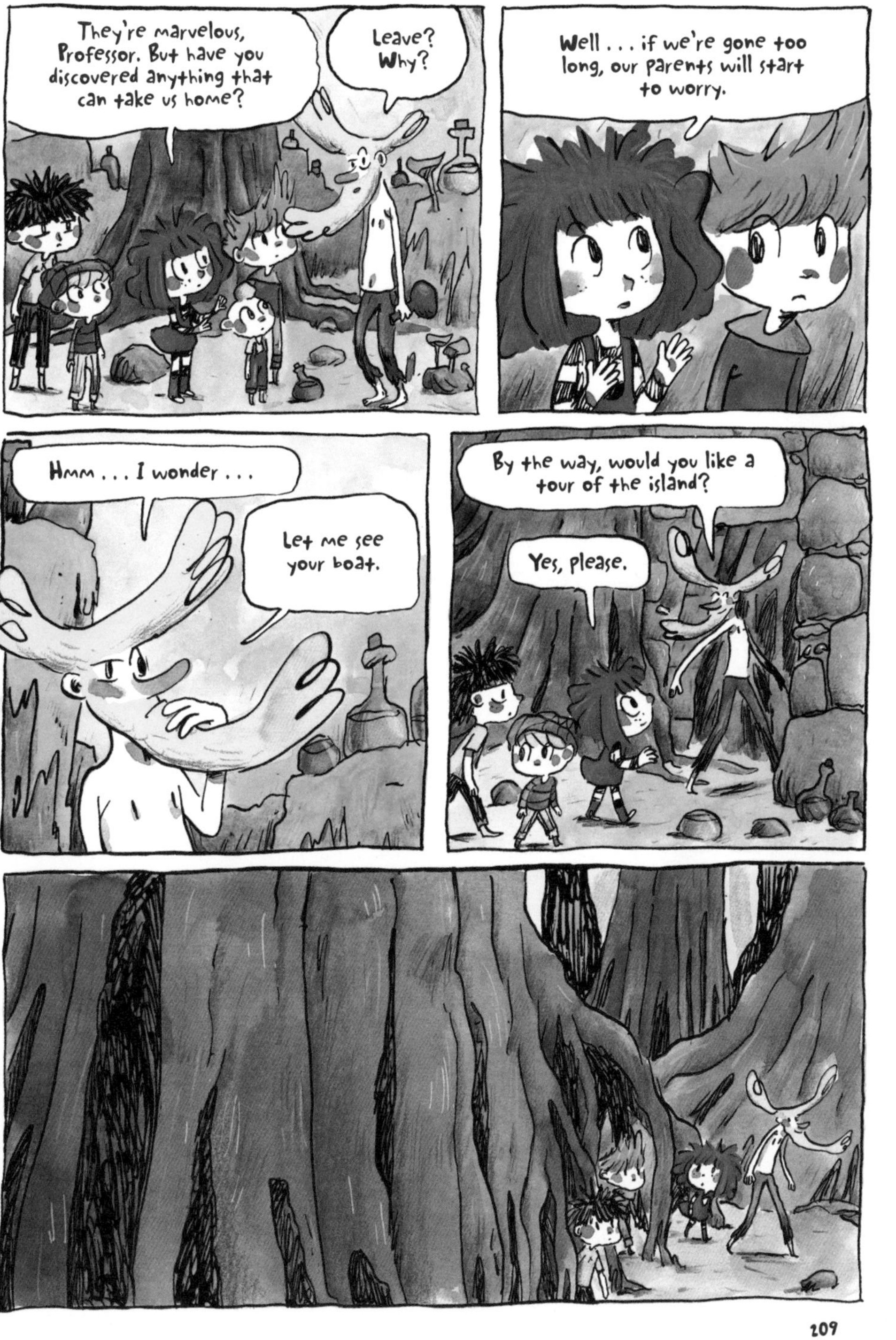
They're marvelous, Professor. But have you discovered anything that can take us home?
Leave? Why?
Well . . . if we're gone too long, our parents will start to worry.
Hmm . . . I wonder . . .
Let me see your boat.
By the way, would you like a tour of the island?
Yes, please.

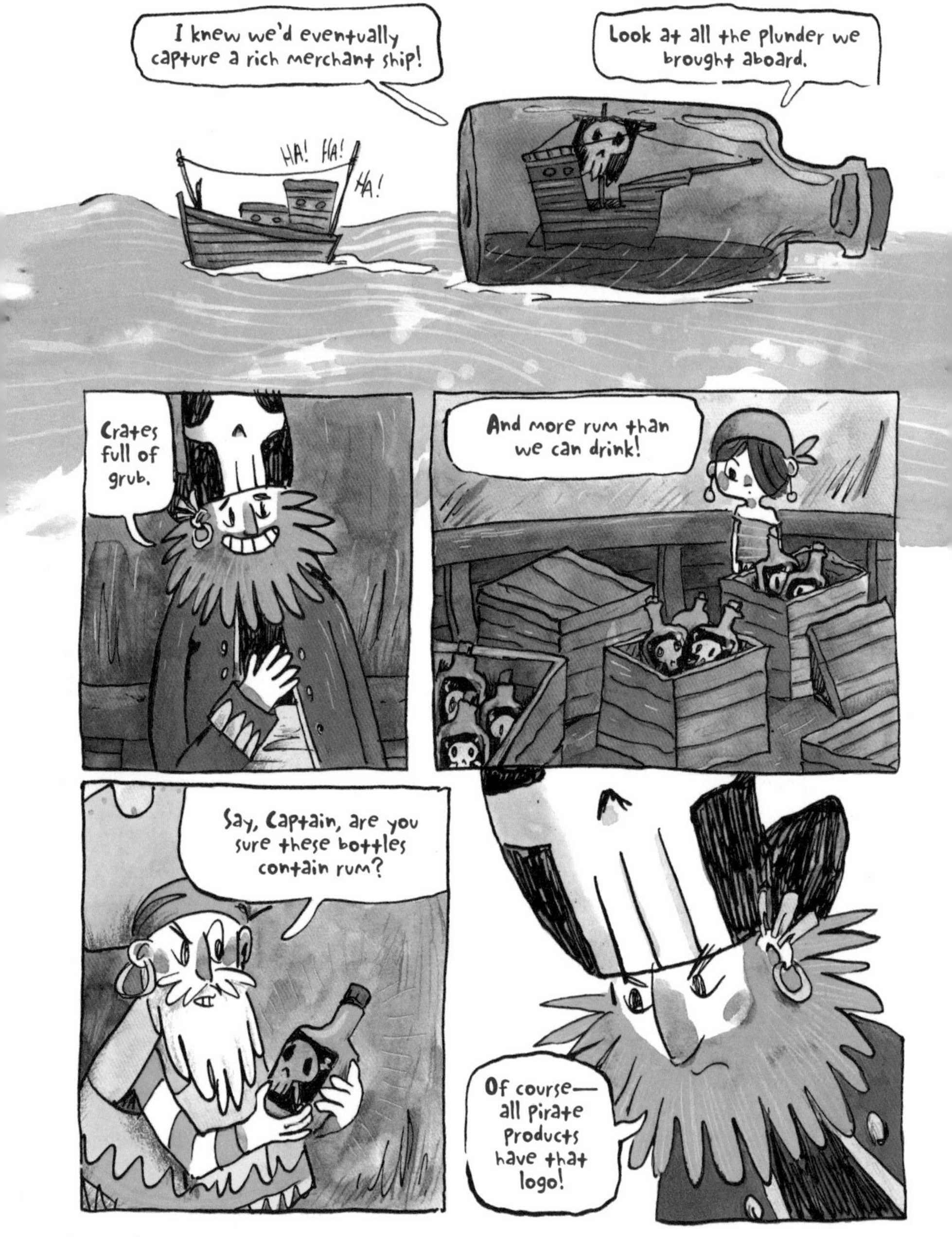
I knew we'd eventually capture a rich merchant ship!
Look at all the plunder we brought aboard.
HA! HA! HA!
Crates full of grub.
And more rum than we can drink!
Say, Captain, are you sure these bottles contain rum?
Of course— all pirate products have that logo!

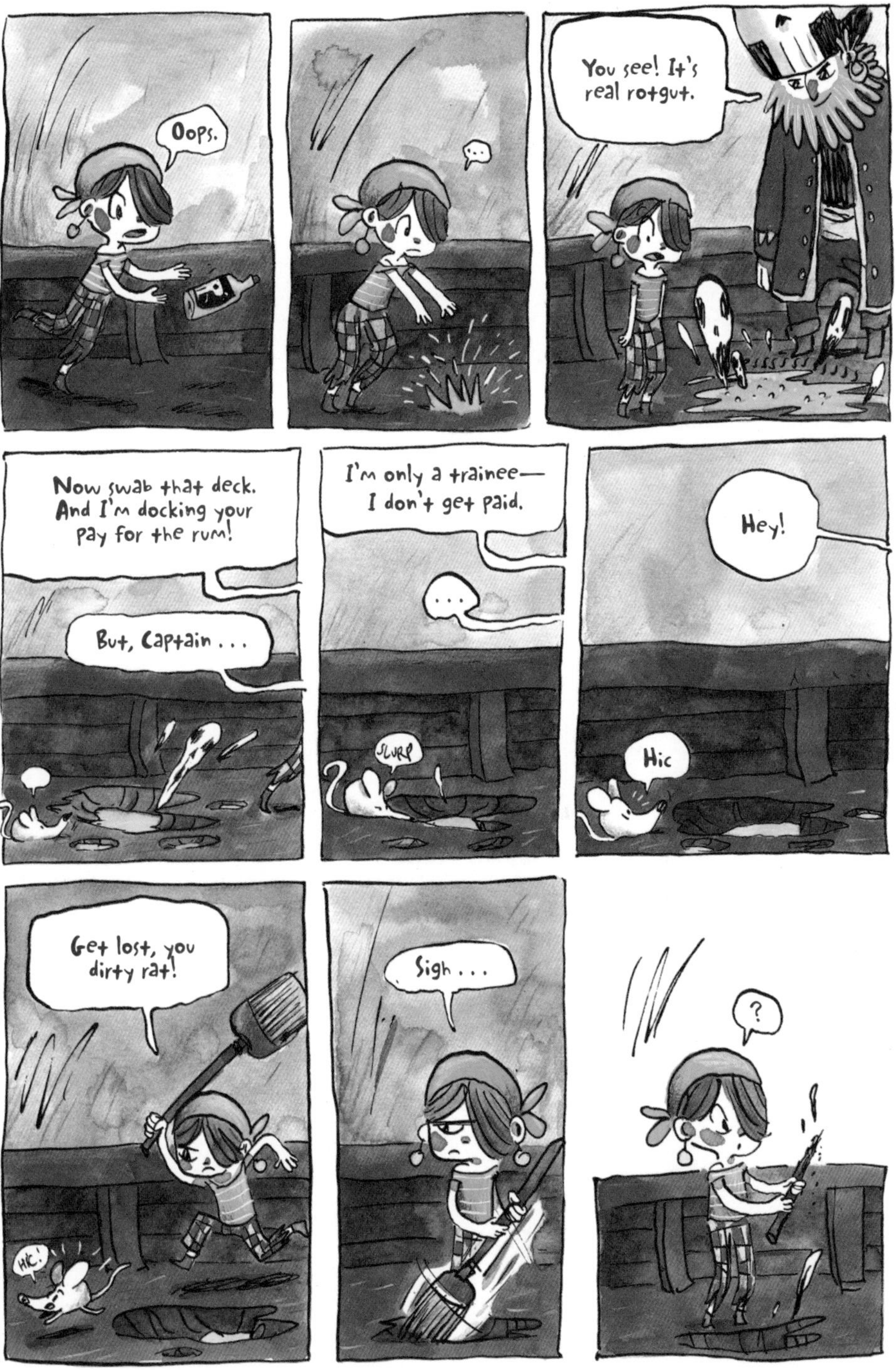

Oops.
. . .
You see! It's real rotgut.
Now swab that deck. And I'm docking your pay for the rum!
But, Captain . . .
I'm only a trainee— I don't get paid.
. . .
SLURP
Hey!
Hic
Get lost, you dirty rat!
HIC!
Sigh . . .
?

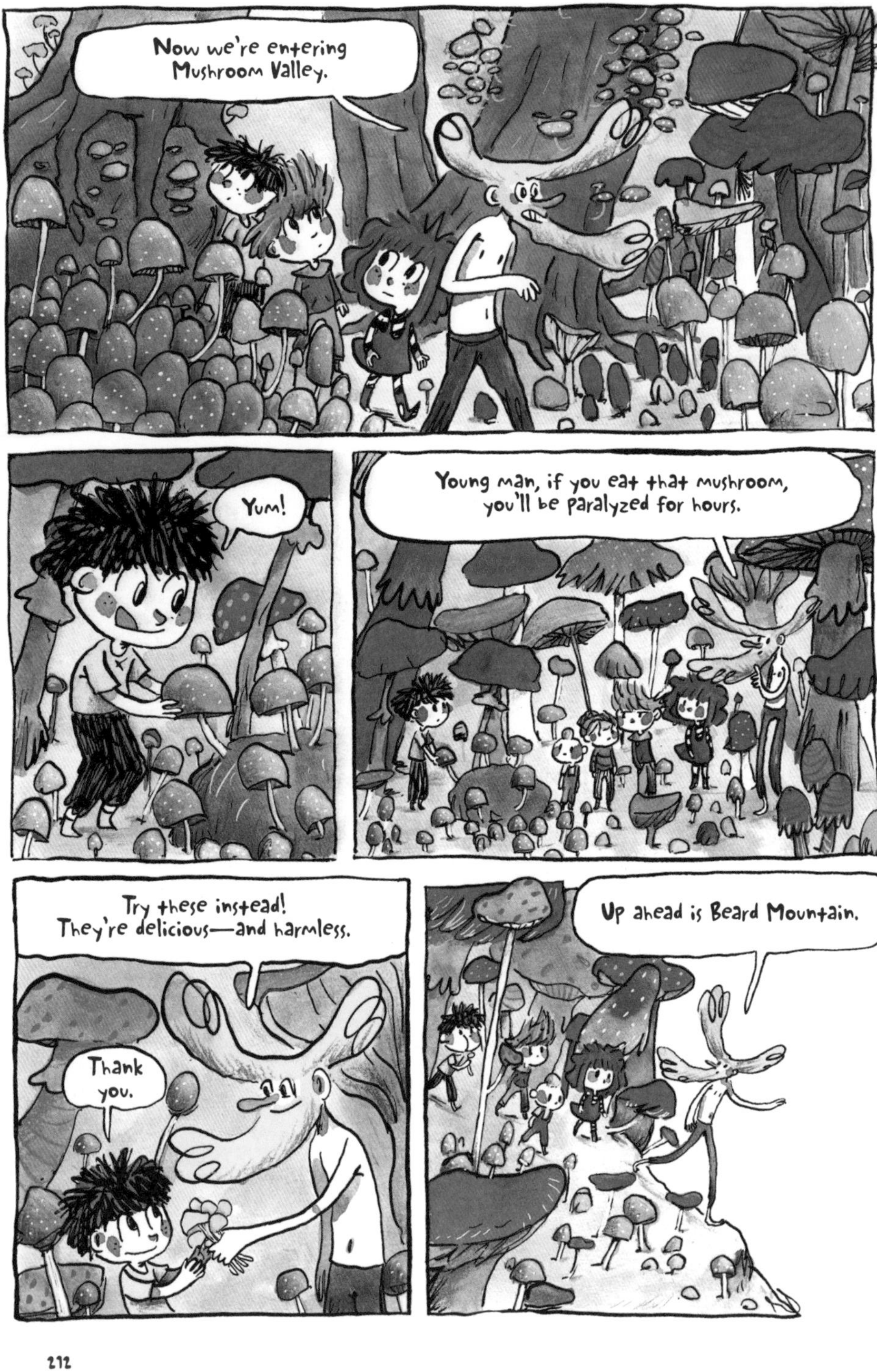
Now we're entering Mushroom Valley.
Yum!
Young man, if you eat that mushroom, you'll be paralyzed for hours.
Try these instead! They're delicious—and harmless.
Thank you.
Up ahead is Beard Mountain.

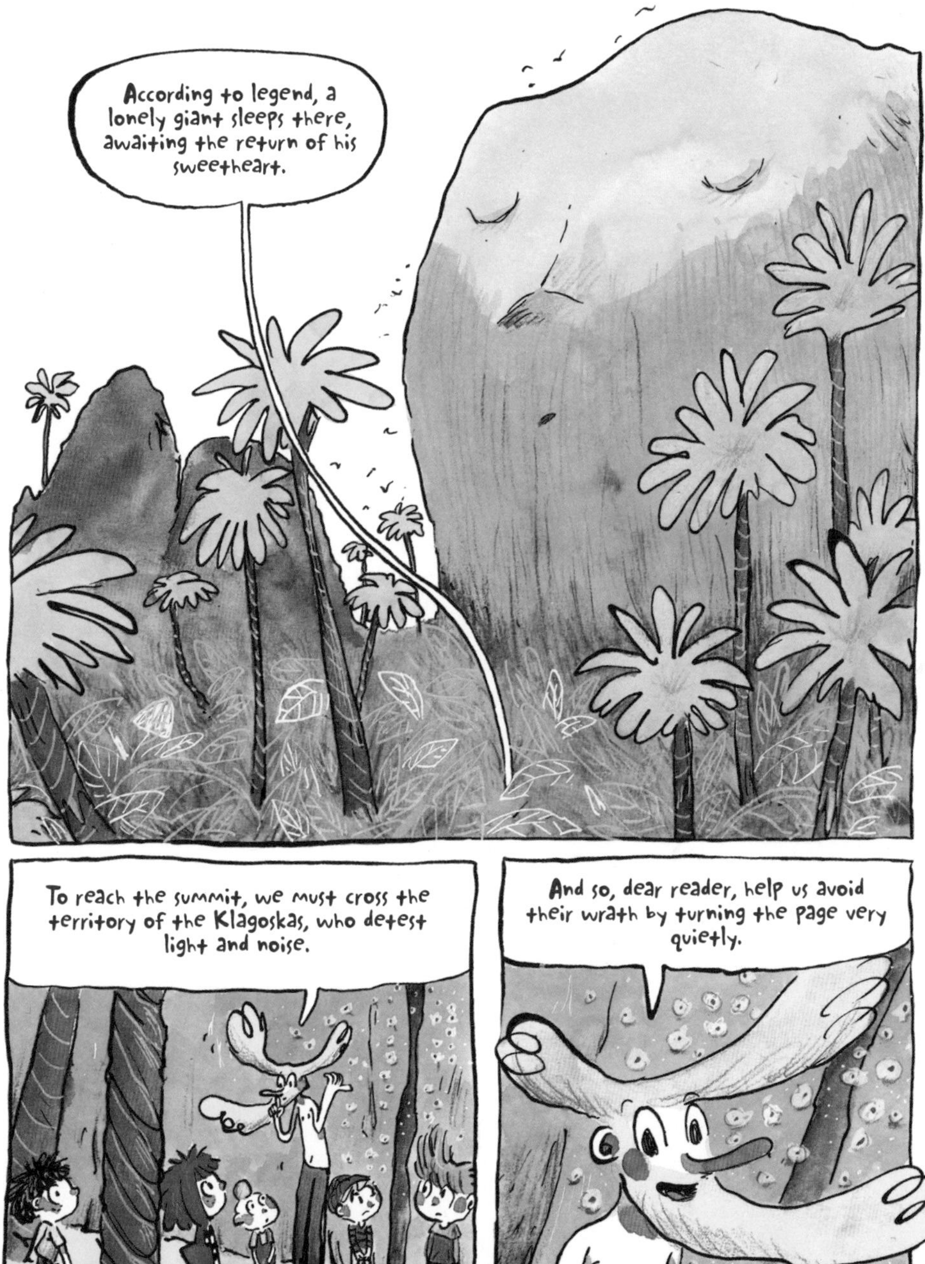
According to legend, a lonely giant sleeps there, awaiting the return of his sweetheart.
To reach the summit, we must cross the territory of the Klagoskas, who detest light and noise.
And so, dear reader, help us avoid their wrath by turning the page very quietly.

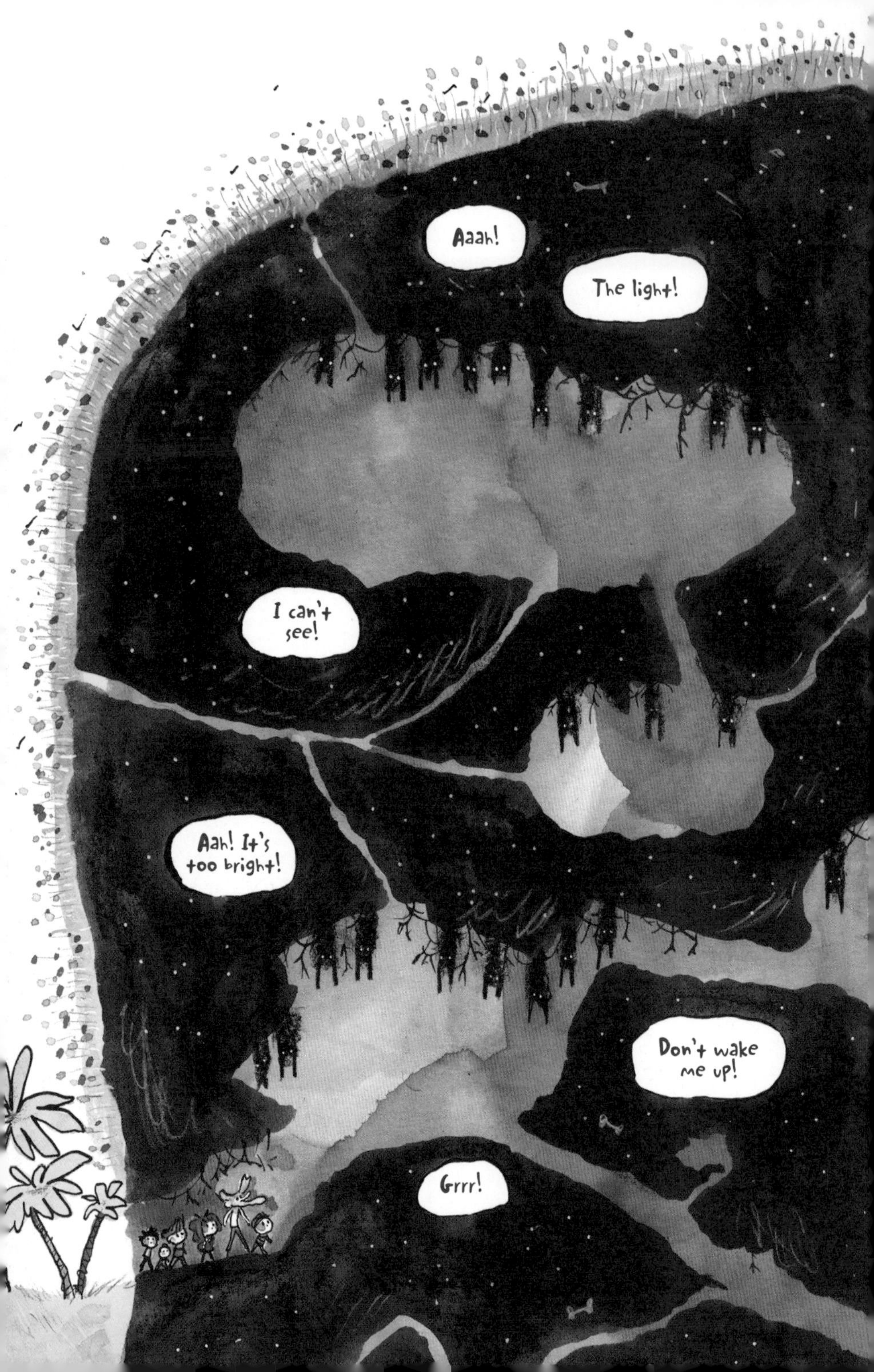
Aaah!
The light!
I can't see!
Aah! It's too bright!
Don't wake me up!
Grrr!

Put out that light!
Let's hurry!
Aaah, my eyes!
Let's get out of here!
Flee, pathetic mortals.
They're in a bad mood.
Is breakfast ready yet?

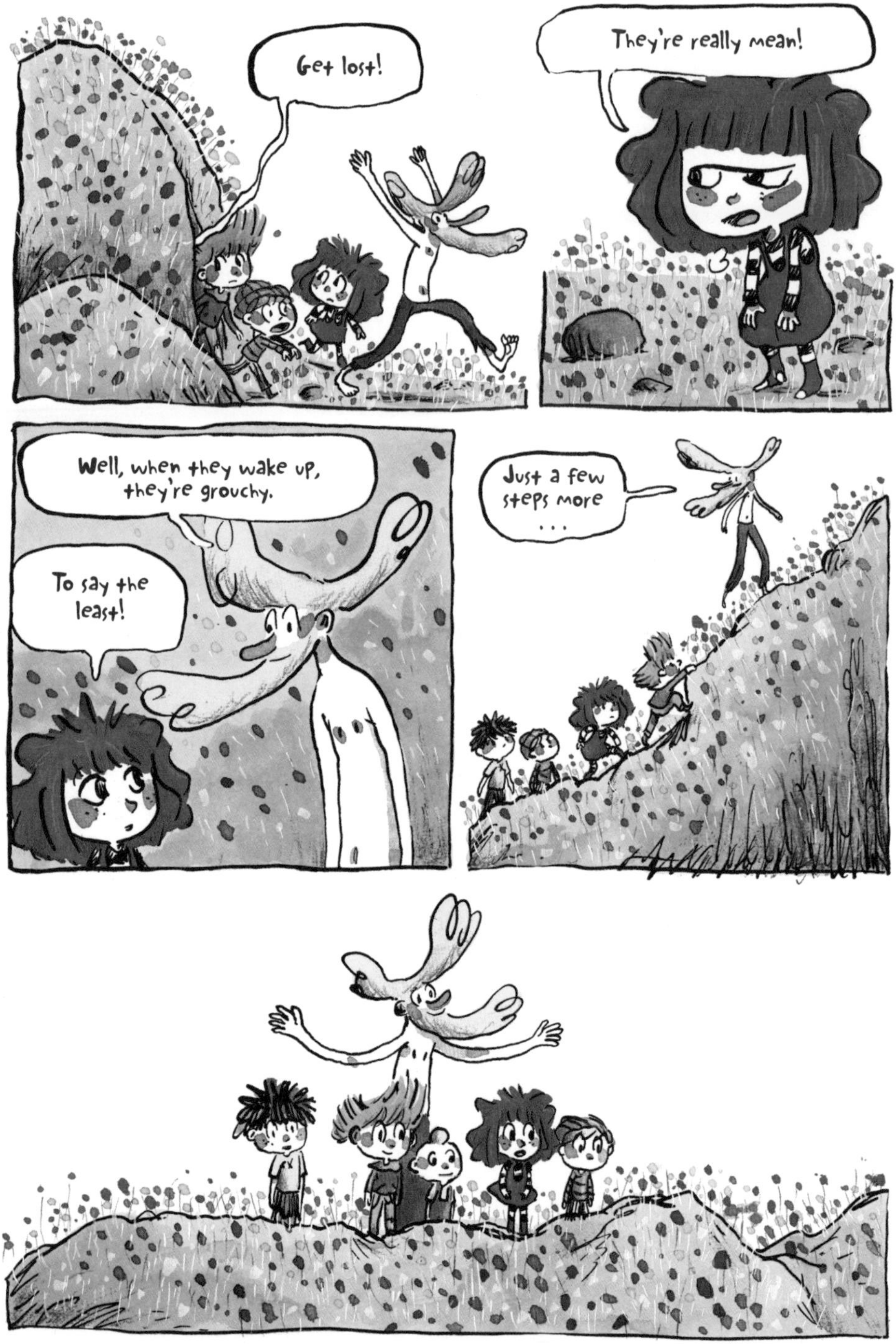
Get lost!
They're really mean!
Well, when they wake up, they're grouchy.
To say the least!
Just a few steps more . . .

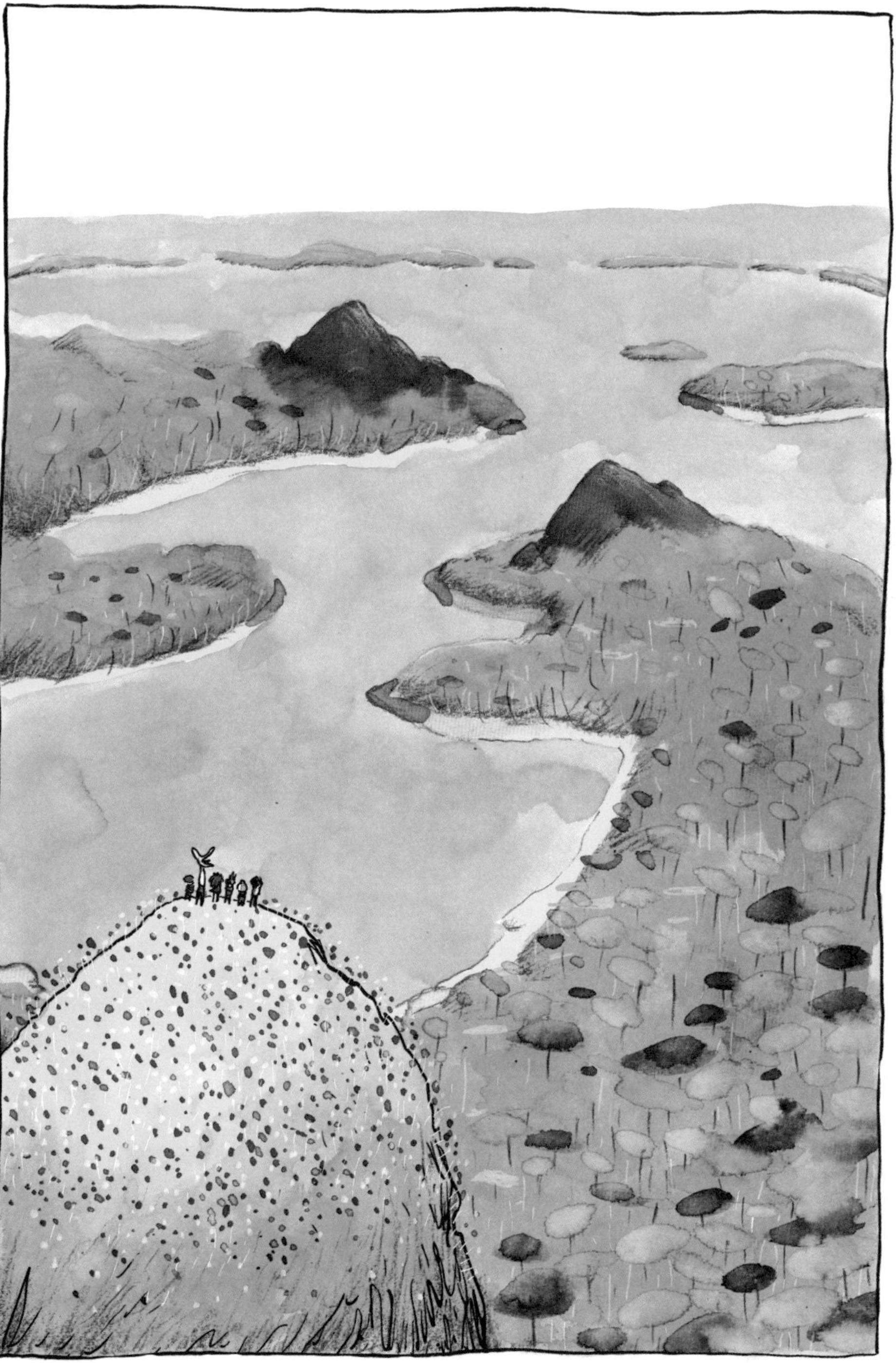

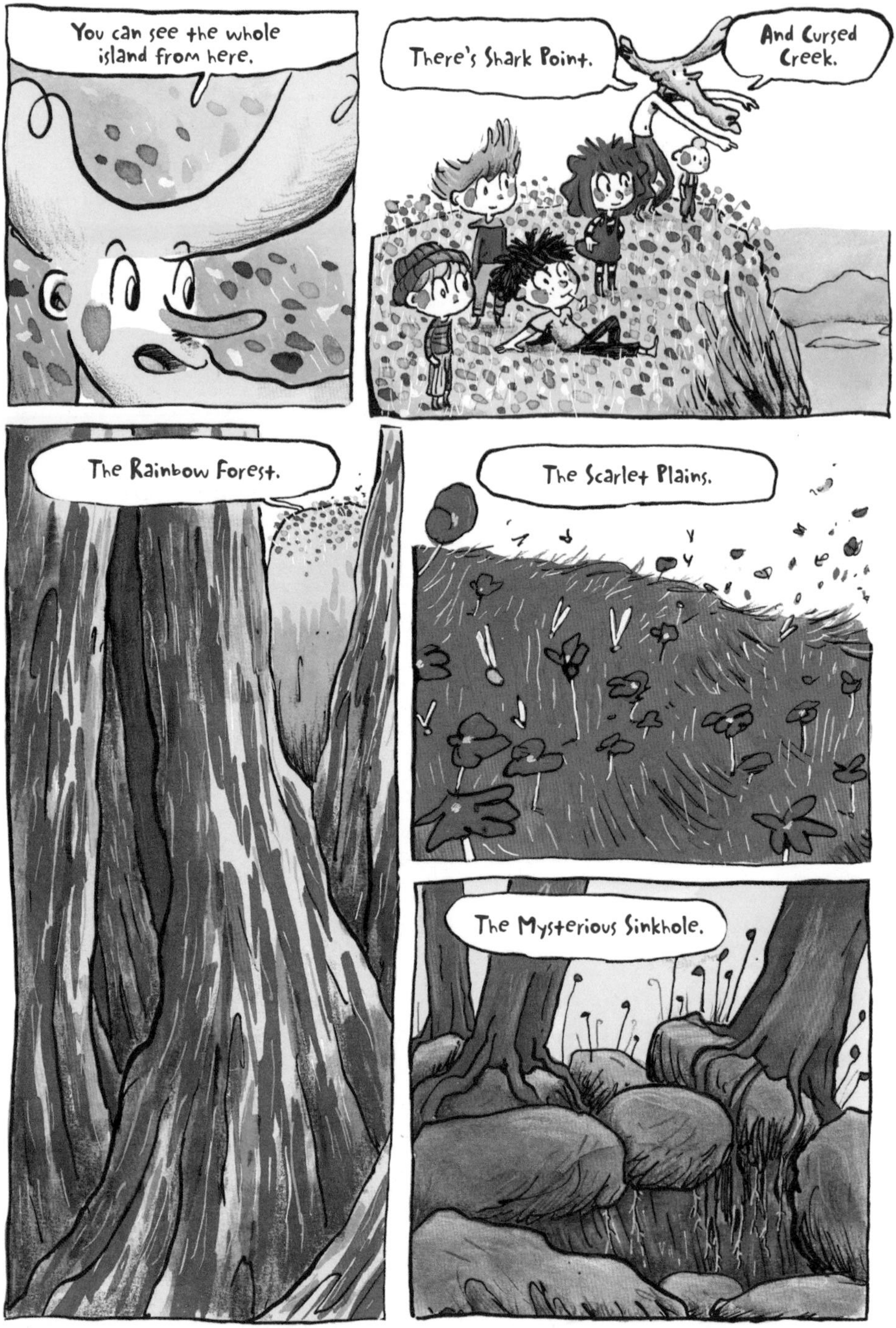
You can see the whole island from here.
There's Shark Point.
And Cursed Creek.
The Rainbow Forest.
The Scarlet Plains.
The Mysterious Sinkhole.

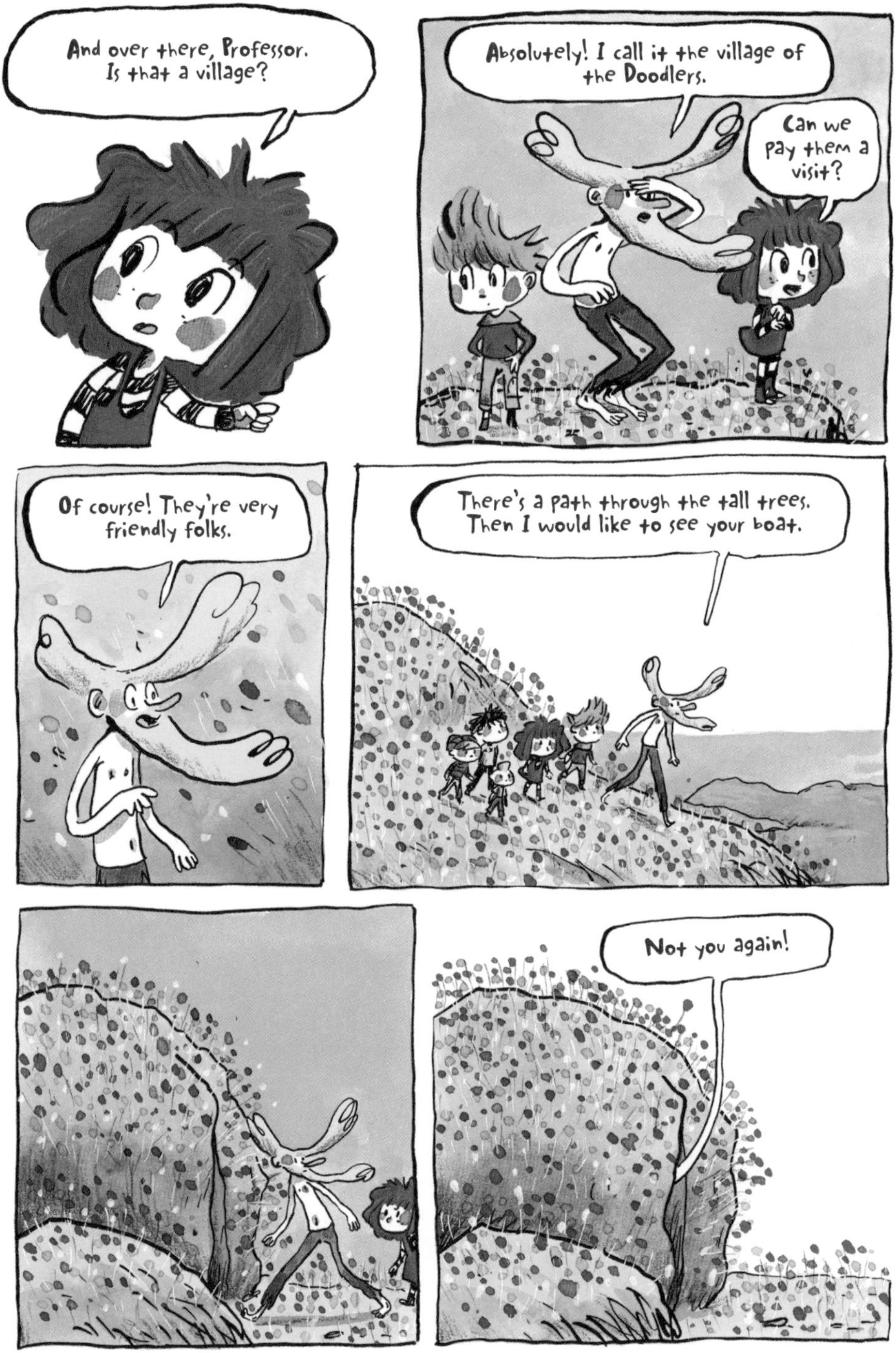
And over there, Professor. Is that a village?
Absolutely! I call it the village of the Doodlers.
Can we pay them a visit?
Of course! They're very friendly folks.
There's a path through the tall trees. Then I would like to see your boat.
Not you again!

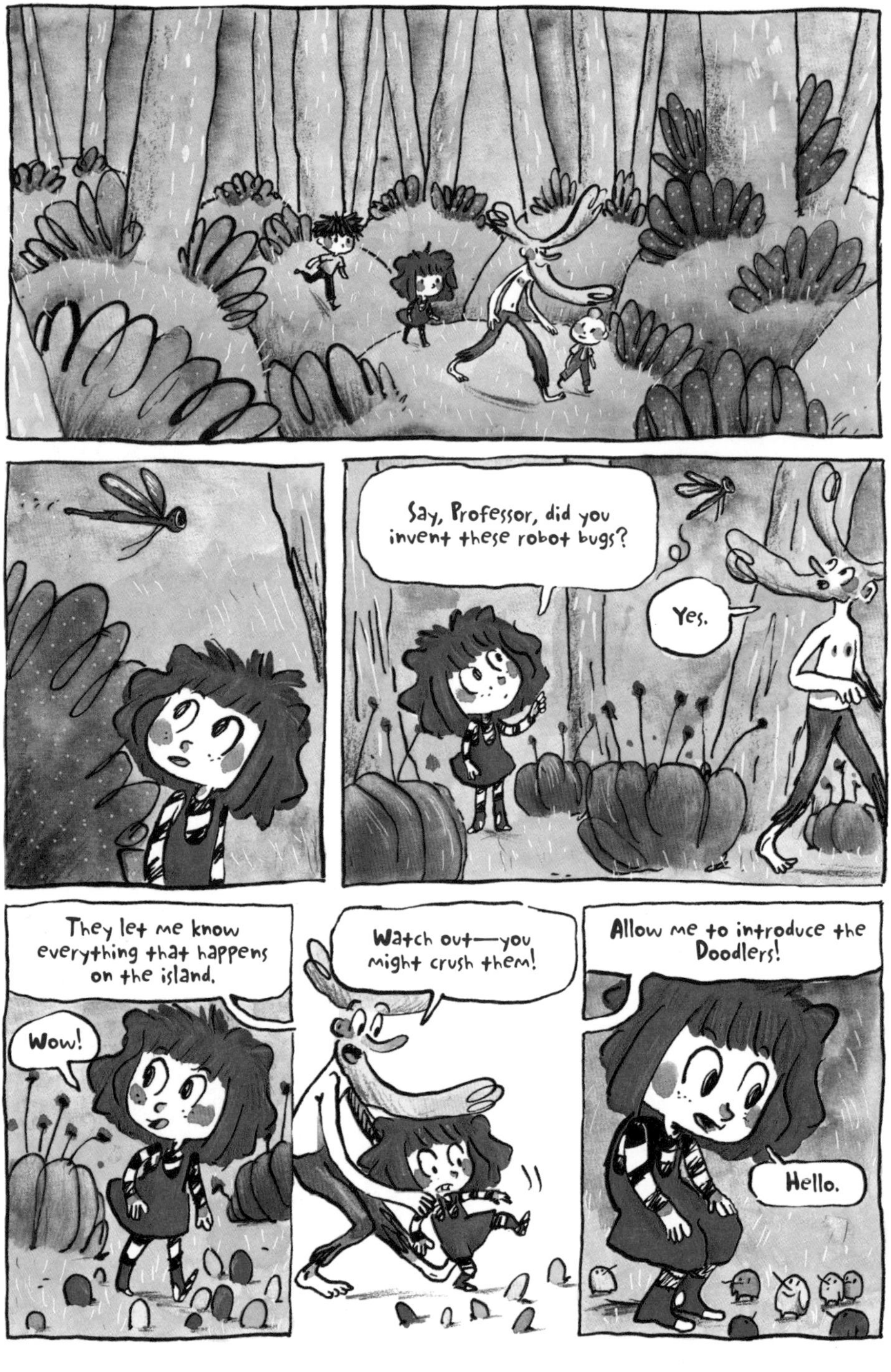
Say, Professor, did you invent these robot bugs?
Yes.
They let me know everything that happens on the island.
Wow!
Watch out—you might crush them!
Allow me to introduce the Doodlers!
Hello.

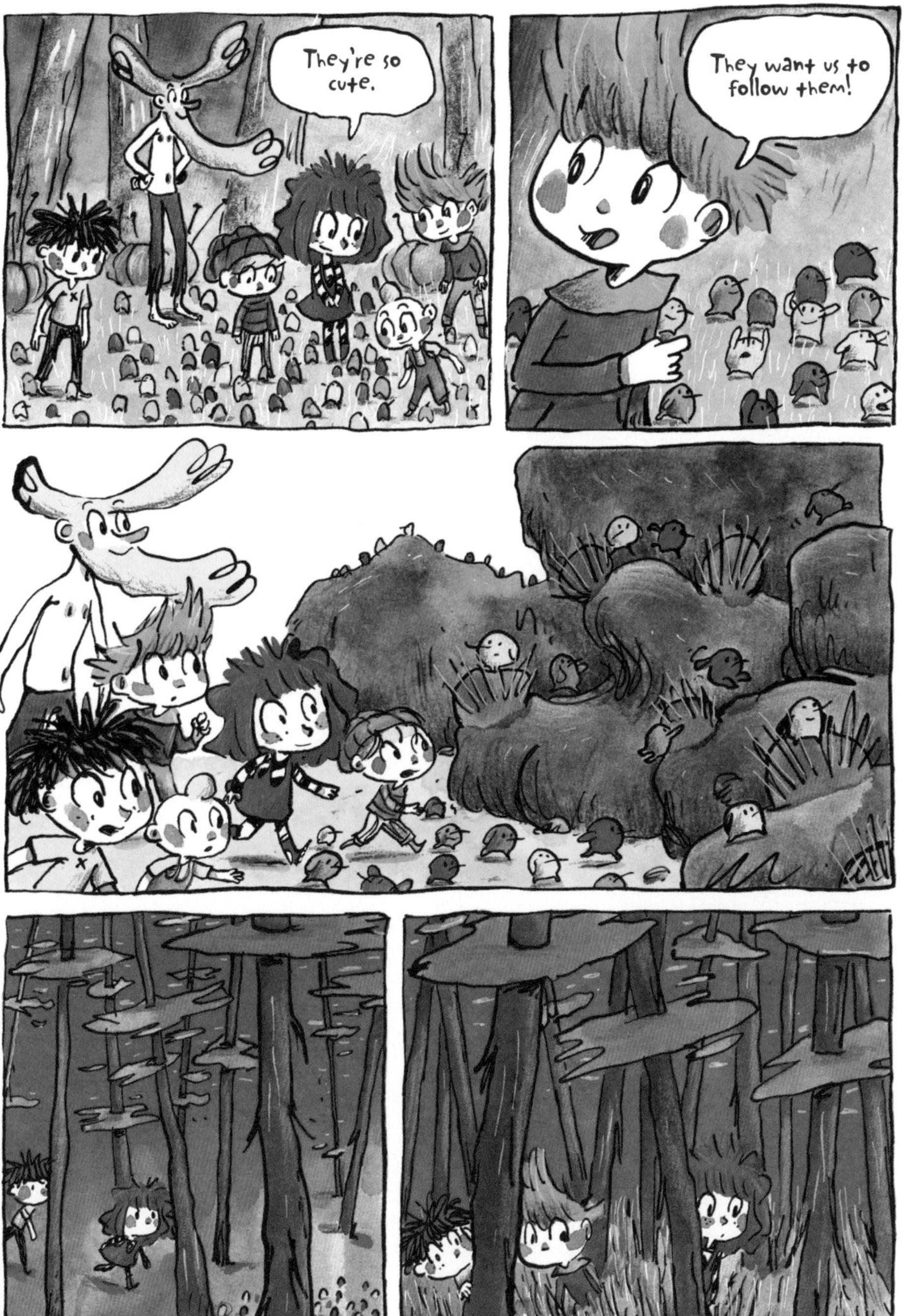
They're so cute.
They want us to follow them!

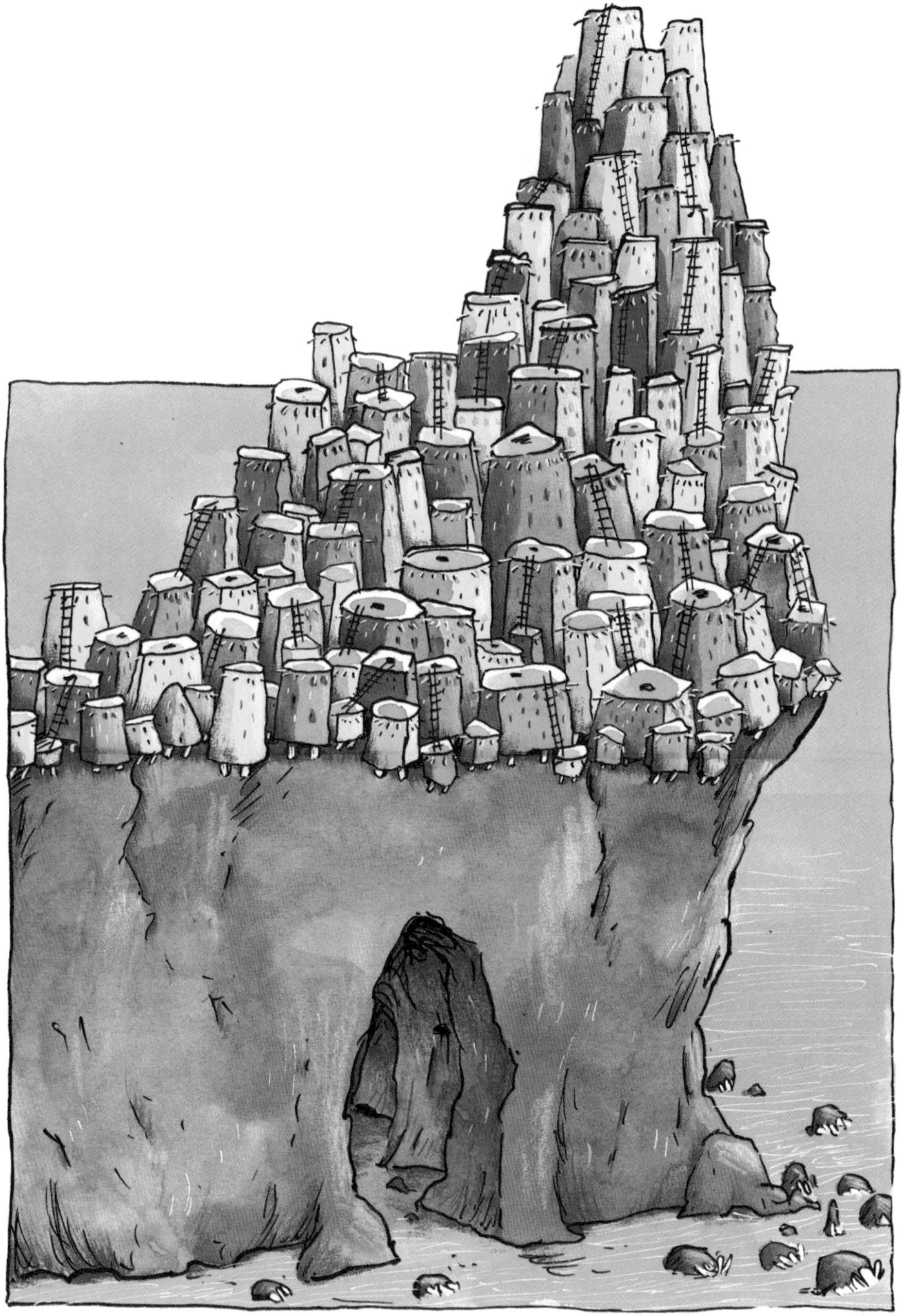

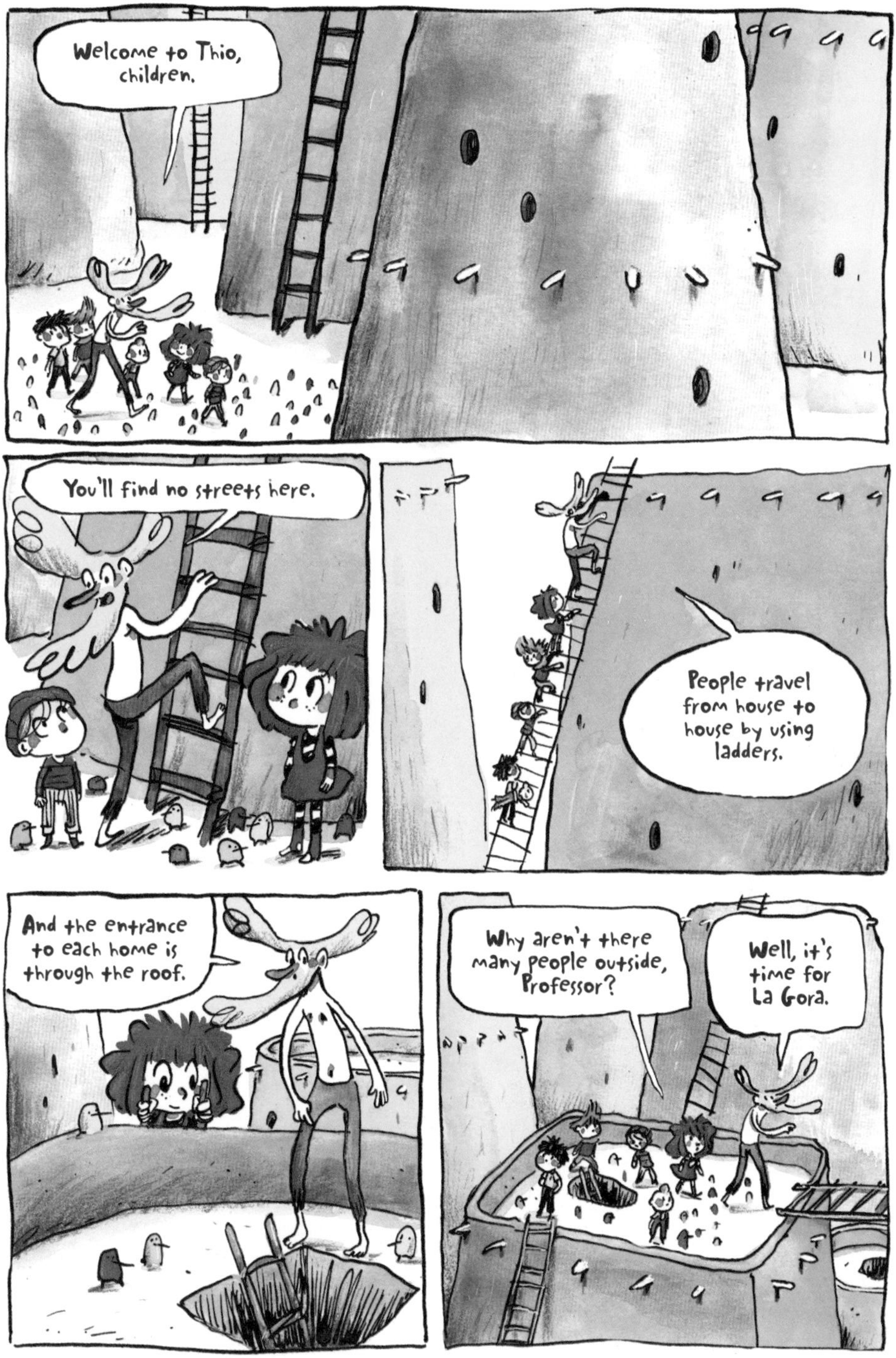
Welcome to Thio, children.
You'll find no streets here.
People travel from house to house by using ladders.
And the entrance to each home is through the roof.
Why aren't there many people outside, Professor?
Well, it's time for La Gora.

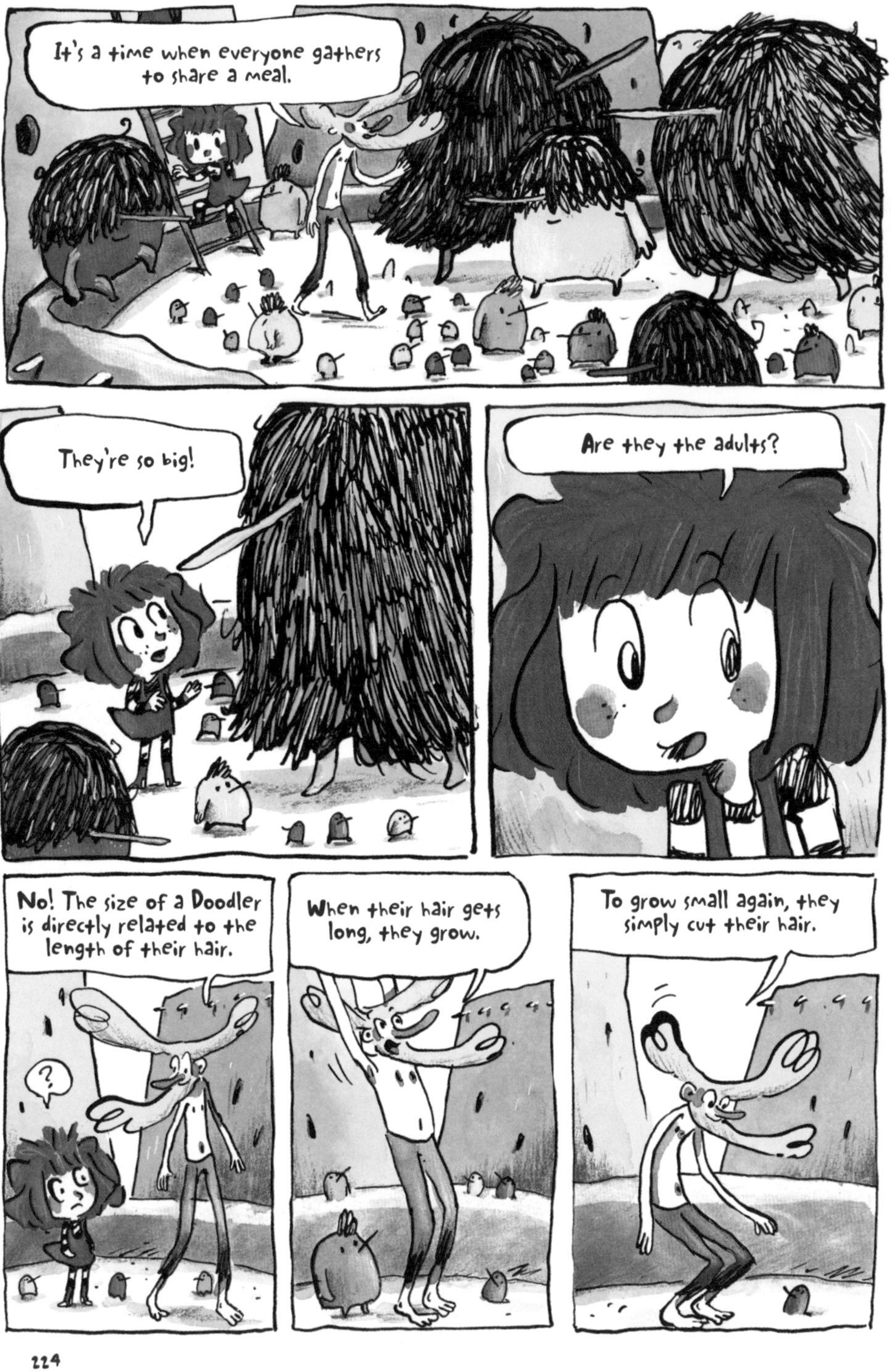
It's a time when everyone gathers to share a meal.
They're so big!
Are they the adults?
No! The size of a Doodler is directly related to the length of their hair.
?
When their hair gets long, they grow.
To grow small again, they simply cut their hair.

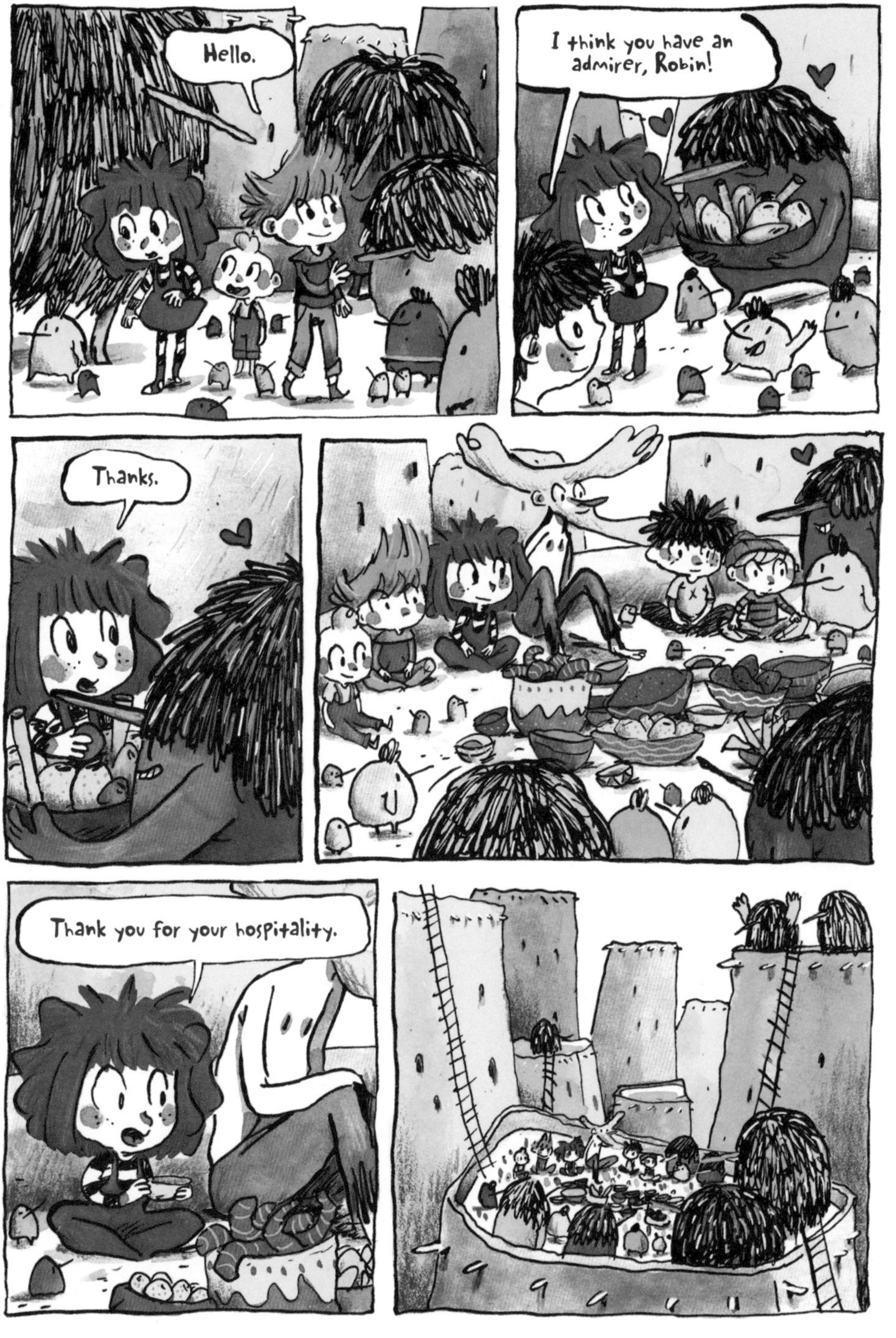
Hello.
I think you have an admirer, Robin!
Thanks.
Thank you for your hospitality.

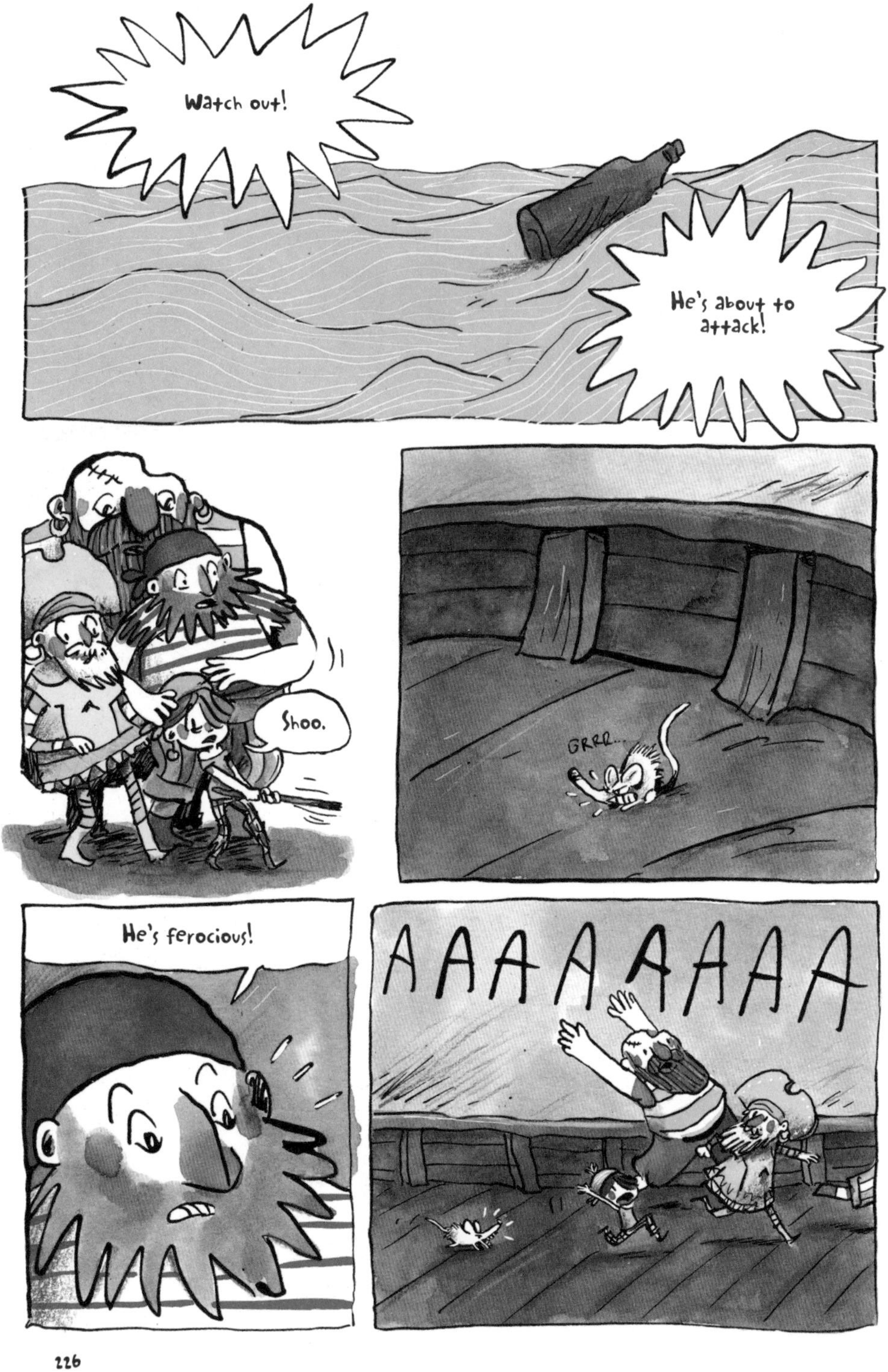

Watch out!
He's about to attack!
Shoo.
GRRR...
He's ferocious!
AAAAAAAA

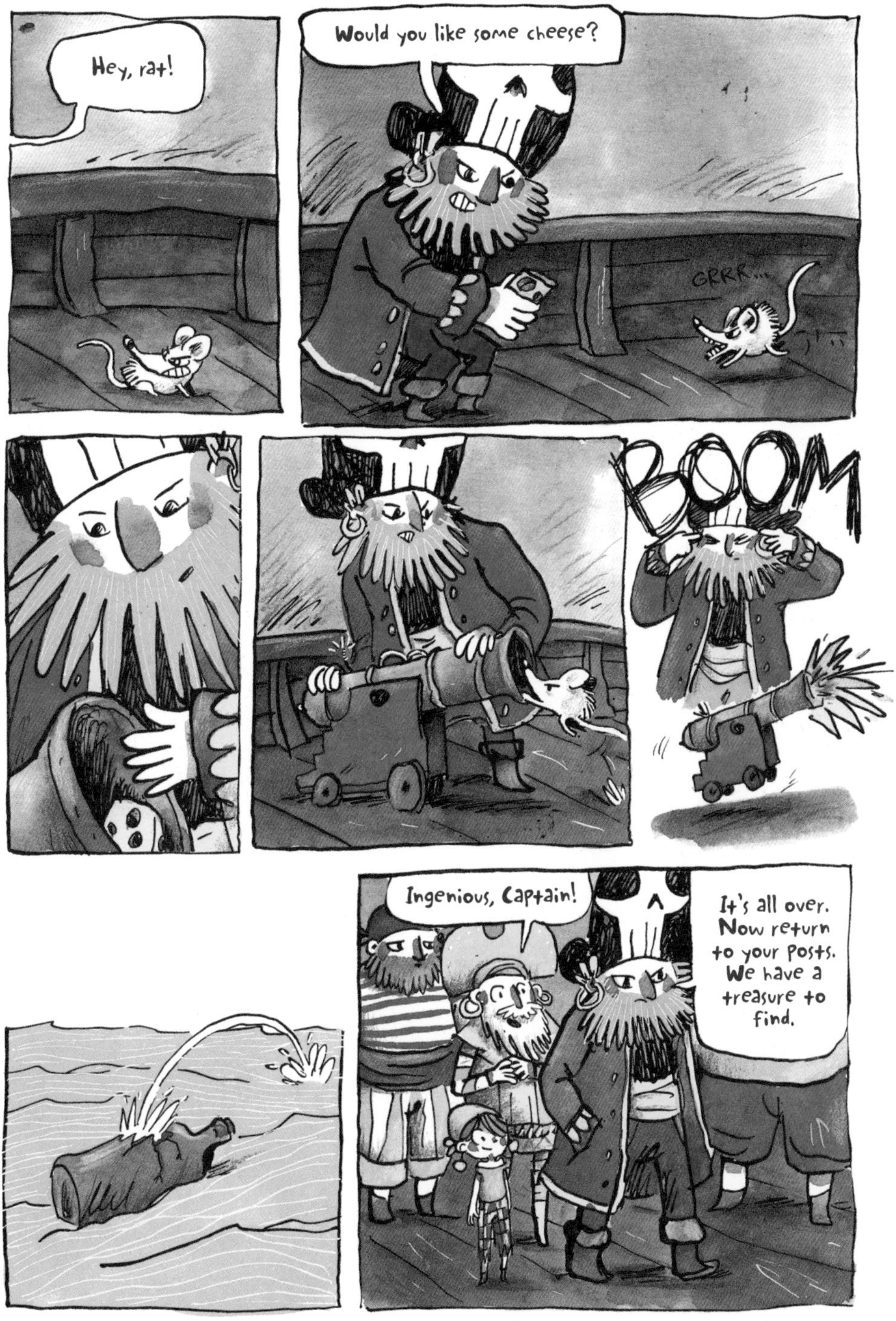
Hey, rat!
Would you like some cheese?
GRRR...
BOOM
Ingenious, Captain!
It's all over. Now return to your posts. We have a treasure to find.

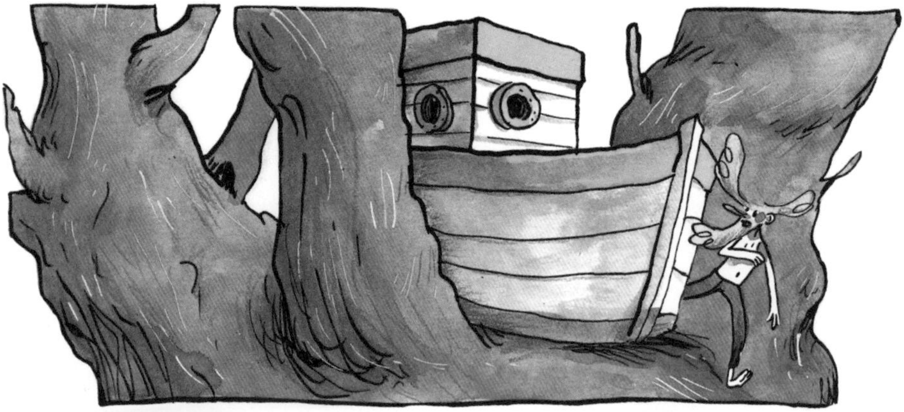

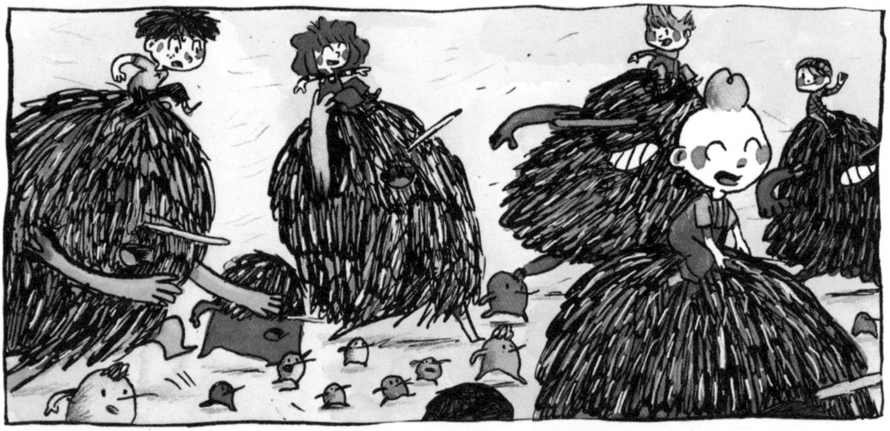

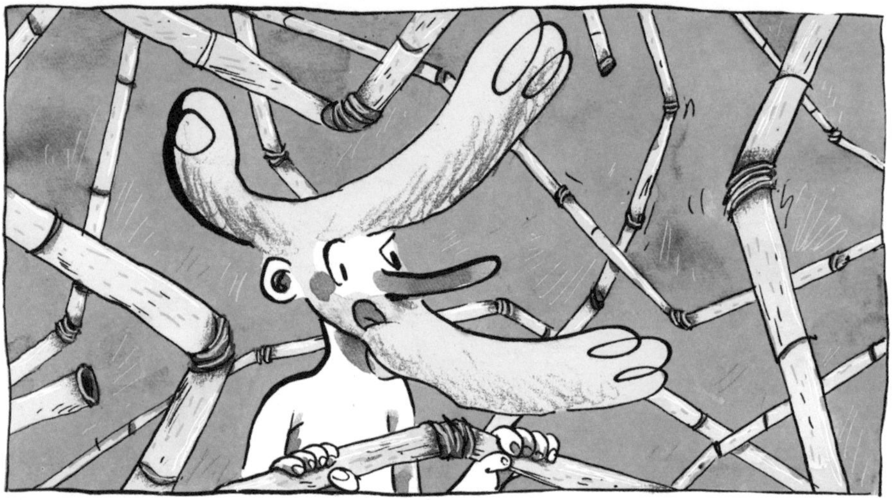

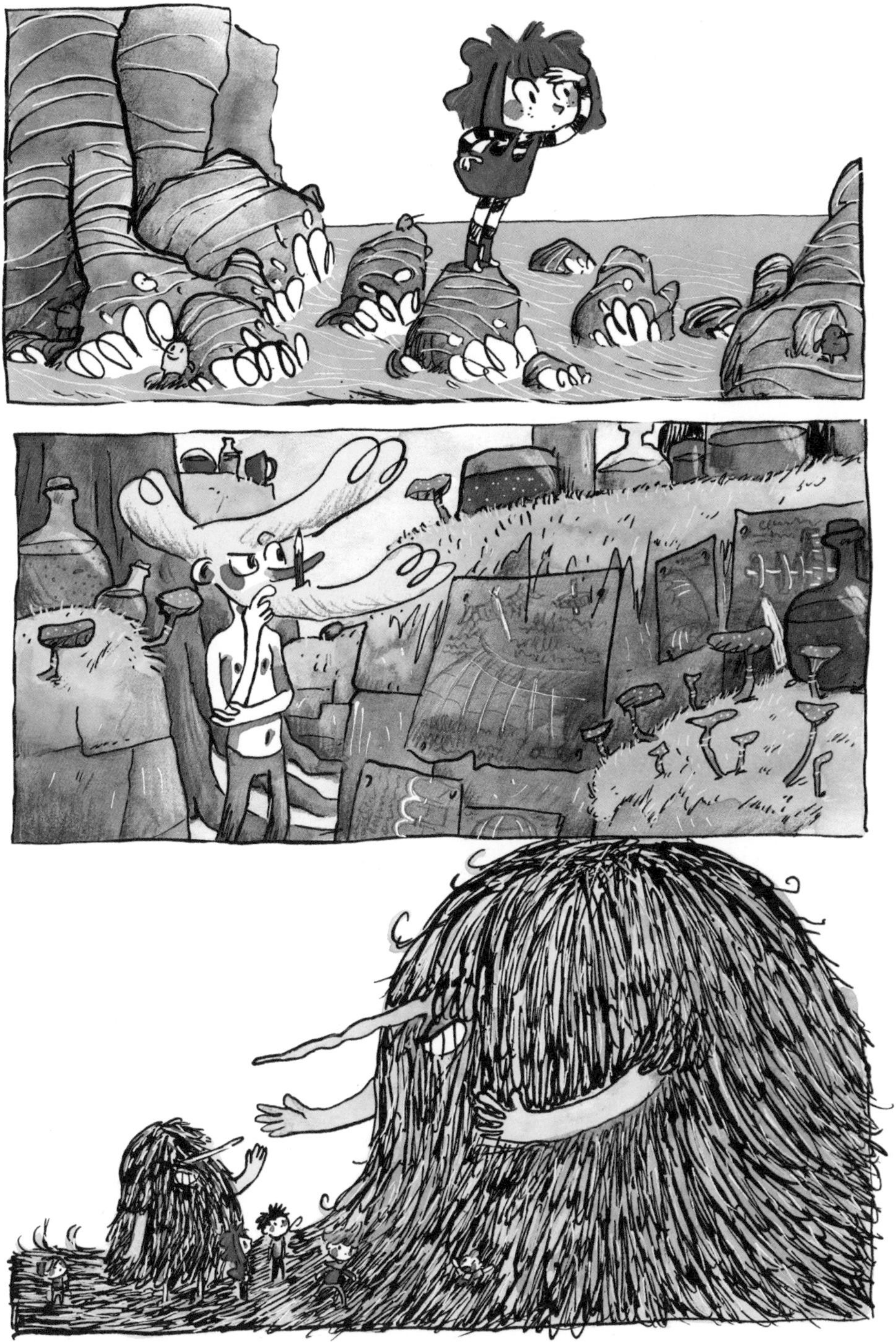

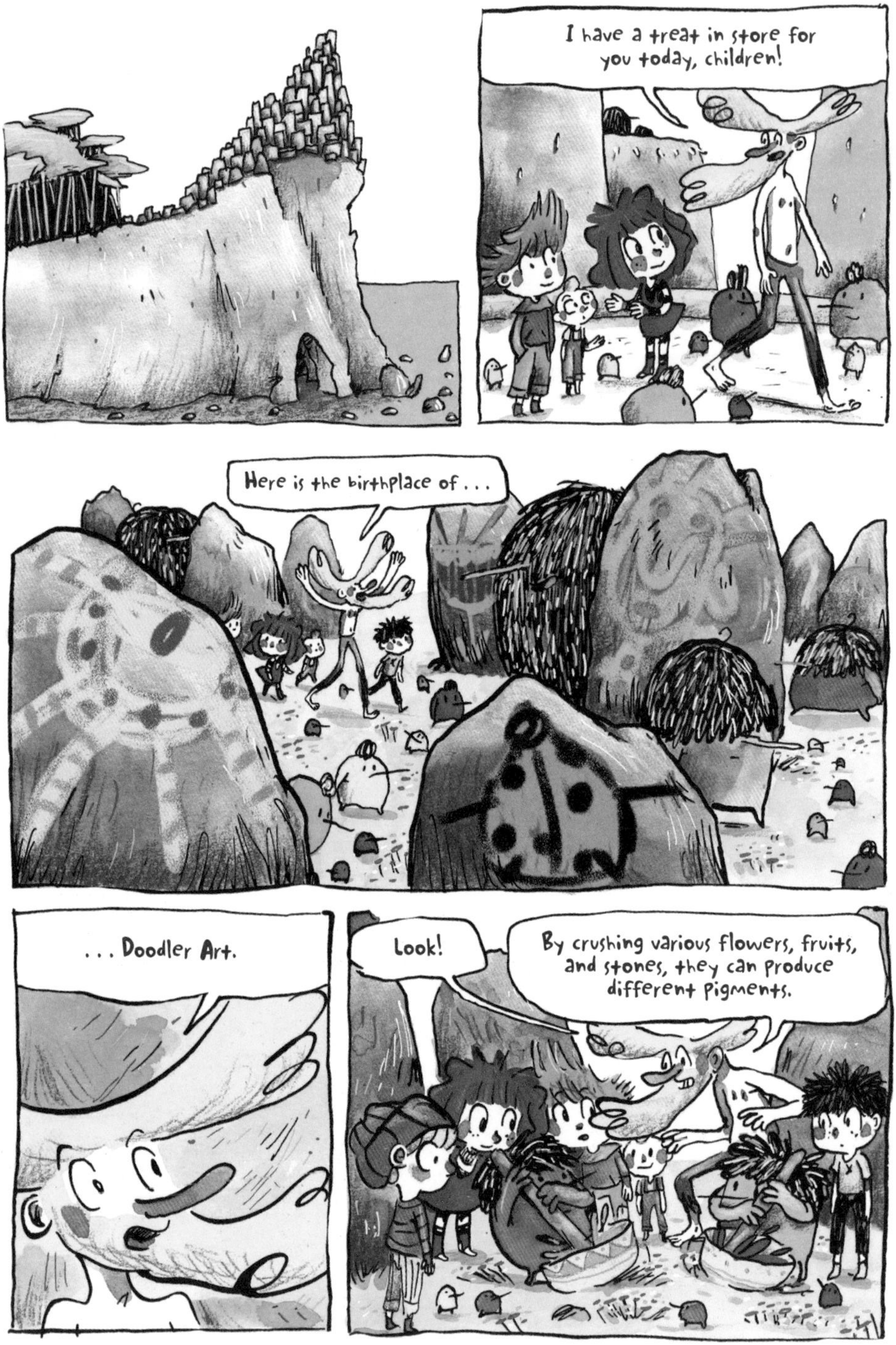
I have a treat in store for you today, children!
Here is the birthplace of . . .
. . . Doodler Art.
Look!
By crushing various flowers, fruits, and stones, they can produce different pigments.

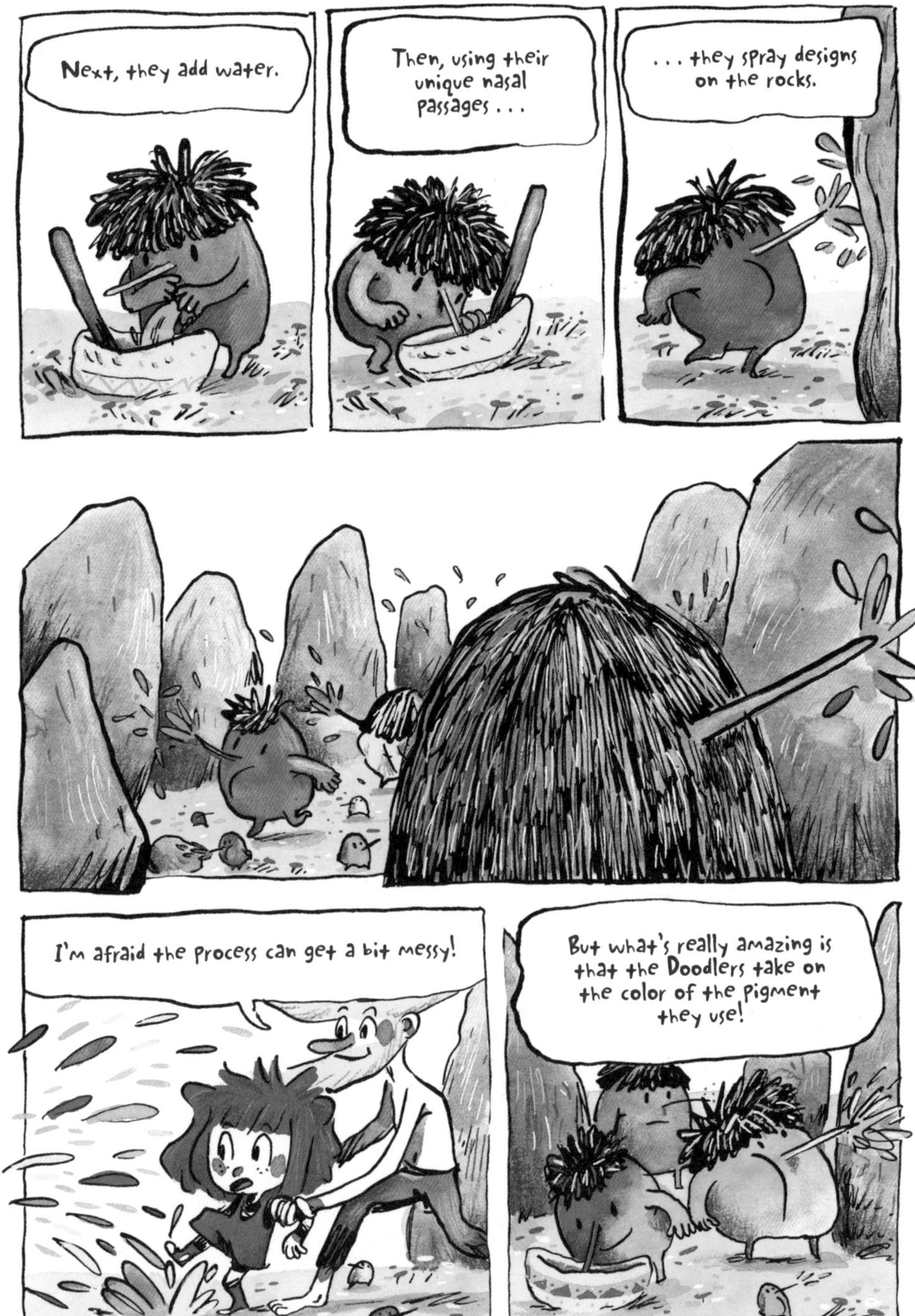
Next, they add water.
Then, using their unique nasal passages . . .
. . . they spray designs on the rocks.
I'm afraid the process can get a bit messy!
But what's really amazing is that the Doodlers take on the color of the pigment they use!

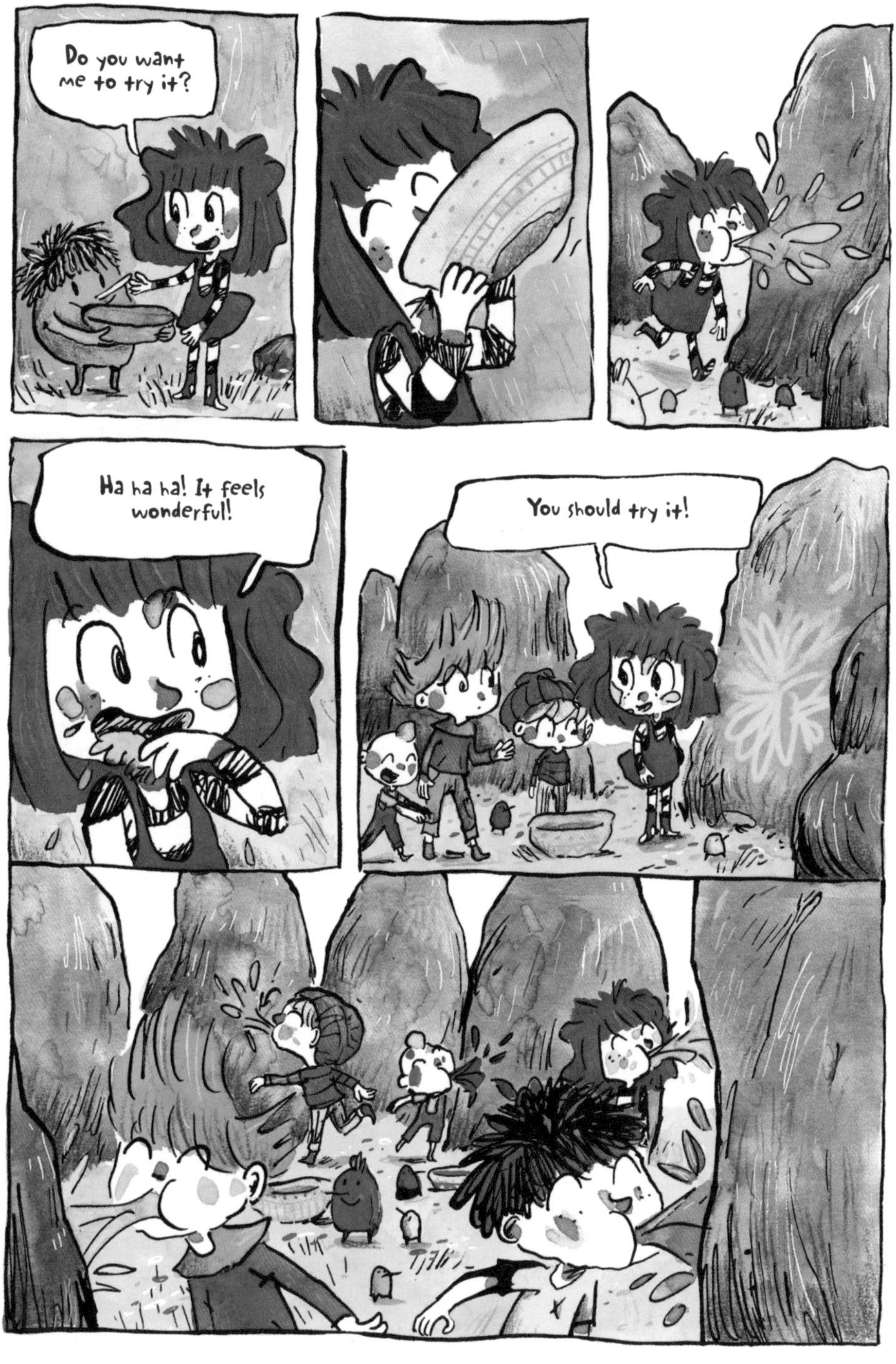
Do you want me to try it?
Ha ha ha! It feels wonderful!
You should try it!

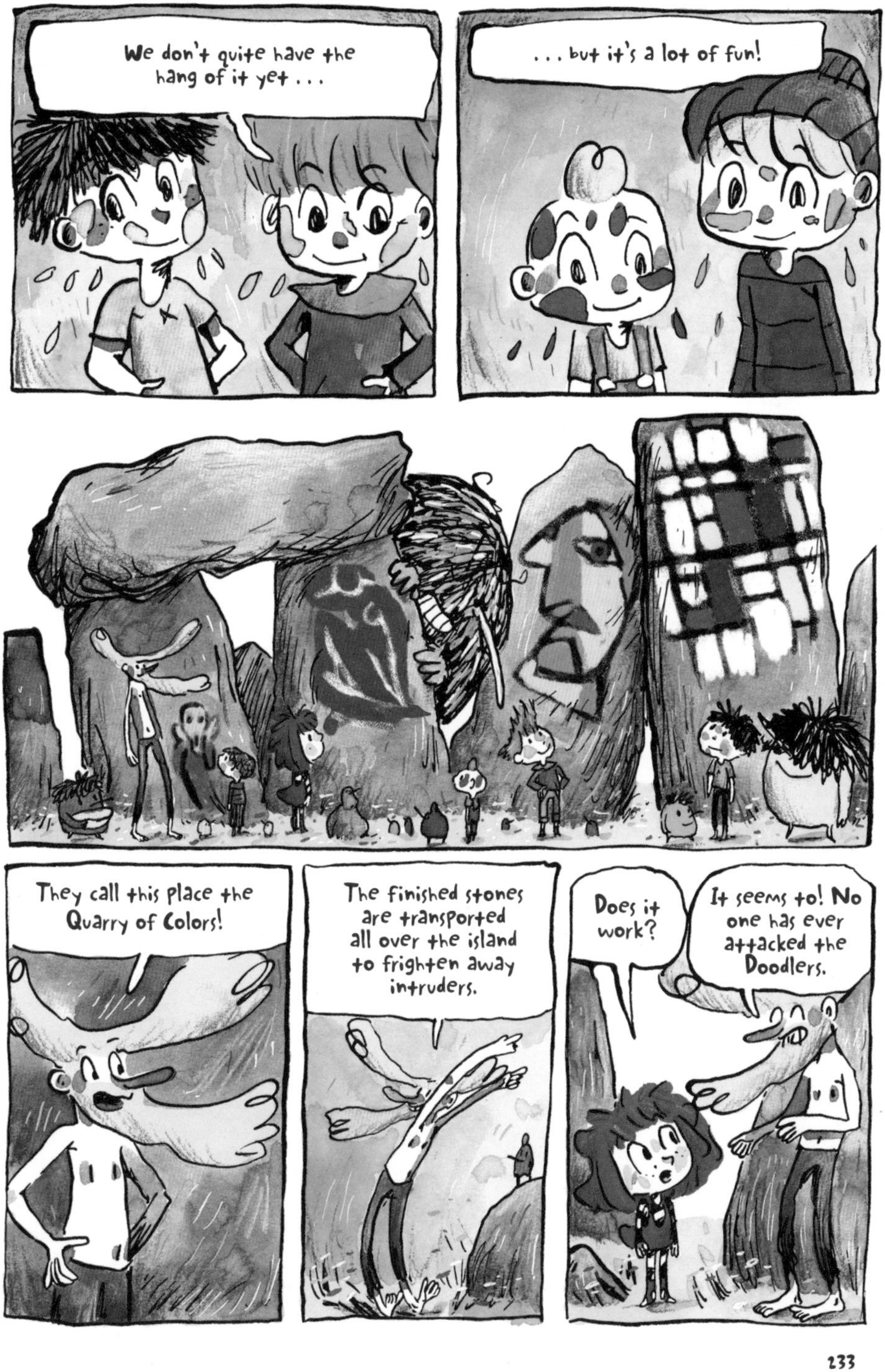
We don't quite have the hang of it yet . . .
. . . but it's a lot of fun!
They call this place the Quarry of Colors!
The finished stones are transported all over the island to frighten away intruders.
Does it work?
It seems to! No one has ever attacked the Doodlers.

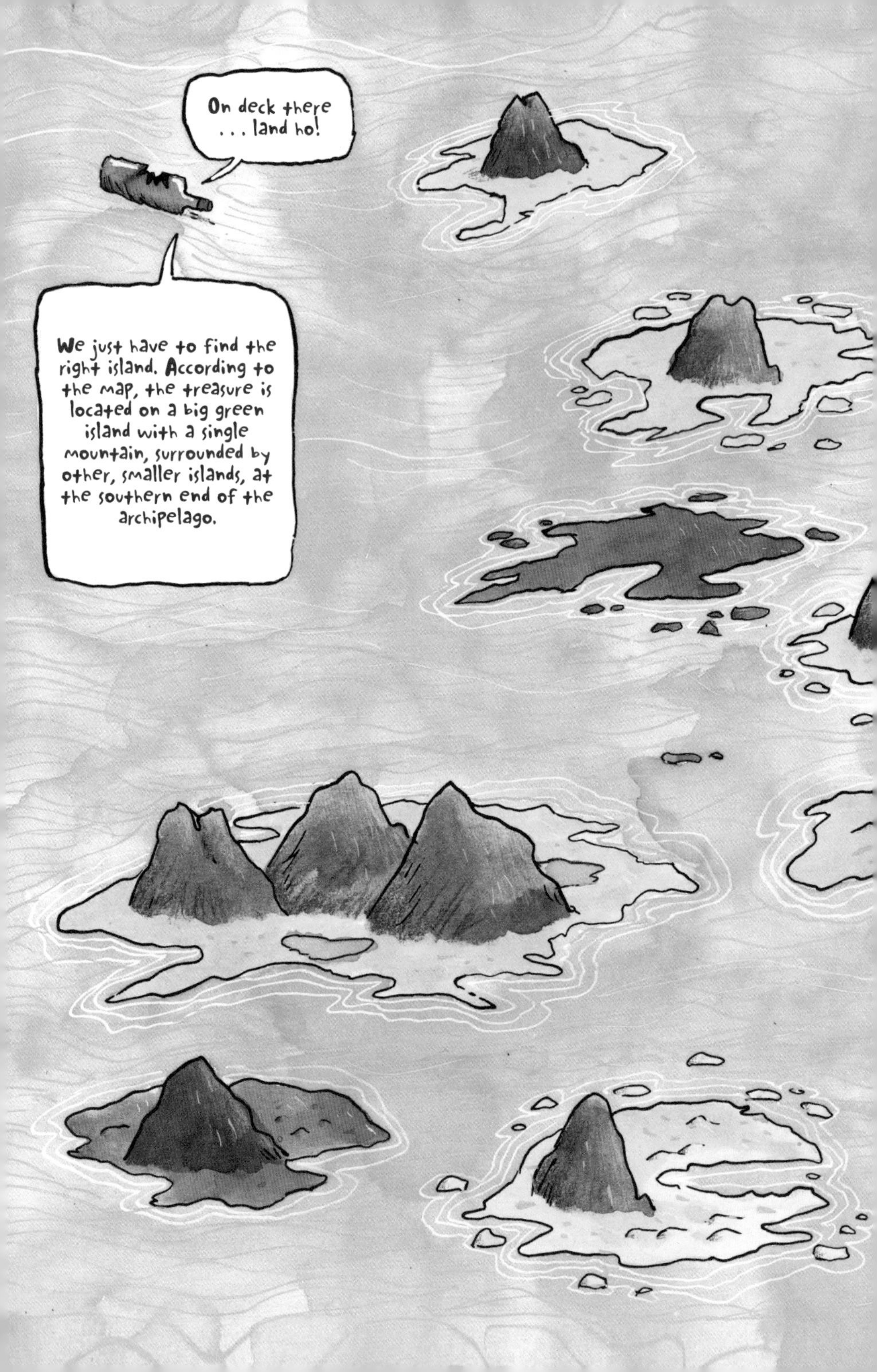
On deck there . . . land ho!
We just have to find the right island. According to the map, the treasure is located on a big green island with a single mountain, surrounded by other, smaller islands, at the southern end of the archipelago.

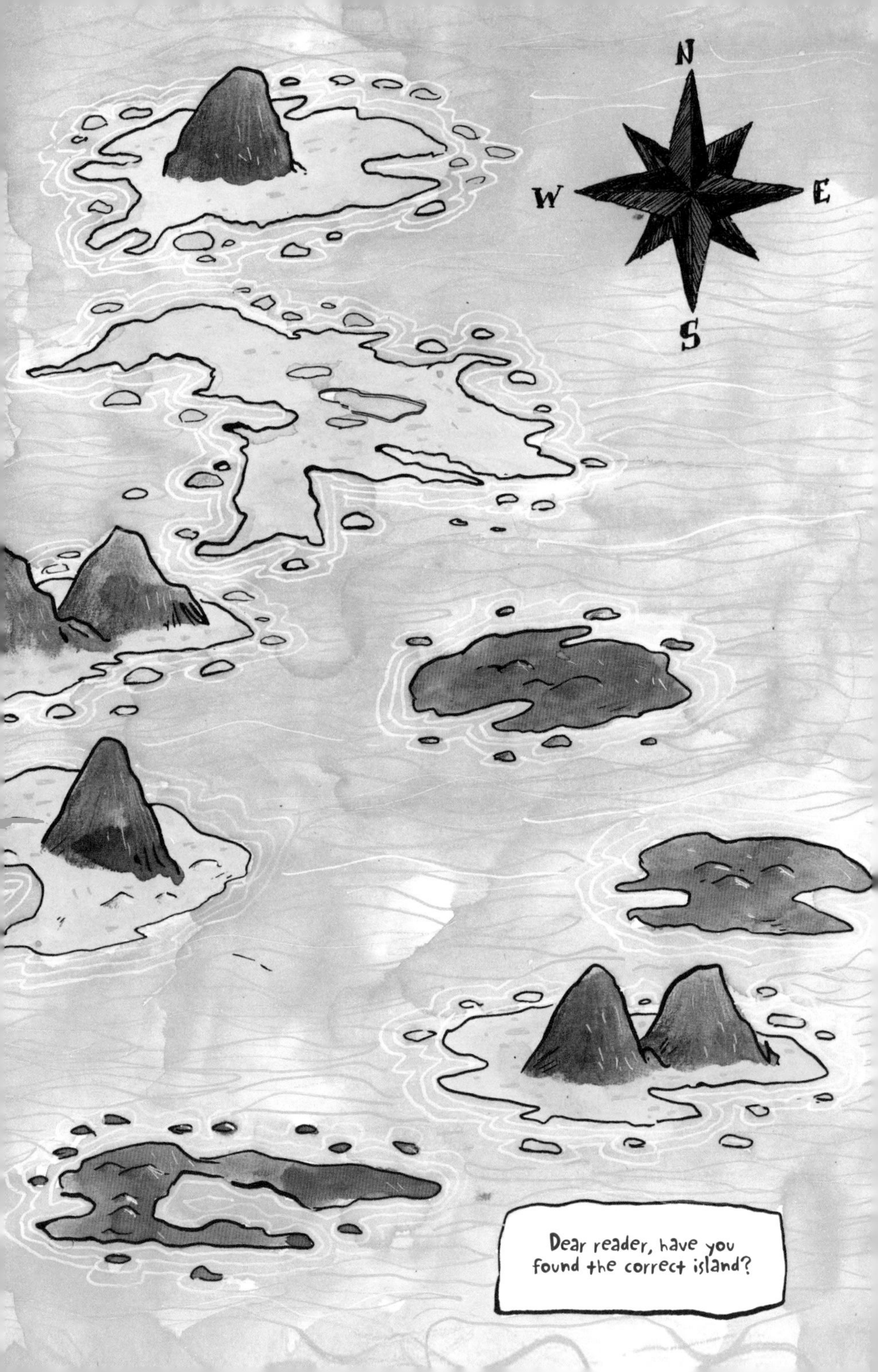
N
W
E
S
Dear reader, have you found the correct island?

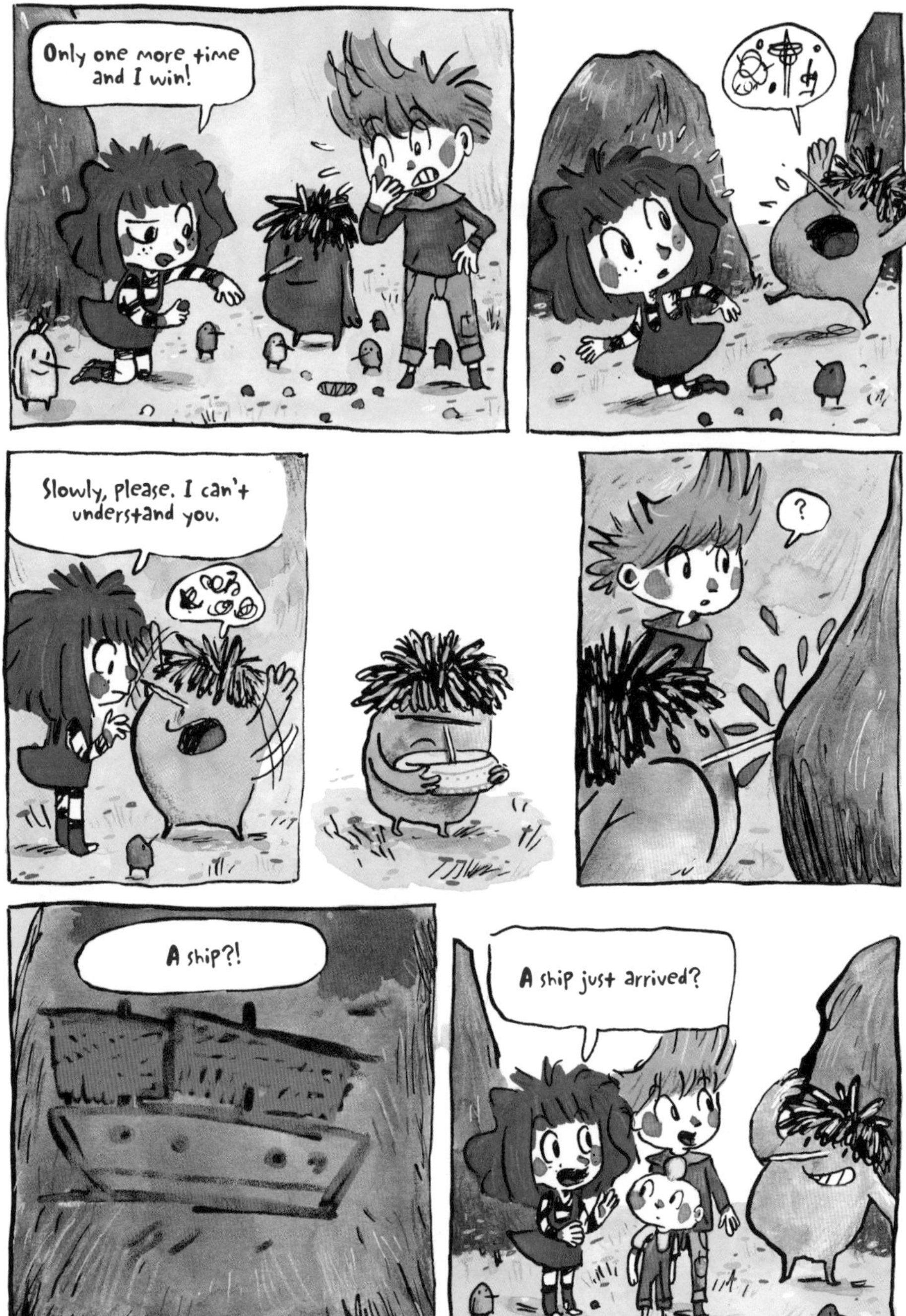
Only one more time and I win!
Slowly, please. I can't understand you.
?
A ship?!
A ship just arrived?

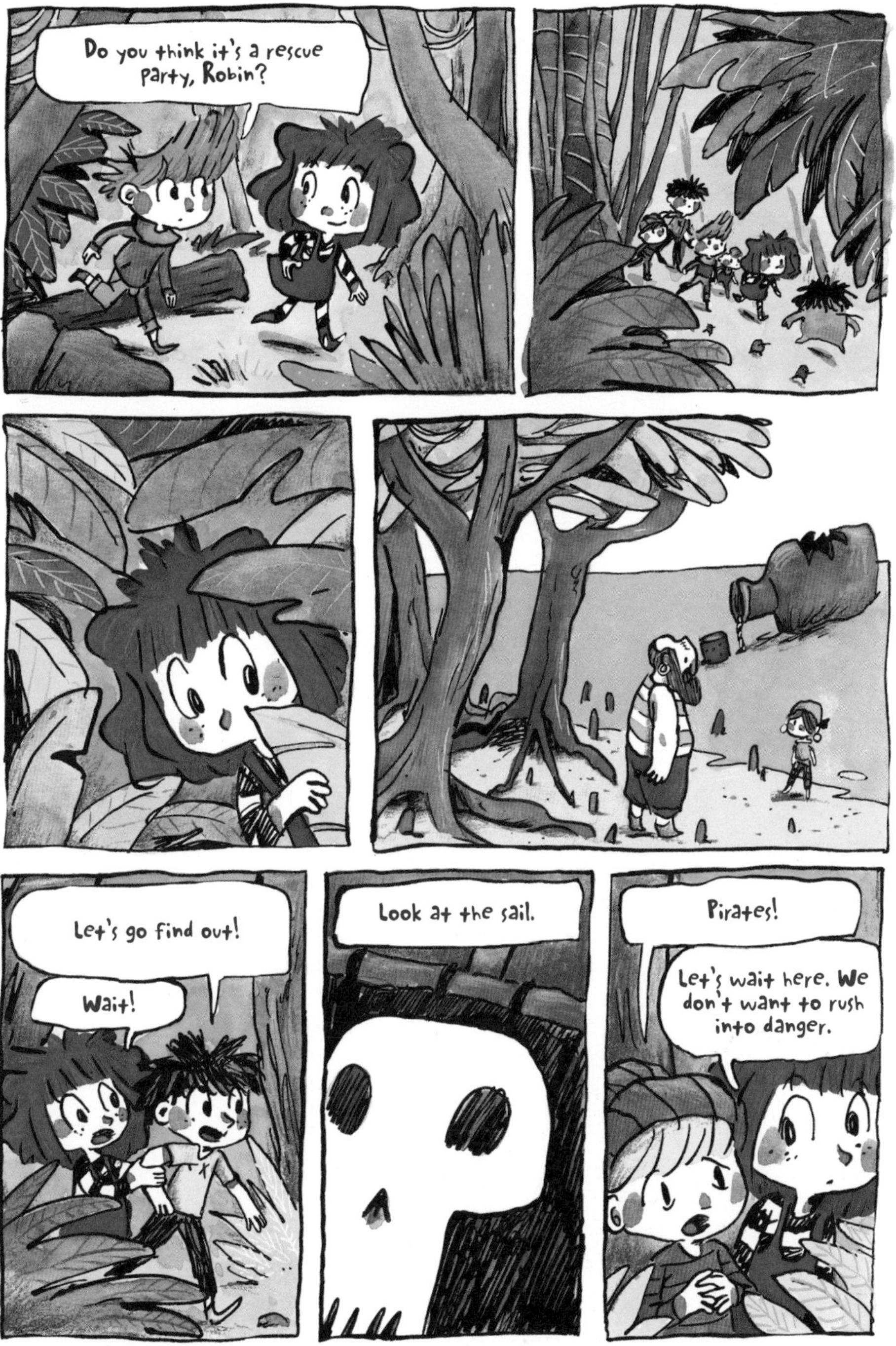
Do you think it's a rescue party, Robin?
Let's go find out!
Wait!
Look at the sail.
Pirates!
Let's wait here. We don't want to rush into danger.

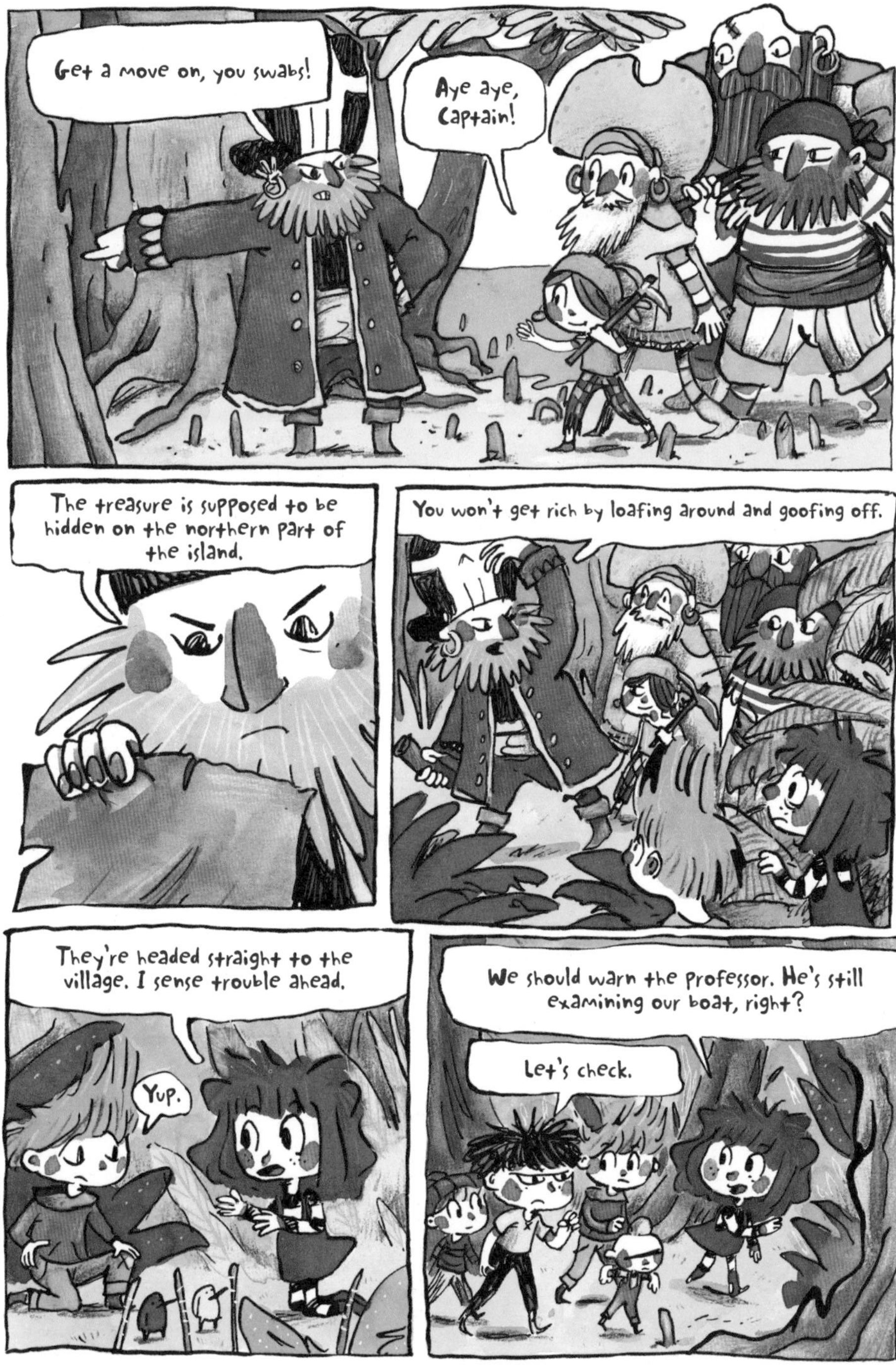
Get a move on, you swabs!
Aye aye, Captain!
The treasure is supposed to be hidden on the northern part of the island.
You won't get rich by loafing around and goofing off.
They're headed straight to the village. I sense trouble ahead.
Yup.
We should warn the professor. He's still examining our boat, right?
Let's check.

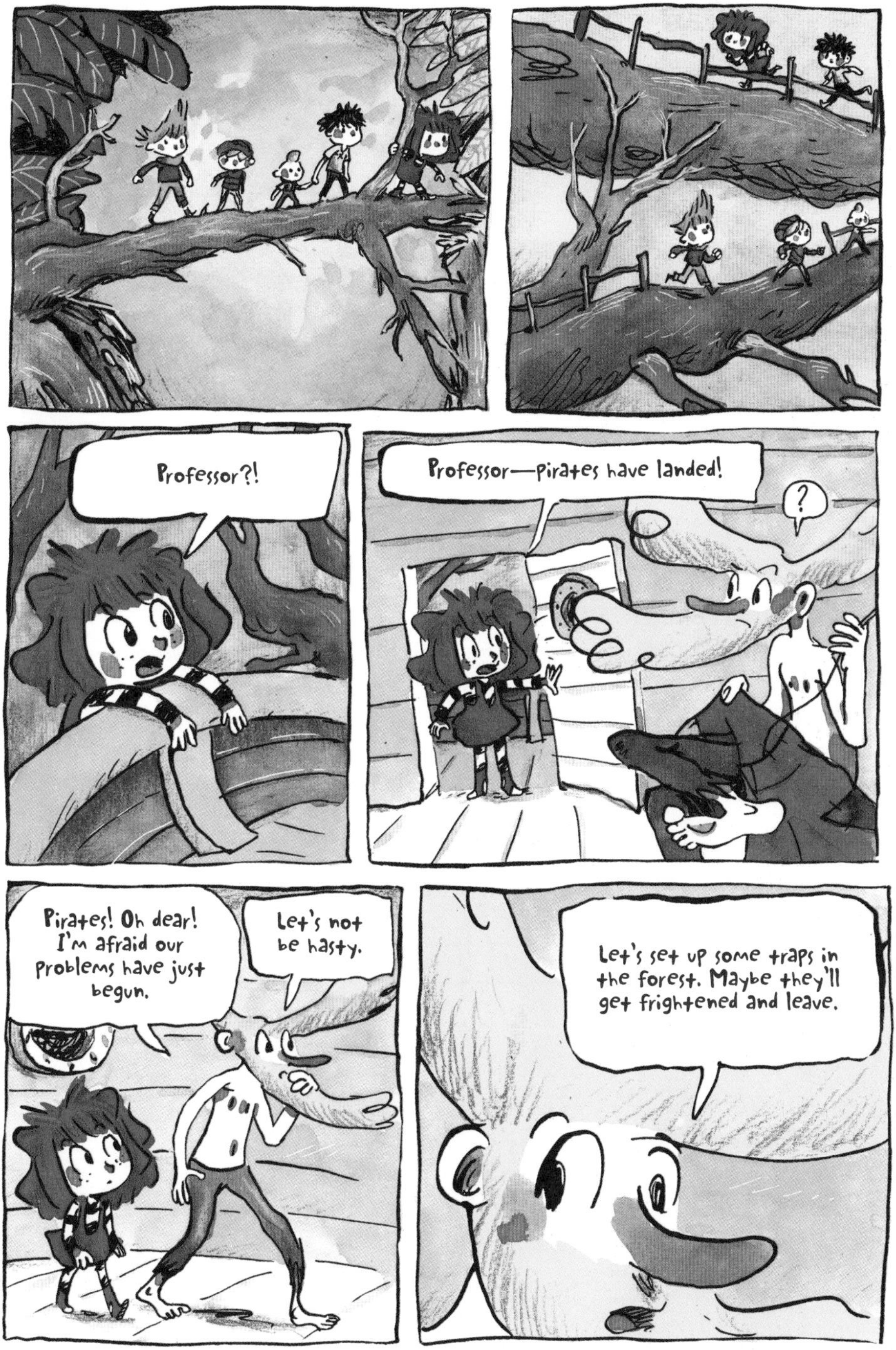
Professor?!
Professor—pirates have landed!
?
Pirates! Oh dear! I'm afraid our problems have just begun.
Let's not be hasty.
Let's set up some traps in the forest. Maybe they'll get frightened and leave.

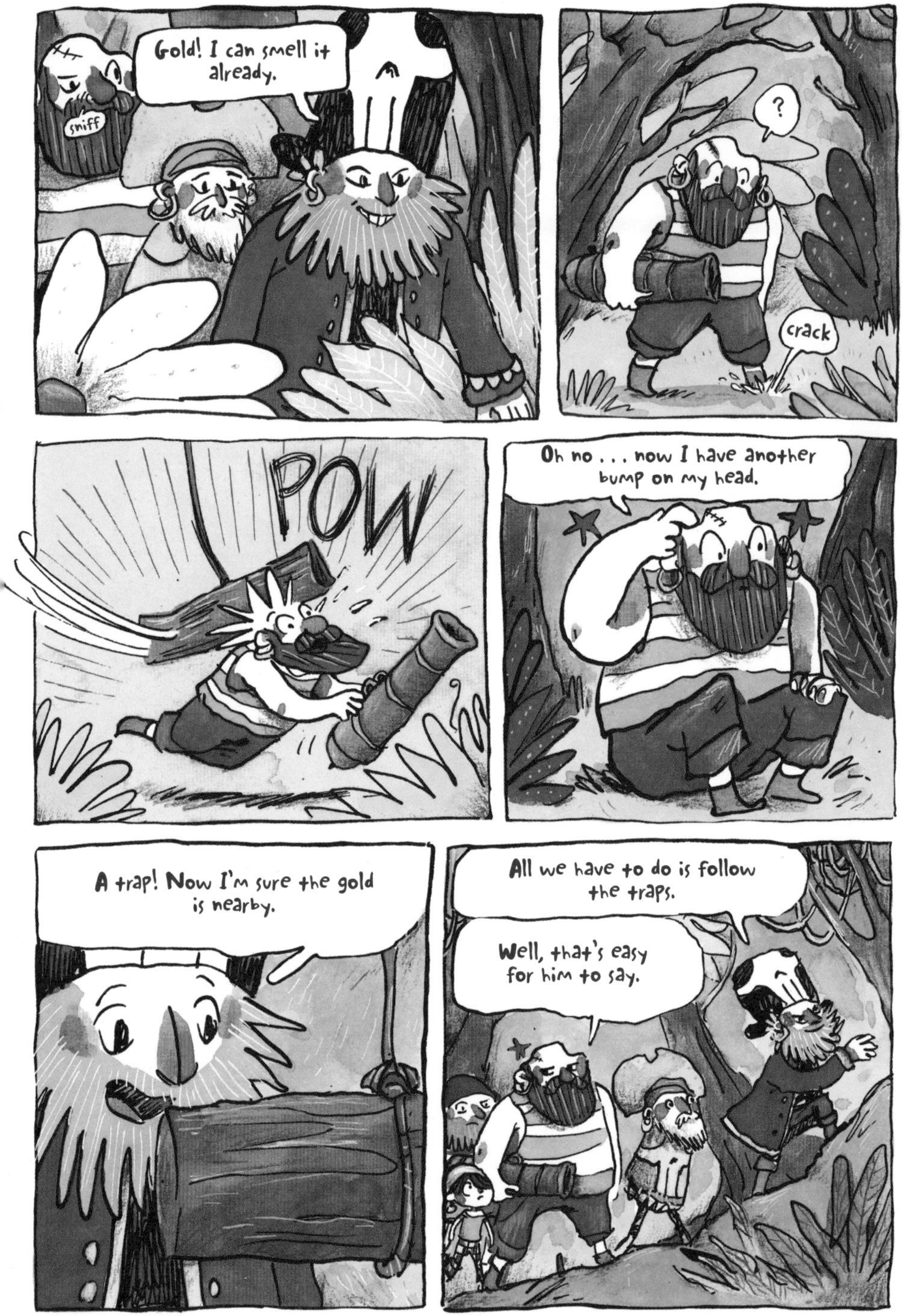
Gold! I can smell it already.
sniff
?
crack
POW
Oh no . . . now I have another bump on my head.
A trap! Now I'm sure the gold is nearby.
All we have to do is follow the traps.
Well, that's easy for him to say.

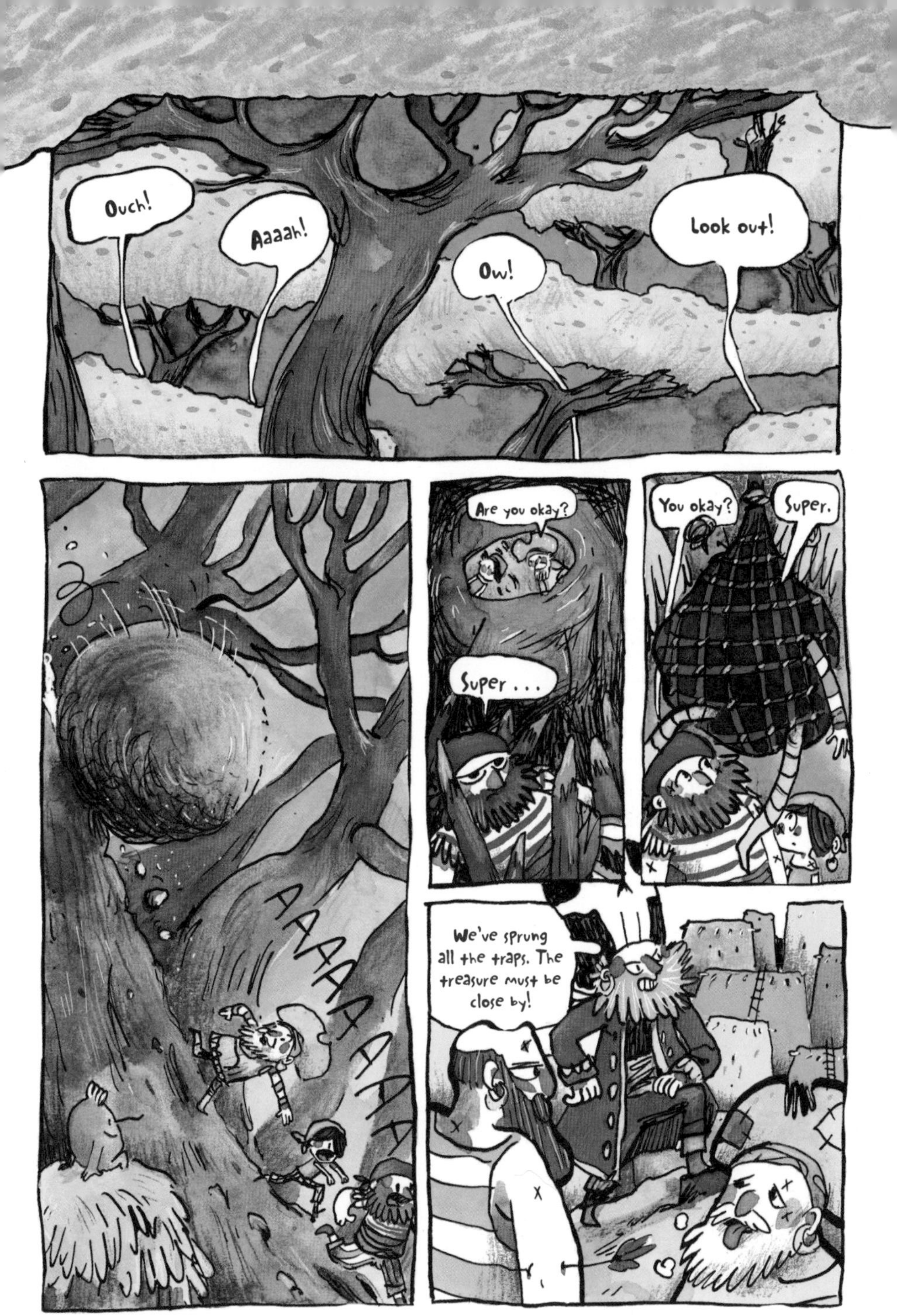
Ouch!
Aaaah!
Ow!
Look out!
AAAAAAAAA
Are you okay?
Super . . .
You okay?
Super.
We've sprung all the traps. The treasure must be close by!

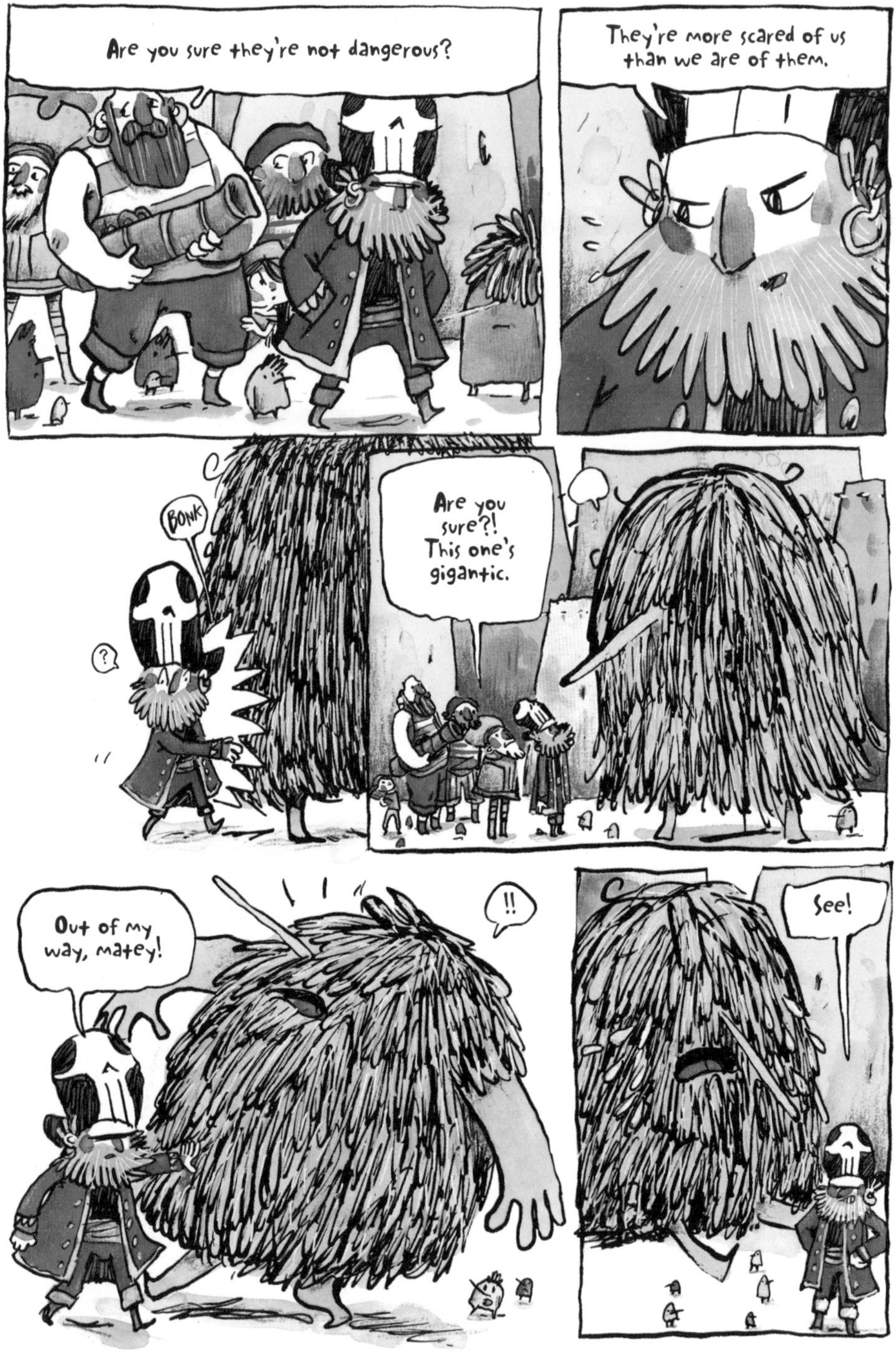
Are you sure they're not dangerous?
They're more scared of us than we are of them.
BONK
?
Are you sure?! This one's gigantic.
Out of my way, matey!
!!
See!

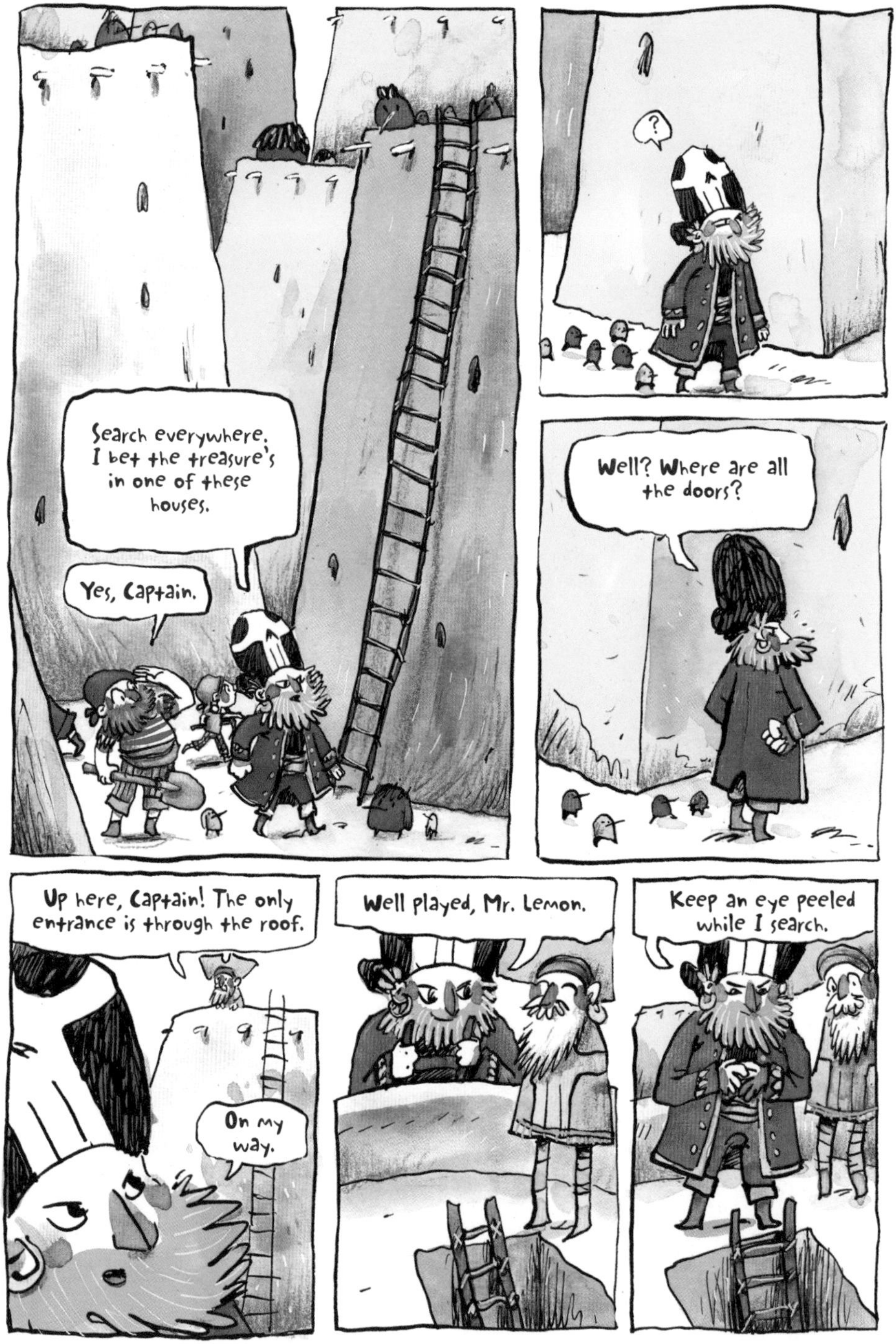
Search everywhere. I bet the treasure's in one of these houses.
Yes, Captain.
?
Well? Where are all the doors?
Up here, Captain! The only entrance is through the roof.
On my way.
Well played, Mr. Lemon.
Keep an eye peeled while I search.

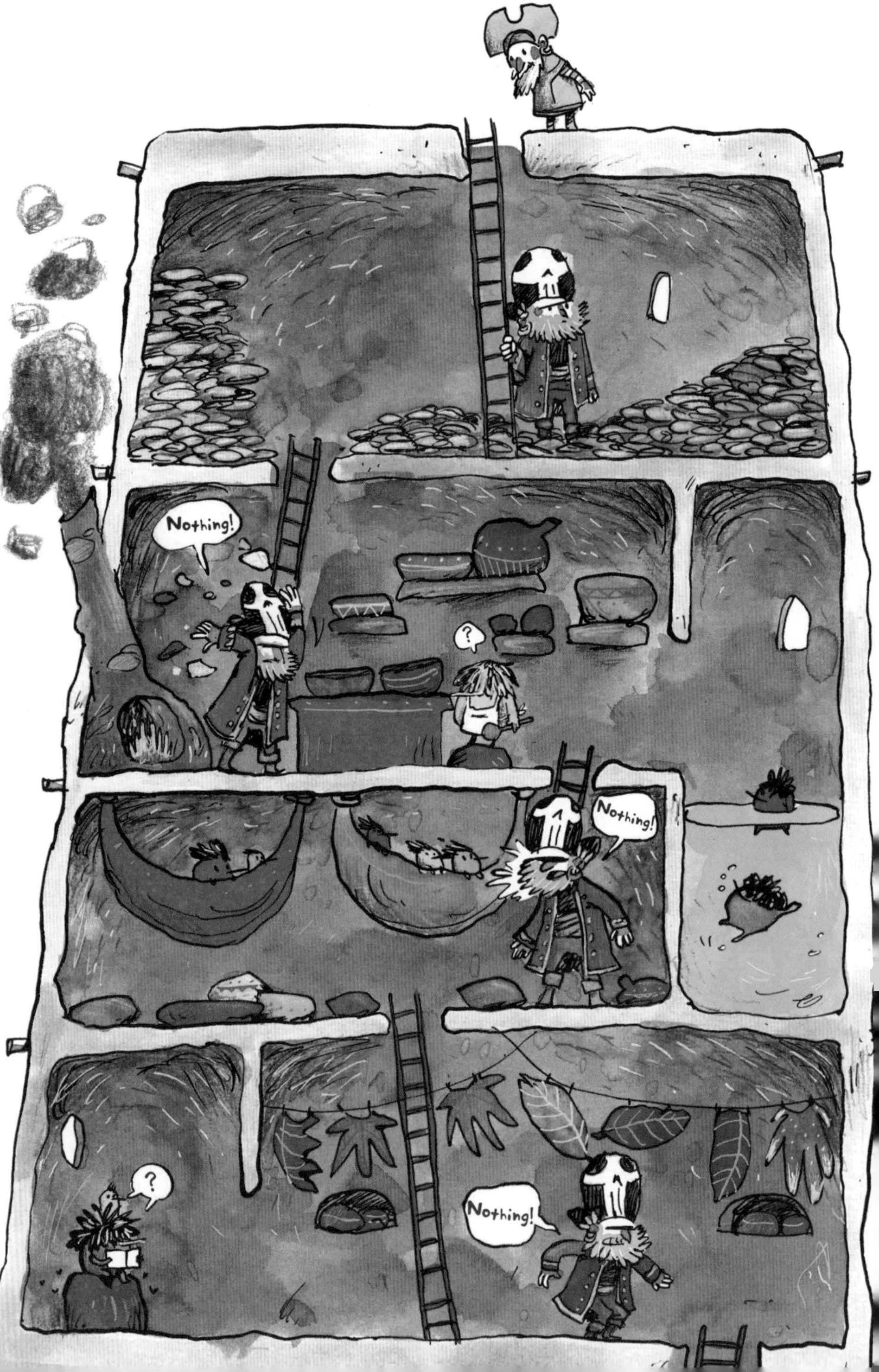

Nothing!
?
Nothing!
?
Nothing!

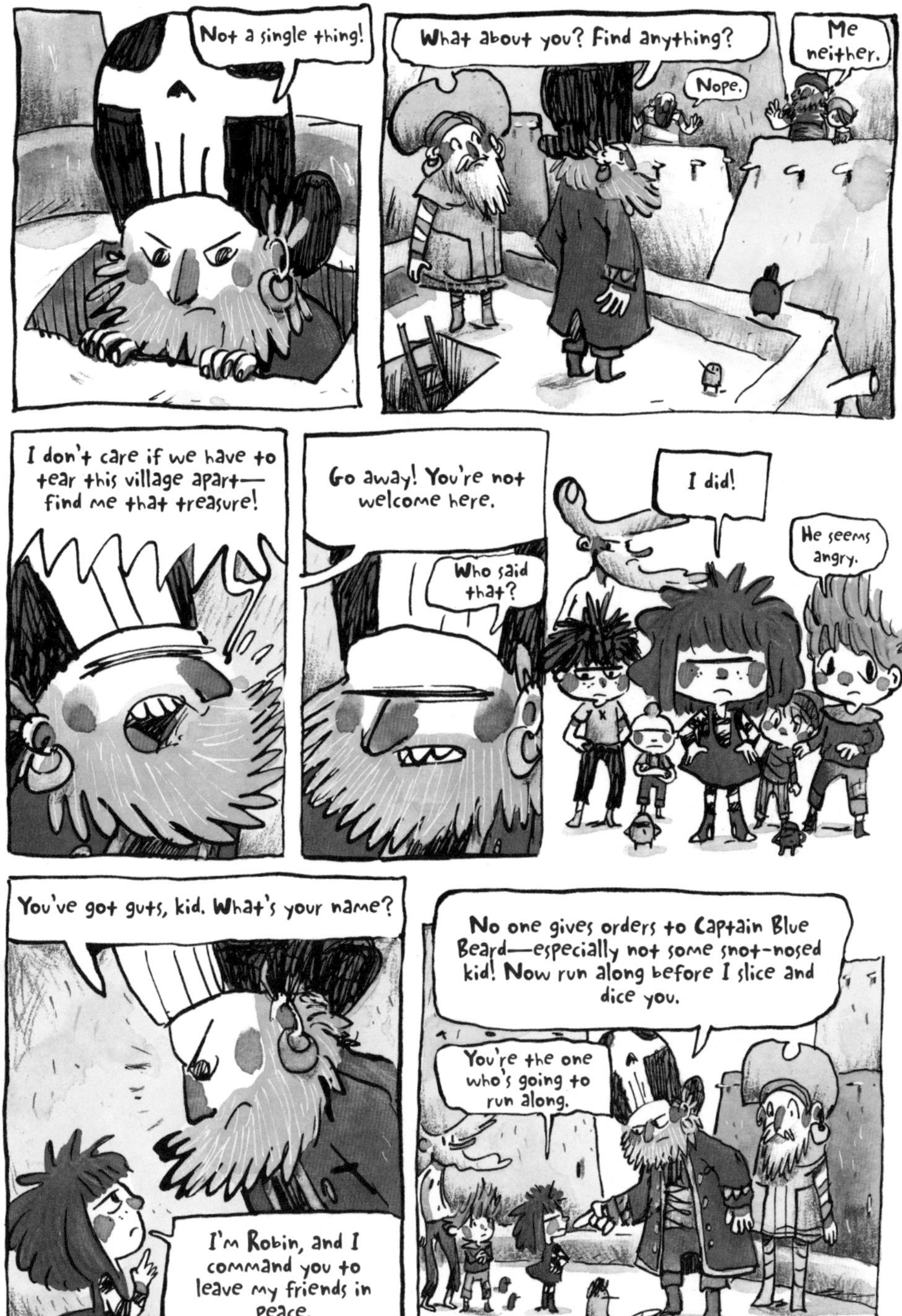
Not a single thing!
What about you? Find anything?
Nope.
Me neither.
I don't care if we have to tear this village apart—find me that treasure!
Go away! You're not welcome here.
Who said that?
I did!
He seems angry.
You've got guts, kid. What's your name?
I'm Robin, and I command you to leave my friends in peace.
No one gives orders to Captain Blue Beard—especially not some snot-nosed kid! Now run along before I slice and dice you.
You're the one who's going to run along.

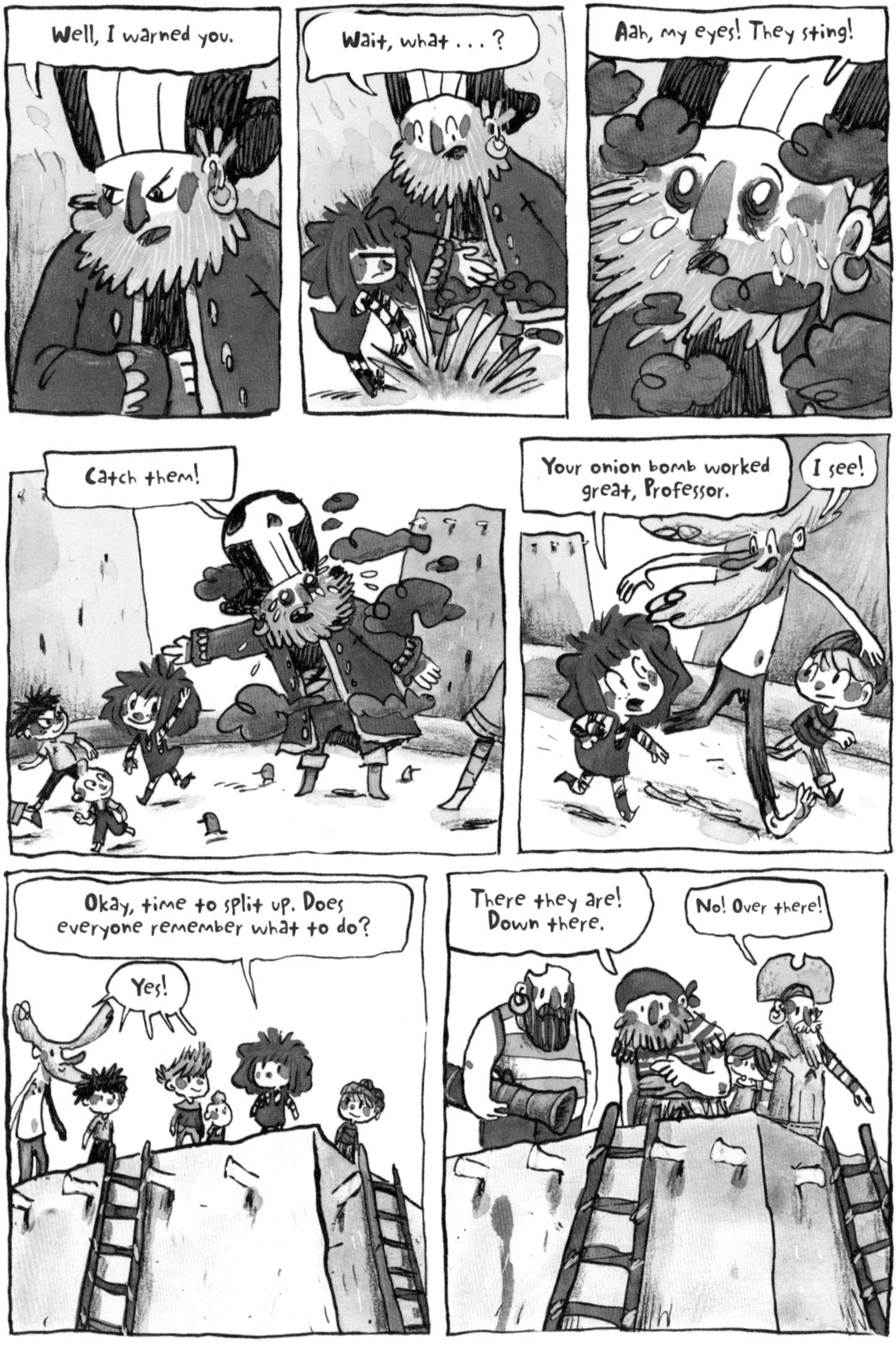
Well, I warned you.
Wait, what . . . ?
Aah, my eyes! They sting!
Catch them!
Your onion bomb worked great, Professor.
I see!
Okay, time to split up. Does everyone remember what to do?
Yes!
There they are! Down there.
No! Over there!

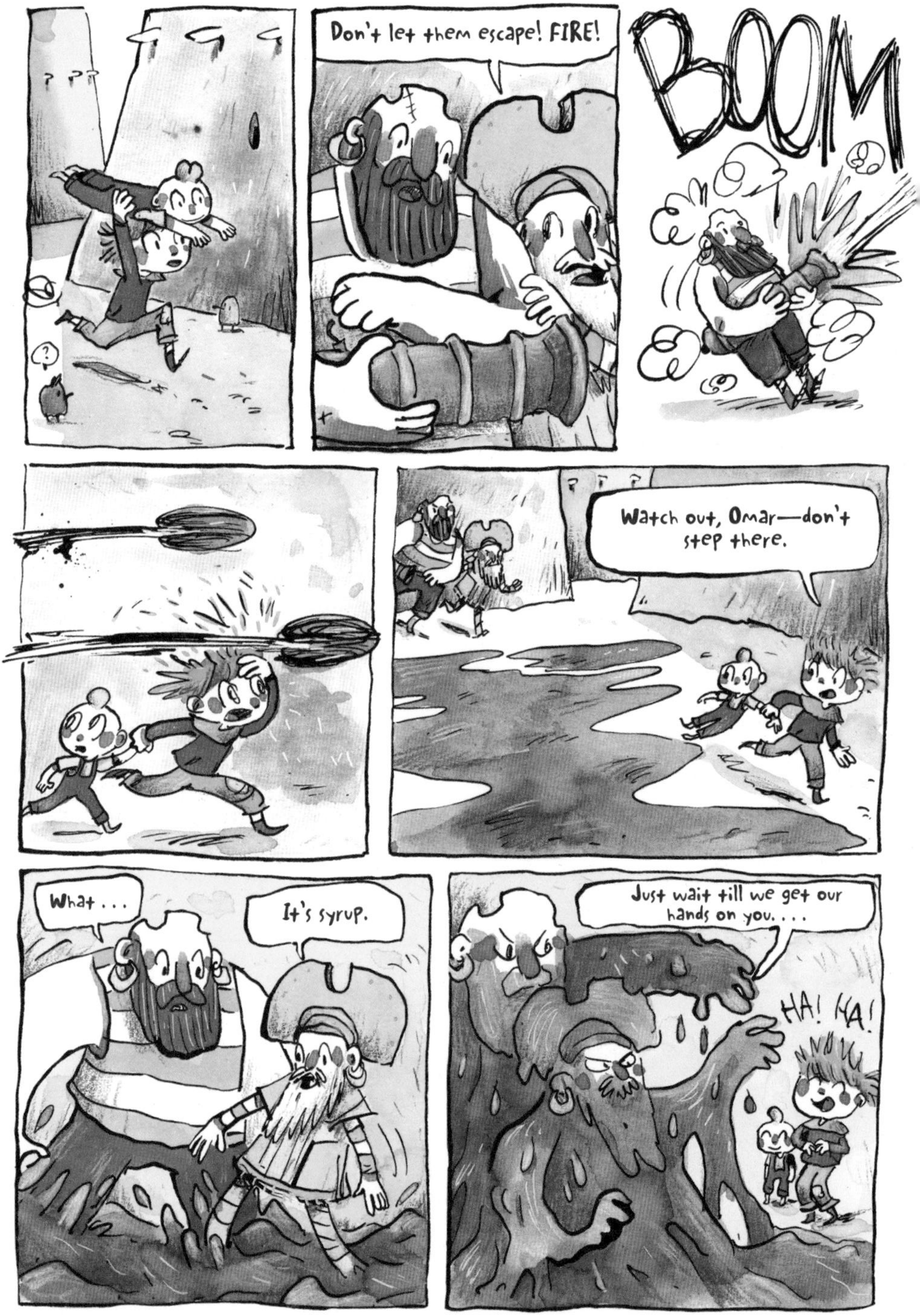
Don't let them escape! FIRE!
BOOM
Watch out, Omar—don't step there.
What . . .
It's syrup.
Just wait till we get our hands on you. . . .
HA! HA!

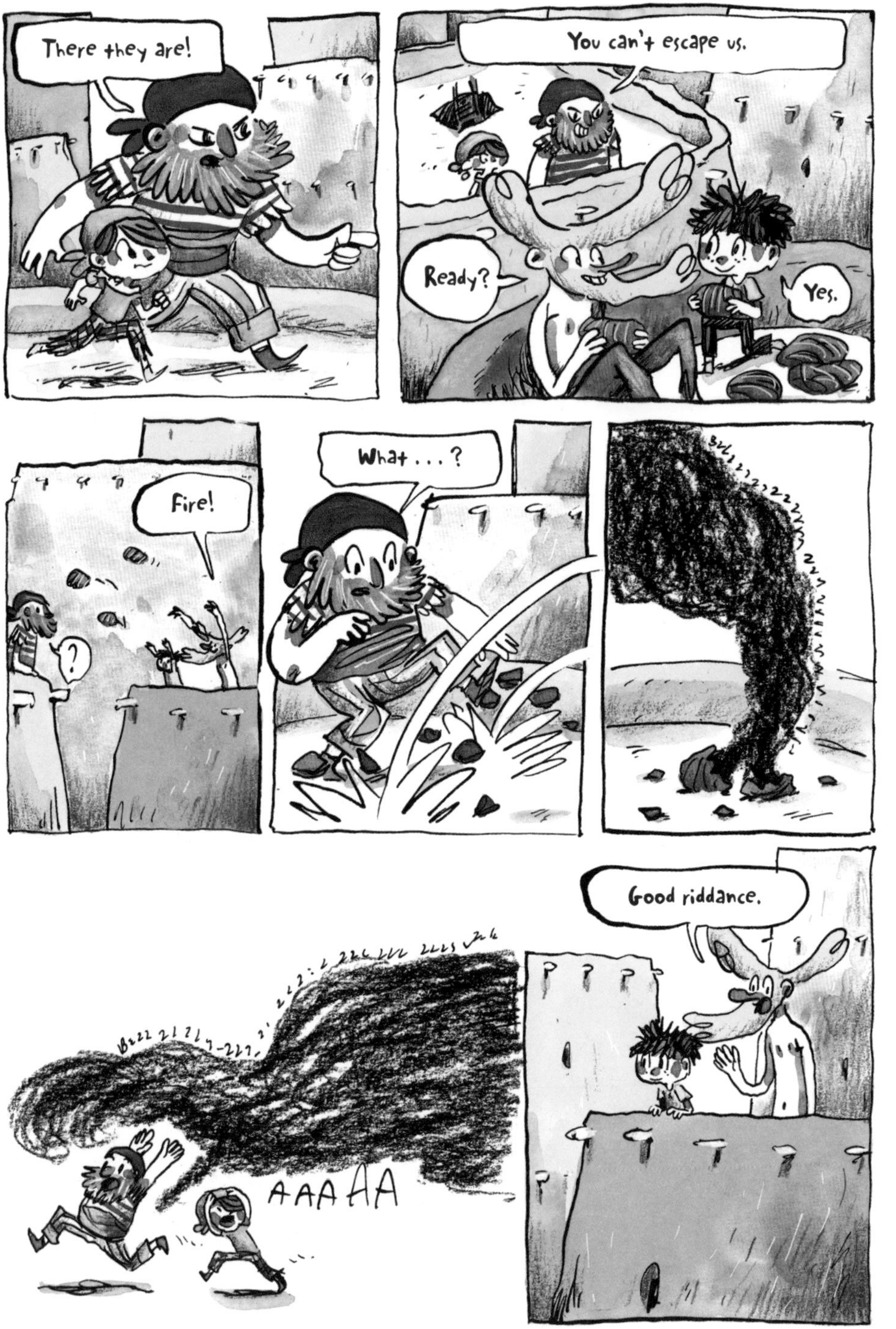
There they are!
You can't escape us.
Ready?
Yes.
Fire!
?
What . . . ?
AAAAA
Good riddance.

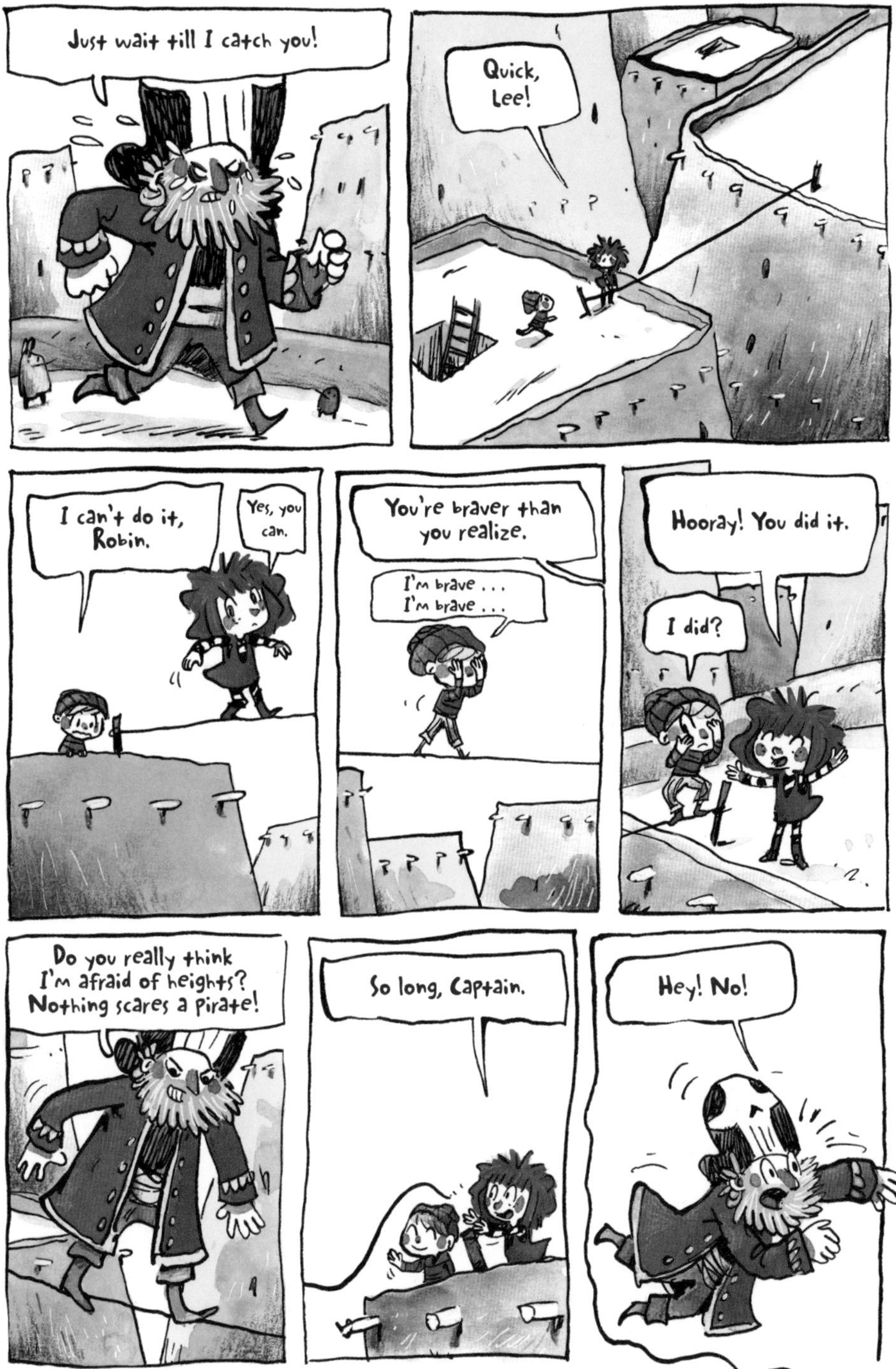

Just wait till I catch you!
Quick, Lee!
I can't do it, Robin.
Yes, you can.
You're braver than you realize.
I'm brave . . .
I'm brave . . .
Hooray! You did it.
I did?
Do you really think I'm afraid of heights? Nothing scares a pirate!
So long, Captain.
Hey! No!

Grr . . . those rotten kids are starting to annoy me.

They're making us look bad.

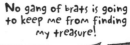

No gang of brats is going to keep me from finding my treasure!

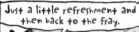

Just a little refreshment and then back to the fray.

I wouldn't drink that if I were you, sir.

Remember the rat. . . .

Nonsense! It's fine!

I'm not touching that stuff.

Bottoms up!

Hic! That's awful strong.

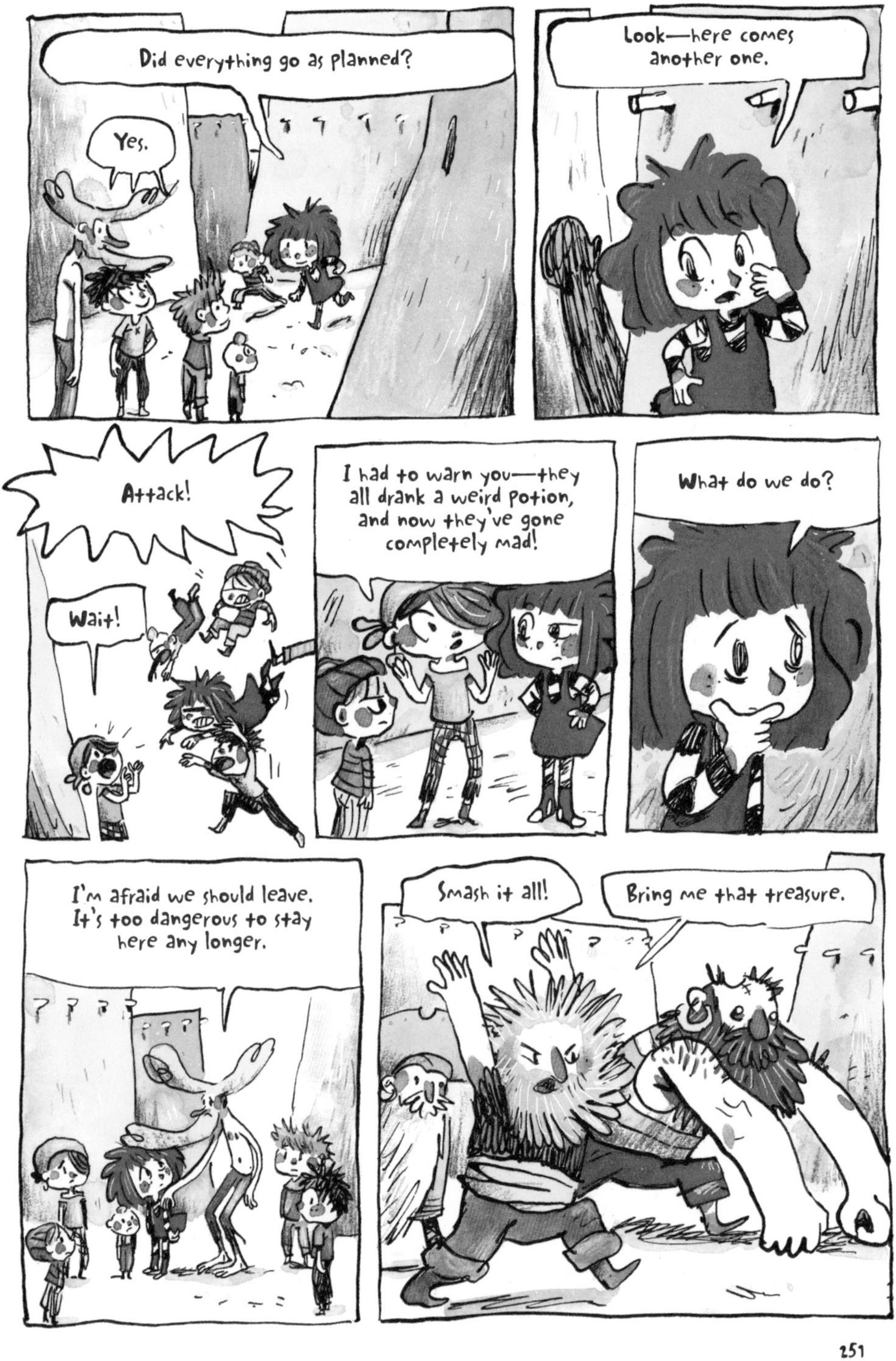
Did everything go as planned?
Yes.
Look—here comes another one.
Attack!
Wait!
I had to warn you—they all drank a weird potion, and now they've gone completely mad!
What do we do?
I'm afraid we should leave. It's too dangerous to stay here any longer.
Smash it all!
Bring me that treasure.

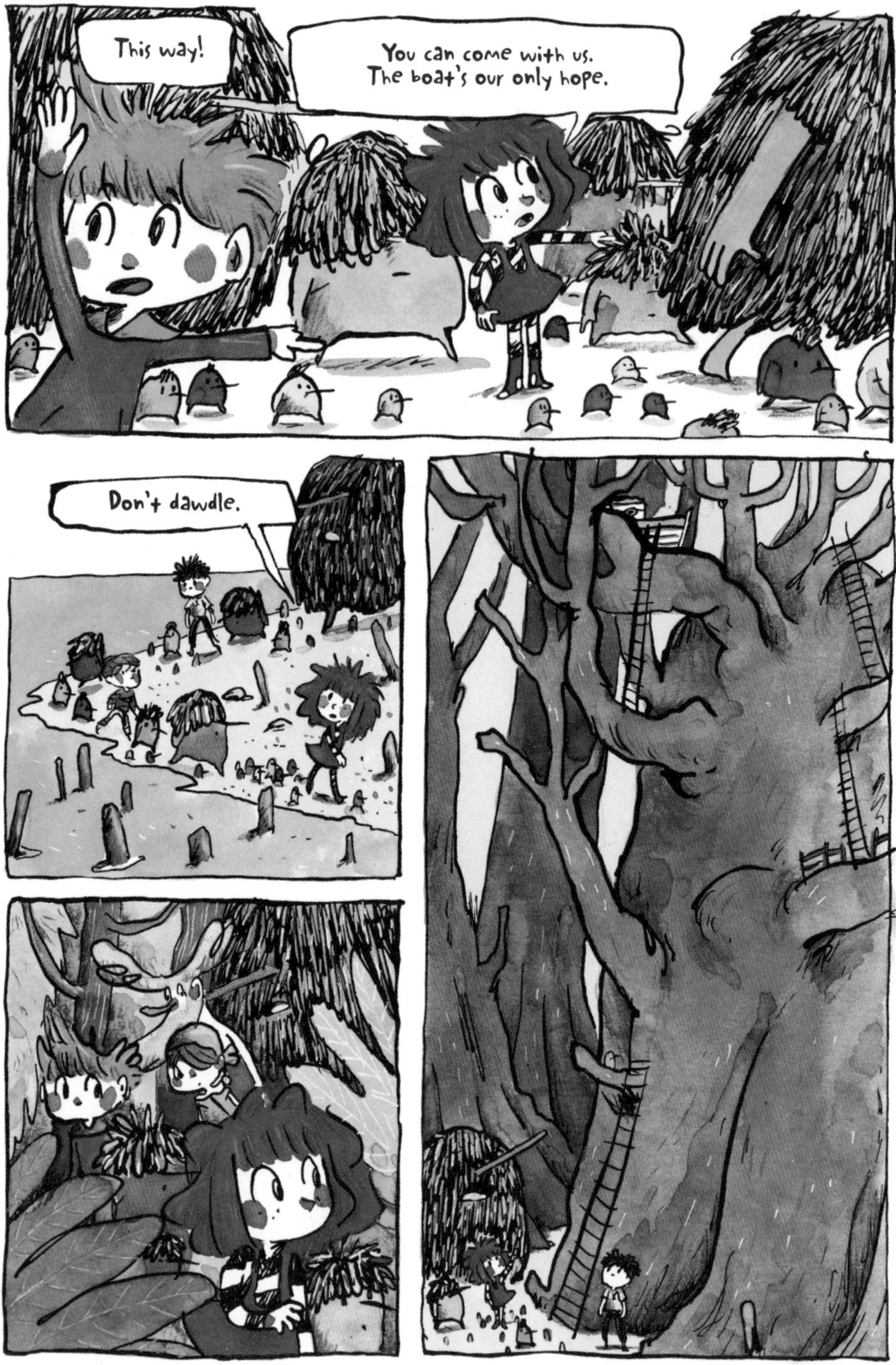
This way!
You can come with us. The boat's our only hope.
Don't dawdle.

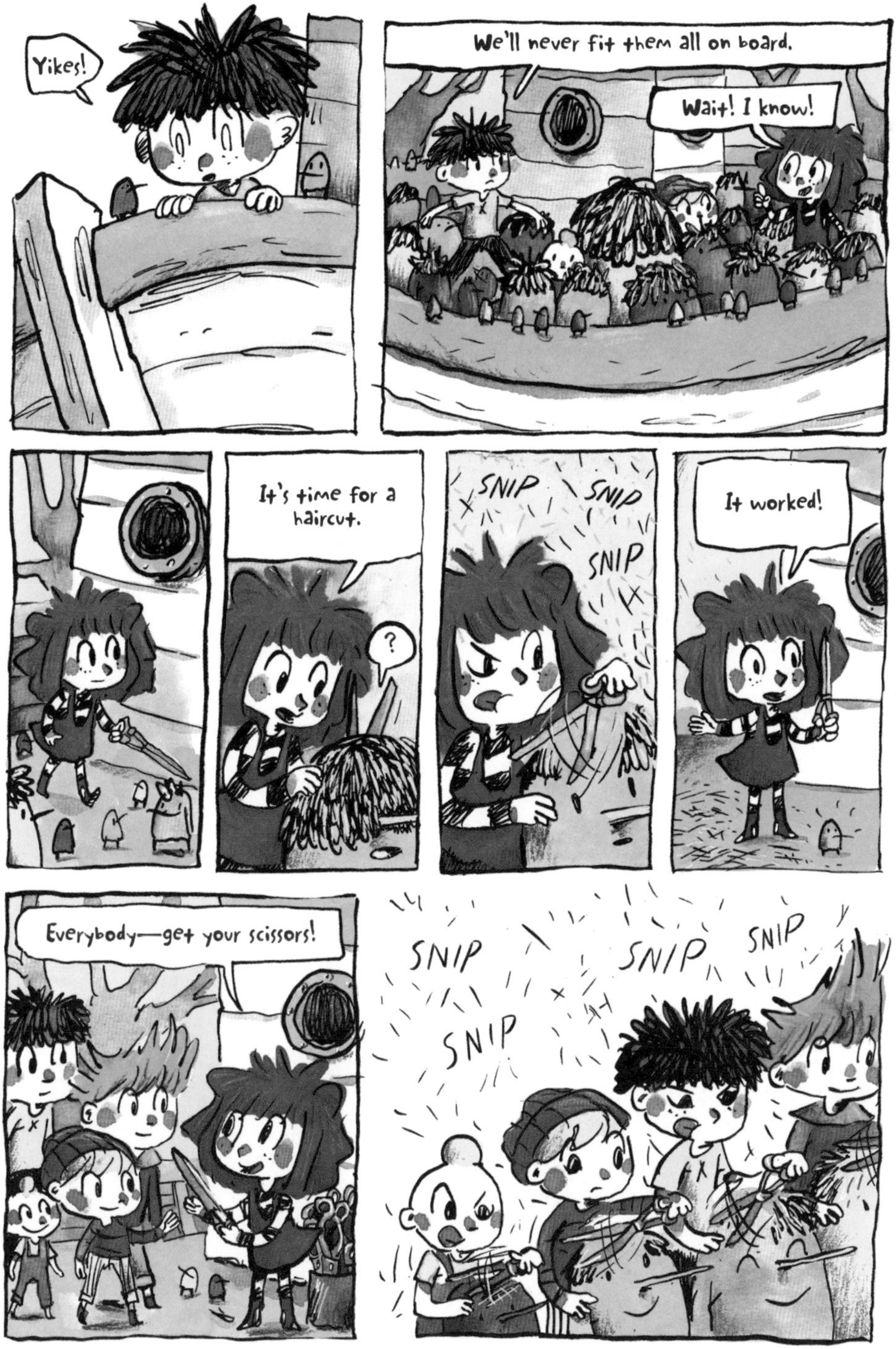
Yikes!
We'll never fit them all on board.
Wait! I know!
It's time for a haircut.
?
SNIP
SNIP
SNIP
It worked!
Everybody—get your scissors!
SNIP
SNIP
SNIP
SNIP

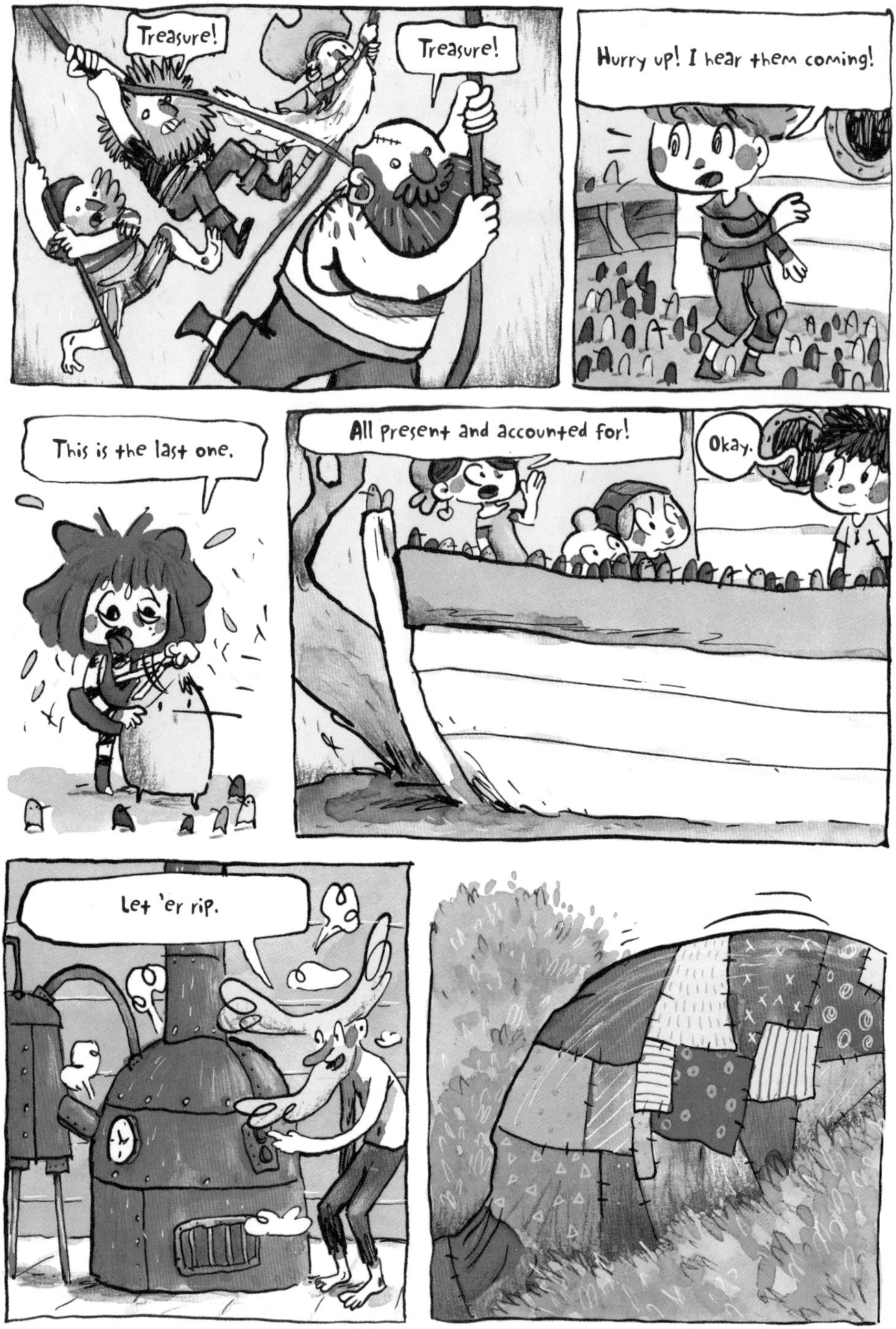
Treasure!
Treasure!
Hurry up! I hear them coming!
This is the last one.
All present and accounted for!
Okay.
Let 'er rip.

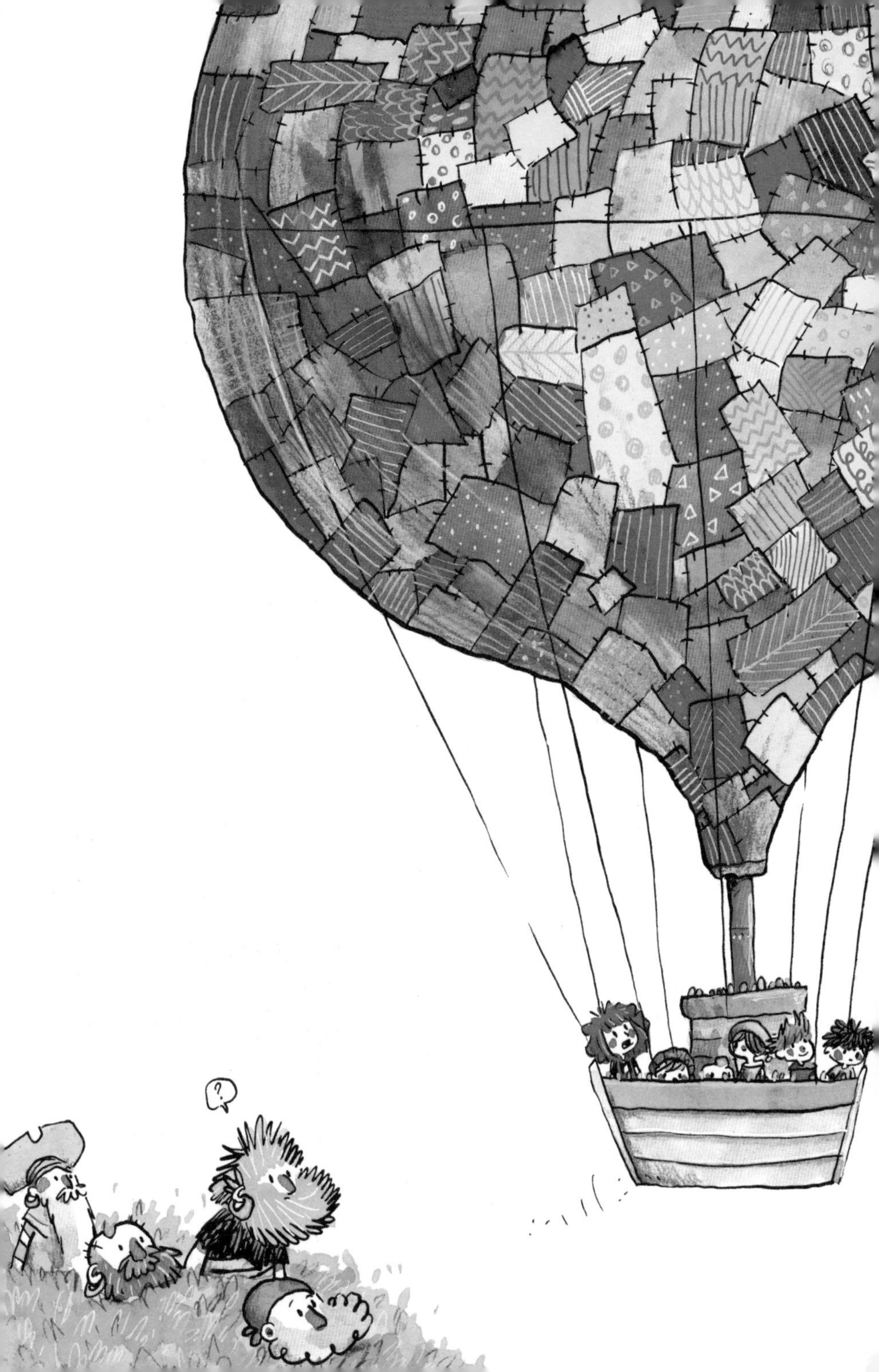
?

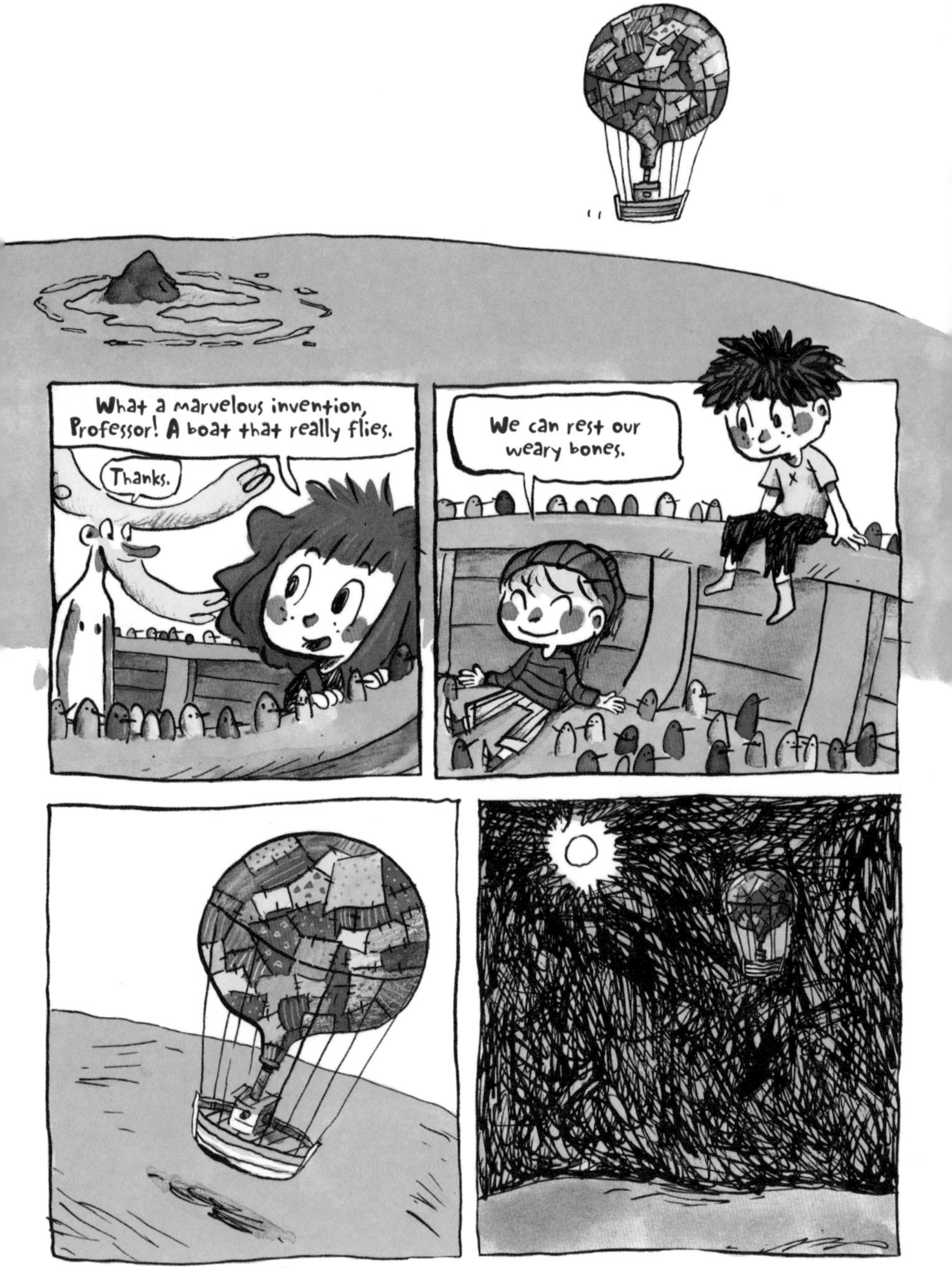
What a marvelous invention, Professor! A boat that really flies.
Thanks.
We can rest our weary bones.

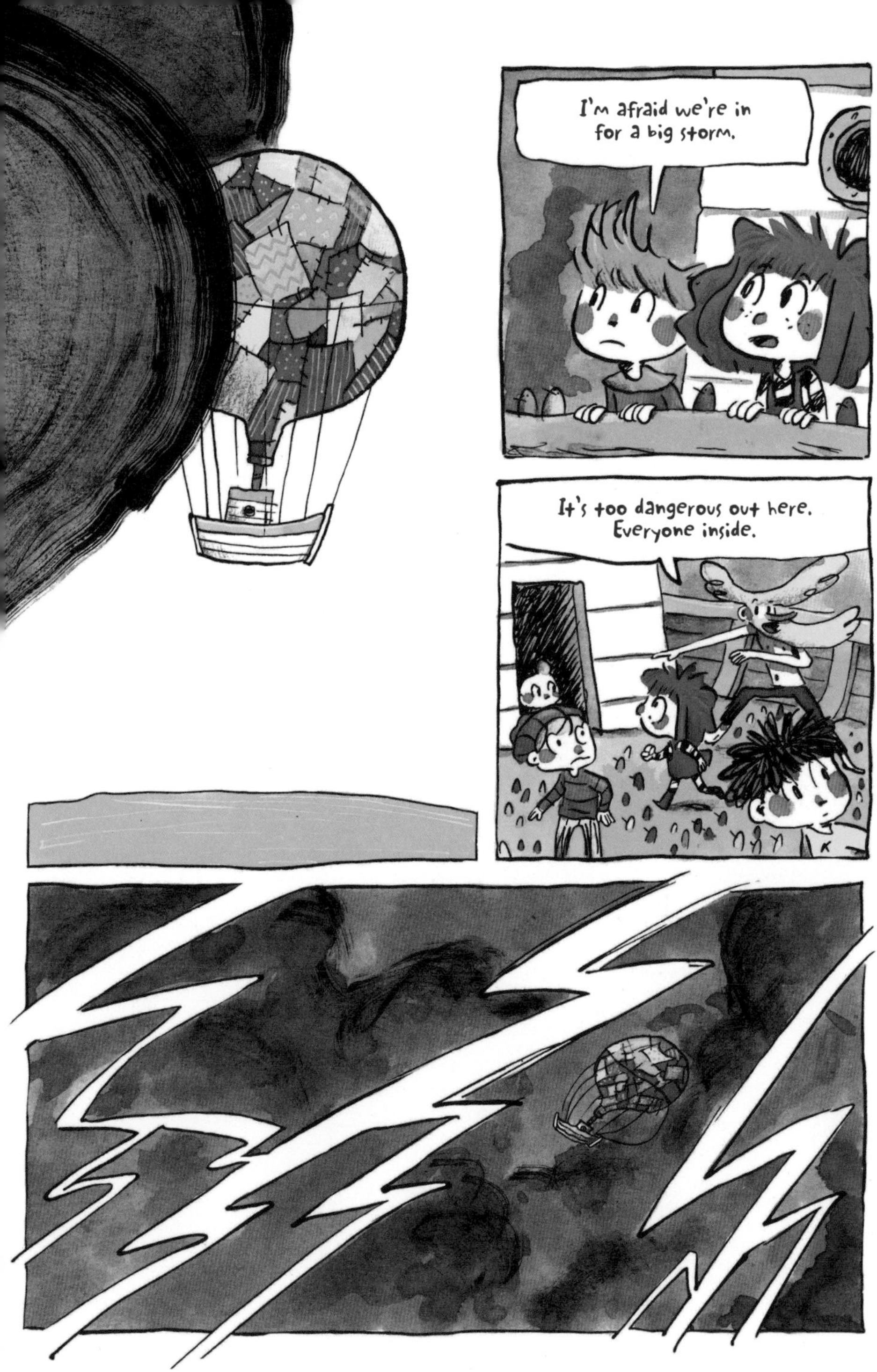
I'm afraid we're in for a big storm.
It's too dangerous out here. Everyone inside.

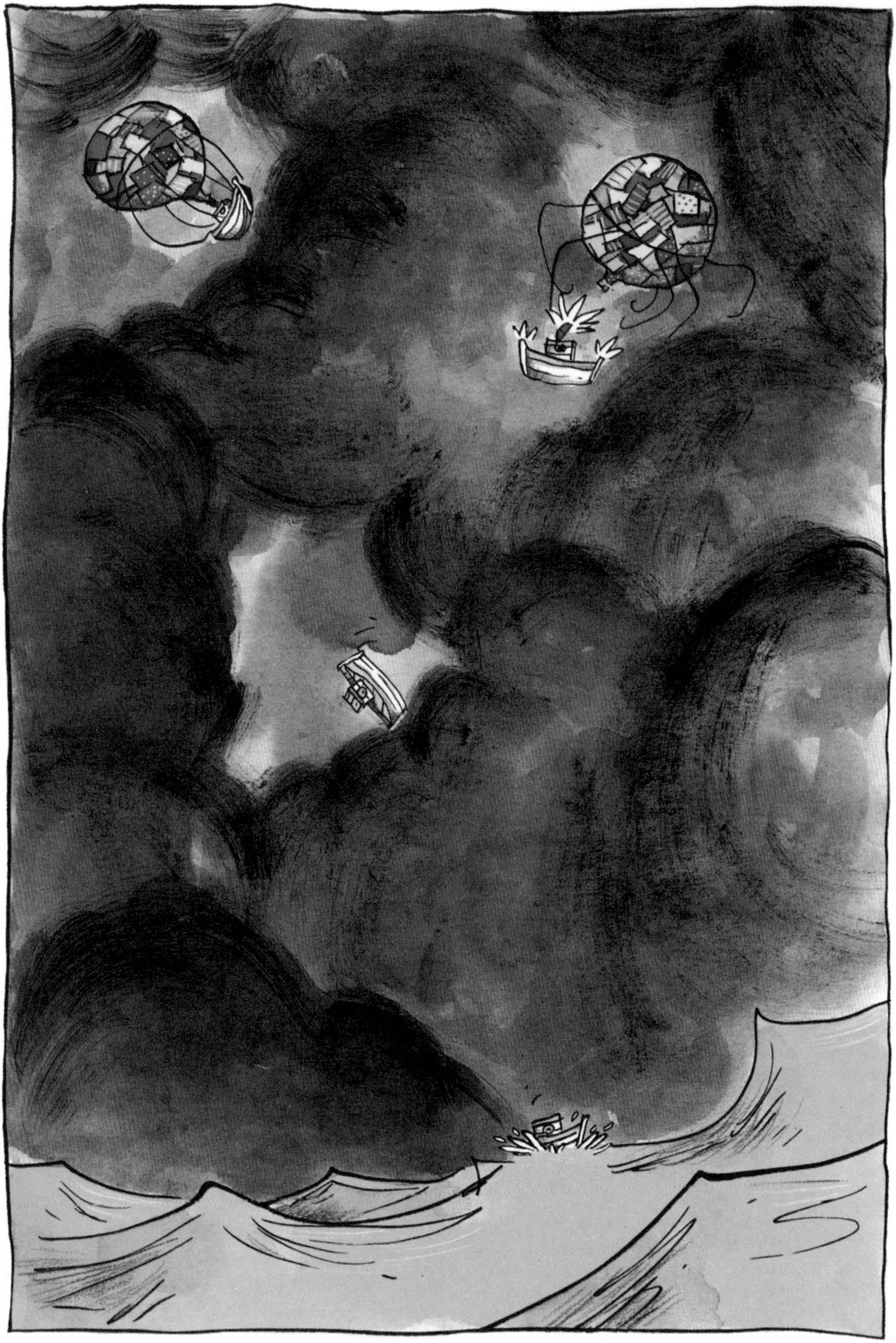

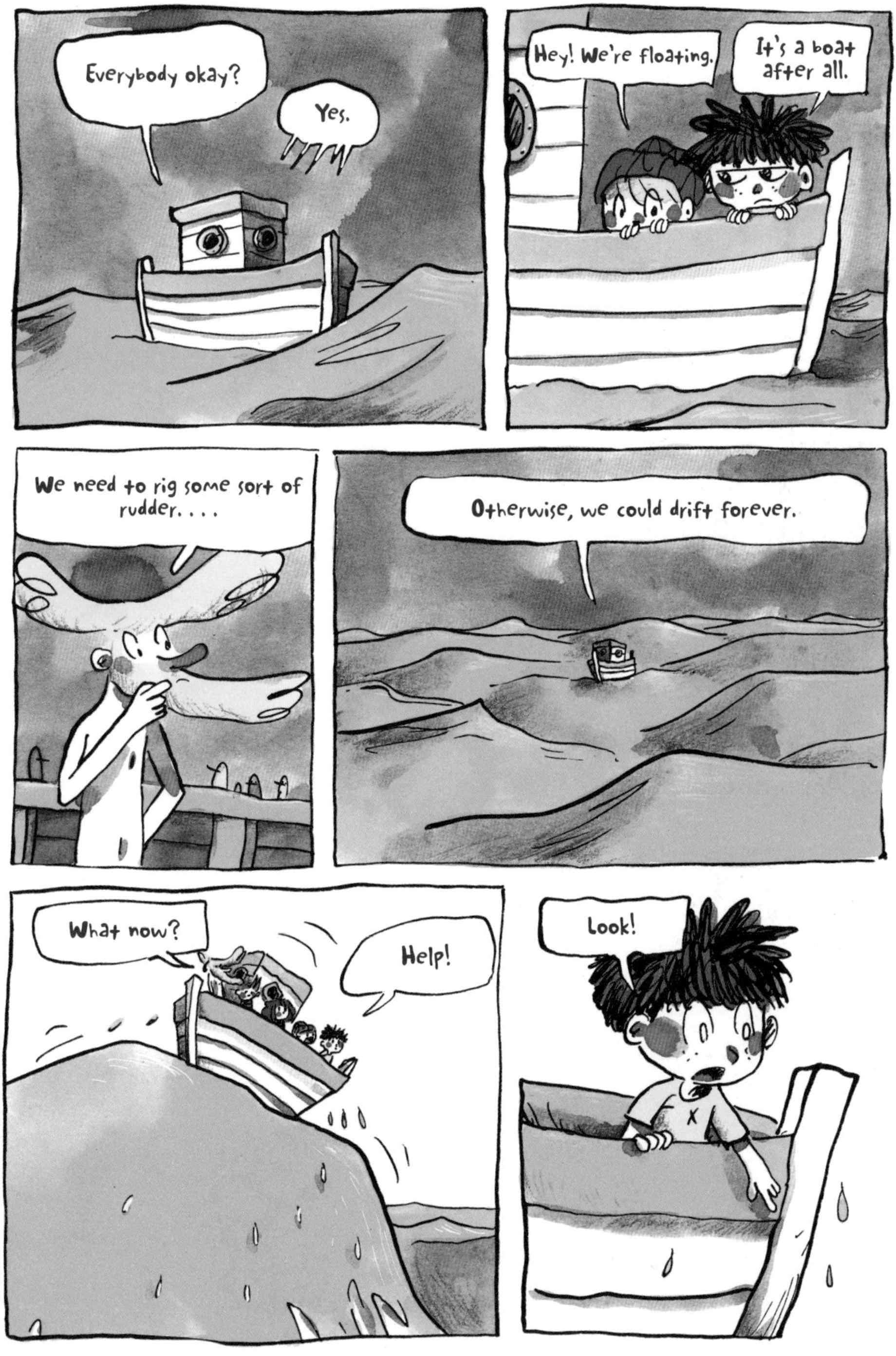
Everybody okay?
Yes.
Hey! We're floating.
It's a boat after all.
We need to rig some sort of rudder. . . .
Otherwise, we could drift forever.
What now?
Help!
Look!

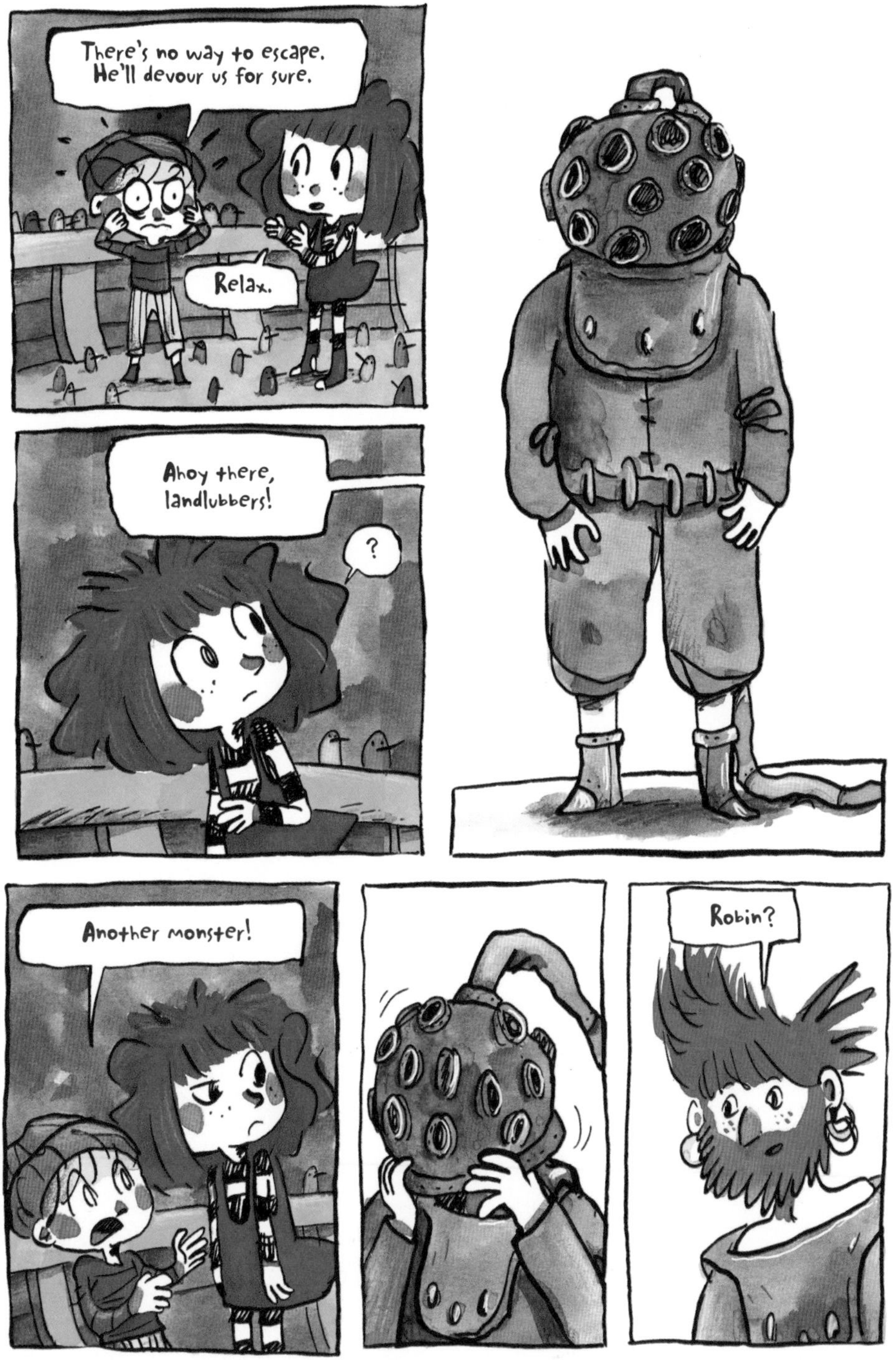
There's no way to escape. He'll devour us for sure.
Relax.
Ahoy there, landlubbers!
?
Another monster!
Robin?

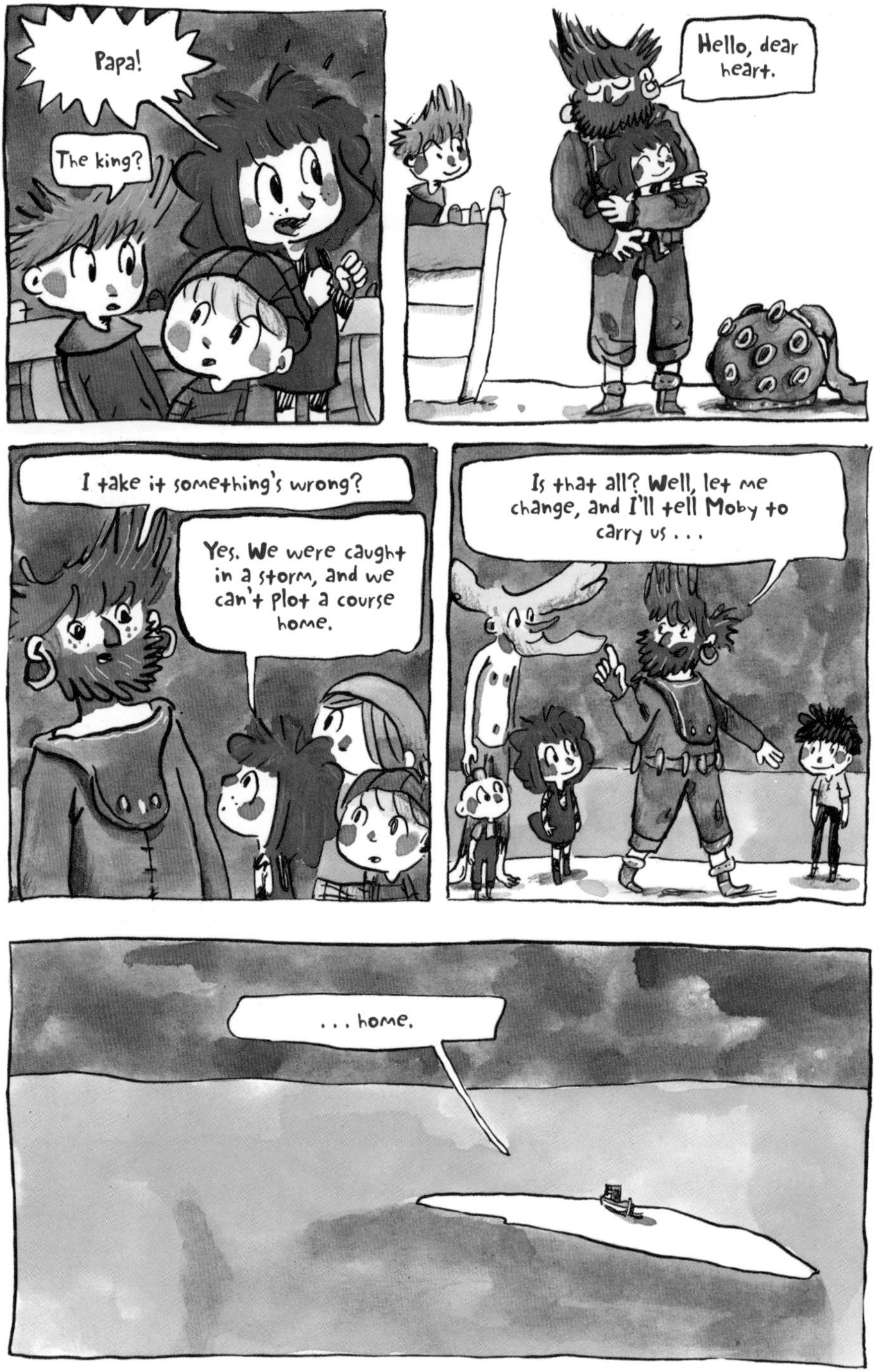
Papa!
The king?
Hello, dear heart.
I take it something's wrong?
Yes. We were caught in a storm, and we can't plot a course home.
Is that all? Well, let me change, and I'll tell Moby to carry us . . .
. . . home.

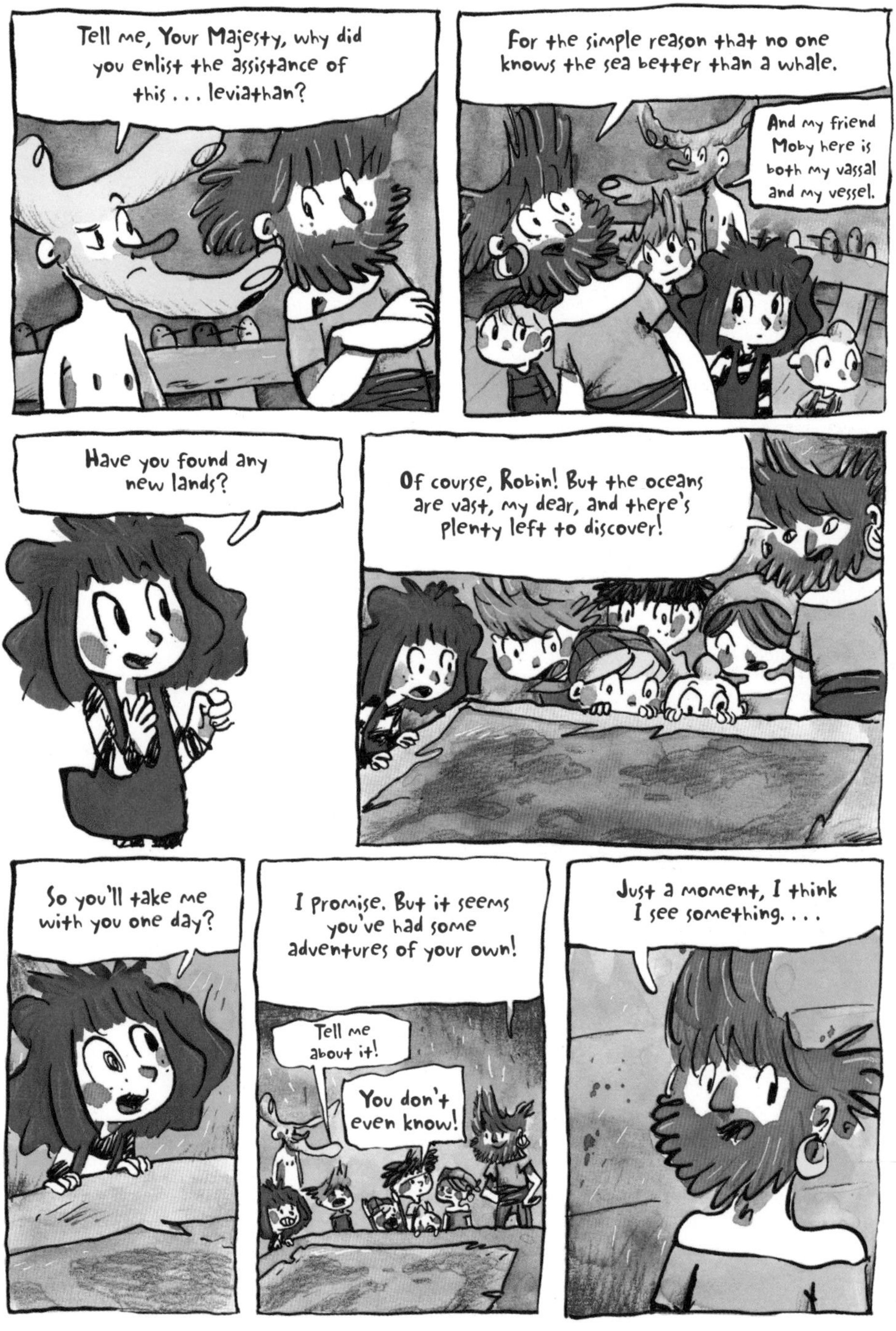
Tell me, Your Majesty, why did you enlist the assistance of this . . . leviathan?
For the simple reason that no one knows the sea better than a whale.
And my friend Moby here is both my vassal and my vessel.
Have you found any new lands?
Of course, Robin! But the oceans are vast, my dear, and there's plenty left to discover!
So you'll take me with you one day?
I promise. But it seems you've had some adventures of your own!
Tell me about it!
You don't even know!
Just a moment, I think I see something. . . .

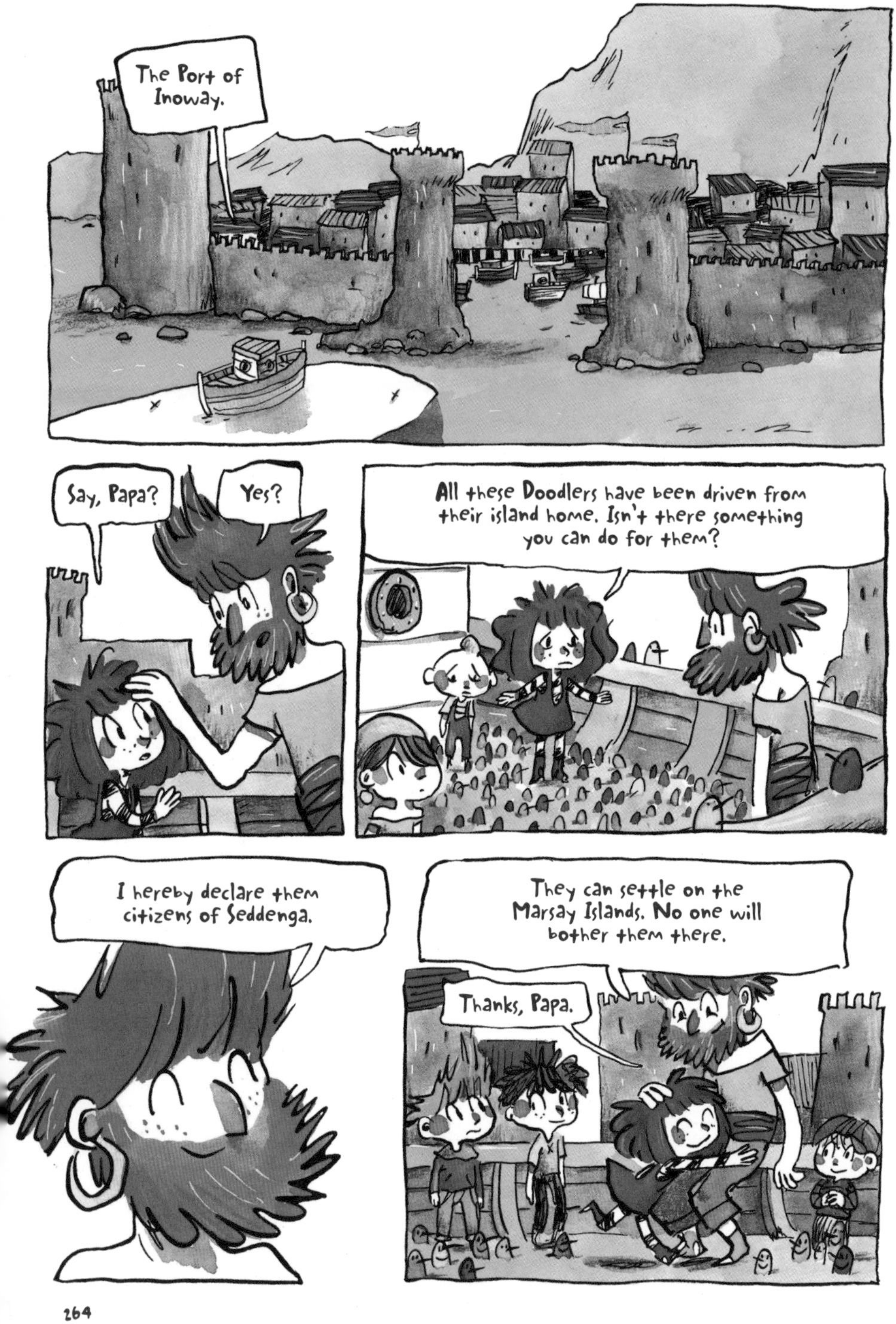
The Port of Inoway.
Say, Papa?
Yes?
All these Doodlers have been driven from their island home. Isn't there something you can do for them?
I hereby declare them citizens of Seddenga.
They can settle on the Marsay Islands. No one will bother them there.
Thanks, Papa.

What about you, Professor? If you wish, you can move into the palace and continue your research.

I would be deeply honored, Your Majesty.

Super!

And you, young lady? What would you like to do?

All I want to do is sail the open sea.

Perfect! On my next voyage, you can serve as cabin boy aboard my royal yacht!

Yippee!

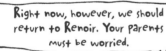

Right now, however, we should return to Renoir. Your parents must be worried.

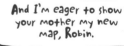

And I'm eager to show your mother my new map, Robin.

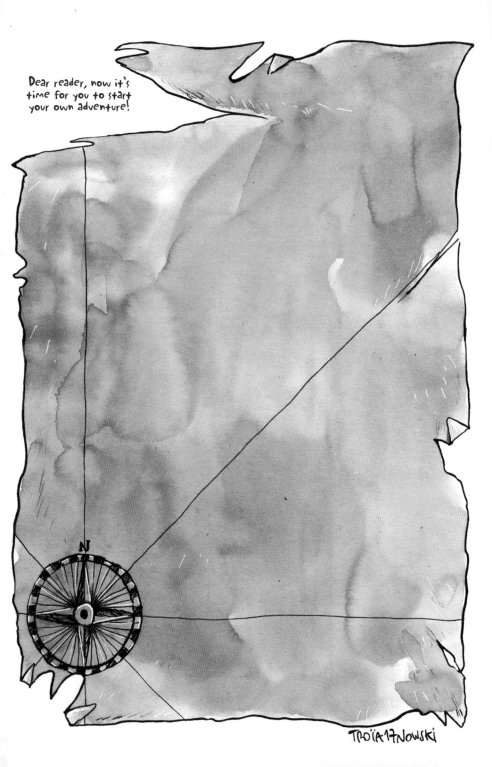

Dear reader, now it's
time for you to start
your own adventure!

Character sketches

# Behind the page! Original sketches

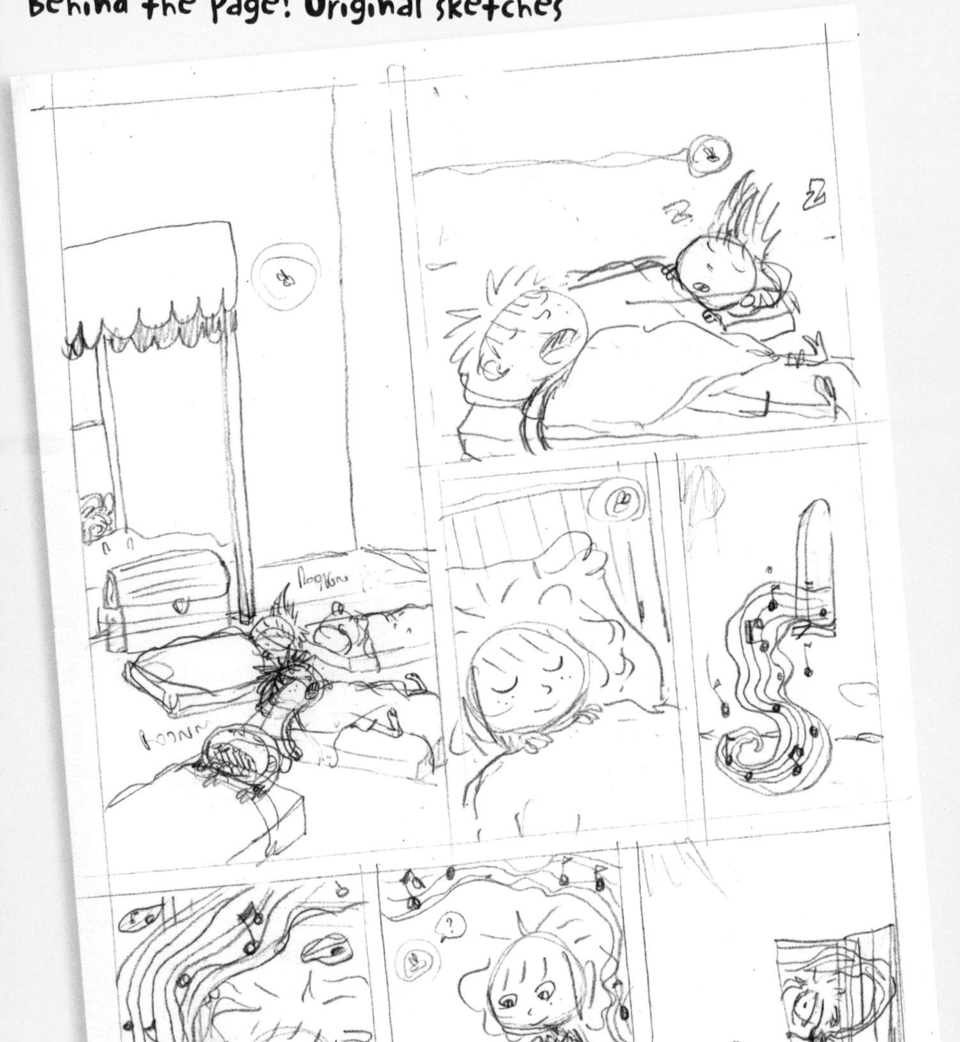

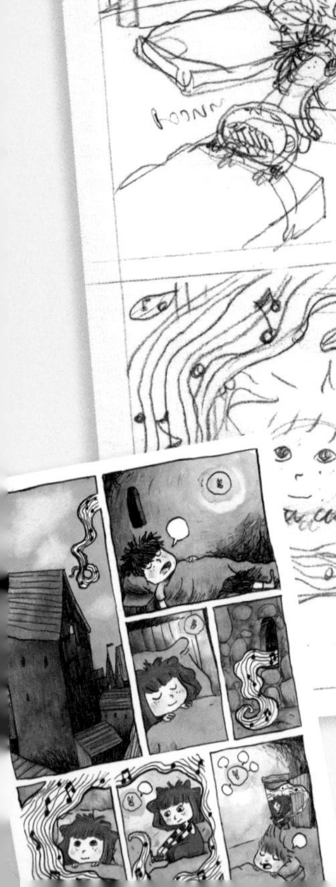

page 113

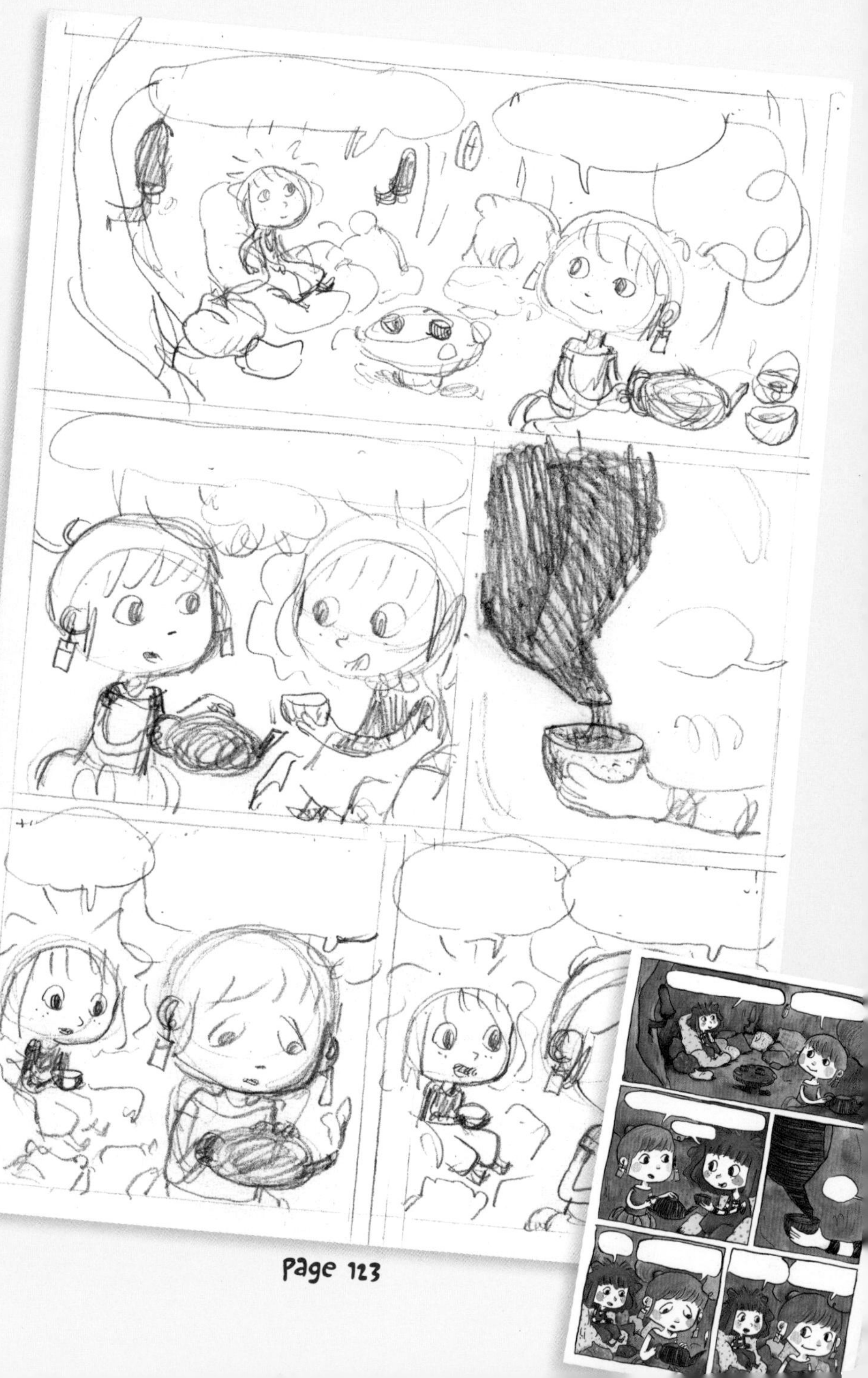

Page 123

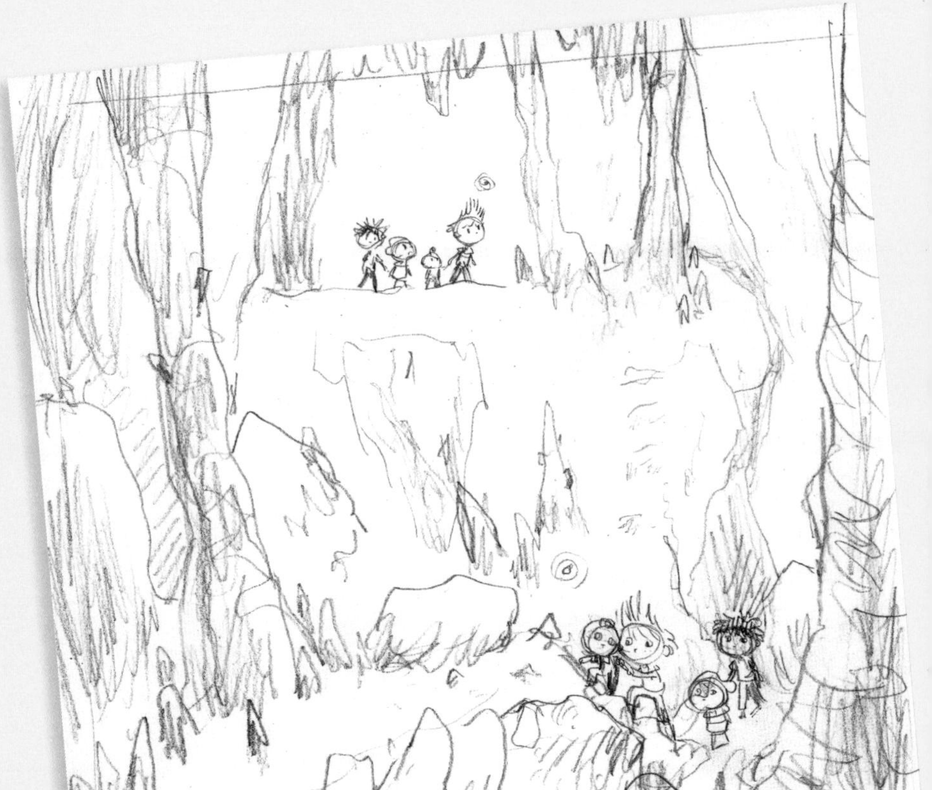

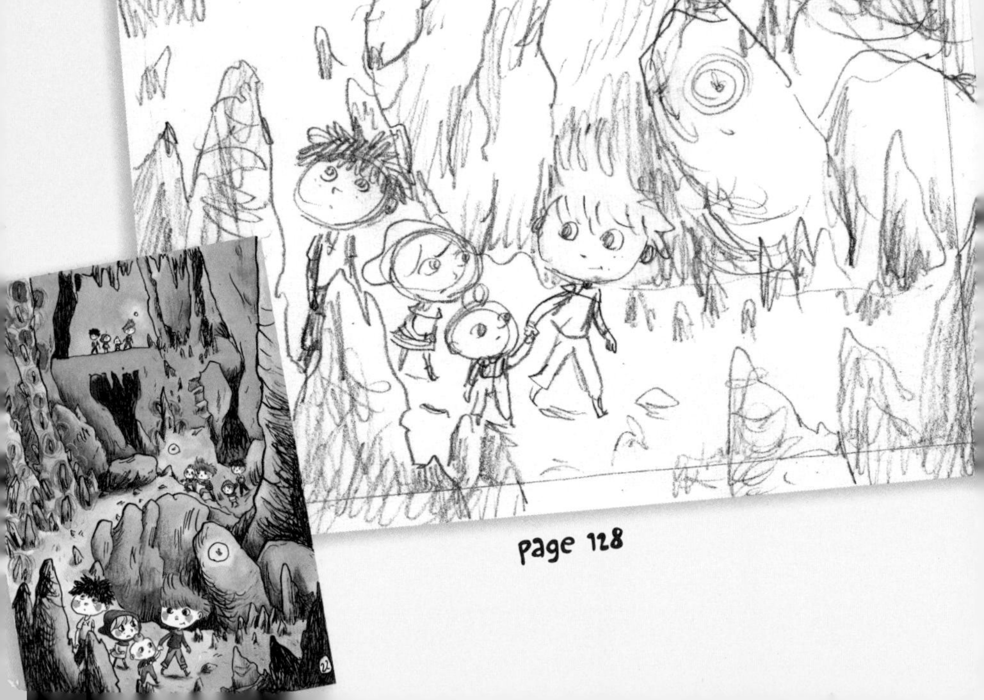

page 128

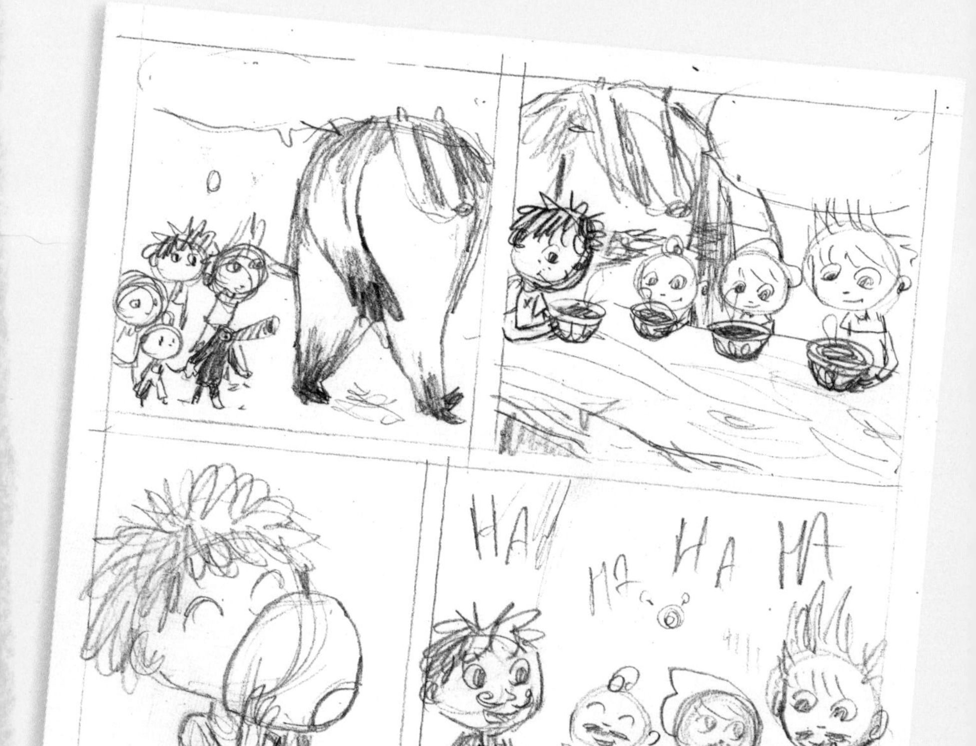
HA
HA
HA
HA

Page 146

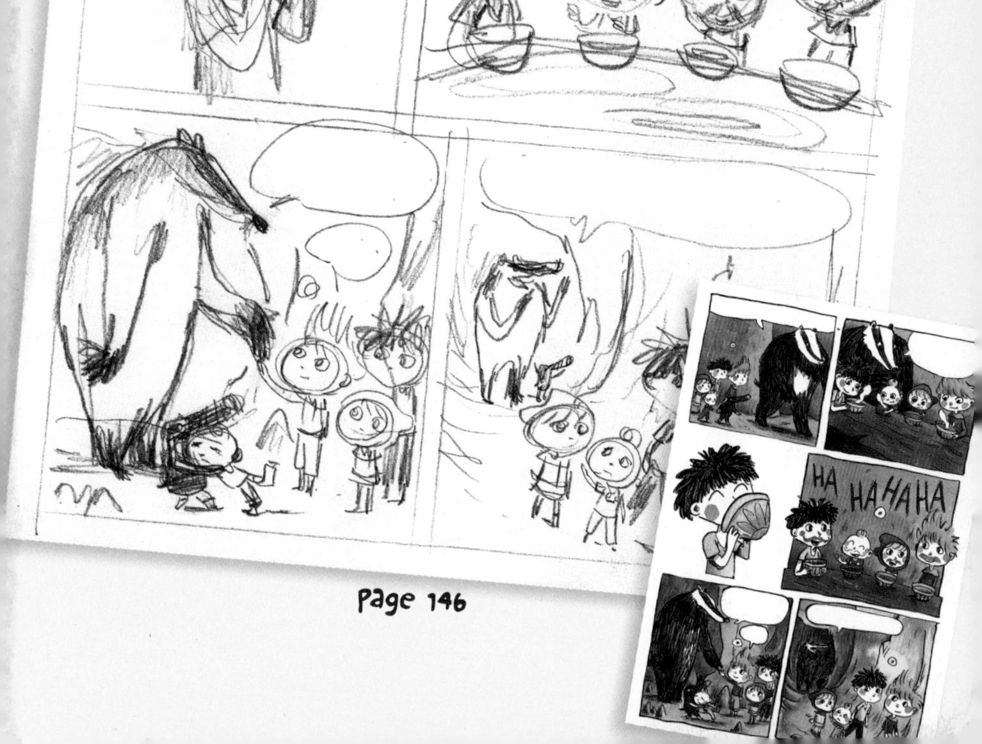
HA
HA HAHA

# RH GRAPHIC
# THE DEBUT LIST

## BUG BOYS
By Laura Knetzger

Bugs, friends, the world around us — this book has everything!
Come explore *Bug Boys* for a fun, thoughtful adventure about growing up and being yourself.

Chapter Book

## THE RUNAWAY PRINCESS
By Johan Troïanowski

The castle is quiet.
And dull.
And boring.
Escape on a quest for excitement with our runaway princess, Robin!

Middle-Grade

## ASTER AND THE ACCIDENTAL MAGIC
By Thom Pico & Karensac

Nothing fun ever happens in the middle of the country . . . except maybe . . . magic?
That's just the beginning of absolutely everything going wrong for Aster.

Middle-Grade

## WITCHLIGHT
By Jessi Zabarsky

Lelek doesn't have any friends or family in the world. And then she meets Sanja. Swords, magic, falling in love . . . these characters come together in a journey to heal the wounds of the past.

Young Adult

# FIND US ONLINE AT
# @RHKIDSGRAPHIC AND
# RHKIDSGRAPHIC.COM